OBLIGATION
AND
REDEMPTION

AN ALTERNATIVE JOURNEY THROUGH
JANE AUSTEN'S
PRIDE AND PREJUDICE

GEORGIA MCCALL

ALTERCONTE

AlterConte Publishers
alterconte@mindspring.com
Memphis, TN 38111
USA

Cover design by Dianne McCaulla and Carolyn Vaughn.

Additional quotes obtained from public domain.

Note from the Author

It is a truth not so universally acknowledged that a sinful man, in need of redemption, must be in want of a Saviour. However little known the understanding or views of such a man may be on this privation, this truth is so well fixed in the Holy Writ, that he is considered the rightful property of the One who destines to fulfil that need, no matter the trials and tribulations which might bring such an extraordinary happening about. Of course, the means of securing such a fixed arrangement can come in many forms, and regrettably oftentimes such forms consign the object to misery and despair before a more blessed outcome might be realised. Such is the case of Fitzwilliam Darcy of Pemberley in Derbyshire. That a woman of inferior birth, little recognised beauty and with no apparent accomplishments to recommend herself, could bring about such a miraculous, yet precedented, happening should in no way be minimised or diminished in the telling. Elizabeth Claire Bennet, of Longbourn, in Hertfordshire finds herself in the unexpected yet coveted position of being the agent of reducing the proud man, so that he might be regenerated as one full of hope and humility. If you find yourself in the category of one who would not wish to acknowledge the plight in which our hero finds himself, do not be dismayed, for the telling of such a remarkable event holds many diversions and pleasures of its own accord. However, for the reader who might find some connection with our characters' condition, out of a similar experience or understanding, be reminded yet again of our great need, no matter outward appearances. And for the reader who discovers the exquisiteness and grace of transformation into the realm of the faithful,
Soli Deo Gloria.

The greatest happiness of life is the conviction that we are loved; loved
for ourselves, or rather, loved in spite of ourselves.
Victor Hugo

Chapter One

Do nothing from rivalry or conceit,
but in humility count others more significant than yourselves.
Let each of you look not only to his own interests,
but also to the interests of others.
Philippians 2:3-4

Although dawn, the sky remained black as storm clouds quickly invaded the awakening countryside. Fitzwilliam Darcy urged his mount to an even quicker pace as he attempted to race the storm. Lightning had been flashing in the distance as he skilfully steered Hermes, his black Arabian, through the woodland along the leaf-covered path.

Darcy had guessed, upon setting out, that he had about an hour before the storm clouds would overtake him, and he meant to make the most of that time. He had relieved his mind of all thought, except the path before him and the exhilaration that came from a brisk pace on the back of his spirited mount. He was himself while unaccompanied, without the need to perform or succumb to the expectations of others. Darcy could feel the escalating cold air sting his face but rejoiced in the sensation. He could forget his sister's near ruin and subsequent pain; he could escape from conniving mothers and daughters; he could forget his own feelings of loneliness and his expected pending courtship. When riding, he was liberated.

Darcy urged his mount faster and had just come around a bend when he saw a sudden flash of colour. By instinct, he squeezed his legs tighter and steered Hermes off the pathway. Just then, a flash of light lit his surroundings and sent a tingling sensation coursing through his body, but he did not have time to consider his danger as his world turned upside down, and true darkness enveloped him.

Later, Darcy would have vague recollections of the following few hours of that transformative day. The pain was immense, as he would open his eyes periodically to take in his location. He knew he was being dragged slowly underneath a canopy of trees blown forcefully overhead. The pain in his ankle surged with each rock or root that dared to get in his way. But that was nothing compared with the relentless throbbing in the back of his head that threatened additional episodes of spinning followed by retching as he was pulled along.

Initially, Darcy thought that he was alone – that the transgressor who startled his horse along the pathway had succumbed to his stallion's ferocity. But he soon understood this was not the case. Darcy knew someone, or perhaps several, were moving him through the woods, whose mercy he, perforce, depended upon; he just hoped that his guardians wished him no harm. At intervals, when he opened his eyes, he would feel a surge of nausea overtake him, so that he could only take in the conflicting sounds and smells of his journey. Occasionally, he would get a scent of flowers sometimes followed by a woman's voice, reminding him of the woman he was to marry. He supposed that he must have been dreaming as his mind sought an escape from his suffering.

In his recumbent position, the rain fell hard upon his face, sometimes making breathing difficult, while the chill of the blustery wind blew against his frame, causing him to shiver as the journey to nowhere incessantly persisted. Minutes passed, or possibly hours, during his journey when nothing but a blur of pain mixed with nausea and misery consumed his conscious thoughts.

Darcy awoke to a dimly lit room with dark walls. He knew for certain that a woman, whom he vaguely recognised, was caring for him; her hands were gentle and her voice calming as she worked to soothe his aches. She spoke kindly to him as she changed the dressing on his head. She had tried to solicit a response about something having to do with the dreadful cold, but he could only imagine his words, being unable to rouse enough to be present to the task. He wondered where the others had gone and hoped he and the woman had not been left alone – a situation he had always stringently avoided.

Without clarity, Darcy would later remember his guardian assisting him onto a bed or cot of some sort and soliciting his help. The pain in his head and ankle was intense, so he cursed out loud, retching yet again with the movement. The indignity of his condition was lost on the misery he felt. If the room would stop spinning, he could assess his predicament, but as it was, he just wanted peace, quiet and warmth. He could handle any discomfort from his ankle, if his head would just stop pounding. The calming effect of her ministrations soothed him back to the land of Morpheus, which was fortunate, as it spared him from another episode of retching.

The next thing that Darcy recalled, however, stayed with him. He had been sleeping, but heard a rustling as he awoke. He opened his eyes and thought that he must have met his end and an angel was before him, dressed in white, with a glow from behind. He tried to focus as the fuzzy haze cleared into a distinct picture of exquisiteness. Before him, not five feet away, was a woman in nothing but her chemise stuck to her frame, showing her shape and curves to perfection. He could clearly see her abundant assets, as he could not pull his eyes away from her. He must have unconsciously made a sound with his sharp intake of breath because she abruptly turned around to gaze at him. He had attempted to turn away quickly, but that only made him more dizzy and confused, and he had to reach up to cover his eyes. She said something, which he answered in the negative without comprehending her words. Darcy was of course mortified that he had nearly been caught staring at her. Could she have known how alluring she was in the wet chemise? Was that her design, to seduce him into a compromising position?

Now that he looked back on the encounter, he understood that that must have been exactly what she had been doing. Her curves would have been intoxicating had he been well enough to appreciate them. Her wet hair had cascaded down to the spot just above the lower curve of her back, drawing his eye to her round bottom. He could just see her breasts through the thin, wet garment. He could not have imagined a more delightful sight, howbeit brief. That vision would haunt his waking and slumbering dreams for many nights to come. But no matter how lovely she was, he could not, and would not, be lured into this nobody's lair. Many more beautiful women had attempted a seduction of him, and no one had been successful.

Focusing on something other than the woman before him, his eyes landed on his coat hanging on a hook by the fire. In an instant Darcy came to realise that he himself was in a state of undress. She had been undressing him! This woman had laid hands upon his person and removed his clothes! He began to fumble under the blanket and was relieved to feel that his shirt and pants were still on, if somewhat damp, which was likely why he still shivered despite being by the fire and under a blanket. This woman, whoever she was, had thought that she could force a compromise and coerce a marriage with him. That was certain never to happen. He had enough money to get himself out of any scrape that might come his way, and he would not succumb to her contrivances. She may have the body to seduce, but he would not fall prey to her purposes. His head was pounding as his pulse raced in outrage. The exertion was exhausting to his body, weakened by blood loss and physical stress.

Being cold slowed down his senses and ability to stay awake; therefore, he gave in to sleep, fitfully at first, but then deeply as his body attempted to escape the pain. Darcy did worry about what this woman might do while he slept but could do nothing to stop her deeds.

THE STORM CLOUDS WERE WELL TO THE WEST when Elizabeth Bennet set out on her daily walk. Although, the temperatures had been unseasonably warm over the past week, at well above the average for October, a cold breeze had begun to stir the night before. She was anxious to put on her walking boots and take in the landscape surrounding her country home in Hertfordshire. She had been unable, in recent days, to partake in her customary routine of walking at dawn along the grounds of Longbourn, and willingly faced the possibility of rain in order to work out her pent up energy in active pursuits.

As the clouds grew more ominous, Elizabeth was lost in thought. Her eyes stayed to the ground, so she would not trip as she walked within a less-travelled part of her father's estate. The leaves had begun their descent onto the woodland bed, so the ground was a carpet of reds, browns and yellows. "Such beauty, such joys!" she exclaimed without restraint. As a wood nymph, she glided down the lane, occasionally reaching down and tossing up a handful of leaves. Autumn was her delight, and not even the exceptionally cold wind that had begun to blow in force could mar her spirits.

When Elizabeth noticed that she was some distance from home, and that the clouds might break soon, she picked up her pace in the direction of the house and began to run down the path. This is just what she needed. She laughed in transport as she attempted to race the storm to come.

The thunder had made a gradual approach but was now all around. Elizabeth was becoming concerned as she finally looked up to the sky through an opening in the trees and saw blackness, well past the time for sunrise. The darkness had now changed the foliage to a dull colour, and she began to worry that she would not make it home before getting wet, as she was still some distance away. This would not be the first time she found herself deep in the woods when a storm developed, but it would be the first in some years, and she did not relish being wet and cold, nor did she look forward to her mother's reproof.

At a running pace, Elizabeth was just rounding a bend, when a tall, black horse nearly trampled her. She tempestuously screamed, and just at that moment lightning struck a tree not one hundred yards away. The immense horse reared as the rider attempted to avert her position, throwing the man to the ground. Unfortunately the rider's left foot was caught in the stirrup, so when the horse bolted, he was dragged over the rough terrain some distance into the woods before his foot was freed when his mount reared again.

This all happened within a moment. Elizabeth, being a sensible woman, ran to the gentleman, whom she recognised to be their new neighbour's guest, Mr. Darcy. He was already bleeding steadily from his head, which alarmed her greatly. Elizabeth called his name, but he remained mostly unresponsive. She knew she had to stop the bleeding, so she tore two large strips of fabric from the bottom of her petticoat, one to roll into a bandage and the other to secure to his head. This took her some time to accomplish, and by now the rain had started coming down, first a few drops that soon turned into a downpour.

Elizabeth considered running home to seek help, but knew her father would not allow her back out into the dangerous storm; he would send a missive to the estate where the man had resided the past week, but the delay could prove disastrous for Mr. Darcy. Elizabeth could go straight to Netherfield Park herself, which was about the same distance as her home, but in the opposite direction; however, like with her own father, she doubted that she could sufficiently describe Mr. Darcy's location and would likely be required to stay behind like a proper lady, thus increasing Mr. Darcy's peril.

The lightning and gusts of wind demanded that she remove him to safety soon, but in the stress of the moment Elizabeth could not bring to mind any shelters nearby, as remote as they were. Then she recalled her father's hunting lodge that had been without use for quite some time. They were a fair distance from where it stood, if her memory served her, and she would have to consider whether going through the woods would be the most expedient way, or if she should follow the path. The woods could cut the distance in half, but the difficulties in traversing uneven terrain may not be worth the effort.

Elizabeth again attempted to wake the unconscious man, who moaned periodically but did not open his eyes. She looked around for his horse, somehow hoping that its presence might prove beneficial, but it was long gone. She would have to somehow get him there herself. Even if the lightning and strong winds were not a threat, staying out in the cold rain was. Since she had left the house, the temperature had dropped significantly and continued to fall as the showers came down hard around them. She said a quick prayer and attempted to hoist him from under his shoulders. Elizabeth had never touched a man, other than her father, outside of the necessities of dancing and greetings. She had not noticed how large Mr. Darcy was, until she tried lifting him. She concluded that the move would be more difficult than she had anticipated. *We will have to take a more direct path, I'm afraid.*

4

Before moving him, she decided to check the passage she planned to take to ensure that she remembered the area correctly and that there were no obvious obstacles along the way. The rain was coming down in sheets by now, making her short journey more difficult, but she finally did see the cabin and realised it was closer than she had originally thought.

Elizabeth wasted no time in returning to the man who was still unconscious. The sound of the rain was only superseded by blustering winds, swaying the trees dangerously overhead. She heard a loud crash in the near distance that shook the ground underneath her. The darkness and rain made it impossible to see the cause, but she suspected her danger, moving all the more quickly. When she reached her charge, she eyed him warily, attempting to figure how she could move a man nearly twice her size that far away. "Mr. Darcy, sir, I am going to get us to safety," said Elizabeth as she stooped low and put her arms under each of his shoulders, trying to lift him enough to shift him into the needed direction. She planned to walk backwards while holding him up, thereby gradually making their way to the cabin; however, now she doubted her ability to move him anywhere.

After little progress was made with her first effort, Elizabeth reconsidered the options of waiting out the storm or leaving the man in order to seek help, but in the end felt uncomfortable with the idea of either. They were a good ways from both Longbourn and Netherfield, and the storm around them was quite severe. She determined that she must do her best to try to move him to safety and leave the rest in the hands of Providence. If Elizabeth eventually found the task impossible, she would then consider alternatives. As it was, she was growing cold and knew that Mr. Darcy, who was not exerting himself, would be feeling even colder. They needed shelter, and it would seem that she was the only one who could get them there.

She attempted to lift him again and was able to take two steps. She immediately tried again, gaining three more. She continued on in this manner across the forest floor aiming towards the cabin hidden in the woods. Elizabeth tripped and fell several times along the route and had never felt more fatigued as she was during their journey to safety. Tears sprang to her eyes, but she resisted letting them fall; she was wet enough and refused to add to the deluge any more than was already streaming down her face. Frustration had found her and mocked the pride she had always placed on her adeptness while in the open air. Elizabeth had never wished for the robustness of a man, until now.

Mr. Darcy would rouse and moan in pain periodically along the way. She had to stop and rest often, rechecking his bandaging as was needed. In this manner, she continued on over the course of the next two hours. While moving him thus, the rain continued steadily, but the lightning had passed into the distance. Elizabeth kept expecting that perhaps someone would come looking for one of them, but all she heard was the constant strain of the torrent around them. By this time, Mr. Darcy was more often awake than not, but groaned with each step. Elizabeth was as gentle as she could be, but the movement caused him obvious discomfort. At one point, she lifted him higher than usual, and he was relieved of his stomach contents, suggesting a concussion. Elizabeth had

had her share of injuries and knew that if this were the case, he required rest, quietude and medical attention to assuage his discomfort.

Elizabeth, with her burden, finally arrived at the cabin. By this time, Darcy and Elizabeth were soaked through. His overcoat could not withstand the rain, especially in light of his essentially travelling across a ditch and through the muddied water along the way. Elizabeth easily opened the door; howbeit, getting him up the steps was no small task. Darcy would occasionally ask where he was going, where was his friend, Bingley, or calling other indistinct names, but otherwise his words were limited to imprecations and oaths.

Elizabeth's former dealings with this gentleman left her with varied impressions. He was haughty, certainly, giving offence to all of Meryton in one evening alone, an admirable feat to be sure. However, she must admit that he was quite intelligent, and as it may be, somewhat handsome. Perhaps he gave offence wherever he went because the populace was wont to oblige him, thus reinforcing his ill behaviour. Although Elizabeth was not one to hold grudges and quickly forgot offences, a trait inherent in living with an off times disparaging mother, she found it difficult to forgive *his* vanity, as his had sorely injured her own.

At the Meryton Assembly, Elizabeth had been obliged, by the scarcity of gentlemen, to sit down for two dances; and during part of that time, Mr. Darcy had been standing near enough for her to hear a conversation between him and Mr. Bingley, who came from the dance for a few minutes to press his friend to join it.

"Come, Darcy," said he, "I must have you dance. I hate to see you standing about by yourself in this stupid manner. You had much better dance."

"I certainly shall not. You know how I detest it, unless I am particularly acquainted with my partner. At such an assembly as this it would be insupportable. Your sisters are engaged, and there is not another woman in the room whom it would not be a punishment to me to stand up with."

"I would not be so fastidious as you are," cried Mr. Bingley, "for a kingdom! Upon my honour, I never met with so many pleasant girls in my life as I have this evening; and there are several of them you see uncommonly pretty."

"You are dancing with the only handsome girl in the room," said Mr. Darcy, looking at Elizabeth's elder sister, Jane.

"Oh! She is the most beautiful creature I ever beheld! But there is one of her sisters sitting down just behind you, who is very pretty, and I dare say very agreeable. Do let me ask my partner to introduce you."

"Which do you mean?" and turning round he looked for a moment at Elizabeth, till catching her eye, he withdrew his own and coldly said, "She is tolerable, but not handsome enough to tempt me; I am in no humour at present to give consequence to young ladies who are slighted by other men. You had better return to your partner and enjoy her smiles, for you are wasting your time with me."

Mr. Bingley followed his advice. Mr. Darcy walked off, and Elizabeth remained with no very cordial feelings towards him. She told the story, however, with great spirit among her friends; for she had a lively, playful disposition, which delighted in anything ridiculous, and she had at that moment begun to think him so.

Mr. Darcy, unaware of her censure, continued in like manner throughout his brief stay at Netherfield while in the company of the locals. Elizabeth had not desired conversation with the man, and he could not distinguish her from amongst the other ladies present. The irony of her current situation amused Elizabeth. Here was the gentleman who would not dare to tolerate her company, and she was the one who at this moment determined his fate. Had he known the turn of events, surely he would have been more obliging, and maybe even acknowledged her upon first being offered introduction, but such was the turn of events. Elizabeth was not one for gloom and attempted to find the drollery in the situations presented to her; however, this diversion into levity was short-lived when she contemplated the reality of their plight. She had knowingly, but without consideration of the consequences at the time, involved herself in a situation that could have long-term repercussions on her reputation and as a result her future and that of her family.

Elizabeth had always been independent in her ways and thoughts. Her father educated her more like a man than a lady. She had never felt the need for protection and certainly did not see herself so vulnerable or inattentive as to place herself at risk for a compromise. However, here she was in a cabin with a man, not of her family, for an unknown duration.

Elizabeth surveyed this haven that could serve the purpose of either saving or indicting them. The cabin was a single room with a fireplace in the centre of the far wall. In the corner to her left was a bed that had a quilt pulled over the top and a blanket folded at its foot, and beside it stood a side table that had a washbasin and pitcher for cleansing. In the opposite corner sat a table with two chairs. There were four windows, covered with masculine yet simple window coverings, which would have let in ample light had the sky been clear, but here, nestled underneath a canopy of trees on a dismal day, the room was quite dark. The cabin looked as if someone had left things clean and ready for use, but that was likely at least two years ago.

Elizabeth contemplated leaving him in the cabin, now that he was out of the rain, and going for help. Surely, his friends would be able to arrive within a couple of hours. She had decided on this course and was going to check on him one last time to tell him of her plan and make sure his bandages were secure; however, when she went to his side, Elizabeth noticed that Mr. Darcy had begun to shiver rather forcefully. She could see he was experiencing worse effects from the cold rain than she had. After transporting him so far, Elizabeth was quite warm, but Mr. Darcy was soaked through. She realised that she could not leave him in the cold, if sheltered, room alone, at least not without a fire to give him some warmth.

Once her decision was made, she got to the occupation at hand. First, she needed to get a fire going. A few pieces of wood remained by the hearth. Additional wood rested on the porch outside and remained dry, as it had been placed underneath the cabin's awning. She gathered a few loads of wood and some pieces of kindling to start the fire in the cabin's single fireplace, while lamenting the realisation that the supply could last but a few hours. Elizabeth's education had lacked the building of fires; nonetheless, she had watched Sarah at home plenty of times, and she felt up to the task. Indeed, she was able to get a blaze going without too many difficulties and hoped the small fire could warm the room adequately.

Although the fire began to generate some warmth, the cabin's chill was difficult to overcome. Mr. Darcy was lying on the floor before the fire and occasionally moaned and asked in succession who was with him. Elizabeth would answer, repeating herself verbatim with each query, "Mr. Darcy, I am Miss Elizabeth Bennet; you fell off your horse, and I have brought you to safety." She had to suppress a giggle as she considered his repetitions. She knew his situation was serious, but Elizabeth, having learnt to handle hardship with satire, found some bit of humour – the intelligent and august Mr. Darcy with muddled faculties.

After having rested from her exertion of the past few hours, she noticed how decidedly cold was the room. Her layers of clothing would not soon dry, and neither would Mr. Darcy's. He continued to shiver, as Elizabeth again contemplated going for help. She opened the door and noticed that the rain had intensified, not diminished, and that the thunder was increasing in volume, yet again. It was impossible that she could leave now.

If Elizabeth were to adhere to propriety in all its limitations, she considered that she would be safe from the gossips and consequences inherent in spending time alone with a young man. He was obviously unable to compromise her person in actuality, due to his injuries, and surely this would be taken into account by anyone who might discover their location. Unfortunately, if they were not discovered soon, the delay would compromise Mr. Darcy's chance at recovery, if not her reputation.

As long as Mr. Darcy remained in wet clothing, no amount of heat from the small fire could provide adequate warmth. Add to that, the temperatures had been dropping outside. Elizabeth was afraid of his becoming fevered and felt a responsibility to keep him safe. Although realistically, she could not have prevented his accident, she did consider that had she not been in his path, his misfortunes would have been limited to getting caught in the rain on the way back to Netherfield.

Elizabeth reviewed her options. She first considered what Mr. Darcy would want and expect of her. She could ask him, but he lacked clarity of mind, and his thoughts were disordered, most likely not a true reflection of his veracious inclinations. She asked anyway. "Mr. Darcy, I am afraid that your wet clothes will only serve to keep you in a miserable and perhaps dangerous chill. What would you have me do for you?"

"Cold," he moaned as his body shivered, but Elizabeth could not make out the rest of the words.

She retrieved the coverings from the bed to place on him but then hesitated; the blankets remained the one dry option for modesty's sake and for the warmth they could provide, but only if kept dry. While he was soaking wet they would do little to protect him. Elizabeth said a quick prayer for guidance and peace about her decision. This choice, though necessary for Mr. Darcy's wellbeing, could have lasting consequences on her life and peace. She decided to wait a few more minutes, hoping another option would come to her, or that they would be miraculously discovered. But as no other satisfactory alternatives presented themselves, Elizabeth determined that Mr. Darcy's health was to be the primary consideration. If he were to become irrevocably ill, Elizabeth could not escape her culpability, and so she responded accordingly.

Elizabeth bent down to Mr. Darcy's side and told him her plans. She would attempt to warm him by removing some of his wet clothing and then covering him with a dry quilt. As he did not reject her declaration, she proceeded to take off his greatcoat by turning him from one side to the other. Elizabeth found this whole experience rather disconcerting, yet mildly humorous. If her sister, Jane, had told her yesterday that she would be undressing a gentleman today, they would have been excessively entertained by the notion. Elizabeth certainly had never expected she would behave so brazenly at any point as a maiden. Her standards for propriety exceeded that of the most exacting lady. She appreciated the irony of her life on this day, but quickly moved on to more serious thoughts, as she conceded that she was not even particularly familiar with a man's attire.

Elizabeth began to unbutton Mr. Darcy's jacket. She found more difficulty when trying to remove this layer, as his clothing was snug, made more so by the moisture. Elizabeth had often wondered if a valet was truly necessary for the dressing, or in this case, undressing of men. She had never suspected the inherent obstacles, until now. She then tackled his waistcoat and cravat, placing them on a hook embedded within the rocks of the hearth, that they might dry.

So far, Elizabeth felt like she had succeeded in ridding him of his wet garments while maintaining respectability, should their location be revealed. From here on, she must be discreet in her efforts. Taking mental note of his form, she pondered whether he might benefit from more of his wardrobe being removed. She could not help but notice the man's muscular and well-proportioned physique. He would be handsome, if not so arrogant; Elizabeth could not admire a man who felt himself above his company. In the end, she resolved that she could not, and would not, remove any other layers of his attire; a blanket would have to suffice.

Elizabeth recognised the possible benefit of repositioning the bed in front of the fire in order to get Mr. Darcy off the floor. In this way, he would be more comfortable, while keeping the chill of the ground from seeping into his frame. Elizabeth promptly dragged the wooden bed, being more the size of a cot, towards the hearth. "Mr. Darcy, I am going to lift you onto this bed. You will be more comfortable if I can get you off the floor." He nodded and attempted to assist her, which made the task easier for her shaky legs, but unfortunately, the movement brought on more discomfort for the man than the effort may have been worth. She covered him with the blanket and pushed the bed as close to the fire as possible.

She then regarded his left boot and the possible benefits of its removal. His ankle might be sprained or even broken based on the unnatural angle of his foot while being dragged by his horse. Despite being in and out of consciousness during the journey to the cabin, Mr. Darcy's moans and verbal outbursts reflected the pain that had afflicted him. Elizabeth suspected that the snug boot might be cutting off the circulation to his injured foot, owing to the possible swelling in his ankle. It was decided; she had to get the boot off.

Deliberating how best to proceed, she thought to attempt pulling off the offending boot, but in the end acknowledged this might damage his ankle even more. She hoped that Mr. Darcy would have the cognition to help her, so bending down closer to him, she tried to explain the problem. He pointed to the dagger hidden within its mate. Did Mr. Darcy suppose that he might run across a highwayman during his morning exercise? She smiled to herself. Perhaps he did think their ways rather savage.

Forgetting her distracting mirth yet again, Elizabeth got to the task before her. She soon found that cutting off the boot would not be as easy as she had anticipated. She started at the top and methodically began the slow process of splitting the fine leather of his costly Hessian, careful not to touch his leg with the sharp tip. Mr. Darcy was quiet and still as she worked, dozing in and out of slumber. After a full twenty minutes had passed, she completed her efforts and was able to cautiously remove the boot. She was startled by what she saw. Even through his stocking, she could see that his ankle was indeed swollen with dark bruising, and his toes were white and cold. She pulled off the wet stocking and instinctively began to gently rub his toes with her hands in an attempt to enhance the circulation, but any movement to his ankle caused him to yell out more expletives. He was obviously not as refined as he would have others believe him, and Elizabeth, in her love of irony, found this thought somewhat refreshing. After wrapping his ankle in strips of fabric from her petticoat to minimise movement, she raised his injured foot onto a makeshift pillow using his own greatcoat and gently tucked the blanket under him

Elizabeth marked that the bandage on his head was again in need of replacing, so she removed her handkerchief from the sleeve of her pelisse. She folded it into a small square and secured it where the blood soaked strip had rested. His bleeding had abated but would still likely ruin her sister's handiwork – the handkerchief had been a gift from her elder sister, Jane. Nonetheless, the fabric was softer and cleaner than her dwindling petticoat and the perfect size for the task.

Her efforts finally catching up to her, Elizabeth sat on the side of the bed for a moment to rest. Tears again threatened to spill over onto her cheeks. *Please, Lord, take this burden from me.* Determining that she should remove herself from the cot – and the room if it were possible – she stood, now trembling from fatigue and the chill. Nevertheless, thirst and hunger soon overcame any other feeling that she had, as she regretted forgoing the usual breakfast roll that she had done without in her haste to leave the house. But thirst she could resolve as there was plenty of water to be found outside.

Elizabeth looked around the small room for something to use to gather water and spotted the pitcher and washbasin on the small table next to where the cot had been. She opened the latch of the door to take it outside, causing a cold wind to blow into the cabin. Her wet clothes could not protect her from the biting chill, but they must have water, so out she went. Although the rain was coming down steadily and could have provided plenty for her purposes if she would but set out the bowl, she decided to go to the well. She was already wet, and it would be quicker. She was rewarded for her efforts, as she was able to draw up a full bucket of clean water, which she added to the pitcher. By now, her hair had completely escaped the pins of her hastily assembled chignon. She attempted to brush aside the long strands that were determined to cling to her face, as she hastened indoors to get out of the frigid wind and rain, spilling some of her efforts along the way.

With numb hands, she carried the pitcher to the table. Hanging upon the stones of the fireplace was a ladle. Her hands were shaking as she scooped out some water and drank. When Elizabeth had her fill, she offered some to Mr. Darcy, requiring that she help lift his head from behind as he took a sip. After he swallowed, he turned his head aside, saying "No more. Please stop."

Although the water went far to cure Elizabeth's thirst, in the long run it actually made her colder than before. The trip out into the rain renewed the chill that had set in deeply, and she began to shiver uncontrollably while she paced around the room. *If I keep moving, perhaps I can stay warm.*

After a little while, Elizabeth stopped her pacing and glanced over to Mr. Darcy, who, to her, seemed in a deep slumber. If she could but remove some of her wet clothing and hang it by the fire to dry, while leaving on her undergarments, she felt that she could wrap up in the quilt for modesty and warmth. But then the thought intruded upon her that at any moment, they might be discovered, and she would surely be found wanting in propriety, modesty and all things decent. However that may be, her body shook; she could not continue in her present state, and it was unlikely they would be found while the rain continued in torrents. After adding another piece of wood to the fire, Elizabeth removed and set aside the rest of the pins from her hair.

Checking Mr. Darcy again for any sign that he might rouse, Elizabeth was satisfied and began to unbutton her woollen pelisse, which had somewhat protected her from the wind and chill, but could not fight the deep cold. She hung the pelisse on the hook that had held the ladle, and turned it towards the warmth of the small fire. Although her hands were still numb from the chill, she was able to quickly unbutton her dress, which thankfully fastened up the front, as she had prepared for her walk alone this morning. She then dropped it down over her shoulders. Elizabeth watched Mr. Darcy the entire time while removing the garment, and satisfied that he truly was not going to see her, she stepped out of the gown and turned to the fire to figure out how to hang her dress so that it might quickly dry. She saw a broom on the other side of the fireplace leaning against the corner. Using the top of the broom as a hook, she hung her dress there. Since she had quickly dressed this morning and saw no need for a corset, she only had her chemise remaining, as her petticoat had been sacrificed to Mr. Darcy's care. As a result, she was quite exposed. Elizabeth turned to grab the quilt, and realised that in her haste to get out of her wet garments, she had inadvertently left it on the other side of the fireplace; she quickly reached for her covering and put it around herself. Mr. Darcy stirred, and Elizabeth turned around to see if he still slept. He was reaching up to his head and rubbing his temples, eyes open.

"Mr. Darcy, do you need something? May I fetch you some more water?"

"No. Umm I thank you. No," he stammered, face turning red.

Elizabeth was unsettled, suspecting that he had likely been staring at her form. She leaned down and pulled his blanket up to his shoulders since his movement had caused him to uncover himself. He looked away. She wrapped herself more tightly with the quilt and turned towards the fire, certain now that he had regarded her at least for a moment while she removed her wet clothing. In her exhaustion, she felt provoked. She could be home by now warm in her dressing gown by a blazing fire with hot tea to her lips, without consideration for his health. She determined to ignore the man unless he asked specifically for assistance. Turning towards the fire again with the quilt securely around her shoulders, yet open towards the warmth, she leaned into the small blaze, adding pieces of wood as needed.

How long she was standing thus, she did not know, but her chemise had begun to dry. When checking, she saw that Mr. Darcy's clothing was further along than her own, and so was ready to flip over. Elizabeth had been diligently tending to the clothes when he spoke. "Excuse me, Miss uh, Miss…. Well, I am in need of some time alone."

Elizabeth turned his way. "There is no where for me to go, sir. What do you propose?"

He turned scarlet. This was obviously very difficult for him. Elizabeth could not help but inwardly smile at his now feeling the discomfort of the situation, as she had felt since their arrival.

"Forgive me, but I am in need of relieving myself, and I must have some privacy. Can you please bring me the chamber pot, assuming there is one, and then leave me?"

Now it was Elizabeth's occasion to turn scarlet. "Of course. I, well, I don't know." She began searching the room for the requested item or something that could work in its stead. There was a room outside for such things, but with the downpour and his inability to walk, there really was no way to accommodate him. She had exhausted her search of the cabin, and so decided to look outside on the porch where she had remembered some pieces of tin. She opened the door and found on the porch, under the awning and next to the remnant of firewood, a tin bucket. *Well, this will have to do.*

With embarrassment, she brought the bucket to him. As she handed it over, she looked away. "And what is this for?" he asked, incredulously.

"This is not Netherfield, sir. We are in a cabin, a usually uninhabited cabin, in the woods. There is a place outside for those who need privacy, but I am afraid this is all I can offer you under the circumstances. You can make use of what I have provided, or you can wait out the storm; I care not."

Mr. Darcy had never been spoken to by anyone in this way, ever, not even by his cousins, who were equal to him in every way, and he was incensed. "Miss…"

"Elizabeth Bennet."

"Miss Bennet, you must leave."

"I can step outside for a moment and leave you to your privacy; then you may call out to me to return. I just ask that you make quick work of things, as it is quite cold outside, and I have hardly recovered from my last excursion." On that note, Elizabeth turned and headed for the door, head held high, as she attempted to sound more in control than she actually was. She had upon first observing the entrance of the Netherfield party at the assembly, thought Mr. Darcy to be quite attractive with or without his fortune, but their few interactions since that initial moment had left her feeling that perhaps her first impressions were at fault. He spoke to no one and had little energy to exert himself for local society, an insult not easily forgiven for a young woman with Elizabeth's confidence.

Elizabeth was shivering again, when she heard him call her from within, having left the door ajar to hear him over the rain. She returned to the room with the last of the firewood and found him, his right arm resting over his eyes, with a pained expression on his countenance. She approached him and he handed her the bucket. "See to this, then you may give me some more water."

Taking a deep, stabilizing breath, Elizabeth walked over to the man who lay by the fire. She collected the bucket and headed back outside to dispose of its contents, feeling fully the degradation of the chore. It is not that she had never emptied a chamber pot before; of course she had at various times when up during the night caring for one of her sisters, but she had never assisted a man, especially one who looked at her with contempt. He was of the upper ranks of society; she knew that contrary to Mr. Bingley's assessment, that Mr. Darcy obviously despised the lower gentry. She could see the disdain in his eyes over dinner and at the local social events of the past week. Nevertheless, as was her nature, Elizabeth determined to find the humour in her present situation. Mr. Darcy resembled everyone else at the base level; everyone needed the chamber pot, no matter how highborn.

Elizabeth drew some water from the pitcher to share with her patient, assisting him in sitting up. He drank all that was there, and then with her help, lowered himself slowly back down, the dizzying effects of sitting up taking its toll on his spirits and patience.

"Now, you may go find help."

"Mr. Darcy there are two things that keep me from following your command – that I am sure you have thought long and hard over. If I could remove myself and not be considered negligent of your care, believe me, I would, but I cannot in good conscience leave you alone. I have struggled with alternatives for many hours now and have come up with no other option but to remain; however, I can assure you that I do not like this situation any more than you do.

"In addition to your present condition, the rain has not abated since we arrived. The temperatures have dropped significantly, and we are two, maybe three miles, from my home, Longbourn, in one direction and Netherfield in the other. Do you propose that I don my wet clothes and take on the storm outside?"

Mr. Darcy muttered with sarcasm, not lost on Elizabeth, "I am sure you speak things as you see them."

"Sir, I am a gentleman's daughter. I do not know what you are implying, but I can assure you that I find the predicament in which we find ourselves quite unsettling; however, what's done is done. Neither you nor I can go back and change what has happened up to this point, so we must make the best of a difficult situation. And that is what I intend to do." Remembering that he too had experienced a rough and trying day, for the time being Elizabeth decided from now on to demonstrate grace and to avoid casting judgement upon his character regardless of the provocation.

AFTER PUTTING THE LAST of the firewood into the small hearth, Elizabeth, keeping the quilt tightly drawn around her, pulled a chair up to the fire and next to the cot. She sat down for nearly the first time since she set out that morning. Hours had passed, but it was difficult to tell how many as the sky remained concealed by the cloud cover and continuous rain. The fiercest part of the storm had passed, and Elizabeth was certain that they would soon be found, if not by her own family then by Mr. Darcy's friends. Their future might depend upon the identity of their rescuer. Seeing that Mr. Darcy was much more lucid, to get her mind off the unwanted circumstances, Elizabeth thought that conversation was in order. "We must have some conversation, Mr. Darcy, though very little would suffice."

"I have no objection to hearing you, but I have no desire to perform my share. Talking increases my discomfort." Must he be subjected to her twaddle?

"Do you like books, Mr. Darcy?" After a pause, Elizabeth continued, "I am in the midst of reading a newly acquired novel." She watched his expression to follow his reaction to the news. She was rewarded with a slight smirk. "I love a novel above all things, and this one in particular leaves me quite distracted. Do you care to know of which book I speak?" This time she waited several moments before resuming. She found that she quite enjoyed observing his reactions to her monologue. He was attempting to show no interest; nonetheless, if he was as bored as she, and as in need of a preoccupation to distract from their predicament, then he was likely listening attentively, if not openly.

"*The Italian.* I find that my favourite stories are the ones that most mimic reality. Finding similarities in stories to match real life can be quite entertaining, if one enjoys observing the characters around us. The author of this particular story has included some outrageous coincidences, which I also find amusing." After some reflection, Elizabeth continued, "The heroine, an upright and moral creature of seemingly low birth, attempts to follow her conscience and keep to her own social sphere as a way to protect herself from the evils of the upper class, but love intervenes. Fortunately for her, the one whom she loves, Vivaldi, is also moral and upstanding, always doing what is right in the sight of God and his own conscience; however, he finds that his heart rules him. He cannot overcome his impassioned love for Ellena. His mother, the Marchesa, maliciously schemes to keep her son and his undeserving lover apart, sending each of them on perilous journeys across the countryside and into the Inquisition and the mercy of a murderer. Ironically, of all the characters, Ellena is the noblest of all and the most deserving of happiness; nevertheless, her rank in their culture would keep her locked away if possible. Of course if she were not beautiful, then her situation would be safe, for who would give up his station in life and family for someone unpleasant to look upon? Will their love survive? In novels, everything comes to good in the end, so I would imagine so. I plan on completing my book, now that I am no longer expected to entertain our guest."

Although Mr. Darcy would not at first acknowledge that he was listening to her chatter, due to the difficulties related to nausea when opening his eyes and his not wanting to give this woman any more attention than she deserved, he was indeed listening. After several minutes had passed, and after Elizabeth was sure that he had fallen back asleep, he said, "I imagine your book was written by a woman of average standing in society. What could she know of the expectations of those with rank, of the nobility? She obviously writes about that which she knows nothing."

"So by your estimation, the author can have no understanding of the character and actions of those who may have different backgrounds from herself? I confess that I have always found that observation of others outside of our own circles could lend enlightenment to their possible actions and motivations. There are those of the aristocracy who lower themselves, at least to a degree, in order to marry their choices. You cannot deny this. And if this is indeed noticed in real life, could the author not also determine that her characters are to enjoy the same advantage?"

"Advantage to whom? Surely not to the Marchesa's son, or his parents. Their standing in society will, of course, diminish. There can be no advantage there."

"I suppose we must define advantage. For surely, having the freedom and will to marry whom one chooses could be considered advantageous by some, if not by most."

"You, miss, have been reading fairy tales. You can have no understanding regarding the personal decisions of those of consequence. Your environs provide little variety with which to make an informed judgement."

"Mr. Darcy, all people have hopes, dreams and inclinations towards finding happiness. Of course, the means of finding such joy may vary amongst people, but in general, no matter a person's station, finding a true love match must have significant value. Even kings and queens have sought felicity in the arms of a sanctioned lover. Dissatisfaction in the marriage state drives men and women alike into the arms of others, due not necessarily to the desire for profligate behaviour, but out of a yearning to feel loved and to show love. Of course, simply a desire to experience feelings of wanton joy does not justify such actions, but I cannot help but wonder if extramarital pursuits would not diminish, if society in general put more value in marrying for love rather than the material advantages."

"And you have learnt by observation about the licentious tendencies of the upper class, Miss Bennet?"

"It is all over the gossip section of the paper." When he sneered, she responded, "Do you find it more improper to read the gossip or to create it? I own that I prefer the former, but then I have never claimed to be in the same league as the upper class when it comes to ability to create gossip." The irritation clearly present on Mr. Darcy's face provided Elizabeth a source of dearly needed amusement. She was not a mean sort of girl, but she did enjoy creating a response in someone so intent on having none.

Darcy was shocked at such a speech from a supposed gentlewoman; that she would express her opinions so openly to a gentleman was unseemly and unheard of. He responded in silent reflection, thus ending the conversation.

Elizabeth, sensing she had yet again gone too far, remained silent as well, rather spending time in contemplation of her escape. The rain had lessened, and she decided that Mr. Darcy was well enough to be left alone while she sought help. Elizabeth considered that the course of events would be better arranged if she were not actually with Mr. Darcy when found. Elizabeth stood to inspect her dress to see if during the course of the past few hours, it had dried sufficiently. When standing, she realised how she had over-exerted herself with no nourishment to replenish her long spent energy. Her legs wobbled below her, a feeling Elizabeth had never had the disadvantage of experiencing, unlike other ladies with less stamina. She leaned upon the chair as the light-headedness passed.

Fortunate to find her gown tolerably dry, considering the fire had dwindled from its already reduced state, Elizabeth looked around the room to determine if there was somewhere that might afford her some privacy as she changed from the draping of a quilt to her clothes. She did not trust this Mr. Darcy, especially after her suspicions earlier, but there was no separation from him to be found. She suspected that although he was quiet and still, that he might yet be awake. Elizabeth would not give credit again to his appearance of sleeping, but still she must dress. Elizabeth checked to see if his coat and waistcoat were ready for him to put on, and although still somewhat damp, could likely be worn without too much discomfort.

"Mr. Darcy, I find that our clothes are no longer soaking wet; we could likely put them back on without too much of a chill. I would be willing to assist you as you need, since I know that raising your head can be rather painful for you, but I also ask that you give me the privacy that I need in order to dress myself first."

"Then go to it."

"As there is no where within the confines of this room, the entire cabin really, in which to dress alone, I need to ensure that you will not look in my direction while I drop the quilt and put on my gown. I need no assistance, except in the privacy, which I beg you will give me."

"I am a gentleman, Miss Bennet. You can be assured of my providing you with whatever privacy you require to put yourself back into a state of decorum. I do not make a habit of sharing rooms with ladies, and I can assure you that I will give you no reason to suspect otherwise."

"That sounds commendable, but how can I know that I should trust you? You, who plead to be trustworthy, have given me no reason to believe in the veracity of such a claim. I have heard how men of means give the appearance of propriety, but behind closed doors, show every sign of debauchery that they can afford, and some they cannot."

16

"How dare you accuse me of impropriety, while frolicking around the room in nothing but a chemise and quilt!" He took a deep breath. "I give you my word as a gentleman; I will keep my eyes firmly closed. I have no desire of opening them just to be reminded of the situation in which you have placed me. I simply ask that you make quick work of things." This speech made his head pound as his anger took hold.

Elizabeth warily placed herself in a position where she could stand behind his head, so he would have to truly strain in order to see her. She suspected this would be impossible for him, as she had seen the effects of moving in one direction or the other. She did not trust this man, after suspecting that he had been gazing upon her, and she was determined to protect her privacy. Upon dropping the quilt, she quickly stepped into her dress, pulling it up to her shoulder, and buttoned the front. The seams had not yet dried completely, but overall, it was satisfactory. She then put on her woollen pelisse and felt much warmer than she had since their arrival, although still rather chilled. Her hair was adequately dry to pin back up, which she quickly accomplished. Feeling more herself, she offered to assist Mr. Darcy with dressing.

He replied to her inquiries, "I do not want help, as I am able to dress myself. You should not have removed my clothing in the first place, no matter how cold I seemed to be; you did so without my consent. I was perfectly comfortable with my clothes on; removing them has created a problem that could have been avoided. I have to wonder why you would have taken upon yourself the charge to doff *my* attire; surely the necessity was not sufficient for such a response. I marvel at your ingenuity in contriving such a gainful situation," said he with an unmistakeable implication of her guilt. "If you could please hand over my waistcoat, I can begin, and finish, hopefully before we are discovered."

Elizabeth was no simpleton; she now fully understood the implication of his words. Mr. Darcy was accusing her of manipulation, of taking advantage of the situation in which they found themselves, perhaps even of manufacturing the business, as ridiculous as that could have been. She removed the waistcoat from its resting place and turned to hand it over to the conceited man before her.

Mr. Darcy attempted to rise to his elbows to accept and don his waistcoat; however, as Elizabeth was handing it over to him, nausea overtook him, and he vomited straight onto her newly dried gown. If not for the vertigo, Mr. Darcy may have felt mortified, but the movement of the room overtook his senses and all he could do was drop back down to the cot, eyes closed.

Tears sprang to Elizabeth's eyes, and this time she could not contain them, but there was no need for concealment now, as Mr. Darcy was far more engrossed in his own misery. She dropped the garment and rushed over to her petticoat, happy that there was still some available. After ripping off another portion, she began wiping off the emission that had landed on her clothing. This was too much to bear. His accusations and disrespect added insult to her efforts to correct the debacle. Having to bear his physical ailments and provide relief to him, all while he condemned her, was beyond her ability to cope. Elizabeth was a reasonable woman; she could easily discern the truth of a situation and give merit and concession when due, but at this point, she was beyond seeing anything other than her own injury. The tears flowed as she cleaned the mess, the odour filling her senses. *Did I err in removing Mr. Darcy's clothing?* Elizabeth had attempted to be reasonable in her decisions concerning his care, but could her judgement have been clouded by her exhaustion? Since entering the cabin, Elizabeth's fatigue unceasingly bore down upon her. Perhaps she had let her usually astute judgement lapse. But there was no going back; what was done was done.

Wearily, Elizabeth dried her tears with another strip of petticoat, which had diminished to only a wide band. As she cleaned the mess on her dress, she again resolved to take action now and leave the cabin to get Mr. Darcy medical attention and, if possible, have him removed to somewhere more comfortable. With languor, she started back to Mr. Darcy's side. Surprisingly, Elizabeth found that this small amount of activity made her feel quite lethargic, as she leaned on the back of her chair. She then noticed her brow was moist with perspiration despite not having exerted herself.

Amongst the five siblings, Elizabeth had always been the healthiest and least prone to illness. She always attributed that to her time in the open air and to her hearty appetite. She seldom developed ailments, and when she did, they were of short duration; this did not mean that she was completely immune to a malady. Recently, her sister Kitty, and before her Mary and Jane, had succumbed to a cold which was introduced into the home by their servant, Sarah. Elizabeth had developed a few sniffles herself, but even that seemed to have resolved.

Although, in the past hour she had begun to demonstrate signs of a resurgence of her illness, she refused to acknowledge the possibility. Elizabeth was now determined to go. Although she had remained chilled throughout her time in the cabin, her shivering increased in earnest, despite having donned her outerwear. Just then, a sneeze from Elizabeth startled her patient. "Forgive me for disturbing you. I am about to leave for Longbourn to find help that will restore you to your friends."

Eyeing her warily, he responded, "In the rain? Why not go to Netherfield if your goal is to seek assistance for my sake?"

"Mr. Darcy, I know you need aid that I cannot provide, and the rain has slowed down to where I believe I can remain protected underneath my pelisse. The fewer people who know of our time alone together, the better. My father and his staff will know how to keep this whole affair checked."

"Or attempt to coerce a betrothal."

"My father is a reasonable man. He trusts me and would be able to discern in but a moment that you have been unable to impose yourself upon me." She sneezed again. "His servants are loyal and able to keep this noisome mess quiet."

"And your mother? Is she as reliable as your father in protecting the interests of visiting neighbours?"

At this, Elizabeth paused, embarrassed that Mr. Darcy had obviously learnt more about her family by observation than she had hoped. "I am certain my father will help to extricate me from this situation. As I am his favourite and as he has promised never to insist I marry someone I clearly do not wish to, I know he will deal with the difficulties. All my mother need know is that I found myself caught in the storm. You will be found coincidentally, and no one need know we were together, alone." While looking for her handkerchief, she sneezed yet again, then again.

"If you go to Netherfield, I am certain Bingley will more quickly and quietly find me aid, which of course will include my valet. No one at Netherfield would desire to spread rumours of our time alone. Can the same be said of Longbourn?"

He had her there. Although she sincerely believed her father would protect her reputation and future at all cost, she could not say the same for her mother, or three younger sisters for that matter, if she could not conceal her whereabouts. Another sneeze interrupted her thoughts. *I really must find my handkerchief.* "The servants at Netherfield, can they be trusted?"

She had him there, but he was not about to relent. He knew that if her father found them, he could push for a betrothal, which Darcy knew would be within his rights. Her entire family could be ruined by her machinations, whether she knew the possible consequences for her actions or not. She sneezed again. "If you do not have your handkerchief, I have one in my coat pocket."

Just then, Elizabeth realised she had used hers earlier, and it currently resided on Mr. Darcy's head. Why this was amusing to her, she did not know. Nothing about her situation was amusing, but her nature was to laugh at absurdities, so she responded with a slight giggle.

"Are you laughing at me?"

"No, I apologise if you thought that I might find something diverting about you. I can see that you do not appreciate a little humour, especially at your own expense. I just realised where my handkerchief is, and thought how silly of me." At his puzzled expression, she pointed to his head. "I used it earlier to control the bleeding. I had forgotten." But then with a frown, she continued, "It was one of several – gifts from my sister, Jane. She embroidered my initials on it."

"Please, then I insist you use mine." As directed, Elizabeth retrieved the cloth from his coat pocket, just as a new sneeze escaped. "You are ill."

"No, a little cold air has never made me sick before. I just have a tickle in my nose," said she, while trying to appear unaffected. Mr. Darcy looked more closely at her and noticed that she looked flushed, and her eyes appeared weary.

"I think not."

"Well, it cannot be helped, either way. I will not argue with you. You need help, and I need to seek it, preferably at Longbourn."

Stubborn woman.

Elizabeth stood and faltered, leaning upon the chair. She glanced at Mr. Darcy, hoping in vain that he had missed that little performance.

"Miss Bennet, although I regret saying so, you must see that you cannot go out in the cold rain without protection in your weakened condition."

"Mr. Darcy, I am not an incapacitated, delicate woman, and if I want to go out in this weather, I will. I appreciate your concern, especially in light of our current circumstances, but I will not wait a moment longer for someone to discover us. I am determined that we will not be found alone together. I will not be moved from my course!"

Yet Elizabeth was too late.

Chapter Two

All men make mistakes, but a good man yields when he knows his course is wrong, and repairs the evil. The only crime is pride.
Sophocles, Antigone

"Papa! Thank God you are here," Elizabeth exclaimed as she turned to the opening that revealed her father. She quickly moved towards the door, bringing on a slight dizzy spell. "And Mr. Bingley, hello. Your friend, Mr Darcy, is within." With a look of profound relief, Mr. Bingley entered the cabin behind her father, along with two servants.

"Elizabeth, you will forgive my intrusion, but your mother insisted I look for you. I have not had a moment's peace since you were discovered missing this morning at breakfast. But, I knew how it would be. You are safe and no doubt, used your wits to make that so." Her father kissed her cheek then surveyed the room. "I do believe you have found your way here before, if I am not mistaken."

Relieved at his teasing tone, Elizabeth smiled. "I do believe you are correct, Papa." She turned to see that Mr. Darcy's friend had found him. "Mr. Bingley, he struck his head when he fell from his horse. He may benefit from a doctor, as I believe he has a concussion. For now, he really must be kept still."

"Darcy, you look awful!" Mr. Bingley exclaimed as he looked down to his friend who still wore Elizabeth's handkerchief upon the side of his head.

"For God's sake, Bingley. Can you lower your voice?" Darcy responded, then added quietly and with meaning, "Are any servants with you?"

"Of course, I brought two footmen. We have been looking for you for hours. When the stable hands notified me of your horse's return without you, I gathered a group of men to begin the search. The others must still be on the east side of the estate. I confess that I was quite losing hope when I happened upon Mr. Bennet here in search of Miss Elizabeth. Apparently, she too has been missing all day. When we heard about her disappearance, we hoped that you might have found her, keeping her safe."

Mr. Bennet smirked. "Yes, well, we can now see that they are safe and secure. Mr. Darcy has done a remarkable job keeping my Lizzy out of harm's way. I believe that with a meal and some hot tea, she will be as good as new." He regarded his daughter and noticed that she looked quite unlike her usual self. Her weary eyes betrayed her worry and encroaching illness.

Mr. Bennet had a quick mind, and upon finding Mr. Bingley along the path, he realised the possible implications of the events of the day. If his daughter and Mr. Darcy happened to be found together, there could be trouble. News of their being alone together for the better part of the day would spread like a wildfire, especially if his wife or youngest daughters were to find out. He believed that he could keep the whole business quiet, but with servants involved, that task would be near impossible. He had left his own servants at home, feeling quite certain he would find his daughter safe somewhere without their help. He had many memories of searching for his second eldest, who would find herself lost when quite young, and up to some trouble as an older child, and more recently, caught outside when losing track of time. Therefore, before he ventured out of his study to look for her, he truly did not consider this to be an occasion to worry over, until he witnessed the disturbing remnants of the storm.

There were razed trees that blocked the main pathways, and some of the more shallow ditches were overflowing. But even the possibility of her having come to harm did not enter his mind, until he happened upon Mr. Bingley. He was not familiar enough with these gentlemen from London to trust either, should one of them find himself alone with any of his daughters. As they searched, at least he reasoned that Elizabeth was his most capable daughter of getting out of a scrape, but unfortunately, also the most likely of getting into one.

When Mr. Bennet had found Mr. Bingley, they were about half of a mile from their current location. Apparently, the younger man had been searching all over the grounds of Netherfield with no success and had ventured onto the property of Longbourn, hoping that perhaps Mr. Darcy had found his way there and would soon be found. As Mr. Bennet was more familiar with the landscape, Mr. Bingley had been relieved to find him and was soon rewarded for his trust in the older gentleman when he directed their path to his hunting cabin upon noticing the small amount of smoke coming from the chimney.

When entering the cabin, Mr. Bennet had been relieved; however, his relief was lessened when he saw that his suspicions were confirmed and Elizabeth did indeed find herself alone with a single man. Discovering that gentleman ill and incapable of causing any physical harm consoled Mr. Bennet somewhat; nonetheless, he knew the implications of her being found companionless with this gentleman, and with witnesses, even if his daughter did not. Of course with a loyal staff, there was a reasonably good chance nothing would come of the situation, but Mr. Bingley's servants were recently hired and likely local men, who would relish nothing better than to be in possession of such provocative gossip. Perhaps Mr. Bennet could persuade Mr. Darcy to pay for silence. Mr. Darcy had already expressed his feelings on Mr. Bennet's favourite daughter, so he knew that Mr. Darcy did not wish for an engagement any more than Elizabeth did. Of course, financially speaking, the match would be brilliant, but he knew his daughter could never be happy with the man, one whom she could not like or respect. He would not push the attachment if a scandal could be avoided.

"Bingley, I need to speak with you in private, if you can ask your staff to wait outside the door."

"Of course, Darcy," said Bingley, sending his men outside to await his summons.

Mr. Darcy glanced over to where Miss Elizabeth and her father were in conference on the other side of the room and then began speaking quietly to his friend, "Bingley, you have found me in a rather precarious situation. You must know that nothing untoward has happened that could justify Mr. Bennet in forcing an attachment with his family. Nevertheless, I have no doubt that he will try. My worth has been bandied about Meryton for the past week, and her father will most assuredly want to take advantage. If there is a way we could silence your staff, perhaps with a payoff, we may be able to avoid a scandal. I am not concerned about local gossip, but if the slander were to reach London, the results could negatively affect my plans and those of others totally unrelated to the Bennets. Bingley, it is imperative that we resolve this before anyone leaves the cabin."

"I see your point, although I am not certain that your assessment of Mr. Bennet is accurate. He seems a reasonable chap to me. Obviously, you have been unable to impose yourself on his daughter, even if it were within your nature."

"We will soon see. Please, Bingley, ask Mr. Bennet to join us."

Elizabeth and her father had been in quiet conversation. "Papa, I know our circumstances look rather dreadful, but I can assure you that nothing improper has occurred. I was on our property running along the path in an attempt to reach home before the worse part of the storm hit, when I was almost run down by Mr. Darcy's horse. When I screamed, the horse reared and so caused Mr. Darcy to fall. I had to get him out of the storm, so I brought him here, and he has been unable to do anything but lie there ever since. I have been seeing to his needs, but I promise, Papa, that *nothing* inappropriate has happened."

"I will own that I was worried when I considered you might be alone with a man. I trust you implicitly of course, but I am a man, and therefore know that men may have unsuitable thoughts, but many also choose to act on them, and with your being alone, you made yourself quite vulnerable."

The father and daughter had had this conversation before; she knew that she should never be alone with a gentleman unprotected. He allowed her walks, appreciating how important they were and also knowing that no one else at Longbourn could keep up with her to provide escort. But neither was of a nature to dwell on what could not be changed, so they determined to work on a solution to the problem. Just then Mr. Bingley invited Mr. Bennet to join his conversation with his friend.

Elizabeth came with her father as they crossed the room. "Sir, if you do not mind, I prefer speaking with you in private," Mr. Darcy stated calmly.

Mr. Bennet looked archly at the young man and emitted a soft chuckle. "I am afraid that your seemingly routine request will not be acceptable in this instance. Lizzy has every right to be included in the discussion that you wish to have."

Now I see where her impudence comes from. "Sir, I wish to have an unbiased discussion with you on the events of the day."

"Are you suggesting that my Lizzy would be anything but forthright?"

"I do not mean to offend, but surely you can see that Miss Bennet should not be included."

"I see no such thing. Lizzy, please join us." Mr. Bennet highly respected his daughter's intelligence, but also her discernment. She had remarkable insight and could likely contribute greatly to the topic at hand, especially in light of her being the only one who apparently had been fully cognisant of the entirety of the events of the day. Her future was at stake; he would not exclude her.

"Thank you, Papa," spoke Elizabeth softly, relieved to finally have her father with her and on her side.

"Mr. Darcy, I am listening," Mr. Bennet stated, in anticipation.

With reluctance Mr. Darcy began, "You must forgive me for not rising. I find that my injuries have left me unable to sit up, without the room spinning terribly. As you can see, and as your daughter can attest, I have found myself completely at her mercy since our encounter this morning, so you can be persuaded with objective evidence that nothing untoward has occurred this day in regards to your daughter. In addition, I can assure you, that even if I had not been injured, Miss Bennet would have been safe with me. I am a gentleman with principles that would forbid me from imposing upon her. I can offer you many character references, if you doubt the veracity of my words. I realise how our being alone for this time period may look to the populace of Hertfordshire – and the society of London, if the details were made known – but I am hoping that we can come up with an agreement that might keep the events from spreading, in order to spare your daughter from ruin, and me from scandal." This was about all the words that Mr. Darcy could string together at the moment. He closed his eyes and attempted to relax, despite his apparent agitation.

"I agree."

In surprise, Mr. Darcy replied, "You do?"

"Of course. My Lizzy has no wish to be married to you, and you obviously have no wish to be married to her, as merely tolerable as she is, so I have no desire to push the match." Darcy, not noticing the slight to which Mr. Bennet had referred, looked noticeably relieved. "However, if word gets out, and this becomes public knowledge, I expect you to perform your duty as a gentleman and as a contributor to this debacle."

"Papa, you cannot be in earnest!"

With a pained look to his daughter, Mr. Bennet replied, "Dear, you know the consequences should your time with Mr. Darcy become public knowledge. You will become the target of widespread gossip. Today's events are like food to a starving man if it gets into the mind of a relentless gossip. Truth means nothing, and no one will believe in your innocence, nor care about the injury that could come of spreading such blather. Once out, the tale will take on a life of it's own, like a cancer that cannot be stopped or cured. And if this becomes fodder for the gossip mill, I am afraid that we will have only one way to respond."

"I do not see that at all!" exclaimed his distressed daughter.

Looking pointedly at her, he replied, "Lizzy, I know that you do. If word gets out, you, as well as your sisters, will be forever ruined in local society. You know that should neither you, nor any of your sisters ever marry well, you would all be at risk of destitution. Now I do not plan on leaving this world anytime soon, but things happen outside of our control. I cannot in good conscience leave you and your sisters to the mercy of the kindness of others. If there were means of surviving the effects of the gossip, if there were an alternative for you, then I would not go this route, but truly, Lizzy, even if there were reasonable options for you as a companion or governess, your sisters do not deserve to suffer a life with no honourable marriage prospects."

Deep down, Elizabeth knew this. She had been contemplating the same conclusion throughout the day, but hearing her father state the truth was unnerving. She had hoped that he could and would come up with an alternative.

Mr. Darcy, witnessing this exchange, was certain that the two Bennets had been planning this to happen, knowing that news of their adventure would find its way into local society. Even in the short week in Hertfordshire, Darcy had heard Mrs. Bennet pushing forward her daughters and gossiping in her turn. All it would take is one word to his own wife, and Mr. Bennet's plan would be in place. "Sir, I believe that we can keep this whole business quiet. The only ones who know that I spent the day with Miss Bennet are Bingley's servants and the four of us. If we can persuade these men to keep quiet, surely no one need know, but if gossip related to this does spread, then the culpability of such an event would be laid squarely at your door. I am confident that I can keep this quiet, but to be honest, I do not trust you or your daughter to do such a thing. You have everything to gain and nothing to lose by spreading the events of today."

"Except my daughter's reputation and future happiness!" an angry Mr. Bennet retorted.

"Which would soon be rectified if I were forced to acquiesce and offer for her hand, which as a gentleman, I would be obligated to request."

Mr. Bennet had a long history of averting unpleasant conversations and was ready to leave this one behind. If not for the seriousness of the implications, he would have found a way to walk out with Elizabeth then, but he had to make his expectations clear to both Mr. Darcy and Elizabeth, as painful as that would be. "Mr. Darcy, you have my word that not a sound of this incident will leave this room. I know that there are those in my family who have weaknesses that might, in their ignorance, contribute to their own ruin. I promise that news of this will not spread by any means that I can avoid. I will do all in my power to escape a scandal, as you will be doing the same. I plan to tell those at Longbourn that Elizabeth was found alone by me on the opposite side of my estate. I will ensure that we return to Longbourn from that route in order to keep up pretences. It is up to you and Mr. Bingley to ensure that Mr. Bingley's men keep quiet; but I warn you, if word does get out, I expect you to do your duty as a gentleman. You were on my estate and nearly ran down my daughter. She has spent the whole of the day seeing to your comfort. I will not have her suffer the consequences of your accident alone."

"Bingley, call in your servants." Mr. Darcy would have preferred having this conversation standing. He was much taller than the average man and found that his imposing stature contributed greatly to his ability to intimidate others into relenting to his cause. Of course, he knew that this was an inappropriate way to achieve his own ends; however, he would use his assets to his benefit if needed, especially if good would come as a result. Unfortunately, today he would have to rely solely on his finances, which were also commanding.

As the men entered, they surveyed the situation before them. They may not have been well educated, but they were quick enough to determine how the following conversation would go. The master's friend had obviously gotten himself into a scrape. When his horse had returned to Netherfield without its rider, the household went into an uproar. Mr. Bingley assembled a search party, but had to wait on the storm to abate, and no one had had any luck finding Mr.

Darcy until now. Based on the circumstances before them, Mr. Darcy was obviously in good hands, safely ensconced in this cabin the entire time. His clothes were hanging up by the small fire, almost dry. A young lady, lovely yet clearly tired, had been attending to his needs, whatever they might be. Also, before them stood a concerned father, who would likely pay well for them to forget the scene in front of them; and if not the father, then the rich, young man who would find himself married within the month without their aid.

As servants, they had no hope to become elevated beyond their present state. Each was content with this knowledge, but having additional capital would add comforts to their lives, and if they played their cards right, could set each of them up for years to come. They waited for the conversation to unfold.

With as much focus as Mr. Darcy could muster, he began. "Men, I will not insult you with explaining the situation before you. As you can plainly see, you have found yourselves with uncommonly beneficial information. You know that I have been missing and have spent these last ten or so hours alone in this cabin with Miss Elizabeth Bennet. Neither of us planned for the events of the day to transpire, and I hope that she and I are in agreement that we would like to forget that they have and move forward with our lives without anyone the wiser. The only people who have any knowledge of our being here alone together are in this room. You are fortunate that I am willing to pay for your silence concerning anything that you have witnessed. Do we understand one another?"

The two servants glanced at one another, nodding when one returned, "Yes, sir. I believe we do."

Mr. Bingley, anxious to be of service to his friend, said, "You must also understand that if the events of today are spread after you have received payment, you will be dismissed without pay or reference."

"Yes, sir, but I must ask, how much are you talking about? We, of course, would not have thought to ask for money for our silence, but since you mentioned it, I am interested in what you have in mind," the other servant boldly asked. He knew that Mr. Darcy was in no condition to make demands and was the type of man to speak plainly.

"Two hundred-fifty pounds for each of you."

Their eyes widened. Not wanting to offend or come across as mercenary, the second footman said, "We accept." And the other nodded his agreement.

"Very well, then. I suppose we have a deal."

The footmen were dismissed to the porch for the time being, while the occupants made their final words. "Mr. Darcy, I thank you for your willingness to go to such lengths to avoid marriage to my daughter. That was very, uh, generous of you. However, I must tell you, that if word of this leaks, I still expect you to do your duty. I will not have my daughter ruined as a result of her attempting to help you."

Mr. Darcy despised the fact that he was vulnerable to the impending events. He was used to money and power paving his way. "There will be no reason for talk of settlements as long as you uphold your end of the bargain, sir. And as an added incentive, I would like to offer you compensation for your discretion." At Mr. Bennet's raised brows, he continued, "I would like to add one thousand pounds to your daughter's dowry as a good faith offering. I want to see this end here and now, and I am certain that you can see the benefit in accepting this financial offer of benevolence."

Elizabeth quickly glanced to her father. As she and her father often communicated with looks and gestures, she was familiar enough with his expressions to observe the anger that the others may have failed to notice. However, this time he chose not to cover his indignation with witticism. "Sir, you offend me. While you may have mercenary reasons to avoid a connection with my family, I can assure you money has no bearing on my choices for my daughter. You do not have enough money to affect my decisions regarding Elizabeth's happiness. And certainly there is no price that I could put on her happiness and wellbeing, which would be in jeopardy if married to you. She is worth more to me than your overflowing coffers. I would ask that you retract your financial offer post-haste before I send you out of my cabin and into the cold rain, despite your wounds."

Darcy preferred being in a position of authority. He had always effectively controlled his life and those around him with finesse and proficiency, and this man before him was attempting to thwart his purpose. Mr. Bennet would not take his money, which left him with no other avenue to influence him while in his weakened state. "Have it your way," is all Darcy said as he closed his eyes without a word to the woman who had been his caregiver for the day. He was anxious to return to Netherfield and to put this whole scene behind him.

In awkward haste, Mr. Bingley thanked Elizabeth for taking such prodigious care of his friend, wished them safe journeys on their way home, and promised to visit when the weather cleared. At that, Mr. Bennet and Elizabeth left the cabin.

MR. BENNET INSISTED that his daughter ride with him back to Longbourn on horseback. Elizabeth preferred walking to riding, but in this instance, she was in agreement. She trusted her father to keep her safe, despite her trepidation of sitting on a mount. She found herself too tired to attempt to walk, and despite the initial apprehension at being found by her father, alone with Mr. Darcy, she was relieved that she would not face the more than two-mile walk back home in the rain. Even she knew that little journey would have been too much for her.

Elizabeth and her father spoke little on the way home, which suited her well, for in her weakened state, she could not bear to hear her father's reproach, which was sure to come. However, prior to reaching Longbourn, he did broach the subject that they needed to discuss before entering the manor. "Lizzy, my dear. I know you have had a busy day, what with saving a great man, but we must make certain your mother and sisters learn nothing of your adventures. You got caught in the rain and remained until I found you. You chose not to come home, due to waiting out the storm."

"And where was I exactly while waiting for the rain to stop?"

"Let's say the stone folly on the south side of the estate, the one my grandfather built for his wife."

"A bit of romantic scenery; how ironic. The folly it is then." After a pause, Elizabeth continued, "Thank you, Papa. You have been very generous with me. I am desperately sorry to have put you in such a difficult situation, having to lie in order to protect me from my own bit of folly."

"You always have been talented at getting into a mess, but you do not deserve to be tied to a man who could not respect you, who would always look down on your origins. You were meant for better prospects, and I promise that I will do all in my power to keep you from a life of misery. But, if the events of today spread, … Well, we will not talk of that. You just take care of yourself; you have had a stressful day and by your appearance, you are becoming ill, a rarity indeed."

As they entered Longbourn, Elizabeth could hear her mother in the sitting room exclaiming, "Is that her; is that Lizzy? She will be the death of me; I am sure. Lizzy, come in this room at once!"

Elizabeth sighed and started towards the sound that was her mother. Her father stayed her, though. "Lizzy, my dear, go on upstairs, and I will explain everything to your mother. Hill, make sure you add wood to Lizzy's fire in her chamber and have hot water sent up. Sarah needs to be available to assist her." A relieved Elizabeth headed upstairs and was surprised to find herself winded with the effort.

Jane came up behind, hugging her tightly, "Lizzy, I was so worried. Are you well?"

"I am fine, just a little tired." Jane opened the door to their shared room and joined Elizabeth, who sat on the bed, leaning on the bedpost. Jane waited patiently for Elizabeth to elaborate. They were as close as two sisters could be and knew if there was anything to relate, that Elizabeth would in her own time.

Shortly after the young ladies entered the room, Hill, the family's faithful housekeeper, brought in some wood for the fire, followed by Sarah, the maid, bringing hot water for washing. "Miss Elizabeth, I will bring up some hot tea momentarily. Would you like anything else to go with that?"

"Some broth, cheese and bread would be lovely. Thank you, Hill." Once the servants had departed, Elizabeth turned to Jane. "I will share the events of the day, but first, I need to clean and change my clothes."

Jane Bennet, the closest to Elizabeth in age and understanding, held a special place in the life of her sister. They were confidantes and friends, despite being so different in personalities. Where Elizabeth was lively, witty and vivacious, Jane was soft-spoken, introspective and serene; nonetheless, there could be no two sisters as close. Elizabeth could trust Jane with any secret, but the question at hand in her mind was whether she should burden her with the events of the day. Elizabeth worried that Jane, as was her tendency, would agonise over something that could not be changed.

Jane assisted Elizabeth in removing her wet clothes and donning a warm dressing gown, after Elizabeth used the warm water to clean off the remnants of her day's activities. Following the arrival of the tea and small meal, she took out a brush and released Elizabeth's hair from the remaining pins. Elizabeth sat by the fire with her hot tea and attempted to find the warmth she had missed throughout the day. "Lizzy, you do look dreadful. Why do you not stay in your room for the remainder of the evening? I am certain Mama would understand."

"That does sound lovely, Jane, but I am afraid that you may be wrong about Mama. She will want me to join the family for supper. I'll just get a little rest in my room before coming downstairs." After a few minutes of Jane's ministrations with the brush, Elizabeth decided to tell Jane all. She selfishly needed someone to share her burden, and Jane was the one to take on that role. "Jane, this morning I decided to take a walk on the far side of the estate. You know that Mama has not let me out of the house since Mr. Collins's arrival, unless he was with me. Well, I was determined to get in some exercise before the storm hit, but I was lost in my thoughts before noticing that I had gone some distance. When I realised that the sky remained dark, despite the sunrise, I was nearly three miles from home. I turned and picked up my pace to run home." At Jane's raised brow, Elizabeth confirmed with a laugh, "Yes, I know, Jane. Ladies do not run across the countryside. And had I taken your advice today, I would have been well served, but as it was, in my haste, I did not notice a horse and rider bearing down upon me until it was too late. The curve in the path did not help either."

"Lizzy, you were unharmed? Who could have been riding at that time of day?"

"I am well, Jane. Please do not worry about that; I am just a little tired. My problems began when Mr. Darcy's horse threw him."

"Mr. Darcy? Poor man! Was he seriously harmed?"

"I believe he sustained a concussion, which can be dangerous, but mostly quite uncomfortable; if you will remember, I have had my own share. Also, his foot got stuck in the stirrup for a few moments when his horse bolted. I do not think that he broke any bones, but his ankle was sorely bruised, and probably sprained. At any rate, he could not walk."

"So what did you do?"

"I removed him from the path and pulled him nearly two hundred yards through thickets and brambles and across ditches and into the comforts of Papa's hunting cabin."

"Do be serious, Lizzy."

"I am in earnest," Elizabeth replied with a slight giggle. She realised how preposterous the whole story sounded. "Poor Mr. Darcy missed the entire adventure, as he was quite incognisant of his surroundings, which is good for him. He would have been quite put out after our rather unseemly trek across the woody countryside!"

"I cannot believe that you were able to move him so far. No wonder you are tired. But how is Mr. Darcy?"

"Actually, I was beginning to worry about him until he roused enough to speak to me, but that was when things really declined." At Jane's puzzled look, Elizabeth smiled and then continued. "I am being ungenerous. Mr. Darcy was in a sorry state. Every time he sat up, he would get light-headed and lose his stomach. At first, he would only stir periodically, but he did improve. In fact, we were having delightful conversations by the time Papa arrived."

"Lizzy...."

"Jane, he will be fine. Remember when I was fifteen and fell out of the tree? Within a week I was back outside. Truly, he will be well. When we left, he was negotiating with the servants to keep quiet about finding us alone together, after he charged my father to relent and not force a marriage, as if Papa would be so mercenary. Believe me when I say, Mr. Darcy will recover, no doubt sooner than he deserves."

"Lizzy, Mr. Darcy is not all that bad. Mr. Bingley thinks so highly of him. Surely, they would not be such close friends if Mr. Darcy were undeserving. Perhaps the injury to his head caused him to say things he would not normally say. You know when you fell out of the tree, you were quite unkind for the first two days."

"Jane, if it makes you feel better, I will try to only think charitable thoughts about the man. I am certain that I would not be so offended by his pride, had he not so completely mortified my own. See, is that not better?"

"But Lizzy, what was that you said about forcing a marriage? Surely you do not want to marry the man. That could not happen, could it? You dislike him so. It would grieve me to know that you would be pushed into matrimony with a man whom you could not love. Papa would never make you marry, if it were not your wish."

"Papa has already told me that he has no wish to force an alliance with Mr. Darcy. He dislikes him as much as I. You know Papa could not condone a man who would offend one of his daughters. He does have his own ration of pride, you know."

"Still, Lizzy, what if someone finds out and rumours begin to circulate? Would Papa not be compelled to make Mr. Darcy marry you?" At Elizabeth's frown, Jane added, "I am sure it will not come to that. Who was with Papa anyway, Lizzy?"

"Mr. Bingley and two of his footmen."

"His servants were with him?"

"Do not worry yourself overly concerning that. Mr. Darcy was prepared to pay quite well for the two to keep silent, and Mr. Bingley threatened their release from service without a referral. So you see, no one would have a desire to disseminate the event of our compromising situation. Everyone would lose and no one could win in such event." Elizabeth finished this with a feigned cheerful smile, which Jane knew was born out of fatigue and a desire to end the discussion.

"You need your rest. I will leave you and let you get some sleep."

"Thank you, Jane. I admit that I am finding it difficult to continue our conversation feeling the way I do. I need to lie down before eating anything, but let Mama know that I will be down for supper later." So Jane left, and Elizabeth crawled under the counterpane for some much needed rest. Elizabeth did not actually make it down for supper that evening, nor breakfast the next day. The events of that morning and afternoon had worn on her usual excellent health, and she was unequal to any activity beyond slumber.

The next morning, Jane became worried about her sister. Not only had Elizabeth not made it downstairs for supper, but she had also developed a fever, which was quite irregular for the usually robust, young woman. The convenience of such an illness, however, spared Elizabeth from her mother's reproofs, but such an advantage came at a heavy price, as Elizabeth felt the full misery of an untreated ailment. Elizabeth slept most of the day while Jane sat by her side, ready to offer a glass of water or some broth when she might awaken, but she woke little. When Elizabeth did arouse, she expressed her apologies for causing Jane such worry. She noticed the strain on Jane's features while she gently reapplied a cooling cloth to Elizabeth's face and neck. "Jane, you must be as tired as I. Please, do not distress yourself about me. This is but a trifling cold, I can assure you. All I need is a little more rest, which will not come easily if I am concerned about you."

"I always suspected you would make a poor patient, Lizzy. Now, you will let me repay you for all of your kindnesses shown to me in my many past illnesses." Elizabeth was too tired to argue, but wondered if her mother had made her way up to the sickroom while she slept, or if she were even concerned about her, as she most assuredly would be if Jane or Lydia were ill. Mrs. Bennet had made her opinion concerning each of her daughters quite clear, having no means to curb her own tongue. Elizabeth had long ago learnt to accept her mother's criticisms with grace, knowing that while she was her mother's least favourite daughter, she was her father's most cherished.

What Elizabeth had not realised was that her mother had indeed come to her room to check on her, mainly to give Jane the break and rest she needed in order to look her best. Mrs. Bennet did not want Jane to become ill herself or to have tired eyes should Miss Bingley or Mr. Bingley call upon the family. Jane would never have left Elizabeth, had she known that her fever would intensify, and certainly would not have left her in the negligent care of her mother.

Elizabeth had seemed to be resting comfortably, so their mother was taken off guard when her sick daughter began tossing in her sleep in a fevered sweat. Mrs. Bennet was about to call for Hill to take over, when Elizabeth began mumbling. At first, her mother paid no heed to the ramblings, but then heard the name Mr. Darcy and something about marriage. Elizabeth had tears falling down her cheeks. Her mother leaned in close and said, "Lizzy, what are you babbling about? Why would you marry that odious man?"

Elizabeth had been dreaming in her sick-induced state, imagining that Mr. Darcy had not spurned her presence. "Mr. Darcy... alone with you." Then there were more indistinct words. "Papa, I had to help him. It was my fault." Her mother began listening quite intently when Elizabeth then said the words, "marry him," and was shocked at what she heard. Mrs. Bennet was constantly occupied with the task of marrying off her five daughters. She had been distracted by the arrival of Mr. Collins and her plans to bring about a marriage between him and Elizabeth. She wanted Mr. Bingley for Jane, and Mr. Collins was quite good enough for her second oldest daughter. Although Elizabeth may not have been her favourite, her mother had to concede that she was the most intelligent of her five daughters and would make a fine mistress of Longbourn some day. Her plans were abruptly changed when Mr. Collins began paying special attention to her least beautiful daughter, Mary. She truly did not much care which of her daughters he married, as long as it was one of them, *and not Jane or Lydia*. She could not have sacrificed them to a man whose only virtue was his future inheritance.

Listening to Elizabeth's stammering, her mind whirled. *Was Elizabeth with Mr. Darcy during that awful storm? But Mr. Bennet said she had been stuck in that old folly. Could they have been in the folly together? How romantic!* A big smile spread across her face. *That clever girl! I knew she was not made to be so sly for nothing.* Mrs. Bennet giggled to herself. *Wait until I tell Sister.*

But, alas, she could in fact *not* wait, so Mrs. Bennet put down the cooling cloth, checked herself in the mirror and set off without delay for Meryton where Mrs. Philips resided, leaving Elizabeth feverish and alone in her sickbed, unaware that the course of her life had just changed.

Chapter Three

"The proud person always wants to do the right thing, the great thing.
But because he wants to do it in his own strength,
he is fighting not with man, but with God."
Søren Kierkegaard
Provocations: Spiritual Writings of Kierkegaard

Darcy found himself quite unequal to any type of manoeuvring for the next three days. His head injury, although not dangerous, made him utterly nauseated whenever he lifted himself. His memory was intact concerning the entire episode on the day of his injuries; however, much of that day had been spent either asleep or unconscious from the fall, so there was little to recall. Two things did replay themselves over and over in his mind, one being the conversation about the novel Miss Elizabeth had been reading and the other, the picture which had become ingrained in his head of her clothed in nothing but her wet chemise clinging to her form. Darcy did not consider Miss Elizabeth to be a beauty in the truest sense of the word, but he could not deny her attractions for man's baser inclinations. As he was a gentleman and was raised to look beyond the commonplace enticements, he attempted to extricate these thoughts from his mind; nevertheless, Darcy was a man, as well as a gentleman, and found his imagination often going back to what he had seen that day. He had much time to dwell on these visions, as he had nothing else he could accomplish without the annoying vertigo. Bingley attempted to make himself useful for his friend, but this only caused Darcy more grief. Bingley's idea of help came close to hovering, and if there could be any action more annoying to Darcy than this, it was Bingley's hovering, accomplished within the midst of his own nausea.

Bingley had sent his servants back to Netherfield in order to retrieve necessities that might make Darcy's tenure at the Bennets' cabin more bearable. They returned with blankets, food, and additional firewood, since the small supply at the cabin had long been consumed. While the servants were on their errand, Darcy asked his friend, "Bingley, how long have these footmen been in your service? Are they the men you brought from London or are they local stock?"

"I believe the butler hired them locally; however, they have performed their duties this past fortnight with remarkable diligence. I have no reason to complain, nor to think that we cannot trust their word."

"Time will tell. We have done all we can to ensure their confidentiality. Now, I find myself in need of solitude. Would I be asking too much if you were to keep talking to a minimum?"

"Not at all, my friend. It would be my pleasure to have an opportunity to serve you for a change. Would you like some water?"

"Just sleep, please."

When Bingley found himself in stressful situations, he tended to let his mouth run faster than his good sense. He knew this failing and how annoying his friend would find him; this was learnt the hard way, on a Sunday when Darcy had nothing to do but listen to his chatter. His own mind began to wander as he considered his friend's predicament. He knew Darcy to be impeccable in his dealings with young maidens, but he did not know Miss Elizabeth's proclivities. Her liveliness was apparent, and she was often engaged in stimulating conversations. In spite of these merits, Bingley had been deceived in the past concerning a woman's virtues. Elizabeth's younger sisters, Miss Kitty and Miss Lydia, flirted shamelessly with the local gentlemen. Could Elizabeth actually take after her younger sisters, or was she more like Miss Bennet? The thought of Jane Bennet brought a happy smile to his face, a common enough occurrence whenever in her company. Miss Bennet and her sister, Miss Elizabeth, were as close as he had ever seen two sisters, certainly closer than his own, and Miss Bennet had spoken of her sister with such respect and warmth. Miss Bennet's manners and words contained true admiration for her sibling, and her own kind manners were without disguise. No, there could not have been intentional foul play enacted by Miss Elizabeth. Miss Bennet admired her too well to believe her capable of manipulation.

Bingley's servants arrived and set to work making the cabin more comfortable. They had no desire to risk their employment and livelihood over spreading a little gossip. The money they would earn to keep quiet could make their lives much more comfortable in the future. As footmen, they would have no other opportunity to earn such a sum, so they agreed between themselves to keep the affair quiet.

The men had returned with a cart and had plenty of wood and coal to last for the next few days. Darcy's valet arrived with the footmen and attended his master with the same diligence he always had. Nelson had been with the Darcy family for greater than fifteen years and was the soul of discretion. His devotion to Darcy had been proven time and again, often placing himself for the night in Darcy's dressing room when away from home, or if any young ladies were staying at Darcy's residence. In this way, he was able to counter more than a few attempts at a compromise by a resourceful lady, young and old alike.

When Darcy awoke, he was relieved that the cabin had finally begun to warm up and that his valet had arrived. The fire earlier in the day provided little heat. His head continued to throb, and he began to notice that his whole body was beginning to ache. Bingley had decided to contact the local apothecary to assess Darcy's ailments and to ensure that all was being done that could be done to bring about a swift recovery; but regardless of his plans, Darcy denied him, as he did not want the events in the cabin to become widely known.

The next few days were spent as miserably as Darcy had ever experienced. The condition of the cabin was altogether rustic with an unpleasant, musty smell and dark, unadorned walls, certainly not up to the standards to which Darcy was accustomed. The only items of any comfort were those brought from Netherfield. His head pounded with a persistent, dull ache that periodically intensified, and he continued to have dry heaves if he attempted to sit up. His ankle caused discomfort when moving his leg, but otherwise the pain was quite lost on a general sense of malaise, as often attended a cold, which he realised he had contracted the morning following his arrival. He had little inclination to dwell upon the events that brought him to the cabin or the young woman who had endeavoured to bring him there – aside from his incessant recollection of her form.

Bingley and the two footmen returned to Netherfield. Darcy had asked that Bingley leave him alone for the majority of his tenure in the cabin with his trusted valet, as Bingley's equanimity had become unbearable to witness when he himself felt so poorly. His valet knew Darcy and his needs as well as he knew his own and was perfectly capable of providing any relief within his power. The outside world was of no consequence to Darcy during his stay at the cabin; all he wished for was a reprieve from his current discomfort.

Nonetheless, after three days, Darcy became determined to return to Netherfield where he might at least sleep in a soft bed rather than a lumpy cot. Lying down for an extended time left him feeling all the aches associated with being bed-ridden and stuck in the same attitude for days at a time. When Bingley arrived for his daily visit, Darcy relayed his wish to leave.

"Are you certain, Darcy? You do look dreadful."

"I insist that you make ready transportation for me. You cannot change my mind," Darcy replied with a scowl closer to his usual appearance.

Bingley smiled, "I do believe you are getting back to your usual self. I'll arrange a gig to pick you up, or would you prefer the cart, so you might recline? The path is too narrow for my carriage."

"The gig will do well enough." Turning to his valet, he continued, "Nelson, please help me prepare to leave while my friend arranges our transportation." With a nod, his valet got to work.

"Caroline will be pleased to finally have the opportunity to assist you. She has been at sixes and sevens over your being here and has been yearning for the chance to prove her merit as a hostess. as well as a nurse," Bingley teased.

Darcy scowled again. "Please, Bingley, I beg of you, keep your sister away from me as I attempt to recover. If she thinks I would appreciate any assistance that she can provide, she is mistaken. Unless she is directing your staff to draw up a hot bath, I would prefer she keep her distance. Nelson will know my needs and is perfectly capable of meeting them, without her involvement."

Bingley put his hands up as if in surrender with a knowing smile. "I know how you feel about her. Still, I think she means well, even though she can be rather tiresome. But I find it funny that when I get sick, she tells me to quit my complaints and move on! And speaking of moving on, I suppose I must if we are to get you home before darkness sets in." Bingley left for Netherfield and to warn Caroline of Darcy's imminent return, with an unlooked for directive to keep away from him while he recovers.

Darcy's arduous move to Netherfield left him exhausted and uncomfortable upon his arrival. He had not sat up for that long since his injury occurred, and he found that this made him lightheaded and nauseated. He was able to keep the contents of his stomach down by sheer willpower. Darcy was determined to enter the house upright by leaning on his friend, but the energy consumed by such a task was nearly too much to bear, and he, in humility, had to allow

Bingley's footmen to support him on either side as he gained the steps to the front entrance. Miss Bingley presented herself at the door of the house, determined to be useful to the man whom she hoped to marry; nevertheless, her efforts were quite lost on him, as he had striven to shut out of his mind all of the bustle going on around him. He was a tall, well-formed man, which had always worked to his advantage; however, these attributes only made the task of assisting him into the manor and up the flight of stairs to the guest wing more laborious for Bingley's men.

With the help of one other footman, Nelson was able to get Darcy into the bath, which to Darcy's relief, Miss Bingley had ordered drawn – an occasion for him to relent that her desire to impress sometimes had its advantages. After soaking in the warm, sudsy water for half an hour, he was ready to put on a soft sleeping shirt and climb into the downy comfort of the poster bed. Only one hour was needed to transport him to Netherfield; nevertheless, that hour came at a price. Darcy knew that the move would likely set him back, but he could not have spent another day in that oppressive cabin or lament the change in location. Darcy's fever did return, but not to the previous extent. He continued to eat little, despite the variety of food ordered for him by his faithful hostess.

As Darcy focused on his recovery, his friend continued to make social calls throughout the neighbourhood. Darcy had asked Bingley to keep his ears open to any gossip, not expecting to hear any, but wanting the solace that would only come in knowing that word of his trials had not been laid open to public scrutiny. What Bingley heard, however, would bring Darcy anything *but* solace.

THE DAY AFTER DARCY'S RETURN to Netherfield, Bingley rode out to Meryton with his sister, Caroline, hoping to encounter Miss Bennet. Not seeing her upon first entering the town, he set off on his own, while Caroline and a maid went to the butcher and then the baker to personally check on the orders for the following fortnight. She did not want any detail to go amiss while Mr. Darcy was in residence. Mr. Bingley was greeted by the local townsfolk with the kindest of courtesies, and he was pleased to have taken a home in such an agreeable area of the country.

Mrs. Philips, the sister of Mrs. Bennet, spied Mr. Bingley strolling down the walkway of Meryton, and quickly came out to the street to pay her respects. Mrs. Philips was much like her elder sister by way of her mouth leading before her mind could catch up; howbeit, when it came to local news, she was as shrewd as any Londoner. "Mr. Bingley, how nice it is to see you on this fine day. We have missed seeing you and your friend this week."

With a bow and a congenial smile, Bingley replied, "Madam, a pleasure to see you as well. We have been rather distracted as of late, but I could not help but make time to come visit with my new friends in Meryton, such as yourself."

"You would not be looking for anyone in particular would you?"

With uncharacteristic shyness, he replied that he was pleased to see any of his new acquaintances.

"I have seen several local people out shopping today, as the weather is so fine. Why I just saw my nieces not fifteen minutes ago walk past this very spot and enter into the milliner's." Bingley could no more stop his eyes light up and a smile spread across his face than he could stop breathing, as he turned his head towards the milliners. So Mrs. Philips had guessed correctly about the direction Bingley's heart was following. Jane Bennet was a lovely girl; how could Mr. Bingley help but fall for her? Upon seeing Mr. Bingley's distracted gaze, and after gaining this bit of insight, she moved on to the next topic on her mind, the one that most held her curiosity. "It is a pity that my niece, Elizabeth, was unable to join her sisters today. Of course, she has been quite ill these past few days. Getting caught out in the rain does not do anyone any good. What she was doing out all alone, I am sure I do not know. But it is a good thing she was out, for what would have happened to Mr. Darcy!"

Bingley quickly shifted his astonished eyes from the milliners to Mrs. Philips. "What would have happened to Mr. Darcy?" Bingley hesitantly replied, as he dared not say anything to confirm or deny the exclamation.

"Of course. He may have been out in the cold rain for hours before you found him, *if* you found him. I daresay, he would have been in a sorry state, if he survived at all."

"I am afraid that you have the advantage over me, madam." Bingley had singularly lost all interest in the lovely Miss Bennet, as he scrambled to discern what she knew, and therefore, what the town was saying, for in the short time he had been in Hertfordshire, he had determined that she was the notorious town gossip.

"Sir, surely you know, for Mr. Darcy is your guest. I heard it from Mrs. Bennet, who heard it straight from Lizzy. She did no less than rescue him and save his life. Mrs. Bennet had been worried to a frenzy about Lizzy, as she had set out at first light and had not been seen until her father brought her home in such a state! He had found her you see at the folly on the Longbourn property, soaked through. She has been sick in bed since that night, feverish and unable to eat or drink. She put her own life in danger trying to save him, I am certain."

Bingley just stared at her. *What folly? Her story makes no sense.*

She continued, "The folly is such a romantic location on the estate. I know of at least two couples to get engaged there, including Mr. and Mrs. Bennet, and now this! How charming!"

Bingley knew he had to intervene but knew not what to say. The less said the better, but how was he to counter her story without giving away the truth of it? "Darcy has not been to the folly. In fact I had no idea there was one at Longbourn. It must be on the other side of the estate from Netherfield is it not?"

"Of course it is, and a lovely location at that, perfect for a rendezvous." She winked at him as if they were in on a great secret.

"Madam, Mr. Darcy was not at a folly, I can assure you." *That was the truth.*

"Well, where is he now? I heard he was ill at Netherfield, just like our Lizzy is at Longbourn. They were found at the same time. You cannot deny that can you, sir?"

"Mr. Darcy is the best person to account for himself on that day, but he is not here. He remains my guest and friend, and as such, I feel as though I cannot discuss his happenings in good conscience."

"Of course you are astute in these matters. I only meant to warn you of what the neighbours are hearing, and more importantly, what they are spreading. I would never have said anything to you, if you were not the personal friend of Mr. Darcy. You know, he could do a lot worse than our Lizzy. She will give him no cause to repine. The Bennet girls are the jewels of the county, they are, and mark my words, Mr. Darcy will find that she is up to the challenge. He is a rather stern fellow for her, but she will laugh it out of him." She continued on in this vein, sniggering as she went.

This is altogether horrible. What will I say to Darcy? He had to try to quench her tongue before they were overheard. Talking as softly as he could, hoping she would follow suit, Bingley said, "Mrs. Philips, surely you cannot believe that Mr. Darcy will offer for Miss Elizabeth? Why, he barely knows her, and as I have said, they were not at the folly together on that day. Now I ask that you please not spread rumours that have no foundation and that can have such a devastating effect on the Bennets, as well as my friend."

She looked at him as if he had grown horns. "Of course Lizzy was with him. She said so herself."

"She told you this?" He could not believe Miss Elizabeth would have actually let this get out. She seemed so sincere in her dislike of his friend. He understood why; Darcy had been a beast since he had joined him in Hertfordshire, standing aloof and haughty. Bingley knew this was just one side of the multifaceted man, but still, the good people of Meryton did not know. Darcy had actually offended Miss Elizabeth at the assembly not a fortnight ago, and Bingley was certain, based on her expression at the time, that she had overheard the insult.

"As I was saying, she told her mother while her mother was caring for her, as she was rather feverish, but her point was clear. She said that she saved Mr. Darcy in the rain and had to marry him. Now she was gone all day, and I suppose he was missing as well. At least that is what I had heard that day. Miss Bingley had sent a messenger into town asking if anyone had seen him, and that he had been absent since early that morning, just like our Lizzy."

Trying to change her mind would be futile. He had to get back to Darcy and get direction from him. "I will get to the bottom of these rumours; you can be certain of that, but I can assure you that Miss Elizabeth and Mr. Darcy are not engaged and have no plans to become so."

"Mr. Bingley, please do not look so distressed. Lizzy is as fine a girl as one could find. I have always been partial to Lydia, as she amuses me so, but Lizzy is as loyal as they come, and she has a good head on her shoulders. I would imagine that she would have been married by now, if she did not scare all the young men away with her impertinent remarks. I believe that she intimidates them, and they do not want to look unlearned in front of her. Your friend may just like a wife who knows her mind."

"Yes, well, I must be going now. Please give my respects to Mr. Philips." Bingley bowed and headed towards Caroline's destination. He saw her coming out of the baker's shop, eyes wide and in distress. She approached him in agitation.

"Charles, you will not believe what I have just heard. It is outrageous!" She grabbed his arm and began leading him quickly to the carriage as she whispered looking around to make sure no one was eavesdropping. "Apparently, there is a rumour, no doubt spread by the Bennets, that Mr. Darcy and Miss Elizabeth spent the entirety of the day of the storm alone together, and that she is expecting a proposal of marriage. How could anyone believe such a tale? He would never offer for someone so utterly beneath him, regardless of how he spent his day. We must do something to stop this slander. To think that Mr. Darcy would align himself to such a woman, such a family!"

"I have heard a similar report. We must get home to warn Darcy and to come up with a plan to counteract the damage. Although I would disagree with you on the suitability of the family, I know Darcy probably would not." The two quickly made their way back to the carriage and departed for Netherfield.

Bingley dreaded the pending conversation with his friend. His worst fears were to be realised. Although Caroline believed that Darcy would not offer for Miss Elizabeth based on these rumours, he was quite certain that Darcy would. His friend had always been the model of probity and would never leave a woman or her family in disgrace if he had somehow been involved. While in the carriage, he admonished Caroline to act as if nothing had occurred out of the ordinary while in front of the servants. As soon as Bingley and Caroline arrived at Netherfield, he went to Darcy's room while his sister sought out Mrs. Hurst.

Bingley knocked on his friend's door and upon receiving a call to enter, he opened it quietly. The room was dark with the windows closed, as bright light tended to worsen Darcy's headache. "Bingley, have you already been into town? You were not gone long."

Bingley closed the door behind him and hesitantly crossed the room, pulling up the chair next to the bed. "I felt a need to return as quickly as I could. You see, I heard enough while in town to make me realise that we have a potential problem before us."

"Tell me."

After a deep breath, Bingley continued. "After Caroline left to ensure our food orders were as she had intended, I went down the main street. I had not gone far when Mrs. Philips called out to me. We exchanged pleasantries, but then she began telling me about how Miss Elizabeth was ill and unable to come into town after being out in the storm," he paused a moment, then continued, "with you."

With controlled fury, Darcy began speaking, "Damn! How could this have happened? The Bennets planned this all along, I know. They are a disgraceful lot. What am I to do?" His breathing became heavy, as he reached up to his temple to rub the pain away. "What else did this woman say?"

"That was the confusing part. She said that you and Miss Elizabeth had spent the day together in some folly on the Longbourn estate, after she had saved you. Then again, Mr. Bennet did say they would tell the family she was found on the opposite side of the estate from Netherfield – but alone. Anyway, she spoke as if she meant to warn me about what people were saying."

"And from where had she gotten her information?"

"From Mrs. Bennet. You see Mrs. Philips and Mrs. Bennet are sisters."

"Blast! That woman is the most uncouth, avaricious harpy with whom I have ever had the misfortune to meet. She no doubt could not wait to share everything she knew, so that she could ensnare a rich man for her conniving daughter."

Although Bingley did not share the same sentiments about the Bennets as his friend, he could not help but see the truth in his assertions that Mrs. Bennet was spreading rumours with the hope of forcing a marriage to the wealthy visitor. Bingley had supposed her to be rather eccentric, but not rapacious. "Darcy, what would you have me do?"

"I need you to return to Meryton and discover what else is being said. Based on the assertion that I was at some folly with Miss Elizabeth, there may be inadequate truth to the claims to bind me." Even as he said this, he knew that even a hint of impropriety could damage Miss Elizabeth's reputation, but he must know all.

"Darcy, Caroline also heard from someone at the baker's shop that Miss Elizabeth was expecting a proposal from you, as you had spent the entire day alone with her. I am afraid that the damage cannot be contained as the general population of Meryton is talking about it." After a few moments of silence from his friend, he regrettably added, "Mrs. Philips said that Miss Elizabeth herself had told her mother about being with you."

Darcy glared at his friend, as if he somehow had transformed into this Miss Elizabeth. "I will not be forced into a marriage to her. She has created her own misfortunes; she will have to manage them alone!"

Could Darcy truly refuse to do his duty? Bingley felt all of the injustice in his friend's situation; to be forced into matrimony with a woman whom he could not even respect was beyond contemplating. His friend had always been above reproach in every situation, and to then be connected against his will to a woman so decidedly beneath him was cruelty itself. Although Bingley thought highly of Miss Bennet, he knew that Darcy's standards for suitability exceeded his own in every way, and that he would never willingly connect himself to the Bennet family, even though gentry. But could Darcy leave Miss Elizabeth to ruin? Surely he was speaking out of turn. "Darcy, before you decide on a course of action, let us consider all of the possibilities."

"What possibilities could there be? Miss Elizabeth Bennet has gone back on her word and has purposely attempted to put me in an untenable position. I have no doubt that was her design all along when she saw me riding out alone."

"Darcy, now you are talking nonsense. She could not have planned for your injuries."

"Regardless, once they occurred, she took matters into her hands in a way that would ensure her own compromise, thereby safeguarding that I would be honour-bound to offer for her." With exasperation, he continued, "I cannot believe that after all of these years of successfully avoiding scandal that it would be a country nobody who succeeded where no one else could. Of all the ladies who have attempted that feat, I would end up getting caught by the very least suitable!" Bingley did not know what to say, so he just listened. "And what of Lady Annette? Before coming here, I had decided to publicly court her."

"Darcy, I am truly sorry."

"Damn her and her family!" After a few moments of silence, Darcy continued, "Forgive me. My anger got the better of me. If you do not mind, I would like to be alone. My head is throbbing and I know not what to think or say."

"Do not regard it, my friend. I will return to town and see what else I can hear." Bingley walked to the door, and with a heavy heart he exited, leaving his friend alone and wishing for a better outcome than seemed to be before him.

MISS BINGLEY HAD RELAYED the story to her sister, Louisa Hurst, upon returning to Netherfield. She was beside herself with anger at the gall of the local inhabitants of this unholy town. How dare they think that Mr. Darcy would lower himself to request the hand of a daughter of an impoverished gentleman? Miss Eliza had no money and no connections and little taste. Her wardrobe was two years behind the current fashion, and she was altogether forward and above herself. She displayed no accomplishments worth noting; she could not even play the pianoforte without missing notes. "I have worked too hard to give Mr. Darcy up to this trollop!" Louisa listened to her tirade, nodding her head to the truth of her words.

"I have to do something to save Mr. Darcy. I feel quite certain that given some time, he would be asking for my hand. This has been the opportunity for him to see me as mistress of a home, and I have mastered the role without a fault. I know that he would want me over Eliza, for she has nothing to recommend herself."

"Caroline, I agree. She is nothing to you."

"I have all of the usual accomplishments; I play the pianoforte, sing, and paint. I know Italian and French and I have proven that I can be an admirable hostess in a large country home. I would be doing him a favour intervening to make him have to declare himself to me before he could lower himself to offer for her."

"But, Caroline, you said that he would never ask for her hand, so there is no need to push him."

"Louisa, I am trying to make this easy for the man. You know how honourable he is; he will feel that he must act, no matter how much he despises the idea. Rumours concerning Eliza are just speculation; however, if he compromises me and there are witnesses, he will have no choice but to ask for me instead. Even though Charles can be rather intimidated by Mr. Darcy, he would never let his friend get away with not offering his hand if we were found out publicly. I just have to think of a way to make it happen."

"I don't know, Caroline. I think you may need to reconsider this idea, or at least wait until we hear more."

"Wait until he feels inclined to offer for her? No, I must act soon. Will you help me, Louisa?"

Louisa was not feeling disposed to help her sister in any plot that could cause trouble between Mr. Darcy and the Bingleys. Due to their family's recent association to trade, their place in society was not as solid as Caroline seemed to think, and if Caroline's plan were unsuccessful, Mr. Darcy could cut them off, which would be much worse than if he were to marry one of the Bennets. In fact, if he did marry Eliza, that would raise Miss Bennet's station sufficiently to make an alliance with their own brother profitable. Louisa reasoned that if Mr. Darcy were planning to offer for Caroline, he would have done so by now. Of course Louisa was not going to tell Caroline this. She had always followed her sister's lead, as she found fighting her to be distasteful and unproductive. Louisa would agree with Caroline, then find a way to thwart her plans. "Dear sister, I will do all I can to help our family and Mr. Darcy."

"I knew I could count on you." They were both silent for some time as Miss Bingley contemplated how best to secure Mr. Darcy. After a few moments she looked to her sister and smiled as the plan was formulating in her mind. Yes, she would put her stratagem in motion in the morning while her brother was gone on his morning ride. She then began outlining the details with Louisa, who listened in astonishment to how conniving her sister could be on such short notice.

BINGLEY REALISED THAT THE SITUATION was graver than he had feared. While Miss Elizabeth Bennet was very well liked and admired in the small town of Meryton, his friend was considered haughty and above his company. The local inhabitants were certain that Elizabeth was being ill-used, and if Mr. Darcy did not ask for her hand, then this would confirm their suspicions that he was the worst of men. This would not motivate Mr. Darcy to act, however, since once he left the area, he was not likely to return, and he would have no desire to make such a monumental decision for himself based on a comparatively few people's opinions, especially since these same people were of no consequence. Although he would hate for Lady Annette to get wind of the scandal, his place in society was not at risk based on his current predicament.

Yet Bingley also discovered that Elizabeth and her family would be in disgrace should Darcy not ask for Elizabeth's hand. Stories were being bandied about that suggested they were seen in an embrace, that he had met her clandestinely, and that they were already secretly engaged and had planned an elopement. Bingley witnessed the sad truth that gossip, with all its power, spread like a fire, while ignoring the harm inflicted on its victims. He was sad for Darcy and for Miss Elizabeth. He, unlike Darcy, could not believe that Miss Elizabeth was the one who began the stories. He suspected that a little of the truth had gotten out, and fiction had taken over. His own sister had let it be known that Darcy was missing, requesting help from the locals. This occurred concurrently to Miss Elizabeth's disappearance. There was no reason for Miss Elizabeth to have been missing for the entire day, as she was not injured and she knew her way home well, but she had not returned. In his mind he could see how others might transform the story, especially in light of Mrs. Bennet's declarations. She was obviously a woman who could not hold her tongue, but she was not malicious and probably did not even consider how her own daughter could be harmed by her reports.

During the course of the afternoon, Bingley learnt that Mrs. Bennet's five daughters had no dowry to speak of and an estate entailed away to the male line; this would motivate any parent to seek husbands for her girls, but he could not approve of forcing a man, especially a principled one, into marriage. Bingley knew his friend was honourable and in the end could not leave the Bennet family to suffer through the scandal that was developing. *If only there were another way.... And what about Miss Elizabeth's elder sister, Miss Bennet?* Bingley had a developing tenderness towards her. *If her mother were mercenary, could she be also? Would* she *join into an unrequited attachment to save her own family?* He could not think this of her. She was without beguilement, even if her mother were not.

CAROLINE AWOKE AFTER A FULL NIGHT OF DREAMING, or at least daydreaming, of being mistress of Pemberley. Mr. Darcy could not help but appreciate the talent with which she would be able to perform her duties. She imagined Georgiana's coming out with herself guiding his sister through the social scene of London, ensuring an expeditious success. Of course, she would insist Georgiana come out the following Season, the sooner she marries, the sooner she would establish her own residence.

Caroline had every expectation of her triumph today. She would give Mr. Darcy consummate reason to feel compelled to offer for her. She even went so far as to pen a note to Mr. Darcy as if answering a request for a liaison, sharing her delight in once again having him visit her chamber. All she had to do was get him there while she was scantily clad. She would be near him as he entered, waiting for the door to close and then embrace him. Her sister along with a housemaid would be at the ready to walk in on them from her sitting room.

Caroline's lady's maid would never go against her wishes for fear of reprisal, yet she was opposed to playing a part in forcing a compromise with the handsome Mr. Darcy. Knowing she could be dismissed without a reference was the only inducement to participating in the scandal. Her job was to go to Mr. Darcy's room and bang on the door asking for help in Miss Bingley's room, that a man was in there trying to attack her. Once she accomplished this task she was to follow Mr. Darcy to Miss Bingley's chamber and then close the door behind him as he entered the room, then lock the door from the outside with her key, so he could not leave once he discovered the trap. Of course he might *not* want to leave after he sees her in her diaphanous lingerie. Caroline was proud of her tall and thin figure that she presented and believed that even if Mr. Darcy were of a mind to find anger in her manipulations, that he would soon approve of her once he observed the revealing nature of her gown. Louisa would have to wait a full minute before entering the room, so that Caroline could lure him towards her bed, which would make the situation irrefutably compromising. Her brother would be told by at least three witnesses that Mr. Darcy had entered her room, and the note would be used as proof that his entrance was prearranged.

What she did not know was that her sister would side with Mr. Darcy if it came to that. Louisa hoped that Mr. Darcy would accept Caroline and be thankful for her manoeuvrings, but if he were not, she would expose Caroline's machinations as deceitful and selfish and completely contrived to entrap Mr. Darcy. She would have to send the housemaid away to safeguard her plan.

Darcy was in a sound slumber. The draught that his valet had given him, not two hours previously, was allowing Darcy to finally sleep. His days and nights seemed to have gotten mixed up since his injuries, as the heavy curtains were drawn with a low fire maintained in order to sustain the warmth in his chamber, yielding a perpetual dim light. His fever had finally broken, leaving the uncomfortable lingering effects of a cold, but his biggest complaint was related to the headache that was amplified by the contemplation of Bingley's report from the previous day. He was now able to sit up longer without the effects of nausea, as long as his efforts were slow and deliberate. Unfortunately, he had found little sleep during the night, as he was agitated about his predicament. Due to his ankle still being somewhat tender and the vertigo that came with quick movements, he had been unable to participate in his usual method of calming, which was pacing the room.

Suddenly, he heard someone banging on the door from the hallway confusing his senses and jarring him from his much needed sleep. A woman's voice came from without calling, "Help, sir; you must come help Miss Bingley. She is being attacked!"

Before Darcy could formulate an appropriate response, he began acting on instinct. His valet, Nelson, had developed a makeshift crutch to help him get around his room if he were alone and had a need. As his ankle was still somewhat sore, he continued to benefit from this assistance; however, in his haste, he had hobbled past it, and opened the door revealing a frightened lady's maid, Miss Bingley's he presumed. "Sir, you must not tarry! He could be hurting her!"

In his muddled state, that was all it took to move Darcy into action. Forgetting the pain in his ankle, and his lack of robe, he moved forward, limping all the way, past the alarmed maid, and headed for Miss Bingley's door, just down the hall and around the corner from his own.

His valet quickly entered his chamber from the dressing room in time to see Darcy hobble out the door. When Darcy reached the open doorway and heard Miss Bingley's screech for help, he rushed in. The lady's maid was just about to close the door behind him to secure it, when his valet followed behind and pushed the door back open. The sight before him made Nelson glad he had been so presumptuous.

Miss Bingley was still screeching but for a reason altogether different from the one that she had originally intended when her plan was set in motion. When Darcy's valet entered the room, his eyes fell upon a horrified woman dressed in a revealing gown that had lost some as its appeal, as it was covered in the vomitus Darcy could not stop from losing due to the unfortunate effect of his continued vertigo. Though his nausea had improved over the past week, the sudden movement could not be tolerated.

Of course, Darcy was horrified that he had done such a thing and briefly forgot about the cause that had drawn him into her room, yet once he looked up and noticed what Miss Bingley was wearing underneath his emission, he realised the true nature of his problem. He had, in his weakened state, forgotten his well-practised diligence that served to keep just such a plight from occurring; nevertheless, his valet had *not* been ill nor had he let *his* guard down. On the contrary, Nelson had contemplated his master's vulnerability and during this visit had made a habit of locking Darcy's chamber door and hanging a bell on the latch that would alert him to any intrusions on Darcy's privacy. He had also left the door to the dressing room open, so he could hear any activity, not trusting the mistress of the manor to refrain from using her own set of keys to enter his room. Nelson knew that Miss Bingley had long wanted to become Mrs. Darcy and was likely reaching a new level of desperation considering the circumstances. Since his master had been ill, Nelson's guard was much more deliberate, as Darcy was open to attack both day and night.

Miss Bingley stood arms outstretched and motionless, except for conspicuous quick and heavy breathing as she attempted to compose herself. If the situation did not have the potentially incriminating repercussions, Nelson would have burst out in hilarity, but as it was, he had to make certain that Miss Bingley knew that his master would not fall into her trap, that he was witness to the entire episode, and would swear, under oath if necessary, that Darcy was innocent of any improprieties. It was at this moment when the expected witness of this farce, Mrs. Hurst, walked in. Instead of the predicted scene, distressing as it might have been, what she saw quite shocked her even more than she could have anticipated. As soon as she hastily assessed the situation, she began to cover her guilt with declarations of how appalled she was at Miss Bingley's state of undress and to apologise for any discomfort Caroline might have caused. She claimed to have come in response to the screams, and verbalised her disapprobation for her sister's machinations.

Caroline was fuming, as she looked towards her sister who clearly would purport her own innocence. If she were not covered in the disgusting discharge, she would have taken issue with her sister's change in allegiance, but as it was all she could do was turn on her heels and run out of the room into her dressing room. Louisa and Caroline's lady's maid followed behind her, the latter unable to conceal her mirth despite the treachery.

Darcy needed to sit down, or better yet lie down, but was unable to get to his room in order to find a safe and comfortable haven. Instead, he just sank to the floor of Miss Bingley's chamber, head in his hands. The sudden movement of arising quickly and hastily – while making his way to her room – threw Darcy into a figurative tailspin. His dizziness left him unable to do anything but lie down right where he found himself. He was there for about ten minutes, while Nelson attempted to apply wet, cool cloths to his face, when Bingley happened to walk by and see the commotion within his sister's chambers. He looked in and discovered the distressing scene of an obviously ill Darcy in Caroline's room, with Darcy's valet in attendance.

With equal parts levity and intent, Bingley said, "I say, Darcy, I feel it is my duty to ask what you are doing in my sister's chamber. My understanding was that you did not feel up to getting out of bed, much less having a liaison in a lady's room." Darcy was Bingley's dearest friend, and he trusted him implicitly, but all the same, hearing something rational on the subject from Darcy would ease his mind.

By this time, Darcy's breathing had calmed. He was on his back, right knee bent with left leg out long; his left arm was crossed over his eyes and right arm stretched out. "Bingley, I will say this one time and one time only. Your sister is a conniving trollop who is not above forcing a compromise on a guest in your home, even one weakened by illness and pain. If you do not take control of her, I will be forced to leave and check into the inn in Meryton. I am too ill to give you details, so I suggest you ask Miss Bingley or Mrs. Hurst what happened. Then if you have any other questions, Nelson can give you a full account." Then opening his eyes and looking at his able attendant, he continued, "Nelson, please assist me to my room."

Bingley would have been offended, and perhaps another man may have taken this as cause to call Darcy out if he were not to yield to his presumed obligations, but he was too aware of his sister's character and his friend's credit. Bingley responded by looking around for Caroline who had remained absent.

Meanwhile, as Darcy's valet attempted to raise him up to a standing position, he let out an expletive and sat back down. Bingley then directed his gaze back to his friend and realised his help was needed; he could consult his sisters later. He went to the other side of Darcy, from where his valet was leaning down, and helped him back to his feet. Although Darcy was able to make his way to Miss Bingley's chamber on his sprained ankle, the movement hither had done its damage. He was again unable to put any weight on his left foot, so the other two men had to support him a good bit. They slowly returned to Darcy's chamber where Nelson quickly got to work making him comfortable. When that was accomplished, Bingley pulled Darcy's valet aside. "Do you want to tell me what happened, or must I ask my sisters?"

Nelson was respectful of Darcy's friend, but would in no way leave any room for misinterpretation. "It would be my privilege to explain to you the events leading up to your arrival." He then gave a dependable accounting of the past half hour's happenings. Bingley listened in horror at the level of deceit that his sister had enacted, not doubting once the veracity of the claims. He was too acquainted with his friend's honour to think otherwise. In addition, the evidence of Darcy's wretched condition was before him. He apologised profusely to Darcy and promised to discipline his sister appropriately, making sure she kept her distance. Bingley left Darcy's room to do just that. But as soon as he shut the door behind him, he let a smile spread across his face imagining his sister's mortification. Of course, he must chastise her for her deception, but he found the idea of natural consequences to be most gratifying.

ELIZABETH COULD NOT TOLERATE many days indoors, especially if those days were spent ill in bed, so when she awoke feeling the near restoration of her health, she prepared to join her family to break her long fast. This happened to occur on the same morning as Miss Bingley's ill-judged attempt to restore Mr. Darcy's freedom to bind himself to her.

Elizabeth entered the breakfast room after her family had already gathered. "Lizzy, " said her mother, "I am glad to see you are well enough to join us, for I have wanted to have an accounting from you about the day of that terrible storm, but your father would not let me disturb you, as he says you needed to spend your energy in recovering. You are healthy enough, and I told him one does not die of a trifling cold, but he would not be moved." She peered at Mr. Bennet, while continuing, "He takes great delight in vexing me."

Elizabeth glanced quickly at her father before answering, "Mama, I am sure I have nothing to add to what Papa has already told you. Perhaps instead, you and my family can tell me what I have missed. I am sure you have more to tell me about the comings and goings since I have been abed than I could conjure up about that day."

Lydia jumped into the conversation certain that Elizabeth was correct in her assumption, "We have such news, Lizzy! The militia has arrived and will be stationed in Meryton for the whole of winter. Is that not grand?"

This distraction was sufficient to divert her mother for a few moments' time, as she also was quite enamoured of the idea herself; nevertheless, when she realised Elizabeth had not actually answered her question, she returned to the topic. "Lizzy, I see that you wish to be sly, but I insist on your telling me everything. How long have you and Mr. Darcy been partial to one another? Last I knew, he found you barely tolerable, and you found him most severe. I knew you did not have your father's wit for nothing. You must have found a way to draw him in."

"Mama! I did no such thing! I am sure I know nothing of which you speak." Elizabeth then turned to her father, eyes wide, and said, "Papa, you told her where you found me, did you not?"

"Of course, my dear. I found you at the folly, quite chilled too. It was a good thing I came upon you when I did, or you may have had far worse than your trifling cold, which has had you in bed these six days."

Looking at Mr. Bennet, her mother said, "I am not talking about what you told me, but about what Lizzy told me."

Everyone's eyes were then set upon Elizabeth. "Mr. Darcy has not changed his opinion of me, as far as I am aware. Mary, could you pass the rolls, please. I am famished."

"Oh, no, Lizzy, you will not change the subject again. I entreat you to tell me what happened."

"Mrs. Bennet, you will refrain from your inquisition. I have told you all there is to tell, now let Elizabeth eat her breakfast in peace. Mary, now pass your sister the rolls. Would you like anything else, Lizzy? Perhaps some butter or preserves?" Jane sat beside Elizabeth and prepared her sister's tea according to her preferences while Elizabeth made ready her food.

After a few moments of silence, Lydia, wanting to return to the previous subject of officers continued, "We will have such a time. Aunt Philips says she is to invite the soldiers to her home, so we may meet more of them! They are ever so handsome and obliging! I have never seen so many men in redcoats."

Mary decided to make her contribution. "A woman cannot be too careful at protecting her reputation; her good name and that of her family could so easily be lost forever." Elizabeth was accustomed to hearing her sister verbalise such platitudes directed at her younger sisters, but was surprised when she noticed that, with apparent condescension, Mary was looking directly at her. Elizabeth glanced around the table curious to see if she were missing something of some importance. Jane had her head down, hands in her lap diligently smoothing out her serviette. Lydia and Kitty were in conference, giggling.

Mr. William Collins, a distant cousin to Mr. Bennet, sat to Mary's left. He had been in residence with the Bennets going on a fortnight now and was to inherit the Longbourn estate upon the death of Mr. Bennet due to an entail that had originated two generations previously. He would be able to evict the Bennet ladies from their home, at his leisure, without recourse, if he so chose, upon Mr. Bennet's future demise. Be that as it may, he had come to make amends in a way that would join his happiness with their salvation. He had heard about the great beauty residing at Longbourn, and knowing that his future inheritance would work highly in his favour, set out to capture the hand of one of his fair cousins. His patroness, Lady Catherine de Bourgh, encouraged him to find a wife, so he had meant to do so as efficiently and conveniently as may be.

Upon first entering Longbourn, he had determined that Jane Bennet, the eldest and most beautiful of the five sisters, was to be the joy of his future life, as would be her due as firstborn, but Mrs. Bennet quickly directed him away from thoughts of her eldest daughter, as she had greater things in mind for Jane and would not sacrifice her splendour on such a man. Mrs. Bennet had encouraged him, therefore, to seek an attachment with Elizabeth, who was next to Jane in both age and beauty. Yet Elizabeth had chosen to ignore his partiality and had perhaps somewhat innocently supposed that by ignoring Mr. Collins, he might take the hint and leave her to herself. However, Elizabeth soon learnt that she had misjudged his discernment. His attentions to her had grown while at Longbourn up until the day before the storm. Like her father, she could enjoy the ridiculous, but it had become more than she could bear, so she had endeavoured to redirect his allegiance. Elizabeth had been engaged in reading her newly acquired novel, when Mr. Collins came upon her in the sitting room. He had much to say on the inappropriateness of reading novels written by women to inspire romantic notions. Elizabeth told him that Mary, her sister next in age, had shared this view with her many times, but that she could not abide by such inclinations. She then took that opportunity to acquaint him with Mary's pious character and hidden appeal.

Elizabeth had seen how Mary admired Mr. Collins and could make him an agreeable, if not ardent, wife. Mary would give him the deference he obviously longed for, but knew not how to earn, and Mr. Collins would have a wife who considered piety above pleasure and would support with diligence his office of rector. Mary also adhered to Mr. Collins's views on rank and would confer to Lady Catherine all of the deference which the noble lady required. Elizabeth knew that she herself could not make Mr. Collins happy, so had encouraged him to image the same.

Although Mary's look was simple and unadorned, improvement would come by simply wearing a becoming colour and rearranging her hair. Mary had readily agreed to Elizabeth's encouragement because, proud though she was, she was also desirous to catch Mr. Collins for herself, for she singularly found him to her liking. When Mr. Collins gazed upon Mary with a new understanding of her character, which he had to that point ignored, and with a new appreciation of her attractions, the plan had been laid in motion, thus freeing Elizabeth to her own diversions.

So following a week of wooing, after Mary's speech Mr. Collins gazed at his new favourite with unguarded esteem, and then said, "Mary, you do honour to your family, for I know that you would follow all of the strictures which are designed to protect a virtuous and wholesome gentleman's daughter. My noble patroness, Lady Catherine de Bourgh, could find no fault in your elegant, yet humble dignity, especially in the face of criticism for your family's failings."

Mr. Bennet then said, "It is a good thing that your patroness holds such high standards for people so utterly unrelated to her. That shows a mark of true grace."

Mrs. Bennet looked as if she was about to open her mouth to say something, but Mr. Bennet's stern glance caused her to uncharacteristically hold her tongue. This went far to silence Mr. Collins as well, for Mr. Bennet rarely exerted his despotic influence upon his family, but when he did, he would not be gainsaid.

The meal continued on in relative silence from this point on while Mr. Bennet remained at the table longer than was his usual want. Elizabeth was glad he lingered, as his presence seemed to be putting an embargo on her mother's inquiries. When at last Elizabeth had completed her meal, her father stood and said, "Lizzy, my dear, do your father a favour and join me in my study. I have missed your company and have felt the privation for sensible conversation during your convalescence."

Elizabeth stood and followed her father from the dining room, and as she left, she heard her mother resume her complaints, "Your father will make a mess of things to be sure."

Her father closed the door to his study behind them, knowing of eavesdroppers in the household; he was not willing to have this conversation overheard. He then guided her to the pair of leather chairs at the hearth. Many hours were spent reading together in similar attitude. Elizabeth's father reached over and gently grasped her hand within his. "Well, Lizzy, how do you fare? I must say, except for having lost some weight and a little pallor, you look your usual self."

Elizabeth smiled while tenderly squeezing his hand, "Papa, is this why you brought me in here? To ask about which you can see for yourself? You are not one for idle chatter, so as you know I am on the mend, why do you not tell me whatever is causing you distress?"

"Yes, well, I did bring you in here to speak about something other than your restoration to good health, but I wished first to ensure that your recovery was in earnest before proceeding to something unpleasant for us both." At her confused look, he continued, "My dear, during your illness, your mother relieved your sister, Jane, and took care of you herself for a short time." At Elizabeth's look of surprise, he added, "Jane was much fatigued and in need of rest; you know your sister would never leave your side without her mother insisting. Anyway, amid the duration of her time at your side, you progressively became more agitated as your fever rose again. By your mother's account, she was standing to call for Hill when she heard you begin muttering words that she at first did not comprehend, but then she took in their significance."

"Papa, what are you saying? Please, I beg you to get to the point."

Her father took in a deep breath, then continued, "You apparently relayed to her that you had been alone with Mr. Darcy, helping him, and something about marrying him. From this your mother determined that you and Mr. Darcy had spent the entirety of the day during the storm alone together at the folly, that you had managed to save Mr. Darcy's life and that he was honour bound to offer for your hand in marriage."

Elizabeth's hand tightened around her father's, eyes wide, brows drawn in. "That cannot be."

"I assure you that she believes that to be the truth of things and will not be moved, since she heard it directly from you."

"I must speak to her and make sure she understands the truth, that..." She faltered. What exactly was the truth? She marvelled at how her mother had been able to come up with such a close resemblance to the actuality. The location was of course incorrect, yet she and her father had directly falsified that information, and she would have no reason to question a difference, but the rest was nearly accurate. She did spend the day with Mr. Darcy, she possibly saved his life, and he was honour-bound, if this information got out, to offer for her. The truth could not get out! "Papa, I beg of you, please tell me that Mama has not gone into town while I have been ill."

"She knew that if she had come to me, I would have forbidden her to speak a word of it to anyone, so she got ready and went into town with the plan of visiting with her sister Philips, proclaiming her triumph."

"But, Papa, surely she considered that he might not offer for me, that my reputation and that of my family would be ruined should he not come forward. He could have left the vicinity of Meryton by now, never to return, and our good name would be extirpated. He has no reason to offer me anything but disdain." She sat there, considering her predicament, and then softly said, "Mary. She was talking about me, was she not?" As her father looked away towards the window, tears came to Elizabeth's eyes. In all her days, she had always maintained the rules of propriety designed to protect a woman and a man from censure. Her father was proud of her prudence when dealing with the opposite sex. She always treated men the same, with kindness, but no apparent favouritism that might cause a gentleman to question her interest and others to question her virtue. She had determined that she would be the one pursued, but within societal boundaries. Like most women, Elizabeth noticed the available men around her, but she never considered participating in any flirtations unsuitable for a daughter of a respected gentleman; the extent of her attentions towards the opposite sex was limited to nothing more than playful teasing.

Mr. Bennet loathed the emotional outbursts of the fairer sex, especially after years of marriage had made him immune to the common effects; nonetheless, his favourite daughter was dear to his heart, and he knew the possible ramifications of his ignorant wife's actions. He got down on a knee, so he could move closer to her and held her close, while she began to weep. "Elizabeth, all is not lost. Perhaps our good friends will not let idle gossip affect their esteem for you. We must give this some time to assess the real damage."

"Papa, what are people saying now? What hope can you give me?"

"I have not been to town, as you know, and the only visitors we can claim are your aunt Philips and Miss Lucas asking about your health. Lizzy, as soon as your mother told me of her suspicions, I restricted her to the house, but I am afraid I was too late to make a difference. Your sisters went into town yesterday and received stares from our neighbours. But really, my dear, that really is no different from usual. Wherever they go, they make sport."

"You cannot jest at a time like this! This is altogether horrible."

"Oh, Lizzy, you are just learning of it, yet I have had time to consider it these three days at least. Surely, our friends know you and would not think the worst has happened."

"But my mother certainly believes the worst, and even more, has chosen to share her beliefs with all of Meryton. I have always understood that I was her least favourite, but to put me in such a position. It is unconscionable!"

"Lizzy, if it makes you feel better, I do believe your mother has acted out of concern for you and our family's future rather than malice. She cannot see the ramifications of her actions. She sees the perfect way to secure your future in comfort and ease, not a misalliance with a man who will always look down upon you, or worse, leave you in ruin. Mr. Darcy must know that I cannot defend your honour, for if I were to fail, Mr. Collins would inherit the house, as well as his pick of the Bennet ladies."

"Did you explain this to Mama?"

"No, I did not. Your mother is single-minded in this affair, and I am not certain I could change her thoughts quite yet. Also, I did not want her to know for certain what she already speculates." Mr. Bennet then decided that this was the time to share the history subsisting between her parents. "Dear, I have been putting a great deal of thought into whether I should share a story with you, and I think that it may help you to understand your mother a little better and what drives her decisions. You see, I grew up at Longbourn, of course, and knew the community as you now do. My father sent me away to school, and I came home on the holidays, as all sons of gentlemen do. Then I went to Oxford for my higher education, so I was not often at Longbourn. While I was away, life carried on, and some little girls turned into lovely women. Of course, I held no interest in the local ladies, no matter how beautiful, for I was to marry an heiress who could contribute to the family's estate.

"But I was not ready to settle, and my father was still quite able to handle the estate on his own. I would go to town during the Season to enjoy the theatre and museums, as well as the soirées. Then my father and mother both died quite unexpectedly when they contracted the flu. I had to return to Longbourn and learn estate management in earnest and in the most difficult of circumstances. I determined then that I needed a wife. I quite enjoyed my time in London and had met several promising ladies, so once the mourning period was over, and the estate was in the capable hands of my steward, I left for town to secure a bride." By now, Elizabeth had quite forgotten her own predicament, as she was lost in the story. She nodded for him to continue.

"There was a lovely daughter of a gentleman from Kent who brought ten thousand pounds with her. But her worth was not in her dowry. Although her intelligence was hidden from me at first, I soon realised through our time together, that she was astute and clever, having knowledge that was superior to most women. I had intended on asking for her hand, a match based on affection and prudence. I returned home in order to retrieve the ring that my father had presented to my mother upon their engagement." He looked at Elizabeth who was absorbed in his tale. Giving her a little smile and a squeeze of her hand, he continued, "I never made it back to London. While home, I carelessly allowed myself to get into a compromising situation with a young, local beauty, not a gentleman's daughter, but the daughter of a lawyer. I had attended a local assembly, having little intention of dancing, but there were fewer men in attendance than ladies, so I felt it my duty to stand up with those in need of a partner. This was scarcely a hardship, as the ladies were in abundance and the music inviting, and having attended previous assemblies with these same ladies, I knew the pleasure that a dance would afford.

"Now you must remember that I was set on my chosen course in London, so I only danced once with any of the women at the assembly and kept conversation to a minimum. In my heart, I would not betray the lady in town. However, when I left, having had more punch than was good for me, I discovered too late that I was obligated as a gentleman to ask for the hand of a Miss Gardiner. I will not share with you the details of the night, but suffice it to say that although your mother may appear lacking in intelligence, she is not at all insufficient in her ability to scheme." Both were quiet for some time before he continued, "I never saw the woman from London again, the one with whom I had fallen in love.

"I admit that I have never quite forgiven your mother for her stratagem, but I must give her credit; she secured a much better match than she had any hope for, despite her beauty. And if not for her scheming, I would not have you or your sisters. Sometimes I forget the blessings that have come my way through my children as a result of our marriage, but I would make the same choice again to ensure your and your sisters' presence in my life. She had no one to defend her honour, as her brother was too young at the time to force my compliance, and her father, not a gentleman and incapable anyway. But when I look at you, my dear, I have no regrets."

"I never knew."

"Of course you did not; there was no need to share such intimate knowledge of our family's genesis, but perhaps you can understand how your mother may have come to the understanding that spreading news of a compromise might be the best course. Although she and I did not start with a love match, we were able to find our own version of love, and she has security, at least until my demise. You can see that her nature to manipulate a situation has not abated."

"Thank you for telling me, Papa. I think I understand you both better. That time in your life could not have been easy for you, losing both of your parents at once, then being thrown into an unequal marriage, lacking in affection, while losing the love you would never know. I have the utmost respect for you and your ability to find contentment in a difficult situation."

"Do not praise me, my dear; I am afraid I have found regret more often than contentment, but I have accepted my lot."

"That is why you retreat to your study."

"Yes, I do." He took a deep breath and then said, "I tried at first to encourage your mother to exercise her mind, but she would have none of it, so I found other ways to seek pleasure in our relationship; I found amusement, instead, and if I could not change her, I could shape the disposition of our children. After my first two daughters, your mother's influence took over. To her credit, she does set a fine table, and if she did not spend so much time and money on frivolous pursuits, she would be credited with a lovely and welcoming home."

"Are you saying that I should accept my lot concerning Mr. Darcy and consider that there may be at least some good to come from a match?"

"No, I am not. I hope for you to have the love match which I never had."

"So what are we to do?"

"I have been thinking on a proper course, and have determined that we will wait. Perhaps the gossip in Meryton will die down, but we will also need to see if Mr. Darcy is willing to do his duty."

"But I do not want him, and you just said that you hope for something different for me."

"I know what you want. We are like-minded, my dear. I would not have you marry that man unless there were no other viable options, but you must see that should the rumours gain acceptance, that we will have to consider a future with Mr. Darcy as a real possibility."

"Must I truly consider marriage to that man? He disdains me; I would know a life of misery. Perhaps I could go to Aunt and Uncle Gardiners' until another scandal takes over the attention of the town. And then...."

"Come Lizzy, you are not silly like your younger sisters. Do you not see what this has the potential to do to your family? I am not one to worry about others' views of the Bennets. What do we live for, but to make sport for our neighbours and laugh at them in our turn?" Elizabeth had seen his account to be truer than she could wish. "I have rarely taken the time to concern myself with my family's security should I leave this world; your mother has adequate nerves to cover the both of us, so why should I? But Lizzy, even I can see the problems that will arise should this continue on its current path; I lived through that myself, you remember. Society does not care what happened in that cabin, or folly, or wherever you find yourself alone with a man. People will judge you based on their own depravity. Nothing would please Meryton more than stopping your mother's gossip by spreading rumours about her own daughters. It is all part of a game such as chess, but with far more cruel intent."

"What have I done?" Elizabeth softly replied as she turned her head and gazed into the hot fire. "I should have left him in the woods. Surely his friend would have found him soon enough."

"Lizzy, you cannot know what would have or would not have happened. You must accept what you did and remember that you did so with the best of intentions. I cannot believe that Providence would be so cruel as to make you suffer for the rest of your life when your intentions were honourable. And you may not remember, but I do; several trees were down around the lane, which made travel through the woods difficult and treacherous during the storm. If this makes you feel any better, I must tell you that I am proud of the way you acted on Mr. Darcy's behalf, despite his condescension towards you. That showed a real strength of character which is rarely seen in this world."

"Truly?" Elizabeth had spent no small amount of time while sick in the bed worrying over her father's judgement of her – in addition to her worry over the possibility of the news of her time alone with Mr. Darcy leaking to the public. Unfortunately, her worries were likely the catalyst that began the rumours, as she must have spoken her concerns out loud, just when her mother could hear.

"I have always been most proud of you." Mr. Bennet stood and assisted Elizabeth to her feet. "If your mother seeks you out, you must continue to stick with our original story. If we can convince her of our claims, we may have a chance with the rest of society." He kissed her wet cheek and sent her out in search of her dearest sister, Jane.

"JANE, THERE YOU ARE. I have been looking for you," Elizabeth said as she joined her sister in the stillroom. Elizabeth was trying to keep up the appearance of cheer for her sister's sake, who would be certain to take Elizabeth's concerns upon herself. On the previous day, Jane, her sisters and Mr. Collins had gone to Meryton in order to take in some shopping after several days of rain. Elizabeth, having learnt of Jane's encountering the local busybodies, was anxious to speak to her to discover the extent of her troubles, but was reluctant, not wanting to upset her with questions.

"Lizzy, I was hoping you would come looking for me. You look as though you are feeling much better today. I have been uneasy about you, since you rarely get sick; you have been in bed for almost a week complete."

Genuinely smiling at her sister's heartfelt tenderness, she responded, "As you see, I am almost back to normal. I appreciate all of the time you spent nursing me. I am sure I can give you the credit for my recovery."

"I was pleased to have the opportunity to repay you for all of your kindnesses towards me. You have always been fortunate in your health. You must have been chilled to the bone that day."

"I could not get warm, as I was soaked through, and there was not nearly adequate firewood to sustain a fire for long. I do not think I got warm until I arrived to my own room with a hot cup of tea."

"I hate even thinking about your being gone for so long. I cannot express to you my worry – my dearest sister out in the storm. But you always know how to take care of yourself. I always admire your fortitude, Lizzy. If I could but be more like you, I am sure I would never be frightened."

"I assure you, Jane, that I know fear. In fact I find myself rather fearful right now." At Jane's look of puzzlement, Elizabeth continued, "Tell me what you know. What are people saying about me? Papa told me what Mama has done. Do I have hope?"

"Oh, Lizzy, I am so sorry for leaving you alone with Mama. I tried to stay, truly I did, but she would not hear of it. She said I needed my rest to look my best in case the Bingleys were to call on us. She would not take no for an answer. You looked so peaceful when I left. You had fallen asleep, and although you still had your fever, it seemed to have improved somewhat. When I returned, you were alone and burning hot. Hill walked in shortly after I did, and said that my mother had sent her in to watch you, but she had other duties that she also had to accomplish and did not know what to do. She apparently had been checking on you off and on over the previous hour." Agitation entered Jane's words, "If only I had not fallen asleep, I may have heard her going up and down the stairs, and could have arrived sooner. I took over from there, of course. You were saying some things about Mr. Darcy, but nothing coherent, really. I do not know what Mama heard or what Hill may have heard. If only I could have persuaded Mama to let me stay." Tears came to Jane's eyes. "This is all my fault."

"Jane, do not be silly. Of course this is not your fault. You have been a devoted sister. My only remembrances of the past few days have been of your taking care of me. I can go through anything just knowing that I have you beside me."

"You are too kind to me, but I will endeavour to be worthy of your faith in me."

As Elizabeth began assisting her sister with the dried herbs, she continued, "Jane, you have not yet answered my question about the rumours. When you went to town yesterday, what did you hear?"

Jane continued diligently working, as Elizabeth waited patiently. She could tell that her sister was agitated and needed time to gather her thoughts, so that rather than helping Elizabeth's nerves, her delay increased her worries. "I went into town with my sisters and Mr. Collins. You will be happy to know that he continues in his attentions to Mary, and we are expecting a proposal any day now. I believe he has only waited this long to ensure your recovery before bringing our family joy." Elizabeth was aware that Jane was stalling, but she was happy for Mary, if this is what she truly wanted.

"We went into the milliner's shop, for you know Lydia and Kitty would not find peace until we did. Mr. and Mrs. Hopkins were both in the shop that day. She came out to us asking if we needed assistance. I could tell she was perturbed with Lydia and Kitty as they made a mess of the ribbons. I began straightening them before she came over to do the same. She noticed you were not with us and asked about your health. Of course, I said as little as I could, saying you had decided not to join us today. Then she indicated that she had heard from Mrs. Taylor, who heard it from Aunt Philips, who heard it from Mama that you were ill due to having gotten caught in the storm with a gentleman, Mr. Darcy to be exact."

At Elizabeth's look of distress, she continued, "I told her that our mother could not know what happened that day, since you have not spoken with her, and that I know for certain that you would not do anything lacking complete propriety. She then just patted my arm with a look of concern and said that I was naïve to the ways of the world, and that a gentleman like Mr. Darcy is used to getting what he wants, and certainly, a lady of your beauty would not be ignored in such a circumstance. I began to defend you, but then Lydia had overheard, and said that you would not spend an entire day with that severe man, especially after he offended you so meanly at the assembly, and that if he did need saving that you certainly would not want to be the one to have to do the task. Then she said, 'We do not care if he is the richest man in Derbyshire.'"

Elizabeth listened in horror to the account of her sister's bringing disgrace to the Bennet family. Sometimes Elizabeth was able to ignore the indecorum of her younger sisters, but then she would be reminded of their unseemliness time and again.

"Then Mr. Collins decided to add his view of the situation. He said that his cousin could not possibly have done anything to help Mr. Darcy, as he is such a strong and capable man, and you are so weak, that it was likely the other way around. Mr. Darcy, being the man of noble lineage would have come to your rescue if any saving were necessary, but that he would never put himself in that kind of position with a woman of less distinction, for Lady Catherine could never approve." Elizabeth rolled her eyes at this, but knew he was probably correct on that point. Mr. Darcy, though likely gallant with the ladies of his own station, would not possibly do any more than was necessary for a daughter of a country gentleman.

"Mrs. Hopkins then said, that for your sake, she hoped Mr. Darcy would do his duty, as no one could respect the family of a woman who would discredit herself for the sake of catching a rich man."

"Jane, she cannot believe that I have done anything disreputable! She has always been so kind to me. She must know that I would not knowingly bring scandal to Longbourn!"

"I told her you would not, and she just shook her head and tsk tsk'd. She then suggested we make our purchases or leave."

After Elizabeth had taken all of this in, she asked, "Did you see anyone else?"

"Yes, we did see Aunt Philips while on our way home from the milliner's. She told us what Mama had told her. Lydia and Kitty giggled and said that if you had to pick someone to save, you should have waited for the officers to arrive. But Mr. Collins did not believe it to be true, that he was certain Mr. Darcy could not have allowed himself to be degraded by you."

Jane looked to her sister with remorse in her eyes for having to be the one to pass on such offensive news. But Lizzy hugged her and said, "Dear sister, you must learn to laugh at the insensibility of others. Mr. Collins is demonstrating his ignorance, rather than my shame. He probably dreams up speeches to declare his place as our saviour and ours as his charity. Surely, you must know that his opinion cannot matter one jot to me."

"But what of Meryton? Surely the opinion of our neighbours must have some weight? Lizzy, what if they believe Mama's words? There is no way to disprove her, and if they continue judging you as I witnessed yesterday, a scandal against our family is inevitable."

"I should go into town myself and make sure that everyone knows that I have no shame and that I am well. Surely a disgraced woman would not show herself in town brazenly. They will know by my demeanour that I am innocent."

"I do hope you are correct, but you must not walk there today; you are not fully recovered. I can tell that you need your rest."

"I am afraid you are correct on that point, so I will wait until tomorrow. Will you join me? You are stronger than you think, and your strength will help carry me through the day."

"I would be pleased to go with you. Now you go rest." Elizabeth hugged her sister again and went to her room for a needed nap. However, sleep would not come to her as she considered how her life was beginning to spin out of control.

ELIZABETH FELT STRONGER THAN THE PREVIOUS DAY, despite a deficiency of sleep during the night. She knew that what she needed most was fresh air and some activity to work out the lingering effects of her illness. The day was proving to be lovely, and the sun was shining, so she put on her spencer, bonnet and gloves and set out to Meryton with Jane.

Mr. Collins watched them as they departed the manor, curious to know where the two were going. Nothing was said of an outing over breakfast, and he felt for certain that Miss Elizabeth had set out to fan the flames of deception that had been ignited by her mother. Mr. Darcy would be a brilliant catch for her, but Mr. Collins was quite certain that his patroness would be horrified by even the hint of any unseemly behaviour displayed by her illustrious nephew, especially in light of his pending engagement to his cousin, Anne de Bourgh. He now realised why Miss Elizabeth had so adeptly caused him to change his allegiance from herself to her sister, Mary. She obviously had had her sights on a more lucrative prey. He quickly donned his coat and hat and headed out after them.

Even in her somewhat weakened state, Elizabeth still tended to outstrip her sister on their trek to Meryton, which was but two miles from home. She was uneasy about what she would find in town. Surely her sister had worried too much concerning the gossip being bandied about. Elizabeth had grown up amongst these people. They were familiar enough with her character to know that although she did often walk without a companion, this was because no one was available, rather than improper reasons.

As they entered town, they slowed their steps, so that nothing would appear amiss. They casually went into the bookstore, perusing the shelves for something unique. Elizabeth had brought some of her saved pin money, so that she would have purpose while in the many shops she intended on visiting. A book would be just the thing to bring her joy while soliciting information about her reputation. The owner of this shop, a man of about her father's age, saw them enter. He kept behind his desk as they shopped. Two local ladies entered together, saw her and smiled. Then they put their heads together and whispered indistinguishable words. Giggling, they left the establishment, glancing back her way one more time.

After about ten more minutes, the proprietor walked up and said, "Miss Bennet, Miss Elizabeth, can I assist you in finding a purchase?"

Elizabeth smiled at the man she had known since she came of age, "Hello, Mr. Thompson, I really have nothing in mind. Is there anything that you could recommend for me? I find that I would like to branch out a little and expand my limited supply of books, perhaps something that a woman would enjoy, for I have all the books of my father's at my disposal."

"How about Fordyce's Sermons?"

Elizabeth almost laughed out loud. What were the chances of this man suggesting the same book that had inspired her insipid cousin so? "No, I think not. I believe there is already a copy of that same book in possession of our cousin who has been visiting these two weeks. We have heard more than our share of that particular book. Perhaps a novel. I have been reading one from Radcliffe that amuses me, but I prefer trying a different author."

"A novel? Why Miss Elizabeth, I never took you for the maudlin type, but I suppose there are many things about you of which I have limited knowledge."

Her cheeks traitorously became scarlet as she considered the unspoken meaning behind his words. "Sir, my hope is that no one unconnected with my family would have a full perception of me, nor would judge my character without complete understanding. A casual observer, such as yourself, should not have the privilege of that much insight. As you would not judge a book by its cover, you should also not judge a person by mere observation or even more, hearsay. But I am sure, you were just considering my usual purchases and considering my tastes, which as you may recall are as varied as the people of Meryton." Elizabeth knew better than to offend, but she wanted to make her point clear, so she smiled charmingly at him to disarm her words, as she usually did when there was a risk of giving offence. If this man, who had known her for several years, was accepting the gossip at face value, what damage could the intermeddlers be instilling in the general population, and was that damage something from which her family could recover?

"If I can assist you in finding any purchases, I will be in the back." He turned and headed into the other room.

Finding his usually solicitous attention lacking, Elizabeth turned to her sister and said, "Jane, I think we have done enough shopping here. Shall we head to the milliner's?"

Jane had been watching the entire interaction between her sister and the bookseller, having an uncomfortable feeling about coming to town. They headed to their next destination three doors down. There were two ladies being waited upon when they entered, a Miss King and Miss Long. They looked up when the bell on the door rang. Elizabeth and her sister entered and went straight to the ribbons on the opposite side of the store. The two ladies and the shopkeeper kept stealing glances their way and whispering. Although Elizabeth had a familiarity with these ladies, she would not count them as friends.

The owner, Mrs. Hopkins, joined the Bennet sisters and asked, "What are you ladies doing in town? I am surprised to see you."

"I cannot guess why, as we shop here regularly, " Elizabeth replied.

"We heard news of your illness of course, but you look recovered."

"As you see." Elizabeth did not like the way this conversation was going either. "Do you have any new green ribbon? I would like some to match my cream satin."

"I received a new shipment last week. You can find the new ones hanging over the table by the window." Then she walked away. In all of Elizabeth's days, she could not remember this woman ever leaving her to shop on her own. Usually, she was fawning over the gentry, and the Bennets in particular.

Then Charlotte Lucas and her younger sister, Maria, walked in. Elizabeth was happy to see a face that she knew would be friendly. Miss Lucas and Elizabeth had been close friends since about ten years ago when Sir Lucas moved his family to the estate adjacent to Longbourn on the side opposite of Netherfield. "Lizzy, I am glad to see you out. Jane, I hope you are well."

"Charlotte, I am happy to see you. What brings you into town?"

She nodded to her sister, "I am with Maria. She wanted to purchase some fashion plates to help her dream up her next gown. I decided to join her since the day is so fine." Maria was looking down at her feet. "Lizzy, I am surprised to see you here." She glanced to the two customers who had stopped talking and seemed to be concentrating most fervently on the selection of patterns.

Not Charlotte too. "I suppose you want to get to your shopping. We will not disturb you."

"Please do not go on my account. I have been looking forward to spending time with you. Did your mother not tell you that I stopped by two days ago? I have been most anxious to see you well."

Elizabeth felt relief. "Charlotte, you are the best of friends. I am feeling back to my usual self, and decided to get some fresh air. You know me too well not to comprehend that a good walk is the best medicine for me."

Charlotte smiled at her friend and then turned to Jane, "Would you be so kind as to help Maria in sorting through the fashion plates? You know that I am greatly deficient when it comes to the latest styles." Jane, suspecting that Charlotte desired some privacy with Elizabeth, readily agreed and led Maria to that section of the shop.

Elizabeth spoke softly, "Charlotte, what is amiss? You must tell me what you have heard. My father said that my mother spread rumours in town, and I can see by the looks I have been receiving that her words have taken root."

Charlotte, looking around, saw that they had an audience. "Let us step outside." After walking onto the boardwalk, Charlotte pulled her aside to the area just between the two structures. "Lizzy, first let me say that I know you, and I have confidence that you have always acted with respectability; there is no reason for me to suspect your behaviour in this instance to be otherwise.

However, my mother has insisted that I not have contact with you until this misunderstanding with Mr. Darcy has been resolved."

"Does she think I have behaved inappropriately?"

"I do not know, but she believes that my association with you can lead to unfavourable outcomes for us. Lizzy, you need not tell me what actually happened that day. I support you as I would a sister, but I must keep my distance or risk censure from my parents, just until this blows over."

"But what if it does not?"

"Lizzy, you are innocent, I am certain. I believe that everything will work out satisfactorily."

"Dear friend, you must tell me. What are people saying?"

After a pause, Charlotte related, "That you had an assignation planned with Mr. Darcy at the folly on your father's estate, hoping to secure him and that a storm quickly arose trapping you there. Apparently one of you was injured while the other had to stay to administer relief. They believe that Mr. Darcy was just using you, while you were attempting to secure your future."

Elizabeth looked on her friend in horror. "But that is not what happened, I can assure you, Charlotte. Is that what my mother is saying about her own daughter? This is unconscionable."

"I do not know if that is what your mother said; I just know that that is the story going around." After a few moments of silence, she continued, "Lizzy, although my mother has forbidden me to see you, I want you to contact me should you need anything in which I may assist you. My dearest friend is in trouble, and I cannot sit idly by while you may need me. I will always be here for you."

Elizabeth hugged Charlotte in an affectionate embrace, then parted before they could be seen. "Your confidence in me will give me the strength to endure whatever may come. I need only think of your steadfastness."

"There is one more thing; I saw Mr. Collins walking around town looking for you. He is asking where you may have gone. He seems to think that he has become your guardian. I tell you this so that you may find a means of avoiding him. The last thing you need is a scene with another gentleman."

"Thank you, Charlotte. I came into town today to discover for myself what was being said and to observe people's reactions. I have not been well-pleased with what I have seen, and your communication has disheartened me." At her friend's look of contrition, she continued, "Be not disturbed by my saying so, I am glad that you have told me. I know I can trust in your good judgement."

"I will go to Jane and send her out to you. I suggest you continue through this alley to the next street. I observed Mr. Collins leaving that area of town earlier." Charlotte then went into the shop. When Jane joined her, they quickly made their way home to share the news with their father.

MEANWHILE, AT MERYTON, Mr. Collins was attempting to find the elusive Misses Bennet. After several attempts at asking the local inhabitants, he came across a new member of the neighbourhood, who was riding into town. With an appropriate bow, he began, "Mr. Bingley, sir, I hate to impose upon you on this beautiful day, which I am certain you have planned to spend in your own pursuits; indeed, if I were a man of leisure such as yourself, I likewise would enjoy the fine weather, but I find that you and I might possibly share the same mission as regards to the future of those we hold dear, and so I am humbling myself before you, one gentleman to another, with the hope that perhaps you could assist me in locating Miss Bennet and her sister, Miss Elizabeth. Of course I know that you are very busy and do not have time to actively assist me in my endeavour, but perhaps you have seen the ladies over the course of this morning."

Bingley was quite astonished at this speech made by a man whom he had met but once, and who was wiping his brow with a wet handkerchief, as he was sweating abundantly. Mr. Collins had uttered his words so quickly that he had only taken one breath through the whole communication, and so had to catch up at the end. As their missions were perhaps somewhat related, Bingley smiled and offered what little input he had available, that he had not seen the ladies, but that he would enjoy the society if he had.

"Mr. Bingley, I must ask that you pass on my apologies to the guest in your home of Netherfield Park, which I suspect is a fine estate in itself, certainly finer than Longbourn of which I am the sole heir, and which estate will pass to me at the time of Mr. Bennet's demise. Of course, there is no residence within the county of Hertfordshire that can compare to the acreage of my patroness, Lady Catherine de Bourgh, which boasts over one hundred windows and grounds that extend beyond the distance one could travel by foot in a day. But I digress; as this reminds me of my errand, for Lady Catherine's nephew, your guest to whom I have referred, Mr. Darcy of Pemberley, is in great danger of being abominably used by my cousin whom I have known but a fortnight, Miss Elizabeth, who conspired a compromise with that gentleman in order to force him into ignoring his duty to himself and to his relations, including Lady Catherine's daughter, Miss De Bourgh who is none other than Mr. Darcy's betrothed. I saw Miss Elizabeth and her elder sister leave Longbourn on their way to Meryton to set ablaze the flames of deceit, for I know that Mr. Darcy would never put into jeopardy his duty to his dear aunt and cousin and make himself vulnerable to a country lady of low birth, such as Miss Elizabeth. If I can find them, I will escort them back to Longbourn and insist that their father, Mr. Bennet, keep Miss Elizabeth away from local society, so as not to encourage further injury to Mr. Darcy's character."

"I thank you, sir, for your interest in the integrity of Mr. Darcy. I will be sure to pass on to him how you are attempting to take such prodigious care of him, despite having never made his acquaintance. I am unhappy to say that I have not seen the Bennet ladies this morning, but if I do, I will certainly warn them." At this, Bingley steered his mount to the side and rode away, leaving Mr. Collins to wonder at the exchange.

Bingley had indeed been attempting to do his duty to his friend, to find information related to the rumours. Mr. Collins's words did not convince Bingley of the veracity of his claims. To be sure, Mr. Collins's speech more likely achieved the opposite of his goal, for Mr. Collins was not one whose words held gravitas. Bingley had also been hoping to encounter Miss Bennet. He found himself thinking about her often, as he had never met a woman with such kind expressions of sincere goodness, and he wanted to know more of her, despite his friend's apprehensions concerning the Bennets. He reckoned that were he to judge Miss Bennet for her sister's supposed machinations, this would be akin to someone casting judgement upon him for his own sister's duplicity in attempting to seduce Darcy, not that he believed Miss Elizabeth capable of such deception herself. After a couple of hours, he found no sign of the sisters and eventually returned to Netherfield, having heard only a continuation of the tales that had been circulating concerning his friend.

He regretted having to share with Darcy the results of his probing. Rather than diminishing, the tales were growing more specific and more indicting. He attempted to deny to the locals the possibility of the claims, but had no proof to offer for his objections. Bingley was regretting having invited Darcy to Netherfield and felt the full weight of the blame. If only he had not let this property! He could not change the past, and thus quickly decided to help his friend into the future.

Chapter Four

And how, when she considered the haughty character of the Marchese di Vivaldi, the imperious and vindictive nature of the Marchesa, and, still more, their united repugnance to a connection with her, how could she endure to think, even for a moment, of intruding herself into such a family! Pride, delicacy, good sense seemed to warn her against a conduct so humiliating and vexatious in its consequences, and to exhort her to preserve her own dignity by independence.
Ann Radcliffe
The Italian

Over the course of the following week, Elizabeth unobtrusively remained at Longbourn with her family. Her mother had finally begun to lament her efficacious skill at spreading what she would have considered at the time splendid news concerning her family. No one had heard anything from Mr. Darcy, as he remained furtively ensconced at Netherfield. Mr. Bingley had been seen on multiple occasions throughout the neighbourhood, at social gatherings and hunting parties; nevertheless, he did not mention his friend, and few had the gall to ask about him.

Mrs. Bennet had taken to her room, claiming her nerves were carried away, and she blamed her least favourite daughter, Elizabeth, for her own predicament. She had forgotten that it was she who had first begun the unsubstantiated tales that now quite possibly could be the ruination of her family. Should Mr. Darcy not do his duty and come apply for her hand, Elizabeth and all of her sisters could expect to be shunned by anyone who might offer a future for them. However, as Mrs. Bennet had remained upstairs, she also persisted in her ignorance of the discussions taking place in Mr. Bennet's study between Mr. Bennet and Mr. Collins.

The visitor at Longbourn had been in residence for the previous three weeks, which had been quite enough as Mr. Bennet reckoned. At first, Mr. Collins provided amusement for the gentleman, but his presence had become wearisome, especially in the face of scandal, as he spent no small amount of time proclaiming to Mr. Bennet, and the rest of the family, the dangers of imprudence. Elizabeth had begun taking meals in her room to avoid the castigation of the man against her character. She avoided him at every turn, so she was unaware of the time he had been spending with her father, and her father had chosen not to share with her the topic of the deliberations, so as not to cause her undue distress.

Mr. Collins attempted to come up with a solution that would enable Mr. Darcy to be free to marry Miss De Bourgh. He held Lady Catherine's plans for her daughter as his greatest concern. If he could secure Darcy's removal from the clutches of Miss Elizabeth, he would be counted as most devoted. And although Mr. Collins could not approve of Miss Elizabeth's methods of attracting a man to herself, he could appreciate that she did *in fact* attract her share. Her sister, Mary, was a pretty kind of girl, yet she did not have the vitality and allure that Elizabeth possessed. In light of this, he had decided to offer for Miss Elizabeth, thereby securing her to himself and freeing Mr. Darcy for his cousin, Miss De Bourgh. The plan was perfect. The Bennets would be destitute upon Mr. Bennet's demise without Mr. Collins's intervention. And although that could be years away, the fear of the eventual certainty of his passing plagued Mrs. Bennet and began to play on the sensibility of them all, thereby ensuring their acceptance of his proposal.

At first Mr. Bennet had steadfastly refused any such possibility; nevertheless, as time dragged on without the great man showing his face at Longbourn, he had begun to fear the eventuality of having to accept Mr. Collins's request for her hand. He did not share Mr. Collins's supplication with Mary either, for he knew that she had developed an unlikely *tendre* for him. Mary had always been hidden behind her sisters' exuberance and beauty. The past fortnight had done much to improve her bearing, and Mr. Bennet would very much dislike seeing her hurt by the likes of Mr. Collins, and as much as Mr. Bennet hated to consider the reality of the situation, the truth of the matter was that his family needed Mr. Collins's security. Never had Mr. Bennet regretted so much his lackadaisical attitude towards his family's future.

Elizabeth was summoned to her father's study one morning just after breakfast. He had been reticent throughout the meal, while Mr. Collins had a look of great satisfaction upon his face. With apprehension, Elizabeth knocked on her father's door and opened it before she heard a response. "Papa, you wanted to speak with me?"

"Close the door, Elizabeth." Her father then rose and assisted her to the chair across the desk from him. He reached for the port and poured out two glasses, one for each of them. Handing one to her, she characteristically lifted an eyebrow in question. Elizabeth could often tell what her father was thinking; regardless, on this occasion, his words would shock her to the core. Although early in the day for wine, she took a drink, knowing he would not have offered fortification without reasoning.

After several minutes of quiet, just when Elizabeth had determined to ask why she had been summoned, her father began, "The rumours seem to have taken on a life of their own, my dear. We have had no callers, so I asked Hill to determine the extent of the effects of your mother's blathering upon our neighbours. We have little hope that the scandal will die down of its own accord. Apparently, news has even reached London, as an enterprising servant related the story to the papers in town. News of Mr. Darcy's shenanigans comes with a high price, you see."

"Who would do such a thing?"

"That is neither here nor there, my dear." Thoughtfully, he continued, "Mr. Darcy will survive the scandal to be sure, as tomorrow's paper will come up with new stories to relay and distract. Many so-called gentlemen of his station use young women and get nothing more than their hand slapped and a reputation of being a Casanova. His wealth will protect him; however, you do not have that luxury. Your virtue makes you an acceptable bride to a gentleman; if that falls into question, your smiles and beauty will do little to attract a suitor worthy of you, especially in light of your small portion. I am afraid that your heroic efforts at saving Mr. Darcy have put you in a tenuous position from which you will not likely recover. If you were the only one to feel the effects, I am certain you could handle the change with fortitude and grace. Be that as it may, your entire family will fall with you. Your and your sisters' dowries are insufficient to protect you in light of this scandal."

Elizabeth's eyes filled with tears as she attempted to hear her father out. He was her protector and she prayed that he had an alternative, a plan to recover what the family once had before her mistaken act of kindness. "Mr. Collins refuses to ask for Mary's hand while the family suffers from disgrace. He has offered an alternative that would save your reputation, secure our family's future and afford you a place at Longbourn."

"Father, you cannot mean what I think. Tell me you are not suggesting...."

"Elizabeth, you must know that if there were any other alternatives, I would not impose upon you in such a way. Your happiness means a great deal to me, but my family's welfare will be vastly affected by how we handle this situation."

"But what about Mary? Although I do not understand her sentiments, she is quite taken with the man. Surely I could not hurt her in that way."

"Elizabeth, he will not ask for her."

"Papa, I cannot marry that man! He is a fool!"

"Fool or not, he makes a valid offer. He will inherit Longbourn. Due to the scandal, he cannot offer for Mary; however, if you agree to marry him, the scandal will be forgotten and your sisters will be able to marry where they will. And you will become mistress of your family's estate when I am gone." At her look of horror, he continued, "Being married to someone whom you cannot respect can be insufferable at times, it is true, but really, my dear, there are amusements that will arise in your daily life that will make living with a foolish man bearable."

"No! I will not!" Tears were now streaming down her cheeks. "Papa, I cannot marry that man. Please, do not make me; I beg of you. Send me away; I do not care where."

"If it were only you, as difficult as that would be, I know I could do that. You are strong and intelligent and would endure wherever you are, but your sisters cannot. Elizabeth, Mr. Bingley surely could not continue in his admiration of Jane. We have neither seen nor heard from his sisters or that gentleman since leaving the cabin."

"But what if Mr. Darcy offers for me? Have you made any effort to contact him, to make him do his duty? Is he even still in the area?"

"Yes, Lizzy, he remains at Netherfield. Yesterday morning I sent a missive to him requesting his presence. Nathan returned and confirmed to me that the gentleman had indeed received my note. Would you prefer Mr. Darcy over Mr. Collins should he make an offer?"

"Papa, I do not want either man, but of course between the two I would be inclined towards Mr. Darcy. But I have always desired to marry for love. Jane and I have agreed to only marry with the strongest of affections. Papa, please. Surely we do not need to make a decision today."

"Mr. Collins must return to Hunsford tomorrow, and he rightly requests an answer. He would like a private interview with you this morning."

"Please, I need time."

"I will ask him to wait until this evening after supper then, to see if Mr. Darcy will do his duty." He assisted her from her seat and hugged her. "I truly regret this course of action."

She stood motionless, angry with her father, yet sympathetic to his plight, that she would be the one to cause him such grief. "I'm going out," she said and then quickly left the study, anxious to remove herself from the house before encountering anyone. In her haste, she left her pelisse, bonnet and gloves at home, not caring for her comfort on this chilly, wet morning and desirous to escape.

Elizabeth had always found great delight in studying people's characters. She shared this penchant with her father, much to her mother's vexation. Mr. Bennet, relishing in the absurdity of others, found contentment in meditating on the foolishness of those nearest to him. Introducing someone new to the household, in the form of Mr. Collins, had been anticipated and provided no small amount of merriment to Mr. Bennet and his favourite daughter; nevertheless, he and Elizabeth both had learnt that small doses of their relation were sufficient to satisfy any proclivity towards this type of amusement. Mr. Collins was equal parts haughty and servile, and where one word would suffice, he used ten. So the thought of being irrevocably joined to such a ridiculous man was causing profound turmoil for Elizabeth and despair for her father.

Elizabeth left from the servants' entrance, eluding anyone's notice, and headed towards the gardens in the back of the house. She started at a quick walk that soon turned into a run when she reached the trees. Had Elizabeth not been so familiar with this path, she surely would have lost her way, as the tears in her eyes obscured her view, but on she ran. Suddenly, as a winded Elizabeth rounded the bend at the top of a slow incline, she came upon a man on horseback. In her precipitance and tear-filled eyes, she did not see him until she was nearly underfoot. Impulsively, she screamed, and the horse reared; notwithstanding, on this occasion the gentleman on horseback did not fall. He had been riding at a slow pace, reluctant to fulfil his obligation, and so was able to more easily gain control of his mount, despite the soreness in his ankle. Elizabeth fell back to the ground, which inspired Mr. Darcy to dismount and reach down to assist her to her feet. He held a cold stare as he reached his hand down to hers, bare to the elements, and easily lifted her to a stand. He noticed that she had been crying as she attempted to catch her breath from her exertion and dismay.

What kind of woman runs across the countryside? Did she not learn anything from our last encounter? Am I to be bound to this chit who has no understanding of the appropriate behaviour and dress of a gentlewoman?

Elizabeth attempted a curtsey, but performed ill, while Mr. Darcy provided a cursory bow. Looking aside she said, "Mr. Darcy, forgive me. In my haste I was not heeding my direction and did not notice your presence until you were upon me." She knew that her lack of bonnet and gloves left her open to his derision.

"Miss Bennet, you are headed out alone? Do you not have a maid or footman to join you?"

Elizabeth heard only contempt from this man who held her future in his hands. "I often walk out alone. I am on my father's property and would have no reason to suppose anyone wholly unconnected to us would be riding across his land. Anyway, we have had no visitors this past week, so why should I expect to run across you this morning? Surely any business you might have had at Longbourn is now long overdue." *How dare he judge my suitability when he himself has been shirking his own obligations?*

"I know my duties and how to fulfil them, Miss Elizabeth Bennet. I believe that we had an agreement which I held to be binding, but which you apparently did not." He continued to stare at her face, red with anger, seeing her tears, but not moved to sympathy. "Congratulations, you were able to succeed where others were not."

"I have only succeeded in saving a man who shows only disdain towards me, that has resulted in a scandal that has tainted my family and provided me a future filled with misery, no matter the course."

"Miss Bennet, do not pretend ignorance of my worth and suitability. There is nary a woman in England, single or married, who would not wish to be in your place. Few can boast of my advantages."

Elizabeth found herself laughing, through her tears, at his arrogance. All of the emotions of the past week were surging up within her, the fear, the absurdity, the anger; and this man had the audacity to speculate that she should be gratified by her position, that she should, by some rational means, rejoice in her suffering! "Do you mean to pay respects to my father, then? Are you to offer for me?"

"I do," he answered in a clipped tone and with visible scorn, as he tried to maintain self-control. His life had taken a decided turn in a direction at complete opposition to the one he had anticipated. Darcy's plans were made; he was to return to town and offer for Lady Annette. As a couple, they would live with mutual regard and distinction, and his wife would assist his sister, Georgiana, through the trying years of coming out into society with grace and poise. Now, through no fault of his own, he was bound to this woman with questionable respectability, who runs across the grounds of her father's estate without proper attire and her dress six inches deep in mud.

"Do I accept a man who humiliates himself with his obsequious banter, or do I accept a man who humiliates me with his conceited disdain?" Elizabeth asked herself through her despair. The answer to this was clearer than she gave credit at the time with the haughty Mr. Darcy before her, looking down upon her. Between the two men asking for her hand, she would rather take arrogance over stupidity; at least there would be something to admire in a man who was well educated, and he was more handsome to look upon, which had its own merits. Yet at this moment, she could not see clearly what would later be obvious. She could bear his presence no longer, and abruptly left to make her way down the path upon which she had been travelling when she had been interrupted. She could only think of fleeing, finding peace in obscurity.

Darcy watched her run down the lane, not understanding her outburst. Many years had passed since he had seen a young maiden demonstrate such activity, and he was appalled, but he knew his duty to his honour. He had no desire to offer for Miss Elizabeth; she had little beauty and no accomplishments. Hoping that by some miracle, the situation would change, he had remained at Netherfield, listening to the reports from his valet and Bingley concerning the gossip of the neighbourhood. Like Elizabeth, he had been hoping for some miracle to relieve him of his obligations as a gentleman.

Darcy knew he could just walk away, but his honour forbade it. When news had reached London, as confirmed by an express from his home in town, he accepted that he had no choice but to offer for her and only awaited the time when he would be able to ride to Longbourn, without the aid of his cane, in order to ask for Miss Elizabeth's hand. In his pride, he refused to arrive looking less than his usual healthy self. He had considered paying the family a settlement to release him of his responsibilities while compensating them for their loss in respectability; however he knew this would worsen the situation for the family, seeming like she was his mistress whose services he had bought. The family may receive an easy pay-off, but the long-term damage to the Bennets would be beyond calculation. He also thought to pay a man of lower station to marry her, but could he really release his duties to another? This went against his character and his pride in every way.

As he arrived at Longbourn, he dismounted and handed his horse to the startled stable boy, who like the rest of the family's servants had been privy to the gossip bandied about Meryton. Darcy instructed him, "Do not bother to take him to the stables. I shall not be long." The young man could not hide his curiosity as he watched the imposing gentleman walk up to the main entry of the home.

After Darcy was greeted at the door by an older man, seemingly the butler, but perhaps a footman, he waited to be directed into the presence of Mr. Bennet. The man returned and asked Darcy to follow him to the room that must have been Mr. Bennet's private study. Books – those not included in the assortment that lined the shelves against two of the walls – were strewn about the room on the table by the fire, on his desk, and some were even stacked upon the floor. Mr. Bennet was seated at a medium sized desk and stood upon Darcy's entrance. They each performed a cursory bow, and then Mr. Bennet directed Darcy to a seat across from him. Mr. Bennet held his astonishment as he offered his guest a beverage from the sideboard on which sat an array of bottles usually untouched until the evening hours.

"I thank you. Perhaps some brandy?"

Mr. Bennet set aside two glasses and poured up his best. Whether or not Mr. Darcy required any fortification to weather the conversation at hand, he did; the small glass of port he partook with his daughter, not nearly adequate for this occasion. After handing the glass to Darcy, he determined to be patient as he awaited the man's purpose in coming. Darcy drank the brandy with appreciation and commented upon its merit. Mr. Bennet merely bowed his head in acknowledgement, as he abided the continued deferment. Mr. Bennet was adept at watching and waiting for the proper moment for intercession, but his imperturbability was waning. This man before him had procrastinated in his duty long enough, and Mr. Bennet was ready to conclude the business at hand.

At length Darcy, having finished his drink, began, "Mr. Bennet, I have no doubt that you apprehend the reason for my call. Indeed, you must have anticipated this interview for some time now." Mr. Bennet stared at the man, revealing no emotion. Darcy took a deep breath and continued, "I have come to offer for your daughter's hand in marriage."

Mr. Bennet was in no mood to let this occasion pass without causing a little grief. "Do you now? And which daughter would you like as your partner in life?"

Confused, Darcy responded, "Miss Elizabeth, of course." He did not like to be toyed with.

"Yes, Lizzy. She is my favourite, you know, meritorious of any present distress that this unfortunate circumstance has caused you. I have no doubt that you will find her admirable qualities worthy of even a man of your heritage."

"As your daughter, I have no doubt that you see her as such."

"Her being the daughter of such an indolent man as I, or silly a woman as her mother, is not what makes her commendable. Had you been found by Lydia, she would have run straightaway to Longbourn to share the tale and forgotten what she was about halfway home, as she began to think about the bonnet she would refashion upon her arrival; or by Mary, who would have offered you her advice on carelessly running across the countryside on an uncontrollable mount, and how putting yourself at risk is an affront to God; or Kitty, who would have stood stock-still crying and wishing her sister, Lydia, were there to tell her what to do. Then there is Jane, who would have held your hand and provided soothing relief until your end was at hand. No, you were quite fortunate that Elizabeth was the one who came upon you. Her determination and courage have served her well these twenty years, and although her mother depicts her as not being as beautiful as the angelic Jane, I confess that I see in my second daughter the charisma and fascination of the divine." Mr. Bennet was determined to let Mr. Darcy know the true value of the woman who would become his bride. "Mr. Darcy, if you allow her to thrive under your care, you will discover a charming lady of both intelligence and grace. You could not in all of England find a woman with more estimable qualities than my Lizzy."

Darcy listened on, showing no emotion in the face of this degree of doltish disillusionment. He determined to display to the man charity because he could appreciate the difficulty inherent upon losing a daughter to a man he felt the need to placate. For all Mr. Bennet knew, Darcy could be one of the many men of England who physically abused their wives and exploited the women for pleasure alone. He was not such a man, and even more, he had steeled himself to give the respect due a wife of an esteemed gentleman, but that could not delude him adequately at this point to forget her origins or to see virtues where they did not dwell. He had just seen her running across the estate in a dishevelled state with dirty hems and tattered slippers. Perhaps in the town of Meryton, such unseemliness was given merit, but not by his standards. "Sir, I can assure you that your daughter will not be treated with anything but courtesy due the daughter and wife of a gentleman."

"Can you promise the same from your family? Will they also treat her with regard?"

"Mr. Bennet, I cannot claim to know how my family will react to this compulsory union. They know that I would never lower myself to marry into a family so decidedly beneath my own without contrivance. How they welcome or spurn Miss Elizabeth cannot be helped at this point. My hope of course is that they will come to accept the situation as it is and learn to look beyond her provenance."

"And what about you? Can you look beyond her origins? Can you in honesty promise to love, comfort, honour and protect her, Mr. Darcy?"

"I promise to do my very best. But you must understand that by marrying your daughter, I am going against the wishes of my friends, family, and indeed against my own inclinations. Forgive me, but disguise of every sort is my abhorrence, nor am I ashamed of the feelings which I relate. They are natural and just. Could you expect me to rejoice in the inferiority of her connections? To congratulate myself on the hope of relations, whose condition in life is so decidedly beneath my own?"

Mr. Bennet felt himself growing more angry every moment, yet he tried to the utmost to speak with composure when he said, "You are mistaken, Mr. Darcy, if you suppose yourself superior in any way, other than consequence, to my daughter. I watched you with much amusement when you arrived into Meryton, peacocking around the assemblies, above your company, exhibiting your hauteur. Elizabeth is not impressed by your vainglorious displays, rather she finds diversion in the absurdity of your pretension."

By now thus affronted, Darcy stood up before the older man behind the desk. "Mr. Bennet, I will thank you to hold your tongue. The pride that you deride is the only thing that has brought me thus today to save your family from the ruination brought about by your daughter's stratagem and spreading of scandalous reports." Darcy began pacing to calm his indignation, the mild residual pain in his ankle forgotten. Finally, when he at last succeeded in calming his emotions, he continued, "I suggest that we call the banns at church in two days' time and then set the date the Tuesday following the final call, giving us just over a fortnight to complete the task. The sooner we conclude this business, the better. You understand that I am a most eligible bachelor, and there will be no peace anytime soon concerning the forthcoming announcement. This amount of time should be adequate to prove to the populace that no issue was derived from the day I spent in isolation with your daughter, while hastening an end to the scandalous rumours. I intend to leave for town Monday morning with the goal of telling my sister and family my plans before the papers can publish the story. When I return to Netherfield in one week's time, I will have the settlement papers prepared and ready for you to review. I am certain you will approve of the provisions that your daughter will receive. Indeed, I plan on being quite generous in spite of the situation."

Mr. Bennet had been sitting, staring at Mr. Darcy's display. He knew that he had lost his temper, something seldom seen at Longbourn. He was attempting to keep his composure as well. At the end of Darcy's speech, he was ready to end the conversation, having no reason to disagree with the proposal that Darcy had obviously already predetermined. Mr. Bennet was astute enough to realise that Mr. Darcy was trying to make good on a disturbing situation, but he could not condone any discredit to his daughter. He stood and walked around his desk, holding out his hand to Mr. Darcy, a silent acknowledgement of the arrangements. "Until Sunday, sir. I wish you the best of health."

As Darcy closed the door to Mr. Bennet's study, Mr. Collins intercepted him with a solemn bow. Darcy's astonishment at being so addressed was very evident to anyone who might have been present, excepting Mr. Collins himself. "Mr. Darcy, you must allow me to apologise for not being available to receive you properly when you arrived at Longbourn. Your estimable aunt, Lady Catherine de Bourgh, gifted to me the living at Hunsford, the paling of which is shared by your aunt's own estate, Rosings Park, surely the grandest house in all of Kent." He went on to observe that he was very fortunate in his patroness whose attention to his wishes, and consideration for his comfort, appeared very remarkable; then he protested that he had never in his life witnessed such behaviour in a person of rank, such affability, as he himself experienced from Lady Catherine. "And, I am happy to report to you that the fine Lady was in perfect health not three weeks ago.

"You may wonder at the coincidence at finding someone connected to your own family temporarily residing here at Longbourn." Darcy was eyeing him with unrestrained wonder, and when at last Mr. Collins allowed him time to speak, replied with an air of distant civility as he attempted to make his way around him to the front entrance. Mr. Collins, however, was not discouraged from speaking again, and Mr. Darcy's contempt was abundantly increasing with the length of his second speech up until Mr. Collins finally got to the point.

"You cannot possibly have come here with any intention of aligning yourself with a family so beneath you, and indeed, unworthy of your attentions. I can see that you have the same admirable qualities as your relation, my patroness, who condescends to guide her humble servant in the manner most befitting a productive member of society. I would have you know, sir, that your unfortunate meeting with Miss Elizabeth will now in no way cause a breach in the alliance which you have long held with your most worthy cousin, Miss De Bourgh. For I have offered to take your place, thus freeing you of a misplaced obligation to consort with the Bennets." He said this with such a look of satisfaction as he took another low bow, that he missed the distaste covering Darcy's visage.

"Sir, do you mean to suggest that I should dismiss my duty and allow a man who is decidedly beneath me to fulfil my own obligations? In what manner can you defend the suggestion that I would ignore my conscience and allow you to pay a debt that is my own?"

"Mr. Darcy, you misunderstand me. I only mean that it would be an honour for me to aid you in escaping a match, which cannot be desirable for you, to a woman of low connections and qualities that cannot compare to those of your lovely and most estimable cousin. I have within my power a way of securing Miss Elizabeth to myself. Her father, just yesterday evening agreed that should you fail to arrive to secure her hand, that he would consent to my offer."

"You and Mr. Bennet must be forgiven your obvious misunderstanding of my character. I would not and could not *fail* in doing the duty that has been laid at my own door. Your sense of responsibility is misplaced, sir."

"But my duty to Lady Catherine demands that I assist..."

He was cut off here, "Sir, you may feel an inclination towards appeasing my aunt, but you have no connection with me. This is a matter which does not concern you in the slightest, so I would thank you to let me by." Darcy made his way around the obsequious man, and then turned with a parting thought. "I will inform my own relations about my upcoming nuptials. Do not let me discover you have taken the task upon yourself."

"But..." Before he could continue, Mr. Darcy had closed the door behind him.

THE BANNS WERE READ as expected on the following Sunday. Darcy made a point to sit with the Bennets. If he were locked into his present course, he would make a good show of it. He sat next to Elizabeth, but as she was looking down, he could not see her eyes as her bonnet obscured his view. Bingley took advantage of the occasion and sat, along with his sisters, in the pew behind the Bennet family. Caroline, indignant about the upcoming nuptials and primed to find fault, showed little civility towards Elizabeth, who found Miss Bingley's behaviour more amusing than offensive. She could not judge Miss Bingley for her disappointed hopes, no matter how contrary to her own they would seem. Of course, Elizabeth had not yet heard the story of Caroline's disgrace, for if she had, she would have found diversion in the highly variable wishes of the two ladies. Miss Bingley's lingerie had been desecrated by Darcy when she attempted to secure him, and Elizabeth's dress when she was attempting to flee the possibility. But as news of this story had not yet reached Longbourn, due to the scarcity of visitors, she remained in ignorance and instead had to concentrate on disregarding the imposing man sitting beside her.

She attempted to listen to the pastor whom she had known for many years now. Although kind, his monotonous way of delivering a message often left her mind free to wander. Today was such an occasion. No matter how hard she tried to attend to his words, she continued to dwell on Mr. Darcy and the upcoming announcement. When Darcy sat beside her upon entering the church, she could discern whispers of acknowledgement from all around her. Those in the pews turned this way and that to observe her reception. She attempted to look serene, as Jane would certainly be, but she was not Jane, and hiding her emotions came difficult for her. Instead, she just looked down, so as to avoid giving cause for more disapprobation from her neighbours or the gentleman.

After church, Mrs. Bennet, having completely forgotten the dire straights her family had faced upon first hearing of Darcy's private conference with her husband, merrily invited the party from Netherfield over for tea, which Bingley readily accepted. That was the last place Darcy wanted to be. He knew that he would marry Miss Elizabeth soon enough, but he had no desire to spend time with her family. He figured that after they married, the two of them would spend little time in the presence of the Bennets. Elizabeth's demeanour would hopefully improve with time away from her noisome relations. He planned to limit occasions that would put her in their presence. Because Bingley hastily accepted the invitation, and as he was Bingley's guest, he had little choice but to join them; refusing would give too great offence.

Miss Bingley felt her advantage when compared to the Bennets and readily derided their manners while on the way to Longbourn. Darcy had forgiven her of her misguided attempt at securing him. Although he had no intention whatsoever of a match with her, he could upon reflection absolve her of miscreant designs. Had she been successful, she could have saved him from an imprudent marriage. Yet what Miss Bingley did not realise was that marriage to her would be no less ignoble. "Mr. Darcy, I hope you will give your mother-in-law a few hints, when this desirable event takes place, as to the advantage of holding her tongue; and if you can compass it, to cure the younger girls of running after the officers. And, if I may mention so delicate a subject, endeavour to check that little something, bordering on conceit and impertinence, which your lady possesses."

"Have you anything else to propose for my domestic felicity?"

"Oh! Yes. —Do let the portraits of your uncle and aunt Philips be placed in the gallery at Pemberley. Put them next to your great uncle the judge. They are in the same profession, you know, only in different lines. As for your Elizabeth's picture, you must not attempt to have it taken, for what painter could give beauty where there is none." She laughed heartily as her brother cast her an exasperated look, disbelieving they could have been derived from the same parents.

Darcy was about to respond with irritation, as Miss Bingley had gone too far, but how had he spoken any more graciously? She felt she could speak thus because he did not disabuse her of the idea. He then resolved to show more moderation in his expressions concerning Miss Elizabeth and her family.

The afternoon was spent in uncomfortable and contrived conversation. Mrs. Bennet had set a fine display of food; however, no one but Mr. Hurst could appreciate the effort, as Mr. Bingley and Jane were too wrapped up in their tête-a-tête, while half of the group either failingly attempted to speak of some commonality while the others looked on in unfeigned discontent.

Lydia, the youngest of the Bennet daughters, was a stout, well-grown girl of fifteen, with a fine complexion and good-humoured countenance, a favourite with her mother, whose affection had brought her into public at an early age. She had high animal spirits, and a sort of natural self-consequence. She was very equal therefore to address Mr. Bingley on the subject of a ball given in honour of Mr. Darcy and her sister, Lizzy. "Mr. Bingley, it would be the most shameful thing in the world if you do not give a ball to celebrate the occasion." His answer to this sudden attack was delightful to their mother's ear, but painful for Elizabeth.

"I am perfectly ready to open my home for a ball, I assure you. How would the Monday prior to the wedding on Tuesday suit?" Mrs. Bennet and Miss Lydia were in perfect accord on the matter, and so the date was set. "And I would like to claim a dance with all of the Bennet ladies, starting with Miss Bennet for the first set and Miss Elizabeth for the following one, if I may be so bold."

Jane blushed and readily accepted the request. Darcy, seeing that he could not escape the affair, turned to Elizabeth and applied for her hand for the first set. He did not go so far as to request another from any of her sisters, however – his discourtesy being noticed by more in the room than just Elizabeth. She felt this to be another proof of his arrogance and she determined, then, that she would find ways to show him that *she* could not always admire him as he felt he so deserved.

Miss Bingley and her sister, reaching a new level of astonishment at the display, whispered together in quiet merriment laced with derision; yet when they finally left and were able to be at leisure for sharing their conversation within the confines of the carriage, they expressed their sentiments openly. "Charles, what could you be thinking? A ball? Surely Mr. Darcy would not want such a spectacle made, seeming to celebrate his union with that uncouth family, would you, sir?"

Considering her own spectacle made at his expense but one week ago, he felt her declarations rather bold and imperceptive of her own position within his forbearance. "I would not wish to draw attention to the event, beyond what is necessary to give the appearance of propriety. Nevertheless, hopefully the ball will do the task of drawing the gossips away from the methods of our attachment and towards the fulfilment of the marriage with all the usual consequence that accompanies a wedding celebration."

"Regardless of the prudence of the idea, we will have a ball, and you, Caroline, will have the opportunity to display your excellent hosting skills, as mistress of my household. Personally, I am looking forward to the celebration in my home, to repay the kindnesses shown to me by the locals," said an optimistic Mr. Bingley.

Miss Bingley, now having a new and enlightened perspective on hosting the event, began planning in her mind how she would demonstrate her skills to Darcy in contrast to Eliza's. He would regret that he did not allow her to save him.

IN KENT, ON THIS SAME DAY, and about the same time, Mr. Collins completed the Sunday worship service at Hunsford. He had not seen his patroness since his arrival late the previous day. Mr. Collins was in an agitated state, knowing that Lady Catherine would be highly incensed with the scandalous occurrences at Longbourn, which put him in the unhappy position of having news to tell her, but not being at liberty to share. He felt that it was his duty to ensure her wellbeing, and having failed in that endeavour by not securing Miss Elizabeth's hand, Mr. Collins knew he would face the brunt of her initial wrath, which would only be amplified by her supposing that he withheld the gossip from her in order to achieve his own felicity. His plans to save Mr. Darcy from the clutches of Miss Elizabeth Bennet did not come to fruition and actually put an embargo on his efforts to serve Lady Catherine through his usual efficient means of communication. Mr. Darcy had made it clear that he should not inform his patroness of her nephew's upcoming wedding. Nevertheless, he did need to share with her his own joy at having offered for – and subsequently been accepted by – the hand of Miss Mary Bennet. He was quite content in his choice of bride, excepting the anticipated wrath of Lady Catherine at his failure to remedy the scandal to her advantage.

After Mr. Darcy had visited Longbourn and made his declarations to honour his duty, Mr. Collins had decided to continue with his plan to marry the third daughter of Longbourn. Having a close connection with the Bennet family would now be to his advantage should Lady Catherine's ire be more than he could manage, since Mr. Darcy might have more to offer by way of patronage in the church. So the evening before his departure from Longbourn, rather than offering for Miss Elizabeth, he had asked for a private interview with Miss Mary and declared his passionate love towards her, and promised that she would participate in all the benefits that an alliance with him could provide.

Chapter Five

"Pride is the chalice into which all human sins are poured: it glitters and jingles and its arabesque lures your gaze, while your lips involuntarily touch the seductive beverage."
Vladimir Odoevsky

Darcy arrived at his home in London early the following afternoon, having left Netherfield as soon as he was able and happy to finally be in his own comfortable dwelling. He was master at Darcy House, in control, and was eager to draw on that comfort. The previous fortnight had been the worst of his remembrance, excepting the time surrounding the deaths of his parents. Between the pain of his injuries and the costly effects to his independence, he had rarely felt so powerless. It was as if some force outside of himself had taken over his life, finding amusement in absurdity.

After refreshing himself, he went to his study to catch up on his correspondence. Anything of significance had been forwarded to Netherfield, so mainly he sifted through invitations, letters of appreciation for prior benevolence and the multitudinous requests for assistance. His steward in town had managed his business affairs that were not important enough to send to Netherfield, but in his illness, he had been unable to fulfil his responsibilities while in Hertfordshire. This would be a busy week for Darcy as he attempted to complete his preceding business and inform his family of his upcoming nuptials. He would also need to meet with his solicitor to draw up the marriage settlement, while his staff got to work readying the mistress's chamber.

Contemplating the preparation of Miss Elizabeth's chamber led him to naturally dwell on the idea that he would soon be married, enjoying all of the physical benefits inherent upon that happy state. The picture of Miss Elizabeth, wet in her chemise, had never left Darcy's mind. He held onto the idea tenaciously even when he knew it was ungentlemanly; if her sensual attributes were to be the only benefit of the union, he would use that thought to keep him sane over the next fortnight.

He determined that in the morning he would begin the day by making a call to the home of his relations, Tromwell House, where he would be able to inform his aunt and uncle Fitzwilliam as well as his sister, Georgiana, of his upcoming wedding. Darcy had spent the journey to town considering how he would break the news of his engagement to them. Likely, his aunt and uncle had already read in the papers about his supposed compromise of a young, country maiden, but hopefully they kept this information from Georgiana. They also were probably unsuspecting of the final outcome, so he expected to face their astonished response.

So as not to unnecessarily upset his sister, Darcy decided to convey that he was in agreement with the marriage, and that Miss Elizabeth would make a fine match, despite her low birth and lack of connections. Georgiana looked up to him with the highest devotion; if she thought for one moment that there was no love match, or that Miss Elizabeth had manipulated him into offering for her, she would go into her relationship with her new sister with a prejudice not easily overcome. He considered that keeping Georgiana in town during the wedding would be for the best. Darcy knew that he was no great actor and in order to keep his sister unsuspecting of the truth behind his regard for his fiancée, he determined to keep her away. In addition, he feared the impact the Bennets would have on her sensibilities. They were an uncouth lot; the less time spent in their company the better. Darcy did not like deceit, so he felt somewhat guilty about deluding his sister, but he was unsure he could pull off the feat. He rarely if ever put on a show of emotions when he had none. *Can I convince her that I have a fondness for my soon-to-be wife when I have none?*

He arrived at their home shortly after breakfast. His sister, forgetting that she was nearly grown, ran up to him for a tender embrace. He found that he quite enjoyed the show of emotion. After the difficult time away, he needed the affection only someone whom he loved could bestow. After an account of Georgiana's time with the Fitzwilliams, he suggested that she practise the pianoforte in the music room, so she could exhibit to him after dinner. Recalling that she was to act the proper lady, she glided out of the room, but with a becoming smile upon her face.

After Georgiana left, closing the door behind her, their aunt and uncle looked at one another in a unifying stance before his uncle spoke, "What is this we have been reading about in the papers, Darcy? Can we hope there is no truth to the scandalous rumours being bandied about town?"

With concern Darcy responded, "Does Georgiana know?"

"Of course not. As you are aware, she does not read the papers, and we kept any visitors away from her hearing."

"Thank you." He stood and paced to gather his thoughts. This is when his relations noticed his slight limp.

"Darcy, why are you limping?"

Looking somewhat confused, having forgotten for the moment the injury that had plagued him previously, he responded, "I sustained an injury to my ankle, as well as my head, but two weeks ago. Actually, that leads me to the answer of your first question." He walked over to the sofa and sat before continuing, "A young woman and I were travelling upon the same path, but in opposite directions early one morning. A storm was quickly approaching from the west, so I picked up my pace. Well, in reality, my pace was rather more speedy than necessary for an early ride on a dark morning. When I came around a turn, I almost ran down a local, genteel woman, who also was trying to make it to her home before the storm began. Unfortunately, I fell off my horse resulting in my wounds."

With alarm, his aunt responded, "How dreadful! But you seem recovered. Are you? And what about the lady? Was she much injured?"

"I am well, as you see. And the lady sustained no injuries... that I am aware of." Darcy, just at that moment, realised that he had never bothered inquiring about Miss Elizabeth's condition after the accident. She was obviously well enough to get him to that wretched dwelling. For a moment, he felt shame for his lack of attention to a lady's needs in a possibly traumatic situation, but quickly overcame his guilt when he considered the predicament in which he now found himself, and at her doing. "She was able to get me safely out of the storm, but in so doing, she put us in a socially damaging situation."

"She is the woman mentioned in the papers who spent un-chaperoned time alone with you, who expects you to marry her?" Darcy's aunt questioned.

"She is."

"Well, of course, you will not marry her. From what we read about the woman, she is the dowerless daughter of a country gentleman. No one would expect you to lower yourself to offer for her, Darcy. Pay her family off for their trouble – she did get you to safety, you say – and be done with it. You have no ties to that county, and your peers are already thinking of other scandals on which to dwell." Darcy remained quiet. "Did James not tell me you were considering courting that young debutante? First Season out, though nineteen? Lady Annette, I believe was her name, was it not, dear?" his uncle said, turning to his wife, "I hear her dowry nears forty thousand."

"Yes, I was considering her, but no more." Darcy disliked people speaking of his personal matters.

His aunt and uncle looked at him in question, "Has she been taken, then? From what I hear from Langston, she was the prize this year, but was holding out for your offer. Did she weary of waiting for you?" his uncle queried with a hint of amusement.

Darcy stood and walked to the window where he peered down to the street below. He had not been looking forward to this moment. His relations would be appalled at his decision, as he well understood. They could not fathom his need to honour his obligations, no matter his distaste in doing so. Of course, the Fitzwilliam side of the family was of noble heritage and always strove to do what was right, to show their superiority to those of lesser birth, but they would not accept his decision to put his pride aside to marry beneath him, with no inducement but his honour and the respectability and future of a family totally unconnected to his own. Darcy then turned and faced his family and said, "You must wish me joy. I have asked for and will soon receive the hand of Miss Elizabeth Bennet of Longbourn, in Hertfordshire."

Silence reigned as his aunt and uncle stood up, mouths agape. "You cannot be in earnest," his aunt said with a countenance of unbelief.

"Darcy, do not be so foolish. You most certainly are not engaged," his uncle scoffingly added.

"Indeed, I am. The first banns were read yesterday. I came to town to make ready the house for a new mistress and to inform my family of my betrothal. I will be meeting with my solicitor this afternoon to draw up the contract, once I have spoken to Georgiana."

"But why? Surely, as your uncle said, you did not have to offer for her, just pay her family a generous sum, which I know you can afford, and be done with the business." Darcy mused that he also had gone over this argument many times on his own.

"Miss Bennet will be my wife. I have chosen of my free will to offer for her, and I hope that you will find it within your hearts to accept my decision, to welcome her, for she will be your niece."

"How can you ask us to abide by your decision? You expect us to tolerate her as a member of our family just because you choose to overlook her connections? Well, I, for one, shall not. The betrothal has not yet been announced, nor has a settlement been signed; you have time to change your mind, and you will," his uncle emphatically stated.

"Please, dear, you must listen to your uncle, for Georgiana's sake if not your own. She will be coming out in two years. You will need a wife who can add to your connections, not diminish them. Surely, you would not wish to harm her prospects."

"Please, I have thought through all that you could possibly say to dissuade me, and I am determined that this is the proper course. I would greatly desire your acquiescence, but regardless of your support, I will not change my mind." Darcy looked directly at each of them with determination. "If you will excuse me, I would like to speak to Georgiana now."

"Is there nothing we can say then?"

"You are assuming that by my marrying the lady that I will be going against some moral sanction. She is a gentleman's daughter and I, a gentleman. Once we are married, she will learn what it means to be a Darcy and the niece of an earl. I beg of you, accept my decision."

"Well, I know that I cannot, but your aunt will likely give in. She always had a soft spot when it comes to you."

Darcy looked to his aunt who smiled fleetingly at him and looked away. "I will write to you after I return to London with Miss Bennet, before the announcement is made in the papers. You should expect us in a fortnight."

"So soon, but why?"

"The sooner I am able to leave Hertfordshire, the better. Delaying will do nothing to ease the transition ahead. The decision is made, so I would like to quench the scandal before Georgiana hears or is affected by it. If you would be so kind, I would like to ask that you keep Georgiana here indefinitely. The first month of marriage would be trying in any circumstance, but I feel that we will need time to get to know one another without interruption. I will come visit Georgiana often while Miss Bennet and I reside at Darcy House, but I think that Georgiana will also need time to become accustomed to having a new sister. Introducing her slowly to Miss Bennet will be the best course, I believe. Maybe by Christmas I will be able to make the introductions to all of my family, and perhaps when we return to Pemberley, Georgiana will be ready to join us. I will not be able to tell James about my engagement in person. I have written to him, though, so that he is not taken by surprise. Since you may see him before I, could you tell him about my plans for after the wedding? He would want to know." After a pause and nods of consent, he continued, "I will leave you now to find Georgiana." And with sincerity continued, "Thank you for taking her into your home." He made a quick bow and left his aunt and uncle dumbfounded and desirous to intervene.

Georgiana was practising fervently on the pianoforte and did not hear his arrival. The music was soothing to his soul and gave him the respite he needed, so he sat to listen to her skilful execution of Bach's Prelude in C Major. Georgiana always played with sensitivity, not often heard by the ladies who attempted to garner his favour in their overt displays to impress. He listened patiently, closing his eyes and taking in the melody. Darcy considered how far his sister had come in the short months following her near ruin. He had failed to protect her from the schemes of a scoundrel and only saved her from misery by luck. Had he arrived to Ramsgate a day later, Georgiana would have been irreparably injured, even if she had later been found. Darcy lived with the guilt that weighed heavily upon his soul and only wanted to foster her recovery of spirit, but instead, in sharing his plans, he might possibly give his sister more sorrow to add to her shame if she were to know the truth.

Darcy started when he heard Georgiana speak. "Brother, I did not know you had entered. I have been practising most diligently since arriving here. I know that it pleases you when I strive to do my best with my accomplishments."

With a sincere smile, he said, "I am always delighted with your efforts, dear sister, and on this particular occasion, I am gratified that you have excelled, as your playing just now has given me a respite from what preoccupies me."

She rushed over to him, concern written upon her face, "Oh, Brother, if I can do anything to soothe you, please know that I would."

He reached for her hand and squeezed it gently, "You are a good girl. I am just attempting to decide the best way to tell you some news which may surprise you, but I hope will delight you." At her puzzled look, he continued, "Georgiana, I am to be married." Her eyes widened and she opened her mouth to speak, but he continued, "Her name is Miss Elizabeth Bennet, and she currently resides at an estate in Hertfordshire a few miles from Mr. Bingley's new establishment."

"But you have only been gone three weeks. How could you have fallen in love so quickly?"

"Many people marry after a short period of courting. In fact many marry when they do not even know their future spouse. Do not let the length of our attachment cause you concern."

She sat quietly for a few moments trying to work out the validity of his statements in her mind. Did he not just this summer chastise her for trusting a man she hardly knew, one who ultimately wished to use her for his own gain? "Do you love her?"

Darcy would not lie to her, but nor did he wish for her to know the truth of the matter. Of course, her learning of his subterfuge later could be equally harmful. He would have to be careful in his responses. "People marry for reasons other than love, but within time, affection blossoms. It was this way with our parents you know, but my memory of them is that only of the deepest devotion."

"If you do not love her, she must have other admirable qualities. Tell me about her." Georgiana silently worried about the type of wife her brother would find. The bride of Fitzwilliam Darcy could destroy or flourish her own existence.

Darcy thought for a few moments. "Well, she is about your height, with chestnut hair, her eyes are the colour of... um, well I do not know the colour of her eyes."

"William, you do not know her eye colour? How much time exactly have you spent in her company?"

"I was in Hertfordshire for these three weeks. I do not notice such details; I am no poet."

"But surely you would have looked into her eyes to mark their colour."

He responded playfully trying to change the subject, "You, my dear, read too many novels. She has four sisters and is the daughter of a gentleman."

"I will have five sisters?" she said in astonishment.

"I do not see that you will be much in their company, Georgiana, but yes, five, the youngest about your age."

"Why would I not see them much? Hertfordshire is not far from town. Surely they would come visit us or we them once you are married."

"Her father does not prefer society, so the family rarely comes to London. Perhaps one day we could invite them to Pemberley for a visit." He looked away from her.

"You are not telling me everything. What was it that led you to offer for her, Brother? You have been around scores of women trying to gain your approbation for years, then you leave to visit your friend in the country and come back engaged to a woman you cannot even sufficiently describe to me. You can confide in me, dear William."

He stood quickly and walked over to the hearth, leaning onto his arm. This was not going as he had hoped. Georgiana was becoming too perceptive for her own good. "The circumstances surrounding our engagement are complicated." He paused; she waited patiently. He despised distressing her after her trying summer and autumn. "I offered for her to save her family from a ruinous scandal. She is a lady, despite her family's lack of fortune and connections. Once we marry, she will improve her standing in society, and hopefully after some time will be ready to help you with your coming out."

"But why sacrifice yourself and your happiness for a family so unrelated to you? You cannot!"

"Georgiana, you must calm yourself. What is done, is done, and I do not regret my decision to offer for her."

"Just explain to me why, please; I must know."

Realising that she would likely find out the assumed particulars from others who delighted in spreading a good tale if he did not relate the truth, he decided to tell her all, minimising the incriminating details, so as not to prejudice her against his bride-to-be. He told her the same information that he relayed to his aunt and uncle ending with the rumours of a compromise, which made him bound to ask for Miss Bennet's hand.

"Did she take advantage of the situation and spread the gossip herself in order to secure you? Could anyone be so cruel?"

"I am not sure how the rumours began, but it would seem that her mother was the first to tell enough of the truth to make escaping the effects impossible."

"That conniver!"

"Georgiana, hold your tongue! You may not approve of my decision or my choice of wife, but you will be respectful." Tears sprang to her eyes, as she turned away. Darcy immediately regretted his outburst, especially as he saw his own words reflected in her own. This could not be easy for his sister; Georgiana had always hoped to gain a sister she could love and respect. "Forgive me. This has not been easy for me, and I see that it will be difficult for you as well. I had hoped to spare you from this pain, but you would know all." He reached for her and held her close. "Thank you for caring enough to be upset. You are one of few in my life who truly cares about me. Sometimes I find it difficult to discern those who genuinely enjoy my company versus those who only care about my fortune. I fear there will be many more who are upset, but for likely different reasons than you display. Many mamas and daughters will regret my leaving the marriage mart. I confess that is one thing I will not miss." He was attempting to ease her pain but with little success. She adored him and an affront to him was provocation for her as well.

"When will I meet the woman?"

He sighed. "That woman will soon be your sister. Please, help me, dear sister. I need your support, not your censure."

With sadness in her eyes, she softly responded, "I will try."

"We will marry in a fortnight at her family home and then come to London. You will be staying on here at Tromwell House while I am gone for the wedding and then for the following month or so. We will remain in London through the festive season, and hopefully by then you, Miss Bennet and I can travel to Pemberley."

"I will not be staying at Darcy House with you? Why ever not?"

"I believe that Miss Bennet and I will need time to become better acquainted without the influence of others." At her look of displeasure, he continued, "This will all be quite new to her. I would like to give her an opportunity to become adjusted to her new role... and to me. I promise that I will come to see you often, though. Perhaps at Christmas Miss Bennet and I could join the family, and you could meet her then."

The seed of resentment had been planted within Georgiana, and she was already determining that the future Mrs. Darcy would never be someone with whom she would choose a relationship. Like the despicable Mr. Wickham, this woman had selfishly manipulated her brother's good name and honour for her benefit. Her brother, who meant more to her than any jewels or land ever could, was being used by this woman, completely unknown to him, in order to raise her position in society, while removing him from his sister, who looked up to him and depended upon him like a father. "Whatever pleases you, Brother," she said while trying to regulate her emotions and hiding her internal thoughts.

Darcy could not see that his efforts to protect Georgiana from the negative influences of Elizabeth and her family would actually cause a schism not easily healed. He knew that the best plan was to keep Georgiana in ignorance to the truth of the match, but Georgiana was too perceptive. Like her brother, though generous and active in providing relief to her subordinates, her temper was what might be called resentful; once her good opinion was lost, it was lost forever.

Darcy bade his sister a subdued farewell, promising to return later in the evening for dinner, then headed to the home of Lord Cunningham. This was the one interview that he dreaded most. Darcy had known that he must choose a bride from amongst the *ton*, preferably a woman of noble birth, and she must bring a sizeable dowry as was fitting a man of his station. His family's wealth and long history along with connections to nobility made him a highly sought after mate, so his choices were plenty. Due to his determination to make a connection before Georgiana's entrance into society, Darcy had contemplated beginning a courtship with Lady Annette Croxley, who was the younger sister of an acquaintance of his from Cambridge, Cecil Croxley – Viscount Wexley. Their family estate was in a county neighbouring Derbyshire, where she had spent the majority of her time, away from the prattle of the ladies and the advances of the gentlemen residing in London. She had met all of his criteria for an accomplished woman who could manage his households with grace. She also had two younger sisters, the younger being Georgiana's age, who would likely welcome his young sister into their own family, giving Georgiana the friendship and sense of belonging for which she yearned.

During the previous Spring Season, Darcy had made Lady Annette's acquaintance at a private dinner party hosted by his cousin, Viscount Langston, while she was in the midst of her first Season. Her brother resembled Darcy in his reserve and his tenacious hold to tradition and chaperoned his sister while their father was at their country estate. Lady Annette had waited until she was nineteen before making her debut, and as such, she had a maturity about her that was lacking in many of the debutantes, which Darcy found pleasing. Lady Annette displayed her physical attributes to perfection with a presumed modesty that held much promise. Her dowry of forty thousand only added to her many charms.

Darcy had begun paying Lady Annette special attention as the summer progressed, before the urgent matter with his sister had distracted him. Unusual to Darcy's wont, he had singled her out at several private balls requesting her hand for a set to either open or close the ball. Darcy had invited her and her family to Darcy House on two occasions to dine and had thought that he would make his interest public; however, with Georgiana's near ruin, he determined to devote his time to his sister until he could be assured of the secrecy of her shame. After his return to London from Netherfield, he had planned to secure Lady Annette's hand and fulfil his duty to his family. Of course, he did not love Lady Annette; that would perhaps come with time, but he knew that he could reside with her with equanimity and confidence in her upholding the dignity of the Darcy name. Her conversation was pleasing, if not stimulating, but Lady Annette always kept her opinions respectable, rarely disagreeing with him, but also not fawning over him with undesired attention, as so many others had. If her opinion was discordant with his own, she held her tongue, rather than practise the deceit of agreeing when she in fact did not.

Darcy had been anxious to make his desires known before someone else acquired a commitment. He would have spoken to her father, Lord Cunningham, before his trip to assist Bingley; however, her father had travelled to his estate in the north, not due to return until after the harvest. He had been fairly confident there was no one else who had garnered her approval, and Darcy was quite certain she had been without doubt as to his intentions. Having his own plans shattered had been bad enough, but knowing he was to cause this family, whom he admired, disappointment left Darcy full of remorse.

Darcy's relations had responded as expected, but he could not predict the scene to come. His coach pulled up to the affluent residence; he thought he discerned Lady Annette looking out a window on the third floor, quickly dropping the drapery back to avoid notice.

Darcy stepped out and walked to the large front door, knocking, and was promptly admitted. He requested a meeting with Lord Cunningham, but was told that he remained in the North. Not wanting to leave without resolving matters, he asked for Lord Cunningham's son, Lord Wexley, and was soon led to the study. Wexley stood and gave a cursory bow to Darcy, who returned the courtesy. "Darcy, now this is a surprise. I thought you to be in Hertfordshire with your friend, the one from trade. From what the papers report, you are in much demand there."

He gets straight to the point. Darcy could appreciate a man who did not mince words, but was not used to being on the receiving end of such discord. After directed to sit, he began, "I had hoped that my friends would not heed everything they read, especially something that would call into question my integrity." The man from behind the desk stared at him, apparently waiting for him to elaborate. "I wanted to come and speak with you in person, hoping that you had not seen the reports in the paper, but ready to explain either way."

"I cannot pretend to know why you would make the effort to come see me; surely you have many friends of closer acquaintance whom you might feel more interested in your tale."

"You obviously wish to make this difficult for me, Wexley. I cannot say I blame you, but you must know that my being here purports my feelings of deep regret that you and your family might have been injured by the reports which are not completely based on facts."

"Perhaps you can explain what the facts are."

Taking a deep breath, Darcy began, "While visiting my friend, Charles Bingley, I decided to ride out one morning; however, a storm came up, and by chance I came upon a woman right at the moment lightning struck a tree nearby. Her scream caused my horse to bolt and me to lose my seat. As a result, I was injured. We then spent the day alone, me in a state of injury at her mercy, and she in a position to take advantage. Her father found us but did not immediately push a betrothal. After a few days, word got out of our compromising situation, some of the information truth and other fiction." Darcy looked away for a few moments before continuing. "As a result, I had no other recourse but to offer for her. We both know that my intentions were otherwise, but that cannot now be helped. I had no other alternative, if I were to keep my honour."

"And what about the respect due a woman of an eminent family? Does she not also deserve your deference? My sister has developed a fondness for you and was greatly disturbed by the news in the papers." His voice rising, he continued, "A gentleman does not pay his addresses to a maiden, only to leave her to the derision of her friends in disappointed hopes. I told her that you would be an excellent match as your distinction exceeded that of any other man of our acquaintance despite your lack of title, and this is the response we are to receive!"

Darcy felt the sting, as he had been condemning himself likewise. "I apologise for the role that I have played in injuring your sister. She does not deserve this misfortune. Lady Annette is an exemplary woman, and I wish her the greatest joy and hope that she will one day forgive me for the disservice which came by my hand."

Wexley stood. "I will convey to her your regrets. I do not believe we have anything else to say to one another."

"Thank you for hearing me out. I hope that when we are able to put this behind us we can still be friends," said Darcy, saddened and without hope of reconciliation any time soon. He left intending to make his way to his solicitor's office, but instead found himself at Antonio's Fencing Academy. The settlement would have to wait until tomorrow, for what he needed was some exertion, and if he were lucky, he would find his just due in a good lashing.

ALTHOUGH ELIZABETH HAD NO WISH TO MARRY MR. DARCY, she had enough wit about her to admit that she was grateful she would not be forced into an embarrassing union with Mr. Collins. And since Mr. Darcy had left the country for the time being, she determined to enjoy the respite from the stress of the past month. In addition to her Aunt Philip's proclamations about the descent of the Bennet family with Elizabeth's ruin, she also had conveyed news of the militia's arrival, much to Elizabeth's little sisters' delight and vexation since they, up until then, had had no share. Yet now that the Bennet family could claim triumph in a match with Mr. Darcy, they were welcomed back into Meryton society with all the alacrity due to them.

Shortly after breakfast, four of the five sisters set out for town, the two eldest to the milliners to seek amendments to their dresses for the upcoming ball, and the two youngest to seek out officers. Elizabeth's mother had insisted that she obtain a new dress for the occasion, but her practical daughter found no need to spend her father's money on such an affair when she would be getting a new dress for the actual wedding. Instead, she would rework her best frock with the green ribbon she had been admiring on her last visit. This time at the milliners, however, she received all the courtesy due a woman who would soon be mistress of her own grand estate.

After Elizabeth and Jane had joined their younger sisters, the attention of each was soon caught by a young man, whom they had never seen before, of a most gentlemanlike appearance, walking with an officer on the other side of the roadway. The officer was Mr. Denny, concerning whose return from London Lydia came to inquire, and he bowed as they passed. All were struck with the stranger's air, all wondered who he could be, and Kitty and Lydia, determined if possible to find out, led the way across the street towards them, under pretence of wanting something in the opposite shop. Mr. Denny addressed them directly, and entreated permission to introduce his friend, Mr. Wickham, who had returned with him the day before from town, and he was happy to say had accepted a commission in their corps. This was exactly as it should be, for the young man wanted only regimentals to make him completely charming. His appearance was greatly in his favour; he had all the best parts of beauty: a fine countenance, a good figure, and very pleasing address. The introduction was followed up on his side by a happy readiness of conversation – a readiness at the same time perfectly correct and unassuming – and the whole party were still standing and talking together very agreeably, when the sound of a horse drew their notice and Bingley was seen riding down the street. On distinguishing the ladies of the group, the gentleman came directly towards them, and began the usual civilities, Miss Bennet being the principal object of his attention.

When Mrs. Philips spotted the group of young people standing outside her home, she opened the upstairs window of her house to greet them and to extend the invitation to Mr. Bingley and Mr. Wickham for that evening's festivities. Mrs. Philips had invited a group of officers and her nieces to her home for games. The invitation was accepted with pleasure and all looked forward to an evening spent in the company of new friends. The officers and Mr. Bingley walked on in their own respective directions, while the Bennet sisters entered their aunt's home for refreshment. The sisters, knowing that if any news were to be had, their aunt would most certainly be in possession of the truth of the matter, began making exclamations and inquiries about the officers, especially of Mr. Wickham. But, she could only tell her nieces what they already knew, that Mr. Denny had brought him from London, and that he was to have a lieutenant's commission in the ----shire. She had been watching him the last hour, she said, as he walked up and down the street and had Mr. Wickham appeared again, Kitty and Lydia would certainly have continued the occupation, but unluckily no one passed the windows now except a few of the officers, who in comparison with the stranger, were become "stupid, disagreeable fellows."

That evening, by the time they entered the drawing room, the sisters had the pleasure of hearing that Mr. Wickham had already arrived along with his comrades and were at the moment in the other room. No sooner did the ladies sit, than the gentlemen, including Mr. Wickham, entered the room. Elizabeth felt that she had neither been seeing him before, nor thinking of him since, with the smallest degree of unreasonable admiration. The officers of the ----shire were in general a very creditable, gentlemanlike set, and the best of them were of the present party; but Mr. Wickham was as far beyond them all in person, countenance, air, and walk, as they were superior to the broad-faced stuffy uncle Philips, breathing port wine, who followed them into the room.

Mr. Wickham was the happy man towards whom almost every female eye was turned, and Elizabeth was the happy woman by whom he finally seated himself. Moreover, the agreeable manner in which he immediately fell into conversation, though it was only on its being a wet night, and on the probability of a rainy season made her feel that the commonest, dullest, most threadbare topic might be rendered interesting by the skill of the speaker.

The games were to begin, and with ready delight he was received at the table between Elizabeth and Lydia. At first there seemed danger of Lydia's engrossing him entirely, for she was a most determined talker; but being likewise extremely fond of lottery tickets, she soon grew too much interested in the game to have attention for any one in particular. Allowing for the common demands of the game, Mr. Wickham was therefore at leisure to talk to Elizabeth, and she was very willing to hear him, for although she was newly engaged, a woman could not help but feel flattered at the attentions of a handsome gentleman. Since being the target of Mr. Collins' recent regard and being the recipient of Mr. Darcy's disdain, Elizabeth consoled herself by innocently allowing Mr. Wickham to stoke her wounded vanity.

After a few moments of idle conversation, however, he surprised her by wishing her congratulations on her recent engagement. At her look of surprise, he informed her that his fellow officers spoke with fervour about all of the local ladies, and since she was one of the most beautiful of the neighbourhood, she had a greater share in their admiration and disappointment at being no longer available to accept the attentions often paid in society. He flattered her with more words of approbation, which she was happy to accept, and then shocked her with his mention of being well acquainted with her fiancé.

"You may well be surprised, Miss Bennet, being an intimate with Darcy and seeing my now lowered place in society. You see Darcy and I have had an extended relationship. Have you yourself known him long?"

"I cannot say that I have, but I do have every expectation that we will soon become more familiar with one another in the near future."

"You are to be married soon then?"

"Within a fortnight." She looked away. Elizabeth had determined that she would be content with her lot, but sitting here in company with this amiable and handsome gentleman brought home to her that she would soon be attached to a man who had little admiration for her.

Wickham, having learnt of the history of the engagement and sensing her disquiet, said, "You are a fortunate woman and must congratulate yourself. You have achieved what no other has been able to thus far, and believe me when I say that many have tried to secure him." At her look of wonder, he continued softly, "Pemberley is a lovely home, well worth any disagreeable circumstances that might accompany the match."

She sensed that he was attempting to communicate more than was actually said, so she cautiously continued, "You know Mr. Darcy well, then?"

He smiled and laughed lightly, "You may wonder at such an assertion; it is true, but I have no right to give my opinion of him. I am not qualified to form one. I have known him too long and too well to be a fair judge. It is impossible for me to be impartial. But I would be curious to know yours. You are soon to be wed, but I sense that the joy, that usually comes with a marriage, is lacking."

His impertinence was lost on her curiosity. "I know very little of my soon-to-be husband, and would appreciate an opportunity to learn more about him. I know his estate is grand, but other than that, I know him only to be a tall, proud fellow," she returned lightly.

"I cannot pretend to express a fondness for him which I do not hold. I would not be surprised if you told me that he was highly esteemed by you and your friends of Meryton, for I believe it does not often happen that he is not. The world is blinded by his fortune and consequence, or frightened by his high and imposing manners, and sees him only as he chooses to be seen."

"He is to be gone a week while he prepares for our nuptials, but when he returns, I do hope you will not be uncomfortable by his presence."

"Oh! No, we are not on friendly terms, and it always gives me pain to meet him, but I have no reason for avoiding him but a sense of very great ill usage and most painful regrets at his being what he is. His father, the late Mr. Darcy, was one of the best men that ever breathed, and the truest friend I ever had, and I can never be in company with this Mr. Darcy without being grieved to the soul by a thousand tender recollections. His behaviour to myself has been scandalous, but I verily believe I could forgive him anything and everything, rather than his disappointing the hopes and disgracing the memory of his father."

Elizabeth found her interest of the subject increase, and listened with all her heart; but the delicacy of it prevented further inquiry.

Mr. Wickham began to speak on more general topics, Meryton, the neighbourhood, the society, appearing highly pleased with all that he had yet seen, and speaking of the latter especially, with gentle but very intelligible gallantry.

"It was the prospect of constant society, and good society, that brought me here after Denny's description of the area. My disposition will not bear solitude. I must have employment and society. A military life is not what I was intended for, but circumstances have now made it eligible. The church ought to have been my profession—I was brought up for the church, and I should at this time have been in possession of a most valuable living, had it pleased the gentleman to whom you will soon be attached."

"Indeed!"

"Yes – the late Mr. Darcy bequeathed me the next presentation of the best living in his gift. He was my godfather, and excessively attached to me. I cannot do justice to his kindness. He meant to provide for me amply and thought he had done so; but when the living fell, it was given elsewhere."

"Good heavens!" cried Elizabeth; "but how could that be? How could his will be disregarded? Why did you not seek legal redress?"

"There was just such an informality in the terms of the bequest as to give me no hope from the law. A man of honour could not have doubted the intention, but Mr. Darcy chose to doubt it – or to treat it as a merely conditional recommendation, and to assert that I had forfeited all claim to it by extravagance, imprudence, in short anything or nothing. The living became vacant two years ago, exactly as I was of an age to hold it, and it was given to another man. I cannot accuse myself of having really done anything to deserve to lose it. I have a warm, unguarded temper, and I may perhaps have sometimes spoken my opinion of him, and to him, too freely. I can recall nothing worse. But the fact is, that we are very different sorts of men, and that he hates me."

"This is quite shocking! He deserves to be publicly disgraced." Elizabeth said this, quite forgetting that she was referring to her future husband.

"Some time or other he will be—but it shall not be by me. Till I can forget his father, I can never defy or expose him."

Elizabeth honoured him for such feelings, and thought him handsomer than ever as he expressed them. "But what," said she, after a pause, "can have been his motive? What can have induced him to behave so cruelly?"

"A thorough, determined dislike of me – a dislike which I cannot but attribute in some measure to jealousy. Had the late Mr. Darcy liked me less, his son might have borne with me better; but his father's uncommon attachment to me irritated him, I believe, very early in life. He had not a temper to bear the sort of competition in which we stood, the sort of preference which was often given me."

"I had not thought Mr. Darcy so bad as this. I had supposed him to despise his fellow creatures in general, but did not suspect him of descending to such malicious revenge, such injustice, such inhumanity as this!"

"I will not trust myself on the subject," replied Wickham, "I can hardly be just to him."

Elizabeth was again deep in thought, and after a time exclaimed, "To treat in such a manner, the godson, the friend, the favourite of his father!" She could have added, "A young man too, like you, whose very countenance may vouch for your being amiable," but she contented herself with, "And one, too, who had probably been his own companion from childhood, connected together, as I think you said, in the closest manner!"

"We were born in the same parish, within the same park the greatest part of our youth was passed together; inmates of the same house, sharing the same amusements, objects of the same parental care. My father began life in the profession, which your uncle, Mr. Philips, appears to do so much credit to—but he gave up everything to be of use to the late Mr. Darcy, and devoted all his time to the care of the Pemberley property. He was most highly esteemed by Mr. Darcy, a most intimate, confidential friend. Mr. Darcy often acknowledged himself to be under the greatest obligations to my father's active superintendence, and when immediately before my father's death, Mr. Darcy gave him a voluntary promise of providing for me, I am convinced that he felt it to be as much a debt of gratitude to him, as of affection to myself. "

"How strange!" cried Elizabeth. "How abominable! I wonder that the very pride of Mr. Darcy has not made him just to you, if from no better motive than that he should not have been too proud to be dishonest—for dishonesty I must call it. How could he have behaved that way to you, and yet be the same man to offer for me – a woman with no connection whatsoever to his family?" Then Elizabeth blushed as she considered that Mr. Wickham must have been privy to the gossip and not wanting him to think that she might have acted with impropriety.

"It is amazing," replied Wickham, overlooking her embarrassment, "for almost all his actions may be traced to pride – and pride has often been his best friend. It has connected him nearer with virtue than any other feeling. But we are none of us consistent; and in his behaviour to me, there were stronger impulses even than pride."

"Can such abominable pride as his have ever done him good?"

"Yes. It has often led him to be liberal and generous, to give his money freely, to display hospitality, to assist his tenants, and relieve the poor. Family pride, and filial pride – for he is very proud of what his father was – have done this. Not to appear to disgrace his family, to degenerate from the popular qualities, or lose the influence of the Pemberley House, is a powerful motive. He has also brotherly pride which with some affection makes him a very kind and careful guardian of his sister, and you will hear him generally cried up as the most attentive and best of brothers."

After many pauses and many trials of other subjects, Elizabeth could not help reverting once more to the first, and saying, "I am astonished at his intimacy with Mr. Bingley! How can Mr. Bingley, who seems good humour itself, and is, I really believe, truly amiable, be in friendship with such a man? How can they suit each other? Do you know Mr. Bingley?" she said looking in that man's direction.

"Not at all."

"He is a sweet-tempered, amiable, charming man. He cannot know what Mr. Darcy is."

"Probably not, but Mr. Darcy can please where he chooses. He does not want abilities. He can be a conversible companion if he thinks it worth his while. Among those who are at all his equals in consequence, he is a very different man from what he is to the less prosperous. His pride never deserts him; but with the rich he is liberal-minded, just, sincere, rational, honourable, and perhaps agreeable, allowing something for fortune and figure. And since you are soon to be his wife, you may very well enjoy these, his more noble and amiable attributes."

Somewhere in the recesses of her mind, Elizabeth had a small doubt as to the veracity of Mr. Wickham's claims. Surely Mr. Darcy could not have the honour to offer for her when he despised the idea, thereby securing a union with a family so decidedly beneath his own, yet not help the friend from his youth, when helping him would not even necessitate constant interaction. However, before this idea took root, she quickly dismissed this possibility. And as Elizabeth recalled the impropriety of such a conversation regarding the man she was to promise fidelity, she attempted to change the subject. Although the conversation left many unanswered questions, she saw the wisdom of inquiring about other areas of Mr. Wickham's life, and determined that he was a most agreeable man, who would henceforth be known as only a fond memory.

When Elizabeth left her aunt and uncle Philips, she had much to think about. She had hoped that the diversion of a night in town would relieve her of her apprehensions about her upcoming matrimony, but contrariwise, it left her in a state of more disquiet. She was shocked to learn that the man she was to marry was malicious and could treat a former friend – who was much like a brother in practice – in such an infamous manner. Tears threatened her eyes, as she attempted to think of other more agreeable subjects. She had two weeks before she would leave her home and all she held dear, and she refused to dwell on such unhappy thoughts. She determined not to share her reflections with Jane, for Elizabeth could not change her situation, and it would only cause her sister pain. Jane was apt to think the best in everyone, and would probably endeavour to make everyone involved innocent. But Elizabeth knew that the interested people could not all be left blameless as Jane would want, and she felt certain just what to think. Wickham, a young man of amiable appearance and kind attentions, has been used abominably ill by his childhood friend, whose pride would not allow him the grace to accept that his father loved another, and so endeavoured to destroy his future prospects, without regard to decency, merit or conscience. For who could deny the justice of Wickham's indignation against Mr. Darcy?

The question that plagued Elizabeth was whether or even how to address her concerns to Mr. Darcy. She knew that Mr. Darcy would soon be her husband and, therefore, her sole benefactor. He would have the means of bringing a great degree of misery to her life, so she had to consider in what manner she should address his decisions. Perhaps after they have been married for some time, she could encourage him to welcome Mr. Wickham back to Pemberley and restore his place as beneficiary of Mr. Darcy's father's wishes.

THE LADIES OF LONGBOURN WERE OFTEN in the company of Mr. Wickham and his fellow officers. The officers were invited to Longbourn for tea after having met the ladies in Meryton, and were therefore able to meet Elizabeth's mother and father, the former of which was highly gratified to see such a handsome man pay her daughters attention, and the latter content for the society of an obviously intelligent young man. The subject of Mr. Darcy's treatment of Wickham was not raised again by either Elizabeth or the gentleman; nonetheless, they did share a knowing look when Wickham's future or his plans for the militia were mentioned. Mr. Wickham paid Elizabeth all of the compliments due a lovely woman, and as he was skilled in this area, he did so with all the finesse that came so naturally. Due to Elizabeth's bruised ego, as a direct result of Mr. Darcy's insult and continued contempt, her vanity was quite starved, and as the nourishment was in abundant supply through a skilled seducer, she naïvely enjoyed her fill. Of course, Elizabeth would never behave in any manner that would be labelled improper. His compliments were not balanced with her own, yet she did admire him in her heart and wished that his future could be filled with all of the blessings that a friendly and engaging man could deserve.

Elizabeth was somewhat surprised one day when Wickham expressed to her his initial surprise upon learning of Darcy's engagement to her, not just because of her lack of connections, but also because of Darcy's long-standing, supposed engagement to his cousin, Lady Catherine's daughter, Anne De Bourgh. Wickham admitted that when they first met, he thought it forward of him to mention so delicate a subject, but after becoming such good friends, felt that he could not in good conscience fail to mention this to her. Mr. Collins had alluded to the attachment when speaking to her father, and so she herself was made aware of the planned engagement, but she had given no credence to the scheme, since Mr. Darcy himself had failed to mention it and had certainly, if grudgingly, offered for her. A man could not legally be bound to more than one woman, so she had thought Mr. Collins' assertions to be ill founded. "Mr. Wickham," said she, "was there much love in their attachment? He cannot be under seven and twenty. Surely if he were going to marry her, he would have done so by now."

"I believe they are both eight and twenty, and no, the attachment was not strong, at least it was not when I last visited there with the Darcy family. She was always a sickly creature, rarely allowed to join in outdoor pursuits. Miss De Bourgh does not have your vivacity or beauty, to be sure."

Elizabeth decided not to think on the matter. She could not change her present course and could not regret his having offered for her instead of his cousin when it saved her own family from ruin.

On the following Tuesday, the sisters again went into town. Elizabeth would not admit to herself her growing regard for Mr. Wickham, for she was promised to another man, no matter her distaste for the situation, so she chose to dwell on her inclination to ease his transition into the militia through her friendship and that of her family. The officers had finished their drills for the day and were making their way through Meryton towards the local pub. Upon seeing the Bennets, the men walked up to the ladies who had just arrived. As usual, Mr. Wickham walked to Elizabeth's side and engaged her in conversation. He had the ability to flatter and the means, by his own charms, to give weight to his approbation. Elizabeth had never felt such mixed feelings of regard and disappointment concerning a man. How could it be that in all of her days, she would now receive the attentions of such an amiable gentleman, just when she was no longer free to accept them?

MR. DARCY HAD ARRIVED AT NETHERFIELD at about a quarter of an hour before dark. He had designed his return at a time when calling on the Bennets would be unacceptable, even for one betrothed. He had enjoyed his time at Darcy House with frequent visits to his family, and spent the week preparing for Elizabeth's entrance into his life. He had chosen a ring at the jewellery store his father had frequented when purchasing gifts for his mother. It was simple yet elegant and a ring appropriate for the wife of a Darcy. He had always planned on giving his mother's ring to his future bride; nevertheless, Darcy could not bring himself to share the intimacy of such a sentiment. He would of course give her access to his mother's collection, but her ring represented the bond of love between his dear parents and to give it to one whom he held little regard grieved him. His solicitor had completed the settlement papers and delivered them Monday morning; he had no reason to remain in town and so had to do his duty.

Darcy had written to his close relations who did not reside in town and visited those who did. During his calls, he had attempted to offset the inherent difficulties of such a match but found it difficult to give pretences that did not exist. Also, Darcy had known that he must inform his aunt, Lady Catherine de Bourgh, and had dreaded the communication. Since she was staying at her estate in Kent at the time, he decided to tell her in writing. Lady Catherine had long held the belief that Darcy would one day wed her own daughter, Anne, thus joining the estates of Darcy and De Bourgh; however, Darcy had long known that her wishes would never come to fruition. He had always dealt with his aunt's presumption towards the match through ignoring and skilfully changing the subject, knowing that at some point he would have to disappoint her. He had expected such a time to occur in the near future with a betrothal to Lady Annette. He had already spoken with Anne about his wishes on the matter, to which she had happily acceded, for she had no desire to marry her cousin, and would be secure financially whether married to Darcy or not. After writing to his aunt, he had expected a quick reply, but had to leave London before a response was received. He had not sent the note by express and was now wishing he had, for he wanted any disagreeable encounters to occur before he brought Elizabeth to Darcy House. But he knew his duty and left for Netherfield, hoping rather than believing his aunt had accepted his engagement. He had no wish to attempt to defend his decision to her, knowing the difficulties he had bourn when defending his resolution to himself.

Bingley had agreed to join Darcy on his visit to Longbourn; he was easily persuaded, as he had been looking for another excuse to call on the family. While Darcy was away, Bingley had been in the company of the Bennets on three separate occasions and was becoming decidedly attached to the lovely Miss Bennet. They set out shortly after breakfast, riding through Meryton as they directed their path to the Longbourn estate. On their way, they spotted the Bennet ladies across the road speaking with a group of men in regimentals. Bingley led them to the gathering and after alighting, bowed gracefully with special attention to Miss Bennet. Darcy was halfway through dismounting when he became aware of the identity of the person speaking with Miss Elizabeth. *What is he doing here?* As his mind searched for possible reasons for his appearance in Meryton, he recalled himself and made a cursory bow to Elizabeth. Wickham had a brief look of confusion when Elizabeth decided to attempt to break the awkward silence.

"Mr. Darcy, I believe you are acquainted with Mr. Wickham."

"I am," he answered, curtly, then turning to look at her, he continued, "Miss Elizabeth, allow me to escort you to Longbourn."

"But, sir, we just arrived. Will you not join us?" she said, not noticing Mr. Wickham's uneasiness.

Darcy reached down to take hold of her hand and placed it on his arm. "I believe your home is this way." He began walking, and she had no choice but to follow. Darcy then momentarily turned back. "Miss Bennet, would you be so kind as to join us?"

Bingley then jumped in, "Miss Bennet, allow me to escort you." He was pleased with this opportunity to walk with her, not noticing the tension that had settled into the group.

"Lizzy!" cried Lydia, "*we* are not leaving yet. You can have Mr. Darcy all to yourself, for we have officers enough to escort us home." Then she turned to Mr. Wickham and put her arm through his.

After Elizabeth and Darcy had left, Wickham smirked. This was going to be easier than he thought. When arriving to Meryton, his new friends had told him about the local inhabitants, focusing on the ladies of the county who had the most to offer by way of society and beauty. The scandal that limited association with the Bennet family was the topic of much conversation, but what piqued Wickham's interest most was the mention of Mr. Darcy. At first he thought that he could not be the same Darcy with whom he had been so closely associated, but then the estate of Pemberley had been mentioned, as well as his wealth, and he knew there could not be two such men. He determined then to meet the woman who was soon to be Mrs. Darcy. His curiosity concerning Elizabeth drove him initially; however, after meeting her, he decided that wreaking havoc on the marriage would be a more worthwhile and entertaining endeavour. Wickham had a healthy fear of Darcy, for he was a powerful man, but he knew that Darcy would never do anything to him that might bring disrepute to the family name, which left Wickham safe from physical harm. Wickham had almost succeeded the previous summer in wooing away Miss Darcy from her vacation home, if not for Darcy's inopportune arrival; Darcy would not want that getting out, which gave Wickham some bit of power over the man's possible avenues of retaliation. If he could draw Elizabeth away, perhaps he would be able to extract a payoff for silence to avoid embarrassing the family, and if not, the tangible motivation of making Darcy a cuckold was too much to resist. He turned his attention to the young girl beside him, "Miss Lydia, your sister is very fortunate in being Mr. Darcy's choice of wife. You and your family must be well pleased with the match."

"Mama is, but I am not sure anyone else in the family cares, for he is such a serious, ill-tempered man. I have only been in his company a few times, but he always looks down his nose at me. Lizzy has shown no fondness for him, and I do not think she would have accepted his offer if she were not obligated."

"I know she does not care for some of his actions, but surely she sees the pecuniary benefits of being married to Mr. Darcy as being worth the small tedium of his company. He can be rather loathsome, but really, she will not have to reside with him unless she wishes, for he has more than one estate and a house in town. Many great men live separate lives from their wives, marrying to secure a substantial dowry and to conceive an heir. After she has done her job, she may do as she pleases. Darcy will not cause her harm like some men." Lydia looked up at him puzzled. "I am sure your sister has her head about her and will find peace with the match. I do hope that she does not forget her friends once she becomes a woman of fashion," Wickham said with a charming smile.

"Lizzy will do as she pleases, to be sure; she always has."

"I do hope that she is able to continue on in that manner. It would pain me to know that she must change to satisfy Darcy's view of how a wife should behave. You will keep me informed, will you not? I would dearly appreciate your sharing with me your sister's success at conforming to his ways. I think too highly of her not to worry."

"You are so gallant to be thinking of Lizzy, but why do we not find something more fun to speak of? Will you be attending the ball that Mr. Bingley is hosting in honour of Lizzy and Mr. Darcy? It is to be held next Monday, you know."

"If an invitation is extended to me, I would be happy to attend."

"Consider yourself invited then."

ELIZABETH'S PACE REFLECTED the irritation in her breast. She had released Darcy's arm as soon as they had departed from the group. *How dare he embarrass me in such a public manner? And poor Mr. Wickham, cut so rudely in front of his friends.* Her sense of justice propelled her forward in agitation, leaving Jane and Bingley lagging far behind.

Mr. Darcy was similarly disturbed as his thoughts wandered to the possible reasons for finding Wickham in the company of Miss Elizabeth. *Could they be working in conjunction with one another, entrapping me in order to gain financial advantage? This will not do.* In the shock of the moment, Darcy had barely noticed Wickham's wearing a redcoat, but upon further reflection, wondered how that had come to pass. *Surely Wickham did not join the regiment without hopes of furthering his financial situation. Could he have known I was here and joined the local troops in order to communicate with Miss Elizabeth?*

Finally, after ruminating over the possibilities, Darcy stopped and looked at Elizabeth. "I do not know how long Mr. Wickham has been an acquaintance of yours or how he has imposed himself upon you, but know this: if I find that you have had any further contact with him before we are married, I will call off the engagement, leaving you and your family to deal with the consequences."

Elizabeth stopped when Mr. Darcy spoke and lifting her chin defiantly said, "Mr. Darcy, I realise that you and Mr. Wickham have your differences, but surely you do not expect me to be your pawn as a means to hurt him more." She knew that she should just agree, but her sense of justice made her temporarily forget her prudence.

Unused to being questioned, Darcy's ire grew. After a few calming breaths he continued, "I demand that you agree to this now, or I will consider our betrothal at an end. Miss Elizabeth, I suggest you consider the repercussions to your family and yourself of such an action before determining your response."

Elizabeth looked away, trying desperately to control her indignant feelings. She considered whether marriage to this man was worth the suffering her family would be certain to experience. If it were just she, the answer would be evident, and she considered giving an immediate response in the negative; however, luckily for her, she spied Jane and Mr. Bingley happily walking around a turn in the road towards them, thereby making her decision much clearer. She looked him straight in the eye and said, "Mr. Darcy, I will agree to your terms for my family's sake. I would not have my family suffer for the position in which you have placed me." At that, she turned again towards Longbourn, not looking to see if Mr. Darcy were following.

As Longbourn was a couple of miles from Meryton, there was still some small distance to traverse to arrive there. To lighten her mood, Elizabeth decided to tease him to see how he might handle such an action. "I see that you enjoy arranging business just as you please, sir. You like to have your own way very well, do you not, Mr. Darcy?"

After a few moments, he responded slowly and deliberately, "I have many people under my care. My decisions affect the livelihood of my servants, tenants, and family as well as their futures. I can assure you that I make no demands lightly and feel no need to explain my motives. I do not apologise for doing so in this case, for either you know Mr. Wickham's duplicity and are in consortium with him, or you do not and would be better served in ignorance." Mr. Darcy was under the conviction that an innocent lady was best left to the direction of those with more understanding and knowledge of the world.

"Mr. Darcy, if not finding the pleasure in the power of choice, you obviously at least have the means to direct things as you will. I wonder at your not being married by now, for the sake of having somebody at your disposal. But I suppose in marrying me you will be able to enjoy a lasting convenience of that kind."

"I do not always find satisfaction in the administration of my duties or in overseeing others. There are instances that I would gladly forego, if not for the need of satisfying my conscience. Miss Bennet, I have faults, but I hope they are not in neglecting the needs of others when I could be of some benefit."

"You think highly of your ability at directing others. Could it be that perhaps, the persons you regulate might know better than you their best course?"

"In this situation, no."

Silence reigned during the balance of the walk to Longbourn. Darcy had intended to take time to present the ring to Miss Elizabeth today, but upon further reflection, he decided to wait to see how Wickham's presence in Meryton would affect his engagement. Knowing that Elizabeth could be in league with Wickham made him concerned that by giving the ring to her, he would be giving Wickham an opportunity to gain possession of it and once again take advantage of him.

Upon arriving at Longbourn and handing over his horse to the stable hand, Mr. Darcy was led by Elizabeth to her father's study, while she herself went to her room. She needed a moment to cool off as she waited for Jane and Mr. Bingley to arrive. Once she saw them from her window, slowly ambling down the drive towards the house, she went to the drawing room to act as chaperone. If one good thing came out of this match, she hoped it would be a union with Mr. Bingley.

Meanwhile, Mr. Darcy met with Mr. Bennet to review the settlement papers and finalise any unresolved issues. Knowing that Miss Elizabeth's actions in regard to Wickham could have a long-lasting negative impact on the Bennets' future, he felt obligated to share with the man about his past dealings with Wickham, without giving away details that Darcy felt were not in his own best interest to share. He also hoped to learn from Miss Elizabeth's father if she had had any previous dealings with the man, hoping to discover if he had cause to fear an alliance between the two. Mr. Bennet eased his mind somewhat by responding that he had never before in his life either seen nor heard of Mr. Wickham and doubted that his daughter had, based on their shared conversations and her usual candour with him. This apparently was the first week of their acquaintance.

Darcy hoped that he had intervened soon enough to stifle any plots Wickham may have planned by using Miss Elizabeth. He related to Mr. Bennet the ultimatum given to his daughter regarding Wickham and received the response that he had hoped for, that Mr. Bennet would make certain that Elizabeth does not have any contact with Wickham, either on her own or through her sisters.

Later, when her father reiterated to Elizabeth Darcy's requirement regarding Wickham, she was upset to realise that she could not send an apology by way of one of her sisters for having to leave so abruptly. *How am I to disregard such a deserving and amiable man? Will I always be required to display Darcy's arrogance and rude precepts to those considered unworthy of his benevolence?*

She determined not to dwell on the negative but to hope for the future. Perhaps after their marriage had taken place, she could in some way alleviate Mr. Wickham's plight and with kind direction of her own, encourage Mr. Darcy to renew his old friendship while softening his conscience.

Chapter Six

He wished to prepare her for measures, which might hereafter be
necessary to accomplish the revenge he meditated, and he knew that
by flattering her vanity, he was most likely to succeed.
He praised her, therefore, for qualities he wished her to possess,
encouraged her to reject general opinions by admiring as the
symptoms of a superior understanding, the convenient morality upon
which she had occasionally acted; and, calling sternness justice,
extolled that for strength of mind, which was only callous
insensibility.
Ann Radcliffe
The Italian

Over the course of the following week, there were several engagements
planned to celebrate the betrothal subsisting between the afflicted, yet resigned
couple. They each had determined within him and herself to bestow upon the
other grace and to attempt to make the best of a trying situation. Darcy attended
social gatherings initiated by the local gentry designed to recognise the couple,
but found it beyond his capability to perform a role in which he did not take
pleasure. The local society lacked not just in fortune, but also in manners and
decorum. Their insipid conversation tried his patience beyond anything he had
experienced in his life. This was most keenly felt when in the presence of the
Bennet family. Although he had to concede that Miss Bennet and his betrothed
were above the rest in many ways, he still saw them as holding a place in society
below that which he would have ever chosen as companions, much less a spouse
for him or his friend. Darcy was not really concerned about an attachment
between Miss Bennet and his friend, for Bingley had been in and out of love
many times, but he worried that perhaps the family might manoeuvre a situation
thus entrapping his friend to misery, as he himself had been. So although he
could not enjoy the celebrations, he could focus on protecting his friend while
pretending, without success, to be pleased.

One such gathering took place at Lucas Lodge, the closest neighbours to the
Bennet family, the eldest daughter of which family being Elizabeth's closest
friend and confidante. Elizabeth and Charlotte were talking with one another
when the Netherfield party arrived. The Bingleys and their guests had made a
habit of appearing at gatherings past the hour expected, so no one was surprised
at the late entrance. Indeed, Elizabeth was glad for the delay that gave her an
opportunity to speak with Charlotte in private for the first time since Darcy's
return. They were speaking on marriage, specifically focusing on the upcoming
weddings within the Bennet family, including those already planned and one that
they were hopeful would come, which would be certain to make Jane the
happiest of creatures.

It was generally evident whenever Jane and Mr. Bingley met, that he did admire her; and to Elizabeth it was equally evident that Jane was yielding to the preference which she had begun to entertain for him from the first, and was in a way to be very much in love; but she considered with pleasure that it was not likely to be discovered by the world in general, since Jane united with great strength of feeling, a composure of temper and a uniform cheerfulness of manner, which would guard her from the suspicions of the impertinent. Elizabeth mentioned this to her friend, Miss Lucas.

"It may perhaps be pleasant," replied Charlotte, "to be able to impose on the public in such a case; but it is sometimes a disadvantage to be so very guarded. If a woman conceals her affection with the same skill from the object of it, she may lose the opportunity of fixing him; and it will then be but poor consolation to believe the world equally in the dark. We can all begin freely – a slight preference is natural enough – but there are very few of us who have heart enough to be really in love without encouragement. A woman had better show more affection than she feels. Bingley likes your sister undoubtedly; but he may never do more than like her, if she does not help him on."

"But she does help him on, as much as her nature will allow. If I can perceive her regard for him, he must be a simpleton indeed not to discover it too."

"Remember, Eliza, that he does not know Jane's disposition as you do."

"But if a woman is partial to a man, and does not endeavour to conceal it, he must find it out."

"Perhaps he must, if he sees enough of her. But though Bingley and Jane meet tolerably often, it is never for many hours together. Jane should therefore make the most of every half hour in which she can command his attention. When she is secure of him, there will be leisure for falling in love as much as she chooses."

"Your plan is a good one," replied Elizabeth, "where nothing is in question but the desire of being well married. But these are not Jane's feelings; she is not acting by design."

"Well," said Charlotte, "I wish Jane success with all my heart, and if she were married to him tomorrow, I should think she had as good a chance of happiness as if she were to be studying his character for a twelvemonth. Happiness in marriage is entirely a matter of chance. If the dispositions of the parties are ever so well known to each other, or ever so similar beforehand, it does not advance their felicity in the least. They always continue to grow sufficiently to have their share of vexation; and it is better to know as little as possible of the defects of the person with whom you are to pass your life."

"You make me laugh, Charlotte; but it is not sound. You know it is not sound, and that you would never act in this way yourself. I would never act in this way given a choice; I never in my life hoped to be in my current situation, where I must marry a stranger, a man with whom I share no commonality, yet hoping for a comfortable marriage."

"Eliza, forgive me for bringing the conversation too close to home, but I do hope to encourage you. You may not know Mr. Darcy now, and truly may have no fondness for the man, but take heart; many start in the marriage state in such a way and then grow in respect and contentment if not in love."

During the course of the conversation, Elizabeth had noticed the arrival of the Netherfield party. Elizabeth saw that Mr. Bingley placed himself next to Jane; however, Mr. Darcy had made no move to greet her. Instead she found that the man was staring at her and Charlotte with an inscrutable mien. Charlotte also noticed the stare and saw disapproval. Although she was trying to encourage Elizabeth as she faced her future with Mr. Darcy, she knew that her friend's playfulness and whimsy would likely suffer under a severe man.

Elizabeth, attempting to ignore his inspection, said playfully, "I do believe my own chances of happiness in marriage to be rather slim, regardless of our lack of familiarity of dispositions. How do I find contentment with a man who belittles me? No, I will have to find my pleasure in learning the byways and passageways of the Pemberley estate. As grand as I have heard it spoken of by Miss Bingley, I fear that I will become lost more often than not. But I do not foresee that that would result in Mr. Darcy's coming to look for me; he would be certain to send one of his many servants for that pleasure. Perhaps I could find a tree to climb to sit and enjoy the spectacle." At this, Charlotte and Elizabeth gaily laughed. Elizabeth had always used levity when faced with difficulties; this Charlotte knew well and attempted to appease her through joining in.

"Well, it looks as though he is looking for you now. I am sure you noticed that he was staring at you."

"He means to frighten me with his harsh looks, but every attempt at intimidation causes my spirit to rise to meet him. Shall I go to make my greetings? I feel I must take courage before I become afraid of him." She said this with a smile and then went across the room to her intended's side. With a curtsy, she began, "Mr. Darcy, a pleasure to see you have made it tonight. I believe that dinner will be called soon, as our hosts were awaiting your arrival in order to begin."

Darcy understood that in her tease, she was scolding him for their late entry. "Then I must apologise to our host. Unfortunately my usual promptness has been undermined on my visit here, but I can assure you that tardiness is a problem for which I rarely must ask forgiveness."

"Is that so? This must occur only in Hertfordshire then," she replied archly.

He tried to decide the most gracious response, while not letting her know that her words had any weight. "Miss Elizabeth, if you will excuse me. I thank you for reminding me of my need to apologise to our hosts. I will procure my friend, so that we might promptly offer amends." He then gathered Bingley from Miss Bennet and looked for his host, just before dinner was announced.

Elizabeth found herself seated across the table from Mr. Darcy, with Miss Bingley to his left and Miss Lucas to her own right. Little conversation was had in that merry group as each attempted to come up with a subject worthwhile to speak upon. Miss Bingley decided to show her superior communication skills and so began her own monologue about London society and how the current company compared to her esteemed friends there. After some minutes of acclaiming the quality of the clothing currently worn in London, Miss Bingley moved on to speak of the accomplishments of the ladies of London, so rarely seen in the country.

"You must comprehend a great deal in your idea of an accomplished woman," said Elizabeth to Miss Bingley, thereby interrupting her soliloquy.

"Oh! Certainly," cried Miss Bingley, "no one can be really esteemed accomplished, who does not greatly surpass what is usually met with. A woman must have a thorough knowledge of music, singing, drawing, dancing, and the modern languages, to deserve the word; and besides all this, she must possess a certain something in her air and manner of walking, the tone of her voice, her address and expressions, or the word will be but half deserved."

"And, Mr. Darcy, do you also agree with Miss Bingley's description of an accomplished woman?"

"Yes, I do comprehend a great deal in it. All this she must possess, and to all this she must yet add something more substantial, in the improvement of her mind by extensive reading. There are very few truly accomplished women of my acquaintance, I daresay not more than half a dozen at most."

"With the extensive list that you and Miss Bingley design, I am not surprised at your knowing only six accomplished women. In truth, I rather wonder at your knowing *any*."

"Are you so severe upon your own sex as to doubt the possibility of all this?"

"I never saw such a woman. I never saw such capacity, and taste, and application, and elegance, as you describe, united."

Miss Bingley cried out against the injustice of her implied doubt, and was protesting that they knew many women who answered this description, while Elizabeth looked down to her food in mirth. "Miss Eliza, please, do tell; what are *your* accomplishments? We know you to be a great walker, as you seem to always be about the countryside, but what else can you add to your list of talents?" Elizabeth knew this was said to make sport with her, but she was not intimidated and determined to respond in truth. Let Mr. Darcy know her failings.

"I confess that I do enjoy walking and even running when the fancy takes hold. I have pleasure in many things, but am proficient in none. I enjoy reading next to walking, and when I can accomplish both in one outing, I am satisfied." Miss Bingley sneered at her, having made her point to Mr. Darcy. If she could not have him, she would make him regret having lost her, anyway.

Miss Bingley had not finished with her intent as she moved on to pile praise onto Mr. Darcy and his choice of estate. "Miss Eliza, you should then be quite content at Pemberley, as Mr. Darcy's estate has a delightful library and the finest grounds to be found in all of England, do you not, sir?" Before he could respond, she continued, "I venture, you will probably be situated there a month straight without having an occasion to see one another, but perhaps Mr. Darcy will not want you removing his books to the open air. His collection is quite fine and worthy of better care than you may be willing or able to provide."

"Perhaps you are right. I will make sure to bring my own, for I would not want to sully anything at so fine a home." Elizabeth smiled sweetly then began a conversation with Charlotte, who had been greatly amused at the exchange going on around her. She knew that Elizabeth was teasing the two dinner guests, but held in her laughter, as she doubted not that the principal listeners were in ignorance of her friend's provocations.

Mr. Darcy's intervention in pulling Mr. Bingley away from Jane resulted in their being separated for dinner. Instead Bingley found himself between Lydia and Mary. Although Mr. Bingley was adept at conversing with most anyone, he found Lydia without need of a partner in her chatter. Mary, sensing the discomfort of the meal as she watched Mr. Bingley stare at her eldest sister across the table, knowing that he wished to be with Jane instead of herself, tried to come up with something sensible to say, but knew not how, so she concentrated on her soup. After a short time, Bingley was roused from his reverie by Mrs. Bennet, just across the table and two up from him, who inquired about the upcoming ball and who was to be invited. He responded that he hoped all of their friends would be able to come and certainly the Bennets could invite whomever they wished, since it was to be given in honour of Miss Elizabeth as well as Mr. Darcy.

"Oh, how generous of you, sir. I have been thinking upon who might come to help us celebrate. You know, the officers have spent some time with our family. I am sure you have issued an invitation there. Dancing can be a difficult endeavour when there are too few men, you know. My girls are especially fond of Mr. Wickham, so you must include him."

Her unrestrained voice was regarded across the table. Upon hearing the name of Wickham, Mr. Darcy looked up. Bingley, not knowing Darcy's history with Wickham nor the need to say otherwise, agreed to the inclusion of all of the officers, as he had found their company pleasant and entertaining, and indicated that he had already issued the invitation. Elizabeth smiled to herself as she considered Mr. Darcy's discomfort at the prospect and secretly hoped to at least see Mr. Wickham at the ball, that he might discover the reason for her incivility and place the blame where it lay.

Dinner passed in like manner for the rest of the meal and was followed by a short separation of the sexes, the men staying in the dining room and the ladies retiring to the drawing room. Mr. Bennet used this time to approach Mr. Darcy to enquire about his plans for after the wedding. "I intend to take Miss Elizabeth to London for the festive season, then on to Pemberley until spring."

"Will you be returning for Mary's wedding before you depart for the North? Lizzy would not like missing a day so important to her sister."

"I have made no plans for such an occasion, and have only learnt of the engagement earlier this evening over dinner," responded Darcy and then paused before continuing. "Allow me to congratulate you on your fortunate alliances. I understand that my aunt's rector is the one soon to be your son. You must be proud for two of your daughters to make advantageous matches."

"Indeed, I admire both of my sons-in-law highly but cannot decide which of you is to be my favourite." He paused here as if in contemplation before recalling himself. "I do hope for Lizzy's sake that you make plans to bring her or at least let her come on her own. Although she and Mary are unlike in manner and interests, Lizzy loves her and would be sorry to miss the occasion."

"I will take that under advisement, sir." Darcy looked around to see if anyone was listening, and finding that the others were occupied in their own conversations, he continued, "Mr. Bennet, while I have this opportunity, I would like to reiterate my wishes regarding Mr. Wickham. Your wife specifically asked my friend to invite him to the ball. Bingley knows nothing about my former dealings with the man, and so did not exclude him from the invitation. I have every reason to doubt his attendance; nevertheless, I would ask that you do your part to ensure that he not be encouraged by your family to make a showing. I stand by my threat to you and your daughter. If she has communication with that man before the wedding, I will walk away from this business without remorse."

"I am curious as to your connection with Mr. Wickham. You have asked me to ensure my family's distance from him, but have not told me the details behind the reason for our lack of civility. If I am to listen to the constant complaints of my family on this matter, you can at least give me justification for such a course."

Darcy did not know Mr. Bennet well enough to trust his confidence in this matter, and so replied in general terms about his toying with respectable ladies and those of the lower classes, as well as his amassing sizeable debt wherever he goes. Before Mr. Bennet could ask more specific questions, Sir William announced that it was time to join the ladies. Mr. Bennet had no reason not to agree to Darcy's terms, except perhaps the peace that he longed to keep in his home. He knew that all he had to do in this case was to let his wife know that avoiding Wickham was a wish of Mr. Darcy, and it would be done. Her desire to please the man was greater than her desire to attach Wickham to one of her other daughters, especially as he had no fortune.

The men joined the ladies, and the night continued on in congenial, if not completely pleasant, conversation. Mr. Darcy knew his duty and remained by Miss Elizabeth's side; therefore, when she was summoned by her friend to play and sing for the company, he offered to turn her pages and make a show of affability. He would not have considered her playing to match that of his sister's, and he would agree with her own assessment of herself – that she was not proficient in the art. However, Elizabeth did not shrink from her presentation, and although not accomplished, she had pluck and did not cower in the face of a challenge. And although he usually esteemed men with courage such as this, his feelings were too coloured by resentment to truly acknowledge the idea as yet in her case.

ON FRIDAY MORNING, but four days before the expected wedding, Mr. Bennet sat at the breakfast table finishing his meal when he calmly but decisively announced to the ladies of the home that Mr. Wickham was not to visit Longbourn, nor were any of them to speak with him in the village until after the conclusion of the wedding. He had told Mrs. Bennet the details of the edict the evening before, and after a heated exchange, achieved her final acquiescence – due mostly to the ultimatum given by Mr. Darcy. Mr. Bennet was explaining to the younger family members what his expectations on the matter entailed when their attention was suddenly drawn to the window by the sound of a carriage.

They were astonished to see a chaise and four driving up the lawn. It was too early in the morning for visitors, and the equipage did not answer to that of any of their neighbours. The horses were post; and neither the carriage, nor the livery of the servant who preceded it, were familiar to them. Mr. Bennet who was never fond of company made his escape to his own study before he could be detained, rejoicing in his propitious evasion of the expected complaints concerning Mr. Wickham's dismissal from their society. The conjectures amongst the ladies relating to their unexpected caller continued, though with little satisfaction, till the door of the breakfast room was thrown open, and their visitor entered. She was announced as Lady Catherine de Bourgh and with her walked Mr. Collins, her vicar.

The ladies were of course all intending to be surprised, but their astonishment was beyond their expectation. The guests entered the room, Lady Catherine with an ungracious air and Mr. Collins with his own form of condescension, and sat down without saying a word as Lady Catherine prepared to burden those assembled with her reason for coming. She turned to Mr. Collins, who was standing beside her and said, "Which of these ladies, may I ask, is Miss Elizabeth Bennet?"

Elizabeth, finding it nonsensical not to reply herself, indicated very concisely that she was the one to whom she referred.

Turning to Miss Elizabeth with a glance to Mrs. Bennet, she continued, "This is your mother?"

"Yes, Madam."

"And these others I suppose are your sisters. Which one of you is to marry my parson here?"

Mary did not know to be intimidated by a grand lady and so spoke up without trepidation, "I am Mr. Collins's betrothed. He has told me much about you, but I own that I did not think you so solicitous as to plan to bring him here in an unannounced visit before we were to be married." Mr. Collins was too afraid to say anything in his defence, and so remained unusually quiet.

"I am not here to see you; I have come to speak with your sister, about whom my nephew has written to me. Miss Elizabeth Bennet, there seemed to be a prettyish kind of a little wilderness on one side of your lawn. I should be glad to take a turn in it, if you will favour me with your company."

"Go, my dear," cried her mother, "and show her ladyship about the different walks. I think she will be pleased with the hermitage. We can enjoy the unexpected visit with Mr. Collins."

Elizabeth obeyed. After running into her own room for her parasol, Elizabeth attended her noble guest downstairs. As they passed through the hall, Lady Catherine opened the doors into the formal dining-parlour and drawing room, and pronouncing them, after a short survey, to be decent looking rooms, walked on.

Her carriage remained at the door, and Elizabeth saw that her waiting-woman was in it. They proceeded in silence along the gravel walk that led to the copse;

104

Elizabeth was determined to make no effort for conversation with a woman who was insolent and demanding. *Now I see that contemptuousness is a family trait not limited to Mr. Darcy alone. What can she mean by this audacious visit?*

As soon as they entered the copse, Lady Catherine began, "You can be at no loss, Miss Bennet, to understand the reason of my journey hither. Your own heart, your own conscience, must tell you why I come."

Elizabeth looked with unaffected astonishment. "Indeed, you are mistaken, madam. I have not been at all able to account for the honour of meeting you without the benefit of Mr. Darcy's introduction."

"Miss Bennet," replied her ladyship, in an angry tone, "you ought to know, that I am not to be trifled with. But however insincere you may choose to be, you shall not find me so. My character has ever been celebrated for its sincerity and frankness, and in a cause of such a moment as this, I shall certainly not depart from it. A letter from Darcy reached me three days ago. Although I was already aware of your sister's plan to marry my rector, I was told in writing that you, that Miss Elizabeth Bennet, would be united to my own nephew, Mr. Darcy himself. I know it must be a scandalous union, for he would never shirk his duty to his own family. Though I would not injure him so much as to suppose his own complaisance, I instantly resolved on setting off for this place, that I might make my sentiments known to you and demand that you release him from this ridiculous connection."

"I wonder at your coming all this way to make this request, madam. You know Mr. Darcy better than myself, I will wager. You must realise that he is his own man and makes his own decisions. If he asked me to marry him, and I accepted, what business can that be of yours?"

"Miss Bennet, do you know who I am? I have not been accustomed to such language as this. I am almost the nearest relation he has in the world, and am entitled to know all his dearest concerns."

"But you are not entitled to know mine; nor will such behaviour as this ever induce me to do your bidding."

"Let me be rightly understood. This match, to which you have the presumption to aspire, can never take place – no, never. Mr. Darcy is engaged to my daughter. Now what have you to say?"

"Only this; that if he is so, he would never have been free to make an offer for me. However, he has offered, and I, in turn, accepted."

Lady Catherine hesitated for a moment, and then replied, "The engagement between them is of a peculiar kind. From their infancy, they have been intended for each other. It was the favourite wish of his mother, as well as of hers. While in their cradles, we planned the union; and now, at the moment when the wishes of both sisters would be accomplished through their marriage, it is to be prevented by a young woman of inferior birth, of no importance in the world, and wholly unallied to the family! Do you pay no regard to the wishes of his friends, to his tacit engagement with Miss De Bourgh? Are you lost to every feeling of propriety and delicacy? Do you hear me say that from his earliest hours he was destined for his cousin?"

"Yes, and I had heard it before from Mr. Collins. But what is that to me? If there is no other objection to my marrying your nephew, I shall certainly not be kept from it by knowing that his mother and aunt wished him to marry Miss De Bourgh. You both did as much as you could in planning the marriage. Its completion depended on others. If Mr. Darcy is neither by honour nor inclination confined to his cousin, why is not he to make another choice. And if I am that choice, why may not I accept him?"

"Because honour, decorum, prudence, nay interest, forbid it. Yes, Miss Bennet, interest; for do not expect to be noticed by his family or friends, if you wilfully act against the inclinations of all. You will be censured, slighted, and despised, by everyone connected with him. Your alliance will be a disgrace; your name will never even be mentioned by any of us."

"These are heavy misfortunes," replied Elizabeth. "But he has asked, and I have accepted. There is nothing that you, your family, nor anyone unconnected with me can say that will cause me to rescind on my acceptance of his proposal."

"Obstinate, headstrong girl! I am ashamed of you. You are to understand, Miss Bennet, that I came here with the determined resolution of carrying my purpose; nor will I be dissuaded from it. I have not been used to submit to any person's whims. I have not been in the habit of brooking disappointment."

"That will make your ladyship's situation at present more pitiable; but it will have no effect on me."

"I will not be interrupted. Hear me in silence. My daughter and my nephew are formed for each other. They are descended on the maternal side, from the same noble line, and on the father's, from respectable, honourable, and ancient, though untitled families. Their fortune on both sides is splendid. They are destined for each other by the voice of every member of their respective houses; and what is to divide them? —The upstart pretensions of a young woman without family, connections, or fortune? Is this to be endured? But it must not, shall not be. If you were sensible of your own good, you would not wish to quit the sphere in which you have been brought up. All of Darcy's relations and friends will know you to be a mercenary harlot, who seeks to raise herself by entrapment."

"Your nephew's holdings mean nothing to me. And in marrying your nephew, I should not consider myself as quitting that sphere into which I have been raised. He is a gentleman – I, a gentleman's daughter. So far we are equal."

"True. You are a gentleman's daughter. But who is your mother? Who are your uncles and aunts? Do not imagine me ignorant of their condition."

"Whatever my connections may be," said Elizabeth, "if your nephew does not object to them, they can be nothing to you."

"Of course he objects to them! But you have entrapped him, giving him no choice in the matter. He does what he supposes to be honourable, but in so doing, has left my daughter to the derision of the world. I demand that you promise me that you will release him from this farce of an engagement."

"I will make no promise of the kind."

"Miss Bennet, I am shocked and astonished. I expected to find a more reasonable young woman. But do not deceive yourself into a belief that I will recede. I shall not go away until you have given me the assurance I require."

"And I certainly never shall give it. I am not to be intimidated into anything so wholly unreasonable. Your ladyship wants Mr. Darcy to marry your daughter; but would my giving you the wished-for promise make their marriage at all more probable? Would my refusing to accept his hand, make him wish to bestow it on his cousin? Allow me to say, Lady Catherine, that the arguments with which you have supported this extraordinary application, have been as frivolous as the application was ill judged. You have widely mistaken my character, if you think I can be worked on by such persuasions as these. How far your nephew might approve of your interference in his affairs, I cannot tell; but you have certainly no right to concern yourself in mine. I must beg, therefore, to be importuned no farther on the subject."

"Not so hasty, if you please. I have by no means done. I see that you will be unreasonable with respect to duty or honour. You desire monetary compensation. I knew you would not capitulate without financial remuneration. I will offer you ten thousand pounds to break the engagement with my nephew." She paused to let the young woman consider the amount. "You must know that this is more than you deserve or could ever hope to gain in any other situation."

"You offend me, Lady Catherine. Do you think I would accept a bribe to break an engagement, to put my family in an untenable situation that would ruin me – and them with me – thus forfeiting any future happiness that comes from respectability, which might come our way? You are mistaken, madam, if you think I can be worked on in this manner."

"It is best that you accept my offer and be done with Darcy. If you choose to move forward with this marriage, your life with him will be one of misery and loneliness. He will never respect you, much less have affection for you. He will of course keep a mistress to provide comfort in an indifferent union, while you are left alone to bear him an heir. Be reasonable. Your family would get over it soon enough, as my vicar, Mr. Collins, will marry you instead. He joined me today to make his intentions known. As you are aware, he will one day be master of Longbourn. With ten thousand pounds, your sisters need not be destitute from your scandal."

"You are suggesting that I ask my sister to give up her own plans to marry Mr. Collins so that he could marry me instead? Are you mad? Why on earth would I agree to a plan so ridiculous? You say that Mr. Darcy's friends and family would regard me as mercenary; would accepting your proposal not confirm this allegation? And if I were mercenary, why would I give up Mr. Darcy's ten thousand a year for a one time payment of such a comparatively small amount and a future with an absurd man?"

"You are then resolved to have him? You will continue with your plans to ruin the lives of so many with this scandalous endeavour?"

"I am only resolved to act in that manner, which will, in my own opinion, constitute my family's own happiness and wellbeing, without reference to you, or to any person so wholly unconnected with me."

"You refuse, then, to oblige me. You refuse to obey the claims of duty and honour. You are determined to ruin him in the opinion of all his friends, and make him the contempt of the world."

"Neither duty, nor honour," replied Elizabeth, "have any possible claim on me in the present instance. No principle of either would be violated by my marriage with Mr. Darcy. And with regard to the resentment of his family or the indignation of the world, I have not one moment of concern, for Mr. Darcy and I are acting in a way that absolves each of us from all censure. If this cannot be seen by those who claim a connection to either of us, I can have no cause to repine."

"And this is your real opinion! This is your final resolve! Very well. I shall now know how to act with regards to Darcy. Do not imagine, Miss Bennet, that your ambition will ever be gratified. I came to try you and to give you an alternative that would acquit you of your guilt. I hoped to find you reasonable; but depend upon it, I will do my part to ensure the desolation that will naturally come to you if you continue with this course."

In this manner Lady Catherine talked on till they were at the door of the carriage, when turning hastily round, she added, "Tell Mr. Collins that I will not wait for him. He must come out at once. Now, I take no leave of you, Miss Bennet. I send no compliments to your mother. You deserve no such attention. I am most seriously displeased."

Elizabeth made no answer; and without attempting to persuade her ladyship to return into the house or to allow Mr. Collins some time with Mary, walked quietly into it herself. She informed Mr. Collins of his lady's imminent departure, apologised to Mary for his hasty removal, then proceeded upstairs. Her mother impatiently met her at the door of the dressing room to ask why Lady Catherine would not come in again and rest herself while Mr. Collins visited with Mary.

"She did not choose it," said her daughter, "she would go."

"Lady Catherine is a very fine-looking woman! And her calling here was prodigiously civil! For she only came, I suppose, to meet the ladies who would be joining her family and her neighbourhood, and of course to allow Mr. Collins time with our dear Mary. She is kindness itself. I suppose she had nothing particular to say to you, Lizzy?"

Elizabeth was forced to give into a little falsehood here; for to acknowledge the substance of their conversation would only bring her mother pain and a fit of nerves, and Elizabeth further indignation. Her mother would surely need her vinaigrette and Elizabeth, quietude.

Although Elizabeth's fortitude did not abandon her during Lady Catherine's attack, when alone in her room, she gave her distress free rein, as she considered her future life with such a family. Even though Mr. Darcy was conceited and arrogant, she had supposed that after their marriage had taken place, he might soften towards her – that they might one day find some measure of felicity. Elizabeth could not deny his attractions and with a little teasing might one day find some semblance of pleasure in their union, but what of his family? How could she withstand their vitriol in light of the tenuous hope of Mr. Darcy's future regard? And could her words be true? — Might Mr. Darcy take a mistress, disparaging her and their marriage in such a manner?

LADY CATHERINE HAD BEGUN to pull away from Longbourn when Mr. Collins came running out the front door, waving his arms erratically. Although she was in no mood to wait for him, she halted the carriage hoping for a positive report from his visit with Mr. Bennet. She had instructed him to attempt to reason with Elizabeth's father in case she herself was unsuccessful with the doxy who ensnared Darcy. If Miss Bennet could not see reason, perhaps her father would.

When Mr. Collins entered the chaise panting, she enquired as to his success. He then told Lady Catherine what Mr. Bennet had told him. "'Mr. Collins,' said he, 'my Lizzy is to marry Mr. Darcy and you, sir, will soon be united with Mary. If you choose to dishonour our understanding into which you willingly, and legally I might add, entered, I will sue you for breach of contract. And sir, if Mary hears anything about this conversation, I promise that I will live to be a hundred rather than have you inherit Longbourn.' Yes, I believe that is how he put it. He cannot legally do that, can he?" She gave him a look of contempt, as the dose that was Mr. Collins had been quite enough for the day.

"But, Lady Catherine," he continued, "after I left Mr. Bennet's study, I joined the ladies. That is when I overheard Miss Lydia and Miss Kitty complaining about not being able to talk to a man by the name of Mr. Wickham again until after the wedding. They were quite loud in their protestations, so I easily took notice of what they had to say before I entered the room. I heard the younger one say that it was not fair that they could not talk to Wickham when it was Elizabeth whom Mr. Darcy would not let speak to him. The two youngest girls are far too forward, and I was glad that Mr. Bennet was making an attempt to rein them in, but I began to wonder what Mr. Darcy had to do with the business." He looked at this patroness for guidance as to whether to continue or not. After she nodded, he resumed. "So, after I entered the room, I sat next to my Mary. I questioned her about the source of the girls' concern, and she told me that Mr. Darcy had told Elizabeth and Mr. Bennet that if Elizabeth had any communication with that Wickham man before the wedding, that he, Mr. Darcy that is, would call off the wedding and leave her in ruin. Miss Mary did not know why this was the case, but she speculated that perhaps the man named Wickham admired Elizabeth, and Mr. Darcy, in his jealousy, would not share her with him."

Lady Catherine listened to all that Mr. Collins had to say, as he continued to add details to his dialogue with his betrothed. Her lip curled up into a half smile, as she began to formulate a plan, should she not succeed in changing Darcy's mind. *Perhaps he may need added motivation to do his duty to his own family.*

They arrived at Netherfield so that Lady Catherine could give Darcy her opinion on his plans and ensure that he reconsider his familial obligations and stop this abhorrent arrangement to ruin the names of Darcy and De Bourgh. This time, she left Mr. Collins in the chaise with the task of considering alternative ways to change the mind of his cousin Elizabeth. She did not think that he would actually come up with a new idea but felt the exertion could only be good for him. Lady Catherine was soon announced to those in the drawing room, which included Miss Bingley, Mrs Hurst, Mr. Hurst and her nephew, Mr. Darcy.

Looking directly at Darcy, she said, "I must speak to you at once. These other people must give us privacy." She then looked around to the gathering waiting for a speedy response.

Darcy was embarrassed by his aunt's officious and offensive display and spoke to recover some semblance of decorum. "Lady Catherine, allow me to introduce my hostess, Miss Bingley, and her brother and sister, Mr. and Mrs. Hurst. Miss Bingley has been gracious during my visit to her brother's home."

His point was clear, so his aunt, though not in the mood to recognise yet another of Darcy's acquaintances tainted by trade, gave a small nod, and said with a peevish look upon her face, "It is a pleasure." Then turning back to Darcy demanded that he take her somewhere to speak privately concerning a most alarming subject. Miss Bingley would have felt offence at the slight, if not secretly pleased at the obvious reason for her visit, and wished her all the luck that could be sent her way.

Darcy led her from the public area to Bingley's study and offered her a seat, which she refused. Instead she began making her point. "Darcy, what can you mean by engaging yourself to that...that... trollop! Have you lost your mind? Have her arts and allurements caused you to forget yourself, what you owe to your family, to your own honour?"

Darcy desperately wanted to diffuse the situation without giving his aunt hope for a change in circumstances. "Madam, please be seated and let me order tea. You must be in need of refreshment after such a journey. I am sure we can discuss the matter as two civilised adults."

"I will not be distracted. Tell me, do you plan to go through with this farce? Or can I hope that you have seen reason?"

"Aunt, I can assure you that I have put no small amount of thought into my decision to marry Miss Bennet. Our plans stand. The wedding will be Tuesday, and if you are willing, you may stay until then, so that you might wish us joy."

She looked at him as if he had declared that he was to become a monk. "Have you no sense, Darcy? Your mother would be ashamed of you, as I am ashamed. You are to marry *my* daughter, as you well know. Truly, you have known since you were a child what your obligations to the family are."

"No, Aunt, I will not be marrying Anne. I am bound by neither duty nor inclination to join with my cousin." His aunt was about to speak, until he held up his hand to stay her. "And you need to know that my marriage to Miss Bennet has no bearing on the *supposed* engagement to your daughter. My attachment to Anne is limited to that of a cousin. I have never intended to marry her; this she knows, as Anne and I have previously spoken on the subject." He did not mention that he had in fact spoken to Anne due to his desire to offer for Lady Annette rather than Miss Bennet. "If you asked her, you would know that she has no desire to marry me either."

"What she wants does not signify, just like what you want does not. You are to join the De Bourgh fortune to that of Pemberley, thereby making our family one of the wealthiest in the kingdom. It is your duty to make this happen."

Of course Darcy had heard this before, but he had never witnessed his mother or father speak of growing the fortune by way of marrying his cousin, Anne. In fact, his father had told him that he must make certain to marry a healthy woman who would be able to bear him children; he needed an heir far more than additional fortune, and Anne was too weak to accomplish this task. "I am sorry that you travelled so far to be disappointed in this way, but I will not be moved. I can only hope that you will accept my decision and welcome Miss Bennet to our family."

"Do not mention her name to me again. I have already spoken to that strumpet and she cares nothing for you. She told me that she is only acting in a way that will bring herself happiness without regard to anyone else. Miss Bennet cares nothing for you, Darcy, yet you defend your choice to marry her. She means to enjoy your fortune and save her family. I told her that no one in your family or of your acquaintance would recognise her, but instead would scorn her; however, she remained unmoved."

In indignation, Darcy said, "You went to Longbourn and spoke with Miss Bennet on my behalf? You take far too much upon yourself, madam. Whom I choose to marry is no concern of yours. If you cannot respect my wishes as they stand, I ask that you keep your opinions to yourself. You have placed a burden upon my duties that can only make my future a greater trial. I would ask that you give your apologies to Miss Bennet if I felt that it were within your power to do so. As it is, I must ask you to desist from your censure of her and of her family."

"Darcy, you cannot be putting her concerns above your family's!"

Irritated but also with contrition, he answered, "Aunt Catherine, you are my family, and I respect you and your position in my life; however, I cannot have you threatening the future Mrs. Darcy. I apologise if I have not been sufficiently forthright with you. In attempting to avoid conflict, I have created an even more unpleasant situation for us all. You could not have known my mind regarding Anne, of course, and I have disappointed your hopes. But I can assure you that I am only acting upon the noble inclinations that were instilled within me by my most excellent parents. I believe that they would not have had me leave a family in ruin when I could do something to help, especially when I would be the central figure in their destruction." His speech became softer and more beseeching as he spoke. "Dear Aunt, please do not make this more difficult, I beg you."

Lady Catherine was a woman who wore her nobility with pride. She was arrogant, critical of others and happy to be of use to her subordinates through directional instruction. However, she also did have a sincere affection for her nephew and could not continue in this manner. She determined then that she would take upon herself the task of saving him from a marriage to a woman unworthy of the Darcy name, a woman whose maternal heritage had no consequence whatsoever.

Lady Catherine took her leave of Darcy, departing Netherfield without the common courtesy to say goodbye to his hosts. She entered the carriage, telling the footman to take them to the militia officers' quarters.

When they arrived, she had her footman discover the location of Mr. Wickham. It had been years since she had last seen the son of Mr. George Darcy's trusted and reliable steward. Mr. Darcy loved the younger Wickham – as he had admired his father – for reasons that Lady Catherine could not understand. Years before, Mr. Darcy had come to Rosings for his annual visit and brought his son and Wickham with him, as they were friends, of about the same age. The young men were at Cambridge together, and Mr. Darcy wished to acquaint his son with the estate management concerns at Rosings. He brought Wickham along to liven the more sombre atmosphere surrounding his deceased wife's sister.

Wickham was summoned and brought to Lady Catherine, who was waiting at his commander's office, having left Mr. Collins in the carriage.

"Lady Catherine, how delightful to make your acquaintance once again. I must say that you look as lovely as ever. To what do I owe this visit?" Wickham's charms were on full alert to make the most of the interview.

She asked him to close the door behind him and when that was done, said, "I do not have the time nor inclination for small talk. Instead, I want you to tell me what you are doing in Meryton with the militia and what my nephew has against you that he would warn Miss Elizabeth Bennet's family against you."

Her look of contempt was not lost on him, but he was used to being looked down upon and had learnt to use it as a strength. He smiled and said, "Indeed, my circumstances are reduced from what they were when last we met. I was then a student at Cambridge looking forward to a living at Kympton, as my godfather, my dearest friend, had told me that he intended for me; however, I do believe that his son became jealous of his love and affection for me. I knew that I was not meant for the church and asked and also received some small compensation that I was happy to have. I tried to get more, to obtain a sum equal to the living, but he would not agree. Instead he dismissed me without hope of a future means of supporting myself. Since his father's demise, he has exacted his revenge upon me by thwarting any hopes of a fruitful alliance.

"When I entered this county and joined the militia, I of course did my part to become acquainted with the local society. When I discovered the happy coincidence of the Bennet's connection with Darcy, I hoped that he might lay his jealousies aside, that we could renew our friendship. That is all. I obviously misread him, I am aggrieved to say, but I can assure you that I hold no ill will against *him*."

"Do you dare to question my nephew in front of me? I see how it is. Miss Bennet obviously uses her captivation to entice men of all stations. If you truly have financial need, I believe that we can come up with an understanding that might benefit both of us." She paused before continuing, "I have reliable information that indicates that if Miss Bennet is found to be in any type of communication with you, Mr. Darcy will break his engagement with her. I am willing to offer you a financial reward if you are able to ensure that this happens."

This surprised Wickham, that Darcy would actually break his public engagement just for Miss Elizabeth's connection with himself. *Darcy must fear where her allegiance lies.*

Not wanting to seem too keen on this proposal, Wickham replied that he would not think of doing anything that might cause a disturbance for Darcy, the son of the man whom he admired above all others. After much negotiation, however, it was decided that Lady Catherine would pay him three thousand pounds, if he were successful in seducing Miss Elizabeth, at least to the extent of causing her to communicate with him prior to Tuesday, thereby calling off the wedding.

This was better than he could ever have hoped. Not only would he have the joy of drawing a beautiful woman away from Darcy, he would be well compensated. He knew Darcy would never marry Anne De Bourgh, but he would not reveal this sentiment to Lady Catherine. If she were willing to pay him to do her bidding in such a pleasant endeavour, he saw no reason to disabuse her of the notion. *This should not be too difficult.* He knew that he had already earned Elizabeth's admiration and trust; all he had to do was get her to speak with him, as she had done several times in the recent weeks; and if things were to go farther, better yet.

Lady Catherine left Wickham to come up with a plan to entice the lovely Elizabeth. She could not have found a more willing and reliable man to do her bidding in this venture. His greatest attributes would come into play, and he could not wait to make his move.

The great lady then decided to leave her faithful rector in Hertfordshire to help the undertaking by being the one to cry foul when the occasion occurred, if Darcy were not present to witness the treachery. She had her coachman return to Longbourn, dropping him off without exiting the carriage herself. Her parting words to Mr. Collins were instructions for the following four days, assisting Mr. Wickham as needed, and how he was to return to Hunsford by posting coach when his task was accomplished.

THE FOLLOWING DAY brought rain which left most people indoors, the Bennets finishing wedding preparations, the Netherfield party despondently attending to preparations for the ball, and Wickham anticipating his earnings at the card tables within the lodgings of the officers. On Sunday, the final banns were read as Darcy once again sat with his intended. There was no sign of Wickham within the church; indeed, Wickham had not made a showing within a church in many years now and had not considered that particular location as a possible means of gaining his reward or at the very least, antagonising Darcy. Mr. Collins, having been left behind by Lady Catherine, was staying with the Bennets and, therefore, attended the weekly worship, taking his place beside Mary but in view of Elizabeth. He had been instructed to observe Elizabeth closely, so that he might move quickly should she have any contact with Wickham. After church, Bingley, his family and his guest were invited to return later in the evening for dinner. He enthusiastically accepted, not noticing the appalled looks on the faces of his sisters. So the entire party was obligated, yet again, to an evening of insipid entertainment at Longbourn. It was during this visit that Darcy's concerns related to Bingley's growing attachment to Miss Bennet were to reach new heights. He always enjoyed Bingley's easy manners at social gatherings, in that they helped to ease the burden of conversation; yet now, Bingley was of no use as he sequestered himself away from the group with the lovely, eldest Bennet sister. While watching Bingley in the corner, he determined to separate the two after the wedding by keeping him in London. Darcy could not bear to see his friend shackled as he had been. Bingley was easily swayed by Darcy's advice, so the task should not be too difficult. Also, as town held much diversion, Bingley would easily forget the woman he would leave behind.

Mr. Wickham attempted a visit at Longbourn the following morning, the day of the ball. He had gathered a small group of officers to join him, making his entrance difficult to refuse. He suspected that he would not be welcome given Darcy's ultimatum and the Bennets' need, if not desire, to adhere to his demands. Because he was on high alert, Mr. Collins had spied Wickham walking up the lane that led to the manor house of Longbourn. Mr. Collins then made his way downstairs where he could observe Wickham's admittance and Cousin Elizabeth's response. Mr. Collins had not considered where his loyalties should lie. In his eyes, his patroness was all that was regal and commendable, while the Bennets behaved shamefully, all except his Mary, of course. Mrs. Bennet, knowing the ramifications of Mr. Wickham's entrance into her home, but not knowing how to intervene without causing offence, ran up to her room and demanded Elizabeth attend her. This same daughter was mortified at her family's response to his visit. She could not let him know in words or looks that she lamented the turn of events, that she wished she could somehow make things right between him and Mr. Darcy, and that she had the highest regard for him as a friend, if not favourite.

Elizabeth later found solace when she learnt that her father had invited Wickham into his study, while the other officers visited with the ladies of the house. Mr. Bennet had asked Wickham to keep away from Elizabeth and her family until the wedding was completed, and that she was essentially in the care of Mr. Darcy. "Mr. Wickham," said he, "you must not find fault with my Lizzy on this score. We must abide by the wishes of her fiancé in this instance. Surely, you would not want any harm to come her way as a result of your acquaintance, brief as it has been."

"Mr. Bennet, please know that I hold your daughter in the highest esteem. If I were but able to save her from her present situation…" Looking away as if in anguish, he continued, "but I must not have wishes that will only torment me. You are right; I must not do anything that would cause the great Darcy to transpose his dislike of me upon an innocent, especially one as amiable and kind as Miss Elizabeth – whose very future depends upon his benevolence."

"Yes, well, I am glad we understand one another." After a few more minutes of meaningless conversation, Mr. Bennet escorted Mr. Wickham to the front door, sending him on his way.

Elizabeth observed his departure from her window, sorry for not being able to say farewell to her friend, but cognisant that her burgeoning tender regard for him was not appropriate for a woman about to wed another man. She determined that she would think no more of the handsome Mr. Wickham and got to the task of packing for her departure from Longbourn that would take place the following day and then preparing for the evening ball.

Wickham left frustrated, but not without hope, as he had more than one plan in place. This time the following day, Elizabeth would be marrying Darcy unless he had a means of being alone with her, or even near enough to encourage her to speak with him. He had known that she walked alone in the mornings across the countryside. In fact, Wickham had gone out early this same morning to intercept her on her rambles, but after two hours in the cold morning air searching for her without success, he had found nothing but disappointment. Wickham had been out very late the previous night meeting up with a barmaid after having gambled away some of his planned earnings, and he was not in the mood for failure. He came to the realisation that success would not come unless he made greater effort; he must make a showing at the ball that evening. He had hoped to avoid that venture; he hated Darcy, but had a healthy fear of him, nonetheless. But the more he thought about the idea, the more he liked it. At the ball, surely Darcy would not make a public display against him. Wickham decided that if he attended the ball, he could easily attempt an assignation with Miss Elizabeth. He would have many opportunities to catch her off her guard. And surely Mr. Bennet would not fault him for attending a gathering with all of the fellow officers.

Chapter Seven

"Pride is a very common failing, I believe. By all that I have ever read, I am convinced that it is very common indeed; that human nature is particularly prone to it, and that there are very few of us who do not cherish a feeling of self-complacency on the score of some quality or other, real or imaginary."
Jane Austen
Pride and Prejudice

The Gardiners, who were the brother and sister-in-law of Elizabeth's mother, arrived just before tea, having left their two youngest children at home, but brought the older boy and girl to witness the wedding of their favourite cousin. The wedding was to be a simple affair with only Jane and Mr. Bingley as the attendants, but Elizabeth desired that her young cousin, Anna, a girl of six years precede her down the aisle as flower girl. Considering that Mr. Darcy might disapprove of the daughter of a tradesman participating in their wedding, she chose not to tell him. He would learn soon enough.

Mr. Gardiner was Mrs. Bennet's junior by ten years. He was a handsome man, as was his sister, but added to his physical attractions were his keen intellect and amiable nature, as was unlike his sister. All of these qualities combined to make him an astute and profitable businessman. Due to his successes in the trading industry, he was able to provide his family, which included his nieces, opportunities to enjoy the cultural offerings in London.

His wife, née Margaret Eleanor Pennington, originated from the small town of Lambton in Derbyshire, a daughter of the local rector. After her father's death, her family had moved to town to live with her grandfather on her mother's side. She was admitted into a school for ladies, the same as Bingley's sisters, and upon coming out, met her future husband at the theatre. They had attended with mutual friends and during the same Season, became engaged. Theirs was a love match, but advantageous to both, for he had already begun to amass a fine living, and she had the education, decorum and benevolence to support him in all of his endeavours. Mrs. Gardiner held on to her youthful beauty and natural elegance.

Since Elizabeth and Jane had come out into society, they had each spent no less than three months per year in town visiting the Gardiners. This arrangement was mutually beneficial, for the Bennet sisters had the opportunity of exposure to a family where decorum and kindness were in abundant supply. The Gardiners received a reprieve from the pressures of rearing children and enjoyed the company of two thoughtful and intelligent young ladies.

Although Elizabeth longed to have time for a private audience with her aunt Gardiner, she found no opportunity during the course of the afternoon. Elizabeth had hoped to gain insight as to her duties as a wife. Her mother had not yet spoken of such matters, which although providing some relief from the woman's vulgar commentaries, left Elizabeth in complete ignorance and apprehension as to the prospects on the occasion. Elizabeth's aunt knew her well and had planned on making time to explain what to expect on the wedding night and to provide some sense of solace for her innocent, yet inquisitive niece. As it happened though, Mrs. Bennet, not usually in tune with others' needs, monopolised all of Mrs. Gardiner's time with talk of the wedding and the wedding breakfast.

Elizabeth and Jane each had taken exceptional care when preparing for the ball, but for different reasons. The latter wished to inspire the attachment to which her heart had already been bound. The former had determined that even if she were not handsome enough to tempt the illustrious Mr. Darcy, she would make a good showing nonetheless. Perhaps after her obligatory dance with her fiancé, she would find other amiable partners who might overlook her deficiencies. Elizabeth felt that she needed one final day to enjoy the felicity of being a carefree maiden. She had been obliged to remain indoors that morning as her father forbade her from walking out alone for fear of the possibility of encountering the handsome Mr. Wickham. She had seen him once before on one of her morning jaunts, and although she understood her father's caution, she was despondent about the deprivation. She had been unable to walk out on several mornings due to the heavy rain and had hoped to have one last opportunity to say goodbye to her favourite haunts that she knew quite as well as her own chamber at Longbourn.

Fortunately for Elizabeth, preparations for the ball took her mind off of her disappointments of the morning. Elizabeth wore a white satin gown with a low, yet modest décolletage that was highlighted by small ivory coloured flowers made of silk, stretching across the squared neckline, and below the bosom, the green ribbon that she had recently purchased contrasted beautifully with the gown, while complementing her eyes. The dress gathered in the back below the high waist with a grouping of similar silk flowers, but larger in size. The sleeves were short with a slight puff, carrying the same theme as the rest of the gown. The dress was overlaid with a sheer and shimmering netting, one of her recent additions to reform the ensemble. Her white silk gloves reached to three inches below the edge of the sleeves. Her hair was held in place by pins tipped with the same silk flowers that balanced exquisitely with her chestnut locks. Her curls framed her face in the front with one long curl cascading down and across her right shoulder. She felt uncommonly good-looking and considered that she might even surpass the elegance of the Bingley sisters. Elizabeth gazed at her reflection in the looking glass and was pleased with what she saw. Jane came up behind her, smiling, and said, "Lizzy, how lovely you are. Mr. Darcy cannot help but admire you."

Laughing, Elizabeth replied, "Jane, I am afraid you may be overestimating my appeal, but please continue. I must not see myself through his eyes, but yours, as you, dear, were always my faithful admirer. Oh, Jane, what will I do without you to make me feel pretty?"

"What can you mean? Mr. Darcy is not so blinded by his pride not to notice his beautiful bride. You must not take his remarks as a personal affront to you. He is a man used to having his way. This must be difficult for him. Mr. Bingley says that he is master of his own estate in Derbyshire, but also has a home in Dover as well as the one in town. Mr. Darcy has hundreds of servants and tenants who answer to him and whose livelihoods depend upon him. Surely having no say in whom he will marry must come heavily for him. We must show him grace not anger, Lizzy. If you are to have a happy life, surely you see that you must exert kindness not judgement."

"Sweet Jane. Leave it to you to find something charitable to say to soften my heart. For your sake, I will not assume that he will look down upon me. And whether he does or not, I will attempt to avoid censuring him based on his past assumptions against me."

"I know you will. You have always been fair and willing to move past disagreements."

"Jane, since when have we had disagreements? You are the most amiable person I know. If I had any troubles with you to overcome, I am sure I do not remember them."

Jane smiled and hugged her. "You are the best of sisters, and I will miss you terribly."

"Perhaps his friend will soon make you an offer, so that we might visit more often than otherwise. I fear that I will not be spending much time at Longbourn in the future. I doubt that I will be allowed to see my family at all."

"Surely not! He is too honourable for that course. Mr. Bingley has spoken to me of his fairness and generosity to all under his care. He could not require his own wife to disown her family for his sake."

"You must be right, Jane." Elizabeth finished the conversation, not wanting to disagree with her sister, thereby causing each of them pain. Jane could not think less than the very best of all of her fellow creatures, no matter the situation, and Elizabeth was not keen on disabusing her of the notion on this particular occasion.

The Bennets were required to travel by two trips to Netherfield, as there were too many people to fit in the carriage at one time. They decided that Mr. Collins would go in the first group with Jane, Elizabeth, Mary and Kitty. The carriage would then return for Mr. and Mrs. Bennet, Mr. and Mrs. Gardiner and Lydia, who complained bitterly of the misfortune of arriving after the others. The ball was to start earlier than the usual hour due to the early wedding the following day; however, due to the lateness in the year, it was full dark before they left Longbourn. Mr. Collins somehow managed to sit next to Elizabeth on the rear-facing seat; Elizabeth thought it odd that a man engaged to one woman would choose to sit next to another when given an opportunity to do otherwise, but she soon forgot about it owing to her understanding that Mr. Collins would always be an oddity to her. She sat across the carriage directly in front of Jane but could not see her. Usually Mr. Collins would rattle on concerning whatever happened to enter his head, for if he were to think it, it must be news of some import. However, on this evening he was rather silent. The four others in the carriage were grateful, for although Mary was pleased with her fiancé, she did have her limits, and he had been unusually agitated since his unexpected arrival.

The silence in Mr. Collins' quarter allowed Elizabeth and Jane the opportunity to converse on the evening's prospects – Elizabeth, expecting many lively dances with her long-held acquaintances, and Jane, without giving too much of her feelings away, upon the pleasure to be had in the company of Mr. Bingley and his sisters. While they were chatting over the sounds of the carriage and horses, Elizabeth did not notice that Mr. Collins had placed two folded pieces of parchment into her reticule.

When Mr. Wickham had arrived that morning for the call, Mr. Collins watched diligently to see if Elizabeth would give in to her base longings and speak with Mr. Wickham, as Lady Catherine had directed him to do. While watching out of the window to see Mr. Wickham leave, he saw the man's obscure summons, quickly exiting the house from the service entrance and going into the shrubbery, where Mr. Wickham waited for him. Mr. Wickham had devised a backup plan to ensure success before the day was complete. He had written two correspondences to Elizabeth, declaring his unabashed feelings for her with a hope of future assignations, and planned to find a means of placing them onto her person before the ball. One was dated for the day of the ball and the other from two days prior, with a broken seal to make it look as though she had already received and opened a letter from him, sentimentally keeping it with her. Lady Catherine had told him to use her parson as was necessary, that although Mr. Collins was betrothed to join the Bennet family, like a hound, he was loyal to his benefactress.

He instructed Mr. Collins in detail concerning when and how to place the private missives into Miss Elizabeth's reticule. Mr. Collins had only to wait for the moment most conducive to success, which he found in the darkness of the carriage. Once this was accomplished, he need wait until Wickham had been at the ball for at least an hour before telling Mr. Darcy of his witnessing a note being given to Elizabeth from the man. Once Mr. Darcy sought for and received the evidence, he would be free from the Bennet family. Of course, Mr. Collins was insensible to the adverse effect this would now have upon his own betrothed, as well as himself should Mr. Wickham find success, but he had not thought through Lady Catherine's directives to that extent, as he was not a sagacious man, trusting her implicitly.

As the carriage approached Netherfield Park, its inhabitants admired the general splendour of the well-lit structure. Each window of the home emanated light and beckoned those arriving to enter and join the festivities. Due to Mr. Bingley's giving the ball in honour of Elizabeth and Darcy, Elizabeth was to arrive just prior to its opening. The Longbourn party was greeted upon entering by Mr. Bingley and his younger sister. Although Mr. Bingley's welcome was gracious and anticipatory of a pleasant evening, Miss Bingley's greeting contained only the barest of civilities. They remained in the receiving line with their hosts, chatting amicably with the master of the home, until more of the guests began to arrive. Elizabeth and Jane then entered the drawing room, which was well lit and arrayed with seasonal flowers, while Kitty made her own explorations. As Mr. Collins and Mary found the nearest seats against the wall, the elder Miss Bennets kept to themselves facing the entrance to witness the arrival of the neighbourhood. All were bedecked in their finest attire.

When Charlotte entered the room, she walked over to her friends who were smiling and waving in her direction. "Eliza, Jane, you both look splendid this evening. Your men will be anxious to take a turn with you, I will wager."

"Oh, Charlotte," said Elizabeth with a laugh, "you amuse me. You must remember that I am *barely tolerable* according to the man to whom you refer. However, perhaps other gentlemen will find me handsome enough for dances when I have completed the obligatory one, and that will satisfy me and my wounded vanity." Elizabeth said this in jest; however deep down, she hoped that her life would not be filled with the insecurities that come when one cannot find favour with a spouse. She had seen this between her parents daily; also she had been found lacking repeatedly in contrast to Jane, and happily accepted the comparison, for who could be more beautiful than Jane in countenance or character? But to always be found wanting by a husband – that would be a sore trial to bear.

The three chatted about the happenings since last they met, then moved on to examine the other guests who had been arriving at a steady pace. This was the grandest ball that the market town of Meryton had witnessed since Elizabeth had come out in society at sixteen, and all invited wore their best and wished for her well-doing in a good natured way, forgetting that they had ever scoffed at Elizabeth's predicament betwixt the storm and her engagement. To be sure it would have been more for the advantage of conversation, had Miss Elizabeth Bennet come upon the town without hope of an attachment; or, as the happiest alternative, been secluded from the world, in some distant farmhouse. But there was much to be talked of in marrying her; and those who also had the benefit of an invitation to the ball to celebrate the union lost but little of their spirit in this change of circumstances because with such a husband, her misery was considered certain, despite his wealth.

Elizabeth had not yet encountered Mr. Darcy, and she began to wonder if he might not make his expected showing. She had almost given up on the pleasure when he approached from behind. "Miss Bennet, Miss Elizabeth, and Miss Lucas, you all look lovely this evening," said he after an appropriate bow. Turning to Elizabeth he continued, "May I retrieve some refreshment for you and your friends before the dancing begins?"

Elizabeth was astonished at Mr. Darcy's attention, but then remembered his tardiness and chose to tease him. "You may, sir. I am surprised though that I have not yet seen you. I remember your recently telling me that you are usually prompt in your concerns. I am afraid that you are teaching me not to believe a word you say. That is not a fruitful way to begin the marriage state."

"I apologise. I hope I have not alarmed you," he replied, hiding any emotion he may have felt at her censure.

"No. However, I did arrive early myself, as you and I are to be the honoured guests. Have you forgotten?"

She had a way of annoying him with her teasing. Of course, it did not occur to him that this was due to the usual veracity of her assertions. Mr. Darcy disliked being scrutinised by people in general, but especially those beneath himself.

He had lingered overlong in the family sitting room with the Hursts before making his entrance shortly after the arrival of the first Bennet carriage, but then had been caught by Miss Bingley, who in favour of his company, had rudely left the receiving line to let her brother perform the hosting duties on his own, while she occupied Mr. Darcy in an adjoining room, out of the view of his fiancée.

Miss Bingley had become quite irritable over the course of the past week since Darcy's return, and was seeking solace upon that same man's arm. She meant to make this evening as unpleasant for Miss Elizabeth Bennet as she could and had been whispering words of disparagement concerning that lady and her friends in attendance. Miss Bingley was comparing their social skills to her own fine abilities, the absurdity of the analysis completely lost upon herself.

Darcy had finally been able to extricate himself from Miss Bingley's hold upon his arm and then look for his bride-to-be. He had found her on the opposite side of the room, facing the doorway that led to the entrance. She was laughing at something her friend, Miss Lucas, had been saying. She certainly seemed to be enjoying herself thus far, which was more than he could say of himself. *For someone who claims to be unhappy about the marriage, she seems to be happy enough.* He had longed to have this evening come to an end and would have made an even later entrance if duty had not obligated him to join the festivities. Knowing he could not delay any further, he had crossed the room to her discourteous enquiries, and thus the conversation continued.

"I have not forgotten. Please, excuse me; I will procure some refreshment for you and your companions." He then made a quick bow and departed to complete the task.

"Eliza," said Charlotte, "you must not be so severe on Mr. Darcy. I think he is trying to be solicitous. Rather than tease him so, perhaps you should try to show a little affection and respect. A man needs to feel as though his partner admires him."

Elizabeth laughed. "Charlotte, since when have you become an expert on the male disposition? I think Mr. Darcy gets enough of that with Miss Bingley. I know you mean to help, but truly, I cannot be someone different than I am in order to gratify a man who has no fondness for me. We must, each of us, learn to accept the eccentricities of the other, and that, my friend, will be difficult enough for me without having to pretend feelings that I do not possess."

"But, surely you see that you will have to change to accommodate his own requirements. He could make your life uncomfortable if he has a mind. Mr. Darcy is not your father; he may not appreciate a woman who asserts her own opinions so decidedly."

Jane felt that she needed to defend them both. "I believe Mr. Darcy to be a considerate gentleman, for Mr. Bingley thinks so highly of him. Also, his manners show him to have a kind regard for others. And Lizzy has a compassionate heart," said she, gazing fondly upon Elizabeth. "Given time he will not fail to notice your amiable qualities."

"I grant you that I should not push the man so; really I do. I just find I can't help myself when he looks down his nose at me. It is a shame he is so handsome himself or I could claim equal disappointment!" Her companions' eyes then darted behind her, and presently Mr. Darcy returned with the beverages, so the ladies' tête-à-tête came to an end.

Darcy soon noticed that a group of officers entered for they were difficult to miss in their scarlet regimentals. He observed Elizabeth's apparent discomfort when she too noticed the arrival. Elizabeth attempted to look unaffected, concentrating on the dull conversation at hand. With relief she marked that Mr. Wickham did not make a showing. Elizabeth had thought about how she should handle his coming, if in fact he did decide to attend the ball, even though her father had suggested that he not. She had come to understand that should Wickham impose himself upon the company, she would have a difficult time not taking his notice and so thought it best that he stay away. His being there was not worth the risk to her family in losing the protection of Mr. Darcy.

Before long, it was time for the dancing to commence. Bingley approached the group and offered his hand to Jane, while beaming unreservedly. "Miss Bennet, I believe this dance is mine." She smiled becomingly and joined him as he led her to the dance floor.

Subsequently, Darcy turned to Elizabeth and said, "Shall we?" She placed her hand in his and could feel the assurance that matched his bearing, as they moved to the head of the line. Even through their gloved hands, she felt an unanticipated frisson of attraction that she could not so easily ignore; nonetheless, Elizabeth hoped she was able to admirably hide her perplexing, singular reaction, and indeed it was so. They were situated beside Mr. Bingley and Jane, and on the other side of them were the Hursts, then Miss Bingley and Mr. Byron Jamison, a local man who recently inherited his uncle's estate. Although Mr. Jamison had a pleasant countenance, Miss Bingley only had eyes for Mr. Darcy and watched him through the simple movements of the country-dance, taking comfort in Darcy's unwavering severity. She was unable to discern the conversation for there was little to be had, but she strained to hear anyway. Her partner attempted to make conversation, giving up once he realised her object.

After some moments of silence, Elizabeth fancied that obliging Mr. Darcy to talk would punish him more than no words at all, so with some amusement she began, "Mr. Darcy, we must have some conversation, though little would suffice." This sounded vaguely familiar to him, as if they had had this conversation in the past. As he was trying to recollect when that might have been, she smiled and said, "You might comment on the number of couples or the general splendour of the room."

"I will comment on whatever it is you wish. I await your pleasure."

Elizabeth replied, "That will suffice for now," as she elegantly passed in front of him, flawlessly moving to the flow of the music. Darcy noticed her graceful execution of the familiar dance and was grateful that at the very least she would perform well in a London ballroom. After crossing her with two sweeps, he was able to recall the occasion during which she had spoken the same words. They were in the cabin when Elizabeth had attempted to engage him in conversation.

"What say you to books?" said Darcy remembering that she had been reading a novel.

"Books! Oh, no, I am sure we never read the same, or not with the same feelings. I cannot speak of books in a ballroom."

Darcy was surprised by her response and struggled for something else on which to speak. Not caring for the awkward position in which she had placed him, he said, "Do you talk by rule then, while you are dancing?"

"Sometimes. One must speak a little, you know. It would look odd to be entirely silent for half an hour together, and yet for the advantage of some, conversation ought to be so arranged as that they may enjoy the opportunity of saying as little as possible."

"Are you consulting your own feelings in the present case, or do you imagine that you are gratifying mine?"

"Both," replied Elizabeth archly; "for I have seen a great similarity in the turn of our minds. We are each of an unsocial, taciturn disposition, unwilling to speak, unless we expect to say something that will amaze the whole room, and be handed down to posterity with all the éclat of a proverb."

"This is no striking resemblance to your own character, I am sure. How near it is to my own, I cannot pretend to say, though you must think it a faithful portrait undoubtedly." Elizabeth smiled and then looked away.

After parting and coming back together she continued, "Few words pass your lips while in the company of others, unless of course that is only while in the presence of new connections. Perhaps you are easier in the company of your equals."

"It is true that I do not find speaking of inconsequential matters to be pleasing, nor beneficial, in order to form a lasting acquaintance. Where there are like minds, there will always be something stimulating of which to speak."

"But, sir, how can you get from not knowing a person to talking on the deep topics that have meaning to you, without going through the necessary small talk to discover what the commonalities might be? Do you greet a person upon first meeting and then ask his *or her* views on the war in France or perhaps the inhumanity of slavery, or do you first ascertain the person's views upon the proffered punch or song selection, to gauge whether he has formed opinions, and then skilfully move the observation to more pleasing and stimulating topics? I find that when small talk stifles the interaction, then perhaps moving to a new partner is preferable. However, agreeable conversationalists will move the subjects along, much like a dance, weaving in and out of ideas, coming together then diverging along the way. The clothing your partner wears or the school in which he or she learnt the dance has no bearing when executed by both with facility and grace."

"You, Miss Bennet, are naïve," Darcy said as he acknowledged her criticism.

Elizabeth's ire was increasing, yet again. She had determined, for Jane's sake if not her own, to be forbearing with the man, but she found his arrogance to feed her anger. "My level of naïveté is irrelevant. Where two people are open and engaging, there can always be something of which to speak, even if one is ignorant of the topic, for the best conversations occur when learning something new. My father would never let me sit idly when stimulating dialogue was going on about me. He would ask my opinion, and I learnt to give it with confidence. I hope you, sir, do not mind a wife with a mind."

"I prefer a wife who knows her place, whose mission is to support her husband, not to attempt to make him into a fool."

"Well, then, you are safe from me. I feel no need to help you in making yourself appear a fool." She looked away trying to hide her smile in vain, eyes lit with mirth.

He looked at her in disbelief. *Is this the woman to whom I will be forever bound?*

Sensing she may have gone too far in her jest, she said, "I have always supposed that an educated man would not be intimidated by a wife who enjoys spirited teasing." After seeing his unhappy mien, she relented; she must learn to curtail her taunts until he got to know her better. "I cannot say that I did not mean to provoke you, but I can say that I regret having done so." The dance separated them as they continued down the line. She glanced his way to see how he accepted her apology.

"Are you always this exasperating, Miss Bennet? Can I expect to be treated with the same discourtesy your father receives from *his* own wife?" This cut Elizabeth to the quick. *He compares me to my mother*! She had never seen herself in anyway like her mother.

"Mr. Darcy, are you not to be laughed at?" asked Elizabeth. "That is an uncommon advantage, and uncommon I hope it will continue, for it would be a great loss to have many such acquaintants, especially to be married to one. I dearly love a laugh."

"The wisest and the best of men, nay, the wisest and best of their actions, may be rendered ridiculous by a person whose first object in life is a joke."

"Certainly," replied Elizabeth, "there are such people, but I hope I am not one of them. I hope I never ridicule what is wise or good. Follies and nonsense, whims and inconsistencies do divert me, I own, and I laugh at them whenever I can. But these, I suppose, are precisely what you are without."

"Perhaps that is not possible for anyone. But it has been the study of my life to avoid those weaknesses which often expose a strong understanding to ridicule."

"Such as vanity and pride."

"Yes, vanity is a weakness indeed. But pride – where there is a real superiority of mind – pride will be always under good regulation."

Elizabeth turned away to hide a smile, and when she had schooled her features she looked back his way. "You have convinced me, sir, that you have no defect. You own it without disguise."

"No," said Darcy, "I have made no such pretension. I have faults enough, but they are not, I hope, of understanding. My temper, I dare not vouch for. It is, I believe, too little yielding, certainly too little for the convenience of the world. I cannot forget the follies and vices of others so soon as I ought, or their offences against myself. My feelings are not puffed about with every attempt to move them. My temper would perhaps be called resentful. My good opinion once lost is lost forever."

"That is a failing indeed!" cried Elizabeth. "Implacable resentment is a shade in a character. But you have chosen your fault well. I really cannot laugh at it." She thought of Mr. Wickham's being the object of his resentment, and her heart went out to him.

"There is, I believe, in every disposition a tendency to some particular evil, a natural defect, which not even the best education can overcome," said he.

"And your defect is a propensity to hate everybody."

"And yours is wilfully to misunderstand them." He looked away before continuing, "Certainly, there are other forms of entertainment on a dance floor than discussing the faults of each other's dance partner."

"We have tried speaking upon two or three subjects already without success, and what we could talk of next I cannot imagine. Perhaps we can now give our attention to the steps of the dance." Instead of focusing on the dance, however, Elizabeth could not keep her mind from wandering to the handsome gentleman whom she had given a piece of her heart most unwillingly. Mr. Darcy had all but admitted that he held on to resentment; Mr. Wickham would forever remain in his disfavour, without recourse. Elizabeth was relieved that he had not shown up, for the risk of his attempting to communicate with her in front of Mr. Darcy was too great. Regardless, she was saddened that she might never see Mr. Wickham again, and she knew that she would always remember him with fond regret.

During one of the lulls in the movement, Elizabeth noticed that her sister Mary was dancing with her own fiancé. Poor Mary, who rarely put herself forward to be asked to dance, looked embarrassed by his missteps and poor timing. Mr. Collins seemed to be stepping on more toes than just Mary's. Darcy noticed the display as well. Elizabeth felt his judgement of Mr. Collins's clumsy execution fall to her own family. Elizabeth could do nothing about Mr. Collins, but be grateful that she had not been obligated to marry that man instead. Her salvation stood in front of her, but she could not appreciate him as Mr. Darcy gave her his austere stare; so she held her head high, steadily regarding him until it was again their time to join in the promenade.

The dance finally came to an end, and Darcy led Elizabeth to the side of the room where stood her friend, Charlotte, who had been obliged to sit out the first set of the evening. Bingley and Jane also arrived so that Bingley might claim his formerly requested dance from the guest of honour, Elizabeth. Darcy knew his duty and so invited Jane to dance with him, thus leaving Charlotte alone to sit out the second set. As they were walking away, Elizabeth turned back to see Jane being led to the floor by Darcy, yet Charlotte left alone. Mr. Bingley also turned, happy to see that his friend had been kind enough to ask Miss Bennet to dance, but noticed that Elizabeth did not share his satisfaction. He said, "Miss Elizabeth, you do not look happy that Darcy has asked your sister to dance, unless I am mistaken."

She smiled at his perceptiveness. "No, I am happy that he has taken this opportunity to ask her. I am just sorry to see my friend, Miss Lucas, again without a partner. I guess I had hoped he might request a dance from her instead, since Jane has just finished one."

"I would be happy to dance with Miss Lucas on the next set. Oh, look, your cousin, Mr. Collins, is asking her."

"Oh, dear." Elizabeth recalled the previous dance and felt for her friend.

"Miss Elizabeth, we are all here to enjoy ourselves. Do not be troubled by how others might judge a performance that is not perfect." Mr. Bingley's countenance was as sincere as his words, and Elizabeth returned the expression.

"Thank you, sir. You are all that is cordial and a most gracious host. If I have not yet done so, let me take this time to thank you for hosting a ball in honour of my upcoming marriage. Mr. Darcy is fortunate to have you as a friend." *As different as you both are from one another,* she might have added.

"No, it is I who am fortunate. His friendship has benefitted me in countless ways, and I am happy to respond to his own generosity towards me."

By now they were in line and the dance had commenced. Being the host and she, one of the guests of honour, they were at the head with Jane and Darcy next to them. Elizabeth longed to ask Mr. Bingley about his understanding of Mr. Darcy's dealings with Mr. Wickham, but could not ask while in close proximity to the man in question. Also, she did not want to say something that might make Mr. Bingley uncomfortable, so she just enjoyed the dance while speaking of pleasing topics that always seemed to lead back to the angelic Jane.

Mr. Darcy then danced with Miss Bingley and Mrs. Hurst, as he knew to be right, but chose not to dance again until the supper dance with Elizabeth. He disliked the activity, but understood it to be his duty to ask his hosts. He noticed throughout the evening that Elizabeth seemed to be enjoying herself immensely, even if he were not. She accepted every dance and enjoyed all of her partners' smiles. He could tell that she was popular amongst the local gentry. Elizabeth would peek his way on occasion, raising her brow as if to mock him. Twice he saw her glance at him while giggling to her friend, Miss Lucas. He despised the frivolity and was certain she was making a joke of him. After tomorrow, this would be over; he would then exercise his authority. The one source of amusement came when Mr. Collins requested a dance from her. The look on Elizabeth's face when she turned around to see who had tapped her on the shoulder provided Darcy with much entertainment. *Miss Elizabeth's expressions are so animated; she wears her feelings candidly. At least in that way, there is no artifice.*

Elizabeth had planned on enjoying herself at the ball, and so far her success had been sure, up until Mr. Collins tapped on her shoulder, thus startling her into grief. Of course, she had to accept. She had avoided him by keeping a full dance card and crossing the room when she would see him approach, but she could no longer evade him, thus she made her way to the line-up. Elizabeth could see Mr. Darcy smirk as she glanced his way, and she knew that he was enjoying the exhibition. She found merriment in the follies and foibles of her fellow man, but her mirth was sorely tried when she joined its object, especially when the proud Mr. Darcy watched on quietly laughing at her. Her only comfort lay in knowing that she had not been the only victim.

The dance finally ended, and Mr. Darcy approached to claim the supper set as previously arranged. She noticed him smile for likely the first time. His attractions increased significantly when he looked amused. Of course, Elizabeth despised the fact that it was at her own expense that he found pleasure, so she was determined he would not see her discomfiture. In light of her assumptions about his diversion, Elizabeth would have been surprised to learn that Darcy could not help but admire her ability to keep up pretences in spite of her humiliation and had actually found satisfaction in finally relieving her of her mortification.

Their second set proceeded without discord, as they seemed to have reached a truce of sorts. Elizabeth's character was not prone to vexation, and she dearly loved to dance. She had to admit that he was proficient in the art, even if he were silent and brooding. Darcy also conceded that the attraction of Elizabeth's smile exceeded the average he had seen, and he could not find fault in her dancing; nonetheless, he had not yet found it within himself to call her handsome.

Since Darcy and Elizabeth danced the supper set, they also were to eat together at the table of honour, along with their hosts and Elizabeth's father. Her mother had chosen to sit with the other matrons, so she could spend the time gloating over her triumph in securing two eligible men for her daughters, and most likely a third, if Mr. Bingley's attentions to her eldest were to be her guide. Because Bingley had also danced with Jane prior to supper, she joined him in her mother's place, sitting between her sister and Mr. Bingley. The conversation was lively, as was usual when Bingley was in attendance; nevertheless, Mr. Darcy remained reticent throughout the meal. He was courteous to Elizabeth and solicitous to her needs, but it was obvious that his brief gallantry in saving her from her cousin's footfalls had ended, and he again found no pleasure in bestowing his attention.

Elizabeth's aunt and uncle Gardiner had arrived, along with Elizabeth's parents, after the first set had begun, so Elizabeth had not yet had the opportunity to introduce them to her fiancé. Elizabeth knew her Gardiner relations to be ones about whom she need not blush and wanted Mr. Darcy to see that although in trade, they were perfectly fashionable and knowledgeable. "Mr. Darcy, you have not yet met my family from London; they arrived just today for the wedding and are in attendance this evening. Perhaps after supper, you would allow them to make your acquaintance."

"As you wish." Darcy had no desire to meet her relations from trade. He had heard about them from Miss Bingley who had it from Miss Bennet. But Darcy supposed that he would need to meet them eventually. It did not signify that he would have to continue the relationship. His approval won him a pleasing smile from his betrothed. She had rarely smiled at him.

Elizabeth soon became alarmed when hearing her mother from the table next, speaking loudly about the great matches that her daughters had achieved. Her words were vulgar and boisterous, so that her meaning was easily discerned from anyone within two tables' distance. Mrs. Bennet was sitting next to Lady Lucas, speaking freely and openly, and her theme had made its way to the expectation that Jane would be soon married to Mr. Bingley. It was an animating subject and Mrs. Bennet seemed incapable of fatigue while enumerating the advantages of the match. His being such a charming young man, and so rich, and living but three miles from them, were the first points of self-congratulation; and then it was such a comfort to think how fond Elizabeth and Jane were, and how being married to such good friends would allow them to spend more time in one another's company. And how grand it would be that when Jane went to visit Lizzy, she herself could join them, so as to save Mr. Bennet the expense of travelling. She concluded with many good wishes that Lady Lucas might soon be equally fortunate, though evidently and triumphantly believing there was no chance of it.

Elizabeth caught her father's attention and with pleading eyes, begged him to intervene. He just looked at her in his usual manner, signifying that he thought it all a good joke. *Can he not see how this must look to Mr. Bingley and Mr. Darcy?* In Mr. Darcy's silence, Elizabeth could perceive that he had overheard the chief of her mother's discourse. She glanced his way and saw indignant contempt change to a composed and steady gravity. Elizabeth was glad when Mr. Darcy requested if she would like more of her beverage, giving him a reason to walk away for a time. As soon as he stood and left, she endeavoured to speak to her father in a hushed tone across the table, making sure Jane and Mr. Bingley were in conversation, "Papa, you must check Mama! What advantage can her display be to Jane? She is making our family look to be mercenary, which can do naught to recommend us." Nothing that she could say, however, had any influence. Her father would let her mother rattle on. This distressed Elizabeth, but Mr. Bennet did not think that Mr. Bingley noticed the prattle, and discomforting Mr. Darcy was the added benefit. Elizabeth could endure the drollery, and would come around to see the humour in the scene in front of them.

Darcy returned with the punch. He had needed to get away from the Bennets and while gone had taken some needed air outside on the balcony. If he had had any doubt about the avaricious nature of his engagement, he had no more.

At length Mrs. Bennet had no more to say; and Lady Lucas, who had been long yawning at the repetition of delights, which she saw no likelihood of sharing, was left to the comforts of cold ham and chicken. Elizabeth now began to revive. But not long was the interval of tranquillity, for when supper was over, singing was talked of, and she had the mortification of seeing Mary, after very little entreaty, preparing to oblige the company. By many significant looks and silent entreaties, did Elizabeth endeavour to prevent such a proof of complaisance, but in vain. Mary would not understand them; such an opportunity of exhibiting was delightful to her, and she began her song. Elizabeth's eyes were fixed on her with most painful sensations; and she watched her progress through the several stanzas with an impatience which was very ill rewarded at their close; for Mary, on receiving thanks from the tables, and in particular praise from her betrothed, began another. Mary's powers were by no means fitted for such a display; her voice was weak, and her manner

128

affected. Elizabeth was in agony. She looked at Jane, to see how she bore it; but Jane was very composedly talking to Bingley. She looked at his two sisters, and saw them making signs of derision at each other, and at Darcy, who continued impenetrably grave. She looked at her father across the table to entreat his interference, lest Mary should be singing all night. He finally took the hint and when Mary had finished her second song, said aloud and across the room, "That will do extremely well, child. You have delighted us long enough. Let the other young ladies have time to exhibit."

Elizabeth felt sorry for Mary at her humiliation with her father's public speech. But true mortification arrived when her two youngest sisters came bustling into the room being chased by young officers. The girls were squealing in a delight that was not lessened when Lydia tripped and fell onto the lap of Mr. Collins. To Elizabeth it appeared that had her family made an agreement to expose themselves as much as they could during the evening, it would have been impossible for them to play their parts with more spirit, or finer success; and happy did she think it for Bingley and her sister that some of the exhibition had escaped his notice, and that his feelings were not of a sort to be much distressed by the folly which he must have witnessed. That his two sisters and especially Mr. Darcy, however, should have such an opportunity of ridiculing her relations was bad enough, and she could not determine whether the silent contempt of the gentleman, or the insolent smiles of the ladies, were more intolerable.

If she could have been privy to the thoughts that truly assaulted Mr. Darcy, she would have been mortified to the extreme and would perhaps have been more solicitous of his predicament. But happily for her, she was spared that knowledge, and unbeknownst to her, the situation was about to go from very bad to even worse, for there was a new addition to the festivities, who had quietly entered Netherfield, unseen as yet by the honoured couple.

MR. WICKHAM had planned his arrival to occur during the supper set. He watched as the scene played out like a comedy on the stage. He could not have been more delighted at Darcy's discomfiture and would have thought twice about attempting to disengage him from Miss Elizabeth and her ridiculous family had he not had three thousand pounds before him as a reward for his success.

Mr. Collins noticed Wickham standing by one of the columns and nodded to communicate his success in stowing away the missives in Elizabeth's reticule. Wickham would still attempt an assignation with Elizabeth for good measure: nothing that might cause an angry father to push another engagement once the other had been terminated, but his success was riding on Mr. Darcy's discovery of her holding onto communication from him. Mr. Collins would soon make the accusation that would result in Darcy's release.

Mr. Darcy was leading Elizabeth out of the dining area when her eyes were arrested by the appearance of Mr. Wickham. She blushed and looked flustered in the extreme, thereby bringing Darcy's attention to the object of her disquiet. There in the corner stood Mr. Wickham displaying a charming countenance as he stared at Elizabeth.

Ire immediately rose in Darcy's chest, and he had to use all of his fortitude to avoid walking across the room and tossing Wickham out the door.

Elizabeth's anxiety increased to distraction as she realised that both men were watching her to gauge her reaction. She could not determine why he chose to attend the ball, in light of her father's disclosure to the man about her and her family's strictures. She could only assume that he did not fully comprehend the risk. Elizabeth tried to remain calm, but Mr. Wickham's unbroken gaze made her flush all the more. Mr. Darcy broke the silence saying, "Miss Elizabeth, it would seem that you have an admirer. Were you aware that Mr. Wickham was to attend the ball this evening?"

"How would I have known that, sir? I have not spoken with him in a week's time, and my father requested that he not come."

"Then why is he here?"

"I cannot account for his comings and goings. Perhaps you should ask him yourself." Mr. Darcy then left towards the man in question, and Elizabeth was sorry she had suggested such a thing. She turned to walk away when she was solicited for a dance by John Lucas. Elizabeth accepted, hoping for a distraction from her current circumstances. When she looked over and saw Mr. Darcy speaking with a man in uniform, she noticed that the officer's hair was not dark as Wickham's was, but fair. He was a man whom Elizabeth had not seen before, and Mr. Darcy was speaking in an unusually animated manner with him.

After the set was over, Elizabeth excused herself from her partner and found Charlotte. She needed a friend rather than another man requesting a dance. "Charlotte, have you seen Mr. Wickham? I must keep my distance from him, and I worry that he will try to speak with me. Mr. Darcy intended to make him depart but now he is with another officer. I am afraid he may be attempting to cause further trouble for Mr. Wickham."

"I did see Mr. Wickham when leaving the dining room, but I did not see Mr. Darcy speak with him, if that is what you are afraid of."

"I am not sure what disturbs me more, Mr. Wickham's attempting to speak with me or Mr. Darcy's throwing him out. This is all so vexing! Why could he not stay away?"

"Calm yourself, Eliza. Why can't you speak with Mr. Wickham?" After Elizabeth explained Darcy's ultimatum, Charlotte continued, "Mr. Darcy is a gentleman, and Mr. Wickham knows your opinion of him. And even if he does not, really, Lizzy, you will be married tomorrow. You cannot be concerned about another man's feelings towards you."

Elizabeth looked thoughtfully at her friend. "You are right, but I find it difficult to convince my heart." When Charlotte looked at her in question, she continued, "Do not suppose that he has won my allegiance or my heart in full, but I do admire Mr. Wickham and want the very best for his future. I cannot help but feel for him when Mr. Darcy has treated him so abominably."

"Are you certain that Mr. Wickham is the victim, Eliza? Could it be that there are two sides to the story? Perhaps, Mr. Darcy could be exonerated of wrongdoing if you knew all the particulars. I know that I am not acquainted with the whole of the tale, but Mr. Darcy seems an honourable man. He has been honourable to you, has he not?"

"But Charlotte, there was truth in all Mr. Wickham said. He gave details and reports completely consistent with Mr. Darcy's character, as he has so openly displayed."

"Then why is Mr. Wickham here? Your father asked him not to come. Could he be goading Mr. Darcy to drive him to retaliation in order to show his true character? Or perhaps another reason altogether?" Then Charlotte noticed his approach saying, "Eliza, you must go to your father. Mr. Wickham is coming this way. You must not let Mr. Darcy see him with you. I will intercept him until you can get to Mr. Bennet." Elizabeth thanked her friend, and then went in pursuit of her father.

Charlotte was able to detain Mr. Wickham until Elizabeth had disappeared into the adjoining room, but Elizabeth could not find her father there. When she turned to exit into the next area, she saw Mr. Wickham motioning for her to join him on the balcony. She quickly diverted her eyes, knowing that she must appear exceptionally rude, but could do nothing else. *Shame on Mr. Darcy for making me behave this way!*

The gentleman started in her direction, so Elizabeth moved towards her sister, Jane, who was talking with Caroline Bingley, of all people. "Jane, excuse me for interrupting, but I must speak with you in private."

"Jane, dear, you must not let me detain you. Your sister seems in need of your assistance in some way," Miss Bingley said sweetly.

"Thank you," Jane said to her friend, then turned to Elizabeth and said, "Let us go into the room set aside for the ladies to refresh. We can speak there." There were two older women who were departing as they entered, thus leaving them quite alone. "Lizzy, what has you upset?"

In hushed tones she said, "Mr. Wickham! He is here!"

"You have seen him?"

"Yes, he was coming towards me when I approached you. What can I do? If I go back out there, he will surely try to speak with me. He already motioned for me to meet him on the balcony."

Jane's eyes widened, "What did you do?"

"I looked away and sought you," Elizabeth said as tears threatened her eyes.

"Lizzy, come sit down with me, and we will try to figure out what to do."

AFTER DARCY HAD SEEN WICKHAM, he began to cross the room to let him know that he was not welcome and to demand that he leave the gathering. However, he was stopped in his path by a site that truly astonished him. His cousin, Colonel James Fitzwilliam, stood before him in his full regimentals and wearing a warm smile, pleased to see his best friend again. Had they been in a more private location, they would have embraced, as they truly loved one another as brothers more so than mere cousins. "James, what an undeniably pleasant surprise! I cannot believe you are here. I had no expectation that you would come."

"What and miss my best friend's wedding? I am hurt you should think so."

"I just know how your family feels about my decision, and I thought that you too might express your disapproval by not wanting to come."

"My approval should have no bearing on your decision concerning whom to marry. Surely you do not suspect that I would censor you for your choice in bride. I am concerned, however, of how all of this came about. You must admit that this is unlike you, Darcy. I never thought that you would marry a woman without rank or fortune. She must be exceptionally lovely."

"What did your parents tell you about her?"

Fitzwilliam grinned, "My parents! They sent me to try to talk some sense into you." At Darcy's grave expression, the colonel laughed, "You look like a bear with that countenance. Of course, I would never presume to talk you into or out of anything. I know you better than that. But, I would like to hear what would cause you, a man of your scruples and exacting ways, to change your course and ask a country maiden to marry you. I could not have been more shocked, when I received your letter, had Bony surrendered France to England. I would have made it here sooner if I could have gotten leave." Fitzwilliam stared at him waiting for the story, but was unprepared to hear what Darcy would say next.

For a moment, Darcy had forgotten his pursuit of Wickham, but then recollected. "Fitzwilliam, did you just see Wickham? He was here not a moment ago."

"What? That blackguard is here at *your* engagement celebration?" He began looking around the room.

"It is a long story, but yes; he was over in that corner, but I do not see him anymore," said Darcy as he scanned the area. "James, you take this room, and I will look in the game room. If you find him, escort him to the main entrance and wait for me. We will meet there, and once he is gone, I will explain what I can of this mess."

A little later, Darcy found Wickham coming in from the door that exited onto the balcony. "Darcy, nice party! I had no idea that you had so many friends!"

"What are you doing here? I believe you understood that you were not invited."

"Au contraire, my friend. I received an invitation from Miss Bennet herself, not to mention Mr. Bingley. Nice gentleman he is, too." Wickham *had* indeed received an invitation from a Miss Bennet; Darcy need not know which one.

"Then your welcome has just ended. Would you like to leave of your own volition, or should I assist you to the door?"

"Darcy, do not be so uptight! I will leave if I am not wanted, but you may disappoint more than one lady. Your Elizabeth may not look kindly upon your treatment of me."

"Miss Elizabeth's desires will be under regulation soon enough and are no concern of yours. Now, are you walking out on your own, or do I throw you over the balcony?"

Wickham looked at the balcony doors as if to consider the idea, but then began walking towards the entry, followed closely by Darcy. Colonel Fitzwilliam stood there waiting for them and looked questioningly at his cousin, whose countenance did not betray his resentment. Wickham made a gentlemanly bow to both men and departed Netherfield.

Fitzwilliam was the first to speak, "Now do you want to tell me what the hell is going on here?"

Darcy led him over to an area of the room where they could not be overheard and began softly, "When I returned from London last week, I discovered that Wickham had joined the militia stationed in Meryton. He must have learnt of my engagement to Miss Elizabeth because before I came back, he had insinuated himself into her good graces. I know not what lies he has told her about me, but I suspect she believes them."

"Darcy, she is to marry you. Surely she knows not to trust a word that miscreant would say."

Darcy just looked at him and sighed. "No, I do not think that she does, and furthermore, I cannot be certain that Miss Elizabeth has not known him longer than just this past fortnight."

"You think they may be somehow allied against you?"

"I do not know what to think, Fitzwilliam." He looked away trying to consider what to say. "I have known her a month. I am ignorant to her former ways and connections. She was chafed when I told her she was to have nothing to do with him, but I could not tell if that was because she does not like to be commanded what to do or because she has some biding affiliation with him."

"Perhaps you should start at the beginning for me. I find that my confusion over your relationship with this woman has me unable to account for your concern over Wickham."

"Your parents, no doubt, told you about my accident and how I came to be in a situation that compromised Miss Elizabeth and her family's reputation. I had no choice but to act honourably." Darcy's sombre mien told Fitzwilliam that his speculations were on the mark, that Darcy had finally been forced into a marriage that he could not want.

"And the lady, is she so bad?"

"She has no connections, no dowry to speak of; her family is obscene, and her mother's relations are in trade."

"Is she pretty?" Darcy rolled his eyes at his cousin. "Seriously, man. Is she attractive? You cannot say there is no value in a handsome face, for your children may grow up to look like her." Fitzwilliam was trying to bring some levity to the question; as a soldier he knew that sometimes it is the small things that one needs to grasp upon to survive the difficulties in life.

"She is not ugly, if that is what you want to know, but she traipses across the countryside unsuitably attired, stepping in puddles and covering her shoes and clothes in mud. She is positively wild, James." He said this with vehemence that Fitzwilliam found amusing.

"Sounds captivating to me, but I am a military man. My tastes in women have changed dramatically to what they once were when I was at Cambridge. That is why I will never marry. The women whom I desire would never be acceptable as the daughter of an earl, so I am forever doomed to bachelorhood. And very few have the dowries to entice me anyway." After a few moments of reflection, he continued, "Tell me about your engagement. I want to hear it from you rather than from my parents." So Darcy began the story starting with his ride on that stormy morning.

ELIZABETH CAUTIOUSLY OPENED THE DOOR to peek into the corridor. When she saw that it was clear, she slipped out into the hallway and made her way to the drawing room, looking for her sister who had departed the ladies' room just before her. Miss Bingley had interrupted the sisters' private conference after they had been in the ladies' room not a quarter of an hour, resulting in Jane's early removal while Elizabeth remained alone. Jane had planned to search for their father who would best know what to do given the circumstance of Mr. Wickham's attentions.

While scanning the house, Jane came up to Elizabeth and reported that her father and mother had left. Due to the wedding's early start in the morning, their mother had asked to be taken home. Mr. Bennet took her and the Gardiners to Longbourn and would return the carriage for the rest of the party. Jane had not yet seen Mr. Wickham and volunteered that perhaps he had left when he saw that she was avoiding him.

Elizabeth hoped this was the case, and was also sorry that Mr. Darcy would not have the occasion to meet her aunt and uncle this evening, but was most distraught that her father had left. This meant that she would have to depend upon Mr. Darcy. Her heart lurched once again when she saw her fiancé talking to a man in regimentals, but she observed that he was the same man with whom he had been speaking previously. Elizabeth hesitantly joined him by his side, letting him know of her presence.

"Miss Elizabeth, allow me to introduce you to my cousin, Colonel James Fitzwilliam. Fitzwilliam, this is my fiancée, Miss Elizabeth Bennet of Longbourn." The Colonel bowed as Elizabeth curtseyed. "The colonel is my cousin on my mother's side. My mother and his father were siblings. His father is the Earl of Matlock." In provocation, Darcy continued, "Miss Elizabeth, you look somewhat distraught. I cannot claim to understand your feelings on the matter, but you may want to know that Mr. Wickham has left."

Elizabeth stared at him in surprise, that he would be so bold in front of his cousin, but saw that he was looking for her reaction. "I thank you for letting me know about Mr. Bingley's guest. Will you also be telling me about the rest of the invitees as they depart?"

"You appeared as though you were looking for someone a moment ago, and I thought that perhaps Mr. Wickham might have been the object."

"I was indeed looking for someone, my father, but Jane has since told me that he, along with my mother, aunt and uncle, departed after supper. So, you see that that gentleman was not the one whom I sought; therefore, you can rest easy tonight. The wedding shall go on as planned."

"I am glad to hear it."

She looked at him archly, and then turned to Darcy's cousin whom she was already predisposed to like, for although appearing not much older than her fiancé, his cousin's laugh lines spoke of his good humour. "Colonel Fitzwilliam, it is a pleasure to make your acquaintance. Did you just arrive, or has Mr. Darcy sequestered you away somewhere?" She smiled while glancing at Mr. Darcy to see how he took her tease.

In good humour, he replied, "I only just arrived before supper. I was able to clean off the road dirt and make myself presentable in time to ask you to favour me for the next dance, that is if you are available? I would never assume that a lady as lovely as yourself would have space on her card so late in the evening." *She is quite beautiful, my cousin, as is usual with women around you, and she can also hold her own, which is not so common.*

"I am delighted to join you, sir, for I have the next two dances free."

"Excellent!" Fitzwilliam continued, "And as this dance seems to be at an end, shall we line up for the next?" She took his arm and walked away with him. He was not as handsome as Mr. Darcy, few were, but his pleasing manners and congenial personality predisposed her to think highly of him.

They found their place in line, and before the dance began, her sister Lydia came up and said, "Lizzy, who is that handsome man with you? I thought I knew all of the officers, but I daresay I have never seen him before." She said this more loudly than was necessary, thus embarrassing Elizabeth, as Colonel Fitzwilliam did indeed overhear her.

"Miss Elizabeth, please be so kind as to introduce me to this lovely, young lady."

Lydia thrilled at the distinction. Hoping that her sister would not say something silly, Elizabeth made the introductions.

"Miss Lydia, if you are not otherwise engaged, would you join me in dancing the following set?"

She agreed with alacrity and moved on with her partner to the far side of the line. "You are a brave man, Colonel. My sister's exuberance often grows as the evening progresses, and as you are an officer, I am afraid that she will find your company much to her liking."

"I will be happy to get to know her since you will be my cousin after tomorrow." Then Colonel Fitzwilliam entered into conversation directly with the readiness and ease of a well-bred man and talked pleasantly. Elizabeth very much enjoyed the dance, as he was skilled at the art and seamlessly led her through the more intricate steps accompanying this particular set. His manners were easy and inviting, and Elizabeth could not believe that he and Mr. Darcy could come from the same family and told him so. "You find my cousin and myself to be so different, do you?"

"Yes, I do."

"I imagine that Darcy is rather quiet amongst the local society, unless he has changed recently," added Colonel Fitzwilliam.

"So, he is usually distant and aloof?" said Elizabeth with an unabashed directness.

"No, he is not that. Well, I can imagine that he could be when surrounded by unfamiliar people, but when around friends and family, he can be good-humoured enough." Elizabeth looked surprised. "Pray let me hear what you have to accuse him of!" cried Colonel Fitzwilliam. "I should like to know how he behaves amongst strangers."

"Would you like to hear about the first time I saw him or of the fateful day that we encountered one another upon the path on my father's estate?"

"Both if you are willing to share."

"You shall hear then, but prepare yourself for something very dreadful. The first time of my ever seeing him in Hertfordshire, you must know, was at a ball, and at this ball, what do you think he did? He danced only four dances! I am sorry to pain you, but so it was. He danced only four dances, and only with his party, though gentlemen were scarce; and, to my certain knowledge, more than one young lady was sitting down in want of a partner."

He laughed heartily. "I can well imagine!" She was a little surprised by Colonel Fitzwilliam's jesting at the expense of his cousin. "So, did you actually meet him at the ball, or was it on the path?"

"We did not meet at the assembly; it was a public gathering, and he did not wish to be introduced, " said Elizabeth gauging his cousin's response. Pleased to discern he meant no ill-will, she continued, "We were in company on two other occasions, but I do not know if he remembers or not. We actually first met on the path, or more accurately, in the cabin, but I am sure he has told you what happened on that day, as he was able to remember it anyway."

Colonel Fitzwilliam then said, "Darcy did give me some of the particulars, but admitted that he was not well and only has a few recollections that he could share with me. I was hoping that perhaps you would fill in the blanks."

"So, are you trying then to determine whether I am a mercenary upstart taking advantage of your cousin who is honour-bound to act the gentleman, or are you open to hearing the events of the day from the perspective of someone you neither know nor trust, hoping to obtain some reason why your cousin would take such a drastic measure as to form an engagement?"

He appreciated her directness. So far, he had no reason to dislike her. "Why do you not tell me? I would like to think the latter, but as you say, I do not yet know or trust you. I mean no offence; I have known you these ten minutes and would like to form an opinion based on something other than my cousin's perspective, which may be biased, or my parents', who have never met you and are most certainly biased."

"Well, let me see. I was on my father's estate early one morning attempting to get in some much needed activity, as it had been several days since I had been able to get out. You see, I dearly love a long walk, but I noticed that in my musings, I failed to recognise the storm clouds, so began to run towards our home." At Colonel Fitzwilliam's raised eyebrows in question, Elizabeth laughed. "Tell me, sir, what would you have done had you been nearly three miles from home, and an ominous storm was coming upon you?" After he conceded her point, she continued. "When I rounded a bend, I came upon a large stallion galloping with a gentleman rider who had no regard for the possibility of encountering someone along the road. Of course, any local inhabitant would have been aware of the possibility of the landowner's daughter walking through the countryside early in the morning, but perhaps Mr. Darcy had not yet known to be so vigilant, so I must forgive him for his recklessness." She smiled at him and continued her tale. "In shock at such an intimidating sight, I screamed just as lightning struck not one hundred yards away. The great horse reared throwing the rider, your cousin, to the ground; however, his foot remained in the stirrup, causing him to be dragged at least thirty feet into the woodland. I, of course, did not know that Mr. Darcy was the horseman until I reached him to see if he were injured.

"When I came upon him, I knew that I had but three choices. I could leave the man, who had insulted me at the local assembly, there to face whatever fate might come his way in the fierce storm, as I felt for a very brief moment was his due. I could go to Longbourn, my father's estate, or Netherfield to seek aid; however, I knew that I would not be permitted to assist in his rescue, and it would be very difficult to describe sufficiently where Mr. Darcy could be found. Or I could attempt to get him to safety before the storm caused further injury. I, in my anxious state, chose quickly to attempt to get him to safety before seeking help. I am afraid that is what sent us down the road that has led to this night. I realised that Mr. Darcy was too ill to leave there in the cabin alone, and the storm was too dangerous to attempt to find aid, so we were left without a chaperone for the whole of the day.

"I was relieved when my father arrived because I knew that he would never make me marry a man for whom I had no fondness, but he brought with him Mr. Bingley and two of his servants. Mr. Darcy was kind enough to offer the servants a large sum of money to avoid marrying me, which may have worked had not my mother been factored in to the equation."

"Your mother? Your story gets more and more interesting," he said with a chuckle.

"We had all agreed to keep the entire affair quiet, for this is the one outcome in which Mr. Darcy's and my wishes united. However, when I reached home, I came down with a fever, after having spent the day in cold, wet clothes. The fever overcame my senses, and my mother overheard my saying something that aroused her maternal instincts. In my sleep, I spoke out loud about marrying Mr. Darcy. Unfortunately for me, I do have a history of talking in my sleep, but my unrest contributed to by utterances to an even greater degree than usual. My mother rather astutely surmised that I had been with Mr. Darcy during the day rather than alone; she may be lacking in other areas, but her matchmaking skills are always on high alert, you see. Having five daughters unattached and an estate entailed away, she endeavoured to secure my future through the only means within her control; thus the rumour began.

"You must understand that although my anger has been directed at my mother for her officious meddling, I know that she interfered due to her concern for my future, so I must forgive her, but I cannot myself approve of this way of obtaining a husband, and would never have agreed to such a scheme if given a choice. So, there you have my story." She boldly looked him in the eyes throughout her speech as they made their way through the dance, stopping and starting her tale as they progressed down the line.

Elizabeth then declared, "You find me shocking."

"I find you delightful."

She laughed. "You, sir, may find yourself quite alone in your opinion. So tell me about yourself. Mr. Darcy said you are a son of an earl? Your uniform would suggest you are not the firstborn."

"I am the second son."

"I see that we have something in common then."

"You are the second daughter?" At her nod, he said, "I have one other brother and a sister. My brother, being the firstborn, will inherit my family's title and holdings, so I joined the military and have the privilege of wearing my regimentals to attract the ladies."

Elizabeth laughed. "You do cut a dashing figure in your red coat, but you might find yourself in an undesirable position, having worn such a fine ensemble." He looked at her questioningly. "As you saw a moment before, my younger sisters are rather fond of a man in uniform. You might find their attentions to be a heavy burden for being thus distinguished."

"What about you, do you like a man in a red coat?" His presumption caught her off guard. Colonel Fitzwilliam then clarified his point. "Have you known Mr. Wickham for long?"

"About a fortnight," Elizabeth responded as she gazed about the room.

"I see that you do not want to speak of him."

"You are engaging *and* perceptive." Within a few moments, the dance allowed them to speak again, so she continued, "I know that Mr. Darcy and Mr. Wickham have their differences. What I do not know is why I have to be put in the middle of those differences. Mr. Darcy can disapprove of Mr. Wickham without involving me. Mr. Wickham has only been kind, and has expressed his desire to reconcile with Mr. Darcy, who by the way has admitted to me just this evening that he does not easily forgive the faults and vices of others. So, you see, I have decided to give each of the gentlemen the benefit of the doubt."

Colonel Fitzwilliam knew that Wickham was a wolf in sheep's clothing, whose only mission was to further his own desires and to fill his pockets with funds squandered from others. Wickham was gifted in his craft, no mistake, but Miss Elizabeth seemed more astute than the average lass. He debated whether or not to try to convince her of Wickham's guilt, but felt that it was Darcy's place to reform her views, not his own, so he decided to end with one last remark on the subject. "I care about my cousin, Miss Bennet, and so I ask you not to let Wickham impose himself upon your union. He is not a man to be trusted and would enjoy nothing more than to bring misery upon Darcy by insinuating himself with Darcy's wife."

Elizabeth liked Colonel Fitzwilliam, but could not abide hearing her friend spoken of so cruelly. To keep peace, she only said, "I thank you for your concern. I will consider what you have had to say, but perhaps we can spend the remainder of our time together with your telling me more about your family." The conversation then continued through the balance of the set with his sharing stories of his family and home.

While Colonel Fitzwilliam and Elizabeth were thus engaged, Mr. Collins approached Mr. Darcy, who had been distracted from his approach by studying the animation revealed upon the countenance of Miss Elizabeth as she spoke with Fitzwilliam. After a low bow, eyes fixed to Mr. Darcy's cravat, Mr. Collins began, "Mr. Darcy, sir, if I did not know that this would ultimately bring you joy, it would pain me to share with you the news that I am prepared to reveal. I am a loyal servant of your aunt, the honourable Lady Catherine de Bourgh, and it is my duty to inform you of a great transgression that has been wrought against you by your fiancée, my cousin, Miss Elizabeth Bennet. I saw, within this past hour, pass from the hands of Mr. Wickham into her own a written correspondence that should condemn them both in the eyes of the church and Lady Catherine herself. Miss Elizabeth has disgraced you in accepting a letter from not only another man, but also one with whom you have forbidden her to have any communication. I tell you this not for my own gratification, although I can assure that anything done in the service of my patroness or her family does indeed give me pleasure, but so that you can achieve your freedom by the procurement of the missive from her clutches, thus confirming her offence against you, before she has time to dispose of it. Proof of her duplicity is within her grasp inside the confines of her reticule at this very moment."

Had Mr. Collins looked up into Mr. Darcy's eyes during the course of his rehearsed speech, he would have seen indignation that was brimming over into fury staring back at him. If asked, Darcy would not have been able to determine whom he most despised at the moment, Wickham, Mr. Collins, or Miss Bennet herself. How dare this man weasel himself into Darcy's business time and again! Yet, if his aunt's parson were telling the truth, Darcy should be grateful to this obsequious fool to have been given this chance, before the wedding has taken place, to discover the extent of Miss Elizabeth's relationship with Wickham.

"And where did you see this supposed rendezvous occur?"

Mr. Collins answered in as few words as he was capable that he had seen them on the balcony. Mr. Darcy recalled that he had seen Wickham coming in from outside and cursed himself for not walking out to see if Wickham had been alone. Darcy had not seen Elizabeth for over thirty minutes leading up to her introduction to Fitzwilliam. He had to determine if Elizabeth were in possession of a letter from Wickham. Darcy would not abide being married to a woman who could not obey him on a point so crucial as this. Her family would have to suffer for her treachery, if what Mr. Collins was saying were true. Darcy told Mr. Collins that his services were no longer necessary, but if he needed further disclosure, he would seek him out. Mr. Collins departed, secure in the knowledge that he had gained immeasurable favour from his patroness.

Shortly, Elizabeth and Colonel Fitzwilliam ended their set and joined Darcy as he stood by the refreshment table. Darcy had been watching them, hoping somehow that her manner would help elucidate Elizabeth's character. Fitzwilliam was just complimenting her on her graceful execution of the dance as they walked up. "Thank you, sir," Elizabeth said with a heartfelt smile upon her face. "Dancing with a partner such as yourself enhances my own performance."

"Miss Bennet, would you like some refreshment?" asked Colonel Fitzwilliam.

"I thank you, yes." However, it was Mr. Darcy who performed the honours of procuring her a glass of punch just before requesting that she join him in the library so that they might have a few moments of privacy before she left.

"Fitzwilliam, we will return momentarily. You do not mind my taking your dance partner away do you?" After an affirmation that he indeed did not mind as he had already promised the next dance to another, Darcy offered his arm to his intended and led her out of the room.

They walked without speaking down the hallway and into the library. Elizabeth looked around and noticed that the room was sorely lacking in books. She laughed to herself thinking that this is just what she would have suspected from Mr. Bingley. The fireplace held the only light, but the blaze was large, thus keeping the room comfortable in the November chill. They stopped before the fire and Darcy motioned for her to have a seat on the sofa. She did as he desired and waited expectantly to see what he might have to say. After a few moments of waiting for him to speak, she impatiently said, "Mr. Darcy, you wished to speak with me?"

He had been considering Mr. Collins's speech and what he would say to obtain the information he desired without causing offence should the unusual man have led him astray. "Yes, forgive me; I was considering my words. Are we both, Miss Elizabeth, in agreement that should you accept communication from Mr. Wickham, the wedding would be called off."

"I agree that those were your terms, and I have upheld your request."

"Where were you during the time between supper and the introduction of my cousin?"

"Of what are you accusing me, sir?"

"I am merely wanting to know your whereabouts. I have no recollection of seeing you and am asking that you account for your time while Mr. Wickham was here."

Elizabeth knew of her innocence but was angry at his officious demands. "I was in the ladies' refreshing room with my sister. You can ask Miss Bingley to confirm what I say, for she was with Jane when I sought her to come with me and then joined us later."

"Miss Elizabeth, please empty your reticule, so that I can see the contents."

Elizabeth wanted to deny him access to her personal belongings, but it was best to give him full and unyielding access in order to prove her innocence, rather than attempt to deny him, thereby increasing his doubts. "Mr. Darcy, do you remain standing to intimidate me with your height? If you sit down, I will give it to you, so you may open it yourself."

Darcy had chosen to remain standing in order to produce just such an effect to which she alluded, but seeing that she was without disguise, he sat, and after being handed the bag, he opened it to search its contents. Not finding anything of interest other than a shoe rose that Elizabeth explained had fallen off during her dance with Mr. Collins, he handed it back to her. "Did Mr. Wickham give you a letter this evening?"

How could he know? She considered her response then decided to tell him all that she knew and hope for the best, so after a deep breath, Elizabeth began, "As you well know, earlier this evening after supper, I saw Mr. Wickham while in your company. When you walked away, I was asked to dance with Mr. Lucas, our neighbour. After the set, I was talking with his sister when Mr. Wickham motioned for me to meet him at the balcony. Instead of following his lead, I looked away."

Elizabeth could tell that Mr. Darcy was battling to maintain his usual control as she continued her narrative of the events leading up to finding a letter in her possession earlier in the evening.

While in the ladies' room, Elizabeth had begun to consider the improper situation in which she had placed herself. Due to the brimming tears that had begun to make their appearance, Elizabeth had withdrawn a handkerchief from her reticule, and as she did, a folded piece of parchment had fallen out of her small bag. Elizabeth had not noticed it until Jane reached down to pick it up and hand it to her. They had both observed at the same time that it was a letter with Elizabeth's name written in a strong but elegant hand. "Jane had inquired if you had penned it, sir – that perhaps it was a sign of your growing affection." Nonplussed, his brows knit together, causing her to smile despite her predicament.

She continued, "Without breaking the seal, I tossed the parchment into the fire. I was uncertain as to who may have written the letter, but based on the strong hand, suspected it to be from a man. Rather than open it to find out, I destroyed it." Elizabeth could not accept a correspondence, for if she did, then Mr. Darcy would be justified in ending the betrothal. A woman engaged to another could not by any moral standard accept a note from another man. "I never accepted the letter and have no way of knowing who wrote it. Nor do I know how it got into my reticule which has been in my possession since leaving Longbourn."

"Your story does not make sense, Miss Bennet. You had to have known it was in there. Perhaps you did not want your sister to know of your treachery – that you would do something to endanger your family?"

"Why would I risk my family's future in that way? I admit to enjoying the man's company, but to jeopardise my sisters' prospects for so selfish a motive is unfathomable." Elizabeth took a deep, steadying breath as she considered not mentioning a second letter that she had also found since Mr. Darcy did not seem to have knowledge of it but thought better of keeping any secrets from him and disclosed the rest of the events.

"We then planned to go to Papa to tell him what had occurred. If I could not find him, I thought to join you. But when I opened the reticule to place the handkerchief within, I was dismayed to find another folded piece of parchment, this one with the seal opened. That's when Miss Bingley entered with the pretence of asking about me, but Jane was able to get Miss Bingley to leave the room with her. As soon as the door was closed, I took out the second letter. As the seal had been broken, it would have been easy to glance at the words to confirm its author, and my curiosity almost won out, but I know what is right, Mr. Darcy, so I walked over to the fireplace and dropped it in." She recalled how she had watched the edges curl as the flames consumed it, along with its secrets. "Jane had planned to look for my father but told me when I joined her a few moments later that she was unable to find him – that they had left for home. So that is when I joined you and Colonel Fitzwilliam. You can ask Jane or Miss Bingley if you wish, and they can verify their parts of my account."

Some minutes went by while Darcy stood and paced before her. He was reviewing her story in his mind and trying to find any holes that might prove her to be misrepresenting the truth. Mr. Collins had approached him and declared that he had actually seen an assignation, but could the strange man be trusted? What motive might he have to lie? Did he hope for a chance with Miss Elizabeth despite having formed an attachment to her plain sister? He had already claimed to be in the service of Darcy's own aunt; might he have a misplaced sense of obligation – to attempt to intercede in the stability of his own relations to find a means to gratify his patroness? "Your cousin, why would he lie?"

"Sir, it is beyond me to enter into the mind and motivations of a stupid man. Perhaps he has some understanding with your aunt and seeks to free you of your duty to me and my family. Although an imprudent choice that could only hurt himself in the long run, I doubt not that his blind devotion could teach him to ignore reason."

Darcy could not reject that assertion. "You did not read any of the letters?"

"I did not. You seem to think they are from Mr. Wickham. I certainly cannot confirm or deny the possibility. However, I can say that he has always behaved honourably with respect to me and our betrothal, so I have no reason to suspect that the letters were written in his hand. After your account, I rather suspect Mr. Collins as the author."

"Miss Elizabeth, you have known Mr. Wickham no more than a fortnight. You cannot comprehend his character in so short a time."

"So you believe that a person's character cannot be sketched so readily?"

"In this case, yes I do."

"Do you distinguish then between one who seems moral but is in actuality corrupt from those who seem corrupt only be found virtuous? Should you not give equal credence to both possibilities?"

"I hope that I always judge in a manner that seeks justice in such cases."

"Then I have now found two things in which we are of like mind." He gazed at her countenance, hoping for some sign that she might fall into the latter category. "Jane can likely be found with Mr. Bingley, I should think."

"If you will excuse me, I will seek her out." He left the room to find Miss Bennet. When he returned with Jane, her eyes were wide with concern.

Elizabeth looked upon her sister with tenderness and said, "Jane, Mr. Darcy would like an accounting of my time from supper until now. Tell him everything that you know. Hold nothing back, for I did not." Jane's gaze passed from her sister to Mr. Darcy, and she began from the point when Elizabeth had come to her until she told Elizabeth that their father was no longer in attendance. This confirmed to Darcy Elizabeth's story, and so he chose not to involve Miss Bingley, who would take great delight in being privy to more talk of scandal.

Elizabeth and Darcy returned to the ball as it was coming to a close. The last dance was called and the carriages began arriving at the front of the estate. The gathering ended much earlier than was usual due to the early morning for all of the principle members of the wedding party and their guests.

Darcy was relieved for the evening to finally be over. Tomorrow he would marry and leave this God-forsaken town. He wished his cousin goodnight then retired to his room, doors locked.

By the time Elizabeth entered Longbourn, those in the first carriage were already gone to bed, so Elizabeth was unable yet again to speak with her aunt. It would have to wait until morning. She climbed the stairs considering how little faith her betrothed had in her integrity – that he would require another's account in order to trust her own. Before their union had even taken place, their relationship already lacked the foundation for a healthy marriage.

Wickham would soon discover that his attempts at stopping the wedding had failed, but he would not give up his ambitions for cashing in on Darcy's predicament as long as he could keep Lady Catherine hopeful and desperate for his success. Perhaps he would be able to fleece even more money from the rich and meddlesome termagant if he played his cards right. She would certainly not be the first harpy to fall prey to Wickham's deceptive charms.

Chapter Eight

So they are no longer two but one flesh.
What therefore God has joined together, let not man separate.
Matthew 19:6

The afternoon had become quite cold by the time Darcy and his bride left for London. Darcy had planned on spending the following month in town, so that they could spend Christmas near his sister, who would be staying with their aunt and uncle Fitzwilliam who lived within a mile of Darcy House.

Elizabeth had no opinion on where their first days of married life would be spent. Of course, Miss Bingley had raised her curiosity about Pemberley, and she anticipated seeing the estate and its surroundings for the first time, but nothing could stir her to think joyously on the prospect while her spirits were so marred by the elusive, upcoming events that would take place as a married woman.

Elizabeth sat across from her new husband in the well-appointed carriage as it swayed to and fro with the blowing of the wind. She was truly exhausted after a night of dancing at the ball with little sleep to recover, and closed her eyes for a rest. Her new husband sat staring out of the window in silent contemplation. She could only imagine what he was thinking.

She reviewed the past eight hours. *Can it truly have been so short a time thus far?* Having tossed and turned the previous night, she had finally dozed off three hours before time to rise again. Jane had retired with her, making very little movement as she dreamt of the handsome and amiable Mr. Bingley. Elizabeth had finally calmed while reflecting upon her dear sister's being so happy. Although Elizabeth was not made for gloomy thoughts, she was incapable of pulling herself out of the foreboding that she felt as the upcoming day had approached. Her life would change in ways that she could not even fathom. Miss Elizabeth Bennet would no longer exist, and she felt as though that woman were being shackled and chained to a drowning ship. She was determined to go down into the deep with calm and poise, to be resurrected as a new and formidable creature to serve as mistress of the great Pemberley. But during the night, she had remained unwillingly insecure and distressed about the day ahead.

ELIZABETH HAD PREPARED FOR THE WEDDING, donning her new gown made of ivory silk, simple yet elegant in its design. The local modiste had fashioned the gown based on Elizabeth's restrained specifications. Her hair was pulled up into an intricate style that took most of an hour to prepare. Sarah, the young abigail to Elizabeth and her four sisters, had a great deal of experience in fashioning styles to complement each of the Bennets and did not fail to impress on this occasion. Even though her hair would be mostly hidden by the wedding bonnet, her curls were tamed to frame her face beautifully. In front of her, upon the vanity, sat her bouquet of white roses, newly arrived from the hothouses of Darcy's home in London. Elizabeth had arranged the small token using the flowers her fiancé had delivered to her the previous day, but added her own favourite wild flowers and herbs that were still in bloom along the lanes of her father's estate. Except for the dark circles under her heavy eyes, she felt that she looked the part of expectant bride. Since an exhausted Elizabeth had slept late, her sisters were dressed first, leaving Elizabeth and Jane to prepare last.

Planning to summon her aunt Gardiner to come to her room and hopefully alleviate the apprehension that threatened to bring her to tears yet again, she had turned to Sarah to make the request, but then her mother came in the room to "explain your duties as a married woman." Elizabeth groaned inwardly. This was the exact thing she had been attempting to avoid these past two weeks. "Now, my dear, I have been meaning to talk to you about what you can expect once you are married. I think it a shame that a young girl cannot be warned about her duties before she has made an understanding with a man, for I believe many with means would choose a different path if that were the case. But this is our lot. First I must tell you that men are all very different from women."

"Mama, really...."

"Shush, child. Do not interrupt me. This is hard enough without your attempting to divert me as you are wont to do." Taking a deep breath, she continued, "Now, as I was saying, men are different. They have needs that women do not have, but it is your duty to meet those needs, at least until an heir is conceived." Mrs. Bennet began fanning herself with her handkerchief as a blush crept up her neck and onto her face. Elizabeth remained quiet. "Now, tonight Mr. Darcy will come to you. I suggest you have some wine before he arrives to calm your nerves. It is best to have as little light as possible, so that he will not be prone to want to look at you. Men like to look at women in a state of undress if at all possible, but you can resist this by dressing modestly." Elizabeth began feeling sick.

"When he comes, you need not do anything unless he asks something particular of you. Just lie still and he will do all of the work. There will be some pain; it is just the way of it, but it will soon be over, and he will leave you to clean up."

Elizabeth felt more confusion than she had before her mother had entered her room, and as she had a habit of expressing her feelings upon her countenance, her mother noticed the uncertainty. "Do you have any questions, Lizzy?"

"Mama, what exactly will he do to me?" Elizabeth felt like she could experience some relief to her agitation if she could just know what would happen to her. The anxiety related to her ignorance was hard for the usually controlled Elizabeth to bear.

Her mother looked at her wide-eyed trying to determine how exactly to explain something so personal, yet disagreeable, to herself. "Well, he will lie atop of you and spread your legs apart, so he can place himself betwixt them. Do not scream out in pain the first time. I learnt that men do not like that. Really, Lizzy, you live on a farm with animals. Surely you have seen what they do!" In her mortification, Elizabeth decided to ask no more questions.

"The good news is that men of means are prone to obtain a mistress to satisfy their carnal appetites; he likely already has one, so you need only be available when attempting to conceive children. You must do better than I did and give Mr. Darcy an heir. I have heard it told that different positions can help determine whether you have a boy or girl, but I would never be so bold as to suggest a thing with your father, despite needing an heir!" The blush on both women's faces intensified.

"Mama, I see this is as difficult for you as it is for me. Thank you for attempting to alleviate my concerns." Elizabeth desired that her mother leave and meant to send her out and obtain counsel from her aunt. As her mother left, she pulled the cord for Sarah to return and ask Mrs. Gardiner to come to her room.

As Sarah had moved on to Jane's toilette, it took several minutes before she could arrive. Instead, Mrs. Hill made a showing. "Oh, Miss Lizzy, you are a picture! Sarah has really come along, has she not?"

"Thank you, Mrs. Hill." With melancholy, Elizabeth reached out to hug the housekeeper who had once turned her over her knee when she had gotten into some trouble or another growing up. "You have always been so good to me, I will miss you dearly." Elizabeth had a wave of despondency come over her as tears again threatened to spill over and ruin the impression of the eager bride she was trying hard to maintain.

"Miss Lizzy, you were always the strong one. I know that you will do well. Just remember to continue to be kind towards your inferiors, and you will earn their devotion. And keep that confidence that has always guided you, so as not to let those in high positions perceive you are vulnerable. In other words, stay true to yourself."

"But what if Mr. Darcy insists I not. I fear Miss Elizabeth Bennet will no longer endure after today, that I will become but a vestige of my former self." Elizabeth despised being so vulnerable and needed the comfort of the mother figure found in Mrs. Hill that her own mother could not provide. But she could not speak with Mrs. Hill of the anxieties that most plagued her. "Mrs. Hill, could you possibly send for my aunt to join me in my room?"

"Of course, she had been asking about you earlier. I believe she was concerned about your not yet coming down for some tea."

"Oh, yes, could you have some tea sent up please? I do not think I could eat a thing, but tea would be nice."

"In a jiffy, miss." At that Mrs. Hill quit the room to complete Elizabeth's requests. However, she could not find Mrs. Gardiner, for Mrs. Bennet had sent her on to the church to make sure everything was made ready for the wedding. The message to this effect had been sent up to Elizabeth, whose agitation increased in the extreme. *What if I am unable to speak with Aunt Gardiner before the wedding?*

The family had gone to the church, which was but two hundred yards from the manor house. Although the distance was short, Elizabeth had taken the carriage to ensure her dress did not suffer the effects from road dirt. Even though she had tried to talk her mother into letting her go early, Mrs. Bennet insisted she not arrive until right before she was to walk down the aisle, so as not to risk being seen by the groom. "Lizzy," she had said, "if your Mr. Darcy sees you before the wedding, your marriage will bode misfortune!" Elizabeth could make no argument on that point; her conference with her aunt would have to wait until the wedding breakfast.

The service transpired with little deviation from the expected and well-known order. Although the ball had included the entire populace of Hertfordshire who might have some association with the Bennets, the wedding itself was a small affair with only close friends and family in attendance. As they recited the wedding vows, each considered the rebellion within their own individual hearts. Promising to love and honour seemed an impossible oath to recite, but in order to marry, one must make the vows, and so recite them they did.

Within half an hour, Mr. and Mrs. Darcy were signing the registry and proceeding to Longbourn for the obligatory wedding breakfast. Mrs. Bennet, being gifted in the art of hosting and exhibiting, had performed her part remarkably well. Longbourn was fêted up as if the aristocrats of London might be in attendance, as indeed might have been the case had Mr. Darcy's relations come. As it was, only the second son of an earl was present, but his showing had a singular effect upon her mother as well as Elizabeth's younger sisters, as they flirted and cooed over him. Elizabeth would have been embarrassed by their behaviour had she not been distracted by her own ruminations.

She approached her aunt and uncle and expressed her desire to introduce them to her new husband. "Aunt, Uncle, will you not join me to meet Mr. Darcy? Since you live in London, I hope that we will all have opportunities for mutual society."

"I hope we may, dear, but you know that you will be running in very different circles than the one in which we associate."

"Nonsense. I am sure, once I live there, that we will have many opportunities to be with one another. You cannot live more than a thirty-minute carriage ride from Mr. Darcy's home." Elizabeth reached for her aunt's hand, "I will need my family to help me survive being away from home. Please say we will see one another often and soon."

"Of course!" Mrs. Gardiner had replied; however, Elizabeth could not know her thoughts about such a scheme. Her aunt perceived the unlikelihood of their being accepted into Mr. Darcy's home, even if Elizabeth did not. Even though Mrs. Gardiner had known the Darcys from her time in Lambton, she was now *tainted* with trade. Although comparatively poor, Elizabeth was a part of the gentry and therefore held a higher position in society, not experiencing the class distinctions that pervaded London. Whenever Elizabeth had visited town, she kept to her relations' friends and social activities, so she could not possibly understand by experience the chasm between the classes. And although Mrs. Gardiner's ancestors were of noble lineage, the *ton* would not accept her association with trade.

Elizabeth led her aunt and uncle over to where Darcy stood talking to Bingley. "Mr. Bingley, I believe last night you already made the acquaintance of my aunt and uncle, but Mr. Darcy, allow me now to introduce to you Mr. and Mrs. Edward Gardiner. They are my family who reside in London. Aunt, Uncle, this is my new husband, Mr. Fitzwilliam Darcy, of Pemberley, in

Derbyshire." They bowed and curtseyed before Elizabeth continued, "I am hoping that since you have a home in London, that I might have the opportunity to see them more often than I have in the past."

"Yes, well, we may spend little time in town, except during the Season."

"You said that we would be going to town after the wedding and remain until the festive season ends, did you not?"

"Yes, I did."

"Wonderful, then I should be able to spend time with them for the next few weeks anyway." She smiled a genuine smile, relieved that she would not be sent up North without friends or family until after she had time to adjust with the support of relations.

Although Mr. and Mrs. Gardiner could easily pass as members of the fashionable set in London, Elizabeth did not realise that Mr. Darcy could not see past their being in trade. Money earned from the workings of a warehouse in Cheapside could not bring the respect that a long history of familial lineage would offer. As it was, Mr. Bingley was just one generation from making a living in trade and reaped the benefits from his hardworking predecessors, but because he did not labour himself and lived off the work of generations before him, he was respected as part of the elite. This dichotomy did not seem to affect Mr. Darcy, for he had no reservations with Bingley's friendship, despite his unsavoury forebears.

"It is a pleasure meeting you. Now, if you will excuse me; I need to ensure that the carriage is ready for our departure." Thus excusing himself, Darcy walked away. This greatly disappointed Elizabeth who had been hoping that Mr. Darcy would acknowledge that she had some family with whom he could find pleasure associating.

Nonplussed, Elizabeth turned to Mr. Bingley who had attempted to rectify the discomfort, occasioned by the removal of his friend, by asking Mr. Gardiner about his business ventures in town. Elizabeth thought there could not be a kinder gentleman than Mr. Bingley and rejoiced that at least her sister might have a marriage based on love and respect, for there was no one more worthy of happiness in matrimony than Jane.

While the men were talking, Elizabeth turned to her aunt and quietly said, "Aunt, I have been hoping for time alone with you, but I find that there must be some outside forces attempting to keep us apart!" She laughed lightly. "Might you be able to speak with me now before we depart?" Anxiety was etched on Elizabeth's brow.

"Oh, Lizzy, I knew you would wish for an opportunity to be alone with me. I have been trying to work out having a moment to meet, but others seem to demand either my time or yours. How about we go up to your room?" Thus they had attempted to escape to Elizabeth's room so she could speak with her aunt in private.

On their way up the stairs, however, Mr. Darcy interrupted them saying, "Mrs. Darcy," how odd that sounded to her ears, "we really must be leaving. Potts says that rain is imminent and we have at least a three-hour ride in front of us. With the drop in temperature and the possibility of a storm, we really should get on the road."

This request had greatly disappointed Elizabeth. She turned to her aunt so Mr. Darcy could not see the fear evident in her eyes. "Aunt, I really was counting on speaking with you."

"Lizzy, my dear, why do I not help you with your pelisse and wrap, and we can talk while I assist?"

Elizabeth looked to Mr. Darcy for his approval. "We need to leave within ten minutes." This declaration disheartened Elizabeth, but she turned to her aunt and put on a cheerful smile.

"I had hoped for time to change into travel clothes."

"We really should be going. As you may recall, a storm can make travel treacherous, and we have already stayed longer than I intended."

Elizabeth turned to her aunt, "I suppose we should hurry then, Aunt." Elizabeth led the way up to her room to get her last minute things." As soon as the door closed behind them, Elizabeth grasped her aunt's hands and said, "Please tell me all will be well!"

"Of course, dear! I know that tonight must have you uneasy, but let me assure you, Lizzy, all *will* be well. Being intimate with your husband is a natural event. God created a husband and wife to be as one in this way. With time, you may find that you enjoy his physical advances."

That was too much to consider. "But what about tonight? I confess that Mama has left me frightened about what to expect."

"Let Mr. Darcy take the lead. I am sure he will be kind to you." Elizabeth doubted her aunt's assertions and would have continued her questions, but it was time to go. Her limited counsel had to suffice.

Elizabeth rocked with the carriage as the thunder rolled outside. She attempted to sleep, but her musings of the morning would not let her rest. Her conversations with her mother and aunt did little to calm her fears. She was not used to feeling this way, out of control, with no diversions to calm her. Elizabeth hoped that Mr. Darcy might understand her worries and not ask her to consummate their marriage on the first night. She had contemplated making such a request and tried to formulate the question in her mind before actually asking him, but could not make herself venture onto that topic and literally paled at the thought. For the first time in her life she felt truly unnerved.

It was not as though she had never considered what her wedding night might be like, for she had. Of course, she did not know exactly what it was she should be imagining, for she was gently bred and gently bred ladies did not talk of nor learn of such things until married. However, she had always imagined marrying a man for love, one whom she could trust to provide solace and comfort to soothe her uneasiness. Her lone musings caused a new blush to cover her face, of which she was unaware. She, Elizabeth Darcy, née Bennet, afraid! She was determined to put her annoying cowardice behind her. Every woman who has been married has gone through this; surely she can too without giving in to panic. Mr. Darcy was a handsome man and when he smiled on rare occasions, he did draw her in. What woman would not want a husband such as he?

Elizabeth recalled how he appeared in the cabin when she had begun to undress him – his strong, masculine frame – but then recollected how this same man had insulted her and found her unable to tempt him into a simple dance.

DARCY SAT ACROSS FROM HIS BRIDE, his occupation varying between staring out at the countryside and gazing upon his new wife. As expected, it began to rain within an hour of leaving Longbourn. He had desired to leave earlier, but understood that his new mother-in-law had gone to a great deal of trouble to provide a wedding breakfast fit for a lord. He had to do his one last duty in Hertfordshire and patiently wait for an appropriate time to depart that would allow them to arrive in London before dark. He glanced at Elizabeth who appeared to be sleeping except for the occasional change in mien. Her expressions transformed from smiles, to frowns, to blushes, to pallor, but most commonly alighted upon sadness. A time or two, a tear escaped from her eyes. The darkness of the day made her countenance difficult at times to discern, but he appreciated this occasion to study her without the obstacle of being noticed. He knew very little about the woman in front of him, but he did perceive that she wore her emotions openly, at least so it would seem. He had been able to tell from across a room if Elizabeth were happy, indignant, embarrassed, frustrated or forlorn. Yet he also remembered occasions when he was unable to decide if she were sincere in her words or just teasing him.

Darcy had noticed that she held good qualities that would certainly be beneficial once their life together began in earnest. Elizabeth was able to dance gracefully, as he had witnessed the evening before, and she seemed to be comfortable in company, even with those whom she had never before met. He remembered her engaging conversation with Fitzwilliam as she danced. Darcy could not know at the time of what they were speaking, but she did so with animation and vigour. And she certainly did not back down from Lady Catherine, a rarity in any social class, which showed great fortitude. She had a pleasing figure, which he had observed on that fateful day of the storm. How could he *not* have been aware of her form when she was wearing so little clothing? He had always suspected that she knew what she was about and had designed to tempt him into a compromise. But how he could have taken advantage of her in his condition, thereby sealing the deal, was beyond him to comprehend.

Although he would never admit it, her captivating shape had haunted him since the storm, and on this journey, the thunder in the distance kept bringing him back to that fateful day with whatever memories he had been able to retain. He wondered, not for the first time, if she were indeed a maiden. There was no rumour to suggest otherwise; however, the town folk who had known her the entirety of her life, seemed quick to judge her as having lost her virtue with a stranger. Tonight would reveal the truth one way or another. Of the whole business, being intimate with an appealing woman held the most promise. She did not have the figure most fashionable women strived for; she was rather slender and of diminutive stature, but she still had the curves where they counted to please a man. He supposed that he could be doing worse. His cousin's remarks about marrying a pretty woman did have some merit, but he did not think he could go so far as to call her pretty, for as Miss Bingley had so rightly articulated in the past, she had little style and would likely raise children to run wild. He would have to keep her and any progeny under stern governance.

This led him to meditate upon his dear sister, Georgiana, whom he loved with all of his heart. He had thought he was being scrupulous and disciplinary in her upbringing, but then she attempted an elopement with a blackguard. His failure in protecting her worked knots in him whenever he considered it. Darcy knew how the general populace of men were, but he deemed Wickham an especially profane cad. Darcy would need to be forever vigilant and endeavour to keep both of the ladies in his life under regulation. At least his sister respected him and would obey his strictures; his wife was another matter altogether. She would have to learn the propriety that is expected as mistress of Pemberley. He would have many social requirements during which Mrs. Darcy must act the part of dutiful and respectful wife. Elizabeth would have much to learn and little time in which to master his instructions. Darcy could only imagine the stack of invitations awaiting them at home from supposed friends who desired to scrutinise her every fault. He took in a deep breath, slowly releasing it as he sought to dispel his dread. A headache was coming on. *I should go back to more pleasant thoughts,* and so he did.

According to the standards of his contemporaries, Darcy lived an uncommonly priggish life. His father had warned him repeatedly of the dangers related to gaming and women. Darcy's family name came with no small measure of pride. All of his actions bore witness to his familial responsibilities. He valued temperance and attempted to live within the bounds of propriety that his father had instilled within him. Losing money at the gaming tables put his estate and holdings at risk, and sacrificing his health just to gratify his lust could also reap significant liabilities. Darcy already had to deal with Wickham's known offspring and in so doing risked censure to himself, for there would always be people who considered him to be the responsible party, no matter his own innocence, just for providing aid.

However, despite his restrained exterior, inside he was like any other man of lascivious inclinations. He was proud of his self-control despite his inner struggles, but now that he was married, he could enjoy all of the benefits that lie therein. He considered the night ahead and smiled to himself. He had considered at one point taking a mistress to satisfy the desires that all men face, but he reflected upon what his father would think and then the possibilities of what could happen to this woman when he married. Would he keep her on or set her up somewhere with all of his illegitimate children born through her? And how would a history with one woman affect his future wife? This was a common enough practice for his fellow peers, but he had higher standards for himself. And what if he somehow developed feelings for the woman? Of course he could never marry her. No, he could not have taken a mistress, and deep down inside he had known this to be the case. But all of those struggles were now unnecessary.

The new Mrs. Darcy would do well enough for meeting his needs and providing an heir. She was healthy with a strong constitution as evidenced throughout the past month, and she had the form to mollify his carnal pursuits. While his mind remained preoccupied with satisfying thoughts, a niggling idea came into his mind. He considered again that she might not have had sexual relations with a man before, which certainly was his hope, but if that were the case, how would she respond to his advances this night? They, of course, must consummate their marriage tonight. Not only was it the custom to do so, but he also wanted to. Add to that, the servants would bear witness to the evidence on the sheets that would confirm that he did not ruin her in the cabin or in some secluded folly, as was the popular belief. Breaking her maidenhead would be the proof of his own innocence, and that proof had value to him, and it should to her as well. Yes, she would not want to wait either if she is innocent of past indiscretions. He would explain this to her at the proper time and make sure that she knew to expect him.

ELIZABETH WAS AWAKENED by Mr. Darcy's baritone voice. "Mrs. Darcy, we will be pulling up to Darcy House in about five minutes." She had been in a deep slumber, her exhaustion finally consuming her. How strange to have been in close quarters with Mr. Darcy for a full three hours with no other interaction than this. Elizabeth attempted in vain to stifle a yawn. The carriage held little light due to the dark clouds of the storm and the late hour of the waning day, so she could not see Mr. Darcy's amused look upon his face.

"Forgive me; I must have fallen asleep." She then looked out of the window to see imposing homes pass by the carriage. Her stomach filled with knots as she saw the reality of her plight. Within a few moments she would enter her new home as Mrs. Darcy. How she disliked that name! She would ask him to call her Elizabeth. They were married; surely that would be appropriate.

Darcy noticed her unease and said, "When we arrive you will have time to freshen up and to change into something more comfortable. I know that riding in your wedding gown was not your wish; I hope it has not been too disagreeable." She shook her head in the negative and continued to look out the window as they made their way past Hyde Park. The dreary scene outside the window mirrored the trepidation within her breast.

The carriage came to an abrupt stop, and the door was opened by a footman who had been awaiting their arrival. Elizabeth, with distraction, wondered if he had been waiting out in the rain, for he was punctual in his services. After Darcy's departure from the carriage, another footman reached up to hand down the new Mrs. Darcy; her husband's relinquishing that honour was not lost on Elizabeth. Two footmen held umbrellas over the Darcys and delivered them into the dry entrance of Darcy House.

The butler stood just inside of the doorway to greet Mr. Darcy and his new wife as the footmen removed their damp outer garments. As Darcy was about to make the introductions, the housekeeper joined them. "Mrs. Darcy, allow me to present the butler of Darcy House, Mr. Horace Franklin, and the housekeeper,

Mrs. Edna Johnson." Then turning to his staff, he continued, "Franklin, Mrs. Johnson, this is Mrs. Elizabeth Darcy."

Franklin had been the butler since Darcy was about ten, having moved up the ranks quickly due to his efficiency and ease at leadership. His height nearly matched Mr. Darcy's and his hair was thick, but greying above his ears. He had a severe look upon his face that seemed to display his natural state. Mrs. Johnson's head was covered in a cap, but her hair that was visible held its brown colouring from her youth. As such, despite her wrinkle lines, it was difficult for Elizabeth to determine the housekeeper's age. Elizabeth provided the appropriate greeting to each of them, then said with sincerity, "Mrs. Johnson, it is a pleasure to make your acquaintance, and I look forward to time in your company during which I hope to take advantage of the wisdom you have earned while in your position." Elizabeth had been thinking of Mrs. Hill and hoped with her heart to have a housekeeper at Darcy House with whom she and her children would one day think upon as nearly family.

"Of course, madam." Disappointed thus far, Elizabeth looked to Mr. Darcy who requested that Mrs. Darcy be escorted to her chamber.

Then turning to Elizabeth, he stated, "Mrs. Darcy, Mrs. Johnson will take you to your chamber. She has assigned a temporary lady's maid to assist you in your toilette and also to unpack your trunk, thus seeing to your needs. If you still feel fatigued, I suggest you take a nap. I will come to your room to escort you to dinner at seven-thirty." He bowed and turned towards his study. He desired a brandy to give him needed warmth while perusing the recent mail before heading to his room.

As Elizabeth ascended the steps to the family quarters, she attempted to engage the housekeeper in light conversation but gave up trying when she only received curt answers in the affirmative or negative. The house was much quieter than that to which Elizabeth was accustomed. She felt a chill both from not having worn her travelling clothes and from the cool welcome she had thus received. Elizabeth hoped that the lady's maid would be more promising in her reception.

Elizabeth's room held potential, with its greens and champagne on the walls and counterpane and touches of rose hues throughout the chamber, reminding her of a scene from the countryside displaying flowers along the paths. She saw a fireplace to her right, from which a small blaze glowed, with a settée upon a soft rug and a door to the left of the hearth. A large canopied bed filled the space to her left against the wall. On the right side of the bed was a closed door, and on the wall directly opposite to her current position there were two large double windows that would bring in plenty of daylight; however, the dreary, rainy day currently brought in little to cheer her. Between the windows was situated a writing desk supplied with parchment, ink and quill pen. She smiled in heartfelt pleasure.

The housekeeper had watched her inspection of the room with attentiveness. She had heard the rumours being bandied about town, just like everyone else. Mrs. Johnson could not feel any level of joy about this new mistress who had risen above her station in marrying Mr. Darcy, but she would have to show her the obligatory deference that was due her. She was determined to meet all of the new mistress's expectations but would go no further. Walking to the door beside the bed and opening the latch, the housekeeper indicated the entrance to her dressing room.

Elizabeth walked over and was surprised to see a servant inside already unloading her truck. She entered saying, "Hello, I am Miss, um, rather *Mrs.* Darcy. Will you be serving as my maid this evening?"

The woman curtseyed and said, "Yes Ma'am, I am Laura Carpenter, and I will be helping you until you decide upon a new lady's maid."

"I am pleased to meet you, Laura, and happy to have someone handy to help me out of this dress! I have never been so ready to remove a gown in my life," Elizabeth said hoping to break the ice somewhat. She suspected this lady's maid would witness Elizabeth's own personal shortcomings and would be privy to her secrets, thus she hoped to gain a friend before anything noteworthy occurred. Elizabeth had only lived or stayed in comparatively smaller homes with not more than six servants, so she was unfamiliar with the types of relationships that might develop between the domestics and the master and mistress. She would have to navigate these new waters with discernment, without sacrificing her own self to the altar of privilege.

Elizabeth thanked the housekeeper for the tour and dismissed her with a smile. Then turning to Laura said, "Now, if you could get me out of this dress and corset, I would be obliged." Laura got to work and in no time, Elizabeth was able to retire to her room and crawl under the counterpane while Laura closed the window coverings. "Could you wake me at seven to prepare for dinner? Mr. Darcy is to escort me down at seven-thirty." Laura assented and left the room to finish her task of settling in the new mistress until she was next needed.

Laura had worked at Pemberley and Darcy House for the past eight years, ever since she was widowed after the death of a local merchant from Lambton. Having the distinction of serving Mrs. Darcy on her first night was a true honour. Mrs. Johnson had picked her due to her strong loyalty to Mr. Darcy and her hard work ethic, but Laura's previous marriage was particularly advantageous. Of course all of the staff was loyal, but this attribute was especially important for a newly married couple when the master held his privacy in high regard. There was speculation that Mrs. Darcy might not be a maiden, and if the rumours were true, any evidence to this possibility had to be concealed. Laura could be counted on to perform her duties with discretion.

As soon as Elizabeth's head had touched the pillow, she was asleep. When Laura returned to awaken her, Elizabeth was confused as to her surroundings, but when seeing her maid's kind face, she remembered she was to get ready for dinner. She had left little time to prepare because she was so tired and wanted to sleep for as long as she could. If it were possible to skip dinner and stay abed, she would certainly have chosen that course. Her appetite had left her this morning and had not yet returned. Just as Laura was putting the finishing touches on her hair, she heard a knock upon a door in her chamber. She stood and walked into her room as her maid left out of the servant's entrance.

Elizabeth called to enter, and it was at this moment that she realised that the door next to the fireplace was Mr. Darcy's private entrance. She blushed scarlet when he entered. A man had never been in her room before, and this left her feeling exposed.

She instinctively lifted her hand to her bosom and to cover the look of surprise said, "I am not yet familiar enough with my room. I did not imagine that door led to *your* room."

"Well, in actuality, it leads to our shared sitting room, but my chamber is on the opposite side." He looked around her chamber, not having seen it since the new window and bed coverings had arrived.

Elizabeth noticed his perusal and said, "This was your mother's room."

"Yes, but it has been some time since I have been in here. Are you pleased with the colours? I told Mrs. Johnson that you enjoyed nature."

She smiled at his thoughtfulness, "Yes, I like them very well."

"Shall we?" He held out his arm for her to lead her to the dining-parlour. They descended the stairs in silence. This was the first opportunity Elizabeth had taken to observe her surroundings. She noticed that his style was elegant and refined without being ostentatious, as she would have supposed. The furniture pieces were suitable to the fortune of their proprietor, well made but not uselessly fine. In this Elizabeth had found something else for which to be grateful, aside from a comfortable bedchamber. They entered the small dining room, used for family meals, and although modest in size compared to the home's formal dining-parlour, it was still on a larger scale than where her family took meals at Longbourn.

The footman pulled the chair out for Elizabeth placing her to the right of Darcy's seat at the head of the table. The meal progressed with little conversation, which resulted in Elizabeth's mind continually going to the night ahead. Her anxieties increased with each moment, thus diminishing her appetite to the extent that made eating nearly impossible, so she pushed her food around, like she did as a child trying to get out of eating her peas.

She was startled from her musings when she heard Darcy say, "Mrs. Darcy, do you not care for pheasant?"

Embarrassed for a moment that she had been caught playing with her food, she said, "No, I do like pheasant; I just find that I am not very hungry."

"Mrs. Williams will be disappointed. She will think that you do not care for her cooking," Darcy returned, unsure himself if this might be the case. He had never seen her shy away from eating like other ladies with whom he had dined. Elizabeth looked alarmed; she had no wish to offend. "But, truly, if you are not hungry, I would not have you push yourself. But I do not believe you ate much earlier today either. Surely, you must need *some* sustenance."

"Forgive me, but I truly do not feel I can take another bite."

"I will ask that dessert be held until later then." Darcy nodded to the footman and sent him to relay the news to the kitchen. "Mrs. Darcy, I did not ask earlier, but were you able to rest?" *Perhaps she is just tired.*

"Yes, I was. The bed is very comfortable, but please, sir, will you not call me Elizabeth?"

"If you wish when we are alone, but in public, I will use the appellation Mrs. Darcy. And what name would you prefer in addressing me?"

Elizabeth thought for a moment and said, "Mr. Darcy, I believe."

His eyebrows shot up in question, "Yet you ask that I not call you Mrs. Darcy?"

"I have always called you Mr. Darcy and still think of you as such. Once a name gets in my head and attaches to a person, I have a difficult time making the change. But you have always referred to me as Miss Elizabeth or Miss Bennet, so surely calling me Elizabeth cannot be a burden to you."

"As you wish." Then there was silence as he finished his plate. Standing, he said, "*Elizabeth*, will you join me in the music room. I would like for you to play for me." She had a wave of relief flow over her. Although not a great musician, she felt playing for him to be familiar ground, so she readily agreed to the scheme. They made their way towards the music room, "I will give you a tour tomorrow when it is light outside, so you are able to see the house better."

"So far, everything I have seen is lovely."

They continued down the corridor and entered a well-lit room that held a pianoforte and a harp in the corner. The abundance of mirrors allowed the small amount of light to reflect giving a warm glow. Elizabeth walked to the pianoforte and ran her fingers along the top. "What a fine instrument you have, sir. Do you play?"

"I once took lessons to please my mother," Darcy said, the corners of his mouth upturned. "But my sister, Georgiana, is the true musician in the family. She practises most diligently and plays remarkably well."

"Then I fear you will be most disappointed in my performance," Elizabeth returned with a smile.

"I have heard you play. You lack practice to be sure, but I plan to have my sister's master provide lessons for you. Now that you have access to a fine instrument, you can have no reason not to improve." He did not miss the brief flash of pique in Elizabeth's eyes but also noted that she withheld any commentary. "There is some sheet music that you can look through unless you have something else you might want to play."

"Oh, how nice, you are letting me choose," she replied saucily, which she quickly regretted. Mr. Darcy likely did not even comprehend how his words offended. Elizabeth looked through the music. She was familiar with a few of the songs, but not so familiar as to play them for an audience, and so she chose to perform something she knew by heart. She began playing, and as the song continued, she closed her eyes and felt the music flow through her. The song she had chosen had a melancholy air that reflected the sadness of her heart. She had not decided upon that song in order to display her feelings; it was more like the song had chosen her, and she reflected the emotions therein with her playing. She was so caught up in the music that she did not realise that tears had begun trickling down her face. Darcy had not noticed her quiet reflections either at first, for he had leaned his head onto the back of the sofa on which he sat. However, at a particularly lovely part of the song, he glanced towards her and saw that she was crying.

Darcy held his emotions in check and rarely showed his vulnerabilities to others; nonetheless, he did have a soft heart, the evidence of which was not often witnessed. This had been a trying and painful day for him, which was likely why he had also gotten caught up in the mournful melody that Elizabeth had been playing. It occurred to him that she might be experiencing some morose sentiments related to the events of the day. She had cried silently in the carriage when pulling away from Longbourn, and there had been evidence of tears at the wedding. But, she had chosen this path, and now she must make the best of it. He would attempt to help her, but she must deal with her own choices. Fitzwilliam had relayed to him after the ball a large part of the conversation that had taken place while dancing with her. Elizabeth had said that her mother overheard her talking in her sleep and from her utterances surmised the whole scandalous tale. What mother would purposely put her family at risk by spreading such unfounded rumours? No, Elizabeth had to have been a part of the dissemination of the report or must have at least told her mother part of the truth, hoping for this outcome.

The song ended and Elizabeth sat there looking at the keys, wiping her tears away, chagrined that she had given in to her emotions in such a display. She began sifting through the sheet music again, trying to provide a distraction to her musings and giving a place for her eyes to rest. Elizabeth jumped in alarm when Darcy's hand touched her arm. "Come, sit with me. We should talk." Elizabeth glanced up to his eyes and looked away, ashamed of her weakness. She allowed him to lead her to the sofa where he had been sitting. She took her seat and placed her hands in her lap, not looking at him.

"Elizabeth, has your mother spoken to you about what to expect on the wedding night?" She turned scarlet, mortified at his implication and nodded in the affirmative. Elizabeth could not see his blushes or she may have found some irony to divert her. "Do you have any questions?"

After some moments of nervous agitation, she said, "I was hoping that... that is to say, I thought we might...." She took a deep breath and said, "Can we not wait until we have gotten to know each other better?" Elizabeth looked up to him, hopeful in his response.

He stared into her imploring eyes for a moment, and then said, "No, we cannot."

"Why ever not?"

"Elizabeth, we are married. You are asking me to put off the inevitable."

"I was just hoping for some time. We barely know one another, and what could it matter to wait?"

"One, the consummation of a marriage traditionally occurs on the wedding night; two, the evidence of this consummation is important to establish our innocence in the affair; and three, I want to." She looked at him with a puzzled expression, brows knit.

"What evidence? I do not understand."

"Your mother did not tell you?"

She blushed anew, looking away, then stood and walked to the window on the opposite side of the room. "My mother spoke to me this morning, but I could not comprehend. She has difficulty expressing herself with clarity at times. I intended to speak with my aunt, and was on my way to do so, when you insisted we leave. So, to be perfectly clear, I do *not* know." She turned, boldly looking at him in the eye as she finished her mortifying speech. She would have seemed unaffected except for the tears that had sprung anew.

He stood and walked to the mantle from where he turned to look at her. *If she is not an innocent, then she could make her life in theatre should the need arise.* "Elizabeth, when a woman loses her, um, virginity, she has some pain due to the breaking of her maidenhead." In his discomfort, he could not help but find diversion in the irony of his explaining to his new wife about her own body, but that was the way of things. A woman was left in ignorance up until her marriage, thus making her more fearful of her husband than was necessary or wise. "There will be some blood," her eyes widened, "but that is only the first time. The blood will serve as evidence of your chastity before marriage."

"You need this, this… evidence?" she asked in incredulity.

"My honour demands that I am proven innocent in my affairs with you that promoted this scandal. I am sorry if you do not see the necessity of such proof to be known of yourself, but I do."

"But I know that I am a maiden. Who else matters? And how would blood from my body make any difference to anybody else? Would you hang the sheets up outside the front door for all to see?" Elizabeth could not believe she was having this conversation, as she had gotten past her embarrassment and moved on to anger.

"Of course not, but you may be surprised to learn that that is exactly what was historically done in some parts of the world. Confirmation of virtue has always been of value; servants talk." As she turned away, he continued, "Elizabeth, you may not care about who knows or does not know the truth of what happened in that cabin, but I do. My honour and family name demand that I be vindicated concerning this outrageous scandal. You owe me this much!" His voice had been steadily increasing as the seeming justice of his argument overtook his sagacity.

Elizabeth felt sick. She knew he had the right and the inclination, even if his argument did not have justice to her own sensibilities. She also felt that her request was juvenile and selfish, but she could not stop the trepidation in her heart.

Darcy saw her nod in understanding. "You are tired, I know. I think it time that we prepare for bed. I will take you to your room and give you an hour to prepare. Will that be adequate time?" She nodded again and began walking towards the door. "Elizabeth, one more thing; leave a candle lit on your bedside table." She stopped walking for a brief moment.

He means to humiliate me.

WHEN SHE ENTERED HER ROOM, Laura was waiting for her and had hot water ready in her copper tub. This was a luxury for Elizabeth who was used to bathing after her sister Jane and not more than three times per week. The fireplace in the dressing room provided some measure of heat as she immersed herself into the welcoming water. Laura suggested she pick one of three scents to add to the bath, and she chose lavender for its calming effect. While she was washing, Laura came in with a glass of wine and handing it to her said, "Ma'am, Mr. Darcy requested that I give you some wine to soothe your nerves." Elizabeth was surprised at Mr. Darcy's solicitude to her needs; he was certainly an enigma, an advantage for she truly enjoyed the study of an intricate character.

"I thank you," Elizabeth said as she blushed at the implications of having a servant know what was to take place. The bath and wine had a soothing effect upon her and she was grateful for the consideration. She could not feel at all sanguine about what was to come, but she remembered her aunt's words, trusting that he would be kind. She had a brief thought of how she might be feeling if she had been forced to marry Mr. Collins instead. Fortunately for Elizabeth, this thought was just what she needed to appreciate the man to whom she would give herself this night.

Once Laura had finished assisting Elizabeth to dry off, she showed her two nightgowns to choose between. They were both white linen gowns with no embellishments, hardly the provocative trousseau most would have considered, but Elizabeth had not thought to purchase anything different and was glad for this provision. With the high neckline and long sleeves, she would be covered more than she had been in her wedding dress. "Ma'am, how would you like your hair? Shall we leave it down? I could brush it for you?"

"No, a simple plait will do well, and you will thank me in the morning; I can assure you." Elizabeth amicably responded. This woman had known her less than six hours, but to Elizabeth, they would always share the bond that comes when two people go through a trauma together – at least to Elizabeth's sensibilities if not the maid's. After completing her task, the maid assured her that she would return promptly if needed later, showing Elizabeth the location of the bell pull.

After Laura left, Elizabeth blew out all of the candles excepting the one next to the bed. The light from the fireplace gave off plenty of light so that she could not see the advantage of the candlelight that Mr. Darcy had requested. The only sound was the crackling of the small blaze in the fireplace, and although the room was plenty warm, she was shivering underneath the bed coverings. Elizabeth was physically and emotionally exhausted. She was simultaneously hoping that the night would end soon but fearing for the next step to begin. She knew this feeling well, as it reminded her of waiting to receive her just punishment for getting into some scrape or another when she was a little girl. Her father never meted out the punishments; it was always her mother or Mrs. Hill, and usually when she was getting her new dresses muddy. Her mother would have her get a switch from the willow, and then she would use it to whip her bare legs. Elizabeth remembered that it was never as bad as she feared and was quickly over. She would hope for the same in this circumstance.

It was not as though Elizabeth did not admire her new husband. He was a handsome man, strong, sure, but her appreciation of his person could not overcome her trepidation. If only he had expressed some level of regard for her, as a woman, as a partner, she felt she could be more welcoming, but as it was,

Elizabeth understood that he merely considered her to be an acquired possession to be made available at his whim.

DARCY HAD ENTERED HIS CHAMBER after taking his new wife to her own and sat down on the chair next to the fireplace. He stared at the flame, reflecting upon Elizabeth's response to his insistence. She seemed genuinely discomfited. He had no desire to take a woman who did not want him, but concurrently, he had no remorse for what was to take place. She brought nothing of value to the marriage except what she could offer in her bed. *Is it unsound to require she oblige me?* He poured himself a brandy and quickly swallowed the drink, letting it burn on the way down. The next glass, he consumed more slowly. His man had his bath ready and as he was helping him with his coat, Darcy said, "Nelson, please get a message to Laura Carpenter, Mrs. Darcy's temporary maid, to make certain to offer my wife some wine. There should be a bottle in the sitting room that would be suitable. While you are gone, I will see to myself." Darcy quickly undressed and gingerly got into the hot water. As he waited for Nelson's return, he continued to nurse his brandy. Soon, he would be able to take his pleasure. This brought a smile to his face. *It has been long enough.*

AFTER ABOUT TEN MINUTES of quiet reflection, there was a knock upon the door from the sitting room. Elizabeth's eyes flew open as she stared at the barrier separating her from her new husband. She managed to squeak out an "Enter." He was wearing a robe and underneath that a nightshirt. His legs were bare. Elizabeth looked away. She was certain that she was crimson from head to toe. Her husband said not a word. Elizabeth continued to shiver underneath the covers, willing herself to remain calm, but with little success. He stood next to the bed staring at her, for how long Elizabeth knew not, for time had become relative; she only suspected his eyes rested upon her, for she saw from the corner of her eye that he was not three feet away and facing the bed.

He took off his robe and placed it at the foot of the counterpane. He lifted the covering that Elizabeth had been holding to her shoulders and climbed in. She closed her eyes, determined not to weep. She began reciting poetry in her head, the ones that she had difficulty remembering, to use for distraction. Unfortunately, the only ones that came to mind were of a romantic nature, which only succeeded in reminding her of the unfortunate circumstances of her marriage.

Darcy continued to stare at her face and wondered what must be going on in her head for she seemed to be concentrating most diligently. A tear escaped her eyes. He had not done anything yet. *Maybe she is prone to crying. I hope she will not turn out like her mother.*

Elizabeth felt him grab the bottom of her nightdress and slowly pull the hem up to her waist. How dreadful that this man whom she could not abide was touching her in this way, and yet the slight graze of his hand felt like a searing brand, marking her as his own. She may have even found some pleasure in Darcy's unfamiliar touch had he thought to grant the possibility, but he had not.

Then she felt his heavy weight descend upon her as he separated her legs—just as her mother had warned! She could not tell what Darcy was doing, but she felt pressure betwixt her legs. He was breathing deeply in her ear. She noticed that he smelt of liquor and wondered if he needed drink as much as she had. Then there was a sharp pain that almost made her scream out, but she remembered her mother's warning and she strove to hold in her lamentation, grabbing the sheet under her hands and squeezing the fabric. She knew that she was no longer Elizabeth Claire Bennet, maiden. As much as she attempted to divert her attention, she could not leave the moment. The pain was burning and felt like she had been sliced open, but that was nothing to the mortification that consumed her. As much as she tried not to cry, the tears would come. She whimpered as she took in shallow breaths. His breathing also changed as his exertions began to build.

Through Elizabeth's pain, she could still tell what he was doing. She was reminded of what her mother had said about living on a farm. She remembered the dogs and how they would make the same movement. How similar men must be to the hound. This idea would give her amusement much later, but for now it simply gave her a disgusted view of man. The pain was relentless until finally Darcy stiffened and cried out, his breath held. After a few moments, he rolled off of her and sat up. She felt the bed lighten as he stood. Elizabeth's eyes stayed clamped shut as she tried to forget what had just happened. Then she heard the door open and close, and he was gone.

Darcy had anticipated this night for a long time, having the pleasure of his own wife to take as he desired and needed, but he did not anticipate feeling that something was wanting. Of course he had heard men speak of the simplicity of going to a brothel compared to their wives. A courtesan asked for nothing but payment, but a wife would expect favours in return for her own. What he did not expect was to feel the emptiness that he now experienced. As soon as he had closed the door he heard her weeping. Elizabeth had held her crying in while he was in the room, but he could tell that this was traumatic for her and that he had hurt her most decidedly. Her cries increased, and he almost went back in to check on her, but stopped himself as he placed his hand on the door handle; she would not want him. It was best for her maid to take care of her. He stood there a few moments longer listening to see that she recovered. Elizabeth continued her sobbing for several more minutes, then he heard another woman's voice, so he left for his room to give her privacy.

Sitting by the fire, he considered the strange dichotomy of lovemaking that left him confused. *Elizabeth's body felt incredible; she was most definitely a maiden, unblemished, and her body's grip stimulated me beyond imagining. How can a man's intense pleasure, to the point of distraction, cause so much hurt and despair for the woman?* Darcy had tried to be gentle, only touching when necessary, but soon got carried away, unable to hold back. He had heard of females enjoying the attentions of men, mistresses who fall in love with the men who hire them for pleasure, but could it all be an act, all part of the titillation she offers? And could it be true that gently born ladies should not experience passion as a man does? And if this were the case, was her response normal and to be expected from now on, or would she become more accustomed to his visits with time? Unless she had been exaggerating, the satisfaction of his libidinous desires came at the high price of her unaffected pain and agony on this night. But even knowing this, if he were aroused again, he would return and do it all over again, just for his own satisfaction. However, somewhere in his breast, he felt this would be unsuitable. Yes, she belonged to him as his wife, and yes, he deserved her offerings, but surely he could wait a little longer until she came around. He was no beast who responded without thought to physical cravings, and he took pride in his self-control. Darcy would give her time to recover physically and become better acquainted with him as she had requested. But after that, she must make herself available.

Chapter Nine

When a woman is talking to you, listen to what she says with her eyes.
Victor Hugo

Elizabeth awoke to the stirring of the fire occasioned by her maid adding some logs to the hearth. She had slept little, yet again, after her traumatic evening on the first night of her already bleak marriage. With little sleep, many tears and a fair amount of wine, she felt poorly and uninspired to arise for the day. Elizabeth watched without moving as Laura quietly replaced the poker to the rack. She could not motivate herself to get up, so she lay there despondently reflecting upon the previous night's events.

Emotions warred within her, each trying to take dominance over the others: shame for her lack of fortitude in such a common-place event, for all women who married had undergone the same ordeal; sorrow for her former life to which she could never return; despair for her loss of hope in ever being loved as she had so longed; and fear for their next encounter. *How can I ever look him in the eye? He has managed to single-handedly knock all of the whimsical impertinence off my face.* Elizabeth kept her eyes closed hoping her maid would not notice that she had awakened.

Laura finished her task that was usually reserved for the housemaid, and departed into the dressing room, allowing her mistress to continue to sleep in privacy.

On the previous night the maid had been on alert for the mistress to summon her after Mr. Darcy's departure. She could tell that Mrs. Darcy was frightened about the events to come, no matter how secure she tried to appear. As soon as she had heard the bell, she hastened to the mistress's chamber. She was disheartened to see the look of anguish on Mrs. Darcy's countenance. Laura rushed over to her mistress who was kneeling on the floor by the bell pull, concerned about her distress. "Mrs. Darcy, are you well? Let me get you something to drink. Wine, may I get you some?"

Elizabeth leaned into this woman who in so short a time had become her sole source of comfort. Laura was about ten years Elizabeth's senior and quite lovely. She had a compassionate countenance about her that reminded her of Jane, and Elizabeth felt that she could become a loyal servant if not confidante. Due to the difference in circumstances, they could never become close companions, but they could establish a relationship built on mutual respect. Whatever the future felicity between the two might bring, on this night Elizabeth needed a friend. She did not immediately respond to her maid's questions as she allowed the woman to embrace her, providing soothing words of comfort. Elizabeth could not betray her vows to her new husband so quickly into their marriage by dishonouring him with expressions of her dismay concerning the momentous event that had just taken place, the event that stripped her of her innocence. Elizabeth must make certain that the woman before her would only consider Elizabeth to be experiencing the physical pains that losing one's chastity would inflict.

"Forgive me for my weaknesses. I am well." She continued to lean into the maid. "Perhaps a little wine."

"Of course, ma'am." Laura departed to poor a glass and handing it to her said, "I have some wet cloths to clean you up a bit. Allow me to get them for you." Elizabeth then looked down to where the maid's eyes had veered and saw that she had blood on her gown. She could not disguise her look of horror.

Elizabeth stood and hobbled to the dressing room, "No, I will come in there." As Elizabeth stood, she glanced to the bed where the soft glow of the single candle illuminated where she had lain. In dismay, she saw the evidence of Mr. Darcy's visit; blood stained the sheets as if she had begun her courses during the night. She could no longer wonder at the physical discomfort as she bore witness to the evidence of her affliction. Her face turned crimson when she glanced to the woman before her.

"Mrs. Darcy, you are now a married woman. The consummation of your marriage is perhaps a burdensome undertaking, but you have no need to feel shame or embarrassment with me. I am here to help you to recover. It is not just my duty, but also my pleasure. Please allow me to help you without feeling unease."

"You must think me a silly creature," Elizabeth said with an unsuccessful lightness, then continued in earnest, "I thank you for your solicitude." Elizabeth slowly followed her maid into the dressing room. "You remind me of my sister, Jane. You have her kind eyes." Laura looked to her with a small smile and nod. No other words were spoken while the maid helped wash away the evidence of her former virginity that Mr. Darcy had valued so highly. After cleansing Mrs. Darcy, Laura stripped the bed of the sheets. A replacement set was waiting in the dressing room. Laura performed the task quickly and efficiently, for her usual duties included that of a housemaid. As an intelligent, educated woman, Laura was being groomed to one day follow in the housekeeper's footsteps. As such, she had been given a variety of duties that would train her to supervise all aspects of managing a household, including lady's maid.

About an hour after Laura had been summoned, she turned to leave Mrs. Darcy to her own ruminations. "Mrs. Darcy, if you have want of anything during the night, you need only ring the bell." At that she left. After hearing nothing from her mistress the following morning, she attended the room, trying hard not to wake Elizabeth, who had been up most of the night, unable to sleep after her emotional and physical trauma.

Without consent, Elizabeth's mind kept replaying the scene. She felt like she could never face the man again. The mortifying truth, however, was that she would have to face him each day of her life, and that he would likely repeat the heinous act before she could recover from this one. Elizabeth was not fashioned to give in to despondency, but she had rarely, if ever, felt this degree of hopelessness – to be married to a man whom she could not respect, giving him her body in a most humiliating manner – it was too much. She attempted sleep without success and finally fell into a fitful slumber after having heard a distant clock strike four.

Two nights of fretful sleep had given her a languor that kept her fixed to her bed. She could not think of one reason to rise except for nature's call, which would not be silenced, so she sat up and stumbled her way to the dressing room. Laura offered assistance, but Elizabeth expressed that she only wished to return to the bed. "I will have some water brought up for a bath when you feel that you are ready to start the day. I can have a tray brought to your room as well."

"Perhaps later."

DARCY HAD ARISEN AT HIS USUAL TIME, which was early for being in town, and entered the small dining room where they had eaten the evening before, and where he usually broke his fast. He did not expect his new wife to be there so early; he had informed her where breakfast would be served and thought that she would eventually make her way down. After drinking some coffee and reading the paper, he began to wonder if she would come down at all. He suspected she was an early riser based on their initial encounter, but perhaps he had judged incorrectly. Darcy was hungry but did not want to begin his meal without her, so he sent a footman to enquire as to when Mrs. Darcy might make a showing. The footman returned to inform him that his wife was still asleep and likely not to make it down for breakfast, so he ate alone and then went to his study to continue sifting through his pile of correspondence and invitations.

When she did not appear for a light luncheon, Darcy had a message delivered to her to ensure she would make a showing for tea in the afternoon. Darcy could not know that his request would cause such anxiety for his wife.

She had received the summons while she sat at her writing desk in her room. Elizabeth felt unequal to facing Mr. Darcy and cowardly kept to her own chamber, hoping he would not venture there. She had eaten not a thing since waking up despite her maid bringing in trays for breakfast and luncheon. The only thing she could accomplish was a bath in which she lingered until the water became tepid. She had felt a need to soak and clean. How does one go from feeling shame when confronted with physical attentions from a gentleman to acceptance after a thirty-minute marriage service and a name change? No, it would take her time to get past her feelings of defilement, no matter their lack of justification.

When it was time for tea, Laura approached her yet again as Elizabeth gazed into the fireplace. "Ma'am, I thought you might want to know that 'tis tea time, and as you are aware, the master requested your attendance. May I help you prepare?"

After a cursory look of panic, Elizabeth quickly took control of her expression and smiled at her maid's continued kindness. "Can you wait a moment?" The maid nodded and Elizabeth sat at her desk and penned a short note informing Mr. Darcy of her inability to attend him at tea, but that she would join him for dinner. She handed the note to Laura who was not privy to its contents. "I will not be going down to tea but will try to make dinner. Can you come to assist me thirty minutes before it is time to go down?"

Laura looked somewhat flustered but knew her place. The servants of Darcy House and Pemberley were not accustomed to their master being denied. "Yes, ma'am," she said as she curtseyed and departed.

Darcy was a little peeved at Elizabeth's obvious avoidance of him, but was just as content to spend the day alone catching up on letters of business and pleasure. He went through the stack of invitations and requests that he had only perused the day before. Far too many so-called friends of the *ton* were anxious to meet the new Mrs. Darcy. He moaned inwardly by the weight of it all. Of course they would have to forgo the vast majority of the invitations, if not all, until Elizabeth obtained a new wardrobe. He would have to schedule time in the next few days to get her to a modiste capable of completing a large number of gowns in a short amount of time. She would also need outerwear that could sustain her through the cold Derbyshire winter. Darcy reflected upon the fortunate wisdom of remaining in town for the next month, for it would take no less time to complete the momentous undertaking.

AT SEVEN-THIRTY, Darcy again knocked on his wife's door prepared to take her down to dinner. She opened the physical barrier that lay between them, looking rather flustered, and as he offered her his arm, she paused a split moment before lightly taking hold. She flushed scarlet, remembering her mortification the last time she had been in his presence.

Elizabeth had been talking herself into accepting her role and bringing her natural confidence with her, but all was for naught when she heard the gentle rap on the door. She reluctantly joined him in walking to the dining room where they had taken their meal the night before. She had eaten scarcely a bite of food in the past two days and although weakened by lack of nourishment could not bring herself to consume any part of the feast before her.

Elizabeth had not had the pleasure of enjoying the exercise to which her body was accustomed, and between that and her aversion to her circumstances, she could not move herself to eat. Darcy again noticed her lack of zeal at the table and questioned her about it. "I simply find that I have no appetite. You must know that I usually exercise in the countryside, and since I have not had that pleasure in more than a week's time, I simply am not hungry. I woke up late and have since taken my meals late, so I find that I am unable to eat dinner." She sighed and then continued, "Please, sir, at least give me the freedom to know when I am hungry."

He stared at her for a few moments as she pushed her food around, then continued eating. If she chose to be stubborn, he would let her reap the consequences on her own.

Silence reigned throughout the meal. Elizabeth could not bring herself to look at her husband, and he was content to sit in peace. But then, at the conclusion of the meal, he decided to discuss with her his plans for the week. "Elizabeth, we were unable, as you know, to get in the tour of the house today. I assume you would like to become familiar with your new home." He paused, awaiting a response. When she realised he was expecting one, she nodded. "Very good, perhaps tomorrow then." When Elizabeth indicated that she would indeed enjoy the prospect, he continued on. "That will not take so very long, as will your tour of Pemberley, so I have scheduled an appointment for you to meet with the modiste in the afternoon in order to begin the task of procuring a new wardrobe."

Elizabeth looked directly at him in confusion. "A new wardrobe, sir?"

Darcy assumed that she would enjoy the endeavour and reiterated his plans with upturned lips knowing at least in this he could please her. He was shocked to hear otherwise.

"I need no new wardrobe, Mr. Darcy. To be sure, two to three gowns for entertainments would suffice, but other than that, I am perfectly content with the wardrobe I brought with me." Elizabeth was offended that he would think that she endeavoured to use his wealth to gain new clothes and comforts. She wanted nothing from him but solace. And she did not want to feel beholden to him in any way, as might a kept woman.

Darcy could not understand her meaning, for it was beyond him to consider a woman who would not desire more clothing, especially when the coffers seemed limitless. "Perhaps, I was unclear. Tomorrow, I have scheduled an appointment with the modiste for you to be fitted for new clothes. You no longer need to limit yourself to the clothes that you wore at Longbourn. Moreover, you need new gowns in order to attend the numerous gatherings that will take place within the next six months, over the festive season and also the Spring Season in London. Not only that, but you need outerwear for the winter in Derbyshire. You will find it to be much colder at Pemberley than what you are accustomed to since Pemberley is situated in the area of the Peaks."

"Like I said, I agree that a few new gowns would be beneficial and perhaps outerwear; however, I do not desire a complete change in my wardrobe. I am perfectly content with the gowns I currently own."

"You cannot continue to wear the same clothing that you did as Miss Bennet. You are Mrs. Darcy now, and *Mrs. Darcy* does not wear dresses two years out of fashion." Her eyes flashed in anger at him. "I do not understand the problem. Surely you see the need for new gowns."

"I do not. I like my current clothes, and I will continue to wear them. I did not marry you so I could go on a shopping expedition," Elizabeth said with conviction.

"Are you always this contrary? Of all things…."

"No, I am not. I simply like the dresses I wear, which is why I wear them, and no matter how much you desire it, I will not be turned into some fashionable paragon who adorns your arm." She looked away affronted.

"I in no way need a wife who hangs on my arm." *I get enough of that with Miss Bingley and the rest of her sort.* "What I need is a wife who is cognisant of her new station in life and dresses the part."

"Like an actress in a performance."

"We are all of us on stage, Elizabeth. You can learn the lines and play the role intended for you, or you can flirt with chaos and bring condescension upon your name. But since your name is now Darcy, I will not have you dressing like a country hoyden. You will purchase new clothes, and that is that," Darcy ended with a petulant huff.

Elizabeth, although offended greatly at his remarks, chose to remain silent, slightly amused, as his countenance betrayed that of a spoilt child. Her best course of action would be inaction. She would have time enough to prudently reflect upon his request and her own reaction.

Darcy stood, and a footman immediately moved behind the chair of Mrs. Darcy, ready to assist her when she followed suit. "Elizabeth, I would like for you to play for me again."

This simple request on this night brought panic to Elizabeth's mind. *Please, God, don't let this be a replay of yesterday!*

Darcy noticed her brief look of discomposure and could not fathom the reason. He thought she enjoyed performing and would welcome the diversion. "Unless you would rather not?"

"I was just hoping.... That is to say... Of course, I will play. Perhaps something more lively today."

"You may choose as you like."

They walked down the passageway to the music room and Elizabeth immediately went to the pianoforte and began a lively song that she hoped would raise her spirits. However, after about half an hour, she attempted without success to hold back a yawn.

"You are tired? I thought you had slept most of the day."

"Indeed, I have had very little sleep." He studied her while she looked down to the instrument and began playing again.

"Since you are tired, why don't we retire?" A look of alarm overtook her countenance that did not go unnoticed by her husband. "You need to rest and I have a book I have been meaning to return to." She gazed his way, trying to determine if he were communicating that he would not be visiting her on this night. He did in fact realise her discomfort, and the likely catalyst, and meant to calm her fears. Darcy did not wish to cause her agitation; on the contrary, he wished to have a wife who welcomed him into her bed. He knew she needed a little time and was willing to give it to her. He always considered himself a gentleman, no matter the reception. Darcy also apprehended that a wife who did not fear him would welcome him readily enough. There would be more awkwardness for Elizabeth eventually, but for now, he could wait.

ELIZABETH SLEPT BETTER THAT NIGHT, mostly out of sheer exhaustion. She had eaten very little. Her body told her that she needed food, but every time she took a bite, nausea precipitated by her distress would overcome her. Again, she slept in, and again she missed breakfast. Her lady's maid began to feel some concern for her, knowing that she was not eating throughout the day and hoping that perhaps she had eaten a good dinner.

The thought of beginning a new day disheartened Elizabeth, but she did look forward to the tour of the house that Mr. Darcy had promised. She requested tea from Laura who suggested she take a muffin as well, which Elizabeth declined.

Elizabeth chose a simple morning dress and sent word to her husband that she could begin a tour at his convenience.

Fifteen minutes later, she heard a knock from the sitting room. Elizabeth opened the door to Mr. Darcy's expressionless visage. She curtseyed and said, "Good morning, sir." He bowed in return.

"I hope you have been able to catch up on some rest. I assumed that you would keep country hours, but I see that you have already taken on London habits." Although said in jest, his wife took it as criticism.

"I prefer early mornings, especially when coupled with a morning walk, but I find little to motivate me while in town."

"Would you prefer an early morning walk then?" Again, Elizabeth thought he was making fun of her country ways, provoking her.

"The only thing I prefer over walking is running." She waited to see his reaction to the news. It was true that she enjoyed the thrill of running down a country lane, but she would never dream of doing so in London. But he did not know that, and she awaited his rejoinder with calculated mirth.

He cocked an eyebrow. "Indeed," was all the response she could invoke.

Overcoming her disappointment, she smiled and said, "I believe you wished to take me on a tour of your home. I await your pleasure." They started with the shared sitting room. Elizabeth had not ventured anywhere that would bring her closer to Mr. Darcy's own room, so although her chamber was adjacent, she had remained ignorant to its contents. As they entered, she noticed a door on the far side, which she presumed opened to Mr. Darcy's own bedroom. After confirming her supposition, he mentioned that he had rarely spent time in this room since his parents died, only enjoying its comforts when his sister was in residence. Their shared sitting room had a door into the hallway from whence the tour began in earnest.

Elizabeth's heart was cheered at her surroundings. The home was finely adorned, but comfortable. The tour took longer than Elizabeth anticipated, for the home was larger than she had originally thought. Darcy made it a point to give small histories of the artefacts and collections that arrayed the rooms. She had to admit that she was impressed by his comprehensive knowledge of his own home and that he was skilled at communicating this knowledge in an entertaining and thoughtful manner. Elizabeth's inquisitive nature took over as she questioned him about what she saw, thus demonstrating a true enthusiasm rather than an ostentatious show of interest. When explaining where his family had acquired a vase, she sought all the particulars: Who had purchased it? Was it gifted? At what time period was it acquired? What was the style? Did he have any others from the same collection?

Darcy was pleasantly surprised by her curiosity, for he had given the same tour on several occasions to many friends and acquaintances, and never had anyone shown such interest. He looked at her puzzled.

"Sir, you have a strange look upon your face, and I cannot make it out."

"Do you always ask so many questions?"

"If you would rather I not, I can always take your lead and be taciturn and reticent."

169

He was about to say that he would not have her change on his behalf, but was that not exactly what he *was* hoping for? Rather, Darcy suggested they move on to the next room, which happened to be the library, and in the case of his London home, also his study. She entered, delight written all over her countenance. Elizabeth walked around the room running her finger along the shelves as she slowly perused their contents. Suddenly she turned to him and exclaimed with true joy, "How marvellous!" Darcy could not help but smile, the first genuine smile – that was not at her expense – she had ever seen on his handsome face. Slightly unnerved by the prospect, she looked away, back to the selection of books. "You must spend all of your time reading! How could you not with such temptation before you?"

What he found most tempting at that moment was not the supply of books. To hide his wayward thoughts, he put on a stern visage that left Elizabeth in confusion.

He truly is an enigma. She shrugged her shoulders and began searching for her first selection. She mused that a person could endure a great deal in order to have access to *this* library.

"If you enjoy this room, you will be pleased to know that the library at Pemberley is no less than four times as large." Elizabeth turned around to him, mouth agape, then realising her faux pas, quickly closed it and gave a slight blush along with a raised brow.

"Then I look forward to experiencing such a spectacle."

"We have seen most of the house and can finish on another day, if you would like to take time in here." Darcy was truly pleased at her genuine delight upon experiencing his favourite room of the house. Although also his study, where he must perform business, in general he found the room to be a haven of sorts.

"I would like that very well."

"Then I will leave you to it. We will depart for your appointment at the modiste in an hour."

"You are coming with me then?" She could not imagine he would have any desire in joining her shopping. *He must want to make certain I buy appropriate clothes for my new station in life. I wonder if he will always be so troublesome.*

"Yes, I plan on joining you this time. The modiste will need to be informed of my expectations and your needs for the upcoming seasons."

"Will you also be picking out the fabric and cut of the gowns?" Elizabeth asked with a challenge to her voice.

He had planned that very thing, but her asking him in that saucy manner made his plans seem an absurdity, even to his own mind. So, instead of replying in the affirmative, he only said that he would be happy to assist in choosing the most becoming colours for her complexion.

Before he left the room to give her some privacy, Elizabeth asked, "You said this is also your study?" He nodded. "Then please, do not let my being here keep you from your own pleasure. You will not disturb me in the least if you choose to stay and see to your own responsibilities."

"Perhaps later." Staying in the same room with a woman, who by all rights and privileges was his for the taking, while she admired his domain with sincere transport, was too much for a man determined to give her time before enjoying her again. "I will see you before we depart."

"ELIZABETH, you must have at least seven winter gowns for use at Pemberley and another ten for spring that would be appropriate for social events and also enough day dresses to get by until we are able to return to purchase more; not to mention nightwear and undergarments." This brought a deep blush to her cheeks, but Darcy continued on. "You also will need outerwear for the frigid Derbyshire winter, along with shoes, bonnets and gloves. You must be reasonable!" He had become increasingly frustrated at Elizabeth's attempts at thwarting the purchase of her trousseau. She refused to see reason.

"I am not in need of so many dresses. Truly! I am perfectly content with what I already have. I will own that having something new to wear to balls or the theatre would be of benefit, but I need no day dresses. I prefer a simple style, without all the embellishments that adorn the ladies of the fashionable set. I will feel like a peacock!"

The seamstress looked on the couple that had excused themselves to the other side of the room for a private conference. She found amusement in the irony of what she witnessed. Never in all of her years had she experienced a customer who was arguing with her husband that she needed *fewer* clothes, for it had always and often been the opposite. She noticed an exasperated Mr. Darcy calling her over, so she joined them. "Madame Alexandra, I apologise for our delay, but I believe we are ready to begin again."

At the end of the long afternoon, they had picked out Darcy's requisite number of gowns, but at Elizabeth's unwavering insistence, with limited ornamentation. However, Darcy was able to convince her to purchase some gowns of his own choosing, one in particular that would be daring in the drop of the décolletage and stunning in colour. The dress would be made from a midnight blue silk that made her skin look like cream and her eyes like emeralds. Elizabeth blushed at the thought of wearing such a dress and blushed anew at the implication behind Mr. Darcy's desire for her to wear it.

The visit to the modiste took much longer than either had planned, so the remainder of her purchases would have to wait for another day. They arrived at Darcy House, each ready for some respite before dinner. The remainder of the evening was similar to the one before, with a meal followed by Elizabeth's exhibition upon the pianoforte. There was very little conversation throughout the evening as each had exceeded his and her own fill of the other over the course of the afternoon. In many ways they had to agree to disagree, but in the end, it was Darcy who had the upper hand, for Elizabeth no longer had the freedoms that she had enjoyed as a Bennet, freedom to choose her own clothes, walk when and where she pleased, eat as much or as little as she wished; no, she was bound to someone who had not her benefit at heart but his own selfish needs. Elizabeth bristled at the idea that despite her opposition, in the end Darcy would have her become a wife of his own choosing.

Elizabeth was becoming accustomed to taking tea in the morning within the confines of her room. Her hunger was real, but her appetite continued to be in opposition to her needs. Elizabeth was by nature a social creature, so she had begun taking this opportunity to get to know her temporary maid. She had learnt of the woman's struggles and successes and how Mr. Darcy's estate had fit into her life. Elizabeth learnt that Laura had been married at the age of seventeen and lost her husband nearly five years later. She had lived in Lambton, the same town in which her aunt Gardiner had grown. Elizabeth was surprised to learn that her maid had known her aunt as girls, attending school and playing in the fields together.

It occurred to Elizabeth how unfair life could be, that every individual exists at the mercy of chance. Her aunt had grown into a woman of wealth and means by the benefit of her birth and through her marriage to a resourceful man, while this woman was now reduced to being a servant, due to the untimely death of her husband whom she also had loved. Elizabeth considered her own situation and how she had arrived there by no design of her own, or Mr. Darcy's for that matter. She felt remorseful, after hearing her maid's tale, for all of her own petulant thoughts and behaviours. She had spent the previous day complaining about having to buy so many gowns, and this woman was reduced to having to dress her in them. Elizabeth promised herself to think more gratefully. She now lived in an elegant home, all of her needs met and a library full of books. Elizabeth would dwell on her many blessings! It was a good thing that she had recovered some of her inherently cheerful nature, for the next month would bring trials to test even the most sanguine of creatures.

BINGLEY ARRIVED IN LONDON AS SCHEDULED. He brought Colonel Fitzwilliam with him, thus saving him from having to ride in the open air again in the late fall chill. The two were only acquainted by association with Darcy, but both were of an amiable disposition and got along admirably. Bingley had planned his trip to town in his usual manner, giving no more than three days' notice and leaving his sisters behind, as he was planning on returning after his current affairs were in order. He had decided to make a formal request to secure Miss Bennet as his own. Coming to London would allow him to retrieve the ring that his father had given his mother two years before her early demise. Bingley reflected upon that ring and its significance to his parents' relationship at the time. His father admired and cherished his mother, who although somewhat spoilt by the man, was also in love with him. The stone was a sapphire, the colour of the sky on a summer day, and would nicely complement Jane's own reflective, azure eyes.

He had been giddy with delight as he considered his plans and was unable to contain his enthusiasm with any degree of success. Colonel Fitzwilliam patiently listened to Bingley's exclamations of joy and transport the distance from Netherfield to Tromwell House, where Colonel Fitzwilliam would be staying for the following week. The colonel had noticed the beautiful sister of Mrs. Darcy, for how could any man with eyes not? She had a sweet disposition and a demure affect that held no symptoms of contrivance. If Bingley could afford such a match, he would be fortunate to take the opportunity.

Darcy, knowing that Bingley was to arrive in London, and suspecting his mission, was greatly disturbed by the prospect of his friend's becoming ensnared by the lovely Miss Bennet. He had heard many times the effusions of Mrs. Bennet and how she rejoiced in her success in a connection to, not one, but two rich men. Even if Miss Bennet had any feelings for his friend, could Darcy in good conscience not warn Bingley away from being trapped in a life attached to such a vulgar family? Darcy had the distance and temperament to ward off the interference of such a mother-in-law, but Bingley did not. He would be vulnerable to her schemes and forced to sponsor all of the younger sisters in London society. Darcy could not bear to think of such a future for his amiable and unguarded friend.

Before leaving Netherfield, Darcy had conspired with Bingley's sisters in a plan to extract him from Miss Bennet's grasp. The sisters were to come to town one day after Bingley's removal with the use of Darcy's own equipage. He would send it to them, so that they, along with Mr. Hurst, could travel in comfort without having to hire public transportation. The house would be closed for the winter and the service help discharged from their duties, giving references and payment through the end of December to the unfortunate employees losing their positions. This, Darcy insisted upon, despite the disinclination of Miss Bingley. Darcy would then, at leisure in town, meet with Bingley warning him of all of the arguments and grounds for severing his relationship with Miss Bennet and her unsuitable family.

The day after their shared shopping excursion, Darcy planned to make calls. He had informed his wife the evening before that he would not be home the majority of the day. As his absence meant her respite, she did not inquire as to his destination nor ask when he might return. Instead she spent the morning enjoying the delights to be found in his library before her errands in the afternoon.

Darcy arrived at Bingley's home on Grosvenor Street at the appropriate calling time. To say that his friend was surprised regarding his visit would be minimising the effect. Bingley had always supposed that a man newly married would have other endeavours as occupation. The reason for his unaccountable call would soon be revealed.

During the course of the two-hour visit, Darcy delineated the many obvious and obscure reasons to break his attachment with Miss Bennet, not the least of which was his suspicion that his new sister held no true affection for him, and as Bingley was of a modest inclination and dependent in most all circumstances upon the judgement of his friend, he capitulated and soon gave up all hope of a life with Miss Bennet. The effect on Bingley was great; his despondency after the visit was keenly felt. Because his sisters had closed the home, he had no alternative but to trust the revered judgement of his best friend, nay, the one whom he depended upon most in the world. This would bring an overwhelming melancholy over Darcy's friend that would affect his disposition more than Darcy could have foretold, for Darcy had never known what it meant to love as Bingley had.

With a heavy heart, yet pleased with his success, Darcy left Grosvenor Street and then headed to Tromwell House. He had intended on visiting his sister upon first returning to London, but had been distracted by Elizabeth's odd schedule. When he arrived, he found his sister to be in a state of agitation, for Fitzwilliam had arrived two days previously, and she had not yet had a word from her brother himself. She had gleaned all of the details that she could manage from her cousin regarding the wedding and the new Mrs. Darcy, and she longed to speak with her brother to discern his capacity to endure such a horrid affair.

When Darcy was announced, Georgiana quickly went to the sitting room, anxious to see her dear brother. When she entered, Georgiana rushed to his side where Darcy stood to embrace her. "Brother, I have been so worried for you! James said that you were well, but I have been so uneasy and eager to see you for myself. I thought you might come yesterday. What has kept you?"

"Georgiana, all the questions! As James said, I am well. I have no battle scars of which to brag as he has. I have been tied up at home, not able to get away until today. But I promise you, I am sound." He then asked how she fared.

"I am well, except for worrying about you. Tell me all." She wondered how his new wife had succeeded in keeping him from his own family these three days.

"I am married, not in prison, love. I have nothing of which to complain." He sat down and motioned for his sister to do the same. "I was surprised when Fitzwilliam arrived at the ball at Netherfield. I had supposed none of my family would be in attendance."

"Oh, but I would have come, if only to provide help, had I been allowed."

"Yes, I know, but it was best that you not attend." Darcy thought about Wickham's unexpected presence in Meryton and was relieved he had made the decision to keep her away. He would not burden her with Elizabeth's conceivable alliance with the scoundrel. At least in that capacity he had not failed his sister.

"Her family is that bad? James only said that they were a lively bunch, but that was enough to make me concerned for your spirits. I know that you find light-hearted groups wearisome."

"That I do, but I can assure you, there are no blemishes to show for the tedious company. We must all of us learn patience when exposed to inferior society."

Darcy's aunt and uncle entered during the visit and assured him that although they could in no way condone his marriage, that they would always welcome him into their home. "When will we have the satisfaction of meeting Mrs. Darcy? Are you still thinking of making the introductions at Christmas?" questioned his aunt.

"Christmas seems as good a time as any. The whole family will be there, so we can take care of everyone at once. Tell me, is Lady Catherine to be in attendance?"

"No, she is to remain in Kent. You know she despises London in winter."

"Well, that is good. I am afraid that she has already met Elizabeth, and from what I gather, the ensuing experience was rather unpleasant for both ladies. I will not have my relations making her feel unwelcome." He looked pointedly at his mother's brother. "She is now my wife, and I must insist on your showing her the respect due that position."

After silence from his uncle, his aunt spoke for them all. "Of course, dear. We understand."

Darcy asked his aunt where his cousin might be. "James is at some meeting taking place at the War Office. He was hoping to catch you, but does not want to come to Darcy House. I will let him know you inquired after him. We don't know how busy he will be in the upcoming weeks since he will only be staying on here for a few more days. He may very well be unavailable for much of the month."

"Then I am grateful I was able to see him in Hertfordshire."

The visit continued on as they enjoyed topics of import and insignificance until it was time for Darcy to leave, promising that he would come often, to the satisfaction of his sister, for her concerns were in no way mollified by the visit, and she hoped to continue to provide him with solace despite not being in residence with him.

WHILE DARCY WAS PAYING CALLS, Elizabeth went shopping to pick out the requisite shoes, gloves, stockings and other feminine accoutrements. She was content in having the opportunity to shop without the tedious company of her husband, who felt it his duty to regulate all of the purchases pertaining to her trousseau. She blushed at the thought of his choosing her undergarments and so was relieved when he informed her of his plans and her mission.

Her temporary maid, Laura, joined her, as well as two footmen who monitored their coming and going from a distance. With the revelation of Laura's having once been a friend of Elizabeth's aunt Gardiner, Elizabeth felt a camaraderie with her not often known between the classes. They enjoyed the afternoon that was declared a success by Elizabeth.

Laura, too, felt a freedom that she had not enjoyed in years. Although being a servant was not conscripted, she had few options available to her as a widow. Her master had been kind in making a position available to her under the circumstances of her husband's demise; however, the burden of accommodating the likes of Miss Bingley and other privileged women of society, who had visited Pemberley and Darcy House through the years, grieved her on more than one occasion. The new Mrs. Darcy was fresh, kind and, when not overcome with the enormity of her new life, vivacious.

"Laura, perhaps on one of my visits to my aunt's home, you could join me and renew your friendship. Would you like that?" Laura's eyes went big as she searched around her to see that they were not overheard. "What is amiss, Laura? Surely I can share my aunt's company with a faithful servant."

"Madam, you are truly one of a kind. Mr. Darcy's friends, and perhaps Mr. Darcy himself, may not know what a treasure you are, but let it be known, that I see your true worth. I can tell that you have the love of your Maker in your heart." Elizabeth did not know what to make of her remarks, so just smiled and grabbed hold of her hand with a squeeze."

"You are too kind. And I am ready for a break! What do you say we return to the house for some rest?" A smile lit Laura's face as they climbed into the carriage.

THAT EVENING brought Elizabeth and Darcy together for the first time that day. He questioned her about her purchases wanting to know every particular. Elizabeth thought it strange that he would care so much about the minutia of her day, but finally concluded that he wanted to make certain that she was fulfilling his mandates to redesign her life. Elizabeth would play her part until his oppressive ways became unbearable; but until then, she would wear a smile and find amusement in the absurdity of it all.

After the meal concluded along with the accounting, Mr. Darcy proposed adjourning to the library instead of the music room. He had wanted to get back to his book where he might lose himself in its pages. Elizabeth readily agreed, but said she was still reading another tome that she had in her room. She excused herself and went upstairs to retrieve the volume. When she entered the library, Mr. Darcy was sitting behind his desk going through a few of the invitations that he had set aside. He thought this might be a good opportunity to review his plans with her for the upcoming month's activities.

"Elizabeth, please have a seat by the fire. You will find it more comfortable there." She did as she was told, but what Darcy did not anticipate was her taking off her slippers and nestling her feet under her dress in a relaxed manner. She did not notice his distraction as he imaged what her feet might look like.

He had moved on to remembering the feel of her legs when she interrupted his reverie. "Mr. Darcy, will you not be joining me? You look so serious there behind your desk. I begin to be afraid that you might be planning on reprimanding me," said she, brow raised in drollery, thus shaking him out of his distractions.

"Forgive me. We have received a few invitations that I thought to consider." Elizabeth watched him, distracted in wondering her role in the planning. "We will spend Christmas Day with my family here in town, the earl and countess, which I thought would be a good time to introduce you to the rest of my family. I spoke with them today, and they are planning on our attendance." He paused, "I know you might be uneasy with the prospect, but I can assure you that they will not treat you the way Lady Catherine did. She is not to be there, for she dislikes town in the winter, so you will be safe from her intrusions."

Diverted by his eagerness to predict her response to his family, she decided to calm his fears. "I look forward to making the acquaintance of your family. I found Colonel Fitzwilliam to be an amiable man, and I would be happy to be in his presence again. I anticipate finding the rest of his family just as cordial." Darcy hoped rather than knew that to be the likely outcome.

"There is also an invitation to a ball, and we are to be the honoured guests. This will take place on New Years Eve." At her smile he continued, "I plan to

176

accept, considering this might be a propitious way of introducing you to society. You will wear the ball gown that I picked out for you, the deep blue one."

"And how shall my hair be worn?" His puzzled expression led her to suppose that her little bit of mischief had missed its mark. "I am sorry; please continue."

"In accepting the invitation, I considered when your gowns would be completed. I also wanted to be certain that you would meet my family before exposing you to my other acquaintances. The ball is to be at Tromwell House; my family will be hosting the gathering, and they hope that we will use this opportunity to show society that I am fortunate in my marriage and that I did not marry a savage, as they are want to believe."

"Well then, I will make sure that I do not eat with my hands, for there may be some in attendance who would snigger at such a sight." He took in her jest.

"Are you laughing at me, Mrs. Darcy?"

"Oh, no. I could not laugh at someone with such insight and nobility. I bow to your better judgement on the social niceties of your peers. I will only speak when spoken to and will perform the dance with precision and finesse. You see, I have already learnt the art of social engagement from your fine example."

Darcy rolled his eyes while pursing his lips. *Will she ever learn to hold her tongue! That, my dear, is the true menace!*

She laughed lightly. "Truly, the look on your face...."

"Enough!"

She looked away in order to hide her countenance, which beheld equal parts mirth and vexation. "Don't mind me. I will quietly move on to my book." Elizabeth opened its pages and began to read where she had last left off earlier that morning within the privacy of her chamber. She wished that she could return there now, for her husband's company always left her annoyed and perplexed.

After about an hour, Elizabeth yawned with a gentle stretch, and closed her book. She stood and expressed her wish to retire to her room for the night. After Darcy looked fixedly at her, she became concerned that perhaps he was contemplating joining her later. Without realising it, the anxiety at such an idea played out upon her face clearly enough that Darcy was not left to wonder what her sentiments would be on the subject.

"Will you at any point be joining me for breakfast? I ask because if you do not desire my company first thing in the morning, I could save my staff and myself the trouble of preparing the breakfast room for the possibility of your gracing us with your presence."

Her eyebrows knit together. She was ashamed that she had not contemplated how her refusal to join Mr. Darcy for breakfast might affect other people. Elizabeth, always quick to admit her faults, apologised for her lack of consideration and expressed her desire to break her fast in her own room.

Darcy suspected she would convey that to be her wish. He did not mind either way, but as he preferred to have oversight within his home, he at least desired foreknowledge of her intent.

Elizabeth was walking through the door, then stopped and turned back to him. He had been watching her leave. "Mr. Darcy, as it has been several days since I have had the pleasure of walking, might I be able to take my exercise in the morning? I noticed that Hyde Park is nearby, and I am in much need of trees and sunshine." Darcy's initial fears were somewhat allayed when she continued, "I promise not to run, sir. I merely need a long, brisk walk." At his delay in answering, she continued on. "I cannot sit idly like other ladies; I will go mad. I beg of you, allow one of your footmen to join me; I will try not to overexert him," she finished this with an unconscious tilt of her head and a charming smile.

This last statement, said in earnest, amused Darcy. He was picturing in his mind Clark, his first footman, running behind Elizabeth as she marched onward around the Serpentine. Then he recalled the idea of such a walk to be uncouth and decided that he would be the one to join her, insuring she did nothing to bring censure upon herself. "What time would you like to leave? I assume you prefer an early morning walk, but you might want to wait until the sun warms the day."

"I prefer walking at dawn. Will that be acceptable?"

"Yes, I will make sure someone is waiting at the front door to escort you."

Chapter Ten

Humility is the foundation of all the other virtues hence, in the soul in which this virtue does not exist there cannot be any other virtue except in mere appearance.
Saint Augustine of Hippo

Elizabeth endured another night of tossing and turning and awakened about an hour before dawn. She did not want to call Laura so early, so Elizabeth had told her the night before about her plan to walk out and that she would take care of herself. She had dressed for walking without the aid of a servant her whole life and did not need to start now, especially when it would mean putting a burden upon her only friend in the house. The plan was for Laura to meet her after the conclusion of her walk to help her bathe and dress for the day. She would take breakfast after her return at the usual time.

After lingering a bit in bed, Elizabeth dawdled as she donned her clothes and outerwear. The days of no exercise and little to eat had left her weakened physically and emotionally. Elizabeth felt as though her mood, like the season, was becoming darker and darker. She needed sunshine and fresh air. As soon as she noticed the approaching dawn, Elizabeth left her room and headed towards the front door of the house. There with a footman was Mr. Darcy. Elizabeth approached, a little confused about her husband's presence but supposed he wanted to introduce her to the footman. "Good morning, Mr. Darcy. Is this my escort?" Elizabeth said as she glanced to the man in livery.

"Actually, I am to be your escort. Clark is here with my greatcoat and top hat. I was waiting for you to descend the stairs before I donned my outerwear."

Elizabeth attempted to hide the shadow that had come over her face. *Does he mean to ruin my walk?* "But sir, surely Clark here is capable of walking with me. He looks to have a strong constitution."

"I am sure he will be able to perform the task when his time comes. But for today, I am to be your guide." She took in a deep breath as she attempted to calm her irritation.

"Very well." It was either Mr. Darcy or no one, so she decided that today she would acquiesce; another day perhaps she would go alone. After putting on his greatcoat and hat, Mr. Darcy with his wife left through the front door and got a slap of cold air on their faces that put a large grin on Elizabeth's as she exhilarated in the chill of the morning. There was nothing like the cold to get her moving, so Elizabeth descended the steps to street level with small hops. Darcy walked down the length following her. "Come, sir, will you not keep up?"

"I will have no problem keeping up, I can assure you, madam." Her juvenile affect fascinated him. *Does she ever moderate herself?*

He offered her his arm and she laughed, continuing to move forward. He raised his brow and followed along. He was surprised that she in no way exaggerated her ability to traipse as she traversed the park. Her pace was quick and her smile infectious. At one point she actually laughed out loud when she saw Darcy struggle to maintain her speed. His legs were longer, but she the more adept. After about three miles out, he spoke for the first time, "Do you always walk this far? We have gone nearly three miles and still have yet to return."

"You cannot be having difficulty in keeping up?" That was the only answer he was to receive as he contemplated just how far they were to go. Fortunately, as it was cold and as London society tended to sleep until a more presentable hour, they encountered only those of the lower classes. When they finally reached the farthermost point of their walk, she stopped to look at the trees and the waning fall flowers as the sun shone down upon their faces. Elizabeth was in her element and her expression could not conceal her joy. "Is this not marvellous? What transport! What joy!" She laughed and spun around with her arms out. *Judge me if you dare, Mr. High and Mighty Darcy!*

She could no more contain her delight than she could walk on the cold water. After nearly two weeks of forced containment, she was incapable of remaining still. He stared at her mesmerised. She was certain he was looking to find fault, as his mien was impassive and placid. *How can anyone remain so dispassionate after a morning like this?* Elizabeth could not comprehend the unexcitable Mr. Darcy.

But what she mistook for stoicism was actually a man attempting with all his might to hold in the emotions that were warring within. He felt embarrassment and disgust at her plebeian behaviour, yet at the same time he was exhilarated and overwhelmed. The brilliancy of her eyes that were brightened by the exercise discomposed him, and he wanted nothing more than to take her animalistic inclinations to his bedroom and devour the untamed essence of her being. When he finally felt that he was able to speak with coherency he queried, "Have you finally reached the point from which you plan to return?"

"If I must." Although not her mission, Elizabeth did hope that perhaps the reality of the nature of her walks would encourage Mr. Darcy to leave the job of escort to someone else. It had quite the opposite effect, but Darcy could not acknowledge this to himself. Instead he displayed a look of indifference upon his face.

"Would you prefer taking my arm for the return? You must be tired." He assumed that she was likely hiding her fatigue.

"I thank you, no." And off she headed back towards whence they came.

They had been gone for well over two hours and Darcy could not even estimate how far they had gone. He felt fatigued and energised at the same time. "Will you come to breakfast today? I figured that since you were up and about, you might join me."

"No, I think not. You may eat at leisure without my intrusion." When he looked surprised, she smiled. "You have had enough of me for the day; I am certain. I thank you for the walk." So as they entered the house, Elizabeth went upstairs.

He almost followed behind but then caught himself. *She cannot know what she is doing to me, and I am certain she would not welcome my advances, especially in the light of day.* After a few moments he climbed the stairs behind her towards his own room to clean and dress for the day.

THEY WERE NOT TO SEE ONE ANOTHER until that evening at supper. Darcy had visited his sister again and had tea with his family, and then went to his club, Whites, in the afternoon. He was hoping that he would run into Bingley for he worried about his friend's acceptance of giving up Miss Bennet, but he only saw superficial acquaintances who chose to pry him for details of his wife and reasons for his marriage.

This wearied him, so after about an hour he stood to leave but then noticed Wexley, who had been sitting at a table with mutual friends. As Wexley watched on, one of his companions said, "Darcy, what brings you to Whites? I figured with your new wife, you would be engrossed in other pleasures than consorting with men. Tell me if the stories are true, for I have heard that she must offer you more than just a beautiful face to have taken you away from more suitable prospects." He glanced at the viscount, who after a brief nod to Darcy, had chosen to look to the other side of the room.

"You flatter me. Now if you will excuse me, I am reminded of a pressing engagement, for as you say, I do have a new bride." As soon as he left, the aggravation inside was given free rein. If he were to be married to the woman, at least he should take the liberties due him. This whole affair was insupportable to his sensibilities. He decided to go home and hopefully later enjoy the favours of his wife about which he had thought all day.

Upon first entering his home, Darcy went to his study, as was his custom, for upon his desk would lay his correspondence that needed immediate attention. On top of the small pile was a note of feminine script with "Mr. Darcy" written on top. He opened the short missive and read.

Dear Mr. Darcy,

I will be unable to join you for dinner this evening. I find that my day of shopping has left me fatigued and in need of quietude. My hope is that due to my refreshing walk this morning, I will find more sleep tonight than I have for the previous week. Please accept my apologies. I have informed the cook and Franklin who will send a tray up to my room should I become hungry.

ED

Blast! Darcy swore to himself. Her timing could not have been worse after the morning walk which had enticed him and the teasing of his peers at White's reminding him of not just his rights but his desires. *I can't go to her tonight. Not only would she not welcome me, but she may be truly ill after that heinous walk this morning.*

Not wanting to eat in the dining room alone, he too decided he would have a tray sent to his study. He picked a book to distract him from his present situation. He normally enjoyed quiet nights alone; indeed, he often preferred them. However, on this night he felt rather isolated. His cousin, and closest friend, was tied up with his life in the military, with the real possibility of being shipped off to the battlefield. He had unwittingly hurt his other dear friend by dashing his hopes for felicity in marriage to a woman who was unsuitable. His family had to keep their distance for at least the next month as he enlightened his wife to her new role. His other friends were jesting him with questions of his motivations for marrying. And his wife was closeted away in her room and had a wall of stone built around her that would not easily come down, if in fact he wanted it down. To his dismay, he would soon find this to be a long and lonely night.

ELIZABETH WOKE UP FEELING somewhat refreshed. She had begun the previous day with an invigorating walk; however, she had begun to decline as she shopped for the third day in a row. The tiresome task of fitting for dresses and standing all afternoon coupled with very little food and liquids, along with inadequate sleep, made her unequal to any exertion, including dressing for dinner, as she had been overcome by a headache. Her maid brought her tea, but could not induce her to eat, for Elizabeth felt dizzy and morose. She had penned the short note to her husband and hoped he would understand and not demand that she attend him anyway.

This morning, she decided that a walk might help in furthering her recovery as it often had at Longbourn, but she had not planned for a footman or Mr. Darcy to attend her. Elizabeth debated upon the best course of action knowing that should she go out alone, Mr. Darcy might be angry. She thought to wait until the household awoke, but was anxious to get started, so she donned her pelisse and gloves and headed downstairs. She was about to walk out of the front door, when Clark, the footman whom she met the day before, walked by. "Mrs. Darcy! Is Mr. Darcy coming down to join you? He had not informed me that he was, but if I need to get his greatcoat, I can be back in a trice."

Realising she was caught and unable to take her walk alone as she longed, she confessed that she had planned on walking out alone and was only to go a short distance. "Mr. Darcy would send me packing if I let you go out without an escort. If it would be acceptable to you, would you be willing to wait right here while I grab a coat for myself and inform Franklin of our plan to walk?" To his credit, he took only a moment to gather his outerwear and return with a smile.

They went in the same direction as the day before, but halfway to her previous destination, she began feeling lightheaded and sick to her stomach. Clark noticed her discomfort and made her sit down on a bench in the park. He continued to stand and offered to retrieve her something to drink. Elizabeth was indeed thirsty and would have sent him on his way if not for the risk in which she would be placing him with his employer for leaving her alone. Instead she made light, merry conversation with him, learning his history with the Darcys. Elizabeth did not feel well but thought that if she sat there long enough, she might begin to improve. After perhaps thirty minutes, she decided to try to make her way back to Darcy House. The morning cold was having a different effect upon her on this day than the one before, for during her rest she had begun to shiver. After standing, Elizabeth took the arm of her escort, for she truly felt ill.

"Mrs. Darcy, if you don't mind my saying so, you look very poorly. When we get back to the house, I will ask your maid to get you something warm to eat and drink. A good meal from cook can do wonders."

"You are considerate. I am happy to know that my husband's home has such proficient and valuable employees. I would imagine there are few homes that can boast such fine young men keeping things afloat." He smiled down at her. Elizabeth had a way of disarming most all people with her easy manners and engaging personality. No matter the class, Elizabeth treated all people with the same consideration and respect.

The walk home took about twice as long as the one out, and by the end, Elizabeth was ready to lie down and get some much-needed rest. While climbing the steps to the house, her pulse sped up. *What is wrong with me? I have never felt this way before.*

As they entered the foyer, Elizabeth was holding onto the footman. The butler approached them requesting if help was needed. Clark opened his mouth to reply when Elizabeth, not wanting to bring attention to herself, said, "All is well. If you could just have Mrs. Johnson send Laura to my room." Elizabeth's pallor was evident to all but herself. She headed to the stairs and began slowly climbing them towards her room.

When she reached the top, she held onto the railing to catch her breath, and it was at this time that Mr. Darcy came up. Seeing that she was struggling, he walked over and put his hand under her arm for support. Stunned, she looked up to him. "Excuse me, sir, but I am fine. If you will just allow me to go to my room."

He heard the coldness in her voice, but pressed on. "You don't look like you are fine. Truly, you look ill. Where have you been?"

"As you can see, I have gone out for a walk and have just returned."

"Alone?"

"No, Clark was kind enough to accompany me."

"That is his job, Elizabeth, not kindness."

She focused her eyes upon him, incensed at his tone of voice, but too tired to do anything about it. So instead, she said, "If you will excuse me, I have need of my maid and a bath." Elizabeth realised that she had no reason whatsoever to be affronted by Mr. Darcy, but in her weakened state, she was incapable of doing otherwise. His touch discomposed her, and not understanding her sentiments while feeling poorly, she hoped to extract him from her person. His close proximity unnerved her and she just wanted to be left alone. She stopped to apologise; however, Darcy had already moved on, as he too was chafed at her own tone of voice.

Elizabeth entered her room and was immediately accosted by Laura, who had been worried about her since the night before. "Mrs. Darcy, where have you been?" Now this was the same question she had just heard from her husband, not two minutes before, but to Elizabeth's ears now, it resounded with compassion rather than pique.

"Laura, I just need a warm bath and perhaps some tea. Could you have some water brought up?"

"Right away, ma'am, and perhaps something hot to eat as well. I bet the cook can prepare some eggs and toast."

Elizabeth crinkled her nose. "No, truly, I just want tea."

"Mrs. Darcy, I know it isn't my place, but I feel I must tell you that I think you are not eating nearly enough. Your body is getting weak, and I am afraid you will soon be ill if you aren't already." Elizabeth was unable to argue against Laura given the current evidence in support of the maid's claim.

"I will try, but you must understand, I truly feel sick when I take a bite."

Laura would have suspected that perhaps her new mistress had been experiencing the ill effects of a previously inopportune pregnancy; however, she was witness to the evidence on the wedding night. That, coupled with the obvious pain and distress of her mistress on that occasion, gave testament to her innocence in that regard. She was thankful for Mr. and Mrs. Darcy's sake that there was sufficient proof to demonstrate otherwise, for she knew the staff would be making sport with Mrs. Darcy's nausea. The common belief was that Mr. Darcy had been forced into marriage due to a weak moment when alone with the lovely Miss Bennet. Laura was relieved to know this was not the case, but today, she worried about what might be causing the young bride to experience such unfavourable physical symptoms. One thing she knew: if Mrs. Darcy did not begin to eat, she would surely continue to suffer.

DARCY CONSIDERED HIS DAY AHEAD in light of Elizabeth's illness. She was definitely unwell, no matter his previous thoughts that she might have been attempting to get out of an evening with him. She had walked too far the day before; he would have to put an end to that kind of behaviour, which was obviously not to her benefit.

He would go see his sister and hope to visit with Fitzwilliam, whom he had not yet seen. Then later, rather than go to the club, he would make his way to Angelo's for his own exercise. He had gone without the company of a woman for so long, how could he find himself so weak in managing the deprivation of just a few days? It was not that he had feelings for Elizabeth; her faults were glaring. But he had physical desires that he had managed by sheer willpower for years; however, now that the floodgates had been opened, the wave of overwhelming passion, in addition to Elizabeth's availability and allure, was diminishing his physical control.

As it happened, his cousin was at Tromwell House and would remain there for the next two days, then return to his regiment until Christmas. Darcy asked if Fitzwilliam would join him at Angelo's, as fencing was a common diversion for the two, thus giving them a chance to visit without the benefit of family nearby and also the chance to work out frustrations against a skilled adversary. Fitzwilliam was anxious to hear how life with Mrs. Darcy fared for his cousin and so promptly agreed to attend him.

On the carriage ride from Tromwell House to Angelo's, the two spoke concerning the previous few days. "So, Darcy, how have you been? I have

184

heard of your visits this past week. Georgiana has been beside herself worrying over you. I tried to calm her fears telling her what I knew about Mrs. Darcy, but she still sees the melancholy in your eyes. You know it would be easier for her if you tried to show a little cheer."

"You ask too much. Each day when I see her, I try to prepare myself to present an air of contentment, but Georgiana reads right through me. The truth is that I am despondent. I cannot help but feel that I have disappointed her and our parents, had they still been alive. I told myself that I married Elizabeth to fulfil my sense of honour, but have I not at the same time diminished the family name, including Pemberley, as well as Georgiana's chances for a good match? When I try to sleep at night, I go over and over in my mind all of the reasons why marriage to Elizabeth is a disgrace brought about by my own failings."

"You could not have prevented the marriage, Darcy, not with a clear conscience."

"Yes, but was it worth the price?" Darcy continued in contemplation.

"Perhaps rather than dwell on her deficiencies, you could consider her fine attributes. I daresay she is a pretty lass."

Darcy looked up at him as if trying to recall her visage. "I suppose in the common way."

"You jest, man!"

"There are many beautiful women in the world, Fitzwilliam. She has no accomplishments to speak of. And beauty means nothing when there is no pleasure to be had." Fitzwilliam's brows shot up.

"She was a maiden, I presume."

"Yes."

"Does she not welcome you?" Darcy stared at him; being a private man, he did not want to discuss the matter. "Give her time." After a few moments longer, Fitzwilliam continued, "You know that lively women make the best lovers."

"Really, Fitzwilliam! Don't be so coarse."

"I am just trying to encourage you," Fitzwilliam responded with a chuckle. "But seriously, this must also be hard on her. I suggest patience, and before long she might come to you instead."

"Are you the expert now?"

"It doesn't take an expert to realise that a maiden who marries needs some time to become accustomed to her duties. Men count down the seconds until the next encounter, but not women, at least not most women. They don't even know what is about to happen to them when they marry. And the wedding night for a maiden is nothing but painful embarrassment, even when she loves the man whom she has married. I have no doubt that Elizabeth will come to respect you; how could she not? And maybe one day she will even love you. Regardless, patience is the key with women."

"You have been reading novels."

"What if I have? It gives great insight into a woman's peculiar thinking. Romance is what they want, or in her case, perhaps not to be looked down upon."

"She knows that she comes from inferior birth. That is not my doing."

Fitzwilliam looked at him in wonder. "Darcy, what a ladies' man you are! Your wife must be enraptured by your charms by now!"

Darcy ignored his cousin's jest at his expense. "She will learn the ropes soon enough; being married to me raises her station considerably. I will just need to keep her from her family." At his cousin's surprised countenance, he continued, "They are barbarians, James. I know you saw it."

"But they are *her* family. You would actually forbid her to see them?"

"She cannot desire their company. I saw her exasperation at the ball. She was mortified."

"Before you start getting all dictatorial, consider how she might perceive your regulations.'"

"More lessons on how to manage my wife?"

"I would never presume to tell Mr. Darcy of Pemberley in Derbyshire what to do. Ah, we have arrived at Angelo's. Get ready to be bested!" They alighted from the carriage and then spent the afternoon enjoying masculine pursuits and familial camaraderie.

ELIZABETH LAY IN BED FOR SEVERAL HOURS and over the course of the afternoon began to gain back some of the strength that had dissipated over the previous day. Laura had encouraged her to take tea and juices, which seemed to revive her. Elizabeth agreed to dress for dinner, even though her appetite had not yet returned. She would try her best, so as not to bring attention upon herself. She had always been a hearty eater, due in part to her level of activity, but also because she loved food; however, even her favourite dishes currently held no appeal.

While Laura attended Elizabeth, she expressed her thoughts. "Mrs. Darcy, when my husband died, I felt like my life as I knew it was over. I had to leave my friends and security and go to Pemberley. I was near home, but when you are in service, there is not much time to get away. I was and still am grateful for my situation, but the sense of loss, not just for my man, but for my former life, was overwhelming at the time. I could neither eat nor enjoy my former pleasures. I lost quite a bit of weight during those months, but after time, I was able to make my way and accept my lot, which ended up being not so bad after all. Now I miss my husband; he was a good man, but I find that I am quite content with my life."

"You think that my physical complaints are related to my circumstances, to being away from home?"

"Now, I don't know your situation and I don't want to know, but maybe with some time and acceptance, you will find that you feel like your former self."

Elizabeth smiled at her and touched her hand. "Thank you. I will keep in mind all that you have said." Elizabeth knew there was likely some truth to what her maid surmised. Getting past her despondency would be difficult. But what gave her most pause was the fear that at any moment Mr. Darcy would knock on her door. Elizabeth Bennet had always been independent, strong and valued. She was mourning her previous life to be sure. How long it would take to fully accept her new position in society and her place in her husband's life, she did not know.

Elizabeth did make it to dinner that evening and tried to look cheerful, but Darcy had begun to read her eyes and facial expressions, and knew that her sunny façade was only a mask. He would not come to her tonight. Darcy knew it would be wrong. He was a man accustomed to having what he wanted when he wanted it, but he also was a man of empathy and courtesy. His mask of indifference would often hide abstruse sentiments that would plague him with concern.

"Elizabeth, you do look better than this morning."

"I thank you. I do *feel* better as well."

"I think it would be best to avoid your long walks in the morning."

Elizabeth looked at him flabbergasted. "You jest!"

That is the second time someone has said such a thing today. Do I look facetious? "Indeed, I do not. You must admit that your walk was the primary reason for your illness."

"I have walked in like manner my whole life. I can assure you that my walk is not the problem."

"I disagree."

"You don't even know me. How can you make such a declaration?"

"It is simple reason, Elizabeth. You walked nearly two hours yesterday and by evening, you became ill. This morning on your subsequent walk, you almost didn't make it back. There will be no more extended walks and no more walks without me."

Elizabeth's breathing increased in rate and depth as she tried to calm herself. *How dare he? How can he be so cruel?* Tears came to her eyes and she stood. "Excuse me; I have lost my appetite." She dropped her serviette beside her plate and then headed towards the door. Darcy stood belatedly, confounded by her show of low breeding through her lack of respect for him, leaving during the middle of the meal.

Walking is not the sport of a lady. She needs to learn to ride. That will give her the exercise she desires with controlled exertion. She must learn to be a lady, not a hoyden.

Elizabeth had tried to eat and was doing well. The cook had remarkable talent, and Elizabeth tried to appreciate it. After her talk with Laura – or rather Laura's talk with her – she decided to take more effort at accepting the place in which Providence had placed her. Elizabeth had forced herself to eat and found that upon really trying the fare with a favourable sentiment, she was able to renew her appetite. But all of her efforts had now come to naught. She could not bear his company, his dining room, or his food a moment longer. Mr. Darcy was officious and condemning. *Will he interminably punish me for this miserable marriage?*

SUNDAY CAME AND ELIZABETH had expected they would attend church together, for she had always attended with her family no matter the weather or season. Mr. Darcy, however, decided that they would not attend services until Elizabeth had been introduced to his family. He felt it was not proper to present her to the public when his family had yet to make the acquaintance. Also, none of her new gowns were completed, so he could not in good conscience bring her into society, even church, when she would so obviously fail to impress.

"Do you not attend services, Mr. Darcy?" she asked at breakfast, her first in his company.

"Of course, I do, but I thought that we would perhaps wait until January."

"Are you more acceptable in His sight at the new year?"

Finding himself more accustomed to her teases, he replied, "That has nothing to do with it. My plan involves your meeting my family at Christmas. It would not be proper to introduce you to the neighbourhood before meeting my family."

"Will they not be there?"

"Yes, which is another reason I prefer to wait. A public presentation cannot be good."

"Then why don't I meet them before Christmas? Are you ashamed of me, Mr. Darcy?" she asked lightly with some provocation, but the question had merit.

"Of course not." *Yes.*

"What is to happen Christmas? Am I to receive a new façade?"

"We have been through this before. That is just the time that I felt was best to introduce you to my family. That decision was made a month ago, and for your benefit, so you can become more comfortable with me before being thrown into the politics and stress of my family."

"You told me they are not all like Lady Catherine. Is that so?"

"She and my uncle are sister and brother. Of course they are alike in many ways, as was my mother, but they also have their differences. Would you not say that although you resemble your sister, Miss Lydia, that you are different as well?"

She thought of the many times she had tried to calm her sister's indecorum. "I do see your meaning," she replied with a small smile of understanding. He was not condemning her family at this moment, just making a valid point. "Then, may we go to my aunt and uncle Gardiner's church? The rector there is quite engaging and surpasses many in intelligence."

"No."

"Just 'no'? I can see no reason you might have not to attend there. Are you afraid of running into someone you know before conducting the formal introductions to your family?"

"We will wait. That is all."

"Why?" Then she continued in exasperation, "I am not a child to be spoken down to, sir. Why will you not attend church with my family? It is the Sabbath; we apparently cannot attend your church. Do you think that God will not show up on that side of town?"

"You cannot possibly understand. We will leave it at that."

"Then may I attend without you? I have wanted to see my family and this would give me a chance to visit. Your carriage could take me, and my uncle's could bring me home later in the evening. Please say you agree." He saw her look of longing. He had no real reason to refuse; this he knew.

"I will call the carriage to be prepared."

Elizabeth then squealed with delight. "Oh, thank you Mr. Darcy!" He looked over to her beaming eyes. He had heard that the eyes were the mirror into the soul and felt this sentiment to be justified on this occasion. "Will you not join me, sir?" Elizabeth so wanted him to become better acquainted with her London relatives.

The allure was lost. "Of course not."

"I know that you might not believe so, but I do think that you might find that you have quite a bit in common with at least my aunt."

"No, Elizabeth!" replied an exasperated Mr. Darcy. He then directed that he would send his carriage to retrieve her before the dinner hour, so there was no need to trouble her uncle to convey her home. "Now if you will excuse me." He stood, bowed and left the breakfast room. Elizabeth could not find it in herself to be angry with the man for his sullenness, for she would soon see her dear aunt and uncle.

SHE GREETED A SURPRISED MR. AND MRS. GARDINER just as they were about to leave for church. Hugs were exchanged to everyone's pleasure. "Oh, Lizzy, we have been so worried about you."

"Aunt, thank you for loving me so." Elizabeth then leaned in and gave her another embrace full of tender regard. "I have been longing to see you."

"Are you to join us for church?" At Elizabeth's nod, her aunt continued, "And what about Mr. Darcy? Is he with you, dear?" she said as she looked around her.

"He would not come." Elizabeth blew out her breath with a sigh. "I am afraid that his pride would not allow him to venture forth into the wilds of Cheapside. I wonder if he has even been to this part of town."

"Well, let's not be hard on the man. He has plenty of reasons to be proud, and perhaps he will warm up to us on a future occasion. Now, if we are to make church we must be on our way."

After the service, Elizabeth enjoyed the afternoon with her cousins and their parents. As she did not have time alone with her aunt, Elizabeth was unable to discuss anything of consequence that two women might speak of when in company after such a momentous week for a new bride. The carriage arrived for her, and she hoped that perhaps Mr. Darcy had come after all in retrieving her, but he had not. It was not that she longed for his companionship, for she felt she had enough of that as it was; she wanted him to see that her relations were superior society, and if he would just give them a chance, he might learn that he indeed enjoyed their company. This could only be an advantage for Elizabeth herself.

When Elizabeth arrived home, Mr. Darcy was nowhere to be seen. She had determined that she would show him all of the gratitude that she felt at being allowed to spend the day with her dear family. The time away from Darcy

House disposed Elizabeth to recover some of her natural good cheer, and she was more than willing to pass that geniality on to her handsome husband.

She did not ask about his whereabouts but instead went to her chamber to rest a bit and prepare for dinner. In but one week's time, she had learnt that Mr. Darcy would arrive to her room promptly at seven-thirty to escort her to the evening meal. Elizabeth laughed to herself when considering her husband's strict adherence to a schedule and began to think that perhaps he was telling the truth in Hertfordshire when she teased him for his perpetual tardiness.

WHILE PREPARING FOR DINNER, Elizabeth told her maid, Laura, about her visit with her relations. "Oh, and I asked my aunt if she remembered you. You must have been quite close, for she not only remembered you but also told me stories of your time together. I did not realise that your father and hers died in the same carriage accident. That must have been hard on you both – for my aunt to have left so soon for town. I would imagine that you were each in want of the comfort of the other."

"That it was, but I soon married and learnt to depend on my husband. My Jack had known my father and missed him as I did. Margaret and I did write, but we soon lost touch as people are wont to do when moving about."

"I hope you don't mind that I told her about your having been widowed and under the employ of Mr. Darcy." Until that moment Elizabeth had not thought that Laura's pride might bristle at her old friend's learning of her drop in station.

"Oh no, ma'am, for Margaret was always kind. I am not ashamed of my place in the world."

"Laura, would you like to join me on my next visit with my aunt?"

"Oh, I don't know. Mr. Darcy might not appreciate my mingling with your relations. He does believe in maintaining the strict lines of social order."

"Let me deal with Mr. Darcy. I plan on asking if I can return next Sunday for services. You can join me then."

"If Mr. Darcy agrees, then I would be happy to come," Laura replied, giving Elizabeth genuine delight.

At that moment and as expected, Mr. Darcy knocked upon the door of the sitting room. With a smile still on her face, Elizabeth crossed the room and opened the latch allowing her husband entrance. He was somewhat taken aback at the felicity that greeted him. "Elizabeth, to what do I owe your obviously festive mood?"

"Thank you for noticing," she responded with a curtsey. Elizabeth then took his arm as they left the room. They spoke not a word until they were seated for dinner.

"Mr. Darcy," said his wife in good cheer, "I must express to you my appreciation for your allowing me to attend services with my family. We had the most enjoyable afternoon."

Darcy noticed the light in her eyes as she conveyed her sentiments on the matter. She was truly happy which manifested itself in her buoyant conversation that followed. She ate heartily, asking him about his day in unaffected interest. *Is this the same woman who arrived at Darcy House not seven days ago?*

"I was thinking that perhaps tomorrow, you can begin your duties as mistress to the house by meeting with the cook to select the menus for the week." He had been thinking that it was time she assumed her role in earnest.

"I would be happy to meet with Mrs. Williams. My mother valued the presence of a master in the kitchen and taught us to do the same."

"Very well. I will request that she make time for you in the morning." Elizabeth smiled at his giving her the opportunity to participate in the workings of the house.

During the course of the meal, she teased in a light-hearted manner and gave him the attention that she would of anyone sharing scrumptious fare amongst friends. He began to think that perhaps tonight would be the night he could return to her room. Then she said, "I have discovered the most delightful intelligence. My aunt Gardiner and my lady's maid, Laura, hail from the same town in Derbyshire and were once friends as young girls. I could not believe the coincidence." She did not notice the look of hauteur that overspread his countenance as she continued on, speaking of the hope that they would soon have a chance to renew the acquaintance.

"Elizabeth, desist from this line of talk. Do you not know that it is unseemly for a servant to fraternise with family in this way?"

Elizabeth was silenced by the unexpected retort. After a few moments of reflection, she found her voice. "I fail to see how one's station in life determines her value as a friend. My aunt and Laura were playmates, no different than you and Mr. Wickham, I suppose. But perhaps that is the problem. You look down upon anyone with disdain, no matter the previous intimacy of the affiliation, when that person no longer has anything of significance to offer you."

"Do not mention that man's name in my house again."

"Oh, don't worry; I can be silent on whatever issue it is that earns your disapproval. I can avoid speaking of my family's residence, my maid's history, my love of walking, my distaste for ostentatious show, my lack of breeding and connections and my opinion of you. In fact, I feel quite able to take your lead and not speak at all." Elizabeth then set her fork down upon her plate, daintily wiped her mouth with her napkin and said, "I find I have lost my appetite, if you will excuse me, I wish to retire early after such a pleasant and eventful day." She stood as the footman rushed over to assist, and departed. Had she looked back, she would have seen Darcy's mouth in a tight line with eyes aflame with ire.

How dare she speak to me that way in my own house? She must learn some humility and respect. After the display, Darcy himself had lost his appetite and decided to go to his study for a brandy and reading to calm his anger. He had a fleeting thought of going to her room anyway, as he felt it was important for her to understand who was master of this home and master of her, but quickly left that notion, recognising it for what it was and the poison that would begin to fester in their marriage if he went down that path.

THEIR ONE WEEK ANNIVERSARY came and went as any other day might, Elizabeth in her rooms most of the day and Darcy taking care of his letters of business with visits to his family and friends. Elizabeth did meet briefly with the cook as planned but could not give any input into the week's meals for she herself had no appetite and everything seemed to be in hand. She also had more shopping to be done, but decided to put it off until she knew not when. Elizabeth had no mind for the activity and could not force herself to take on the task. Instead, she and Laura spent the afternoon sharing tales of their respective youths. Elizabeth marvelled at her aunt's former antics, laughing outright when Laura told the story of their getting stuck in a large tree near the blacksmith's place of business. "Mrs. Darcy, you should have seen the look in Margaret's eyes when her father marched up with the ladder. Oh, we were a sight. I don't believe her father let her near a tree for a six-month."

"I can well believe it! Now I see why my aunt, more than any other, seems to have more patience with me!" Elizabeth looked distracted as she smiled. "My aunt and I have always been close, kindred spirits as it were. While growing up I felt as though she understood me more than anyone else, be it family or friends." Then she turned to Laura, "Please, Laura, will you go with me on Sunday to visit?"

"Oh, I don't know if that would be wise, ma'am. Mr. Darcy might not like your putting me in the company of those outside of service. He might suppose I am trying to raise myself above my station."

"Well, you and I know the truth of the matter. Surely he cannot object to your spending time with friends while in the company of your mistress."

At about five, Elizabeth received a note from her husband informing her that he would not be joining her for dinner that evening and that he was to eat with his sister who begged his company. Elizabeth's husband was often away from home pursuing his own pleasure. Although content to be left at home, she could not help but be curious as to his whereabouts throughout the days and evenings or with whom besides his family he spent his time.

Darcy had at first declined his sister's request, but Georgiana's pleading eyes swayed him to join her. Darcy knew that he was not welcome company for his wife at his own home, and so was easily persuaded to stay. Colonel Fitzwilliam arrived for dinner and was surprised at Darcy's presence in the dining room of Tromwell House.

"Darcy, what brings you to my parents' table for dinner? Does your cook no longer have the special touch?"

Darcy looked at him with a smirk and replied, "Can a brother not spend time with his sister without further motive? I have missed Georgiana, and plan to spend a little extra time with her this evening."

Fitzwilliam knew his cousin well and surmised that there was more to tell, but left the questioning for another time. They just exchanged a look of understanding and moved on to less obtrusive topics. Georgiana continued to worry for her brother and took every opportunity to express her affection and esteem for him.

During the separation of the sexes, while the colonel, his father and Darcy remained alone in the dining room, cigars and brandy aplenty, the subject that was on embargo with Georgiana present was soon broached by the colonel, "So,

Darcy, last I was in your company, you were in need of some physical exertion to assuage the frustrations of married life. Have things improved for you?" He was guessing not, based on the fact that Darcy was at Tromwell rather than Darcy House.

"I have no complaints." Then Darcy went on to change the subject asking his uncle what he had heard about an investment into which they had mutually entered. Fitzwilliam decided a more private interview was in order and planned to go by Darcy House on the morrow to see for himself how things fared for his cousin. Fitzwilliam loved him dearly, but knew that unless Darcy let go of some of his fastidious ways and resentful temperament, he could not be content with a vivacious woman, especially Elizabeth. Fitzwilliam genuinely found her delightful on the occasion of the ball and wedding and knew that she could make a fine wife for such a strong personality as Darcy possessed, but going from loathing to loving would be a rocky road for each of them. Perhaps he could help them along with some gentle prodding. He would call at Darcy House and see the two of them together and decide for himself if the struggles of matrimony had indeed calmed.

Elizabeth had not seen Mr. Darcy since the evening of the disagreement over dinner. She was disappointed with herself for the way she had spoken to him. Even though she felt that he was unreasonable and arrogant, she should not have lowered herself to speak to him so. She had never in her life found her tongue so difficult to tame. The loss of control of her life left her feeling like a dog being cornered in an alley, gnashing out at its owner who tried to put a leash over its neck. But knowing she was behaving inappropriately and doing something about it were two entirely different matters. She knew deep down that she would lash out again given equal provocation.

THE NEXT MORNING CONTINUED Elizabeth's now usual routine. She had begun sleeping later and later, as she did not have a walk to look forward to. Of course, she could have taken a short stroll with Mr. Darcy but was not equal to his company and decided to wait until another time. Breakfast was brought in by Laura, which Elizabeth ignored, choosing to take only tea. Tired of being in her room, Elizabeth decided to go downstairs to the library and pick another book, perhaps a novel this time, to while away her day. She was apprehensive about possibly interrupting Mr. Darcy, but she found that he was not in the room. After picking a book from the large assortment, she went to the family sitting room on the same floor as the library to read. She needed a change in scenery and this room was comfortable and opened to the east for good morning light.

While ensconced in the sitting room, a visitor was announced. Elizabeth rose. In walked Colonel Fitzwilliam whom Elizabeth greeted with true pleasure. "Colonel, welcome. What a delight to see you again. I almost didn't recognise you without your regimentals on. Have you been long in town?"

"I returned with Mr. Bingley. I believe he had pressing business that he was anxious to perform, and he graciously allowed me to join him. I daresay, that man is like a puppy with a new toy. His exuberance was infectious, and I find I am just now calm enough to pay a call to the staid Darcy."

Elizabeth laughed, eyes dancing in merriment. "Yes, Colonel, I wager that Mr. Darcy would not appreciate your coming in here with your tail wagging, risking knocking over one of his priceless vases." She pictured Mr. Bingley's excitable nature and Jane's calm exterior hiding a heart that overflowed with joy, and could not help but smile in satisfaction. They both laughed at the picture of Bingley's infectious mien.

"And how is my new cousin? You are another whose charming face diffuses gaiety, positively affecting those nearby."

"You are too kind, sir. I would not go so far as to agree with you, but it is true, I cannot conceal my humour or my chagrin when I feel them. Do have a seat and I will call for tea." She stood and rang the bell. When a footman entered, she requested that tea and biscuits be brought into the room. The conversation continued on in a light-hearted manner as Fitzwilliam conveyed stories of his life in the military, refraining from the more heinous tales of battle, and Elizabeth added anecdotes of her imaginative youth. Elizabeth again pondered the apparent incongruity that the colonel and her husband shared the same family. As Darcy was quiet and taciturn, the colonel was charming and loquacious.

They were enjoying tea and considering whether a game of charades or a formal dinner were more conducive to judging someone's character when Darcy entered the room. He was unnoticed at first as he stood staring at his wife blatantly flirting with his cousin. Elizabeth was laughing and beaming that beguiling smile that he had seen directed to himself on but rare occasion. Darcy had to admit that she did have a becoming smile at times, when she was not chastising him.

After a few moments of gazing at the two having a pleasant conversation, he gave a light cough to signify his entrance. "Don't let me interrupt the two of you, as you seem to be getting along famously without my presence." Colonel Fitzwilliam and Elizabeth stopped speaking and stared at him, each with his and her own thoughts, the latter wishing he had stayed away if he were going to be tiresome, and the former wondering why his cousin had that daunting visage. Surely Darcy would be happy that his cousin was making an effort to spend time with his new wife, as he attempted to welcome her into the Fitzwilliam family. The poor lass had been locked away in Darcy's home long enough. Surely she needed some social diversion.

"Darcy, I hope you don't mind my coming over while your knocker was still removed from the door. I came to see you and was pleasantly distracted by your beautiful bride. Won't you join us for tea?" As Fitzwilliam spoke, he saw that Darcy eyed his wife with a serious look of displeasure. Elizabeth focused on making tea and refilling cups.

Elizabeth stayed a few moments more, but after feeling the vexation of her husband, she said, "Well, if you are both happily settled, I will leave you to your visit. I am certain that you have more manly subjects to explore than you would be able to with my company."

"Mrs. Darcy," said the colonel, "please don't leave to gratify my desires. I prefer you stay. Darcy here does not have your penchant for storytelling, so you would be sorely missed."

"You are too kind, sir, but I am afraid that my stories are not ones becoming the mistress of the house, so I leave you to share similar antics with the greater share of approval." She curtseyed to the two men as they stood, and she left the room. Elizabeth had enjoyed her visit with Colonel Fitzwilliam, but knew she could not continue with the same pleasure while her husband was in attendance. He had been giving her glowering looks since he entered the room, making clear his disapproval of her speaking with his family. Elizabeth was certain that Mr. Darcy condemned her for her high-spirited conversations.

Both men watched her leave with differing feelings. Darcy had a sensation that he had not felt in years and was not aware what it was, but the remembrance brought him nothing but perturbation. What he could not perceive in his innermost being was jealousy, last experienced when his father had paid unrelenting and enraptured attention to Wickham. Darcy who had none of the easy manners and witticisms of Wickham would look on to a similar scene with the two sharing the bond of camaraderie while he had no part. Elizabeth's enticing smiles were all for other men be they Fitzwilliam, Wickham or the countless others whom she charmed with her demeanour and conversation. If he were to perceive that what he felt was actually jealousy, he would have had a hard time deciding which of the two he coveted more: Elizabeth, for her ease in wrapping his cousin into her web of wiles or Fitzwilliam, for being the one upon whose smiles Elizabeth bestowed. Fitzwilliam on the other hand was deep in disturbing thoughts concerning the relationship, as he just witnessed it, between his cousin and new bride. In nary a week, they seem to have gone from a resigned acceptance to outright animosity. Fitzwilliam could not bear to see his cousin tied to a life of misery like so many others. *Darcy deserves more and frankly, so does his wife.*

The colonel was the first to speak. "Darcy, what a charmer you are! You have her eating out of your hand already." His cousin gave him a stern look then took a sip of tea to hide his vexation. "I must say, Mrs. Darcy and I were having a pleasant visit until you arrived. Why do you suppose she left so abruptly?"

"How would I know? As much as you seem to think that I dictate her, I do not keep watch over her every move, nor do I seek her motivations."

"Don't be so testy, Darcy. I only mean to help." After a few moments, he continued, "I came by to see if you wanted to go to Angelo's. I have a mind for some exercise and thought you might not object to my besting you today. Are you up for it?"

A slight smile came across Darcy's face, "I believe that is exactly what I need. I'll call the carriage."

On the way to the fencing academy, they spoke of Fitzwilliam's plans for the next month. This would be his final day at Tromwell House until Christmas. Darcy invited him for dinner that evening, looking forward to his company, especially in light of his and his wife's recent poor communication. They worked up a vigorous sweat over the next two hours and after cleaning up climbed in the carriage for the short ride to Darcy House. On the way home, Fitzwilliam managed to bring the conversation back around to Elizabeth and their marriage. "Darcy, earlier when I was speaking with Elizabeth everything seemed fine until you walked in. What happened?"

"I suspect she wanted to give us time alone."

"I am not exactly asking why she left. Why did her mood change so drastically upon your entrance? One moment she was smiling and laughing, and the next she couldn't get away quickly enough."

"What do you want from me, Fitzwilliam? What would you have me say?"

"I am just concerned about you. Look, I know that your marriage is in name only. I just hope for more for you, that you might one day find contentment in ways that have nothing to do with your coffers."

"I know you mean well, but truly, I am content. Of course, I do wish that I could have married someone who was able to bring more to the settlement than Elizabeth has, but overall, I cannot say things are different than most arranged marriages. I suppose there will be a time of transition before she learns to accept her new life. Until then, I will try to be patient in directing her into her role."

"That's just it Darcy; a wife should not be a possession. You cannot mould her into the perfect mistress of Pemberley. Try to accept her for who she is and go from there."

"What do you expect me to do? Invite her family to town for the Season and give her mother free rein over my staff? We could sponsor her sisters, so that they have access to other *rich men*."

"I do not think that is what Mrs. Darcy would ask at all. Have you thought to inquire from her what she wants out of a marriage? Do you know what her desires are?"

"Must I remind you that she got what she wanted? She is the author of this entire debacle."

"Are you certain that she got what she wanted? She does not seem too content to me, and based on what she told me on the night before the wedding, this marriage did not at all fulfil her desires."

"I'm not certain of anything. I cannot even know if she does not continue to be in consort with Wickham."

"Surely you cannot believe that Mrs. Darcy is in league with that man. It doesn't seem within her nature." There was silence except for the sound of the horses clopping on the cobblestone pavement outside the window. "Well, I for one do not believe that she could do anything as duplicitous as Wickham has done, and if she is in any way involved with him, it is likely under pretext of some deceit on his part. And if that is the case, you would do well to disabuse her of his manipulations rather than condemn her."

"When the time is right, I will speak with her, but for now, I don't believe she would be open to any revelations I might share. And I most certainly will not tell her anything about that blackguard's designs on Georgiana."

"No, of course not. But you might find she is more open than you think if you were to treat her as a respectable spouse." Darcy shot him a menacing glare.

"I don't mean for that to sound sensational, but there is some validity. Do you treat her the same as you would have Lady Annette?"

"Lady Annette would have come into the marriage with an understanding of her responsibilities and the grace to fulfil them."

"Are you so certain that Mrs. Darcy does not?"

"I am certain that she has no suitable clothing, and when I attempt to fix that problem, she resists; I am certain that her family has no connections to add to my own, and not only that, their behaviour is abominable; and I am certain that she cares not a whit about me, my home or my family. She only has the security and fortune that I can provide in mind." Even as these words left Darcy's lips, he knew he was exaggerating her faults.

"What if you are mistaken? Do you see how your treatment of her will only increase the conflict that seems to be growing between you?" Darcy made no answer. "Darcy, you are right; I am no expert on relationships, but I do know how to treat someone who is below me in rank and how to help them meet expectations. Treating her as if she has no value will not make her happy, and believe me, if she is not happy neither will you be."

Darcy wanted to say again that he was perfectly content with his life as it stood, but that would be a lie to himself and to his cousin. He was miserable and therefore willing to listen to his cousin's wisdom on the matter. But he was not so humble as to admit his acquiescence quite yet. Add to that, he was not ready to hear of how that might play out in his day-to-day life. All he knew was that he needed a change. He could not carry on with a woman who despised him.

They went their separate ways once reaching Darcy House. Dinner would be served in two hours. Fitzwilliam withdrew to his usual room while in residence there in order to get some rest after the vigorous exercise, and Darcy went to his study for some needed time alone.

SEVEN-THIRTY CAME, and punctual as usual, Elizabeth heard Darcy's knock on the shared door. This time she nodded for her maid to open the door in her chamber, as she looked in the mirror in her dressing room trying to add some colour to her unusually pale cheeks with a little pinch. Had Colonel Fitzwilliam not been invited to dine, she considered coming up with an excuse for not joining her husband for dinner, but she knew this would be a blatant dereliction of duties with his cousin in attendance, and having him there as a diversion for both would help the evening to pass with greater ease. She entered her chamber, and while avoiding his eyes, she walked towards him. They descended the stairs in silence and went straight to the dining-parlour where Colonel Fitzwilliam awaited their arrival.

Standing, Colonel Fitzwilliam said, "Mrs. Darcy, you look lovely this evening." She did indeed hold an attraction for the man with her dark hair and green, kind eyes, but he had to admit that her appearance lacked some of the lustre that it had even earlier in the day. He was surprised to see that Darcy let the footman pull the chair out for her; Darcy had always been fastidious in his attentions bestowed upon a lady. In fact, Fitzwilliam had been present more than once when witnessing Darcy's solicitous behaviour towards Lady Annette in attending to her comforts himself. As he witnessed Darcy's interactions with his wife, Fitzwilliam's sense of foreboding increased.

"Thank you, sir," Elizabeth responded to his compliment. "Did you enjoy your afternoon with Mr. Darcy?"

"Yes, we went to Angelo's, the fencing academy. Has Darcy told you about our shared passion for fencing?"

"No, I cannot say he has. But don't feel like he has been neglectful in his duties to myself. I am sure he has told me all I need to know in order to faithfully admire him," said she with a sidelong smile.

Colonel Fitzwilliam joined in her amusement saying, "You too, then? That happened to me years ago," which elicited gentle laughter from Elizabeth.

"James, please do not encourage her so."

Elizabeth then turned to Fitzwilliam with a wink and said, "So, will you not tell me which of you was the victor?"

"As we are pretty equally matched, we were equally divided in our successes. I would have come out ahead had Darcy not gotten his second wind. Have you ever seen the sport?"

"Fitzwilliam! She is a lady. Please do not suggest otherwise."

She looked over to Mr. Darcy archly, and then turned to the colonel, "Yes, as a matter of fact I have." Fitzwilliam's countenance lit up with the intelligence. "My uncle, you see, used to fence, until he received a knee injury three years ago. Jane and I once secretly watched him practise with a friend of his in the mews at his home. I am quite certain he knew we were there, but did not reprimand us. Instead, he gave me a book on the topic, so I could study more about the sport. Unfortunately it was written in French, so I had to learn what I could through the pictures. You see, my French was never very good! But I found the sport fascinating, nonetheless."

"And so what did you learn from those pictures?" questioned the colonel.

"I learnt that men and women are not so different after all. Men have their own lists of accomplishments and like to show off every bit as much as women. The only problem is that they display this talent in front of men alone. It is a shame that women are not invited to watch."

"Mrs. Darcy, that would be most inappropriate," said her shocked husband.

"And why is that, sir? Why can a woman of discernment not watch the sport, for I daresay it is every bit as much art as sport?" Then she turned to the colonel with a gleam in her eye, knowing she was about to alarm her already disturbed husband. "My uncle knew the adventurous side of me and asked if I wanted to learn a little about fencing hands-on. Of course I wanted to, so he carved a stick about the length of a foil, if a little bulkier, and taught me the various moves. When my mother found out, she threatened to keep me from visiting London, so there ended my days as a swordswoman." Elizabeth said this as nonchalantly as she could manage, knowing she was causing great aggravation for her husband.

"That is some story, Mrs. Darcy! And so you can add that to your list of accomplishments," said the colonel, joining in her game as he considered that her teasing nature might be just what his cousin needed in his life.

"I suppose I can, but I am afraid not everyone would have your enthusiasm for its inclusion. I will have to stick with keeping that particular one amongst us alone." She held an engaging smile as she took a sip of wine while Darcy sat dumbfounded. He was hoping to learn more of his wife, but this was extraordinary.

The colonel continued, "Your uncle sounds like an interesting fellow. Tell me about him."

Elizabeth glanced to her husband to see how he would bear her indulgence; then not seeing reproof, as his countenance was unreadable, she began her description. "Thank you for asking. My uncle Gardiner is my mother's younger brother, born at least ten years after her. While still young, his mother, my grandmother, died so my grandfather desired to find husbands for my uncle's sisters, the older marrying his clerk (for he was a solicitor in Meryton) and the younger a country gentleman, my father. My grandfather was lonely and desired a mother for his son, so he found a wife, fortunately of some means, for she was a widow herself. Her family had owned a warehouse and ran a business into which my uncle was then destined. After school and completion of his studies at Oxford, he returned to his father's home to become a partner. The next year my grandfather died and the following, his wife. Since that time Mr. Gardiner married and had four children and now resides in London, on Gracechurch Street, so that he can live near his warehouses."

"And he enjoyed the sport of fencing?"

"I suppose he did, but his real love is fishing. Unfortunately, London holds few places where he can indulge that particular passion. He has spoken of purchasing a country home where he could have lakes full of fish for the sport, but life as a father and businessman seems to have distracted him from that particular goal."

"Are your mother and brother close?"

She smiled, "Not in age or temperament. But they do love one another as family should, and he indulges her by taking in her daughters to attempt to educate us in decorum." Then she laughed, "Some of us must need more work than others, for he invites Jane and me often."

"I am sure he invites you for your engaging company," said the colonel. Elizabeth glanced to her husband who was paying close attention to his plate.

"Well, I cannot claim to know his motive, but I do know that he is a kind man who seeks to further his place in the world through diligent work. And he is generous enough to share his success with all of his family."

Darcy changed the subject, "Speaking of family, Fitzwilliam, how is your sister? Will she be in town for Christmas?"

The colonel knew Darcy could answer this question better than he himself and saw that it was a ploy to change the conversation, which he did with finesse. Elizabeth listened on in heightened interest as the two gentlemen spoke of family and the upcoming festive season. Elizabeth had rarely heard Mr. Darcy speak so openly and loquaciously. Usually he sat quietly while the conversations around him ebbed and flowed without his participation.

There was no separation of the sexes that evening, for if there had been, Elizabeth would have made her exit for the night. Fitzwilliam suggested they withdraw to the music room so that Elizabeth could perform. He was interested in her ability even though she herself had never given reason to suppose she was a great proficient. Darcy on the other hand had insinuated that she was inferior to the ladies whose company he had most often enjoyed.

When entering the music room, Elizabeth walked over to the pianoforte. Again, she perused the sheet music, remembering that there was a song that might fit the occasion. She decided upon a lively Irish tune that she had not played in a while, but with Colonel Fitzwilliam in attendance, she felt to be appropriate as he was a lively sort of man. He offered to turn pages for her, which she accepted happily. Fitzwilliam was pleasantly surprised at her competence. Elizabeth played with feeling and zeal, and he had to stop himself more than once from clapping his hands to the tune along with her. Elizabeth laughed at his enthusiasm for the performance as she finished the song with a flourish. Fitzwilliam was finally able to clap in earnest for her lively rendition, and although she had missed a few notes perhaps, her spiritedness more than made up for the mistakes.

"That was marvellous! And do you sing? I would dearly love to hear you sing," said the colonel. Darcy had heard her sing once before and could not remember anything extraordinary about her performance.

"I can sing, but how well I sing will be for you to judge." And so she began a love song. She did not need him to turn pages for she knew the song by heart, so Fitzwilliam stood in front of her where he could study her countenance. He had always believed that one could learn a great deal about a person by the subtle changes in his or her mien while engaged in an activity, be it drill formations in a regiment or a woman's eyes and smile while performing. He came to the same conclusion that Darcy had long ago, that Elizabeth wore her feelings in the open for all to see, but he also saw something Darcy had not. Elizabeth's voice, though not perfect, had a sincerity that drove the song forward bringing the hearer along with her, sharing the emotions that consumed her. The words conveyed such a longing when accompanied by her melodious voice that he was completely bewitched by the end, as a sailor lost to the song of a siren. When the last note ended, silence reigned for the next five long seconds; then he burst forth with applause.

"Mrs. Darcy, I confess that I have rarely heard anything so lovely. Don't you agree Darcy?" Fitzwilliam turned to his cousin and saw a look of puzzlement. "Darcy, does the cat have your tongue? Would you not say your wife performed exceptionally?"

The other two in the room looked at Darcy, expectant of an answer. "Elizabeth has talent to be sure, but she will not play really well without practising. I plan to ask Georgiana's music master to begin lessons with Elizabeth on Friday, so she will have plenty of time to prepare for Christmas when she will want to play in front of your family."

Fitzwilliam looked on with wonder. How could his usually well-mannered cousin be so obtuse? "I daresay they will love her performance with or without a master's input. Do you know any Christmas songs, Mrs. Darcy? We have a tradition of singing carols at our gathering. Georgiana and my brother's wife play, but I do believe they would welcome your contribution."

Elizabeth looked down to her hands before answering, "Indeed I do know many carols and would be happy to play and sing. We, too, have traditions at my home in Hertfordshire that include music. My sister, Mary, will be the only one this year to provide the accompaniment for my family's entertainment, so she for one will appreciate my absence, for she loves an audience." Then she laughed lightly, but melancholy had entered her eyes, not missed by the two gentlemen. "Shall I play another?"

"If you are willing; I would love to hear more," said Fitzwilliam.

"Mrs. Darcy, won't you play the one that you played for me a week ago, on your first night here?" She blushed at the recollection of that night and their conversation that followed the song, but quickly acquiesced to Darcy's request and began playing, but this time, Elizabeth added the words, for she felt that perhaps she was equal to the challenge the song would place on her emotions. At the conclusion, both men sat mesmerised while she stared at her hands trying to keep her emotions under regulation. Elizabeth then ventured looking up and saw a pained look on the colonel's face. Mr. Darcy had stood up and was facing the fire in the hearth. Not knowing if the gentlemen had approved of her playing, she stood.

"Well, I believe at that I will leave you to your own entertainment. If you will excuse me." She curtseyed and walked towards the door.

"Mrs. Darcy," said the colonel, "that was lovely. Thank you for indulging us." She smiled and bowed her head in thanks and continued out the door.

After a few moments of silence, Fitzwilliam spoke, "Darcy, you didn't tell me your wife played so beautifully. I have a feeling that she is full of surprises."

"Yes, I believe you are correct. What could her uncle have meant by teaching her to fence? I was appalled."

"Man, do you hear yourself? You are going to drive a wedge between the two of you – if you have not already – that will not easily come down. Truly, you must stop placing judgement on her and her family. My own father once played pretend swords with Vickie when she was eight. She had been watching my brother and me as we contended with one another and asked if she could join in. When we told her to leave us, she went straight to Father, and rather than tell her that swordplay was no place for a little girl, he got out two stick swords and played until her curiosity was satisfied, and she never asked to play that particular game again."

Darcy looked away not wanting to agree with his cousin, but convicted of his own mental attacks against his wife. "Darcy, your wife is a lovely woman with a true passion for life that could so easily disappear under a domineering influence. Rather than try to change her, why don't you consider the benefits to such a wife. Her passionate nature could mean many nights of pleasure for you."

"Must you be vulgar?"

"I'm not. I know you would never take a mistress or pay a visit to the courtesans, which means that you must find that passion at home. Rather than be her master, why not try to be her guide and friend? I would bet that she would begin to welcome you in her life, and bed, if you showed her the respect that she deserves." After a pause with no input from Darcy, he continued, "Give it a month. Try to be solicitous of her needs as you would any other lady of our circle. Pull her chair out for her rather than leave that pleasure to a footman, pay her compliments, praise her performance rather than degrade her."

"I do not degrade her. She knows she can do better with practice; she said so herself."

"Don't be so obtuse. She only says that for fear of disappointing you. If she sets you up to believe that she is incapable then she won't be offended when you criticise her. She would just say that she told you so."

"That's absurd."

"I am telling you, Darcy, if you do not begin to show her your approbation, she will never open herself to you. I suspect you will find multiple attributes to admire."

"Fitzwilliam, you are speaking of my wife, not some debutante. I begin to think that you might admire Elizabeth a little too much."

"Don't be ridiculous; she is your wife, as well I know, but if you do not show her some deference, someone else will. How do you think Wickham got into her good graces?"

"I am trying, truly I am, but I cannot get past her origins and possible artifice related to Wickham. I would ask that you not pass judgement on my actions until you are in my position."

"I am not judging, just wishing for your wellbeing." Darcy walked over and poured them each a brandy. After a few more moments of reflection, Fitzwilliam continued, "Just something to think about: give her a month to get comfortable with being Mrs. Darcy without demands for change, or anything else you might desire." He held up his hand to stay Darcy from interrupting. "That will take you to the new year. During that time, take opportunities to verbally appreciate her attributes, while exploring them yourself. If after that time, you find that nothing has improved, then go back to doing things your own way, and I will stay out of it."

"You should stay out of it anyway."

"Perhaps, but I care too much about you to sit idly by. You know I won't be available for the next few weeks, but I hope to see things much better by Christmas."

"I will consider what you've said. I can promise no more." After a pause, Darcy continued, "So, we have the rest of the evening to ourselves. How about some billiards?"

"Certainly! I am feeling quite lucky tonight," replied his cousin and from there did not revisit the topic again.

That night Darcy pondered what his cousin had had to say, and although he could not agree with all, he did know that he was not looking forward to a life with a woman whom he could not respect. He would try to look for virtues that he could admire rather than concentrate on aspects that were lacking. As far as abstaining from marital relations, that one came the hardest to consider.

Intimacy is the only contribution that she could possibly bring to the marriage, so how do I find ways to appreciate her?

ON THE FOLLOWING DAY, Elizabeth met with the cook again while Darcy took care of business in his study. In the afternoon after sharing tea, they set out together, Darcy dropping off Elizabeth with her maid and a footman for shopping while he spent the afternoon with his relations and then on to White's. The evening was spent together over dinner followed by entertainment consisting of Elizabeth performing on the pianoforte. This day became the norm for each subsequent day over the following few weeks, varying between evenings spent in the music room or in the study reading.

Darcy endeavoured to follow his cousin's advice and keep to his own chamber at night. As the days wore on this became easier, especially knowing, as he did, that she would spurn him should he attempt to come to her. On one evening while in the music room, he decided to allude to the possibility of joining her later, in order to gauge her reaction. "Elizabeth, at one time you asked me to give you time to become comfortable with me. Do you remember?" A look of alarm covered her open countenance. "I see that you do. Well, of course you do." He looked to the hearth for the words, but found none there; however, he carried on. "Do you suppose that you would say that you have become more accustomed to our marriage?"

Elizabeth's face paled as she began to fidget with her dress; she attempted to speak, but no words came. How does she tell him that the very idea frightened her, and she knew not when that would change? Did she dare give him hope, so that she could perform her duty no matter her reluctance? "I... um, I cannot say that I am quite comfortable... that is to say, if you need..." She stood and walked to the other side of the room, so that he could not see her face as she attempted to gather her thoughts for a sincere yet accommodating response.

"You have said quite enough." Darcy did not say these words in anger or in rebuke. No more was mentioned on the subject that night, as Darcy knew that now was not the time. His cousin was correct in that he would not want to return to his wife without her willing consent, for although he did feel that in a sense he had bought her through the marriage – in that she, by law, became his possession and he had a right to her person – he would not take her again against her wishes. This he now knew and planned to adhere to. And so he would remain in his own bed, in his own chamber while exercising as much patience as he could muster.

WHILE DINING WITH DARCY one night, Elizabeth asked if she might return to her relations' church the following day for the worship service, to which he grudgingly agreed.

"Thank you, sir. That is most generous of you," replied a sincere Elizabeth. "Will you not join me this week?"

"No, I will remain at home. But if you feel that I will be eternally punished for missing church, I promise to read my prayer book in its place."

"I am not worried about your eternal whereabouts, I was just hoping that you might be willing to spend time with the Gardiners, since they are my family, and I hope that you will one day share my regard for them."

"I believe I did meet them at the wedding breakfast."

"Yes, you were introduced, but you spent no time in their company."

"Elizabeth, I will not keep you from your family during this time of transition for you, but do not ask me to welcome them into *my* life. I cannot attend services in Cheapside. I will not. Please do not ask again."

"Have it your way. As long as you allow me to go, I suppose I will have to get used to doing things on my own. No matter, I am not so difficult to please, and I will have time with those who truly love and respect me." Darcy started to respond, but remembering his cousin's advice, decided that silence would be best.

So the next morning while she prepared for church, she insisted that her maid, Laura, join her for services. "Oh no, ma'am, I do not think the master would approve."

"Nonsense. I am your mistress, am I not? And I say that you will attend with me as my companion. There is nothing for which Mr. Darcy could disapprove." Then Elizabeth told her that she was to pick out one of her own gowns, from her time at Longbourn, so that she need not feel uncomfortable while in the company of the Gardiners.

"I could not do that! Please do not ask that of me."

"Why ever not? Mr. Darcy cannot complain about your wearing my dresses when he desires that I get rid of them. And anyway, he need not know. He will not be joining us. Please say you will; that would make me so happy."

"If it pleases you, than I will agree," the maid responded hesitantly. "I think I am just nervous about seeing Margaret again. We have gone down two very different paths since last we saw one another. What if too much time has gone by?"

"Don't be absurd! Trust your friend. She has not changed in essentials, and I would wager, neither have you."

And so Laura joined Elizabeth in her visit to the Gardiners and enjoyed a day filled with the pleasure of reminiscing. Elizabeth learnt much about her aunt and maid, the two women in her life, as she now knew it, who provided relief to her lonely days. When the two returned to Darcy House, they entered through the front door, quietly laughing about a story revealed earlier in the visit. Elizabeth could not have been more pleased with the events of the day. Laura and Elizabeth's aunt had met again as many friends do, who upon seeing one another again after years of separation, find that it would seem as if nary a day had gone by. They laughed and cried and found the greatest joy in each other's company despite their large change in circumstances; it was as if they were back to being young girls, not yet out in society but anxious to begin their lives. This pleased Elizabeth, to see the happiness that the visit brought to each woman, and she rejoiced in having played her part in bringing the two together. However, as they were beginning to mount the stairs leading to Elizabeth's room, they were intercepted by the master of the house.

"Mrs. Darcy, please send your maid on to your room and meet me in my study." Elizabeth glanced at Laura who had a look of dread on her face as she turned to continue up the stairway. Elizabeth followed closely behind her husband unsure of what she should expect. Her husband's visage was grave, but unlike her maid, she could not figure out what she might have done to cause such a response. As they walked through the door to the study, Darcy motioned for Elizabeth to sit in the chair in front of his desk while he walked behind it. Elizabeth had a sinking feeling that she was about to be reprimanded for something heinous, but knew not why until he finally spoke.

"Would you please tell me why your maid accompanied you to church this morning?"

Elizabeth almost rolled her eyes but caught herself. "Well, most people attend church to worship, but I suppose, there are those who might attend for more nefarious reasons. Laura specifically came *with me* on this day for the pleasure that my aunt and she might share in renewing their acquaintance. I believe that I told you they had grown up together."

"Do you not see how inappropriate that was?"

"No, I do not."

"Elizabeth, you cannot fraternise with your maid in public. It is unseemly. Surely you know this."

"Sir, I do realise that you look upon those beneath you with apathy and disdain, but I do not. Laura is a lovely person whose life has gone down a different path than my aunt's by no fault of her own. Your father was very generous in taking her in and giving her employment when her husband died, but in essentials she is no different than my aunt."

"Do not think that comforts me."

"I do not feel a need to defend my actions, sir. I highly regard each of those ladies, and I will not apologise for bringing them together for the purpose of renewing friendships. Neither of them regrets the visit, nor do I."

"Mrs. Carpenter will not return with you."

"Why are you doing this? Just because you think it wrong to renew the friendship of someone who has dropped in station, this does not mean that I should follow suit. I certainly do not agree with your treatment of those outside your station on this score, but I suppose you will do as you please without consideration to others' wishes, or needs for that matter."

"Are you speaking of your maid or someone else entirely?"

"Neither; I am speaking of you and your abominable pride. I really do not see how we can reconcile our differences when we see people of this world so differently."

"You joined my world; I did not join yours," replied he, clearly affronted by her insults. "Maybe you should have considered our differences when you first began your designs."

"You continue to persist in your belief of my trying to ensnare you." Elizabeth locked eyes with him, yet he did not respond. "I see; well then, if you will excuse me." She stood and started towards the door. She stopped as she put her hand on the knob and then turned back. He had stood and was watching her with an indiscernible mien. "I believe that I will be taking my dinner in my room this evening."

"If that is your wish," Darcy replied. Then Elizabeth opened the door and left him to ponder how he might most easily manage this new barrier to their marital felicity.

THREE DAYS LATER, an unsuspecting Elizabeth was shocked to be awakened in the morning by a maid completely unfamiliar to her. She had been sleeping quite well since Mr. Darcy's question about her being accustomed to the marriage. He did not come to her the evening of his inquiry, which told her of his forbearance despite his wishes. This revelation of his character comforted her, for she realised that although he was taciturn and difficult to bear at times, Mr. Darcy did at least consider her feelings on the matter now that the first night of their union was behind them. Elizabeth finally felt as though she could relax when entering her bedchamber at night and so had slept a full night uninterrupted by strange sounds.

"Good morning, ma'am. My name is Janette, and I will be serving you. Mr. Darcy has hired me as your permanent lady's maid."

"What about Laura? I mean no offence, but I had become accustomed to her."

"Oh, but Mrs. Carpenter cannot serve you any longer for she left this morning for the country estate."

"Without saying goodbye?" Elizabeth wiped the sleep from her eyes, as she looked around puzzled. "I am sure she would have said something. She cannot have left."

"But she has. I saw her leave myself. Mrs. Carpenter told me about your preferences and asked me to tell you that she thanks you for allowing her to serve you, and that it was her pleasure. But now that I'm here, there is no need for her attending you, so she left for the winter."

Elizabeth was silent as her now fully awakened mind took in the news. *How dare he send Laura away without a word to me, or a chance to say goodbye! How long must I endure his punishments?* "Did Laura say anything else?"

"Not that I recall."

So this is it? This is all I am to know on the matter. "Please pick a frock for me; I plan on going down for breakfast this morning." Elizabeth was determined to give Mr. Darcy her own opinion. She knew this was his punishment for taking Laura to Cheapside with her, and she would have her say.

Darcy was stunned when Elizabeth walked into the breakfast room, a look of determination upon her brow. He stood quickly and performed a heedless bow. "Elizabeth…"

"Mr. Darcy, how are you this morning?" She continued to the sideboard and added a boiled egg to her otherwise empty plate. Darcy watched her as she crossed the room and then sat at her seat, head held high.

"I am well. Thank you for asking. This is a fine surprise having you join me."

"Do you like surprises? For I confess I do not, especially when those surprises are of the unpleasant sort." Darcy began to realise that her purpose was not to enjoy an early morning breakfast in his company. He had suspected that she would not take kindly to his interference in the selection of her lady's maid, but he also suspected that had he not taken the initiative, Elizabeth would have desired keeping Laura on, who though kind and comforting to a new bride on her wedding night, could not possibly fulfil the role of abigail to a lady trying to impress the *ton*. Also, Darcy did not care for the bond Elizabeth seemed to be forming with the woman. He would not have his wife in close conference with a servant, no matter the association with her relations. Darcy expected a backlash and was ready for her onslaught.

"I am sorry if you have experienced any unpleasant surprises while at Darcy House. I can assure you that none were meant to be so."

Elizabeth chose to remain silent looking at the servant and back to Darcy to communicate her desire for some privacy. Darcy, also not desiring an audience, dismissed his servant with a nod of his head. "Did you wish to speak with me?"

Having not touched the egg before her, she gently put down her fork while saying with quiet determination, "How dare you send my lady's maid away without consulting me or even telling me for that matter? I always supposed that the wife of a gentleman, no matter her previous rank in society, at least had the prerogative of choosing or dismissing her own lady's maid." Her eyes communicated the ire that her tone did not.

"I pay Mrs. Carpenter's salary; she has been in my employ for many years now. Of course I have the right and inclination to direct her responsibilities. With Mrs. Johnson, I chose her to serve you as your maid until I found a replacement. I believe you were told that she was temporary on that first day of your arrival." Darcy's eyes unwaveringly held her own until she looked away. "Well, I hired a replacement, so Laura joined a small group of servants who were destined for Pemberley just this morning. I saw no need to delay her departure, since there would be no other servants leaving until after Christmas."

"I knew she was temporary, but I had decided that I would like to keep her on. Is that not *my* prerogative? On that first night, Laura said that she would be serving me until I chose a new lady's maid. I have not done so."

"I understand your desire to choose your own maid, but I knew that moving forward in hiring another would come difficult for you, so I took over the task and hired a woman with much experience and pristine references. You might not know how few skilled, reliable *and discreet* lady's maids there are available to choose amongst. I found out about her availability and interviewed her while you were out shopping yesterday. We were fortunate she could begin so quickly. Within a few days you will have forgotten about Mrs. Carpenter and begun to see the practicality of this situation."

"But Laura has been the one light for me during this dark time, and you send her away without even a chance to say goodbye?" Elizabeth was becoming more impassioned as the conversation continued. "I can see you are pleased with your interference in this matter. You suppose that you know better than my own mind what is best for me, even in such intimate concerns as which person will dress me." Elizabeth's eyes were hot with tears as she considered the justification for her anger. "Your face betrays you, and now I can only wonder at my own surprise concerning your level of connivance in my affairs."

"Elizabeth, I did what was best for you and Mrs. Carpenter. She knew that you were becoming too attached to her; you put her in an untenable situation."

"All you see is a servant when you look at her. I see a person with a history, feelings, and hopes. I would never have caused her to feel any less than the kind woman that she is."

"And I replaced her for *you* and your entrance into society. Elizabeth, do you suppose that there is a female in London who would not tear you apart at the first sign of inadequacy? Your *friend* does not have the experience or skill to prepare you for your introduction into society, considering the monumental hurdle you have to overcome on the basis of your origins. Even now, the vicious mamas and daughters, jockeying for their place in society, are sizing you up, ready to judge every article of clothing that adorns your body and every motion you make. And men will be even less forgiving in their assessment as they attempt to determine how you were able to ensnare the master of Pemberley. All of them will be looking for your every flaw, and as my wife, I am determined to circumvent their endeavours against you."

"That is what this is all about – how you will appear in front of your so-called friends. You know, I bet you don't even like those people. You keep me tucked away from your family and social engagements while you go behind the scenes trying to prepare your connections for the undeserving Mrs. Darcy. You have probably told them that your abounding goodness and great mercy constrained you to the exalted humiliation of joining yourself with a mere gentleman's daughter. And now they have only to see how your benevolence will prepare me to take my place beside you and your accomplished sister."

Darcy's eyes darkened at her mention of Georgiana. "How dare you speak of my sister when you don't even know her?"

"Yes, of course I do not know her; she is living not four blocks away and yet you have kept us apart, not desiring to even make the introduction. You are ashamed of your token obligation to the point that you refuse to even present me to your younger sister."

"You can have no understanding of my motivations or desires on the matter." He stood, dropping his serviette beside his plate. "I will not continue this conversation while you attempt to put yourself at odds with me and my sister. You will thank me, Mrs. Darcy, when you make your debut, and until then there will be no more talk of Mrs. Carpenter." Darcy then departed the room while struggling to maintain his composure in light of her ill-judged attack.

Elizabeth was left to her boiled egg. She sat there focusing on the plate before her, but she was miles away in thought. When Elizabeth entered the breakfast room, she had not planned for the conversation to progress as it had; she had not thought ahead to what her words might convey, but she realised that she had antagonised him with her notorious temper. Elizabeth had always been one to lose herself to anger quickly, but then just as quickly she would regret her words. She had never been afraid to speak her mind especially when she felt justified in her opinion, but she often regretted such hasty words of vehemence directed towards her unsuspecting victim. But no matter her regret concerning how the conversation had progressed, she was most disappointed in the outcome. Laura would continue to Pemberley and Elizabeth was left to having no companion with whom to spend her days. Now she was quite used to entertaining herself through many activities and could rightly be said to have little need for input from others for her pleasure; however, more than a fortnight of marriage to the distant Mr. Darcy had left her in want of a friend. Of course, Elizabeth did not see that the very same man whom she labelled as distant was also in want of a companion, and had he known himself better, would have openly welcomed her intrusion into his life, but neither was ready for such a move and so would continue down their rocky path together, yet each alone.

DARCY LEFT FOR TROMWELL HOUSE to spend a few hours in his sister's company. Georgiana noticed her brother's disturbance but knew not how to offer aid, for every time she would ask to be included in his melancholy, he would deny having any such feelings. He had always been unreadable to most; however, Georgiana and he were close despite their difference in age. He was like a father to her, thus she looked up to him in respect and love, but he also let his well-toned guard down with her, so that she was one of very few who could discern the sadness reflected in his eyes. So Georgiana spent the morning and afternoon trying to cheer him up. She played the harp so that he might notice her improvement, for indeed her skill had blossomed, and then she moved on to the pianoforte.

Darcy sat on the sofa with his head leaned back upon the cushion as he attempted to clear his mind of all thought of marital disharmony. However, as one cannot always control the progression of the mind, he could not keep from reviewing the argument that he and Elizabeth had shared earlier in the day. Although he knew that he had done what was right and best for his wife, he saw the pain in her voice and even more so, her eyes. Elizabeth had grown in a few short weeks to depend upon Laura, and he regretted having to separate the two, but in order for Elizabeth to progress in her journey to becoming the proper Mrs. Darcy, she had to sever her dependence upon a servant, no matter her worth and value as a person and friend. And without a skilled lady's maid, her entrance into society would be in jeopardy. Elizabeth could not possibly understand his reasoning and he did not know why he had even attempted to explain it to her, but he wished he had spoken more kindly, so as to soften the loss for her.

Darcy had experienced Elizabeth's anger on multiple occasions. Indeed their entire relationship could be defined by animosity and dissension, but on this particular occasion, he noticed something that he had not seen before, or at least not admitted before. Her impassioned defence scintillated her countenance in such a way that, had Darcy not been so angry, would have drawn him in. In retrospect, he could dwell upon the picture she presented with unbiased reflection. Darcy had to admit to himself that her fervour with respect to each facet of her existence stimulated him, even when the sentiment was indignation against him. He reflected upon her long walk and the brightening of her countenance, the light in her eyes when dancing and the impertinent pique that played across her face when she was rankled. Darcy considered the many visages that he had witnessed throughout the course of their turbulent relationship and had the dawning of appreciation for the passion – or was it beauty? – reflected thereupon. And how could he be thinking along this vein when she had just greatly offended him and his motives as her protector? Was he in fact behaving as protector of her or of himself? The tumult of his mind was great as he let his mind wander over his relationship with his vulnerable yet admittedly vivacious wife.

So while sitting there Darcy resigned himself to follow Fitzwilliam's advice and explore more of Elizabeth's qualities while doing his best to prevent more confrontation, unless it could not be helped. In so doing, he left in better spirits than he had on arriving, which Georgiana attributed to his spending time away from his wife and with his abiding family.

Elizabeth had decided to spend her day in practice upon the pianoforte in anticipation for her upcoming obligatory master lessons. She knew that her skill could advance considerably with a little motivation, and although Mr. Darcy's assessment of her playing offended her exceedingly, she could in truth see the advantage to his declarations of her needing application towards her improvement.

As such, when they joined for dinner that evening, each had resolved to think more highly of the other and to attempt to bring reconciliation. Darcy determined to find ways to compliment her as his cousin had suggested and began with her new frock, which verily looked quite becoming upon her. However, the effect of his words of approbation only led her to further coldness as she supposed that he only noticed her new and expensive gown which she would not have chosen if given the option, for she had always preferred the simpler, classic styles as opposed to the one she currently wore. Her new maid was indeed a proficient, however, and was able to present her to greatest advantage with a becoming hairstyle and adornments. Darcy could now say in truth that Elizabeth did have a natural beauty about her that was improved upon with the benefit of an accomplished maid and fashionable accoutrement.

Although Elizabeth's first impulse was to feel peevishness towards his noticing her wardrobe as being superior to her usual, she decided that she would not give in to emotion. "Indeed your choice of gown does improve the picture, does it not?" she said while smiling sweetly. She took his offered arm, while he silently reflected on her strange response. They spent the evening in inconsequential conversation but they also explored the weeks leading up to Christmas and his plans for them. The piano master was to attend her in two days' time. Elizabeth expressed her gratitude for having the opportunity to improve herself, and although she did sincerely appreciate the chance to cultivate her skill, especially in light of her upcoming introduction to his family, she felt a slight indignation at its suggestion that she was in need of improvement. Then she laughed at herself for finding disapproval in his every motive. They were a fine pair, silently finding fault in one another with the sanctioned goal of trying to find contentment.

Now that a few of her new gowns had arrived, Darcy thought that an outing or two would not go amiss in helping to ameliorate their marital accommodation. He disclosed to her his plan of taking her to the theatre, which gave him immediate satisfaction, for her response was one of unaffected delight. "Truly? I love the theatre, Mr. Darcy. Thank you! When will we be going?"

"In five days."

"I see what you are about. You desire that I wear one of my new gowns and so take me out in public. Well, I will let you manipulate me in such a shameless way, for I dearly love the theatre, and the opera, if you can find one more occasion to put me in another new frock." Darcy was unsure how to take her remark for he was not used to being teased by anyone other than Fitzwilliam, so he continued in giving her details as to the name of play and its whereabouts. The rest of the meal proceeded with tales of prior performances each had seen in the past, and they realised that they had on occasion attended the same productions. This was the first enjoyable evening that Elizabeth had spent in the company of the usually taciturn Mr. Darcy. Rather than exhibit in the music room, Elizabeth suggested they adjourn to Darcy's study, as she felt she had played quite enough for one day. Although few words were shared upon entering the book haven, they sat in comfortable quietude.

The day had indeed begun on treacherous waters, but with each endeavouring to do his and her part towards finding a commonality, the Darcys could retire in their separate chambers knowing that a tenuous truce of sorts had been reached.

ON FRIDAY MORNING, Elizabeth awoke to the anticipation of meeting with the piano master for the first time. Although she rarely considered that her inadequacies on the pianoforte held her back in any significant way, this morning she keenly felt her lack of accomplishment, as she did not wish to embarrass herself in front of a discerning ear. Therefore she had practised most diligently the previous two days, which to her mind had made a significant difference, for she was now able to present him with a larger variety of songs for his critique.

Elizabeth was happy to have survived the lesson with her pride intact. Mr. Carrington had praised her affectation, if not her actual execution, and pronounced that she was indeed adequately proficient to benefit from a master such as himself. He told her because she had an inherent sensibility, that he would be able to improve her playing with diligence and practice. This gave Elizabeth something upon which to focus her days while left alone in the grand house, which pleased her more than she would have thought.

Darcy had secretly listened to Elizabeth's first lesson from behind partly closed doors, and he perceived an improvement in her performance beyond that which he had heard before. Indeed, if truth were told, he had to admit that she was much better than he had given credit in the past. He pondered that had Elizabeth the benefit of a master in her formative years and time spent in practice with a good instrument, that she would have been the superior of even his own sister. He rejoiced in the occasion to add to the accomplishments of his wife, which in turn would add to his own esteem. These lessons would indeed be an investment with a significant payoff.

At the end of the lesson, Darcy entered the room, "Mr. Carrington, it is a pleasure to see you again. I am certain I join my wife in thanking you for sharing your expertise."

"Teaching your wife has been a pleasure. As you already know, she has an inherent skill upon the instrument that delights despite lack of formal instruction, and due to this, she will, with training and practice, become a most proficient musician."

Elizabeth glanced to Mr. Darcy to see how he took the news. She had always suspected that he held her skill, as he did everything else about her, in derision, but she was surprised to perceive his look of pleasure as he said, "I thank you. Mrs. Darcy will flourish under your tutelage, just as Miss Darcy has." A few more moments of conversation upon the virtues of constant practice ensued before Mr. Carrington made his departure. Then Darcy turned to Elizabeth and said, "How did you enjoy your lesson, Elizabeth?"

"Very well indeed."

"I am glad to hear it, for your enjoyment will make the upcoming lessons easier to bear."

"And what if I had said that they were sorely endured, would you scold me for my failure to recognise the benefit of a master and send me to my room to ponder the graces bestowed upon myself?"

"I find no pleasure in scolding a woman and hope that you would see the benefit without my having to point it out to you."

"How fortunate for you that I am astute enough to agree with you," said she with a smile. "I find that I am almost overwrought with the idea of working with Mr. Carrington. I have never been one much for practising, as I have always found something else more agreeable to do, but having a diversion while alone in this big house suits me admirably."

"He will be coming three days a week until we leave for Pemberley, so you should improve significantly enough to carry on without his assistance until we return for the Season."

"How propitious."

"Yes, well, I will be in my study should you need me."

"Of course." And so they parted ways for the day. Elizabeth was truly anxious to apply her newly learnt lesson on the pianoforte and so devoted herself to another hour of playing, after which she met with the cook and sat down to write some long overdue letters to her family. She had received a letter from Jane, which spoke of her distress at the departure of the Bingleys shortly after Elizabeth's own removal from Meryton. Apparently, Mr. Bingley had come to town as expected one day after the Darcy wedding; however, on the following day, his sisters joined him, closing up Netherfield for the winter. What greatly upset Jane was that Mr. Bingley had not only said that he would be returning to the neighbourhood within the week, but he had also agreed upon having dinner at the Bennets on the fifth of December. That day had come and gone without a

212

word from the man, and now the whole family was in upheaval over the dereliction of his promise.

The news of these events shocked Elizabeth exceedingly as she considered what this would mean for Jane whose affections had been long engaged by the seemingly kind attentions of Mr. Bingley. Could they all have been wrong about his intentions or perhaps even his character? Elizabeth decided to ask Mr. Darcy if he had heard from his friend in order to determine the truth of the matter.

WHILE SITTING AT DINNER THAT EVENING, Elizabeth said, "Mr. Darcy, by chance have you had the opportunity of seeing your friend, Mr. Bingley, since his arrival in town?"

He looked up from his soup and calmly answered, "I have had the pleasure."

"Oh, good. And did he happen to tell you of his plans on returning to Netherfield? My family was under the impression that he would be coming back to the neighbourhood, as he had accepted a dinner invitation, but to their disappointment, he did not show up. I know he once said that when he would leave he would be gone in a trice, but really even for him, to close Netherfield without so much as a *by-your-leave* is most abominable. Has he given you any reason to suppose that he would not be returning to Meryton?"

Darcy hated disguise of any sort and was sore to know how to respond to this unexpected attack. "I am sure I do not know his intentions. Did he write to your father explaining his plans?"

"He left the day after our wedding and has not spoken or written to anyone at Longbourn since the breakfast. His sister, Miss Bingley, however, did write to Jane and related to her that the family was bound for London and planned closing the house for the winter with no expectation of returning any time in the near future."

"Then I suppose his plans are to remain in London."

"Do you not see how his marked attentions to Jane have left her in the difficult position of having a regard for a man – with expectations of a declaration – who would subsequently leave her without the hope of ever returning? I admit that I had thought more highly of Mr. Bingley than that. Could he be so capricious as to disregard all respect due a gentleman's daughter? — And one whose kindness and generosity of spirit cannot even now think ill of him for his undeniably discourteous behaviour towards her?"

"Mr. Bingley has many friends in town, and I believe he did say that if he were to leave Netherfield, he would probably be off in five minutes, and that whatever he does is done in a hurry. That has certainly been my experience with the man."

"But he also said that he was quite fixed there and promised to return within a week. His attentions to Jane could not be mistaken. Upon my word, even you cannot deny his inclination on that point."

"I have seen Bingley fall in and out of love so many times that I cannot give credence to any such thing. He has always given his attentions to the most beautiful woman in a room. I cannot say that he behaved any differently around your sister than any other lovely woman." Darcy knew that he was stretching the truth somewhat, but he did not want Elizabeth to suspect that Bingley might have an attachment to her sister, for it could be disastrous when next they saw one another, which was sure to happen at some point, but hopefully not until the Spring Season.

"Then shame on him for toying with the emotions of women who would form an attachment with him based on his attentions. I daresay I never suspected that he could be so cruel." Darcy truly felt affected by his wife's insinuations regarding one of his dearest and most valued friends, for there truly were few more worthy of esteem in regards to a steadfast and abiding devotion to his friendships, but he could not in good conscience expose his wife to his own interference, nor could he expose his friend to the scheming of the Bennet family. He would not let his friend suffer alongside him, no matter the deceit he must enact in the process.

"I can assure you that he had no intention of hurting your sister. He is not of a malicious sort; he just likes the company of beautiful women. Perhaps I should have warned you while in Meryton, but I suspected that his overt and excessive flirting would be seen for what it was, an enjoyable way to spend a holiday in a country village. You don't think that a man of his wealth could truly have designs on a poor gentleman's daughter?" As soon as he said the words, he realised his mistake, but as they could not be taken back, he decided to stand by his assertion, even if the truth were to hurt. He had always been forthright and chose to be clear as to his meaning; surely Elizabeth could see the justice in his words for she was a discerning woman, regardless of where and how she was raised.

Elizabeth's emotions upon hearing his speech left her unprepared for a coherent response for some moments as she attempted to take in his full meaning. Her breaths increased in depth and intensity as his implication dawned on her. "You, sir, have said quite enough." She looked him in the eye and continued, "A man of integrity, one who is *worthy* of esteem, would not let a woman's net worth determine if his attentions would result in an offer of marriage or simply a wounded heart. He would be best to leave her to her own form of amusement rather than trifle with her affections. As there are few men, and apparently none of my acquaintance outside of my extended family, who could have honourable intentions towards a woman of small means, I expected that I would never marry and was content to live my life in service to my sister's family when she were to find her joy. However, I never suspected that there could be so cruel and despicable a man as to toy with a woman of Jane's kindness, generosity, benevolence, nay all that is proper and good in this world. But you have made it clear that no man can be trusted with an innocent nature. Now I begin to wonder if I did not make the improper choice between you and Mr. Collins. I considered your intelligence and understanding to make you a superior husband to the ridiculous man, but perhaps I was wrong. At least he actively and openly looked beyond my lack of dowry, attempting to do what was honourable even if only to please his patroness."

"You compare me to that drivelling fool? I, who laid aside my family's expectations, my duty to my estate and sister and my own inclination to do what was the most difficult but honourable choice for you and your family's benefit alone, and you dare insult me in this manner?"

"Mr. Darcy, you blatantly state that I was mercenary in entrapping you into a marriage with no proof or basis whatsoever as to my own guilt, yet you openly support the idea that any respectable man of wealth – even one dear to you as a friend – might toy with a woman's affections, raise her hopes of happiness without any inclination towards an offer, on the sole basis of her financial status. How can you pass judgement upon me when your own friend's only motivation for following through with his brazen flirtations is a woman's dowry? So, not only does he put value in a woman's outward appearance over her character by choosing the most beautiful woman in the room, but also he uses her abominably for his own amusement. You agree that a man of wealth could not possibly have any honourable designs on a woman who may be all that is lovely, kind and good, and yet you denounce *me and my good family* as mercenary?"

This conversation was hurting Elizabeth more than she was willing to admit to Mr. Darcy or to herself – that her own husband could say such cruel things to her and that Jane should be the one most wounded. How could she bear a life with a man who would never value her due to her family's comparative lack of fortune? This was too much for her as she began to feel sick to her stomach. In a look of flustered confusion, she stood and gave her regrets, but that she would not be able to stay.

Elizabeth did not make an appearance for the entirety of the following day, owing to lack of sleep and a headache. She spent her time in contemplation of her situation and in dedicated correspondence with her sister whom she attempted to placate with her kind words while trying to let her down with care. She could not tell Jane of Mr. Bingley's perfidy, his reckless and misleading attentions in a long line of others, but she had to help her sister to abandon any hope for Mr. Bingley's return or renewal of his insincere regard. She chose to confirm her sister's own knowledge of the events, that Mr. Bingley would not be returning and that perhaps she should attempt to move beyond her attachment. Elizabeth reassured her that she was in no way at fault for Mr. Bingley's inconstancy and that her behaviour was at all times above reproach. Although Jane always appeared serene and composed to the general populace, Elizabeth knew there hid a profoundly affected young woman whose sentiments ran deep, and Elizabeth feared for her sister's recovery from Mr. Bingley's attentions. If Jane were to find out the extent of Mr. Bingley's disregard, Elizabeth doubted she would at all recover.

Darcy, too, felt keenly the disagreement that had taken place over dinner the evening before. Elizabeth's words denigrated his character, and he could not easily forgive the offence she laid at his own door while he attempted to defend his friend. Darcy had not a forgiving temper, and he spent many hours during the night fuming over his wife's attack. He unwillingly regretted, not for the first time, following his principles and meeting the obligation into which he had found himself while in Hertfordshire. Darcy found it a weakness to lament a decision done out of righteous duty, but still his feelings would not obey his conscience, especially after the confrontation with his wife.

Rather than withdraw to his study, he decided to go to Angelo's for a few hours, and then go to his club. What he needed most was time in the company of men who understood the man's world in which he dwelt. He chose to dine at White's and so returned home well after dark, leaving Elizabeth to wonder, not for the first time, what Mr. Darcy did with his time while away from home.

The next day, Elizabeth attended church with the Gardiners again, this time not asking for permission; however, the carriage had been made ready upon her request and waited for her outside the main entrance to the house. She had longed to spend time in the company of her family, people whose values coincided with her own. Elizabeth spoke to her aunt about Jane's disappointed hopes and her own revelations concerning her husband's and his friend's characters. Even though her aunt attempted to lay aside some of her distress, having lived in the harsh world longer than her niece, Elizabeth would not let go of the anger that had been building within her heart.

THE DAY ARRIVED for the Darcys to attend the theatre. Shakespeare's *Twelfth Night* was running through the month of December, and as this was a light-hearted comedy, Darcy thought it to be a suitable first outing as husband and wife. Having spoken with his aunt and uncle, he knew them not to be attending the show on that particular evening. Darcy truly wished for a private place for his family to meet Elizabeth, and as the past weeks had been much more difficult than he anticipated, he hoped to put it off for as long as possible, which at the latest would be Christmas, one week hence. Elizabeth had not been as accepting in her new role as his wife and mistress of his homes as he had hoped, and he was concerned about the response from both Elizabeth and his relations when the time should come.

Elizabeth had been looking forward to her first trip to the theatre as Mrs. Darcy. Although she had fought with Mr. Darcy about the prospect of purchasing a new wardrobe, in truth she liked having new dresses; she just did not like Darcy's officious way of insisting she leave her own style behind while at the same time accusing her of marrying him only for his money – which if she were to go on an extensive shopping excursion would only add weight to his point. She had chosen a creamy yellow gown made of a smooth silk with a crossover front showing her curves to advantage. However, as she was preparing for the evening, in light of their most recent heated exchange, she became apprehensive about being in close quarters with her husband for the entirety of the night. And for Elizabeth, on this evening, a comedy lacked its usual lure given her continued despondency over Jane's disappointed hopes.

Her new maid, Janette, had just put the final touches on her hair and had turned to pick out the accessories when Mr. Darcy stepped into the doorway holding a blue velvet box. He dismissed the maid and took in the captivating vision before him, for indeed Elizabeth Darcy presented a lovely picture with her dark hair adorned with fair ribbon to complement the yellow dress. Elizabeth looked at him through the mirror and then glanced down to her hands in front of her. They had not seen one another, nor spoken for the past three days, and neither had forgotten the harsh words that were said in anger, each feeling the former indignation but in a more controlled manner. Darcy and Elizabeth had each determined to try to move forward, for the essential issue of the argument was a difference in the quintessence of their values, which would not be easily overcome and certainly not before the show that evening, so they divested themselves of their enmity for the time being with the hope of appearing pleasant to one another. While entering society for the first time as man and wife, they would be scrutinised in detail, and both were in concert with the realisation that they had to look the part of a content if not happy couple.

"Elizabeth, you look lovely this evening." She gave a small smile as she thanked him. "Forgive me for intruding on your privacy, but I have come to give you something from the Darcy jewellery collection. May I?" At her nod, he opened the box and pulled out a simple yet stunning strand of diamonds. He stood behind her while she remained sitting and placed them around her neck, clasping them in the back, causing a slight frisson to extend down Elizabeth's back at the slight touch. Elizabeth's eyes widened at the sight as she instinctively raised her hand to touch the shimmering gems.

"They are exquisite," she said softly. "I've never worn something so fine."

"There is more." Darcy then handed her the opened box where she saw the matching earrings and bracelet.

"Oh my." Then looking at him archly, she said, "Are you sure you trust me not to lose them as I skip down the stairs of the theatre?" He just smiled at her, recognising her teasing yet again. Darcy then watched as she placed the earrings and bracelet onto their respective places. "And how do I look? Am I tolerable?"

Darcy had long forgotten those misplaced words that had been spoken as a defence from those around him at the Meryton assembly. He had made a habit of ending any pursuit of his person by speaking words of dissention to those within hearing. So that particular occasion did not stand out in his mind. He most definitely found her more than tolerable on this night. In fact, he found her quite pretty, despite his initial inclination to think contrariwise. If asked now, he would have to admit that her beauty exceeded that of the average lady of his acquaintance, but her temperament and singularity left her wanting in terms of his admiration. "I daresay you are more than tolerable. You look charming." He was then at a loss to understand the significance of Elizabeth's arch look accompanied by her enticing upturned lips.

They arrived at the theatre before the usual fashionable hour. Darcy wanted to avoid as much of the scrutiny as he could, so they were able to make their way to his box without interruption. Elizabeth knew what he was about, and as she did not care a whit about meeting anyone of his acquaintance, she said not a word, even to tease. Instead she devoted her time to watching the theatre patrons as they entered the auditorium, commenting occasionally on what she observed. Darcy watched her in quiet amusement. Upon entering her dressing room earlier, he noticed that her usual animation had been missing; Elizabeth had seemed most despondent. However, as she gazed upon the people below filling the seats, her radiance returned, and he wondered if she had any idea of how her delight showed forth for all to see. He had always held his emotions hidden behind a mask of indiscernible hauteur; in so doing, he could keep those attempting to take advantage of his every action under regulation. But here was his wife, clearly enjoying the spectacle, and the show had not yet begun.

The room filled to about half capacity when the performance began. The lights were dimmed and Elizabeth focused on the spectacle upon the stage rather than the audience. She was familiar with *Twelfth Night*, having read it more than once, but this was the first time she had actually seen it represented by professionals on a stage. She found herself quickly absorbed into the light-hearted drama, laughing more than once out loud, quite forgetting her own melancholy from earlier in the day. When the intermission arrived, she said, "I have always found pleasure in reading this play, but I confess that seeing it executed on the stage makes it all the more entertaining! Have you seen *Twelfth Night* before?"

"I have, but perhaps not with as much pleasure as this time." He would have said, "while in your company," but he was not quite sure that it was her company that made the difference. Regardless, he did indeed savour this particular display over any others in the past. "Would you like some refreshment? I can get you some if you like."

"I would enjoy some lemonade or punch."

"I will be back in a moment then." At this, Mr. Darcy left the box. As a studier of character, Elizabeth had found many perplexities concerning her new husband's personality; however, she noticed that in other ways she could read him like a familiar book. She knew that he did not desire her attendance with him outside the box and likely hoped that no one would venture her way for an introduction. Elizabeth also knew that her husband had not yet recovered from the blow of marrying a woman of poor means and low connections, and although her pride was bruised by the idea, she could not truly fault him, as he had been taught to value wealth and station his whole life. So Elizabeth decided to find diversion in the idea instead and meant to tease him a bit should the opportunity arise.

While gone, Darcy encountered several of his acquaintance, who were wishing him well and seeking an invitation to return with him to his box to meet the new Mrs. Darcy. He was always good at subverting any attempts from the society of London at ingratiating themselves into his life. He used this same skill – that generally gave him the reputation of being arrogant for those who did not know him – in keeping away the unwelcome acquaintances of the *ton* on this particular night. Due to the delays, it took him slightly longer than Elizabeth had expected, so that when he entered, she said in a voice of feigned reproach, "Mr. Darcy, I had almost given up hope that you would return. I thought this to be an unexpected means of losing a wife, simply not returning. Of course a public scandal would have ensued, but hasn't that always been our lot?"

"Elizabeth, you jest and are speaking opinions which are not your own."

"Perhaps," said she with a smile, then she looked around the auditorium and seeing many eyes fixed upon them said, "Mr. Darcy, how you must tire of always being the centre of everyone's attention. I do believe we are being watched by every female within purview of your box. I have begun to wonder if

I have something upon my face with all the scrutiny! You would tell me would you not?"

"You appear to great advantage, Elizabeth." He then glanced out over the crowd and continued, "Of course they are curious about you. There has likely been great speculation about the wife of Mr. Darcy, and this is everyone's first opportunity to take stock of you. The women with fans over their mouths whispering to one another, while taking glances our way, are in great agony over your part in usurping their designs."

She looked at him and saw a slight smile on his lips and a glimmer of a sparkle in his eyes and realised that he too could tease. "I guess then for your advantage, I should not do something obscene or to cause ridicule." She then imagined the idea of waving in an uncouth manner to two particular ladies, deep in conversation who were boldly staring at her in disdain, and laughed. Elizabeth had always been the model of propriety and would never do something so ridiculous, but the thought did give her some diversion. Her laugh earned a questioning look from her partner. "Just my own variety of droll humour. I find little ways to amuse myself within the confines of my mind; some things are best left unsaid, you see."

"I do see. I have made great effort to avoid saying things that might cause offence or might give the wrong impression when in public."

"Indeed?" She said, one brow raised. Then she laughed despite her desire to keep a straight face.

"Are you finding something else about which to laugh? Do *I* perhaps have something on *my* face?"

"Oh, no. Remember, you are a man without fault. You can have nothing about you that would cause me to make light." He had the distinct impression that she was in fact making fun of him in the privacy of her mind, and not liking to be the focus of a jest, he was about to change the subject when a knock was heard on the doorway into his private box. Darcy opened the entrance and saw a most unwelcome sight.

"Bingley, I had no idea you were to attend the theatre tonight," said a flustered Darcy, who had a very distinct memory of the unpleasant conversation with Elizabeth concerning this same gentleman but three days previously.

"We saw you and Mrs. Darcy from across the way and decided to come pay our respects." With him were Miss Bingley and Mr. and Mrs. Hurst. Elizabeth could not pretend to find pleasure in seeing him or his family, so she curtseyed, spoke a few words, and then attempted to continue her observation of the seating below. Mr. Bingley, who had always been a great favourite amongst men and women alike, found this new and uncivil response quite puzzling, especially coming from such an amiable woman as Elizabeth.

Miss Bingley had come with her brother searching for ways to disconcert Mr. Darcy's new bride and found Elizabeth's cut a perfect opportunity to show her brother how uncouth the Bennets were in actuality. "Mrs. Darcy, how do you enjoy your first performance at a grand theatre? *Twelfth Night* seems an appropriate initiation into the London culture."

"You are mistaken, Miss Bingley. I have been to the theatre on many occasions in the past, although this is the first time I have seen this particular play. Though I cannot say I understand your meaning about its being an appropriate initiation."

"I just thought you might appreciate the art of deception in order to make a match."

Darcy himself meant to make a show of defending his wife, but before he could, Elizabeth spoke for herself. "Of course. I understand you, Miss Bingley. I realise that you know all too well how to ensnare a husband and would now be in my place enjoying Mr. Darcy's private box for yourself if not for the intervention of Mr. Darcy's own valet. I must say that your stratagem was a good one. Your creativity truly should do your brother proud and matches perfectly in the expectations provided by your education." Miss Bingley gave Elizabeth an insolent scowl. Apparently Elizabeth had heard about her noble endeavours to free Mr. Darcy from his now wife, whose laughing eyes told her that she also knew of Mr. Darcy's indelicate response onto her person.

Mr. Bingley's eyes widened in shock, while Mr. Darcy worked very hard to hold in the laugh that almost unceremoniously escaped his mouth. *Touché, Elizabeth.* As Mr. Darcy looked on in wicked amusement, Mr. Bingley realised that his family had somehow offended Elizabeth. However, as they had made the curtain call, he could not explore how until another time and so departed in dispirited contrition, for he had the distinct impression that it was not just his sister from whom Elizabeth had found offence.

Elizabeth's glance to her husband communicated more than any words. She remembered their heated argument to be sure and meant to punish poor Bingley who was unaware of the malice that had arisen as a result of Darcy's own deceptive words. Darcy felt the guilt imposed upon his friend most keenly and would have disabused Elizabeth of her notion of Bingley's transgressions had he not known that he was doing his duty to protect his friend. Instead, he tried to make light of the interruption, "So, news must travel quite propitiously in Meryton."

"This you knew." Then she nonchalantly said, while looking towards the crowd, "And I thank you for providing my family with no small amount of diversion when we heard of the unfortunate event. But it would seem Miss Bingley recovered, and I thank you for persisting in your obligation to me in the face of such a scheme." Darcy inclined his head in acknowledgement. The lights were dimmed and the second half of the play began.

Overall the evening went quite well for the Darcys. They each felt that their first public appearance was a success. They had slipped out before the majority of the crowd by leaving five minutes before the conclusion of the play, and the carriage was waiting, as Darcy had previously specified. Elizabeth was disappointed to miss the very end, but understood that Darcy had no wish to face the onslaught of the crowd in the theatre's lobby. She had never been an object of scrutiny and could not say that she enjoyed the prospect of being in close quarters with a relentless group of people vying for Mr. Darcy's attention and her acquaintance, especially for the purpose of finding fault. She began to realise that her husband indeed lived a life of close observation by others and that perhaps his impassive mien held a productive purpose after all. She determined not to judge him too harshly in the future for this perplexing part of his character.

Darcy enjoyed his evening more than he had anticipated. He had almost cancelled the outing, especially in light of the disagreement from a few days previously, but was glad that he had not. Mrs. Darcy performed remarkably well in her new role when the few who did boldly approach them received an introduction. She was self-assured and affable, showing no signs of discomfort. Perhaps she would be ready in a week's time to meet his family.

Chapter Eleven

The passions are the seeds of vices as well as virtues, from which either
may spring, accordingly as they are nurtured. Unhappy they
who have never been taught the art to govern them!
Ann Radcliffe
The Mysteries of Udolpho

Elizabeth had noticed that very few Christmas decorations adorned the walls of Darcy House and meant to ask Mr. Darcy if this was by design or if she might make some alterations before the festive season began in earnest. There were just five days until Christmas, so she planned to ask him before the end of the day. Since the time of their theatre outing, Elizabeth had completed her preparations for her own family's Christmas presents, buying some and making others, and all were ready to give to the Gardiners, so that they could deliver them to the family on their annual holiday visit. She was in the couple's shared sitting room, preparing the packages to be sent when Mr. Darcy entered, surprised by her presence.

"Good afternoon, Mr. Darcy, you find me finishing up my packing for Longbourn's Christmas, and I am glad that you are here, for I wanted to ask you about your usual preparations in your home for the holiday."

"When I am in town, my housekeeper usually takes charge of the task. I believe this Saturday will be the day, with all of the staff in attendance to decorate with greenery brought in from Pemberley."

"How marvellous! Do you assist?"

"I did as a child, but have not in years."

"I see." Elizabeth pondered. "Do you mind if I help? I dearly love the hanging of the green."

"You are now the mistress of the house; you may do as you like."

"Will you join me, then?"

Darcy was taken aback by her request. As it had been years since he had participated—since his mother's death, in fact – he did not know what the endeavour would entail. "If you wish me to."

"Of course."

"I came to tell to you that I plan on introducing you to my relations on Saturday, perhaps after our decorations are complete." Elizabeth looked at him bemused, as he continued. "I had planned on waiting until Christmas, for Fitzwilliam would be in attendance, and I considered, since you and he had met and seemed to enjoy one another's company, that you might find comfort in his presence, but I realise that you do not need a comrade as I had once thought. Your comportment at the theatre impressed me with the idea that you will do well with only myself as your attendant."

This speech was made in sincerity, but it puzzled Elizabeth exceedingly. He seemed almost nervous. "If that is your wish. I look forward to making their acquaintance. I have long desired meeting your family."

"I must warn you that Fitzwilliam is unlike his family in many ways, for he has been in the service of the King for some time now, which has made him more understanding than his family of the lower classes."

"I am not afraid, sir."

"Of course you are not." He provided a faint smile then continued, "So this box is bound for Longbourn?"

"Yes, our family exchanges gifts each year, and I have finally completed making mine and have only to send the package through the Gardiners."

"And what is your family to receive?" Darcy was curious as to how Elizabeth had been spending her pin money. Elizabeth then told him that her father was to receive a book that she had found at the bookstore on Bond Street, her mother a lace cap that she herself had made, her sister Jane, a novel, Mary, sheet music, and her two youngest sisters, bonnets with ribbons and fabric so that they themselves could adorn them. "I used to make gifts for all of my family, but my father had an overabundant supply of embroidered handkerchiefs, hence I decided to give him something he would truly want, so he gets a book from me now. My younger sisters would rather make their own gifts." He took mental note that there was nothing of great import or expense; indeed there was nothing that would suggest that she had just married one of the most affluent men in England, which somewhat surprised him. He thought of how Miss Bingley would have found plenty of expensive gifts to show off her increase in wealth.

"Oh, and my aunt and uncle here in London, they are to receive tickets to the theatre. I asked Franklin to procure them, and I plan on gifting them on Sunday along with the other presents."

"You give all of your family gifts?"

"I know our tradition might seem a little excessive, but not everyone participates. I see it as a time to do something for my family from my heart, in remembrance of Christ's gift to us. I know my younger sisters just like to receive more bonnets and ribbons, but I believe giving is more about the giver than the receiver. Mr. Darcy, will you not come with me on Sunday? We will not be out in public, just a simple visit to my family to wish them a happy Christmas."

"I plan to attend services with my family and had expected you would do the same since you will be meeting them on Saturday." At her look of disappointment, he continued, "However, I see that I should have said something earlier. For this one last time, you may go with your family. I will have a carriage available for you." Elizabeth was silent, wanting to encourage him to come, if only for a short call at the usual pick up time, but knowing that he might get angry if she persisted. She stood there biting her lower lip as she thought through this and finally came to the conclusion that forcing the idea to accept her family would not work; it had certainly not worked towards herself and their marriage.

"Very well. But if you change your mind, you would be most welcome."

Darcy then made his excuses and departed for the day. He was troubled by Elizabeth's continued association with her family, but supposed after leaving for

Pemberley in the next few weeks that she would be limited in her time spent in their company and would likely, on her own, see the inferiority of the connection and naturally decrease time in their presence when next they were to return to town in the spring.

THE HOUSE WAS ABUZZ WITH ACTIVITY as the servants gathered supplies and ladders to decorate the great home. Upon learning of the plans to adorn the home in greenery, Elizabeth had ordered that hot drinks and other refreshments be made available to the staff as they readied the house for the season. She joined in the activity of hanging the greenery in the low places and adorning the tables. Elizabeth took it upon herself to follow her own inclinations about where and how the boxwood would be placed in the foyer along with the flowers from Pemberley's hothouse that had arrived the day before. Elizabeth had always loved flowers, fresh or dried, wild or from the garden. She had an eye for nature and how to present a display indoors. She had helped to decorate her home each festive season for the past fifteen years. However, the housekeeper had different ideas of how things should be done, for she had been in charge of this custom since Lady Anne died, and she did not take kindly to the new mistress interfering.

Since the arrival of Mrs. Darcy, Mrs. Johnson had continued on with civil obedience to Elizabeth's wishes, which was not too difficult since the new mistress had made few demands and mainly kept to her own chamber and the music room. She was nosing her way into the kitchen, but was mainly just observing and learning the system that had been employed in the home for years by asking questions about her own role to play. The housekeeper continued in her silent derision of the mistress, not willing to give her the respect due her position. However, when Elizabeth had begun to meddle in the decorating, Mrs. Johnson could not stand idly by and watch as she made the house into an indecorous display. "Mrs. Darcy, please allow me to do this for you. We have been preparing the house each year for Christmas and have much experience in how to display the greenery to the greatest advantage. Your help is simply not needed."

It was but the work of a moment for Elizabeth to sum up the meaning behind the housekeeper's respectful but disingenuous words, and not wanting to offend but also desiring to set the boundaries, said, "I am sure you have done an admirable job these many years, for I have seen how well this household is run with your leadership, and I have enjoyed the display of flowers that greet me every morning. But, as this is now my home, I desire to participate on occasion in the fitting of the ornamentation, and this is one of those times. I promise not to interfere too much in your traditional trimmings, but I do plan to play my part in decorating my new home." Elizabeth smiled sweetly to the woman hoping for this to be the end of the challenge. She knew she had every right to play a part in the endeavour and hoped that if it came down to it, Mr. Darcy would agree. Just as this thought came to mind, she heard his familiar voice from the doorway.

"Mrs. Johnson, I see that you have everything running smoothly as usual and my wife has already joined you." Then turning to Elizabeth, he bowed and said, "Mrs. Darcy, I am at your disposal. What shall you have me do? I have come prepared as you wished." Darcy had overheard the conversation going on between his wife and housekeeper and knew this was a pivotal moment in the life of his efficiently managed home. If he were to side with the housekeeper, Elizabeth would lose all respect in her position as mistress; however, if he sided with Elizabeth there was the risk that his home would begin its journey towards a gauche and unfitting dwelling. He decided for the latter, for Elizabeth could be managed in the privacy of their rooms, but if Elizabeth were to ever find respect as the mistress of the house, she must be shown respect publicly by the master.

Elizabeth smiled kindly at him, unsure if he had heard them speaking before he entered, but thankful for his coming, nonetheless. "I was just about to begin in the foyer. Mrs. Johnson was just telling me that she has been at this for years and has a thorough understanding of how best to show the home to advantage, but as I also have been *festooning* Longbourn for many years, I hope to do my part in my new home. I would enjoy your company and assistance, if you are still willing."

"Indeed, I am at your command." With Darcy's consent, nothing more was said concerning the housekeeper, for the point was made. Elizabeth had won this small battle. They enjoyed the majority of the day joining the servants in trimming the home. After a time, while the servants partook of their refreshments, Elizabeth sat down at the pianoforte and played the Christmas songs that she had been practising since learning of her husband's expectations of her playing for Christmas. Everyone was working and making merry, so that by mid-afternoon, the house was filled to the brim with greens, reds and golds.

When all was completed, Darcy had to admit to himself that Elizabeth's work on the house was all done with taste and elegance, and he had rarely seen the home look finer. "You did not tell me you were so proficient in this area."

"Would it have made a difference?" Then she laughed. "I told you that I have few accomplishments, and that is true, for arranging flowers for Christmas cannot compare to speaking French and painting tables. No, I have very little to offer the marriage, so you will just have to appreciate the meagre contributions I *can* make."

"Perhaps you underestimate yourself."

"That cannot be," Elizabeth replied as she laughed becomingly. "Well, if I am to be ready to leave for our visit to your family, I must be off to my chamber."

"I will retrieve you at six-thirty," responded Darcy as Elizabeth left the music room.

ELIZABETH WORE ANOTHER OF HER NEW GOWNS, this time with a set of pearls that once belonged to Darcy's mother. After discovering which of the dresses she would be wearing, Darcy had retrieved them and presented the lustrous strand to her before leaving. Her hair was held in place by pins adorned with pearls at their tips, contrasting fittingly with her hair, making the pearl set an ideal accompaniment.

Elizabeth still found her husband's company trying for he always seemed to be casting a stern, fixed stare her way as if to find fault. But she had been surprised at his acquiescence in decorating that day and supposed rightly that he was trying to make her transition into his life and his home easier.

Elizabeth watched her husband closely in the darkened carriage as they travelled the few blocks to Tromwell House. "Mr. Darcy, you must stop fidgeting, for you are beginning to make me afraid. Tell me, is it to be that bad?" She appeared amused, for indeed she was, but he missed it due to the limited light and thought perhaps she was in earnest.

"Forgive me, I mean not to alarm you. There is nothing for you to fear, of which I am aware. I am a little nervous for Georgiana's sake. She does not often meet people from outside of her sphere and.... Well, she may have a preconceived idea of you that is unfavourable. My aunt and uncle will show decorum despite any misgivings, but my sister, well she is still young. Please understand if she says or does something that might cause offence. I have tried to give her an approbatory assessment of you, but she will doubtless discover fault as she chooses. Georgiana loves me dearly and will likely find it hard to forgive you based on her assessment of how we entered into our marriage." He said all of this as a matter-of-fact and gave no indication that she should think such behaviour odd.

"You mean *your* assessment. For did you not explain to her the conditions of our engagement? Did you tell her that I forced you to marry me?"

"I told her what I knew to be true. If she or anyone else construes the facts to suggest that there was any artifice in the match, I cannot counter their assessment. I have told her that you have in no way behaved in a manner that would suggest a deficiency in character. She will, in time, accept you, I am certain, for she is of a kind disposition and sweet nature."

Elizabeth thought back to Mr. Wickham's appraisal of Miss Darcy's being excessively proud, like her brother. Of course Mr. Darcy would not describe his own sister in such terms for he adores her, but more importantly, she apparently shares his faults, which he could not see in himself either. There was nothing to do but be herself and hope for the best. It was rare that someone should not like Elizabeth, for she was always a favourite amongst the Meryton populace, at least until the scandal brought her low. She would try to find her own peace in showing respect when due, kindness when undeserved, and fortitude when attacked.

When the Darcys were announced and entered the drawing room, everyone in attendance stood, anxious for their first glance at the new Mrs. Darcy. The sentiments of the inhabitants of the room varied somewhat but each was predisposed to think ill of her for ensnaring their beloved nephew, cousin or brother respectively. Darcy knew this, but could do nothing to change their opinion on the matter without a large dose of time and condescension.

Darcy first presented her to his uncle and aunt Fitzwilliam, Lord Matlock and Lady Estella. Elizabeth curtseyed showing the respect due their rank and thanked them for the invitation. She found the earl to be a handsome, older man with stern features. He reminded her of a male version of Lady Catherine. His wife, still lovely despite her years, wore a dress as fashionable as any debutante and looked at Elizabeth with no indication of her inner reflections.

Next, she was introduced to Patrick Fitzwilliam, the Viscount Langston, and his wife, Lady Susan Fitzwilliam, showing the same deference as was due. Elizabeth found that the viscount was perhaps more handsome than his younger brother, but had an arrogance completely lacking in Colonel Fitzwilliam. His wife reminded Elizabeth of Caroline Bingley in her manner and dress but with less to attract. In truth she was quite homely, but did not seem be aware of her deficiencies. Under the man's scrutiny, Elizabeth felt exposed and wished that she had chosen a dress with more fabric across the neckline.

The younger sister, Lady Victoria, stood off to the side and had been whispering to another much younger woman. They both moved closer for the introduction. Lady Victoria was an attractive woman of about five and twenty and more closely resembled the colonel in looks and manner than the rest in attendance. Her husband was not to make an appearance for an undisclosed reason. Then Elizabeth turned to the younger woman who had been watching her carefully and discovered her to be Miss Georgiana Darcy. Miss Darcy favoured her brother but with lighter features, more closely resembling that of the Fitzwilliam side of the family.

Knowing that she was being scrutinised most closely, Elizabeth attempted to curtail her teasing nature and appear as respectful as she could, for she understood well the expectations of the peerage and the Fitzwilliams in particular. The conversation was stilted while Darcy's family took in her appearance. She was a pretty sort of girl, but certainly not a beauty like Lady Annette, and they each felt Darcy's loss most acutely.

Elizabeth was determined to put the burden of conversation upon her hosts for a truly accomplished woman, as the four in attendance, should have the social skills needed to direct and manage what was to be said. Lady Estella had desired to make Elizabeth uncomfortable with the laconism of the group, to see how she held up in the face of awkward silence, but finally after about half a minute that seemed more like ten, the Countess began to ask Elizabeth about her family, her home and interests. Elizabeth answered politely but directly, not perturbed by the reserve or the impropriety. The countess's daughter did not contribute to the conversation but politely listened in. The daughter-in-law stood off to the side with her husband, whispering while cutting glances to the new member of the family. When she was not looking in Elizabeth's direction, she studied the large mirror above the fireplace. Indeed this set the tone for the entirety of the evening where a mirror was to be found. Lady Susan would look at herself, adjust a curl, pinch her cheek, or pucker her lips to her best advantage then return to the group, only to repeat the endeavour. Although Elizabeth paid rapt attention to whomever chose to speak with her, she could not help but find amusement in the woman's self-absorbed eccentricities.

Dinner was called and they adjourned to the dining-parlour. A formal seating arrangement was used despite the gathering being of a small, family nature.

Elizabeth was placed directly across from her husband. Georgiana was her usual silent self when in the company of someone whom she had never met. She observed every remark, look and gesture made by her new sister, who had not failed to notice her staring. Elizabeth could not help but compare the brother with the sister. They both appeared reserved, taciturn and formidable to the onlooker, but their eyes seemed to speak for them, whether it be with disdain or approbation. In this current instance, Elizabeth saw distrust but could not fault Miss Darcy. Given the circumstances of the acquaintance, she could well imagine her apprehension and meant to put her at ease, as she was able. So Elizabeth decided to address her with a sincere yet neutral comment.

"Miss Darcy, your brother tells me that you are quite accomplished on the pianoforte. I look forward to hearing you play, if that is agreeable to you."

Georgiana looked up sharply and attempted to formulate a response to her understood question. She glanced at her brother, who answered for her, "My sister does not usually perform in public, but she will, of course, play Christmas carols with the rest of the family in a few days."

"Then I look forward to Christmas," Elizabeth said looking to Miss Darcy with a congenial smile.

Lord Langston then said, "I believe my brother has already made your acquaintance. He tells me that you are a lively kind of girl. What can he mean by that?"

Elizabeth looked a little flustered, then responded, "I cannot speak for the colonel nor can I comprehend his meaning, but we have enjoyed spirited conversations. Or perhaps he refers to the reel we danced during the engagement ball at Netherfield." The viscount had other ideas of what *lively* meant and made his sentiments clear as he yet again took a quick look down to her décolletage.

"James was always one to stick by Darcy, no matter the justification," replied the viscount, earning a look of reproach from Darcy, which caused the man to smile slyly.

Then it was the earl's turn, "Mrs. Darcy, my nephew tells me that you have four sisters."

"Yes, I am the second of five."

"And no brothers?"

"No, my lord. My parents had always planned to have sons, but the execution of their plan went awry. My mother blames my father, but I am sure that he cannot be at fault," Elizabeth replied with a sparkle to her eyes having always thought the idea absurd, but then, too late, she thought back to her mother's advice on the day of her wedding and coloured, ashamed of where her mind had gone, yet still not really sure what it meant.

"Your father's estate is entailed away, I believe."

"This is true."

"And to a man who was in Hertfordshire seeking to rectify the burden upon your family by an offer of marriage to one of your father's daughters."

Elizabeth glanced at her husband, not knowing if he had shared this bit of information, or perhaps his uncle had spoken to Lady Catherine herself, as she had been the one to encourage her parson's interest in her family. Darcy remained impassive, apparently expecting such an inquiry. "My father's distant cousin, a Mr. William Collins, who is also the rector of Hunsford and appointed by Lady Catherine de Bourgh, came with the intention of offering for one of us. And he found success, for he is to marry my sister next month."

"Did he not offer for you first? That was what I was told."

"He was making his intentions towards me clear; however, my sister, Mary, was more suited as a parson's wife and had an inclination towards the man, so to our mutual satisfaction, he changed loyalties with the alacrity of a man full of fanciful devotion. I believe that it was the day before I met your nephew that he made the new object of his ardour clear."

"So my nephew is to be the brother of my sister's parson?"

"As you say." A look of unfeigned irritation passed over the earl. Elizabeth could neither say nor do anything to change the facts of the matter. She was just glad that her absurd cousin was not in attendance, for she would have keenly felt the humiliation of the situation. Fortunately for Elizabeth, she did not know that the earl had already met Mr. Collins when Lady Catherine paid a visit while trying to resolve the dilemma in which Darcy had found himself; his unfavourable opinion was firmly established.

Then it was Lady Susan's turn, "Darcy said that you were out walking alone when you came across him in the woods. You did not have an escort?"

"I was on my father's estate. The servants cannot be spared when the day begins, so I do often walk out alone. An early morning walk prepares me for my day. While home, I rarely miss the occasion to take in the fresh air."

"But, surely you can see how improper that is."

"I do not," Elizabeth answered in confidence. "I cannot find fault in traversing my own father's estate in a countryside where I have grown up and know as well as the garden outside my window. I find that the activity is invigorating, and up until two months ago had never resulted in an encounter with anyone outside my family or our tenants."

"You will not be able to continue on in such manner, will she, Darcy?" The man to whom the question was directed was trying to stay out of the inquisition. He had known it would come, and best before Christmas, so that the holy day would not be tainted by his family's assault, but he had hoped himself to stay out of the attack. "Elizabeth knows that she must have a footman with her, and as I can afford to provide a servant when her father could not, I see no problem in the matter. Of course she cannot take on so far a distance and is limited in town as to her destination; but at Pemberley, she will be able to roam as she will, as long as she keeps to the main paths so as not to lose her way. Before long, however, she will be riding the estate and will have no need for footpaths."

Elizabeth listened on in wonder at her husband's narration of his expectations for her future. "Your plan, sir, would be a good one, except for the fact that I do not desire to learn to ride and have no inclination towards the endeavour." Everyone looked to Elizabeth and then Darcy. How would he respond to her blatant show of disrespect?

"You know not of what you speak, Elizabeth. Of course you will learn to ride. All Darcys ride."

"I have no intention of riding; however, perhaps we can discuss this at a more appropriate time. I am sure your family has no interest in the matter."

Everyone was then surprised when Georgiana spoke up, as the indignation at Elizabeth's refractory remarks provoked her to rejoin that her brother was a fair and benevolent head of the family and would not ask anything of her that was unreasonable, and that his desire for her to learn to ride was a sensible one.

Elizabeth thought it best to change the subject, for she could tell that Darcy's family was not in the habit of being questioned or disputed. "I am sure you are correct, Miss Darcy." Then turning to the middle of the table, she continued, "Lady Estella, I have not yet had a chance to compliment you on this delicious meal. Your choice of soup is a favourite of mine, which I have rarely enjoyed more." Elizabeth had only been able to eat a small portion of the fare provided, as she had not regained her appetite since her undesirable marriage had taken place and was disconcerted by the obvious planned attack upon herself by her new relations. None of her family would ever treat a guest in their home with such a rude examination.

"Mrs. Darcy, James tells me that you moved my cousin a distance of more than one hundred yards without assistance, in the middle of a storm, over rough terrain to get him to safety," Lord Langston said as he looked around the group laughing. "Do you really expect us to believe you had no help? That is quite a distance," he continued, hoping to entertain the company through her discomfort.

"Near and far are relative terms. You see, when obstacles are in the way twenty can feel like one hundred. I did contemplate leaving him there," she then gave a sly glance over in Darcy's direction, "but Mr. Darcy was quite pitiful, so I could not abandon him alone in the elements; therefore, I remained. Getting him to the cabin was really quite selfish of me, for I myself did not want to be caught in the storm. But I am afraid we experienced the full force of the storm nonetheless. Mr. Darcy was fortunate enough not to remember our journey in the woods. I had never been so glad of my own habit of vigorous exercise, for without it, I could not have gotten him to safety," she finished with a smile.

"You have not addressed my question of having help."

"I told you that we have no servant to walk out with me, and that I was quite alone until your cousin almost ran me over," she said with a small, quick tilt of her head. Her smile was waning.

"Forgive me if I find your story of this feat too absurd to credit."

Darcy had been passively listening to the exchange and realised that he had never questioned Elizabeth as to the details concerning his move to the cabin. He too wanted to know how she could have transported him alone and remembered the suspicion he held on that day – that another had been there to assist. *Wickham!* But then just as briefly thought about the absurdity of Wickham's being present just as he had been going by. Of course she could have been meeting Wickham in the woods, and that man could have rendered the plan upon seeing that the horseman was Darcy himself. He continued to listen, determined to hear the truth one way or another.

Elizabeth reiterated her previous declaration and then directed another remark to the countess concerning the delicious fare, spending the rest of the meal answering questions as succinctly as she could and changing the subject as needed. As Elizabeth was quite skilled in repartee as a defence, she remained confident and never let on her discomfiture and exasperation. In fact, on at least three occasions during the evening, she took pleasure in a silent joke, needing no one to share the amusement but wishing her father had been in attendance to enjoy a private but pointed glance. These small but fortunate reflections made her first dinner with her in-laws bearable, despite their assailment.

During the separation of the sexes, Lady Susan stood by the mantle where she could watch Elizabeth through the mirror while simultaneously stealing glances at herself. Lady Estella was sitting with their guest along with her daughter. She simply needed to determine on her own if Elizabeth was indeed guilty of orchestrating Darcy's descent. "Mrs. Darcy, your husband has told us his part in how your marriage came about. I am sure you understand our concern, that we cannot help but suppose that you might have arranged the whole unfortunate business." She did not say this accusingly, but seemed to sincerely want to know the truth, so Elizabeth responded in like manner.

"Lady Estella, you ask no more than my own family, for they wanted to be certain that I was not taken advantage of while alone with an unknown man obviously accustomed to having his own way." Georgiana opened her mouth to defend her brother, but Elizabeth continued on. "Please understand that Mr. Darcy's and my own connections must see this in two divergent but plausible ways. Neither of our characters was known to the other before the incident. Circumstances outside of our control brought us together, so that neither of us was at fault."

"But your mother, do you deny her role in spreading the rumours abroad about the compromise?"

"I cannot deny that she played her part in the scandal. My mother acted on a perceived opportunity. I do not condone such means of collecting husbands; and I can assure you that this was done against my will, for I was out of my senses in the sickbed, and against my father's will, who knew nothing of her initiative. Unlike many of the single ladies in our society, I am not the type of woman who would seek an attachment to a man who had no regard for me, solely based on his position in society, the size of his estate, or his family name.

"I must forgive my mother, as I am sure many other ladies must forgive their own, for taking the opportunity presented to her to secure the future of her vulnerable family. I don't believe that she acted any differently than many mothers put in like circumstances and certainly undertook her plan without malice. That is not to say that I approve of her intervention, for I do not. Nor do I adhere to the idea of marrying for any motive other than affection or in my present circumstance, to save my family from ruin. Ours is a society driven by pecuniary and status-based considerations when it comes to marriage, which is essentially a business arrangement to benefit one or both parties; you cannot deny it." Then Elizabeth took a calming breath before continuing. "I hope that as time goes on, you will bear witness to my character as proof that I, if not my mother, am innocent of any stratagem that forced Mr. Darcy into an undesirable alliance with me and my family. I *will* do my best to keep him from regretting his decision to protect my family from a most ruinous scandal."

Lady Estella listened to Elizabeth's speech in wonder as she defended herself with poise and conviction. She could not say that she completely believed the young bride's defence, but she could respect her tenacity under pressure. Few women of her acquaintance, young or old, would have borne the attack this evening as Elizabeth had, and with as much intrepidity. And if she were completely honest with herself, Elizabeth's response had merit. She could not dispute the rationale that many marriages of the *ton* were based on mercenary designs. Was that not why her own son married Lady Susan, for her dowry of thirty thousand? Would he have married her if not for her purse and family? Indeed, she and the earl had to practically force the point by decreasing his allowance to a near trifling before he would agree, for he found Lady Susan to be disagreeable in looks and temperament. She had even suspected, much to her despair, that her son assuaged his disappointment with trips to the exclusive brothel on St. James Street.

But the difference in her son's situation was that both agreed to the match with open resolve, not out of force but mutual benefit. In addition to an alignment with the Earl of Matlock, Lady Susan would one day be the countess, thereby putting her in a position of even greater deference than she was as daughter of a baron. And Langston received thirty thousand pounds through the marriage. But Darcy could receive no benefit from such a match as he found himself. Indeed, he took on a liability, for now he was obligated to a family in need of saving and was honour-bound to be of some assistance.

The men joined the ladies, and Darcy went to his sister to discern how she bore the evening, for they had spoken little. There was no way to exclude Georgiana from the family's interrogation of his wife, and he was just glad that those in company had not gone so far as to openly suggest any corporeal breaches of propriety. Actually, having his sister in attendance likely helped to ensure that the insinuations upon his wife did not descend into vulgarity. Ascertaining that Georgiana was well, if not a little distraught over the conversations to which she had been privy, he then joined Elizabeth as a show of support.

Darcy had sat in resigned discomfiture knowing that the interrogation would be long and arduous. He actually admired Elizabeth for her ability to withstand such a direct attack from no less than two peers of the realm and their noble wives. Darcy even began to have insight into her unique humour that had often been at his own expense, but when directed elsewhere, even to his own relations, he was able to appreciate. Her quick wit and intelligence impressed him, as long as his dear sister was overlooked. Darcy was just glad that they would be past the drama before Christmas Day itself. He had hoped that James would be in attendance on this, Elizabeth's first exposure to the Fitzwilliams, but he had to admit that she was quite able to hold her own despite her unfortunate upbringing. And on the way home, within the confines of the carriage, Darcy said, "I hope you were not offended by my family's queries. Their intentions were not to humiliate you, but to calm their own reservations in defence of me."

"Of course not; I would never judge you by your family's manners, as I would not want to be judged by my own family's words and actions. You see, we both have relations who seek to protect us in embarrassing ways."

"Perhaps we have something else in common then."

"Perhaps. So we return to their home for Christmas?" At his agreement, she continued, "You had told me that your cousins have children, but they were not introduced to me. Will we see them on Tuesday?"

"In the past they have been presented during tea."

"Tell me about them."

"Langston has a son and daughter, of six and four respectively. Their names are Edmund and Emily. Victoria has two daughters, Rebecca and Emma, of about the same ages, maybe a little younger."

"I love children. I hope I will be able to spend a little time with them on Christmas. Are they of easy temperament?"

"I hardly know. We see them for about fifteen minutes, and then they are gone."

She looked at him puzzled. "How often do you see them?"

"A few times a year, I suppose. They begin to get fidgety and then are sent back to their rooms where they can play."

"May I give them each a present for Christmas?"

Darcy was now surprised. "I suppose you can, but truly there is no need. Victoria will likely not be in attendance, for her husband, whom you did not meet tonight, will likely take her to his own family's residence."

"I have planned on presenting Georgiana with a gift, if that is acceptable to you. Since I know little about her, I could not give her something too personal, but as my new sister I felt it right. Does your extended family exchange gifts?"

"No, we have never given gifts beyond Georgiana and myself."

Darcy noticed Elizabeth's smile and could not help but ask what it might signify. "You will think me ungenerous, but I was considering that if your family did share presents, we might give Lady Susan a small looking glass to fit in her reticule." At his look of puzzlement, she said, "Surely, Darcy, you could not miss how often she gazes into the mirror at her own likeness." She laughed lightly with mirth in her eyes. "I saw her looking into that large mirror in the drawing room more than once. Indeed while the ladies were alone, she stood with her back to me while facing the mirror, so she could see my reflection without giving herself away, and I daresay I caught her looking at herself more often than at me. I began to feel jealous at the slight."

Darcy smiled at the idea. "I cannot say I have ever noticed."

"You surprise me, sir. I had always supposed you to be more astute than that. Are you not a studier of character? You sit staring at others so much, I assumed your appraisal had a purpose."

"I do observe closely what goes on around me, but perhaps our purposes differ."

"You look to find fault, and me, diversion."

"Elizabeth, you are harsh on me."

"I must speak as I find. But don't take my assessment too severely. I have observed that there are many facets to Fitzwilliam Darcy, including some I quite admire." When she had his attention, she went on, "However, I plan to keep those to myself. You have heard enough of your praises from your many admirers and even the papers if I recall correctly." Elizabeth was smiling as if she held a secret of some import but would not tell.

It was true. Darcy had heard many times the commendation and obeisance of many on his behalf, attempting to garner his approbation and friendship for reasons of ambitious intent. He doubted the sincerity of his admirers and rarely took their praises to be without guile. So why did he want to know what Elizabeth might have to say? She found his failings true enough and was quick to share them with him and his relations. In fact there were very few of his acquaintance, peers or servants, who ever found fault in him, or at least transgressions they were willing to share. His cousin, Fitzwilliam, was the rare one who showed no deference whatsoever, even though Darcy's approval was essential, as he went a good way to making Fitzwilliam's life free of financial stress. Even his aunts and uncle bestowed enough respect on him to keep their negative opinions of him to themselves, if indeed they had any. In his musings something occurred to him, which gave him pleasure. Smiling he said, "Elizabeth, do you realise what you just said?"

"That I might admire some thing or another about you? Surely that could not surprise you."

"Not that, although, indeed it does. You called me 'Darcy.' You've never done that before."

"Have I not?" She asked, somewhat flustered that she had not realised the familiarity. Then she laughed at herself while blushing for being so concerned about the propriety of it, for he was her husband, and she had likely earned the right to such intimacies.

"No, you have not. But I like it. We are married and Mr. Darcy seems so formal under the circumstances. Do you not think?"

Not knowing how to answer, she responded, "It is true that *Mr.* Darcy does sound rather proper for two people in close quarters." She blushed anew at the thought. "But, I cannot say that I feel completely comfortable without the formality, for in many ways we are like strangers, you and I." They then sat in some silence except for the clip clop of the horses' hooves on the cobblestones of the street as they each thought about the evolution of their relationship thus far. It was only a few moments before the carriage stopped and the door opened thus ending their reflections. Elizabeth was uneasy and ready to depart. She had had enough of the Fitzwilliams for one day and only wanted to get some rest.

Elizabeth went to her family's home as expected the following day and enjoyed the time in their good company. The Gardiners bestowed on her their small gift and she theirs including small toys and sweets for the children. She told them about her visit to the theatre and learnt that they had planned to go themselves, making her gift most propitious.

Then she shared stories of her evening at Lord Matlock's, leaving out the painful recollections of the family's rude welcome. She spoke of the home, the meal, and a description of each person, which was enough to fill the afternoon with stories and amusement. Elizabeth wished them a Happy Christmas and entrusted them with her family's presents as well as a note to each person at Longbourn and then left with a heavy heart, saddened by the idea that she would not be with her beloved family for this year's festivities.

CHRISTMAS EVE ARRIVED and the Fitzwilliam family, in addition to the Darcys, attended church in the late evening after dinner. Many eyes rested upon the newly married couple throughout the service. Having been out in public so seldom, the Darcys had become quite the talk. Elizabeth was judged to be comely, unattractive, tall, short, too thin, too curvaceous and by all, undeserving. So as the congregation celebrated the birth of the Saviour, they also made certain their need for one.

Colonel Fitzwilliam had made his showing that evening and would be celebrating the season with his family for the following fortnight. When first seeing Elizabeth, he was troubled by the change in her appearance. Nothing was obvious to the casual onlooker, but to him she appeared to have a more drawn appearance around her eyes, which no longer expressed her inner vivacity, as they had just two weeks previously. Also, Elizabeth had shed a few pounds from an already slender frame. They shared pleasant and congenial words upon their renewed association.

Elizabeth bore the inspection of the congregation well, as she found much to observe herself. Those in attendance seemed to have come to be seen more than to worship. She philosophically began to consider her place within the Fitzwilliam and Darcy families and if divine Providence had played a role in getting her there. But then how could a good God, who was willing to divest himself of his divine glory to add on human nature for the purpose of saving the lost, how could He orchestrate a situation that had only brought pain? But then she contemplated how much better her life was than so many others in London, those whom she had seen many times in the recent and distant past begging for sustenance. How could He let people starve and freeze to death upon the back streets of London, if He were a good and benevolent deity? Thereupon, she recalled that He himself had come into the world poor and with little shelter, pursued by soldiers who meant to kill Him and one day would be left naked to die. Yes, He did understand the plight of those suffering, and Elizabeth had to believe that He had a plan for them, as He had a plan for herself, however doubtful it would seem on the surface. She was interrupted in her musings by the call to worship and began to contemplate the compassionate and joyful attributes of God, leaving the more philosophical explorations for another day.

The next afternoon, before the Darcys returned to Tromwell House to share in the celebration of the holiday, Darcy knocked on the chamber door from the shared sitting room. "Excuse me if I have interrupted your preparations, but I hoped we might have a few moments before leaving." Elizabeth smiled and replied that there was no inconvenience, as Janette had just finished her hair. Picking up a wrapped package laying upon the writing desk, she followed Darcy into the sitting room.

Elizabeth noticed that he seemed a little uncomfortable, but she could not figure out why that might be. After the two sat down before the hearth, Darcy began, "Elizabeth, I first would like to wish you a Merry Christmas. I hope you will find pleasure on this, our first Christmas."

"Thank you, sir." Elizabeth then was surprised at her own discomfort. She looked to the gift on her lap that she had planned on giving to her husband as she fiddled with the ribbons.

"Although I do not exchange gifts with my extended family, Georgiana and I do give one another something to commemorate the day. And as you are now part of our little family, I have a present for you as well." Then handing her the small wrapped package, he waited for her to untie the ribbons. Inside the box within was a delicate chain of white gold. She picked up the dainty necklace and saw hanging from the middle an elegant cross, embedded with emeralds. Darcy then continued, "I know that it is not much, but I noticed that you have nothing for everyday wear, something modest yet befitting Mrs. Darcy. As my wife, you have many worthy jewels that have been passed down through generations to adorn your neck, but you are of an unaffected sort I believe; I do not mean to offend, mind you. I just thought that you might appreciate having a less elaborate piece in your collection." Darcy felt like a schoolboy talking in circles. He was having a difficult time communicating that he noticed her sense of simplicity without suggesting that she was *simple*.

Elizabeth was taken aback. She had not expected such a well thought-out gift, and although it was much more expensive than any jewellery she had ever owned, or could have afforded in the past, the simplicity and thoughtfulness of the gift impressed her. Uncharacteristically demure, she thanked him. "It's beautiful. Your study of me has not been in vain."

"May I?" he said as he motioned for permission to put it on her. At her nod of agreement, she turned so he could clasp the necklace from the back. As his fingers grazed her skin, gooseflesh spread over her body, causing her to shudder with unfamiliar sensitivity. Her smile was sincere as she reached up to touch the delicate cross.

Then Elizabeth's turn came, so as she turned back towards him, she offered the wrapped package that had been sitting upon her lap. "Merry Christmas, Mr. Darcy."

He took the present from her and untied the ribbon, letting the paper open to reveal a book. Darcy looked pointedly up to her smiling face. "Elizabeth…"

"Open it!" So he dutifully responded, revealing the writing on the inside.

"This is a signed first edition of Robinson Crusoe! But how?"

She laughed as she answered, "A woman has her secrets." He raised his brow in response. "I overheard your asking Mr. Capers at the bookstore two weeks ago if he had yet found a first edition for you. When he had not, I decided to attempt to find it myself. And so I did." After having heard what Mr. Darcy requested at the bookstore, Elizabeth had procured a copy from her uncle, who had many connections. It was on her last visit with her family that her uncle was able to give her the book for which he had in large part surreptitiously interceded to pay (Elizabeth being happily unaware). She was thrilled to be able to give

Mr. Darcy something that he did not already have, and even more, that he had wished for. But she would not give her secrets away. Mr. Darcy would learn to respect her beloved family for their inherent value or not at all.

"But this is far too much! Your pin money should be for you to take care of your needs, not in buying me a present that I can well afford on my own."

"I did not use my pin money, so we are safe."

Darcy considered how little she had spent on her own family compared to this precious gift. He wanted to know how she had been able to accomplish what he and his book supplier could not. "Where did you find this? – A signed copy, no less!"

"Mr. Darcy, you ask too many questions. I believe the proper response to receiving a treasured gift would be, 'Thank you.'"

"Have I just discovered another hidden accomplishment?"

"If I had been the one to write the book, perhaps, but as it is, I am only to be acknowledged for overhearing private conversations and contriving without my husband's knowledge, which may bring about the desired result in this case, but cannot be good for a wife in general."

"Thank you, Elizabeth. I will always hold this book dear for your giving it." He reached over and gently squeezed her hand. "And now, it is time that we left for Tromwell House."

To Darcy's surprise, and Elizabeth's relief, there was no repeat of the previous visit's interrogation. With Colonel Fitzwilliam in residence again, Elizabeth found an ally willing to exert more kindness than censure. Seeing that Elizabeth was in the capable protection of Fitzwilliam, Darcy was able to divide equal time between her and Georgiana. Upon arrival, they partook of assorted delicacies and beverages on display in the drawing room while dividing themselves into small groupings. Elizabeth was speaking with the colonel and Darcy with his sister. The only others in attendance were the earl and countess with the viscount and his wife, Lady Susan.

While with Fitzwilliam, Elizabeth noticed that although in deep conversation with Georgiana, Darcy kept looking her way, at first in a distracted manner but then more deliberate as time went on. Elizabeth could not account for such behaviour and remembered their conversation from the other night when he never denied looking to find fault. Their morning had begun in a most agreeable manner; nonetheless, she could not disregard the evidence that he continued to see her as unacceptable, especially while in the company of his family. So she dedicated herself with vigour to her own conversation daring him to be displeased.

Lady Susan had been in close discourse with Lady Estella, but then her mother-in-law departed to check on the progress of dinner. Elizabeth noticed that as soon as Lady Estella had gone, Lady Susan turned to the nearest mirror and began to examine the reflection of her hair, nose, and neckline without consideration for the others in the room. Elizabeth, however, had observed her perusal and reflexively looked to her husband who had quickly but discretely covered his mouth with his napkin with a look of something in his eyes. *Could it be mirth?* she wondered, but he just as expeditiously removed the napkin with his face inscrutable, leading her to consider that perhaps she had been mistaken. When he winked at her and then turned away, she was certain he had seen the amusing performance before the looking glass. Elizabeth smiled then directed her attention back to the colonel who had noticed only a look of merriment cross her face.

The children were summoned on cue to join the adults for a few moments of delightful observation, and then returned to the nursery to eat their own dinner. Elizabeth found Edmund and Emily to be adorable creatures, shy but inquisitive. The girl reminded her of one of the Gardiners' daughters and Elizabeth instantly felt a connection and determined to visit them later with their presents.

Dinner was an impressive display, and with the colonel in attendance, it was much livelier. Elizabeth was grateful to no longer be the centre of attention and unassumingly enjoyed the interactions going on around her while she herself sat quietly unless singularly addressed. Colonel Fitzwilliam attempted to bring her into the conversation more than once by asking her about the play she had seen and her success with the music master; however, no one else at the table seemed to hold the same level of interest, so Elizabeth only made succinct yet gracious replies.

With no separation of the sexes, the ladies who were willing to contribute to the festivities played carols upon the pianoforte while the others sang with token zeal. Overall the afternoon and early evening progressed with little to vex those in attendance, except perhaps Lady Susan who felt the absurdity of Elizabeth's being allowed entrance into a family event, and Georgiana, who could only feel pain regarding her brother's marital connection.

While Lady Susan played, Elizabeth took Georgiana aside and optimistically presented her with a small wrapped package, taking the younger woman by unaffected surprise. Darcy watched the interaction closely, hoping that his sister might take the expression as the catalyst to warm up to his wife. Georgiana felt all eyes on her as she untied the string to release the wrapping. Darcy intently watched, unaware of what Elizabeth had given his sister and curious to see. Georgiana pulled out a small yet simple bottle. Elizabeth blithely said, "That is scented water that I made from the flowers grown at Longbourn, my home. I inquired from Mrs. Johnson about your favourite floral scent, and she told me roses."

Georgiana was at a loss of what to say, so she quietly and tersely thanked Elizabeth and looked away as she set the bottle down, thereby disappointing Darcy who had hoped for a little more enthusiasm if not appreciation. Elizabeth did not seem to notice the slight and instead asked if Georgiana might show her to the nursery, that she had something that she would like to give the children. Georgiana reluctantly agreed to take her, and they departed the room. Darcy was about to excuse himself to join them, but his cousin stayed him and suggested he give the two ladies some time alone.

While they made their way to the nursery, Elizabeth began, "Georgiana, may I have a word?" At the younger woman's reluctant agreement, she continued. "I know that the past month has been hard on you, being away from your home and your brother. If it were up to me you would be with us at Darcy House, but your brother felt that the wisest course was the current arrangement. As he knows your needs better than I, your brother must have taken other concerns into consideration of which I am unaware." Georgiana kept her eyes glued to the floor as Elizabeth spoke. "As you know, my marriage to your brother was not your brother's wish. I do admire him for his sense of honour that would drive him to request my hand despite having no one to enforce him to uphold his duty. I hope that one day Mr. Darcy and I might develop a mutual regard, and that you and I will see one another as sisters. Please know that I will do my best to be a worthy wife and sister, and hopefully one day mother, if God wills it so."

Georgiana could not speak for fear of what she might say. Instead she looked to Elizabeth for several moments before continuing on their way. Elizabeth felt the disquietude in Georgiana's heart and could only hope that one day they would be friends, knowing there was nothing else she could do but wait patiently.

When arriving at the nursery, Elizabeth entered the suite and immediately the two children turned to look at her in wonder. She said, "Hello Edmund, Emily. I hope you don't mind my intrusion upon your privacy." They continued to stare. "I met you downstairs. My name is Mrs. Darcy; you see I married your cousin, Mr. Darcy, and have come up here to get to know you better." She asked them their ages and favourites for a few moments with hushed responses, and then told them a story about a little girl who loved Christmas so much that she would make gifts for all her family, referring to herself. After a few moments, she got to the point. "I thought you might enjoy opening a present that I made for you." At the word present, their stupor was overcome, and smiles came across their faces as they approached her. She brought two identical packages from around her back where they had been hidden.

They each opened the ones handed to them and discovered within a drawing book with pencils and chalk contained in a small pouch, embroidered with each child's initial. Across the tops of the first ten pages of each book were four small drawings demonstrating how to compose a particular picture. The first in Edmund's was a lion – the first of the four pictures containing two circles, one for the body and a smaller one for the head, the second added a mane, the third a tail and legs, and the fourth had the finished picture with eyes, nose and mouth. Emily's first page had a rabbit in like manner. "When I was a child, my aunt used to make me books, such as the ones I have made you, so I could teach myself how to draw. My mother thought I was so gifted as an artist. I never told her that I had help from the drawings my aunt had made for me because after I had practised, I stopped needing help in that way and could make a lion or rabbit all on my own. Do you think you would like to learn to draw too?" To her satisfaction, they nodded and expressed desire to do just that.

Georgiana had immediately left Elizabeth to the children and returned downstairs while trying to find justification for fault in Elizabeth's speech. Darcy saw Georgiana enter and decided to check on his wife to make sure she knew her way back to the music room. When he arrived at the open doorway, he looked in, curious as to what might be going on between his wife and the two young children. He watched as she presented the gifts to them. Elizabeth was smiling and showing great kindness to these children whom she did not even know, children of two people in his family who had been nothing but accusatory and rude to her – and not on display for all to see. Elizabeth's eyes danced in satisfaction at the children's response to her kind gifts. Darcy felt ashamed of how his own sister had disregarded so flippantly the gift Elizabeth had made for her.

"Elizabeth, you have another hidden talent." She looked up intently to him and not seeing censure, she smiled.

"Indeed I do. It is a wonder my suitors were not clamouring at my door anticipating my next talent to be unfolded."

"So *you* made these books?"

"Really, it is just a little something that I enjoyed as a girl, nothing more." Elizabeth was blushing under his stare, unable to discern if he approved or found displeasure in her trifling gift. His family was likely used to giving and receiving much more extravagant presents than these. Then she recalled that the rest of the family was still gathered downstairs. "Perhaps we should join your family."

"Would you like to spend more time with the children? I could stay with you for a few moments and then escort you down when you are ready." She nodded that she would and began helping the children with their first drawings. Not wanting to keep Mr. Darcy waiting, however, she quickly finished her task and stood to depart.

"I have similar gifts to present to Lady Victoria's children if we are to see them in the near future. Do you suppose we might have an occasion to meet them?"

"I am sure we could arrange a meeting."

"I was unable to determine on Saturday how Lady Victoria viewed me. Her husband was not in attendance, and she hardly spoke a word, which is much unlike the colonel, yet you say they are alike?"

"The siblings are both of a discerning nature. Fitzwilliam is gregarious, but don't let his affability tempt you to miss his acumen. I believe they are both open to your entrance in the family. What is done is done, so the proper and right thing is to accept our marriage, giving you the benefit of the doubt. Like Fitzwilliam, she will welcome you, I believe. Of course, to truly approve of you, she would want to know your character and maybe even desire answers, but she is not so set that she cannot be persuaded to accept you. On the other hand, I cannot predict her husband's response. He will believe as he chooses."

Elizabeth was quiet in contemplation. Could her own husband one day accept her? Was there hope for future happiness? "If you seek the truth, you will find it. I guess you have to *want* to seek the truth though," she said quietly, her thoughts moving from his cousins to her husband. Darcy, who had barely heard the last, considered her words. Had he not always valued truth? He followed the evidence in all circumstances and measured it against his own understanding and experiences. An educated man could do no less.

"DARCY, THERE YOU ARE. Georgiana sent me looking for you," came the voice of Langston. "She asked if you would meet her in her sitting room. I believe she had something that she wanted to give you in private." Noticing Darcy's glance towards his wife, he said, "Don't worry, I will escort Mrs. Darcy to the rest of the family."

Elizabeth was uncomfortable to be left alone with this man who wore his privilege – and dislike for her – upon his brow, but she nodded her acquiescence to her husband. When Darcy left, Langston led her continuing on down the passageway, but instead of taking her towards the music room where Elizabeth had expected, he took her down another hallway. Because Elizabeth was not sure of her direction, nor was she familiar with the house, she let herself be led along by the arm down the unknown hallway. The viscount opened a door and guided her in, closing and then locking it behind him while keeping her within his grasp.

"Mrs. Darcy, Elizabeth, perhaps you might be wondering why I brought you here." By now Elizabeth realised her peril. She had allowed herself to be led into a secluded room with this man of privilege who would naturally believe he was entitled to whatever she might have to give him. If they were discovered, she would be the one condemned by his family. Her husband would likely take his cousin's side as well, suspecting her duplicity. Elizabeth grasped that she was completely at this man's mercy. He openly laughed at the look of trepidation in her eyes while he reached up to touch her curls beside her cheek. "What I am wondering is how you were able to induce my priggish cousin, Darcy, to break his overzealous rules of propriety, to tempt him to offer for you – a woman with nothing but her shapely figure to entice."

Elizabeth felt it best not to enter into this conversation and made to leave the room. She was stayed by his grasp. "Sir, I will not remain here and listen to you insult me."

"I am sorry you see it that way, for I meant only to compliment."

"Please, open the door and let me go."

"Not yet; not until you answer my question. You don't have to say a word though; you can show me," said the viscount as his eyes travelled over her.

"Please, whatever you think to be true, I can assure is not, and my husband would not appreciate your keeping me against my wishes."

"You are mistaken if you think your husband cares about you, Elizabeth." The use of her given name made her bristle, even knowing that was the least of her concerns. "He married you for one thing and one thing only. It would seem that even Darcy has his weaknesses. He should have stuck with the paid strumpets, but I guess that is exactly what you are, paid." At this point he was holding one arm in a strong grip with the other behind her back, his face not twelve inches from her own, as she attempted to push him away. "You go from having nothing – no dowry to speak of – to being the wife of one of the wealthiest men in England. Don't tell me you have done nothing to entice my cousin, that you are innocent of seduction. Your story may delude some, but it does not fool me. You are nothing but an alluring charlatan who uses your wiles to entice men. This is the only value you have," he said as he let go of her arm while still holding her in place, bringing his now free hand up to stroke her breast. "Come, you haven't given me my Christmas present yet."

Elizabeth wanted to scream out, but either no one would hear her, or if they did, they would not believe her innocence over Lord Langston's, but she had to try something; she could not let him continue on in this domineering and invasive manner. So, as she tried to remove his probing hand, Elizabeth said, "Whether or not Mr. Darcy cares for me, he would not want your taking liberties with his wife; I am certain. And, as you are aware, I have nothing to lose with regards to your family. If you continue in this manner, I can assure you that I will not keep silent. Your wife, parents and cousin will know of your treachery. You are threatening the wrong person, sir. I will not be manipulated by you or anyone so wholly without conscience." Of course, Elizabeth knew that she was all bravado and that if he decided to try her, she remained as before, unprotected and completely vulnerable to his advances, but she had no other defence.

He laughed again. "You are a lively one. That is convenient because I like lively; the reward is all the more sweet." He then kissed her aiming for her mouth, but she turned her head just in time to avoid a direct assault. With his arm around her back, he picked her up and carried her to the bed, pushing her down with the weight of his body. His mouth began the trek down her neck onto her exposed chest, as his hands enjoyed continued explorations. He had lifted her dress and was moving his hand up her thigh when they heard a voice from the hallway. Colonel Fitzwilliam was opening doors and quietly but emphatically calling out for Mrs. Darcy. "It seems my younger brother has fallen under your spell as well," he said as he sat up, her expression of panic amusing him. "We can take this up another time; I can be patient. I suggest you keep this to yourself. You may think Darcy would believe you over me, but you are wrong. I have known him for years as blood relations, while your character is equivocal with a history of taking advantage of honourable men." He stood up and walked to the door, opening it while peering into the hallway. He stepped back and waved her through gallantly with his arm that not a moment before was exploring her body.

Elizabeth hurriedly exited through the door and towards the music room, adjusting with her trembling hands the stray locks that had escaped their pins as she walked along, clearly shaken by what had just occurred. Her heart was racing, and tears threatened to spill from her eyes as she considered from what she had been saved. Elizabeth needed time alone to recover, but for fear of being found again, she had to return to the company. She slipped into the music room, and finding Lady Susan still at the instrument, she remained in the back, sitting alone. Mr. Darcy and Miss Darcy were yet out of the room, and the colonel was also missing.

Elizabeth considered how she should respond to the viscount's attack. Would her husband believe her if she told him? Certainly, no one else would. Taking deep, calming breaths, Elizabeth finally managed to stop shaking and dried her tears with her handkerchief. Colonel Fitzwilliam sat beside her just as she had gotten control, making her reflexively jump in agitation.

242

"Pardon me, Mrs. Darcy. I did not mean to startle you. I have been searching for you; I was concerned when you did not return. Is anything amiss?" Elizabeth did not look well at all. Her previously gaunt appearance now took on an expression of panic. "Allow me to get you some wine."

She wanted to decline and say that all was fine, but she could not, so instead, she nodded her head. However, while he was pouring her a glass, Langston entered the room and sat next to her, saying loudly so all could hear, "Mrs. Darcy, you do look awful. I deem you could use some time to rest. Allow me to take you to a room; it would do you a world of good." He smiled kindly at her, as a wolf in sheep's clothing.

"Langston, you have taken my seat. Let Mrs. Darcy decide what she is in need of. When Darcy returns with his sister, he can escort her home. Until then perhaps we could give her a little space," the colonel said with a curt nod for him to move. Colonel Fitzwilliam knew his brother well. He was a man who felt entitled to whatever he wanted. Even as boys, he would take his little brother's toys and claim them as his own, for he was the heir. In light of Elizabeth's apparent agitation, Fitzwilliam suspected his brother might have played a part, which was confirmed by the leer that his brother directed towards the woman and her conspicuous discomposure.

The others in the room had watched the exchange but then were redirected by the performance at the pianoforte. Lady Susan knew her husband was attracted to the new Mrs. Darcy, for indeed he was attracted to many women, but she, Lady Susan, was the woman who held the title of the viscountess and had birthed the heir, so she chose to ignore what she could not change. Lady Susan then returned to her rendition of *Adeste Fideles*, which was a favourite of the family's, to draw the attention away from the harlot.

Darcy entered during the song and joined his wife who was now sitting alone. Darcy had been with his sister in her apartment. Not wanting to share the moment with anyone, especially her brother's new wife, Georgiana had requested his presence away from the family. She had presented him with a charcoal of herself rendered by a young artist whom her aunt had hired, Monsieur René Bernard. Knowing that his sister needed his time and attention, he had remained with her in appreciation for her thoughtful gift.

"In my absence, you will have this before you, so you can remember how dear you are to me," said Georgiana after she had given him her likeness. Darcy knew that his decision to marry Elizabeth was leaving its toll on his sister. He hoped that she would soon be able to join them either at Darcy House or Pemberley, but he felt that each woman needed more time to become accustomed to his shared loyalties.

"Mr. Darcy," said Elizabeth in hushed tones to her husband, "we must go."

"It is still early and you have yet to play," he whispered back.

"I am unwell and need to return to Darcy House. I can go alone if you wish to stay, but please do not let anyone else escort me." Elizabeth did not want to give him any reason to suspect foul play, so she continued, "I have a headache and need quietude. I cannot bear to have anyone else in the close quarters of the carriage, and I do not want to disturb your family." At his hesitation, she said, "Please, sir, I beg of you to take me home directly. Return if you will."

There was indeed a great disturbance in her countenance and change in her disposition from but thirty minutes before. "I will make our excuses and call for the carriage." Darcy stood and walked over to his hosts, speaking quietly concerning their imminent departure and need for the carriage. Much fuss was made with supplications to stay for the remainder of the evening. Georgiana overheard the exchange and added her wishes to the Fitzwilliams', but Darcy stood firm. He looked back across the room and saw that his wife was looking more unwell by the minute, as even the surprising solicitude of his cousin Langston could not seem to provide Elizabeth relief.

While in the carriage on the way home, Darcy began to question her concerning the present illness. "I will be fine, I just have a little headache, nothing that quiet and sleep will not overcome."

"You truly look ill, Elizabeth. Did something happen between the time I left you with Langston and my entrance into the music room?"

"Nothing to speak of." Darcy could not see her within the dark confines of the carriage. Tears had re-emerged, and she desperately attempted to wipe them away before he realised her distress. How could she let him know the truth? He would not believe her over his cousin; she was certain.

"Elizabeth, leaving early was really quite rude, if it was truly just a *little* headache. Surely we could have stayed if that were the case. I know Georgiana was disappointed we left."

"You could have stayed. There was no need for you to join me. In fact, you may return if you wish."

"Really, you cannot make a habit of leaving unpleasant situations because of a *trifling* headache. There will be many occasions that you must play your role regardless of your opinion of the company."

"Indeed." The irony almost made her laugh aloud. Darcy's instruction on playing the proper role would have amused her, if she were not so distraught over the events of the evening.

After arriving at Darcy House, Elizabeth went straight to her room, surprising her maid by requesting a bath be drawn for the second time that day. Elizabeth felt intruded upon and soiled by the repulsive advances of Lord Langston, so although it was Christmas and she would never have wanted to put any extra work on a servant on this holy day, she simply could not rest until a thorough ablution was performed.

Chapter Twelve

For everything there is a season...
A time to weep, and a time to laugh
Ecclesiastes 3: 1,4

Elizabeth sat at her vanity as she prepared for the day ahead. She had wanted to remain in her chamber for the whole of the following day, but duty required that she make a showing for Boxing Day in order to participate in the distribution of gifts to the servants. Her husband had reminded her more than once of her obligations for the day. Because Janette was off for the holiday, Elizabeth was left with the task of hiding the remnants of a sleepless night alone. The previous evening's events had left Elizabeth in considerable distress. She felt vulnerable to Langston and had no one whom she trusted to safeguard her from his advances. Her husband would not believe her over his own cousin; he still thought her guilty of manipulating the situation that eventually led to their marriage.

Today would try her ingenuity as she performed as mistress of Mr. Darcy's homes bestowing benevolence and kindness on his servants when her life now brought her fear and misery. At the beginning of their marriage, Elizabeth had determined to do her very best in fulfilling her role as Mrs. Darcy by learning how to manage his homes and being the model of propriety. Although she had conflicting desires to what her new life entailed, she tried to swallow her pride and accept the changes, which came with daily challenges. However, her encounter the previous evening with Lord Langston demonstrated her vulnerability and inability to mesh into Mr. Darcy's world. His family mocked her, his cousin even going so far as to threaten her in his contempt and perfidiousness. And Elizabeth had no one to share that burden or to provide protection. She could not worry dear Jane or anyone else with her disheartening predicament. But Elizabeth was not made for trepidation. She had a role to play despite her uneasiness, so she continued her preparations as she attempted to hide her weariness.

Darcy gave little thought to the previous evening, owing Elizabeth's hasty retreat to her discomfort and antipathy towards his family. Eventually, she would learn their ways and realise the great chasm between her and his noble relations and how they had so generously condescended to recognise her place in his life. Certainly they were a little hard on Elizabeth upon first meeting her, yet they were obviously attempting to get to know her and show kindness to her. Darcy was especially surprised at Langston's show of cordiality prior to leaving. Darcy had always known him to be the epitome of class distinction, much like his aunt Catherine; nonetheless, Langston was attempting to assist Elizabeth in her discomfort, for which Darcy was grateful.

The couple spent the day with the servants, which helped Elizabeth to focus on other people's needs. The afternoon was full of entertainment for the staff. While the Darcys did not need to linger, Elizabeth found the activity soothing to her anxious spirit, so she remained with the servants, as did Darcy, for his wife's sake.

That night, Elizabeth awoke with a start, as she would during many nights over the course of the next few months. She had been dreaming of a peaceful morning at Longbourn, when she would have awoken at dawn and taken pleasure in a ramble to Oakham Mount, a favourite haunt of hers, before her family had assembled for breakfast. Elizabeth had been running along the path, as was her want, when she was unexpectedly intercepted by Lord Langston. On this occasion, he had almost collided with her while on horseback. Jumping down from his mount, he grabbed hold of her around the waist. The vile man began quietly taunting her with words of provocation as his hands made their explorations. Elizabeth was unable to scream, nor was she capable of removing herself from his unyielding hold. Langston laughed as he continued his attack, which ended only in her finally being able to rouse herself from sleep, but not until after a most tormenting assault.

In a panic, Elizabeth looked around the room trying to determine where she was and if her captor were still present. Upon seeing that she was alone and in her room at Darcy House, Elizabeth's breathing calmed as she let her tears fall. The dream had seemed so real just moments before, and Elizabeth wondered if she would revisit the scene if she were to give in to her overwhelming need for slumber. After an hour of trying to remain awake, Elizabeth finally dosed off again but could not find the peace that sleep would customarily grant her.

DARCY PLANNED TO TAKE ELIZABETH and Georgiana to the opera to see Mozart's *Don Giovanni,* which had been much anticipated. Elizabeth donned yet another new gown, one of her favourites, pink silk with squared bodice that was tasteful if a little daring for Elizabeth's sensibilities. As they made their way to the recently restored Theatre Royal, Covent Garden, Elizabeth spoke of her previous visits before the recent fire, her first to see the pantomime clown, Joseph Grimaldi, when she was but seventeen. This would be her first time there since the theatre reopened three months previously, and Elizabeth was delighted to see it restored to its former grandeur.

When the carriage pulled up to Tromwell House to collect Georgiana, Elizabeth was taken back when, after Georgiana entered and sat next to her brother, Lord Langston climbed in sitting next to herself.

"Darcy, how good of you to allow me to intrude on your evening. Mrs. Darcy, I hope you don't mind my joining you."

Elizabeth felt sickened and without words to respond, but found her voice. "I had no knowledge of your joining us until this moment."

Then Darcy said, "Elizabeth, I was so pleased when Langston expressed his wish to come with us. His public acceptance of you will go far to help your entry into London society. Many will see his presence as a sign of his family's support of our marriage. Are you not pleased?"

Elizabeth looked away out the dark window and said, "It seems too good to be true." With the little light in the carriage Elizabeth hoped no one could see her distress. Meanwhile, the viscount began rubbing his leg and foot up against hers, antagonising her with his presence. Rather than quail, Elizabeth became indignant at his offensive perfidy at her expense. The short ride to the opera house seemed an eternity to Elizabeth, especially because of the long line inching towards the theatre entrance. Finally they were able to alight from the carriage, though it was not Darcy's hand that let her down, or the footman as usual, but Lord Langston's. Elizabeth could not ignore the courtesy, since she could not risk slighting him in front of the vast number of people already collected at the door who were observing them with unfeigned curiosity. She released his hand, perhaps sooner than was proper and quickly stepped over to her husband, instinctively taking his arm. Elizabeth coveted his protection whether he knew of her need or not.

Darcy was a little surprised by Elizabeth's meagre but pronounced show of affection, especially in light of their audience, but without thought reached over and put his hand on top of hers. Elizabeth hardly noticed amidst her feelings of umbrage against Darcy's cousin.

This time, the journey through the crowd to Darcy's private box took far longer than before, for they had appeared during the peak arrival time, as was fashionable, so that there would be plenty of people to see them upon entrance. Elizabeth was introduced to each of Darcy's acquaintances who were bold enough to approach him. Elizabeth was almost surprised to see that familiar, yet almost forgotten, look of hauteur that fell upon Darcy's visage once leaving the theatre vestibule where they had divested themselves of their outer garments. By the time they had reached Darcy's box, Elizabeth had developed a healthy appreciation for her husband's imposing demeanour that she had at one time berated. They were still stopped by many fellow patrons eager to meet the new Mrs. Darcy, but most just stared behind open fans whispering to one another their thoughts of approbation or criticism. Elizabeth was to learn that this was to become the usual sequence of events as a Darcy. She had never felt so exposed in her life.

When they reached the box, Elizabeth attempted to sit on the end, knowing that Darcy would of course sit next to her; however before she could, Georgiana sat down in her intended seat and led her brother to her side, "Brother, oh please sit next to me, so we can share the music like we have before."

He moved over to the seat and while standing motioned for Elizabeth to join him. "Elizabeth you may sit on the other side of me, if that pleases you." She had no choice but to concede to the plan and so sat to Mr. Darcy's right. Langston gloated his triumph at causing Elizabeth distress as he sat to her right, but to the others the look appeared as a show of contented acquiescence.

This production could not give her pleasure as the previous outing to see *Twelfth Night* had, but Elizabeth wryly thought the theme of *Don Giovanni* apropos for the occasion.

The viscount leaned over several times during the performance, when the music was loud enough to conceal his words. "Elizabeth," he whispered close to her hear, causing her to jump, "I must tell you that you look bewitching this evening. Your dress shows you to advantage." His eyes travelled from her eyes, down her neck and rested upon her bosom.

Elizabeth could not decide if his words were meant to vex or charm her. Either way, he was up to no good, and if Darcy had known his intent, he would likely be displeased. But as it was, Darcy could not overhear Langston. Many words of cajolery were used to either tempt or repulse her. She could not enjoy the music and longed for the day she would be at Longbourn for her sister's wedding and then on to Pemberley, away from being the object of derision. Elizabeth was determined not to be alone with the viscount and so remained next to her husband's side for the entirety of the night. This was a new experience for Elizabeth, to desire her husband's presence, even though it was as protector, if not lover.

Darcy was pleased that this member of his family, one whom he could not have foretold to do so, made his endorsement clear to the world. He would be forever grateful for the viscount's kind condescension. He hoped to make certain that Elizabeth understood her good fortune and took every opportunity over the next few days to remind her. Elizabeth endured her husband's ignorant but well-meaning words that were intended to alleviate her concerns, but in fact only intensified them.

THE ANTICIPATED DAY ARRIVED when Mrs. Elizabeth Darcy would make her debut into London society in earnest. Her husband anticipated the event with trepidation. He had discovered over the previous month, that his wife had many good qualities, and that he need not blush without limitation in presenting her to the *ton*. Darcy had ensured that Elizabeth possessed the proper clothing, and that she had a trained abigail to give her the style that she needed in order to contend with the other ladies who would be in attendance. He knew that his peers had desired an opportunity to scoff at his choice of bride; he understood their perspective and their curiosity, even if he would never participate in such a display of discourtesy himself.

As Darcy's valet prepared him for the ball hosted by Lord Matlock and Lady Estella, he considered who might be in attendance. He had not seen Lady Annette since before Michaelmas; he had not seen her brother, Lord Wexley, since that day at his club when Wexley essentially cut him in front of their mutual friends. *If only things could have been different.* But he would try not to think on that tonight. Elizabeth was his wife, and he would not look back.

As he had planned on Elizabeth's wearing her new, midnight blue ball gown, he chose for himself his cream breeches, an ivory waistcoat with golden thread patterned in pin stripes and a dark blue coat. His valet usually made all of the decisions for him concerning his wardrobe, yet tonight he had his own ideas about how he and his wife should present themselves. He desired that they demonstrate a unity in their relationship. He was desperately trying to curb the gossip mills by showing harmony both in his home and with his wife. The rich colouring of the dress would show off Elizabeth's porcelain skin and chestnut hair, and her deep green, yet sparkling eyes would communicate her charms.

Darcy had knocked on Elizabeth's chamber door at the appointed time; however, she was not yet ready, so Janette hesitantly informed him that her mistress would meet him in the foyer within the quarter hour. Darcy disliked

248

being late and almost made an authoritative retort, but then thought better of it. He wanted Elizabeth to look her best for the evening, and if a little more time achieved those results then all the better.

Elizabeth nervously prepared for the evening. Sometime during the day, Darcy had left jewels on her vanity to match her richly coloured gown. He had chosen a sapphire and diamond necklace with a comparatively larger stone in the shape of a teardrop in the centre. The stones were of a darker hue than was most often seen; however, the colour perfectly matched her dress, and when paired with the diamonds, was indeed an impressive addition to her ensemble. Elizabeth's gown was truly a masterpiece, balancing velvet with silk upon the plunging bodice with an empire waistline, making her feel quite exposed; however, she was pleased with the effect. The delay related to Elizabeth's adornment for her hair. Elizabeth was adamantly opposed to the use of quills to fashion her coif; however, Janette was equally as adamant that she should wear the feathers. They compromised by adorning the right side of her head with a few small feathers that matched her gown and provided the perfect balancing effect to the long curl draping over her left shoulder. Elizabeth considered that her dark locks would likely mask the feathers anyway.

Darcy stood at the bottom of the stairs anticipating Elizabeth's descent, and to his delight discovered that he was to be richly rewarded for his patience. Darcy was just opening his watch fob to check the time when from the corner of his eye he caught a glimpse of Elizabeth making her way down the staircase. She was smiling somewhat apprehensively. Elizabeth knew she looked better than she had ever before, and although not as beautiful as Jane, she felt certain that she was a long way from just tolerable. Of course, Darcy may have other views on what constituted such a description, and the remembrance of this caused Elizabeth to doubt her reception, but she could not have been prepared for his unbeguiling response.

Darcy's eyes travelled over her form in unrestrained admiration, the look on his face full of intense wonder and esteem. After an uncomfortable full minute of scrutiny, he finally spoke, "Elizabeth, you are truly stunning. I must say that I have never seen you look finer."

"I am tolerable, I suppose, but surely not handsome enough to tempt you."

His brows knit together. Yet again, those words sounded familiar to him, but he could not determine from which occasion. "You are a beautiful woman, and I will be proud to escort you to the ball." This surprising claim caused her eyebrows to shoot up in an expression of disbelief.

"Mr. Darcy, be careful what you say for you do not like deceit, and I know for certain that you cannot intend such pretty words."

"I am sorry you think so meanly of me. You obviously judge what you say to be a faithful impression, but I cannot agree with you. I doubt not that many men will be requesting a chance to dance with you, while I must let them."

Elizabeth immediately thought of the viscount. She would have to diligently avoid him, so as not to anger her husband or his family with a necessary refusal.

"I believe the ladies will despise me for claiming such a handsome and rich man, but nothing can be done for it. I will have to accept their looks of envy with aplomb," Elizabeth said with merry eyes that had Darcy enthralled as he gazed upon her. Elizabeth mistakenly took this to be a look of censure and apologised for her teasing, worried that he might think her in earnest.

Her words broke the spell that had held him, inciting him to carry on. "Yes, well, we must be going if we are to arrive before the other guests. My aunt excused our standing in the receiving line since I promised we would appear early. And I know Georgiana is anxious for us to arrive, for she will have to leave the ball before supper."

THE COUPLE ARRIVED AT TROMWELL HOUSE, each filled with excitement and trepidation but for different reasons. Elizabeth had been without fault in her deportment during the previous visits with his family and at the theatre, but a ball can bring out the worst in people, and Darcy was afraid of how his peers would treat her in such a setting. Elizabeth feared her next encounter with the viscount and hoped that he would find some other woman to mock with his advances.

They passed through the receiving line without incident, greeting Darcy's relations. Georgiana joined the couple as they entered the ballroom. She wore a white silk, modest gown with gold threading. "Georgiana, you look lovely, my dear," said her brother as he leaned down to kiss her cheek in sincere affection that produced a blush and a smile.

"Indeed you do, Miss Darcy," Elizabeth added, receiving a cool response for her trouble. Elizabeth agreed with Mr. Wickham's account of the girl and judged Darcy's ignorance to her faults in keeping with his blind acceptance of her goodness as a Darcy.

The room filled quickly with the invited guests as several came up to make the introduction. Although a little doubtful of her reception at first, Elizabeth began to feel the excitement of the evening ahead. It was at this time that the colonel joined the Darcys as he proclaimed both ladies to be exceptionally lovely. After this, Elizabeth had the opportunity to meet Lady Victoria's husband, who up until this evening had not deigned to meet the new member of the family. Lady Victoria made the introductions; he bowed a cursory greeting, and then departed for the game room. Elizabeth spoke to his wife who remained behind and who was supposed to most favour her brother, the colonel. Standing beside her though, Elizabeth could see little to support the idea on this occasion. As the instrumentalists began to signal the beginning of the dancing, the earl and countess stood before those congregated to again thank them for coming. Couples began making their way to the dance floor behind their hosts. Colonel Fitzwilliam found his chance and asked Elizabeth to dance the second set with him, if she were not already promised to another. Elizabeth replied, "I am available for the first, if you are not otherwise engaged, sir."

Darcy, surprised at her answer, said, "You are to dance the first with me."

"But, sir, I have not been asked by you."

"You are my wife. Of course you would dance the first with me."

"Be that as it may, a woman likes to be asked."

Darcy, unsure of where this would go replied, "Elizabeth, may I have the honour of your first dance?"

She paused, glancing away, and then looking back replied with good humour, "Of course, it is your duty to ask me, and I suppose I am obliged to accept. But truly, how shall I reply? If I say yes, you will take my acceptance for granted; however, if I say no, you will scorn me."

Darcy's features were stern as was usual, but then he saw the mirth in her eyes and realised that she was teasing him yet again. He held out his hand, which she took with a sly look, and as he led her to the dance floor, a lovely laugh escaped her lips, which drew the attention of those around them. Darcy had a definite but small smile on his face as they passed the other guests, and those in the surrounding area of the great room looked on with astonishment. Who was that unknown woman who had defied conventional mores to laugh at such a man as Mr. Darcy? Those aware of the recent marriage got to work with industry sharing their understanding of the events.

Pleased for the occasion, Fitzwilliam then asked Georgiana to dance, as she was limited to the men within the family as partners and followed behind to enjoy the general excitement and splendour of the evening.

The whispers had begun, but Darcy and Elizabeth did not notice as the music drowned out the indistinct chatter. The two stood across from one another waiting for their turn in the dance. Darcy had his eyes fixed on Elizabeth who was determined to be unaffected by his close scrutiny. She had noticed early in their enforced relationship that he often stared at her. At first she found his examinations disconcerting. He held no regard for her appearance, as she unhappily discovered on the first day of their acquaintance. His fixed gazes were severe and abstruse; Elizabeth suspected they were of an unfavourable nature. Howbeit, on this occasion, his survey of her person left her suspecting quite the opposite.

Their turn arrived, and Darcy seemed as if he had awakened to realise he was in the middle of a dance. He recovered quickly and played his part well. After a few moments, Darcy began, "We must have some conversation; do you not agree?"

"Do you wish to satisfy me or your own desires? I seem to remember your being disinclined to converse while dancing. You certainly do not need to entertain me; I find myself quite amused in my present state of observation," she replied with a grin.

"Oh, and what do you find so amusing? Have I taken a misstep?"

"My pleasure does not arise from the discomfiting mistakes of others, but from their follies. I find there is plenty to delight me without resorting to humiliating others."

They were silent as they separated in the dance. When they came back together, Elizabeth spoke, "I wonder why you so seldom dance. You carry yourself with remarkable grace, and I am sure any woman would be pleased to stand up with you." She had rarely rendered him a compliment, so Darcy was trying to determine her motives from her manner when she looked at him inquiringly, so he took her bait and asked her intention.

"You do justice to your reputation, sir. Miss Bingley had informed me of your perfection in all things, and I only meant to confirm your aptitude in the ballroom. Surely you must know that you are an excellent dancer, and that I could not find fault." Somehow, whenever she spoke, Darcy could not be quite confident in her intentions or his own reply. He found himself perplexed and unable to determine her meaning.

"You also dance with elegance, madam. Might I ask how you became so accomplished in this area?"

After a long pause, Elizabeth replied, "This might come as a surprise to you, Mr. Darcy, but my mother does in fact value the social competencies which are customary to attain within genteel society. Do not suppose that because I grew up as a country maiden, that I have not the refinement that one discovers in town."

His cold mask returned. He could not understand how their conversations so often became a battleground, and he was left without a weapon or an understanding of how the first shot was fired.

Elizabeth was aware of how her words affected him. She was unable to hold her tongue and regretted them even before they had escaped her. He may not have meant to offend her by suggesting that her ability to dance was unexpected. She found herself often attempting to defend herself and her value as a wife of someone of his heritage. She questioned whether she had to defend herself to Darcy alone, or perhaps to herself as well. She wanted to apologise, but they became separated again in the dance. He spoke not the rest of the set, leaving her unsettled by the end. She attempted a small smile, but he turned his eyes away while leading her off the dance floor.

The crowd had increased while they were engaged; he held her hand as he led her to Colonel Fitzwilliam. The colonel was all smiles as they approached. He had a glass of punch waiting for her, so she might take quick refreshment before the next two began. She would have to wait to apologise to Mr. Darcy until later, but for now, she was determined to enjoy herself.

Darcy watched as Elizabeth returned to the dance floor with his cousin. Her lively emotions played across her face, as the two left him alone. He now had to admit that his wife was not only beautiful, but also graceful. She had charms that were beginning to draw him in. Vulnerability came hard to him. Could he let himself become susceptible to such a woman?

As he watched his cousin flawlessly dance with his wife, he began to focus on the conversations going on around him when he heard his name mentioned. "Who is that woman dancing with Lord Matlock's son? She does not look familiar."

"She is the new Mrs. Darcy. I saw her dancing with her husband to open the ball. Of course you have heard their story."

"Indeed I have not. Do tell, for I love tantalizing gossip."

"Well, I had it from Lady Farthington, who heard the report from her lady's maid who knows someone who serves at Darcy House. Apparently, he had to marry her; she entrapped him."

"He finally got caught, did he? I know that ladies have been attempting to ensnare him for years; my daughter was one of them."

Mature yet puerile giggles sounded in Darcy's wake as he walked forward to evade the discovery of having overheard the exchange. He was incensed at the insult to Elizabeth and himself. *How dare those old harpies spread such vicious gossip? These malicious rumours of scheming will make Elizabeth's entrance into society more arduous.* Of course, he knew that no one would readily welcome her based on the truth concerning her absence of fortune and connections upon marriage; the *ton* would always find something to cavil at when associating with Elizabeth. Anyone could find a trivial objection to her if seeking a fault, but to purposely make her introduction more burdensome for sport alone was abhorrent indeed. Darcy felt concern for Elizabeth and the welcome, or lack thereof, which she would surely encounter in the drawing rooms of London.

Darcy found himself by the refreshment table and picked up a beverage. So far, this evening had gone amiss. He had hoped that Elizabeth's fine clothing and acceptance from his noble family would ameliorate her launch into society, but overhearing the women reminded him of the difficulty Elizabeth would truly face. Add to that, he had somehow offended her while dancing. He glanced onto the dance floor, and there before him, he saw Elizabeth's eyes gleam as she smiled broadly. He realised that she had never gazed at him with the same joy as she bestowed on Fitzwilliam. *Does she still despise me? Can we ever live together in harmony as I had once anticipated upon marriage? Could Elizabeth have a strong regard for my cousin?* He had certainly seen them happily engaged in conversation and enjoying one another's company enough times in the past for it to seem that way. With these disturbing thoughts circulating in his mind, he decided fresh air was needed.

Moving towards the back windows that flanked the doorway to the balcony, Darcy passed others who attempted to gain his attention. He heard, "Darcy, is that your new wife who..." or a more feminine voice cooing, "Mr. Darcy, please say we are all misinformed, and you have not been lured away by that woman..." He kept walking, ignoring the sounds around him. He needed time away from the crush of people and their injurious insinuations. While walking by a substantial chimneypiece, he noticed Lady Susan looking at her reflection in the large mirror over the mantle designed to diffuse more candlelight. Instinctively, he looked to Elizabeth to see if she had noticed the same, and then remembered that she was dancing with his cousin and was unlikely to have shared the private amusement. He chuckled as he remembered the number of times he had seen Lady Susan take a peek in a mirror and was surprised he had not noticed her quirky ways before Elizabeth had mentioned them.

Darcy slipped out of the door, hoping to avoid being followed by anyone desiring to further the supplication for more information. He was most comfortable in the company of a small group of friends and found idle chatter irksome and the smells of a crowd noisome. Society had always been oppressive to his sensibilities, but tonight caused him more consternation than was usual. His sense of honour and protective instincts were imposed upon. He was truly grateful that his family seemed to accept the marriage, all except Georgiana and perhaps Lady Susan, but that came as no surprise for Georgiana let her thoughts be known from the beginning – and would find fault with anyone whom she felt had somehow taken advantage of her brother – and Lady Susan could not be pleased with anyone.

After a few moments of quiet reverie, his sister intruded upon his solitude. "Brother, I saw you leave the ballroom. Are you quite all right? When you didn't return, I began to worry."

"Georgiana, my dear, sweet sister, I am well; I just needed some fresh, cool air, but come, you must be very cold out here. Let me escort you back inside."

"I am well for now, if you need to talk. I know that you have been very unhappy as of late, due to your change in circumstances. Introducing Mrs. Darcy to society cannot be easy for you."

Darcy smiled and reached for her cold hands. "On the contrary, she seems to be doing better than I at the moment. But we cannot remain outside. Can I have the pleasure of the next dance with my accomplished, little sister?"

"I am not so little any more, Brother, and yes you may." The second song of the set began, so Georgiana and Darcy joined the line, providing sufficient distraction to quell Darcy's immediate unease. When the dance concluded, Darcy watched as his cousin led Elizabeth to the other side of the room and introduced an unfamiliar gentleman to her. They spoke a few moments, and then the man led her to the dance floor for the next set. Rather than dance again, Darcy decided to watch from the side of the room. Several men, some whom Elizabeth had met previously with him and others unknown to Darcy, succeeded in taking her to the dance floor. She smiled, laughed, and spoke in animation with them, so unlike their own dances. Meanwhile, Darcy began to feel indignant at her overt flirtations. She had never, before or after their marriage, been so open with him. Elizabeth was his wife; surely she could show him such attentions. He could tell by the smiles of the men with whom she was dancing that she had charmed them, as was her inclination. *Why must she attempt to antagonise me at every turn but enchant everyone else?*

After several sets, he lost sight of Elizabeth but was determined to join her and shoo away any other man who attempted to approach her. As he was making his way through the crowd, he heard the voice of Caroline Bingley. "Mr. Darcy, you are alone, I see. Well, that is for the best. I know how you despise tedious company, almost as much as I do. So tell me, how are you? I have been so worried." Miss Bingley was wearing a bright yellow gown, not easily missed in a crowd – which was likely by design – and tall feathers atop her head, making her look like a tall canary.

Darcy bowed, "Miss Bingley, it is a pleasure to see you again. You will be happy to know that all is well. I have no complaints about which to boast." He was excusing himself and about to move onward, when Miss Bingley stopped him with a touch on his arm and the words, "We must talk about Charles." She looked around to make sure they were not overheard, and continued in hushed tones, "My brother will not stop talking about Miss Bennet. He keeps lamenting the fact that he left Hertfordshire without saying goodbye to her and that wild family of hers. He says that he should attempt to apologise for his hasty removal. You must talk some sense into him!"

"Now is not the time or place."

"But he is determined to speak with your wife, for it was her ill-humour at the theatre that spurred him on. You cannot let that happen. The truth will surely come out if he does, and then Charles will be furious with us both. He plans on requesting a set from her tonight." Darcy tightened his jaw as he looked to where his wife was standing not five minutes earlier, but he could not determine her whereabouts.

"He is here?" At her nod, he said, "Miss Bingley, I thank you for the warning. If you will excuse me, I will try to intercede before he has a chance to approach her."

"Oh, and one more thing. You absolutely must speak with your wife about manners. Your cousin, the viscount himself, requested that Mrs. Darcy dance with him, and do you know what she did? She refused him outright. Her behaviour was most shocking, and your cousin – a most agreeable man."

Darcy's eyes darkened as he bowed and left her standing there with a smirk gracing her features.

"You could have at least asked me for a dance," she muttered to herself.

Darcy began earnestly searching for his wife, wondering at the veracity of Miss Bingley's claims. He knew that she would like nothing better than to cause conflict within his already precarious marriage, but if Elizabeth insulted his cousin, when he had been so kind to her, Darcy would have to confront her and insist that she apologise.

ELIZABETH HAD BEEN ASKED by several men to dance, and without her husband around to guide her, she had to accept them all; however, when the viscount approached her, she refused to play into his manipulative hands. She just hoped that no one had been witness to her rejection. Unfortunately, he continued to torment her with his presence, laughing at her discomfort. Finally after several minutes of his insinuations at her expense, Darcy arrived. Langston had seen him coming and immediately changed his tact to one of contrition and kindness. "But Mrs. Darcy, I only want to help you. I have no desire to make myself vulnerable, for I am a married man." She looked keenly at him trying to make out his meaning, then with relief she saw her husband.

"Mr. Darcy, there you are."

"Elizabeth, what is the meaning of this?" Then he turned to Langston, "In what ways do you want to help my wife?"

"Darcy, I have been attempting to talk your wife into dancing with me for your sake, but she seems to think that I have some ulterior motive. You will talk some sense into her, will you not?"

Darcy spoke in susurration to her, "Elizabeth, you insult my family in your refusal. Of course you will go with Lord Langston. He is showing you a great kindness in wanting to publicly honour you with a dance."

Elizabeth in a panic looked to her husband and whispered, "But, sir, I do not wish to dance. Please do not make me do that which will pain me."

Darcy than held her arm and pulled her aside, and continued to speak quietly. "Elizabeth people are watching you. I know not why you choose to refuse Langston; he has been nothing but attentive to your needs, but you *will* accompany him to the dance floor." Elizabeth wanted to feel the indignation at her husband's imposing manner, but she could not, in light of Darcy's ignorance to his cousin's faults; she understood his justification. Elizabeth felt her situation to be without hope, so she looked up and resigned herself to dance with the man. At least she was in a public place with him, so he could do little harm.

Elizabeth allowed herself to be led to the line of dancers that was just forming. She was determined to speak as little as possible to the man. Elizabeth could not see Lady Susan watching from across the room, malice in her heart for the woman who induced her husband's inconstancy.

The second dance of the set began, and Langston took the lead, holding her hand longer than necessary and leering at her décolletage as he would make a pass. Finally, he spoke, "Mrs. Darcy, you seem to think that you will somehow escape my notice. I am not in the habit of being denied." She did not respond and schooled her features so that they could not be read.

He continued, "But you must not think on any *attentions* that you might give me as faithlessness. You are aware that our society, the one that you reached for, does not view marriage as the lower classes might. Indeed, you must be very well acquainted with the idea of a marriage being akin to a business arrangement. No one is exclusively bound to his own spouse. I know Darcy is no different, and you do not have any special regard for the man; I see this in the way you look at him." Elizabeth imagined a retort, but kept her mouth closed; she refused to become ensnared in his traps. Instead, she concentrated on schooling her features to appear pleased with her partner and was able to hide her distaste for the man, despite his continued references to inconstancy and betrayal within the confines of her own marriage.

When Elizabeth was led back to Darcy, she saw that he was speaking to a striking woman of about Elizabeth's age, maybe younger, wearing a fine gown of the lightest pink silk in the current fashion; her neck was adorned with diamonds that reflected the candlelight making her whole countenance seem to sparkle. Her hair resembled the colour of honey, her smile graceful and enhanced by her pink lips. Elizabeth saw the two of them alone in close conference and felt distinctly odd interrupting them, as if she were intruding upon a private moment. Lord Langston sniggered and said, "Oh, this will be good." Elizabeth crinkled her brow, as her apprehension mounted. If Langston was pleased, there could be nothing good.

Lord Langston was the first to speak, "Lady Annette, how delightful. I vow you get lovelier each time I see you, does she not, Darcy?"

"Yes, she is quite beautiful."

"Mrs. Darcy and I were just talking about the many allurements around us, and may I be so bold as to say that you are one of them." His audience was not quite sure how to take his remark, excepting Elizabeth, but she would not let him or the others see her discomfort.

Darcy at length found his voice, "Lady Annette, may I present my wife, Mrs. Elizabeth Darcy? And Elizabeth meet Lady Annette Croxley, daughter of the Earl of Cunningham." Langston held an amused expression upon his face as he took in the scene. Lady Annette's open condescension demonstrated her feelings on the matter. Darcy's face had drained of colour, and he looked as though he might become ill.

Elizabeth smiled sweetly, and after curtseying as was proper, she began to ask Lady Annette about her home county, which she discovered to be in the North of England. The answers were curt, revealing to anyone listening that Lady Annette had no desire to further the acquaintance. This could in no way pain Elizabeth, for although beautiful, she found Lady Annette to be supercilious and discourteous. What she did not understand was the woman's relationship to her husband, especially in light of the viscount's offhand remark. *And why is Darcy so fidgety? – So unlike himself.*

After about five minutes of stilted conversation, Lady Annette turned to Darcy, while taking his arm, and said, "I believe this is our set, Darcy." He glanced over to Elizabeth and allowed himself to be led by the mysterious woman to the dance floor.

Elizabeth had almost forgotten with whom she was standing when his salacious voice interrupted her thoughts, "You know, of course, that Darcy would likely be engaged, if not married, to that woman had it not been for your interference in his plans." She looked up sharply and told herself to walk away from the man. Langston wanted nothing more than to upset her and her marriage. But then her curiosity held her feet in place. "Perhaps you don't know. Darcy had all but declared himself when he left for Hertfordshire to visit his friend, Bingley, the only thing keeping him from staking his claim being her father's absence from town. But neither of them doubted his intentions. I don't know if Darcy was more despondent to lose Lady Annette for her dowry of thirty thousand, her title of daughter to an earl – as was his mother – or for her exceptional and unparalleled beauty. Likely all three."

Elizabeth watched her husband with the graceful and alluring Lady Annette and could not help but let a pang of alarm creep up her spine and enter her heart. She was the most beautiful woman Elizabeth had ever beheld next to her dear Jane, and may have been even more so, if not for her condescension, which to Elizabeth would deprive any person of the beauty that had been God-given. Elizabeth began to feel sick and needed to get away from this man, who in a little over a week's time had become her biggest affliction. Not wanting the viscount to know of his success in disconcerting her, she turned to him and said, "Like a viper, your words are poison, but they cannot sting me." Then she held her head high and walked towards the other side of the room.

"Mrs. Darcy," said an unfamiliar voice. When Elizabeth turned to see who had spoken to her, she saw a group of three young ladies, about Elizabeth's age or slightly older, standing nearby motioning for her to join them. She recognised two of them and the third was soon introduced to be a friend of Lady Susan's. "Come join us. It is not often that we have the pleasure of meeting someone new to London society."

Then another spoke, "We seldom see a man of Mr. Darcy's wealth and superiority lower himself as he did in marrying a nobody and then put her on display as Mr. Darcy has done. You must have him hoodwinked. I never thought I would see the man in such a state. Do tell us your secrets." Then laughter reigned for the next few moments.

Elizabeth, in no mood for such frivolous drivel, said, "Oh, yes. But I am sure you ladies know how it is to be done. My mother sent me out on my morning walks every day at dawn, always within the confines of my father's estate, with the hope and expectation that I would find success in obtaining a husband. She had anticipated that I might ensnare a lord, but instead was resigned to accept a man who was just handsome and rich. Her solace for my not meeting her expectations is that I am now mistress of Pemberley, which I hear is a majestic estate, where my sisters can visit often, so that I can send them out on long walks for the same purpose. We hope to have better luck there since we hear Pemberley has more rich neighbours than Longbourn." At their look of shock and confusion, she smiled and excused herself in order to remove to the same balcony where Darcy had just been not three hours before.

She was finally able to escape for a few moments of fresh air. It was bitterly cold out, but this neither bothered her nor induced her to quit this place of respite away from eyes of scrutiny. Elizabeth had enjoyed the attentions she received throughout the evening. She loved to dance, and there was an abundance of gentlemen willing to give her the pleasure, but she felt as though each man was like Lord Langston, just not as overt in communicating his wishes. The gown that Mr. Darcy had chosen for her revealed her assets to be in abundance, and she felt as though each man was taking notice. Then her mind naturally went to the beautiful woman now dancing with her husband. *Can the viscount be in earnest, or is he just trying to disconcert me?* As these thoughts were beginning to play out in her mind, she heard a strong male voice behind her speaking her name. This startled her as she thought that perhaps Lord Langston had followed in order to take advantage of the seclusion of the balcony. However, she was most surprised to see Mr. Bingley.

"Forgive me for frightening you. I had no intention of making you jump at my voice." Elizabeth recollected herself and responded that she was not afraid and that she just did not expect to see anyone. "I am glad to hear that. It is quite cold outside, is it not?" She nodded that it was so, and he continued, "Tell me, how is your family? Are they all still in Hertfordshire?"

Elizabeth considered how her family, and most especially her beloved sister, had been offended and hurt by this man, and yet he presumed to approach her to ask about them. Did he hope to continue his deceit, so that he might return to Netherfield and continue taking advantage of Jane's kind heart? She was determined not to speak of Jane. "My family remains in Hertfordshire, but one of my sisters is to be married, as you know, within the fortnight. After that is accomplished, they will be able to return to the usual state of affairs, which I am sure will please my father exceedingly."

"Your sister, Mary, is to be wed to Mr. Collins, if I remember correctly."

"You do."

Mr. Bingley seemed most disconcerted and had opened his mouth to say more when the door opened and Miss Bingley came out. "Charles, there you are! I have been looking for you. This is the supper set, and I hope that you will sit with me when the meal begins. You know how I despise dancing, which is why I have chosen to sit out the set."

"Of course, Caroline. I will be inside in just a moment."

"Don't stay out on my account. I have decided to return inside. It seems that the cold has caught up with me after all." Elizabeth then excused herself. She was in no humour to listen to what Mr. Bingley might have to say. There could be no defence for the abominable way in which he had treated her family. Her heart broke for Jane, whose only fault was that she was too trusting; she had not yet experienced the wickedness in the world that Elizabeth had come to know, and Elizabeth hoped she could shield her somehow.

When they had returned to the warmth of the ballroom, Miss Bingley took the opportunity to speak to the woman who had stolen her own opportunity for happiness. "Eliza, might I have a word?"

Elizabeth paused. She had no desire to spend any amount of time with a woman who condemned her, but she would also not be accused of incivility by ignoring the request. So turning, she said, "Yes, Miss Bingley. How may I be of assistance?"

"How fortunate you are to have been honoured with a ball! I know to what degree Darcy despises being made a public spectacle, but I see you hold no such qualms."

"It is true that Mr. Darcy cannot abide the effusions often placed on him by supposed friends."

"My, things have certainly changed for you. I remember, when we first knew you in Hertfordshire, how amazed we all were to find you to be a reputed beauty." Miss Bingley then tapped her finger on her chin as if in recollection, saying "I particularly recollect Darcy saying one night about you in particular, after you had been dining at Netherfield, 'She a beauty! – I should as soon call her mother a wit.'" She then covered her giggles with her hand, pleased to see Elizabeth taken aback, but then proceeded on, hoping to put in the final stab, "But afterwards you must have improved in his eyes, for he seems to be showing you off to great advantage this evening. I see that his efforts have not been in vain, for I have heard many a gentleman speak of your substantial, if not respectable charms."

Elizabeth felt the insult most acutely and found herself incapable of replying to such a blatant and contrived attack.

"Caroline, how dare you speak of such things!" retorted her brother from behind. Although the room was full of loud and distracting sounds, Bingley had witnessed the entire episode, having followed the ladies inside.

When Miss Bingley turned an amused smirk to her brother, Elizabeth took the opportunity to escape the Bingleys' manipulative slander aimed at hurting her and her family. She tried to compose herself – to recollect her own innocence in the painful events that had taken place over the past few months, but she could not escape this new offence that had been set before her. She doubted not the recital of her husband's past, insolently spoken words. Elizabeth knew well that Mr. Darcy had found her lacking in attractions and had worked hard to present his wife this night as an improved version of the original, but hearing the words iterated reopened a leaking and festering wound. But Elizabeth would not let Miss Bingley's aspersions affect her mood any longer. She was determined that she would not allow the woman – whose own position in Mr. Darcy's life was flimsy at best – any power over her. Unfortunately, Elizabeth could not claim such a tenuous hold by the woman now in her husband's company.

Darcy was still dancing with Lady Annette. Elizabeth watched for a moment, and then sighing, left the ballroom looking for some refreshment. Once she had taken a cup of punch, Elizabeth noticed a woman sitting alone in a chair against the wall, and as she felt rather alone herself, she decided to join her. Although they had not been introduced, Elizabeth felt it right to speak with her. Through their short conversation, Elizabeth learnt that her name was Miss Grey and she was a companion to a Miss Darling who was currently engaged in the dance with a gentleman, the heir of a baronetcy. Her charge was eighteen and had come out last Season. Elizabeth began to ask her more about herself and discovered that the woman was the second daughter of a country gentleman whose estate had been entailed away. Instead of being one of five daughters, she was one of two. Her father died two years ago, and as she remained unmarried at twenty-five, she was obligated to look for employment. Her education left her with the choice of governess or companion, and thankfully the position, which she now held, came available. They spoke about her former home and the heir who had removed her remaining family from its comforts.

Elizabeth's heart poured out for this woman, but she kept her inner thoughts hidden, realising that she could very easily have had this woman's life. "And do you enjoy your current employment?"

"As much as anyone could in my position, although I find these balls somewhat difficult to bear. I had always supposed I would marry, but that was not to be. My employer is kind for the most part and asks little of me that might make me uncomfortable, unlike other rich fathers who hire companions and governesses for their own convenience." Looking rather disconcerted she stood and continued, "Well, Mrs. Darcy, it has been a pleasure meeting you. But I must find my charge. The dance has concluded and I should attempt to accompany her to dinner."

Elizabeth stood and smiled saying, "Miss Grey, thank you for allowing me to intrude upon your privacy. It was a pleasure to make your acquaintance." As Elizabeth began to walk to the dining room, she considered Miss Grey's words and also what was left unspoken. Elizabeth was beginning to see a theme with the rich men of privilege, who felt it their entitlement and due to expect a woman to give herself over as a plaything for their amusement. She considered Mr. Bingley's toying with Jane's affections and Lord Langston's strong overtures. Even Mr. Darcy, who had been remarkably patient with her disinclination to be intimate, desired her to wear a gown that would provide sweetmeat for his and everyone else's eyes, and on their wedding night took without giving and without her will. Mr. Wickham had been very kind to her and was likely one of the only men of her acquaintance – aside from Colonel Fitzwilliam – who did not expect more from her, and he was the one whom Darcy maligned.

It was with these thoughts that she entered the dining-parlour looking for her husband. She had not spoken with him alone since their dance, and that was done in ill humour, which she regretted, and wanted to make amends. When she spotted him, she realised that he was not alone, that he had escorted Lady Annette into the dining-parlour and was now sitting beside her, in what looked to be a secret conference. On the other side of him sat Lady Susan and Lord Langston. Elizabeth was unsure of her emotions at the time. She was angry to be sure, angry about her new and unwanted position in life, about her having to endure such an evening, angry that her husband would shame her in such a public way in sitting with a previous love interest, angry that Mr. Bingley had the nerve to speak with her in light of his treatment of her sister, and angry that the viscount was witness to her husband's affront. However, Elizabeth was sagacious and determined to give her husband the benefit of the doubt while attempting to keep a courteous mien. She had little else she could do and would not make a scene to embarrass herself or her new relations and give them just cause to denigrate her. She walked over to where they sat.

"Mr. Darcy, I see that you have already been seated for supper. And what were your plans for me? Should I join Mr. Bingley? He did seem most anxious to speak with me earlier." He stood with a pained look in his eyes that made Elizabeth regret her words, but just fleetingly. She was soon returned to the pleasure of being again vexed with him upon seeing his partner's smug look, but she was able to keep hidden her true ire, for she did not want Mr. Darcy or his companions to know of her distress.

Darcy quietly said, "Elizabeth, forgive me. I saved you a seat, but could not find you. My cousin and his wife then sat down, and I of course could not ask them to leave." Darcy had spent the past two months studying his wife's many expressions. She had always laid bare her feelings on her countenance and in her eyes, but on this occasion, he was at a loss.

"What can you mean? Have you done something dreadful for which you need forgiveness?" She stood smiling with arched brow, daring him to confess whatever sins tugging at his conscience. "Perhaps later then. For now, I will join my new friend, the companion of a Miss Darling. I see her alone on the other side of the room. She, like myself, finds the company above her rather tedious to endure, so perhaps we can bolster one another as we watch the disingenuous show being played out before us." She curtseyed and walked away.

IMMEDIATELY AFTER SUPPER, Darcy approached Elizabeth and requested that she dance the following set with him. "Oh, no. I find that I do not wish to dance, so this time you may scorn me." She held his gaze without so much as a flinch. They stared at one another for what seemed like an eternity but was in fact no more than half a minute.

"Elizabeth, please allow me to explain what happened before supper that led to the unfortunate seating arrangement." She smiled sweetly. He took that as license to continue. "I did not realise the dance with Lady Annette was the supper set." *Indeed I had not planned on dancing with Lady Annette at all.* "When supper was called, she took my arm and guided me to the dining-parlour. I had no honourable choice but to offer her a seat. I intended on your sitting to my right and had tilted the chair to save it for you, but then Langston showed up, and I could not deny him the seat. Your absence continued, so I supposed that you had found another arrangement. I should have left with you, but I had the distinct feeling that you would not welcome me. Please, I was wrong and ask that you forgive my slight at your expense."

Elizabeth then did what he had least expected: she laughed in unfeigned drollery. "Mr. Darcy, you look so contrite. I don't believe I have ever seen you grovel before. I say – I believe your neglect may have been worth hearing the apology."

"Does that mean you forgive me?"

"Oh, no, I cannot absolve you so easily. You must atone for your sins by being extra solicitous to my comfort the rest of the evening, then perhaps I may find it in myself to forgive you." His brows knit together as he attempted to determine her implication and realised yet again that she was teasing. "I could study your facial expressions for years and never tire of the endeavour," she said while smiling. Elizabeth remained unsettled by the events of the evening. Her first ball in the company of her husband's friends left her more homesick than she had yet felt. She longed for the comfort of her father's presence, of Jane's kind words, and even her mother's embarrassing remarks, but Mr. Darcy was her husband, and she had to accept the good and the bad, no matter the balance. She would remain strong and not give in to pain or petty jealousies.

Elizabeth continued to refuse to dance with Darcy until the final set. She did, however, leave him many times as she joined other men on the dance floor. Elizabeth was determined not to let her disquiet affect her or let Mr. Darcy see how she had been hurt by so many, including himself, during the course of the evening.

DARCY'S EXPERIENCES DURING THE BALL were quite different than his wife's. Throughout the first half of the evening, Darcy could think of little else than Elizabeth's pleasing form, sparkling eyes, and ready wit. Whenever they encountered one another, she either challenged or ridiculed him. This had become a pattern for the couple. Darcy had never in his life been around a person with so little respect and ambition for his position and wealth. He had always been well liked, or rather well received, based on his fortune and position in society. His estate had forever been his trump card when considering securing a woman's affections, but Elizabeth had asked him very little about his home, except in the context of specifics pertaining to the walking paths or gardens. He still could not trust her integrity in relation to their scandal, for he had no proof to the contrary, but she seemed so little impressed with him that he knew she was not just playing him for favours. Elizabeth did not even show reverence for his relations, as he would expect from someone trying to vie for a place in society. Darcy found himself desiring for the very thing that had annoyed him with other women. He wanted her attentions and approbation. He saw how she expressed her delight in the presence of other men and wanted the same for himself. Darcy was wondering how he had missed her allurements in the past. Elizabeth truly was a striking beauty, and the very thought of her made him want to take her home and ravish her.

Lady Annette had approached Darcy before supper while he was in deep thought about this present discovery of his wife's many attractions. Elizabeth was at the time on the dance floor with Langston, another in her long line of dance partners, when he was woken up from his reverie by a familiar, feminine voice. "Darcy, did you lose something, or perhaps someone?" He then turned to her and bowed, somewhat flustered, which could only be perceived by his heightened colour, and he wondered if she or anyone else could have read his on-going libidinous thoughts about his wife. As it happened, the woman before him had noticed his impassioned visage and vainly misconstrued his musings to be about herself.

"Lady Annette, what a pleasure seeing you again. I was just thinking about… well about the ball. My aunt and uncle have gone to a great deal of trouble to acknowledge my wife." He looked away, clearly discomposed at the unexpected arrival of his former love interest.

"Yes, it would appear they have." Lady Annette took Darcy's discomposure as a reliable sign of his continued regard for herself, which could not change their current circumstances but gave her satisfaction nonetheless.

In little more than a whisper he said, "Lady Annette, I know not what your brother told you. I did visit him after my engagement, but before the wedding, to apologise for any injury I may have caused you and your family through my marriage. You must know that I had to do my duty. I know we had no formal understanding, you and I, but I also comprehend how my attentions were perceived, and indeed justly so."

"My brother told me your tale; however, the way I see it, you must have wanted something much more than my substantial … dowry to induce you to marry a country nobody. You said that nothing happened between the two of you, but I cannot believe that to be so, or why else would you have married the woman? Obviously, she took advantage of you or perhaps you took advantage of her; maybe both of you were at fault, but the truth is that you wanted to marry her more than you wanted to honour our unspoken agreement."

"I understand why you might see things that way. Indeed, if I were in your shoes, I may have felt the same, but I can assure you that I in no way did anything of my own volition to compromise Elizabeth's reputation. Nor did I seek to cause you embarrassment or pain."

"Can you say the same about her?"

"I have to accept that I am now honour-bound to think the best of her regardless of where the evidence points."

She smiled. "I thought so much. Well now you must suffer with a wife who only respects you for what you can give her, and I am certain that you can give her *quite a lot*."

Darcy wondered at her meaning. Did Lady Annette just refer to his money and connections or was she perhaps thinking of something altogether different? Her suggestive, cursory survey of him left him in doubt. It was just at this moment when Elizabeth walked up with Langston. He could tell that Elizabeth was in distress and only supposed it to have been related to the fact that he was in close conference with a beautiful and elegant female of unknown alliance. But before he could ease Elizabeth's mind and make his retreat, Lady Annette suggested that they were pledged to dance. He had a mind to refuse but knew this would cause more conjecture than was wise to allow, so he accepted his fate and danced with his former interest.

Where Elizabeth had then gone, he did not know. Upon finding that he had unknowingly agreed to dance with Lady Annette during the supper set, he was determined to make his escape and then find his wife to share the meal. He had seen very little of her and wanted to resolve whatever concerns had come between them. However, Lady Annette had taken his arm and was not to let him go. Darcy was trying to be conciliatory; he was the one who had caused Lady Annette's grief, but he also knew how her presence with him must look to his wife and his acquaintances. The meal would progress slowly and with discomfort, but nothing else could be done.

When his wife finally arrived at the table, panic took hold. How could he make this right for Elizabeth without offending Lady Annette? Elizabeth demonstrated her true worth when she boldly proclaimed that she would sit with another and schooled her countenance to hide her bitterness.

After Elizabeth had left, Lady Annette giggled. "Your wife is a strange one, Darcy. She seems perfectly content to let you dine with another, more beautiful woman, while she sits with a lowly companion! Either she does not care a whit about you, or she blindly trusts you. Or maybe she does not know that you and I had an understanding of sorts before she came along. Which can it be? You did tell her about us did you not?"

Darcy heard Langston snigger next to him and then said in a clipped tone, "On the contrary, I have no need to tell her about past interests that came to nothing. She would be correct in assuming that she can trust me. I have always behaved with honour concerning her and any other woman of my acquaintance. As to her feelings towards me, that I cannot judge. Perhaps you should ask her yourself."

Speaking quietly, Lady Annette then said, "Darcy, do not show your anger to me. I have done nothing wrong concerning you. I could have any man I desire, and I had chosen you, but you were the one to marry another. You humiliated me in front of my friends. How could you be so cruel? If Mrs. Darcy feels some embarrassment regarding the two of us sharing a dance and a meal, she should consider it as a small penance."

Darcy had been disturbed by her words, but chose to change the subject and hope for the meal to end quickly. He knew Lady Annette would be justifiably angry, but he also felt a sense of obligation to his wife. His protective instincts had awakened and his only desire was to provide support for Elizabeth. The meal slowly crept by, and Darcy began to think that perhaps he was saved from a most unhappy alliance with the woman beside him. She was beautiful, elegant and accomplished and came with a significant dowry; however, he now saw that she had a biting tongue and condescending tone that he had never seen in his wife, even at his own expense.

Although he and Elizabeth had argued, and although she had offended him countless times, she was ready with an apology for losing her temper and was never malicious; instead she would tease. She always seemed to have those less fortunate than she on her heart. Even when she left him to Lady Annette, she planned to join someone less prosperous in her circumstances than herself, rather than attempt to improve her own standing through seeking out more illustrious connections. Elizabeth laughed at the follies of those around her, but she was not cruel or pernicious. Darcy watched Elizabeth as she spoke with Miss Darling's companion. Even her expressions from across the room spoke of her benevolence and consideration for the woman's comfort. Darcy smiled to himself as he contentedly pondered his wife.

Elizabeth's beauty approached that of Lady Annette and in some ways exceeded it, for her smiles were sincere and her eyes the window into her soul. Although of shorter stature than Lady Annette, her shapely figure and active pursuits made her most alluring. As his reflections ran their course, he realised that the physical consequences of such thoughts were beginning to intrude. The past month had been torturous, and so to offset the embarrassing effects of letting his thoughts run away with him, Darcy endeavoured to control his reflections by turning to Langston; however, his cousin only seemed to find diversion in Darcy's discomposure.

When supper had concluded, Darcy could not get to his wife quickly enough. He had to make his apologies and hope that Elizabeth's kindness would overcome her justifiable anger. And then she teased him. How was it that she could exert so much control over his equilibrium? Did she know what she was doing? Was she purposely playing him like a marionette? He did not know whether to curse her or make love to her but was leaning towards the latter.

Elizabeth then danced with five more gentlemen who were not her husband. She smiled, laughed, and flirted with them all. His desire for her was mounting as each set came to a conclusion. *Will she allow me the next dance?* he kept asking himself. Even though she showed attentions to all of those men, he could not justifiably get angry, for did he not show untoward attention to Lady Annette, even if it were not at his initiation? Lady Annette did approach him again and attempted to garner his full attention, but he sensed that her goal was to disconcert his wife rather than to appease him, so he put on his mask of indifference, which signalled to her, as it had so many other women, that he had no further interest.

Finally the last dance of the evening had arrived, and he uncharacteristically hoped that she would grant him the pleasure of joining her on the dance floor. It was true, he could have insisted she stop dancing with the other men and only dance with himself, but he hoped that she would come willingly to him. And finally, she did. "Mr. Darcy, you look very despondent over here in the corner alone. I have decided that I *may* dance the last with you, but I must insist that you request as a man ought, or I will be pleased to accept another partner."

"Mrs. Darcy, may I have the pleasure of the next set?" he requested as he performed a formal bow, unnerved at the novel experiences of meditating upon her delightful charms and hoping, but not altogether certain, she would accept.

She looked as though she were considering his request and then finally said, "Yes, you may, though we must limit our conversation to the weather this time, for I am in no mood to quarrel over the innuendos and misunderstandings we are prone to cherish." Happy to oblige, he offered his arm as he led her to the line up.

They danced with nary a word spoken. Instead, Darcy's eyes explored her sonsy figure, her smooth complexion, her sparkling eyes, her elegant swing, her shiny curls and her pouty lips that on occasion gave him a warm smile. He could not have known that his scrutiny deeply disturbed her, for he himself had no idea of the detailed perusal, as he had been strangely and unknowingly bewitched through the entirety of the set.

All Elizabeth could think on was Langston and Bingley carelessly playing callous games with women and how her new friend, Miss Grey, was fortunate in her position, for many others came with the price of a woman's virtue. She also thought on Lady Annette and what she could still mean for her husband. She did notice Darcy's salacious scrutiny of her person and hoped that his hunger for her would not be satisfied on this night, for how could she know if he desired her or perhaps Lady Annette? Was she to be a surrogate lover? Was she to be the one he touched while he thought of another? The thought made her feel ill, but she was determined to hide her unrest. Mr. Darcy had always maintained that he could read her expressions, but she would not let him into her mind today. She would not show her vulnerability, so she smiled from time to time and concentrated on the dance while she attempted to think on happy thoughts of Longbourn.

THE TIME FINALLY CAME FOR THE DARCYS TO DEPART. Elizabeth was emotionally and physically exhausted, having hardly eaten a bite owing to her solicitude. They entered the carriage, sitting across from one another. Elizabeth did not realise that she was sitting in the direct line of the moonlight as it beamed into the carriage. Her skin fairly glowed and Darcy was enchanted. Elizabeth could not see how his eyes drank in her beauty, for if she had, she might have felt a foreboding for the night ahead. Darcy was unable to control his thoughts as his mind went to places yet to be explored. His body was responding to the salacity that was building with each moment. Tonight was the night. He refused to wait any longer. *Surely, she feels the need as I do. How could she not?*

He walked her to her room and opened the door for her. She was somewhat surprised, as they usually parted between their rooms. Darcy seemed to hesitate, then picked up her hand and kissed it, a slow, lingering gesture that unnerved her. He then looked into her eyes, then her mouth and then lower still. Then he stepped aside and went to his own room. Janette had been able to get some sleep before Elizabeth returned home and was ready to assist in the removal of her gown. She quietly worked as Elizabeth gazed, as if in a daze, into the looking glass of her dressing room. After the removal of her petticoat and corset, her maid began taking down her hair and brushing out each curl before plaiting it for the night. Elizabeth felt exhausted and anticipated her slumber.

It was while Janette was brushing her locks when Mr. Darcy made his presence known within the doorway to her chamber. He was in his shirtsleeves and breeches. His shirt was open at the top, so that his upper chest was bare. This was the first time since the day of the storm that Elizabeth had actually seen him in anything other than full dress, for on their wedding night, she had clamped her eyes shut for the duration. Her breaths came quickly as she realised his intentions. She wanted to shout, "No!" to please desist and let her be, but she knew her duty and she knew that he had needs. She briefly wondered how he had met his needs up to this point but decided to think on it no more. Janette made her escape; Elizabeth wanted to insist she not leave but bit her lip to keep from intervening.

Without a word Darcy reached his hands down and took hers within his own. She looked away and allowed herself to be led to her room. Elizabeth's heart began to race in trepidation for what was to come. She had considered the likelihood of this happening; with some success, she had even attempted to talk herself into acceptance, for in retrospect, she recalled that not all of her husband's touches on their wedding night were unpleasant. But that was before Langston had imposed himself upon her, and her mind would not relent. Surely, he would be kind to her she told herself. Her husband was a most attractive man, as any lady with eyes would attest; his masculinity and fine figure would cause any woman who had breath within her to capitulate happily to his demands. But Elizabeth could hardly be compared to the average, deferential woman, and her experience thus far had left her in a state of agitation. The previous encounter with her husband had caused her pain and embarrassment. Mr. Darcy had come into her room, taken his pleasure and left her alone without a moment's concern for her own wishes or gratification. Would he be equally selfish again this night?

After arriving home, Darcy had walked Elizabeth to her chamber, making his intentions clear with his manner and visual examination before his departure. When he entered his own room, he began pacing as he anticipated the night ahead. He would give her time to undress. He poured himself a brandy and stood by the fire waiting until his valet appeared. When Nelson showed up, he helped Darcy to remove his shoes, coat and waistcoat. After enough time had passed, he walked through the sitting room and gently opened the door into Elizabeth's chamber and glanced inside. He saw the candlelight emanating from the dressing room and rightly supposed that Elizabeth was still with her lady's maid. Darcy quietly went to the door, standing in the darkness, and watched as the maid brushed through Elizabeth's hair. Her eyes were closed as she relished in the feeling. He imagined running his hands through her long thick curls. She was wearing nothing but her chemise now, and he could see her form through the thin, linen fabric. He had not seen her in this way since that day at the cabin and then only fleetingly, for on their wedding night, in her modesty, she had worn a gown more suited to a winter's night of sleep than lovemaking.

Darcy moved into the light and made his presence known. Elizabeth's eyes opened wide when she glanced at him, but then she averted her gaze. He noticed that her breathing increased and suspected that she was as anxious as he; Darcy determined that he had waited long enough. He had adorned her with jewels, entertained her at the theatre, introduced her to high society, and committed himself to saving her family. Eventually she would learn to accept his advances, hopefully starting tonight. He held out his hands and when she did not budge, he gently grasped both of hers and brought her to a standing position. She was looking away, likely shy and nervous, which he found endearing, as he appreciated her innocence. Then he led her into her chamber and towards the large canopied bed.

But before reaching their destination, he turned towards her and put his left arm around her waist. He just wanted to feel her body close to his own, so he pulled her up against him so that they were touching and he could feel her curves against his frame. He bent his head down to kiss her, but she turned her head away, so that he kissed her cheek instead. This only increased his longing, so he trailed his kisses in a hungry fashion down her neck while his right hand reached up to caress her bosom. Darcy felt like a starved man at a buffet when his libido took control. He now had no thought but to take possession of her, so easily lifting the petite woman before him, he carried her to the bed, placing her across the width of the counterpane. He let himself fall on top of her, careful not to hurt her with his weight, but anxious to indulge in her.

His left arm was now free from holding her, so he reached down to lift up her chemise while his right continued its exploration of her breasts. He tasted her neck, shoulder and then down to her fullness. When her gown had been lifted to above her hips, Darcy began to unbutton and release himself from the confines of his breeches. He was overwhelmed with a consuming longing to join with her, and so he gave free rein to his desires. Elizabeth's body was perfection. Every touch, taste and smell brought him ecstasy, and his only wish was to savour her.

All of his thoughts centred on the satisfaction their union brought to his profound yearning. He wanted this time to last forever but needed the fulfilment and completion of a physical climax, so with mixed emotions he finally reached the apex of his desire. Darcy yelled out and collapsed upon his wife, careful not to burden her with his heavy weight.

As his breathing began to slow to a normal pace, he realised that she was taking deep, heaving breaths, and he at first thought that maybe she, too, had found herself caught in the moment. When he lifted himself so he could look at her, he saw that her breathing was not the result of passion but of anguish. Tears were pouring down her cheek and temples. Her eyes were clamped shut; the only thing holding back the sound of her sob, he discovered, was by her biting her bottom lip. A small amount of bright blood was escaping her mouth where her teeth continued to clamp down.

"Elizabeth, are you hurt?" She did not respond, but instead turned her head in the opposite direction, as if to somehow hide her tears. "Relax. You are hurting yourself; your lip is bleeding." He was not ready for what would happen next. She loosened the hold on her mouth and a wail of distress escaped. She began crying in unfeigned turmoil. Darcy did not know what to do. *What have I done but enjoy my wife? Why is she in such distress? She is no longer chaste; she shouldn't hurt.* "Elizabeth, you must get control of yourself." He rolled over to take his weight off of her in case he had hurt her by his large bearing. Elizabeth quickly pulled down her chemise to her knees while covering her chest where Darcy had revealed her breasts. He noticed that Elizabeth was trying to control her distress without success, and for a moment, he regretted coming to her. However, he soon overcame this sentiment.

When Darcy led Elizabeth to her room, it had been like a déjà vu experience for her. Every motion and touch seemed to mock that of Lord Langston. She had closed her eyes to escape the moment, as children attempt to escape the suspected monster under their bed at night, but contrary to child's play, she could not get away from the physical and emotional feelings that had begun to torment her. For the past week, she had woken from nightmares related to Langston's advances. Elizabeth had come a long way from that frightening encounter to overcome her discomposure. She was strong and tenacious and rarely let herself succumb to panic. But as Langston's cousin, Darcy and he resembled one another in ways that were not immediately apparent. They had the same athletic build and stature. Their eyes were the same penetrating blue that leered at her body as if able to devour it with a mere look. Their breathing increased the same way; their weight overwhelmed her, making her feel vulnerable, the same way. And with Elizabeth's eyes closed, Darcy somehow became Langston in her mind. He was the offensive, self-gratifying man of means who took what he wanted. She had no value to him aside from being a toy to manipulate and possess. The only difference between Darcy and Langston is that Elizabeth was legally and morally bound to submit to the advances of the former, but obligated to stop the latter.

Of course, her thoughts were not the rational thoughts of a wife being loved by her husband. This was due in part to the reality that she was not actually loved by her husband. He had taken her into his home and set her up as mistress. Theirs was very similar to a business relationship, as most marriages of the privileged. She could not overcome her treacherous thoughts that seemed designed to hold her in misery, but she was desperate to keep Darcy from seeing her anguish. Elizabeth did not want him to see her weaknesses, nor did she want him to discover Langston's betrayal at her expense. At first she had feared that Darcy would not believe her, but now she apprehended that it was also her shame at being so used that kept her silent.

Without realising it, Elizabeth had bitten down on her lip to keep from crying out. She had tried to detach herself from Darcy's advances. Although not as physically painful as her first encounter with him, still she felt discomfort that became more pronounced the longer he took. She just wanted him to stop, and finally he yelled out, which she knew now to be a sign that he had at last succeeded in his goal of gratifying his physical desires. Elizabeth hoped he would soon leave without noticing her distress, but that was not to be. After asking her if she were hurt and trying to help her calm, the floodgates of her wretchedness opened and she began to cry releasing all of the emotions that she had so judiciously held in check. Elizabeth knew that she had to stop; she tried with all of her might to control her breathing and distress but was failing in her efforts.

"Elizabeth, you must get control of yourself," he said again. When she had finally calmed, he asked her what she was about. "Why the tears?"

"Please, just go. You are done here. Can you now leave me to myself?"

"No, I will not leave you in distress this time. I understood why you were so afflicted on our wedding night, but I confess that I am at a loss now. Have I somehow hurt you? I did not mean to; I can assure you." Darcy was speaking kindly to her, but Elizabeth could not appreciate nor hear his concern as her mind kept going back to Langston's false words of sentiment.

Her distress increased as he continued to stay. Elizabeth just wanted him gone. She felt embarrassment over her state of undress and foolish for her obvious grief. "The discomfort is over now, so please do not concern yourself. It has been a long night, and I want to be alone now."

"You seemed to have an abundance of energy earlier. You cover yourself now, but you were readily flirting and enjoying the lure of other men the entire night at the ball," said Darcy, now induced to pique by her emotional dismissal.

"You may recall, sir, that you were the one who picked such a revealing bodice, not I. If any man gave me notice because of my dress, it was your doing."

"I saw that you enjoyed their attentions, Elizabeth, but scorned mine. I give you a grand home, extravagant jewels, new fashionable clothing; I take you to the theatre and opera. Damn it! I saved you and your family from ruin, and this is the response I am to receive? You spurn my advances, and by your tears you attempt to make me feel guilty for doing what is only natural and within my rights." Darcy's sense of justice began to overcome his wisdom.

"As for giving attentions, I noticed that yours were employed elsewhere as well. Lady Annette is indeed a beauty. Tell me, did you think of her while with me just now?" Saying those words hurt more than she had suspected they would, but she continued on, "I see how it is; you have confirmed my suspicions all along. I am nothing to you but an expensive harlot that you purchased at the expense of my pin allowance and your reputation. I suppose I am beholden to you and must now make myself available at your whim. I guess that is only right since I came at such a high price."

"That is nonsense! You willingly and publicly entered into this marriage, knowing what it would entail. Do not blame me for expecting you to uphold your *God-ordained* part of the bargain. I am not asking anything from you that any other man would not ask of his wife." Darcy tried to keep his calm. "I have been very patient with you for over a month now, yet you accuse me of treating you like a common strumpet. You have offended me and my honour, and I will not have it." He stood while Elizabeth reached for the coverlet at the end of the bed and said before leaving, "Next time you will welcome me as a wife should."

Elizabeth had an equal mix of anger and despair. She again wished that she could go back to that fateful day in the storm and leave the proud, disagreeable man to fend for himself in the woods. Mr. Darcy could take his jewels, clothing, theatre tickets and homes; they held no lure for her. He and his highborn, ignoble relations were her bane. Yes, Elizabeth regretted yet again coming to his aid and began to pray for a way out of her marriage.

Chapter Thirteen

"Behind every exquisite thing that existed, there was something tragic."
Oscar Wilde
The Picture of Dorian Gray

It is a truth universally acknowledged that two people of high intelligence with different perspectives and in close quarters must be in want of a mediator. And since that would be impossible for the Darcys, and as both were too proud to seek aid or listen if they had, their misunderstandings and pain would continue.

Both of the Darcys slept in the following day, as would be expected after a late night ball, a little passion, and a heated argument. Elizabeth rarely ate breakfast anymore and no longer took pleasure in a morning walk, so she had taken the habit of sleeping in. However, on this particular morning, she slept much later than was her usual want. Darcy, always an early riser, did not leave his room until nearly noon. However, regardless of their change in schedules, neither Darcy was inclined to see the other. Darcy had contemplated going to his club that evening for dinner, but after such a late night he was tired and was not certain if he would be in the mood for more society. Elizabeth had also thought to forego dinner, but knew Darcy would expect her to make a showing. She did not want to add any more reasons to increase his vexation.

So, instead of remaining at home in her room the rest of the day, Elizabeth decided to pay a visit to her relations on Gracechurch Street, hoping to hear news concerning her own family from their Christmas visit. Elizabeth asked her lady's maid to summon a carriage for her, and when she descended the stairs there was no sign of her husband. As usual, a footman accompanied her to Cheapside where she remained the whole of the afternoon. She was hungry for information about her family, and more specifically, Jane. Elizabeth was disheartened to learn that her dear sister had yet to recover from the heartbreak that was induced by Mr. Bingley's removal from Netherfield. Jane would not admit that she was in love with the man, for she could hardly own it to herself, but the pain was real, and she had been in a state of listlessness despite the holy day.

"Elizabeth, dear," said her aunt Gardiner, "our Christmas visit was cut short as you know because we plan on returning for the wedding early, so that I can help your mother. She was in a state! So much to accomplish in such a short time!" They laughed in affectionate remembrance of Mrs. Bennet's ways. "Why don't you join us? That way you can visit with your family for almost an entire week without Mr. Darcy's having to spend the duration listening to your mother's vexations and flutterings, should he feel obligated to join you."

Elizabeth contemplated her proposal. She dearly wanted to spend time with her family, especially in light of Jane's languor. As Jane was her dearest sister and friend, she felt a longing to help her out of her doldrums, so that she could find peace again. But then she considered Mr. Darcy. Would he let her go ahead of their already arranged schedule, and if he did, would he actually come to the wedding or just pick her up on the way to Pemberley, so as to avoid her family? He made it exceedingly clear that he had no use for her relations. And if he did not come, would she be bothered by the slight? These were questions she could not answer; all she knew was that she needed her family. "I will mention it to Mr. Darcy. I cannot predict his response, but I hope that he will approve of my joining you. On what day do you leave?"

"As the wedding is on the tenth, we shall leave on Saturday morning, the fifth. That way your uncle need only take one week off, and I will have several days to help your mother. With your being there, we should have plenty of hands to accomplish everything. Your family would love to see you. And if Mr. Darcy need speak to your uncle, I am certain Edward would be happy to reassure him."

Elizabeth doubted Mr. Darcy's concern on her behalf. Indeed, he would likely be complacent if something were to happen to her on the way that might free him of his misplaced obligation. "I will ask and send a note letting you know of his plans."

"Are you all right, Lizzy? You don't seem your usual self. And forgive me, but you look as though you haven't slept in days."

Elizabeth deliberated on what she should, or even could, say to her aunt. She felt a need to confide her difficulties to someone, but was that wise? Could she in good conscience share her secret thoughts concerning her marriage? She decided that her aunt might have some words of wisdom for her, so she opened the topic, careful to avoid any remarks that might shed Mr. Darcy in poor light. "In truth, I have slept very little. When I go to bed, my mind will not rest even though I am tired."

"Is something amiss? Whatever it is, if you need an ear, I am here for you. I hope you know that."

"You are so good to me. Truly, I do not know what I would have done without you these past six weeks." Elizabeth sat there a few moments, considering what to say. "We attended the ball last night at the Matlocks."

"And how was it?"

"I had never been to such a grand affair. The music could rival that at a concert. The array of food and drink must have kept the staff at Tromwell House busy for weeks." Her aunt continued to listen, knowing that the accommodations were likely not the extent of Elizabeth's concerns. "Mr. Darcy's family took great pains to introduce me in the best light possible, for which I am thankful."

"Have they accepted you, then?"

"No, I would not go so far. That is to say, a few have been very kind. Mr. Darcy's cousin, Colonel Fitzwilliam, whom you may remember from our wedding, has always been gracious and endeavoured to make me feel at ease, and the colonel's sister, Lady Victoria, although not overly friendly, has shown no sign of malice. However, her husband must not approve of me, for I have only met him once, and he showed no sign of acceptance. But I prefer that over

Colonel Fitzwilliam's older brother, the viscount." Elizabeth looked away, clearly upset by whatever thoughts related to that man. Her aunt reached over and held her hand. Elizabeth turned back and gave a languid smile. "That man despises me and looks for opportunities to offend and disconcert me." Elizabeth stood and walked to the chimneypiece rubbing her arms, as she had felt a chill come over her.

"What is it Lizzy? What has he done?"

Not wanting to share such an unsettling narrative of her contact with the man, Elizabeth said, "He has not hurt me, only tried to scare me." At her aunt's look of concern, she went on to say, "Truly, I am well, he just does not believe in my innocence as regards to how our marriage came about, suspecting that I might have won Mr. Darcy over with my *arts and allurements*. But as I know the truth, his words cannot hurt me."

"As long as they are only words. Lizzy, you must be careful. Men with titles, yet no conscience, feel that they can take where they please, especially as regards to women. Your marriage to his cousin may not protect you." Elizabeth looked to her with uneasiness. "I don't mean to frighten you, dear. Just make sure that you are never alone with him, or any other man for that matter, without a servant present. As always, women are vulnerable, married or not. You have Mr. Darcy to protect you; have you spoken with him about your encounters with his cousin?"

"No, I am not at all certain he would believe me, and I do not wish to be the cause of conflict in his family. I have been the source of enough problems as it is."

"Has Mr. Darcy begun to show you more regard? Have you been able to get beyond your initial difficulties?"

Elizabeth was still standing by the fireplace, the flames unable to take away the cold reality of her thoughts, which caused her to tremble. Tears welled up in her eyes. "Sometimes I think that maybe he has come to accept me in his life, that he might even hold me in some esteem, even if fleeting, but then we have an argument and I realise that I was completely mistaken."

"Are you upset because you had a disagreement then?"

"Aunt, when Mr. Darcy and I married, you said that all would be well. The truth is that things seem to be getting worse, not better. Will we ever get to a point where we enjoy each other's company? When he can come to my room and I not feel shame and resentment?" This last question opened up the floodgate to her tears. Her aunt quickly stood up and came to her, wrapping arms around her niece.

"Oh, Lizzy, you have only been married a little over a month, and you still know so little about one another. In time you will become more familiar and comfortable with him. Has he done something you felt to be demeaning to you?" Mrs. Gardiner was talking with tenderness now, hoping to soothe and not cause pain.

"I hardly know. I can just tell you how I feel. He has not made as many demands from me as I had expected; he has but rarely come to my room. But what he does to me.... I feel so used, like a plaything. He dresses me up in fine

274

clothing and jewels as if I were a doll to hang on his arm. I guess I should feel grateful that he makes the effort rather than the contrary. But I want to be valued as a person, not a possession."

"When I lived in Lambton years ago, my father would speak of the elder Mr. Darcy with such esteem. Everyone said that his son was just like him, and indeed the few times I was around him, he was respectful of others, even if a little quiet. Although proud, I would be surprised to learn that he would not show a lady the honour due her, especially his own wife." When Elizabeth did not respond, she continued, "To a new bride, the act of lovemaking seems so foreign and perhaps even improper if there is no love between the two. But Lizzy, you must understand that the physical union between a husband and wife is natural and intended by God to be for the pleasure of both man and woman in a committed relationship."

"I have a hard time accepting that God could call what he has done to me good or even respectable, nor do I see what pleasure can be found for a woman."

Her aunt smiled knowingly. "Lizzy, you truly know not of what you speak. You must remember that God made man to be the way he is for a reason. Men desire women because He designed them to be that way. The problem occurs when man attempts to satisfy that need *outside* the bonds of marriage, which I am afraid occurs all too often in our society. But Mr. Darcy is now married to you. I believe that after you have developed feelings for one another, even if just a friendship, that you will find his advances not so difficult to bear, and may perhaps one day enjoy your times of intimacy."

"You must think me silly."

"No, I think you are an independent, secure woman who desires mutual respect and understanding in marriage. You may find one day that Mr. Darcy wants the same thing for you. I can't help but think that you two were brought together for a purpose, that in reality you are a perfect match; you just need time to discover that for yourselves."

"I wish that could be the case. I always wanted to marry for love. If somehow I could hope that one day Mr. Darcy and I might share a tender regard, could take pleasure in each other's understanding and sentiments, I could find the strength I need to continue on, showing kindness for his family despite their opposition, and showing patience to Mr. Darcy when he offends. But I am afraid that my confidence in such an outcome does not exist, or is frail at best."

"On your wedding day, I heard each of you vow to love the other. If love were just a feeling, no one could make such a promise with the hope of fulfilment, for we all, even in good marriages, have times of vexation and discontent. Instead, consider love as something you patiently show and eagerly do for him, even when undeserved." Mrs. Gardiner smiled adding, "— Especially when undeserved, for that is when the feelings come hardest. Perhaps if you demonstrate love, your own sentiments will naturally follow. And Mr. Darcy might take your example and show you devotion in return."

"How does one show love to someone she does not even like at times?"

"By giving him the respect that all men need and hope for in a wife. Maybe you could ask him to join you on one of your strolls or compliment him when he does something admirable. Surely, he has some attributes for which you can praise him."

Elizabeth laughed, "Aunt, he has hundreds of people who clamour for his good opinion. He does not need nor desire that from me, I am sure. And as for respect, I would be happy to give him his due if only he did not demand it of me. Should not a man earn the respect his wife bestows?"

"Just don't let the circumstances of your union keep you from showing him the consideration due him as your protector."

"Thank you, Aunt. I will attempt to do as you say. I long for a marriage like your own – one of friendship and affection, and I know you would not steer me astray."

They spent the entire afternoon together sharing the news of the previous week and had much to speak of. Elizabeth learnt that Mr. Darcy had sent her worn gowns to Longbourn for her sisters' use. She had been wondering what had happened to the dresses from her former life when they disappeared from her dressing room. Her lady's maid could not enlighten her at the time; now she knew, but she did not know whether to be thankful or vexed at his interference. She was sure her sisters would be pleased to gain the gowns, which were still in good repair, and she was happy it was her own family to benefit; nonetheless, his officious meddling bothered her exceedingly.

After an enlightening and ultimately pleasant afternoon, Elizabeth begrudgingly returned to Darcy House. When she entered, the butler welcomed her, as was his duty, and took her outerwear. "Mrs. Darcy, Mr. Darcy has asked me to give you his apologies and to inform you that he will be dining at Whites this evening."

"Thank you, Franklin," Elizabeth said as she started up the steps, then turned and asked that he have her dinner brought up to her room that evening. Elizabeth spent the entirety of the evening writing in her journal. She had planned on putting her thoughts on paper since she had no friend or family in whom to confide her deepest concerns, those not even her beloved aunt should hear. In it, she wrote of all of her fears, longings, and uncertainties, almost as if in prayer to God. She mentioned Lord Langston's advances, her perturbations regarding her husband, how he would not trust her, how she had felt so used and degraded by him, and her sorrows concerning her family. Elizabeth was up well past midnight pouring her grief onto paper. She had planned to burn the pages for fear of their being discovered, but the exercise was so comforting to her that she decided to keep them intact but hidden, at least until she felt equal to disposing of them. She folded the pages and tied a ribbon around them, placing them in her writing desk under other papers of lesser importance.

THE TRADITIONAL TEA BROUGHT ELIZABETH AND DARCY together for the first time since their argument, and remembering how she was attired in only her chemise, two nights previously, brought a blush to Elizabeth's cheeks. Could she ever get used to being clad so in front of a man, even if he were her husband? Darcy stood as she walked in and performed a bow; she returned the courtesy. Elizabeth busied herself, preparing their tea, and then sat in silence for some time as Darcy ate, while she pushed her food around.

"Mr. Darcy," said she after a few moments of silent nibbling, "I have something to request of you after we eat, if I may."

"You can speak now if you wish it."

Elizabeth glanced at the servants. Not knowing how her husband would respond and wanting to keep her affairs private, she requested that they meet after the small meal in either his study or their shared sitting room. They agreed upon his study, so after tea he escorted her into his sanctuary, seating her before the desk, while he took his place behind it. Darcy then waited patiently to hear her petition.

"As you may be aware, I visited my family in Cheapside yesterday." She smiled at the recollection. "While there, they asked me to join them when they return to Longbourn for my sister's wedding. So instead of arriving the day before the event with you, I could spend four additional days there with my family, with your joining me as planned. That way I could see my family, and you would have no need to spend so much time there in order to bring it about." Elizabeth looked at him hopefully.

Darcy said not a word as he deliberated her request. At first it seemed a reasonable appeal. He certainly had no desire to spend any more time than was necessary in Meryton. He had already reserved a room at the local inn for the ninth, leaving directly after the wedding for Pemberley. He knew that Elizabeth greatly desired to spend time with her family. But then again, was it wise for her to spend so much time in their company? He had hoped to limit her time with them. Would she take steps backwards in her progression towards becoming the respectable wife of an affluent gentleman? She seemed to have come far in such a short time. Would the time spent with her family revert her back to her former ways? She no longer walked obscene distances. Would she take on that annoying, perverse habit again, just when they were to go to Pemberley? — And then there was Wickham. "I would rather you not."

Elizabeth sat there shocked. She had fully expected that he would welcome her leaving early. Of course she doubted that he would do so for her sake, but she thought that he would prefer her absence, which would be even more convenient if he need not join her until the last moment to bring it about. "Why? Why would you refuse me?"

"I think it best that you stay here and that we travel together. Elizabeth, we are now married and as such, we should arrive and depart together."

"Your plan would be a good one, if you in fact desired to be with my family, as I do, but since you do not, and since I have means to go without you, I cannot see that the basis for your refusal has any justification."

Darcy saw the logic of her argument. He lamented her skill at inference on more than one occasion, and this was one of them. "I do not even know your uncle. How can I know that you will be safe?" He was grasping.

"My aunt told me to relate that should you need to speak with him in order to discern his aptitude as an escort, you may come visit, or if you would not go there, you could invite him here. But I can assure you that I have travelled between Longbourn and Gracechurch Street on many occasions without one single mishap. Surely, you can have no other reason to say no."

"Why are you so anxious to go to your former home?"

"You have to ask? I see that you truly do not know me." There was silence between them with only the ticking of the clock and the crackling of the flames in the fireplace filling the void.

Darcy took in a deep breath, knowing the repercussions of saying no on their already tenuous relationship. "You may go with your uncle, but I want to know how you will be travelling. If I in any way disapprove, then I reserve the right to change my mind." Elizabeth wondered why he would care so much about the details.

"Thank you. Shall I summon my uncle to come here to meet you, or will you call on him at his own home?"

"You may invite him here for a morning call tomorrow. Is there anything else, Elizabeth?" After she indicated that there was not, he continued, "Then I will see you at dinner." She stood and left the room.

The following day brought her uncle to call on Mr. Darcy about his niece's trip to Longbourn. After finding the arrangements for travel to be agreeable, Darcy bade him a farewell and returned to his study. Elizabeth had some last minute shopping to complete before their trip to the North while Darcy had to meet with his solicitor. He would have plenty of time to call on his family after Elizabeth left for Longbourn and so chose to stay around Darcy House until then.

With the expectation of seeing her family again, Elizabeth's mood improved considerably. Her appetite was somewhat restored, and the Darcys enjoyed congenial conversation over supper. They spoke about Pemberley and the plans related to their travel North. It would take three days to arrive due to the late start on the day of the wedding and the short span of daylight expected this time of year. Darcy assured her that he had rooms along the route reserved and that they would enjoy a large suite, each with their own accommodations. He would send ahead most of her wardrobe, which Janette was to complete packing before she left with Elizabeth for Longbourn.

"Mr. Darcy, I do not need Janette while with my family. I can use Sarah. That will give Janette more time to prepare for our departure."

"I have already arranged for Janette to join you at Longbourn. I sent an express to your father telling him of your early arrival and that your lady's maid would need a place to sleep. Your uncle was in agreement and so everything is settled."

Elizabeth thought to argue the point but then decided that she would not win, and she was too happy with the prospect of going home to let a difference of opinion and her husband's officious nature get her down. She silently decided that she would share her maid with her sister, Mary; Janette would have Mary looking beautiful on her wedding day. The thought made Elizabeth smile to herself. Seeing her happy expression, Darcy mistakenly thought that perhaps she was pleased with his efforts.

THE SUN WAS SHINING BRIGHTLY, so Elizabeth asked her husband if she could go on a walk with Clark, the footman. He agreed, with the stipulation that she would not be gone more than an hour. She donned her outerwear and was about to set out; however, she remembered that she needed to find a gift for Mary and Mr. Collins before she left the following day. She assuaged her disappointment with the thought that she would be back at Longbourn tomorrow and then on to Pemberley. She would have many opportunities over the next few months to get in her exercise. On her way to her room to change, she heard a man's familiar voice coming from her husband's study. The door was partly opened, and Elizabeth would have continued on her way, except for overhearing her sister's name mentioned in context of the recent ball by Colonel Fitzwilliam.

"I was surprised to see your friend, Bingley, there. I assumed he would be in Hertfordshire courting the angelic Miss Bennet."

"They are not courting. He has not returned to Netherfield since my wedding, I believe."

"I am surprised."

"Why should you be? Bingley has plenty to keep him entertained in town. He has likely forgotten all about her by now."

"Then his sentiments have greatly changed since he and I last spoke." Darcy made no response, so he continued, "The man told me that he intended to make her an offer of marriage. I know that he can be rather capricious, but I was sure he was sincere in his affections. His face was beaming with the very idea."

"He may have been, but sometimes Bingley needs guidance; he doesn't always know what is best for him."

"You didn't do what I think you did, did you?"

"If you mean did I warn him away, I did. "

"Darcy! Why on earth would you do such a thing? She is your sister now, and he, one of your dearest friends. What would drive you to separate them?"

Elizabeth could not believe her ears. What caused her husband to do such a despicable thing? She listened on.

"James, you met her family. You know how vulgar they can be. Bingley's compliant nature would not allow him to protect himself from their unrefined influence. Mrs. Bennet would have him sponsoring the two youngest girls in London society. They would make a laughing stock out of him and his reputation, which I might add is tenuous at best already due to his link to trade. Mrs. Bennet would be at his doorstep at every whim. No, I could not let my friend suffer such a fate. It was done and done for the best. I have been kinder to him than I have myself." Elizabeth was in shock; she had to cover her mouth so as not to make an audible gasp.

"You think that you can just play God with your friend's life? This is preposterous. Bingley is of such a humble nature that he probably took your advice as gold."

"He doesn't know what's good for him, and he trusts my judgement. Bingley may have disregarded my advice, though, if not for his own uncertainty about her feelings for him and her mother's proven matchmaking schemes. How could he ever know if she truly cared for him or was just pressed by her mother to make the match."

"Like you and Mrs. Darcy."

"I would not have him in a marriage where there was no true affection or regard. Unlike me, he is like a puppy that gives loyalty unconditionally and craves attention. He could not be happy in an unrequited union. I have saved him from a most unpleasant match."

Elizabeth could not listen to anymore. She quietly went to her room and wept for her sister who was made to suffer at the hands of Elizabeth's own husband. How could he have been so cruel and with no remorse whatsoever? *There can be no justification for what he has done!* She pulled out the beginnings of her journal, untying the ribbon, and released all of her resentment within its pages. Elizabeth's love for her dear sister, the kindest of all people, the most deserving of happiness, drove her on. Elizabeth would gladly give up any possession and any hope of her own prosperity to have Jane's joy restored.

How could Elizabeth ever be content in a marriage to such a man, who could be so vicious in his dictates? She had to stop herself from packing right then and leaving for the Gardiners immediately. How she desperately needed to be with her family, away from her heartless husband. Elizabeth never made it out to buy Mary a gift. Instead, she sent Janette to find something fitting for the occasion. A dinner tray arrived which she could not bring herself to touch; verily she did not want anything provided by the charge of Mr. Darcy. If he came to her this night, Elizabeth was determined that she would not capitulate to his desires.

Darcy did not come to her room, and not for want of desire, but he was concerned about her health and in light of their last joining, he did not want to cause more discomfort for her so soon. He had received word of her indisposition and the need to send a tray to her room. Elizabeth was to leave for Hertfordshire the following day, and he began to regret agreeing to the scheme. He sent word to the cook to prepare a basket of food to take on her journey and requested a meeting with her lady's maid. During the meeting he asked that she would let him know by express how Elizabeth continued to fare. He also charged her with giving Elizabeth extra care, so that she would recover for the journey to Pemberley. He had noticed over the past few days that Elizabeth had lost weight. She was no longer filling out her gowns recently purchased; he rarely saw her eat more than a trifling when they shared a meal. He began to suspect that perhaps she might be with child and experiencing the ill effects. Uncomfortable with such a question, but desiring to know the truth, he asked Janette if Mrs. Darcy had experienced her courses recently. He was informed that she had about two to three weeks ago when Janette had first come on. Then Darcy had the idea to have Janette keep records of Elizabeth's menses, and so he charged her to do just that.

RATHER THAN THE GARDINERS bring their carriage to Darcy House, Darcy planned for Elizabeth and Janette to be taken to Gracechurch Street. Surprisingly, he accompanied the women to make sure that all was in order and safe for travel. The transportation was arranged as Mr. Gardiner had promised.

The Gardiner children were to remain at home with their nanny and the house servants, so there would be adequate room in the carriage. Mr. Darcy said very little to Elizabeth's relations, but did not depart until the carriage bound for Hertfordshire set out. Elizabeth said nary a word to him the whole of the morning. She was stuck between anger at his intrusion into her sister's happiness and relief to be finally leaving for home.

They pulled up to Longbourn just after the noon hour. Elizabeth was overwhelmed with emotion upon first seeing her family as each took a turn bestowing hugs and merry greetings. After time spent in the company of her family – excepting Mary and Mr. Collins who were at the church – and in an excited flurry of admiration for her coat, gown, and bonnet by her younger sisters and mother, she and Jane left to find somewhere private in which to speak. They laughed and cried, each trying to comfort the other, as loving sisters are wont to do. Elizabeth could not share her knowledge of Mr. Darcy's treachery against her own family. That could not assuage Jane's sorrows and would only increase her grief to know Elizabeth was married to such a man. After dinner, Elizabeth went to her father who had been patiently waiting his turn. If he had fully known her grief, he would have cursed himself for insisting on the marriage; as it was, all of Elizabeth's attempts to hide her sorrow were in vain. She had lost weight and no longer had the sparkle in her eyes that had always captivated her dear papa. They played a game of chess as they had so many times in the past, but neither brooked the subject of Elizabeth's marriage and wellbeing.

The following morning, Elizabeth woke up at dawn and for the first time in weeks set out on her long-anticipated walk. She donned a dress that had once been her own, since silk and satin were not befitting the task. Then she put on her coat that had been specifically bought with the Derbyshire winters in mind. Her boots were lined with animal fur, so although it was January, she was able to keep comfortably warm. In fact, she soon became too heated and made note to be less zealous in the future as related to warm clothing on long walks. Elizabeth was out for about two hours yet still had time to change and prepare for church.

In the afternoon, the family had visitors call. Several men of the regiment still stationed in Meryton arrived. Elizabeth was informed that this was a regular occurrence for the young men. After enjoying tea and cakes, the officers asked if the ladies would like to join them for a walk in the gardens. Although no flowers were growing and no note-worthy beauty was to be seen, they set out and found pleasure amongst the pathways. When the men had arrived, Elizabeth was surprised to see Mr. Wickham amongst the group. Later she was to discover from her father that Mr. Wickham's debts had been paid, and there was no obvious reason not to let him visit if chaperoned, except for Darcy's disapproval, which no longer held any weight.

While the other officers entertained Elizabeth's sisters, Wickham approached her. Elizabeth was at first uncertain about her loyalties and that perhaps at Mr. Darcy's previous mandate, she should not entertain the man's company. Nevertheless, she soon talked herself into conveniently forgetting his order, for he specifically stated that she could not see him before the marriage had taken place. Now that this was in the past, and she was secure as Darcy's bride, what harm could come? He was a guest of her family's and in the company of others and a most agreeable and trustworthy gentleman, unlike the many wealthy men from town whom Darcy felt at liberty to thrust into her company.

"Mrs. Darcy, I am happy to see that you no longer spurn my company." With her look of alarm, he laughed lightly. "Forgive me. I am well aware of Darcy's order for you to stay away from me. I was of course disappointed for I had always enjoyed your companionship, but I knew that you could hardly have done otherwise."

"I am happy to know that you forgive me. I so wanted to let you know the reasons for my discourteous behaviour. I valued your opinion of me too much to obey without regret. But it was only right that I followed his wishes."

"And what about now? Do you still follow his wishes?"

"I cannot bring myself to believe that he would approve of our visit. I imagine that he would be very displeased with the idea; however, he did not specifically request on this trip that I keep my distance from you, and as seeing that we are in the view of the house and with company, there can be no serious objections outside of his dislike for you."

"Thank you for your faith in me. With my family no longer living, I find that I have few who would overlook the stories of a man who was once as close as any brother, one whose wealth and influence hold more weight than my own character. His father, my godfather and in many ways closest friend, had faith in me, and when he died, I lost all hope of reconciliation with his son. He essentially paid me to leave him and his family alone, you know. Oh, how I miss sweet Georgiana!"

At Elizabeth's look of astonishment, he said, "Don't tell me she too has spurned me."

"I have no idea about her thoughts towards you. I am just surprised at your little description of her. Tell me, did you know her well?"

"I spent much time at the home for her amusement alone. Her father had even alluded to the possibility that one day I might claim her as more than a friend. Mr. Darcy desired that I become a gentleman; he even educated me as such. With Georgiana's dowry of thirty thousand, I could have one day claimed the life of a gentleman, but after Mr. Darcy's death, nothing more was said about the idea. Georgiana was too young at that time to even suggest such a plan to the son. And now, Darcy has poisoned her against me. Forgive me for speaking candidly. I see that this must bring you pain."

"Why might Mr. Darcy hold to his animosity when his father so clearly loved you?"

"For that very same reason. As I said last autumn, he was jealous of me. As soon as his father died, he sought to remove me from his life and from Pemberley. I received a small pittance for my trouble." At her disturbed look, he continued, "But I will not have you feeling sorry for me. Perhaps one day you might be able to hasten my return to Pemberley, but until then we will talk no more of the business. Tell me, how has married life treated you? I doubt not that you now have enough jewels to set a family up for life," he said in jest. Elizabeth did not much care for such musings, as she would freely give up all of those jewels to be back at Longbourn for good.

Their visit continued with no more talk of Darcy and his officious ways. Wickham charmed Elizabeth with his words of respect and esteem. He made her feel beautiful and worthy, but was careful not to suggest that his regard was owing to her shapely form or her respective fortune. Wickham made a point to see her on the following two days. Elizabeth knew deep down that her husband would not approve, but she hoped to one day convince him to accept the man into his home and family again. Elizabeth was also careful not to say anything that might lead Wickham to mark the degree of her unhappiness in marriage. She trusted the man, but she would not dishonour Mr. Darcy in that manner. Elizabeth could not have known that the perceptive and discerning Mr. Wickham saw in her looks and bearing her true feelings for her husband and was determined to use this information against his adversary.

TWO DAYS BEFORE THE COLLINS WEDDING, Wickham and Elizabeth were strolling in the garden as Elizabeth chaperoned her younger two sisters walking with Carter and Denny, two fellow officers. Jane and Mary, had gone into town with Mr. Collins, and her mother was with Mrs. Phillips and Mrs. Gardiner. Elizabeth's father had escaped to his study with Mr. Gardiner for quiet pursuits. Elizabeth had been thinking it best to forgo Wickham's company, for her conscience had been telling her that she was in the wrong these past few days, knowing that her husband would not approve of her association with his perceived enemy. But as this was the day before Darcy's expected arrival and as her sisters needed a chaperone, and considering no one else was available, she resigned herself to his company one last time.

Wickham had just told her an amusing tale, leaning down to share something in privacy when without warning, Elizabeth's arm was tugged from behind as she was forcibly brought to a halt and removed from Wickham's side. Elizabeth was astonished as she looked to see that her husband had come up from behind and effectively taken control of her.

Darcy's eyes were ablaze with anger, "Elizabeth, go inside!" She hesitated, looking to Wickham, as if for guidance, but in reality she was fearful about leaving Wickham alone to explain the situation to her incensed husband. "Go inside the house, now!"

She did as her husband said, tears streaming down her face. *Oh, stupid, stupid Lizzy! What have I done? –Talking to that man when I knew Mr. Darcy would be furious?*

Elizabeth ran up to her former room, nervously pacing as she awaited her scolding. She knew he was justified in his anger towards her and felt the full weight of her guilt. At least she was at Longbourn and with her family. Of course what good would that do? Mr. Darcy had every right to be angry and to punish her in whatever way he saw fit. He had never hurt her in any malicious way, but she really could not judge his character adequately to know if he might not raise a hand to her with the right provocation. Then she thought of how Mr.

Darcy had hurt Jane and could not find it in her heart to be sorry if seeing her and Wickham together offended him; she was just sorry that he had surprised them with his resentful presence.

Darcy had received an express the previous evening from Janette, as he had requested, letting him know that Elizabeth seemed to be back to her usual self, perhaps even better. She had taken exercise and eaten more than one would expect from a genteel lady, certainly more than Janette had ever witnessed. Not wanting to cause a stir but cognisant of her loyalties, she also told Mr. Darcy about the officers visiting the family and Elizabeth's apparent connection with the young men. She only casually brought it up in context of Elizabeth's health and demeanour, but that was all that was needed to alert Darcy that Wickham might still be in the area and taking advantage of Elizabeth's return to Longbourn. In fact, Darcy began to wonder anew if that might not be why Elizabeth was so desirous of returning home early. So the following morning, he set out at sunrise for Meryton. This was the day prior to his planned journey, and he hoped a room would be available at the inn. Of course, if what the maid said were an indication of Wickham's imposition on his wife, he would likely insist they leave immediately for Pemberley.

Darcy dropped off his manservant at the Inn of Meryton in order to secure their suite of rooms and then went straight to Longbourn. He decided to ride by horseback so that the post horses could rest without causing a delay. Darcy's stallion had been relocated to Pemberley with the servants, so instead he rode a young and spirited mare that had travelled alongside the carriage. Longbourn was but two miles from Meryton, so he made good time. As he approached the manor, he detected the colour red that matched the uniform of the militia from behind the house. His breathing increased as he realised that his concerns were justified. On the far side of the garden against the hedgerow, he saw that Elizabeth was walking with one of the officers. He could recognise that swag anywhere and so knew her companion to be Wickham. *How dare Elizabeth disobey me! Will I ever be free of that man?*

Rather than warn them of his presence, he tied off the mare at the front of the house, then quietly, but with determination made his way to where his wife was engaged by Wickham's charms. He could hear her laughter ring clear in the cold breeze as she ambled, wearing the warm coat that he himself had picked out for her. Just as Wickham leaned down to say something quietly to her, Darcy reached over to remove Elizabeth from the scene. In anger, he told Elizabeth to go inside the house, so he could deal with his nemesis.

Darcy wanted to lash out in physical retribution for all of the pain Wickham had caused his family, for poisoning his wife against him, for hurting Georgiana, for deceiving his father, for shaming the Darcy name with his gaming debts and illegitimate children that Darcy himself now had to preserve. But he held his temper in check. He recollected his location and had no desire to embarrass the Bennets with an attack while on their property, especially in light of the wedding arrangements. This was a good remembrance, considering two other soldiers were in attendance who might not have seen the justice in Darcy's retribution.

Wickham laughed outright at Darcy's dilemma. "Darcy, such a temper you have. I do believe the passionate Elizabeth might have had a stimulating effect on you."

"You go too far, Wickham. I will say this one last time, stay away from my wife." Although he said this in low tones, his contempt could not be missed.

"But Darcy, why does it bother you if I talk to Elizabeth? You certainly have no feelings for her." They stood facing one another, unflinching. "I see how it is; you can't stand for someone to admire me. You have all of the adoration any one person could stand, yet you have always been jealous of me."

"My relationship with my wife is none of your concern. Stay away from her, or I will destroy you."

"Elizabeth would never forgive you."

"Keep Mrs. Darcy out of this."

"You have done nothing but hurt Elizabeth with your imposing manner and self-righteous attitude. You remind her everyday how much better you are than she is, so if Elizabeth did welcome a clandestine seduction, it was your fault, not mine. I can't help it if believing me came easy for her. I sweet-talked her; you despised her."

It took everything in Darcy not to pummel Wickham. They were not two feet from one another, staring eye-to-eye. Darcy was getting his breathing under regulation as he said, "You know nothing." Darcy then turned to walk to the house, incensed and needing an outlet to vent his anger. He kept squeezing his hands into fists as he imagined striking Wickham's pretty face. *How could Elizabeth believe the man's lies? After all I have done for her, she still prefers Wickham. Does she let him kiss her and make love to her?* His thoughts were too much to bear.

Darcy had spent years watching Wickham's deceptive charms manipulate his father and then almost destroy his sister. Since that fateful day of discovering Georgiana's plans to elope with Wickham, Darcy's life had seemed to plunge more and more out of control. The usually disciplined and unyielding man had been desperately attempting to once again gain command of his own existence, and now Wickham was exerting his influence on Darcy's own wife. Darcy had been patient with Elizabeth, demanding little from her, yet when he did, she spurned him – so unlike the smiles and welcome she easily gifted to other men – to Wickham. She was his wife, not Wickham's! He walked into the house and asked the first person he saw, the housekeeper, where Elizabeth was located. After taking his coat, she directed him towards her room.

As he climbed the stairs, he tried to gain control of his vehemence but could not. He kept imagining Elizabeth in the arms of Wickham, hearing her laugh at his false tales. He found the door to her room easily enough, turned the handle and walked in. There she was in tears, as she asked, "What did you do to him?"

"What did I do to him? Why don't you tell me what he did to *you*, or rather *with you*?"

"You think Mr. Wickham in some way hurt me or led me astray? *He* has never hurt me. You, on the other hand, have in countless ways."

"By saving your family?"

"Will that always be the way you shame me into being a good wife to you, by throwing in my face how noble you were in that whole affair. You seem to forget that I may have saved your life out in those woods," she cried, pointing outside. "Does that mean nothing to you?"

"I can't even know for certain if you are telling me the truth about that day. How do I know that you and Wickham did not set me up? That sounds like the kind of thing he would do. You may have been out in the woods meeting him when I came along and decided to take advantage of the situation."

"There is nothing I can say to convince you of what really happened that day. Until you want to know the truth you will continue in your state of mistrust, and our marriage will continue to be tainted by your suspicions."

"I see that you don't deny it, Elizabeth."

"I have nothing more to say to you." She turned to leave the room, but he caught her arm, thus stopping her.

"You will stay here with me." He pulled her close so she was against him, their faces inches apart.

"You are angry with me. I think you should let me leave before we say or do anything we will regret."

Angry is right, Darcy thought – more so than he had ever been in his life, more so even than when he discovered Wickham's plan to ruin Georgiana, but for reasons even he could not fully comprehend, for in his pride and resentment he could not see how his conflicting feelings for his wife warred within his breast.

"Regret? Is that what you feel when we are alone together in your bedchamber? I need a wife who wants me and me alone," he said in quiet outrage, suspecting that Elizabeth had secretly united in a physical and emotional bond with his greatest adversary.

She just stared at him. What could she say? She did not want to make him more impassioned, but she could not say that she had ever desired him, regardless of her friendship with his former friend. Darcy then unexpectedly pulled her even closer and kissed her, not the kind of kiss that showed how he might care for her, but a kiss that declared her to be his. With effort, Elizabeth was able to pull her face away and turn around in his arms to try to make her escape.

Darcy could not have explained rationally what happened to him next; he felt like someone deep inside, who had been repressed for years, had made his presence known in a most uncharacteristic manner. One moment he was staring at his wife, incensed with her and with Wickham's familiar hold on her, the next he was claiming her as his own.

Elizabeth felt like she was reliving a recent nightmare that had tormented her. Her husband of course had every right to be angry, every right to demand that she obey him, every right to expect her to give herself over to his cravings and needs. But despite those rights, Elizabeth's traitorous body and mind could not accept the callous sense of injustice.

Without love or gentleness or anything that might seem like honour, Elizabeth's husband took her.

He certainly did not hurt her physically. He may have lost control of his well-established ability to discipline his passions, but he did not forget for one moment that he was much stronger and more powerful than his wife. But beyond that consideration, he thought only of himself and his need to feel satisfied, to stake his claim on her physically as his wife.

Elizabeth was cognisant of their location – she was in her old room at Longbourn – so she was particularly careful not to let a sound escape her, and concentrating on this goal gave her a distraction. If anyone were below the room, they might have heard the thumping of the bed, but she could not dwell on that. She was certain, regardless, that everyone would see her shame, for that is what she felt, written across her face. When he was done, and she was able to control her mouth to speak rather than lash out, she said four words in hushed, yet enraged protest of his attack, "You are a beast." Then she lowered her skirt and left the room trying to find somewhere to compose herself.

As soon as it was over, Darcy felt an enormous sense of guilt and misery fall on his head, to an extent that he had never known. *What have I done?* Never in his life had he taken a woman against her wishes, at least not in such a manner. Never had he shown any woman anything but the highest respect. Wickham drove him to this madness, and Darcy let him. He fell to his knees on the floor covering his face with his hands. He was supposed to be a man of honour, a gentleman at all times, and he was reduced to savagery with his own wife. *But did she not also have a part to play? She drove me to this, like the country hoyden she is.*

Of course, Darcy was too unreasonable and fraught with perturbation at the moment to make an unbiased assessment of his actions or possible impetus, and there could be no justification for his deeds even if he had. Fortunately for him, even without true understanding, his conscience would not stay silent.

SOME UNKNOWN TIME LATER, Darcy stepped out of the room, and waiting for him in the hallway was Elizabeth. She did not look at him, but said, "I wish to stay with my family another night as planned, if you will let me." He could tell that she had been crying and his heart began to betray his plans, especially in light of his most recent treatment of her.

"You know I cannot let you stay here if Wickham is to come around again."

"It will only be our family for dinner, and I believe the officers have gone. I saw them leave from the window."

"I should speak with your father." Elizabeth nodded and led him downstairs. Darcy wanted to say he was sorry and to ask for forgiveness. That was the right thing to do, but his pride kept telling him that he had no reason to apologise, that Elizabeth had been in the wrong, while he had been exceedingly patient with her for these six weeks; but then he would recall his unjustified harshness with her.

When Darcy got to the bottom of the stairs, he was notified that a missive had come for him. Opening the folded paper, he read that there was only one room available from the two that were reserved for the following night. They would either need to leave for Pemberley this day, forgoing the wedding and causing an even larger breach in their relationship, or let her stay at her home for one more night. His decision took just a moment. "Elizabeth, it looks like the choice has been made. There is only one room at the inn available." At her disturbed mien, he continued, "I know that one room will not suffice. You may stay at Longbourn, but I must speak with Mr. Bennet." She escorted him to her father's study, not once looking at him, and then left him to it.

Darcy knocked on the door. "Enter." And so he went in closing the door behind him. Mr. Bennet was not alone, for Mr. Gardiner was also present. The men had obviously been engaged in their separate activities, one reading a book and the other reviewing the newspaper. Over the next quarter hour, Darcy told Mr. Bennet of his continued concerns over Mr. Wickham as well as Elizabeth's wish to stay at Longbourn. He insisted that Wickham not be allowed back to the home, or he would remove his wife immediately. Elizabeth's lady's maid would inform him of any breach in this plan.

Mr. Bennet coolly replied, "Your business with Mr. Wickham does not involve me, and I dislike being ungracious to a friend of the family at your command; nevertheless, I dislike even more my Lizzy being taken from us sooner than we would wish it, so I will forbid his visits while Lizzy is here."

"Thank you." He started to stand to leave, but Mr. Bennet asked him to wait a moment.

"So, Mr. Darcy, my Lizzy has been here the past few days, long enough for me to see a noticeable change in her. Since arriving, she has regained much of her usual cheerful self, but I cannot help but express my concern for her. So why don't you tell me your perspective. How have things progressed in your marriage so far? How are *you* surviving the ill effects?"

Darcy was a little taken aback by the brazen question. "We are managing as well as could be expected. The *ill effects,* as you put them, are being dealt with as they come. My family seems to have accepted the marriage for the most part, and Elizabeth is admirably learning her role as mistress to my home."

"Lizzy certainly has not been her usual self, though. What can that signify?"

"As I did not know Elizabeth so well before our marriage, I am not qualified to notice the change or the cause. I see no real difference." This was not entirely true, but Darcy was not ready to own it. Darcy wanted to leave his father-in-law's study, and just as quickly forget about any of his wife's adverse alterations, so he stood. "Now, if you will excuse me, I have not had a chance to wash off the road dirt, and my man has secured a room for me at the inn." Mr. Bennet stayed seated and bowed his head seeing that he had gotten all the information he was to expect, while Mr. Gardiner stood. When Darcy opened the study door, he was ambushed by Mrs. Bennet.

"Mr. Darcy, what a surprise! We thought you would not be here until tomorrow. Well, you must stay here. Lizzy said you were to stay at the inn, which is ridiculous when we have Lizzy's room. Why she and Jane can share with the others, unless of course you prefer otherwise," she finished knowingly accompanied with a blush.

"I thank you but no; my valet is already at the inn and has gotten me settled."

"Is Lizzy not to join you?" She looked to Elizabeth as if attempting to insist that she do just that."

"No, she wishes to stay another night with her family, as originally planned."

"Well then you must have dinner with us, isn't that right, Mr. Bennet?" she said looking to her husband who had not stirred.

"Oh, yes. He is family now, and I would wager he has no other engagements, now do you, sir?"

"Thank you. I would be happy to accept your offer."

"Splendid! It is just a small family meal, mind you. I am sure nothing we have compares to what you are used to. I suspect the expensive chefs you employ have likely spoilt Lizzy too, but my table is one of the finest in the county, I'll wager. Nothing but the best for my family," replied the verbose Mrs. Bennet.

"If you will excuse me. Elizabeth, will you walk out with me?"

She looked up, surprised, and saying nothing she turned and walked towards the front door to where his horse was waiting.

They entered the foyer where the Bennet's manservant was waiting with his coat and top hat. After donning his outerwear and dismissing the servant he turned to his wife and spoke quietly, "Elizabeth, I... please, allow me to apologise."

"I cannot think of that now. I must walk back in that room," she said as she looked towards the direction whence they came, "and act as though nothing has happened. It will have to wait." Then she turned and walked quickly away.

Chapter Fourteen

"Why this unreasonable pride of birth!" said she; "A visionary prejudice
destroys our peace. Never would I submit to enter a family averse to
receive me; they shall learn, at least, that I inherit nobility of soul.
O! Vivaldi! But for this unhappy prejudice!"
Ann Radcliffe
The Italian

Darcy arrived at the Bennet home in time for dinner. The house was astir with activity as each had something of value to say about the wedding, the family, a revered patroness, recent visitors, or even the food. This was fortunate. For the first time, Darcy was actually thankful for the large boisterous family, for this left him with little need to say anything. Not for the first time at this table, did he use the Darcy mask that shut out everyone and did not accept discourse. No one seemed to notice. Either they anticipated nothing different from him, or they did not care for his company either.

Unexpectedly, Elizabeth took a page from Darcy's book of airs, as she too sat quietly in seeming introspection. Mr. Bennet, as well as the Gardiners, noticed the difference in Elizabeth from just the day before. Darcy's presence seemed to have a most unwelcome and stifling effect upon her behaviour. She had been smiling, engaging, and tender in her regard to her family since her arrival, but this evening, she was subdued and uneasy. Whenever Mr. Collins would speak, rather than look to her father in a secret jest, she closed her eyes in embarrassment. Elizabeth did not meet her husband's eyes once during the course of the entire evening. She stood by his side, but acted as though he were not there. When it was time for Darcy's departure, she thanked him for allowing her to stay, then went upstairs without walking him out. It was obvious that not only were the two not in love – as was expected by all except for Mrs. Bennet – but they seemed incapable of enduring one another's company.

Mrs. Bennet watched Darcy's departure and determined to speak with Elizabeth about her duties as wife, how she was to venerate her husband to avoid being left in some distant estate on the other side of the realm. "Lizzy, if you do not show your husband more respect than you did this evening, he will lock you away somewhere. I have heard it happening! Mr. Darcy is used to being revered, and you must do likewise to avoid losing his goodwill. We have lost Mr. Bingley; we cannot afford to lose Mr. Darcy's benevolence as well."

"Mama, I understand your concern, but you must know that Mr. Darcy would not lock me up in the tower of a castle anywhere. And if he did, you could send Mr. Collins to save me."

"Lizzy, this is no laughing matter. I insist you treat your husband with the admiration he is used to. These men with money have mistresses, you know. You cannot afford to have him dwell with another woman before you have borne him a son. Do you understand me?" Elizabeth wanted her mother to leave, so she said all of the appropriate words of understanding and accord.

Mr. Darcy kept his distance the following day. Another meal was expected at Longbourn, this time with the Phillips and other close families in the neighbourhood. The thought of such an evening made him weary, and he longed to leave for Pemberley. He sent for Elizabeth and her belongings as formerly planned and expected. Although she knew this to be the prior arrangement, Elizabeth still loathed leaving her family, especially in light of the events from the previous day. Being alone with Mr. Darcy, even with separate rooms, unnerved her as her recent experience with him so closely mimicked her nightmares of late. Elizabeth arrived at the inn and was met by Darcy just outside the entrance.

"Where is your lady's maid?"

"I left her at Longbourn. This is Mary's time, so I decided to have Janette stay there to help her to dress this evening and tomorrow morning."

"But do you not need help?"

"No, I have chosen my gowns with that thought in mind. I can dress myself without assistance. And I have fixed my hair many times. So you see, I have no need for her. My experience tells me that Janette can work wonders, so Mary will be stunning on her wedding day, which is only right, even though her fiancé is a conceited, silly man. Now if you can direct me to my room, I would like some rest before we leave for dinner."

Darcy did as he was told, all the while considering how thoughtful Elizabeth was on her sister's behalf. Truly, he had only seen her actions towards others of less significance – when the person was not marred with conceit as Mr. Collins – in a sympathetic light. And if he were honest with himself, she was kind to him as well, as a general rule, if not always. He thought about the Christmas gift that she had presented to him. She had seemed genuinely excited that day. *Am I too harsh on her? No, she purposely disregards my wishes, which cannot be excused. And when she gave me the book, did she not admit to overhearing me and going behind my back? I barely know the woman; how can I know how to trust her?*

This night mimicked the one before, except that Elizabeth arrived and departed in Darcy's company. They did not speak a word aside from that which was necessary. "Are you ready to leave?" "When shall we depart in the morning?" "Can you pass the potatoes?" The evening could not end early enough. Darcy walked his wife to her room at the inn, wished her a good night and then went to his own.

Mary looked lovely on her wedding day, as every bride should. Elizabeth wore her least becoming dress so as not to outshine her sister and was happy to see that Jane had done the same. Jane stood up with Mary and no one could have been judged too harshly for comparing the two sisters, but Mary had no need to feel ashamed of her appearance. Although she was less beautiful than Jane, she had never looked better, and the exceptional smile on her face fairly lit the room. Fortunately, Wickham and his fellow officers did not show up for the wedding for they usually had very little association with the bride or groom.

Wickham had told Elizabeth that he would likely not attend the festivities since it pained him to be in Darcy's company, but she did not know if he might come to show that he had not been chased away.

The wedding breakfast could not compare to Elizabeth's although more guests were in attendance. However, like her own, Elizabeth did not look forward to leaving her family. She took the time to go around the room to say a special farewell to each person. Charlotte was the only one who brought about a laugh, for she and Elizabeth had always been able to raise the other's spirits. Perhaps that was why they were so close. "Charlotte, you must come visit me some day. If my family makes the trip, you must be one of them."

"If? Why do you say that? Of course they will come visit you. And I would be happy to join them when invited."

"I am not altogether certain that Mr. Darcy would welcome my family, Charlotte. He finds their company tiresome and beneath his dignity."

"But he cares for you. Surely he would overlook his own feelings in order to satisfy yours."

"Charlotte," responded Elizabeth, "I cannot agree with you. We tolerate one another, and you know I am *barely tolerable*." They laughed but without true mirth. "I will do my best to ensure that you, my dearest friend, are able to visit me. What is the benefit of pin money if not to provide transportation for my friends to come amuse me?"

"I will come, Eliza. I promise." The two women hugged. Elizabeth's eyes brimmed with unshed tears as she thought about not seeing her friend for so long a time. They now had very different lives, and it would be difficult to maintain their long-time friendship.

Before the celebration had concluded, the Darcys said their goodbyes. This was a subdued departure since Elizabeth had no wish to upstage her sister's in any manner. Elizabeth silently cried as they pulled away from Longbourn. Although glad to be away from London and the memories of the place that would forever haunt her, she was no longer looking forward to seeing her new home in Derbyshire. No amount of countryside or gardens could induce her to willingly leave her home at Longbourn, especially in light of Darcy's perpetual presence. Never in all her days could Elizabeth remember disliking someone as much as she did her husband. In order to boost her spirits in a way that made her feel useful, she began a wordless prayer. She opened her fears and her thoughts to her Lord asking to deliver her from her misery and to protect her from the harsh realities of life that she had not known existed. She had never put the value of money over her happiness and that of others, so she asked for protection from falling into the despair of having riches as her only solace, for what comfort had they brought thus far? Elizabeth could not have remembered when her petitions ended because sleep overcame her.

THE TRIP TO PEMBERLEY was the most painful of his remembrance. Darcy had always looked forward to finally being at home, in the wilds of Derbyshire, but he found little to provide comfort along the road this time. Marriage to Elizabeth had brought him nothing but antagonism, indignation, and *passion.* Could he think about that while she sat across from him in an emotional breakdown? Never had he felt such a loss of control over his body, his rationale, or his emotions. He was known for keeping himself under strict regulation, but that had seemed unattainable since she came into his life. Even on that fateful day in the cabin, she unnerved him with her wet chemise sticking to her body, that body that he could not stop thinking about. *How am I to make things right? I cannot go on in this manner. Something has to change, and as I am the head of my family, it must be by my hand.*

He pondered for the duration of the first day's journey upon how he might bring about reconciliation, not that they had ever had any kind of amicable understanding, but they, as man and wife, needed healing. He had always wanted a marriage of mutual respect and understanding. Love had never actually been in the equation of his expectations. Most of the marriages to which he was witness united two people of somewhat equal status working together for the mutual benefit of the family and estate at large. Their children were raised for the purpose of continuing the legacy. His parents had a congenial relationship and regard for one another. They each played their roles as expected. There were no occasions for upheavals of which he was aware. *How does one achieve that type of peaceful existence in marriage? Can that even be possible with a woman of such volatile emotions as Elizabeth possesses? She is a passionate woman in every respect except where a man desires it most.*

So the first day of their journey had each of them in deep contemplation, neither willing to talk, both lamenting the life they had together. Elizabeth was pleased that they again would have separate rooms that night, even if sharing a sitting room. She had no desire for nourishment and so remained in her room until daylight when they headed out again. Of course, a man of Darcy's observant nature noticed that his wife was not eating adequately; he could tell by her ever-diminishing size. He noticed upon the beginning of their engagement that Elizabeth ate more than most women of her age. She seemed to enjoy the tastes and savour the delights upon her plate, but now, she could not go so far as to taste what was before her. She could not fool him as she shifted the food around, but he dared not bring it up again for fear of an argument. There was plenty of that as it was.

The second day brought little change in the mood of the occupants of the Darcy carriage. They each looked out of their respective windows as the stark countryside glided by. There was too much to be said to say anything. The warmth of the hot bricks dissipated over time, leaving Elizabeth shivering more as that leg of their journey went on. Darcy noticed her discomfort, so he offered her the rug that he had been using. When she refused, he took it upon himself to cover her with it anyway. No response was expected and none offered. They made stops at regular intervals to reheat the bricks and to exchange or rest the horses. The following day continued likewise; however, the prospect of seeing Pemberley and removing themselves from the carriage brought each of them a building sense of relief.

The landscape had been changing throughout the three-day journey, but now, they were clearly within the area of the Peaks. Around the eighth hour of their journey, Elizabeth noticed the carriage slowing and making a turn into a lesser road at a lodge. She looked to Darcy with unfeigned curiosity, which brought a small smile to his countenance. "This is your new home." Elizabeth turned back to the window, her mind too full for conversation, but she could not help but admire every remarkable spot and point of view. They gradually ascended for half a mile, and then found themselves at the top of a considerable eminence, where the wood ceased, and the eye was instantly caught by Pemberley House, situated on the opposite side of a valley, into which the road with some abruptness wound. It was a large, handsome, stone building, standing well on rising ground, and backed by a ridge of high wood hills; and in front, a stream of some natural importance was swelled into greater, but without any artificial appearance. Its banks were neither formal, nor falsely adorned. Elizabeth was delighted, for how could she be otherwise? She had never seen a place for which nature had done more or where natural beauty had been so little counteracted by an awkward taste. And Elizabeth began to think that being mistress of Pemberley might be something!

They descended the hill, crossed the bridge, and drove to the door; and, while examining the nearer aspect of the house, all her apprehension of being married to the owner and fulfilling her duties returned. The carriage came to a stop and Darcy alighted. This time, instead of the footman handing Elizabeth out, Darcy reached towards the carriage door to do the honours. Elizabeth hesitated for but a brief moment before accepting his assistance. The air was biting, so they hurried to get into the house, delaying the introductions to the staff until they were all safely inside the manor.

"Elizabeth, may I present our housekeeper, Mrs. Reynolds?" At her smile of approval, he continued with a look of affection as he glanced to his trusted servant, bestowing a kiss upon her cheek, "Mrs. Reynolds, this is your new mistress, Mrs. Elizabeth Darcy." Hearing her full name off his lips unnerved Elizabeth, but why, she could not say. She had heard it said many times in the past six weeks. Perhaps hearing it here, at Pemberley, as mistress was what had given her a start.

"Mrs. Reynolds, it is a pleasure to make your acquaintance. I hope we will become good friends, you and I." Elizabeth looked to Darcy to see how he might take her friendly words. Instead of censure, she saw a warm and tender smile. Over the next few months, she would come to understand her husband's familial relationship with the respectable-looking, elderly woman, but at this time, she was puzzled by the approval she could not have predicted.

"Mrs. Darcy, welcome to your new home. After you have had time to settle in, we can meet together at your leisure. I hope you will find Pemberley a place as dear to you as it has been to me these many years."

Then Darcy spoke up, "I will take Mrs. Darcy to her chamber. Please send her maid to join her, so she can get refreshed from her journey."

"Of course, right away. And may I add that it is so good to have you home."

"It is good to be home." Darcy then turned and held out his arm, which Elizabeth obediently took, but she said not a word. He escorted her up the stairs and down a long hallway that split at the end. Turning right, he stopped at a door and opened it to reveal a lovely bedchamber. Elizabeth had not thought it possible to dwell in a room any more fine than that in Darcy's London home; however, she was disabused of that thought upon first entering her room at Pemberley. A fire was crackling in the large fireplace, giving off an abundance of warmth that was a relief after the frigid journey. But the warmth was not limited to the fire. The comfortable yet elegant effect of the room assuaged her initial fears when first arriving at the great home. Darcy was relieved to see the pleasant look upon Elizabeth's face and so had the courage to speak.

"Elizabeth, if there is any part of your chamber that you would like to change, that is not to your satisfaction, please let me know. This is your room and, therefore, yours for the changing, should you wish it."

"I am perfectly satisfied, but if I find anything that needs altering, I will let you know."

"I, too, need to refresh and get settled. Will you be joining me for dinner?" Darcy knew that she must be hungry after the long journey, eating so little along the way.

"If you don't mind, I prefer to eat in my room tonight. It has been a long journey, and solitude is what I need most." He understood her hidden meaning. She needed to be away from him. In the past this might not have unsettled him; however, this time, he knew that he had wronged her, adding to the established divide that had driven them apart.

"As you wish." He turned to leave, but then stopped. "Tomorrow, we must talk, Elizabeth." She nodded her assent, and he departed into the hallway.

Elizabeth suspected that one of the doors before her led to her husband's but was afraid to open any to discover the truth of the matter. Fortunately, just then Janette entered from the dressing room. Like Darcy House, there was a servant's entrance located within. "Your trunks arrived before you did, Mrs. Darcy, so they are ready for me to begin unpacking. If you would like, I can pick something out for you to change into – something comfortable yet appropriate for dinner."

"I will not be going down for dinner, so any comfortable gown will do."

"How do you like your new home, ma'am? I have never seen such a grand estate, and I have been to many."

"I like it very well so far. The grounds are lovely, even in the winter; the frosty landscape has a quiet, enchanted look about it." She walked over to her great window to take in the view. The hill from which they had descended was crowned with evergreen, receiving increased abruptness from the distance. Overall, it was a beautiful prospect. Every disposition of the ground was good; and she looked on the whole scene, the river, the deciduous trees scattered on its banks, and the winding of the valley, as far as she could trace it, with delight. While she gazed out the window, taking in the scene before her, Janette took her leave. How long she stood before the window, she could not say. The light began to dissipate as the colours changed from blues to reds. Recollecting herself, she entered the dressing chamber where Janette had been industriously awaiting her arrival.

Rather than putting on a different dress, she decided to go ahead and change into her nightdress and dressing gown. Her meal arrived while she was writing letters to her family to inform them of her safe passage to Pemberley. After her letters were completed, she moved to her journal that had quickly become a source of solace for her, like a friend who would not judge or threaten to do her harm. She wrote about Wickham and his many kind compliments that made her feel special, about her husband's rage and cutting words, and how she felt when leaving her family behind. Yet Elizabeth could not bring herself to write about Darcy's demeaning defilement at Longbourn, for the memory gave her too much distress.

THE FOLLOWING MORNING DAWNED BRIGHT FOR ELIZABETH. She awoke, and donning her dressing gown and slippers, she walked over to the other side of the room to gaze out of the frosty windows at the wintry landscape. A light snow had fallen overnight, just enough to give a cheerful glistening to the now familiar landscape. Breakfast arrived with her maid, and she ate heartily for the first time in several days owing to the beauty of the wintry scene outside her window that cheered her spirits.

Darcy wanted to clear the air as soon as was possible upon arriving at Pemberley. Up until this point, there had always been servants within hearing, or the setting was not right, but they could not go on another day. The episodes outside Longbourn with Wickham and then later inside Elizabeth's childhood bedroom tormented him for reasons he could not yet fathom. He had not possessed such anger, resentment, and loss of control before. Elizabeth's words had haunted him, as he felt their justification; he was a beast. He was no different than the average rake. What had Elizabeth done to him?

Darcy had been his own master for the past five years, striving to live his life without blemish. Darcy's guidance as master led to an increase in productivity and income on his estate each year since his father died. The Darcy fortune and holdings made him one of the wealthiest men in the realm. He gave to the less fortunate through a long list of charitable associations. He had lived a life of virtue foregoing the usual trappings that lured his peers into iniquity.

Then Elizabeth Bennet entered his life and turned everything upside down. How had everything gone wrong? She was a simple country maiden with nothing of value to offer a man of his station. Yet since he had known her, Elizabeth had caused him to lose his disciplined control. Something had to change, and the change had to start with him, but he knew not how. He needed to know Elizabeth's relationship to Wickham. He needed to direct a course to bring some type of amicability in his home. Darcy sent a message through Elizabeth's maid telling her that he would come to her room to escort her to tea.

Elizabeth knew that she could not and should not refuse the summons, as much as she wished to avoid the man, so she was ready and waiting for him at the usual hour. All she wanted was to get through this meeting with minimal insult to her or through her.

As if on cue, she heard the knock on one of the doors in her chamber. Opening it, she discovered Mr. Darcy standing there inside a comfortable sitting

296

room. "I see you are ready," said he, hesitantly. "Shall we," he continued while motioning for her to join him through the room where he stood. "This is the sitting room which is very similar to the room at Darcy House, if not a bit larger, but the most agreeable part of the room is actually from the outside. The prospect from those windows on this side of the room, you have seen, I believe, from your own windows, but these over here," he said motioning to the other wall, "open up to the river and hills in the distance."

Elizabeth walked over for a glance out; she was overwhelmed with the view before her. After a few moments of gazing out the large window, she said, "It's stunning. You must be very proud."

"I admit that I do enjoy looking out my own window. My room opens up to this view, whereas yours looks out upon the front of the house. I think that is why I have always enjoyed this sitting room." Darcy then walked over to the door to the hallway, from where they departed, heading to the dining-parlour.

Elizabeth was then occupied with the enterprise of analysing every feature and style of the rooms through which they passed. She followed Darcy into the dining-parlour. It was large, well proportioned, and handsomely fitted up. Elizabeth, after slightly surveying it, went to a window to enjoy its prospect. The view was similar to that of her own chamber, and she could not help but enjoy what she saw. Noticing that Mr. Darcy was staring at her, she looked down and walked to the large dining table.

"I thought we could have tea in the dining–parlour, rather than a more traditional space, in recognition of your first meal at Pemberley, or first outside your room rather."

A footman and a middle-aged gentleman were there to attend the couple during the meal. The older man was introduced as Peters, the butler. Elizabeth discovered that the man had been in his position for nearly twenty years. "Mr. Darcy, are all of your employees so dedicated?"

He smiled and said, "If you give an employee no reason to leave, they tend to stay."

"This room is lovely." Elizabeth then moved to the chair that Mr. Darcy had pulled out for her. For such a grand room, the fare was light, in keeping with the time of day. Elizabeth served the tea as they barely spoke a word other than Darcy's questions about the comfort of her room. Elizabeth ate a few bites to make a good show, but still could not do it justice in apprehension of his intent. Elizabeth detested living in this state of constant trepidation.

Darcy completed his meal and shared his desire to speak with her in the privacy of his study. He stood and walked behind Elizabeth's chair to assist. Darcy offered his arm, leading her out of the dining area and down the hall to his own study. Unlike Darcy House, this room was not a part of the library, but was actually situated adjacent to it. Elizabeth entered the room and could tell why Darcy had chosen his study as the location for their conference. The room had a distinctly masculine air about it, with rich furnishings and a large desk centrally located towards the left side of the room, and a large chimneypiece made of limestone to the right. Around the fireplace were located two leather chairs and a settée, the fabric obviously made by a skilled artisan, embroidered in pleasing rich colours. Upon the wall were amateur pictures of landscapes and portraits that Elizabeth suspected might have been prepared by Georgiana throughout the years. She glanced at Mr. Darcy and saw that he was watching her closely as had become his habit. "Your study is equal parts inviting and intimidating. To which characteristic do I owe your summons today?"

"I cannot say I know exactly. What is the effect on you?"

"I suppose the answer lies in the location where you would have me sit."

"You may sit wherever you wish; I will accommodate you."

So she walked over to the hearth and sat down on one of the large, leather chairs. Although the room was plenty warm, she had noticed that she became chilled easily since leaving home and desired the warmth of the fire. Darcy sat across from her on its twin. After a few moments of reticence on both sides, Darcy finally found his voice. "Elizabeth, we have needed to talk for a good many days now. I chose to wait until we were done with our journey due to the private nature of what needed to be said. My delay in no way lessens the significance or the importance of what I have to say. I regret that our journey to the North necessitated the lapse, but I could not in good conscience speak with you at a location where someone might overhear us." Elizabeth stared at her hands during his entire speech thus far, concentrating on his words as she attempted to keep her emotions in check.

"First, I need to complete my apology to you, the one that I began at Longbourn." He breathed in deeply. "Please accept my sincerest regrets. I have no excuse for my ungentlemanly behaviour towards you. Although I behaved within my rights and authority, I did so out of anger and frustration." He watched as Elizabeth sat, seeming to be in distant thought concerning something upon her hand. "Do you forgive me?"

Her breathing increased as she tried to maintain control. Elizabeth wanted to shout out that she could not and would never forgive him for shaming her in that beastly manner. But then would that not also be iniquitous? She was reminded that he had every right to do with her as he would. She considered being the humble and submissive wife, but then the independent, justifiably angry woman inside of her fought that idea. Elizabeth wanted to walk out the door and live her life without his interference. Had it only been her reputation, she never would have married the man, but since she had, Elizabeth was now bound to him until death they part, and as such was obligated to submit to his needs and apologies. A large cloud seemed to descend over her as this thought came to her. "I must forgive you."

"Does that mean you do?"

"My heart cannot yet follow my mind, but I know that you had every legal right to do what you did. I cannot like it, nor will I ever forget it. You were very cruel in your treatment of me, but I know my duty. I will grant you forgiveness for that offence."

"I thank you."

Tears brimmed in her eyes as she looked up at his face for the first time, "I have no choice in the matter, nor any other. You now hold my life in your hands, and I abhor the idea. I am ashamed at myself for feeling that way, but I cannot help it." Her tears spilt over. She stood and walked to the window. It would have been so much easier if he had not apologised. She could continue on in her just indignation at his treatment. But then she recalled all of the other offences against herself and her family for which he had yet to ask pardon, and her scorn was revived.

Darcy had hoped for a simple resolution to their dilemma. He would apologise for his conduct in her room, and then she would apologise for meeting with Wickham. They would each have their say and clear the air, but Elizabeth could not let it go. Her anger was clouding her better judgement. Her passionate nature was showing itself to least advantage. If he were to humble himself enough to apologise, she could too. "I have said my peace, now I believe that you should as well. We will both feel much better when we have had a chance to clear the air."

"What are you talking about?"

"Wickham."

"I don't know what you think happened between Wickham and myself, but I can assure you that I have been faithful to my marriage vows. And in truth he has always been more gentlemanly towards me, treating me like the lady I am, than you were upon first meeting. *Wickham* has never given me the impression that he wanted more than was proper."

"What are you talking about?"

"What I mean is that a true gentleman does not stare at a woman, especially a lady, in a state of undress when she obviously does not wish to be seen!"

"To what do you refer? I have never done such a thing."

"Then your memory loss obviously and thankfully included the time in the cabin when you indecently stared at me in my wet undergarments while I was trying to rid myself of my soaking clothes, necessitated by my endeavours at saving *you*." She could tell that he had in fact not forgotten by the dawning look of understanding upon his face. "I see that you did not forget. So keep your judgements of Mr. Wickham, me and my genteel breeding to yourself."

Of course, Darcy remembered seeing her. For days he could think of nothing else, but until now, he had not seriously considered her discovery of his unseemly behaviour; nevertheless, he could not admit to being at fault, to her or himself. "You knew what you were about that day. You wanted me to see you, as you well know, to entice me."

She laughed. "You continue in your vain attempt to incriminate me; the whole idea is ridiculous! Surely you know me well enough by now to apprehend that I would do no such thing. Once and for all, I did not try to trap you into a marriage! I was wet and cold and was just trying to get warm. You looked to be asleep, so I took the opportunity to try to remove my soaking dress so that it and my underclothes could dry. You tried to hide your fascination with my person, but I saw it. I did not accuse you of anything ungentlemanly because I thought that maybe your injury had addled your senses, but I see that accusations are the Darcy way. Perhaps your own lust was the real reason you offered for me, under the pretext of a more noble obligation."

This was not going well for Darcy, but he knew Wickham to be perfidious and likely to have imposed himself upon Elizabeth at some point. Indeed, Wickham had never been anything but licentious towards the opposite sex, whether with a lady or a servant, so he continued trying to redirect her judgement from himself, especially in light of her supposition having no merit. "I cannot believe that Wickham did not attempt a seduction either before or after our marriage, or possibly both."

"If he did attempt, I was unaware, but I am possibly unskilled in the art as you might be. If you don't believe me, ask Laura Carpenter, if she is here somewhere. That evidence you so valued proves my innocence before our marriage. I don't know what you believe, but I can assure you that I am not the kind of woman who plays with a man's affections or subjects myself to a man's whims. Mr. Wickham has only been my friend, despite your intervention."

"He is not your friend, Elizabeth. He means to set you against me which cannot be to your advantage."

"You, sir, need no help in that endeavour." Darcy, now standing, was attempting to control his temper, so as not to say something he would regret. He was leaning on the mantle with one hand, the other in a fist, his knuckles against his mouth.

"You take an eager interest in that gentleman," said Darcy, attempting to deflect her attack.

"Who that knows what his misfortunes have been, can help feeling an interest in him?"

"His misfortunes!" repeated Darcy contemptuously. "Yes, his misfortunes have been great indeed."

"And of your infliction," cried Elizabeth with energy. "You have reduced him to his present state of poverty, comparative poverty. You have withheld the advantages, which you must know to have been designed for him. You have done all this and yet you can treat the mention of his misfortunes with contempt and ridicule. Despite his reduced circumstances and your amassed wealth, you cannot bear for Mr. Wickham to hold the regard or respect of anyone within your acquaintance. You, a man who has everything, would let jealousy drive you to condemn a former friend."

"And this," cried Darcy, as he walked with quick steps across the room towards her, "is your opinion of me! This is the estimation in which you hold me! I thank you for explaining it so fully. My faults, according to this calculation, are heavy indeed! But perhaps," added he, stopping in his walk, "these offences might have been overlooked, had not your pride been hurt by my honest confession of the scruples that were the only inducement to lead me to offer for you. These bitter accusations might have been suppressed, had I with greater policy concealed my struggles, and flattered you into the belief of my being impelled towards you by unqualified, unalloyed inclination; by reason, by reflections, by everything. But I would not go into a marriage with deceit on my shoulders. Do you suppose that your condition in life could induce me to offer for you for any reason other than necessity?"

"Deceit, sir, comes in many forms," responded she in heightened colour. "You judge Mr. Wickham harshly and seem to be inclined to judge others on that same score; however, your own misrepresentation of facts condemns you as guilty."

"I have not the pleasure of understanding you."

"But you did take pleasure in the intervention you enacted on behalf of Mr. Bingley. Had not my own experiences decided me against you, had they been indifferent, or had they even been favourable, do you think that any consideration would tempt me to honestly absolve a man who has been the means of ruining, perhaps forever, the happiness of a most beloved sister?"

As she pronounced these words, Mr. Darcy changed colour; but the emotion was short-lived, and he listened without attempting to interrupt her while she continued.

"I have every reason in the world to think ill of you. No motive can excuse the unjust and ungenerous part you acted there. You dare not, you cannot deny that you have been the principal, if not the only means of dividing them from each other, of exposing one to the censure of the world for caprice and instability, the other to its derision for disappointed hopes, and involving them both in misery of the acutest kind. Then you lied to me about the whole affair. I remember it so clearly, the night I realised you are not the gentleman you want everyone to believe."

She paused, and saw with no slight indignation that he was listening with an air which proved him wholly unmoved by any feeling of remorse. He even looked at her with a smile of affected incredulity.

"You cannot deny that you have done it; I heard you bragging to Colonel Fitzwilliam of your *noble* interventions into their lives," she said with renewed indignation.

"I have no wish of denying that I did everything in my power to separate my friend from your sister, or that I rejoice in my success. Towards him I have been kinder than towards myself," Darcy responded, his emotions now in check, a look of hauteur hiding the tumult within.

"Jane is your sister now! How could you be so cruel to her if not to your friend?" Elizabeth was not so successful hiding her passionate feelings of outrage and resentment.

"What I did, was done for a friend, and it was done for the best. Your mother would have him sponsoring your younger sisters in town, and Bingley would not have the tenacity to refuse her. He would become a laughing stock amongst his peers. His feelings for your sister would dissipate once he realised that a man of his position in society could not withstand the mockery that would be laid at his door.

"And how was he to know if your sister's interest was sincere? Your mother is highly skilled at the art of marrying her daughters off. Could he even be certain of Miss Bennet's true affections? The mercenary motivations that guide your family would forever plague him. I could not burden a friend with such a life."

Elizabeth gasped. The injury to her was as equal as that to her sister. "You have insulted me and my family in every possible way. You can now have nothing more to say, nothing more to add that could increase the offence." Elizabeth did not remove her eyes from his as she continued, "From the very beginning, from the first moment I may almost say, of my acquaintance with you, your manners impressing me with the fullest belief of your arrogance, your conceit, and your selfish disdain of the feelings of others, were such as to form that ground-work of disapprobation, on which these succeeding events have built so immoveable a dislike; and I had not known you a month before I felt that you were the last man in the world whom I could have willingly married. This places you on equal footing with Mr. Collins and his mixture of servility and self-importance, but with you rather than servility you boast contempt.

"If the scandal had merely ruined *my* respectability, I would have accepted my lot, leaving my family, being satisfied in the knowledge of my own virtue. I could have and would have made a life for myself under the guidance of a beloved aunt and uncle. But I could not let my family suffer for my poor decision. I rue the day I helped you during that storm. If I could have predicted the events to come, I would have left you there to fend for yourself. I have never in my life regretted a kindness shown someone so wholly undeserving until now." After such a speech, the silence seemed so out of place, except for each taking in a quick succession of calming breaths.

"You have said quite enough, madam. I perfectly comprehend your feelings, and have now only to be ashamed of my own part that has been played in this farcical marriage. Forgive me for having taken up so much of your time." He walked over to the door and opened it, clearly dismissing her from his presence. With pique, they each separated, both wanting distance from the other to calm their turbulent emotions.

Unfortunately for Elizabeth, she had no way of knowing how to return to her room, so she started wandering the halls, hoping the servants would leave her alone, but needing assistance in guiding her to her destination. She did finally reach her chamber and was able to let the full impact of their argument overcome her senses.

Elizabeth wept over Darcy's arrogant intervention into her family's affairs, and not only her family's but also into the livelihood of the amiable Mr. Wickham. However, she was surprised to discover later that her greatest discomfiture lay in Darcy's words of disapprobation concerning their marriage and his specific objections related to her. She had known that he had only found her tolerable in the beginning and only married her out of obligation, but she had hoped that perhaps he had come to have some level of admiration for her. Elizabeth had found her husband staring at her many times, which at first she thought to be out of disapproval or to find fault, but she had begun to suppose that he might esteem her, if only in part. Although she despised the man, somewhere deep down, she had begun to appreciate him and his dedication to his duties. The previous month had brought many vexations, but there had also been times of peace and even some degree of pleasure.

Darcy was fuming. He reviewed the scene that had played out in his study over and again in his head. Elizabeth had offended him in every possible way. No one had ever been so bold as to treat him with such disrespect. He resented her for the manner in which she spoke to him, a Darcy. Not even a professor at Eton had attempted to belittle him as she had. Even as a child his parents venerated him. Who did she think she was? It was all Wickham's doing, he knew. He had whispered words of contempt into her pretty head, and she fell for it, and no matter his defence, she would not listen. Darcy then remembered seeing Wickham with Elizabeth in the garden at Longbourn. She was laughing, and Wickham looked fascinated. Darcy imagined Wickham enticing Elizabeth on one of her long walks, and the idea nauseated him anew. Why it could bother him so, he did not fully understand. Was it merely the same old plague rearing its ugly head, Wickham attempting to lure everyone in Darcy's life over to himself, to take what belonged to him and use it for his own amusement, as he had attempted with Georgiana and succeeded with his father? Or could this be an even greater molestation, taking advantage of his wife's innocence and kindness? And then was she really so innocent and kind? Perhaps she continued to deceive him.

Although Darcy was quite unable to reconcile his actions with his honour, he could at length enjoy the benefits that time affords in placating a guilty conscience, as he had at least in part begun to see the justification of his poisonous actions. But, to his benefit, he could not forget the look upon Elizabeth's countenance that would continue to plague him when his guard was down.

The two principals had no desire to see or speak with the other, so Darcy spent his time in his study catching up on months of mail, and Elizabeth stayed in her room, writing in her journal, reading a book, or sleeping. They each took meals on their own, neither caring at the time how this might look to the large staff at Pemberley.

The livelihood of hundreds depended upon the health of Fitzwilliam Darcy and his progeny. The vast majority of the servants, tenants, and even townsfolk rejoiced upon hearing the news of Darcy's finally taking a bride and bringing home a mistress to his estate. However, there were others who knew him like family, who worried about the haste taken in securing a bride, and that perhaps all was not as well as originally thought. Mrs. Reynolds, who had known Darcy since he was four years of age, had taken the news of his marriage with uncertain apprehension. She hoped for the best, that Darcy had found a wife with whom he could find contentment. He always seemed so focused on his duties as master of Pemberley, and his other holdings, as well as being brother and guardian to Georgiana. Darcy strived to do his very best in whatever obligation lay before him, sometimes to his own detriment. He needed a wife who would complement him by being his support and friend. So many clamoured to be around Darcy for his position, his money, to take advantage of his generous nature, or his sage advice; but there was no one to offer him anything of value, that would be a blessing to him, other than perhaps his sister or Colonel Fitzwilliam. Darcy needed a helpmate, and Mrs. Reynolds wondered if Darcy had chosen a bride to add to his assets or to truly help him to prosper and share his burden.

Based on the first few days of the Darcys' being in residence at Pemberley, Mrs. Reynolds began to lose hope for any good to come from the marriage. Her master had dark circles forming under his eyes and had secluded himself within his study, meeting with his steward for long hours and only coming out to retire in the evening. He had requested additional brandy be provided, yet ate little food. His new bride was not seen again by any except her maid, Janette, who would give no helpful information concerning her mistress's state of health or mind. She would offer nothing about the marriage or the felicity existing therein.

Chapter Fifteen

Adversity is the first path to truth
Lord Byron

Five days after their arrival at Pemberley, Elizabeth received a note written in her husband's hand informing her that he would be leaving the following day for London. He gave no reason for his removal, nor did he give a date of his expected return. So on the following morning, Elizabeth looked out of the window to see her husband's coach take him, his valet and two footmen away from Pemberley. This brought Elizabeth such mixed emotions. Relief was the most palpable; she felt a sense of freedom with his leaving. She also felt sadness. Although Elizabeth came into the marriage unwillingly, she had hoped for its success, that she could somehow grow fond of the man, and he her; but seeing him leave brought home to her the naïveté of such an idea. Of course, he could never love her, and he was the last man with whom she wanted to spend time, was he not?

During the five days of solitude, there had also been a dawning of understanding, as Elizabeth remembered her father's story of how he and her mother came to be married. Meeting Lady Annette had been nagging at her for reasons she could not fathom. She had almost forgotten the encounter owing to the disturbing happenings immediately following the ball and her journey to Longbourn. It was only on the trip to Pemberley and the days to follow that Elizabeth was able to explore her foreboding. Elizabeth came to grasp the stark similarities that existed between her parents' marriage and now her own, and the reality hit her like a violent blow. Like her father's having to give up his love to a woman for whom he planned to offer, Mr. Darcy had given up Lady Annette. This all became quite clear to her. When Lord Langston first whispered words of acrimony designed to make her question her husband's relationship with the beautiful woman with whom he danced, Elizabeth thought that perhaps he only said what he did to vex her. But upon reflection, and given time to meditate upon the viscount's words and her husband's behaviour, Elizabeth comprehended the truth. Like her father, Darcy was forced to give up the woman he loved in order to prevent a scandal, and to Darcy's thinking, Elizabeth was no different than her mother; to him, she had entrapped him, forcing him to give up his hopes for happiness with the woman who was in all ways perfect for him.

This awareness brought Elizabeth a feeling of shame and remorse for any part she had played in the scandal. If only she had not become ill and begun talking in her sleep, Darcy would have been free to marry whom he wanted, and she would, even now, be at home with her family. Mr. Darcy had said that he had no honourable choice but to sit with Lady Annette at the ball, but perhaps this was a confabulation designed to forefend Elizabeth's suspicion. Could he even now be on his way to town to see her again? Maybe he had been seeing Lady Annette throughout the entire time they were in residence at Darcy House. Notwithstanding, after days of speculation and conjecture, Elizabeth decided to think on it no more. She could do nothing about Mr. Darcy's activities and surmised that with all of his faults, she could not see him dallying with a gentleman's daughter, especially one of noble heritage.

Darcy's leaving sparked Elizabeth to overcome her melancholy. She had been considering her future and her role as Mrs. Darcy. If she could not have her husband's love and respect, she could at least fulfil her role as mistress to his estate. Secluding herself in her room was no way for a mistress to respond to her position, and she was determined not to follow in her mother's footpath in *that* manner, so after luncheon, Elizabeth left her chamber and began searching for the servants' stairs that would take her to Mrs. Reynolds's office.

Elizabeth passed a housemaid along the way and asked for the young woman to direct her to the housekeeper. They made conversation as they walked, and Elizabeth learnt a little bit of personal information to help her remember the girl – the first of many servants she would come to know over the following weeks.

While meeting with Mrs. Reynolds, who had welcomed her with unfeigned delight – unlike Mrs. Johnson at Darcy house – Elizabeth scheduled time each day to become more familiar with her new home. She was to go on a tour of the main part of the house today and meet with the chef, Monsieur Lambert, the following day. Elizabeth then planned to meet with the full staff, convening with five at a time, so that she would have a chance to get to know something of relevance about each of them. Elizabeth realised that this was a rather odd request from her, but she had such fond memories of her relationships with the servants at Longbourn that she could not help but hope she would have the opportunity to become somewhat familiar with each of them, and perhaps closer with others. Elizabeth had no way of knowing when her husband would return, but she was determined to build relationships and to make the most of her time in his absence.

On the following day, Elizabeth arrived at Mrs. Reynolds's office to begin her tour of the kitchen and meet the chef. She was pleasantly surprised to find Laura Carpenter, her beloved former maid, there as well. Elizabeth was overcome with pleasure to see her friend again. Elizabeth hugged the woman who had been her only comfort during the first days of her marriage. After a few moments of allowing the women some time to catch up, Mrs. Reynolds said, "I see that you have met my protégée. Mrs. Carpenter has been training to take over my position when I retire later this year."

"Yes, Laura, *rather Mrs. Carpenter*, served as my lady's maid when I first married Mr. Darcy." Then turning to Laura, Elizabeth said, "I have missed you. I didn't understand why you departed so quickly, without a goodbye."

"I was sorry to leave that way. Mr. Darcy informed me of his wish for me to leave with the other servants, so I could start my training here at Pemberley. I was only told after you had gone to bed and had to prepare to leave early the following morning while you were still sleeping. I knew I would see you here and was assured of your new maid's kindness."

"But surely you could have come to my room to take your leave. I was surprised and overwhelmed with the prospect of not having you around any longer."

"I was sorry for things to happen as they did, but I agreed with Mr. Darcy. You needed a trained lady's maid, and he was concerned you would not agree to my removal if you knew ahead of time. And it was important that I be here before the new year. You are a strong woman, Mrs. Darcy. I knew you would be fine without me, and I did not want my being there to take time away from your husband."

"I cannot say how strong I am, but as you see, I have survived thus far." Then Elizabeth looked to Mrs. Reynolds who had been listening with curiosity. "Oh, Mrs. Reynolds, forgive me. Mrs. Carpenter was such help for a young bride in need of guidance. You are fortunate to have her following in your wake."

"Indeed I am. I believe Mr. Darcy decided to place Mrs. Carpenter in the position of my apprentice after seeing how well you two got along. Mrs. Carpenter has been a real asset to Pemberley, covering all of the servant positions at one time or another, disregarding how that would place her in the staff's rankings. I confess I had her in mind all along, which is why I had moved her around so much. You can tell a lot about a person by the way they handle change, and Mrs. Carpenter has always been resilient, despite the difficult road that has brought her to this point."

Elizabeth contemplated how poorly she had accepted her own changes to her life and resolved to do better. She smiled at the two women before her. In just these few moments, she had already begun to feel a special regard for Mrs. Reynolds to match the rapport that had been established with Laura Carpenter.

Laura, upon seeing Elizabeth, had been shocked at the change. She had lost noticeable weight and although now in fine clothing, her pale complexion left the effect wanting. Her fears for her new mistress were obviously not without merit. Mr. Darcy's hasty removal from Pemberley did not bode well for the couple's struggling relationship.

THE FOLLOWING FORTNIGHT WENT BY QUICKLY as Elizabeth made good use of her time. She returned to country hours and spent the entirety of each day out of her chamber exploring the house, the estate and the paths beyond, always accompanied by a footman when on the grounds of the estate. Elizabeth also spent no small amount of time meeting with the servants, learning their names and histories. She quickly developed the reputation of being a kind, intelligent and energetic mistress of Pemberley, restoring Mrs. Reynolds's hopes for Darcy's felicity in marriage. Along with the increase in activity came an increase in Elizabeth's appetite. Without the fear of encountering her husband, she had slept better and was, therefore, better prepared to put more time to active and constructive pursuits. Elizabeth had begun to treasure her new home, especially the grounds. When snow covered the property, she was not deterred. She wandered the gardens close to the house and delighted in the winter wonderland before her, as the landscape transformed from a bleak forest to an unending white blanket of snow.

While in London, Elizabeth truly enjoyed the benefit of the master pianist to help her improve on the pianoforte. Also, since becoming a Darcy, she had the benefit of superior instruments.   Without the noise of her family and the competition for practice time, Elizabeth found that she could devote hours each day to the pianoforte without interruption.   With her natural talent as well as these other inducements, she was quickly on her way to becoming a true proficient, much to her surprise and delight.   Playing became a way of expressing her joys, sorrows and gaiety.

Elizabeth received several responses from the letters that she had dispatched upon first arriving at her new home.   She learnt that Jane had decided to return to Gracechurch Street with her relations for the duration of the winter and the upcoming Spring Season.   Her sister continued to pine for Mr. Bingley but had decided to move on with her life.   She could not continue in anticipation of his return to Netherfield, and there were many other men of her aunt and uncle's acquaintance who might wish for a gentleman's daughter, despite her limited dowry.

While at Longbourn, Elizabeth had met with her father and uncle to establish a way of transferring some of her pin money each month into Jane's dowry. After arriving at Pemberley, she directed the steward to make the necessary transactions starting with the lump sum of one hundred pounds, with a promise of fifty pounds per month towards Jane's welfare during her lifetime.   In this way, Elizabeth hoped to avoid future missed opportunities for her sister owing only to lack of fortune.   As Elizabeth had no way of knowing how Mr. Darcy would respond to such an action, suspecting he would likely construe her efforts as mercenary, she chose to keep her husband's steward from being informed about the specifics of the account, aside from the account number and name of the bank where the account was located.

Elizabeth's regret for her sister had increased substantially since she overheard her husband's conversation with Colonel Fitzwilliam, and she felt the full weight of her sister's lost hopes.   Knowing that Jane's heart was engaged to Mr. Bingley and realising the difficulties her sister would encounter in overcoming her feelings, Elizabeth felt anew the resentment previously directed at her husband.   The justification in giving pin money provided for her by her settlement allowed her the means of assuaging Darcy's involvement in her sister's despair.

During the time of Darcy's absence, Elizabeth thought little of her husband, for the remembrance of his presence only brought her disappointment; instead, she focused on those persons around her who needed her leadership and benevolence.   After Darcy had been gone over three weeks, Elizabeth received word of a tenant farmer's family in need of aid, as the wife was expecting her fourth child; the other three were under the age of six.   The local midwife had ordered the poor woman to bed due to bleeding, and there was no one to prepare food and maintain the home.   By this time, Elizabeth had met all of the staff within the great house, and she was ready to move on to the estate at large, so Elizabeth determined to visit the family herself and begin the monumental task of being introduced to those who made Pemberley the great estate that it was. As such, she requested transportation, a footman and Mrs. Carpenter to accompany her on her visit to determine the family's needs. She also had a basket of food prepared along with some sweetmeats to share with the children.

After about fifteen minutes of travel, she arrived at the tenant's home and took stock in the well-kept lodging, seeing that there was plenty of wood to last the winter piled on the side of the house. The footman assisted the ladies out of the carriage, then went to the door and knocked. The blustery wind made walking to the door difficult as the ladies' skirts risked tripping them. A man of about thirty opened the door, and his eyes widened at the lady before him. Elizabeth smiled and reached her hand out to him in greeting. "Mr. Smithton, I am Mrs. Darcy and this is Mrs. Carpenter. I hope you don't mind our visit."

The man found his voice and responded, "Please come in, out of the cold," which Elizabeth and Mrs. Carpenter gladly did. "Forgive me, " he said looking around the small room, "I didn't know I would have such fine company, you see."

"Please, do not be uneasy. I must congratulate you on the upcoming birth of your child. And I see that I must also congratulate you on the handsome family already in our midst."

The man recollected himself and looked back to his two little boys, who were standing behind their father, peeking around him in curiosity. Neither was older than four. "Thank you. I am a blessed man."

"I see you are busy, so I'll get to the point. My housekeeper informed me of your wife's condition and need for bed rest. And I would not have her put herself or your baby at risk by not following the midwife's orders. So I came to see what might suit you as a means of keeping her off her feet."

"I have been trying to keep things going myself, and I think I can manage on my own. I would not have anyone go to any trouble."

Elizabeth looked around the cabin and saw that the man was not as proficient at keeping things going inside the home as he was outside. There were dirty pots and dishes to be washed, and the room needed a thorough cleaning. "I am confident that you are an excellent farmer, for Mr. Darcy has bragged to me about the prosperity so abundantly found at Pemberley. I noticed pulling up that your home is well kept with plenty of wood for the winter. I would wager that your wife has always been able to properly manage the inside of your home, and now you wish to help her."

"As you say."

"May I meet Mrs. Smithton? Or is she indisposed?"

"Certainly, right this way," said the man, obviously uncomfortable with the mistress herself in his home. He led her through a doorway that was covered by a sheet, holding it open as Elizabeth and Laura entered. "Mary, Mrs. Darcy is here to see you." Then he looked back to his guests. "Mrs. Darcy, um Mrs. Carpenter, this is my wife, Mrs. Smithton."

Elizabeth looked towards the attractive young woman reclined on the small bed and the young girl sitting next to her, who had obviously been listening to her mother read. The woman was trying to sit up. "No, please, do not get up on my account. I came to see what I could do to help your family until the baby comes."

The woman looked to her husband, apparently unsure about what to say. Elizabeth, seeing their discomfort, turned to the man and continued, "I can tell that you must be proud of your family and your home."

"I cannot say otherwise."

"Your family is exactly the kind of family that Pemberley needs to thrive, so when there is an occasion that we can thank you for your hard work, we are anxious to do just that. And since this seems to be such an occasion, I hope you will grant me the privilege of providing assistance to make your wife confident that she is not overburdening you by having to remain in bed. I think that will make her rest easier, which can only help the baby."

"What do you have in mind, if you don't mind my asking?"

"When is your confinement, Mrs. Smithton?"

"The mid-wife says the beginning of April."

"Very well." Elizabeth looked to her companion. "Mrs. Carpenter, are you aware of anyone who might take on a position as maid-of-all-work temporarily? Perhaps one of the other tenants has a daughter willing to help before the growing season begins?"

Laura smiled, recalling just such a girl who had worked in the Pemberley kitchen and as a scullery maid on occasion, but was currently not needed in the big house and so lacked employment. This would help her family, as her father was a tenant managing a smaller piece of property. "I know the perfect girl, Patsy Hargrove. We can stop by her home on the way back and see if she would like the work."

Elizabeth then turned to the couple. "Are you familiar with this girl?" They nodded. "And would you find the arrangements satisfactory?" Their look of hesitation reminded Elizabeth that accepting assistance might come difficult for them. "You would be doing me an enormous favour. I find I cannot sleep at night knowing that there was something I could do to help, but was unable. Please, accept my interference!" Elizabeth said with a smile and small laugh. "You will find me quite the bother when I don't get my way. And you are not just letting me help you, but also Patsy who needs work, it would seem."

Then the man spoke, "We accept your help then, but only until the baby comes."

"Thank you. And now, I brought you a basket from the Pemberley kitchen, including some freshly made bread loaves. And for the children, a special treat. I left it on the table in the other room. I will be right back." Elizabeth left the room and returned with the sweetmeats and some bread and cheese for Mrs. Smithton. Not wanting to overstay her welcome, but anxious to learn a little more about the family and other possible needs, Elizabeth sat for an additional fifteen minutes talking to the children and their parents. She could tell that their clothing was in good shape and that the house was plenty warm, which encouraged her, giving her the confidence that their needs would truly be met with the addition of Patsy.

After saying their goodbyes, Elizabeth and Laura climbed back into the carriage and headed for the home of Patsy Hargrove. After a thirty-minute visit, it was settled that the young woman would start in the morning. Elizabeth could see how the extra money would be a welcome aid. What she did not know was that just that morning, the family had taken inventory of their ration of wood and food for the rest of the winter and found it wanting. They had counted on Patsy's being needed at Pemberley with the new mistress but had heard nothing. Patsy's father, a God-fearing man, prayed that their needs would be met somehow.

"Mrs. Darcy, you are an answer to my prayer." Elizabeth smiled, happy to be able to help two families. During the visit she had resolved to use her own pin money to provide the service; this was her idea, and she was unsure how Darcy would take her interference. Hopefully, he would never know.

Just then, the footman, Clark, who had accompanied them opened the door and said, "Excuse me, ma'am. There looks to be a storm coming in from the south. We should be getting back."

Elizabeth felt pleased with the opportunity she had to aid these two families who contributed towards making her husband's estate thrive and endure.

My son, if sinners entice you, do not consent.
My son, do not walk in the way with them;
hold back your foot from their paths
Proverbs 1:10, 15

IN LONDON, Darcy had surprised his skeleton staff at Darcy House by arriving without prior warning. He had considered sending an express ahead, but instead decided to avoid the commotion that would undoubtedly occur. He planned on taking most of his meals at his club, thereby obviating a fuss in the kitchen. It would take no more than an hour to prepare his room, so he felt an express would be counterproductive to his goal of a quiet entry into town. Darcy gave no explanation for his unexpected return to his staff or his family.

Darcy's visit to Tromwell House the next day provided unforeseeable delight for his sister. It was not until later in that first visit that Georgiana began to suspect that her brother might not have come into town for felicitous reasons. When she was able to focus on his appearance, she saw that he looked tired and worn. He made a good show of his complacency, but she soon suspected the opposite. Georgiana encouraged him to confide his struggles she knew were related to his conniving wife, but he continued his stance that all was well. Darcy discovered on this visit that he would see little of Colonel Fitzwilliam for he was no longer in residence. Also, the viscount had remained in town rather than go to Matlock but was residing at his own London home.

From Tromwell House, Darcy went to Angelo's. He needed to work off his abiding anger in physical exertion and was pleased to find that the exercise truly helped his equanimity. Like many of his peers, Darcy had taken meals many times at Whites to avoid eating at home alone. While Elizabeth was living at Darcy House, he had remained there during most mealtimes in order to eat with her, at least the meals during which she chose to join him. With his wife at Pemberley and limited staffing, Darcy planned on eating at his club most of the time, which would give him some companionship but would not necessitate extended visits. He had no desire to let anyone know of his troubles and hoped to avoid the prying questions. This became his routine in town: a visit with family, exercise at Angelo's and evenings at Whites. This kept his mind and body engaged, thus avoiding too many unpleasant remembrances.

DARCY WAS READING IN THE LIBRARY when he heard someone at the door. A few moments later, he noted a familiar voice approaching the room. Bingley was always friendly with Darcy's butler and nearly everyone else he met. Darcy stood in greeting. "Darcy, I had no idea you were in town. I hope you don't mind my coming by. I know that your knocker is off the door, but Jackson was so kind to let me in, risking your disapproval."

Although Darcy admired his friend's easy manners and affability, he dreaded having to bear his company on this particular trip. "I have been here for not quite a week now." Then Darcy motioned to the chair by the chimneypiece. "Have a seat. I'll call for tea. Or would you rather have coffee?"

"Tea would be just the thing." Darcy rang for the footman and ordered tea before returning to his seat.

"How have you been?" Bingley asked his dearest friend. "I feel like I have seen so little of you since our time in Hertfordshire. —You, with being married and me, trying to stay busy."

"I am well, as you see."

"Did Mrs. Darcy return to town with you?"

"No, she stayed at Pemberley as we only just arrived. The journey is quite long and there was no reason to uproot her when she was just getting settled."

"I am surprised she did not go to Longbourn then. I imagine she misses her family. I believe they were quite close, at least Miss Bennet and your wife were."

"I do believe you are right." *Very smooth, Bingley. Not a minute has gone by, and we are already at your favourite topic.*

"I suppose you went to Longbourn recently though, did you not? For their sister's wedding? I seem to recall Miss Mary was to wed that Mr. Collins. Odd fellow, he was."

"You remember correctly."

"And how was the wedding?" Darcy knew his friend was fishing for information about Jane Bennet, but he was unwilling to take the bait.

"A simple affair really. Elizabeth and I left before the conclusion of the breakfast. I do believe the couple enjoyed themselves, but no one more so than Mrs. Bennet. She seems to be an expert at marrying off her daughters. No detail was left undone. I do believe she would give some of the mamas of the *ton* a run for their money, and the grooms." He finished with a roll of his eyes.

"Darcy you are their family now. Do you still think Mrs. Bennet to be so mercenary?"

"Bingley, I have yet to meet another mother more so."

"But her daughters, they cannot be so."

"Whether they are or not, they must follow along or she will force the issue. You were lucky to get away when you did. Even if Jane Bennet had feelings for you, which I saw no evidence of whatsoever, her mother would make your life miserable trying to subject you with the task of marrying off her younger daughters. Not only would society frown upon such an endeavour, they would likely scorn the younger Bennets – and you as well for helping. Marrying into that family would ruin you and destroy Miss Bingley's chances for a good marriage."

"I believe *your* marriage did more damage to Caroline's pursuits." Bingley said with a smile. "I know you are right. Of course you are. But have you experienced any of that yourself?"

"In part, but not as much as you would, Bingley. And of course, I will ensure there is no opportunity for attempting to foist the younger, brazen sisters upon me," he said in derision. "I have a well-established presence amongst society that will not so easily diminish. I cannot know now what affect my marriage will have on Georgiana, but I hope for the best. She will not come out for another year at least. In time perhaps most will have forgotten about our unfortunate alliance. But I would not have that for you. You cannot afford society's acrimony."

They sat quietly for a few minutes staring at the fire, each deep in thought, Bingley about what he might be willing to risk for his angel and Darcy trying to keep in mind all the reasons he felt justified in keeping his friend away from the Bennets.

Bingley broke the silence with an unexpected question. "Darcy, did I do something that offended Mrs. Darcy? When last I saw her at the ball and before that at the theatre, she seemed rather piqued with my family. I can understand why she might harbour ill feelings towards Caroline, but she was quite put out with me as well."

"Bingley, my wife has had a difficult time transitioning to married life. Elizabeth has some good days and some not-so-good days. I cannot always predict what might cause her displeasure. What I can say is that you are not alone as a target of her ire."

"I see. I am sorry. Is that why you are here... without Mrs. Darcy? No, I do apologise. Please don't answer that." Bingley paused, and then said, "She always seemed so cheerful before."

"And I am sure she will again. It will take some time. For Elizabeth, it could not be helped. I know you would not wish the same for Miss Bennet."

"But, I am not so sure the same would happen with her. Jane, rather Miss Bennet, is such a sweet-tempered lady."

"As is Elizabeth. Bingley, you must not look back."

"But Mrs. Darcy may have gone into your marriage with a prejudiced view of you, unlike how Miss Bennet would have felt with me."

"I know she did not care for me. That was clear."

"Well, I cannot say I blame her after what you said about her at the assembly in Meryton when we first came into town," Bingley said nodding his head with a little chuckle. "I am certain she overheard you."

"What are you talking about? What did I say?"

"You remember. I was trying to encourage you to ask her to dance and you said something like, 'She is tolerable; but not handsome enough to tempt me.' Then you said something about not being in a humour to give consequence to ladies who are slighted by other men. You were unhappy about something, which can be your only excuse, because, I daresay, your wife is a lovely woman."

"That was Elizabeth?" Darcy said more to himself than Bingley. He stood up and walked around slowly as he tried to recall the scene described by his friend. He now remembered saying those words and in truth meant to be heard by the lady to whom Bingley referred. He made a habit of saying such things to avoid raising a lady's expectations, but hearing these words from his friend made him sound like an insolent fool. *But of course it was Elizabeth.* He remembered now how she had laughed at him rather than showing offence. *She was making fun of me... as she does all of the follies of the world. Only Elizabeth would find amusement at such a slight.* "No wonder she wanted to leave me in the woods. She said so, you know."

"That's not all, Darcy. I'm afraid my sister may have given further offence at the ball, the one at Tromwell House on New Years Eve."

"Go on," Darcy said, a foreboding feeling coming over him.

"Caroline could not quite get past losing you to one of the Bennets. I'm afraid she may have – well actually she did – tell Mrs. Darcy some unkind remarks that you had spoken, perhaps in an ill-favoured mood, at Netherfield. They were voiced prior to your understanding with Mrs. Darcy, of course, and you likely did not even mean them."

"What did I say?" Darcy asked, not quite certain he wished to know.

"You will recall that the Bennets and the Lucases had been dining at Netherfield, and after they left, we were all in the drawing room having a beverage. I believe you were in need of something stronger than was served while our guests were in attendance," Bingley said with a smile. "Anyway, we were speaking on the reputed beauty of the Bennet ladies when your wife's name came up, then Miss Elizabeth Bennet. You openly disagreed with the assessment. Unfortunately, my sister remembered your unkind words and shared them with Mrs. Darcy."

Darcy sat there, mouth agape, until he thought to close it. "I hardly remember speaking them. Surely what I said was not so dreadful."

"If her reaction was any indication, I would say that they were, but Darcy, her sister has a forgiving nature. Maybe she does as well. She has likely moved on and has forgotten the imprudent slights."

"No, I think not." Both men sat in silence that was interrupted by the footman bringing in the tea. "Would you like to join me at Angelo's today?"

"And suffer the humiliation of being soundly thrashed?"

"I promise to check my exuberance. Come, let's go. You and I will both feel better, and I will be happy to have some company."

THE DURATION OF HIS STAY put Darcy in contact with many acquaintances, but certainly few bold enough to question him about his wife's whereabouts. However, one evening not quite a fortnight into his stay, he saw Lord Wexley with his father, Lord Cunningham, dining at the club. As Darcy entered the establishment, the two gentlemen invited him to join them. Although Darcy felt somewhat awkward at the thought, he acquiesced and sat at their table.

The conversation started on general topics of mutual interest, politics, new trends in farming, but then ventured on to the less comfortable. Lord Cunningham had never spoken to Darcy about the outcome of his interest in Lady Annette and so brought up the point. "Darcy, my son tells me that you went off and married a pretty country girl. Now I know you never asked for the honour of Annette's hand, but we all know, including Annette, that you were well on your way to doing so. I own that I was astonished when I heard about your engagement and subsequent hasty marriage. Tell me honestly, did you find yourself in a position of having to save her from an indiscreet moment of weakness?"

Darcy was nonplussed at such a question, from a lord no less. Not wanting to give offence but equally not wanting to give any more information than had already been revealed to Lord Wexley, Darcy simply stated, "Neither Mrs. Darcy nor I did anything for which we should feel ashamed. Unfortunately, a woman's virtue can decide her future, and if that virtue is brought into question, she is at risk of losing all hope of stability, both for herself and her family. Due to the situation, rumours began to spread that she had been alone with me over the course of an entire day. No one cared that I was physically incapable of causing her ruin; they just enjoyed destroying the reputation of a local gentleman's family. I could not in good conscience let that happen. I do not regret my decision to do what was right."

"You know you did not have to marry the girl. Robert here says that she is tolerable looking. You could have married her off to some farmer, setting him up nicely; then her family would have been saved and your own future salvaged as well."

Darcy's irritation was growing the longer he listened to the lord daring to suppose his way of handling the dilemma was superior to Darcy's own. "Any speculation on alternative solutions is a waste of time. Elizabeth is now my wife and I cannot feel remorse for honouring my duty to her. As I told Wexley, I deeply regret having hurt Lady Annette, if indeed that is the case. She is a beautiful and accomplished woman of untarnished character. She will have many suitors this Season, as she did last year."

"She wasted an entire year with you, and that's all you can say?" said the older man, obviously unhappy at the outcome.

"I will not defend my actions; I was honour-bound to Elizabeth. What's done is done." Darcy paused, looking at both men in the eye. "Now can we speak of something else?"

"Don't get all testy, Darcy. To show you we have no hard feelings, why don't you come to our place for dinner on Saturday instead of eating at the club? You and Wexley can catch up on old times. You were always friends, were you not?" As Darcy had no viable excuse to refuse, he accepted the invitation, then after a few moments more, excused himself attributing to fatigue.

That night Darcy considered his conversation with the earl and viscount. *Do I truly feel no remorse for marrying Elizabeth?* This past month had been the most difficult of his life, even more so than when his father died, leaving him as master of Pemberley and guardian of his then ten-year old sister. The difference was that when his father died, everyone had faith in him to meet the challenge. Yes, he mourned his father, but he had been trained all of his life for the eventuality of one day taking over his father's duties. He had felt insecure in many ways, but was able to prove to himself, his staff and his peers that he could perform.

But now as a husband, he felt the full weight of his inadequacies. Elizabeth seemed to fight him at every turn, and indeed Darcy did not meet his own expectations of what a good husband should be. He had learnt to respect women, to show them the courtesies and protection due the fairer sex and to be a gentleman at all times. Darcy failed at all of these. *How did I go astray to that extent in so short a time?* He began to understand why Elizabeth despised him. The same day he made marriage vows, he dishonoured her. He failed to show her love. Of course he did not love her, but he could have shown her love at some level, or at the very least, kindness. Elizabeth must have been terribly frightened that first night; she had nearly told him so, but he insisted on her welcoming him to her bed. Darcy's rationale for his expectations seemed so weak in hindsight. The memory of her weeping after he had departed troubled him, but he had soon forgotten, too busy anticipating their next encounter. *Was I really so callous? But that was not the only time. I became even more demanding. My God, at Longbourn I practically violated her – I forced myself on her. At the time I felt justified – she's my wife, and I thought she had given herself to another – the very worst of men. But there can be no grounds for my barbaric behaviour. She said she forgave me, but she did not mean it. Elizabeth felt obligated to accept my apology. I can't even say if I forgive myself. How could I expect her to forgive me?*

Then Darcy considered her treachery: Elizabeth welcomed Wickham into her life; she defended him. And he could not forget that she might have planned the whole scandal. If he were completely honest with himself as he sat reflecting, he would have discounted the idea, but Darcy was trying desperately to absolve himself of the overwhelming sense of guilt that had been increasing steadily each day.

Will Elizabeth ever welcome me? Darcy took this time to commit himself to refrain from coming to her room without her willing consent, but before the thought had even taken root, he began to doubt his ability to ultimately withstand the draw. The idea of employing a mistress unexpectedly returned. Other men had married into what more closely resembled a business arrangement, creating an heir and perhaps a couple of other children, then employing a professional courtesan to meet the high demands of a virile man. From what he gathered from peers who spoke too openly at Whites, wives rarely received their husbands gladly except on occasion – primarily for procreation – and were all too willing

316

to share him with a mistress. Darcy had tried to live a life of virtue to avoid the complications that came with a hired courtesan, but was he being fair to himself? Now that he was married, he had hoped that he would finally find satisfaction, but perhaps he had idealised a committed relationship.

Whatever his course, he must take this time away from Elizabeth to figure it out. Darcy did not know how long he would stay in town, but he determined not to return to Pemberley until he was ready to break down the walls of bitterness that had so easily divided him from his wife.

Saturday was several days away, so now he was committed to staying in town for at least another week for he could not travel on Sunday, and the safety of taking leave was weather-dependent. He would continue his visits with family, exercise at Angelo's, and evening meals at Whites.

ONE NIGHT DARCY was at his club and ran into Langston. They eventually joined a small group of gentlemen who were talking about a recently opened establishment that catered to the needs of men. Madame Karina's was located on St. James not four blocks from Whites. Darcy had never paid any attention to the lewd jokes and references in the past, but now found himself drawn in.

"Madame Karina, or so she calls herself, apparently has worked in the profession for years in Paris, but moved to London late last year to escape the war. Apparently, it wasn't good for business." The men laughed at the idea.

"I thought war would increase her business as men sought a way to escape the cruelties of life."

"Yes, but apparently, her business only catered to the elite, and they became unable to maintain her high standard of living."

"She brought a group of young, some very young, ladies with her, trained in their professional arts. She told me herself that whatever you want, she could provide, for the right price."

Langston then had his say, surprising Darcy, "Madam Karina knows her business, and she carefully screens her girls to make sure they stay clean; she only accepts clients through referrals to avoid the undesirables. But somehow she got the list of the members of Whites and will take anyone on that list. That's how she got started. Add to that, she is very discreet. She never uses your real name. Instead she assigns a different one, some quite amusing."

"You seem to know a lot, Langston," said one of the men.

The viscount smiled and said, "No more than half the other members here." They laughed. "We could all go there tonight, that is if any of you are man enough."

Darcy had never enjoyed such conversations and usually made his exit, but he had to admit, the thought had occurred to him more than once since arriving in town. He had heard that the French were adept at the art of lovemaking; Madame Karina's might be just what he needed. He was mulling this over in his head when several at his table stood up.

"Darcy, are you coming with us?" He stared at the man who asked, unsure of what to say. "Come on and join us. We will catch a hackney and will be back in a couple of hours."

Then Langston, entertained with the thought of Darcy playing along, said, "Your wife will never know. And maybe you will learn a thing or two you can share with her when you go back home. Come on. I know the perfect girl for you, and I'll let you have her." All of the men were standing there looking at him, encouraging him with their words and manner.

Possibly owing to the three drinks he had consumed and lack of nourishment to balance, and also perhaps due to his unsatisfying relationship with his wife, but most definitely due to a slip in judgement, Darcy stood.

The group of men left Whites and got into a couple of hackneys to travel the short distance to Madame Karina's, the freezing temperatures a stark contrast to the warmth found in the club. A few minutes later, they alighted at their destination, anxious to get inside.

During the short journey there, Darcy was telling himself why this was a good idea. His wife did not want him and most likely still would not when he got home. In fact, it could be months, if ever, before she welcomed him; and fearing his own impatience, using a courtesan could help stave off his own desire, with the hopes that he would avoid regrettably losing control with Elizabeth again. Many men of his rank and wealth used these services, even those whom he found worthy of merit and respect. Langston himself came often. Many single men even came to avoid a compromising situation with an innocent, which was a noble motivation. *Is it actually breaking marriage vows if you are simply gratifying a physical need, not establishing an on-going emotional and physical relationship?* Apparently this place is very discreet, not using actual names. Except for the men who were with him, no one would know, and they would not tell for they were just as guilty. *Guilty.* And the French were well trained in the art of copulation. He knew that he had limited experience himself. Maybe he could learn how to help Elizabeth enjoy their intimacies.

Darcy was a proficient at the art of persuasion and as such had admirably talked himself into accepting the enterprise as commendable. When they entered, Darcy looked around, curious to see what such an establishment offered. He was surprised to see a fashionable looking home not unlike his own. There were men dressed in the attire of footmen stationed in several locations within his view, as one might see at any fashionable home, taking coats and hats. Their hostess, for that is what she called herself, came up to make the introductions. Recognising Langston as well as one of the other men, she smiled. Madame Karina wore a diaphanous dress with a plunging décolletage, more suited for sleeping than public consumption.

"Madame Karina, you are looking quite lovely this evening," Langston said, while kissing her hand. "As you see, I have brought several friends with me each anxious to meet a lovely paramour. I can vouch for all of them."

She looked over each of them, taking in each man's fine lines. The scrutiny did its work as each man, including Darcy, began to anticipate the entertainment to come. "If you will follow me, I will guide you to your rooms." Darcy noticed Langston whispering something into their hostess's ear. She looked back and caught Darcy's eye and raised her eyebrow in amusement. Madame brought all of the men to a holding room where they were assigned names, written on the back of a card for privacy, and given room numbers along with a key to the corresponding room. She provided each of them with their beverage of choice and then began leading the men, one by one, to their destinations.

As it would happen, Darcy was the final man left; he looked at his card. On one side, embossed in gold lettering, was the address along with Madame Karina's name, but no identification as to the actual type of business was noted. On the reverse side he saw his assigned name to be Adonis, which caused him to chuckle; he wondered if everyone was given mythical names designed to further entice. Since arriving, his conscience that had been his guide so many times in his life began reasserting itself. *Guilty* kept repeating itself in his mind. The thought of wilfully engaging in an activity that brought him into a state of guilt began to plague him. As he sat there waiting for Madame to return for him, he began to feel the full weight of his perfidy. Could he ever hope to achieve a state of marital harmony if he were to engage in such unfaithfulness, for he now understood that it would indeed be adultery, and so early in his marriage, just because things are difficult? He knew that one encounter would open the door for many others. But then again, his wife despised him. What further harm could be done to his marriage?

The door opened and Madame Karina walked over to him. "I saved the best for last." Then she took his drink from his hand. "Monsieur, Adonis," said she with a sly smile, "your friend spécialement requested Aphrodite to serve you, and I know you will be delighted with her performance, non?"

What madness is this? I must stop! "Madame Karina, I do not doubt her many talents, but I am not altogether certain that I should stay."

"Non? I will take you to Aphrodite. Peut être she can change your mind." She then opened the door and took Darcy's arm, guiding him to the farthest door. He could hear passion as it played out in the rooms along the way. This, Monsieur, is your chamber. While gazing into his eyes, Madame Karina took the key from Darcy, caressed his hand and unlocked the door. When she opened it, he looked inside, curious, but unwilling to enter. *Why do I not just leave?* The inner turmoil in his being overwhelmed him.

He stepped to the doorway and there standing before him, was a woman, no a girl, perhaps Georgiana's age or a little older, with long chestnut locks and green eyes, wearing less even than Madame Karina. She stared at him and smiled seductively while holding out her hand. *My God! She looks like Elizabeth! — A younger Elizabeth, but without the innocence and not as beautiful, for she is only a child. What was Langston thinking to suggest this girl?*

He stared at her for an unknown length of time as he battled within. He could stay and pretend she was his Elizabeth – the task would not be too difficult – or he could leave and remain faithful to his wife. After a few moments of deliberation, he determined his course.

"I apologise for any inconvenience that I have caused, and I am happy to pay for my time, but I cannot in good conscience remain. I really must take my leave."

"Mais, Monsieur, s'il vous plait. Do not go. You are unhappy with Aphrodite? She walked up not six inches from him and placed her hands on his chest. "Je peux serve you myself." She nodded for the girl to go out the servants' entrance as she led him into the room. Madame then turned and locked the door behind them.

Darcy was now breathing in quick short breaths. His body was yearning for more, but his conscience was urging him to leave. *Oh, God, help me!*

Madame Karina made quick work of his cravat, with a proficiency seldom seen with even the most skilled valet. She then began to remove his topcoat while coming even closer to place succulent kisses upon his neck and chest. Darcy had not noticed that she had already unbuttoned half of his vest, when he recalled the appearance of the young girl, the one who resembled Elizabeth. *I will never be able to face Elizabeth if I go through with this! I hate deceit, but then if I were to confess, how could she ever forgive me?*

He pulled away, "No, stop, please." He was breathing hard, "I must go."

She began untying the bow that seemed to be the only thing holding her own dress together.

"Please Madame, I must leave this place!" He reached for the door, but it was locked. *Damn!* He then turned back around just in time to see the dress flow to the floor. He could not help but look at her, mesmerised by her unabashed nudity and arresting curves, but then his mind conveniently remembered Elizabeth's body, of which he had seen so little; but his wife's was untouched, pure. No eyes had ever seen her in this way. Darcy could not at this moment consider the possibility of Wickham's having done so. Instead, he was reminded either by his memory – or by God himself – that he was destined for one woman and she was destined for him, for better or worse. He forced himself to turn and quickly found the key on the floor and unlocked the door. He then removed the agreed upon amount from his billfold and dropped it to the floor as he grabbed his clothes and made his escape. He did not look back, but went straight down the stairs.

The footmen looked at him and walked forward to stop him. Darcy suspected correctly that their job was to protect the employees and to make sure everyone paid up. "I have decided to leave. I can assure you that Madame Karina has been paid. Please, my coat and hat." One of the men retrieved his garments and handed it to him, letting him go with no further questions, which threw Darcy off guard. He could not imagine why they believed him without verifying his claim.

Rather than use one of the hackneys stationed outside waiting for the customers, Darcy walked back to Whites, the cold air helping his physical recovery, as he attempted to reassemble his clothing. He went inside to warm up before calling his carriage for home. This night had been like a nightmare for him, unlike his recurring dreams that included his beautiful wife in her wet chemise. *How could I have let this go so far? God help me.*

Darcy arrived at home and went straight to his chamber, calling for his valet along the way. Nelson raised an appraising brow upon first seeing his master's dishevelled appearance but then, as expected, promptly got to work. Darcy remained in quiet contemplation while his man skilfully prepared him for bed. Once Nelson had left and he was alone, he sat in his chair in front of the fireplace staring at the flames. As he finally let his emotions and his feelings come to the surface, Darcy did something he had not done since his dear mother died. He began to cry; gentle tears falling down his cheeks at first, but as his thoughts wandered, Darcy began to weep heavy tears in anguish of what he had become. He was a beast! Elizabeth had it right.

I have always thought that if anyone had reason for confidence, I had more: my lineage, impeccable – born a Darcy, a family that has thrived in England since the Norman Dynasty, my mother, from a noble family of means – a Cambridge graduate, a gentleman, as to integrity, blameless. Under my rule, Pemberley has prospered beyond any point in its history; every decision I have made has affected hundreds of livelihoods for the good. I have been a most conscientious brother, sacrificing so much time for Georgiana's benefit. And then I did what I thought to be most honourable: I gave up my plans for marriage to save Elizabeth and her family from ruin.

But what true good has come from me? Nothing. I am a beast, just as Elizabeth said, no better than Wickham! Oh yes, I married Elizabeth, but look what I've done to her! She doesn't smile or laugh anymore; she's grown thin and gaunt at my hands! And did I marry her to save her and her family, as I have held to so tenuously, or was it the fact that I couldn't get the look of her and that damn wet chemise out of my head? And by marrying her, I have hurt Georgiana! Can she ever come to accept Elizabeth, or will we always have my marriage come between us? Oh, yes, I have plenty of wealth, but for what purpose? So I can get into Madame Karina's and buy a whore? My education has little value, except to show my famed superiority. My parents would be ashamed of me. My pride will be my albatross, always showing me my failings. Wretched man that I am! Who will deliver me from this shame?

The answer came to him. Who had saved him this evening at the brothel? On whom did he finally call?

Oh, God, please help me to be the husband, brother and master you would have me be. Have mercy on me and protect me from such horrid musings that have plagued me! Be my guide, I beg you. Then Darcy fell to his knees, hands in fists on his brow, and sobbed as a child. He lamented how he had failed as husband, brother and man. He had been given good principles but had followed them in conceit. It was as though his eyes had opened for the first time to see how completely wretched he really was. Everything that had bolstered his pride had been given to him. In what could he truly boast?

When Darcy finally stood, he saw his reflection in the mirror before him. As with new eyes, he observed the man staring back at him, and possibly for the first time in his life, Darcy perceived himself as he actually was. On this night, the ugliness of his soul had been laid bare before him. He was reminded of Lady Susan. Since Elizabeth had exposed the woman's constant self-admiration in the looking glass, he could not fathom what Susan beheld that was attractive to look upon. Now he realised that he too had erroneously seen himself without fault, just as Susan had regarded her own appearance – that all along the truth had remained hidden from his eyes. But to his advantage, Darcy now viewed himself as his Maker did and was thankful, for what hope did he have for improvement without true understanding? For the first time he felt his own weaknesses, which comfortingly brought him solace rather than grief.

Darcy spent many hours that night reviewing his behaviour when he was with Elizabeth, taking mental note of all of his misdeeds, slights and criticisms that might have hurt her or led to her own failings or consortium with Wickham. He had been angry with Elizabeth, but Wickham was right, Darcy had openly despised her. Was it any wonder if she had been inclined towards a man who spoke pretty words? She is a vulnerable woman; of course she would yield to Wickham.

When he returned to Pemberley, Darcy resolved to show kindness to Elizabeth and to try to win her favour. He did not love her and was not even sure that could be possible, but he could respect her, cherish her, and show acts of love with the goal of mutual regard. He saw that Elizabeth did indeed have many good qualities to bring to the marriage and he would try to recognise them and provide encouragement. After a long night of contemplation and introspection, he fell into a peaceful slumber.

DARCY ENJOYED EXERCISE AT ANGELO'S AS BEFORE, but ended the day at Lord Cunningham's home rather than Whites. As expected, Lady Annette was in attendance for she served as hostess since her mother had been deceased the past three years. Darcy had been invited to dine at the home on several occasions over the previous year, but in the past he had always come with the goal of learning more about the daughter with the expectation of one day offering for her. Now, he was not sure why he had come, except that refusing would have added further insult to a family whom Darcy had always respected.

When Darcy was shown into the drawing room, Lady Annette, Lord Wexley and Lord Cunningham greeted him with proper civility. Wexley offered him some wine as they waited for their other guests. He informed Darcy that they had also invited Langston and Lady Susan who likewise were close acquaintances and had joined them on several occasions over the past year.

While they waited for the Fitzwilliams, Darcy noticed that Lady Annette must have taken extra care in preparing for the evening, considering how small the party was to be. Her complicated coiffure was suited to attract a man. Long curls extended to the side of her neck enticing a man to touch them. Her cheeks were heightened by colour, likely owing to the discomfort of having her former suitor as a guest. Darcy wondered what she must have thought when told of his invitation. Although they had seen one another since his marriage, the occasion ended in discomfort for both. Lady Annette wore a strand of diamonds with a large teardrop stone, which when paired with the lovely light blue gown boasting a deep-cut décolletage, invited inspection. Her ensemble was obviously designed to attract, as he supposed it always had been in the past. Apparently the trick had worked well for him, for he remembered being smitten by her beauty and assets.

The foursome made light conversation, Lady Annette acting as the perfect hostess, confirming much of what the men said to be true and smiling prettily.

Langston and Lady Susan arrived about a quarter-hour after him. "Darcy, how nice to see you again." said his cousin as he walked over to shake his hand. Darcy looked at him, ashamed of the events from just a few days before. "Don't worry, my lips are sealed," he added in a susurration.

Susan then joined her husband, curtseying to Darcy after having seen to her hosts. "Darcy, so nice to see you," said she looking around, "and where is Mrs. Darcy? Don't tell us you've already tired of her," she continued, sniggering at her jest.

"Not at all. Elizabeth is at Pemberley. I came in town for business and saw no need to uproot her just as she had arrived."

"But you were just here. What business could you have?"

Darcy despised anyone getting into his own concerns, but he had to remember where he was and that the annoying woman was family. "Business that could not be delayed." Then turning to Langston, he said, "I hear James has been tied up with work. Have you had a chance to see him?" and the subject was changed for the moment.

Lady Susan and Lady Annette separated from the men as they spoke of the ball and other recent social engagements. Darcy was listening to the men drivel on about the war with France, his only interest at the time concerning Colonel Fitzwilliam's involvement while in the war office. While the men spoke, Darcy observed how well Lady Susan got along with Lady Annette. They seemed to be in a tête-a-tête of mutual interest. He saw Lady Annette look over to him, then noticing his interest, smile and whisper something to her companion. He had the distinct feeling that their conversation was at his expense. He could not know that the two were considering their shared aversion to Darcy's own wife. Lady Susan had marked her husband's poorly concealed admiration for Elizabeth's figure, and Lady Annette could not properly be blamed for her petty jealousy over Elizabeth's winning the hand of Mr. Darcy, her dislike fuelled by the ungracious reports from her friend.

Dinner was called, and to Darcy's surprise, Lady Annette latched onto his arm to be escorted to the dining-parlour. Darcy found that his hostess had placed him to her right with Langston to her left and next to his wife. The conversation flowed around him, and he even joined in occasionally. He acknowledged that this was not unlike many other evenings spent in the present company and began to suspect the arrangements were by design. During the beginning of the meal, Lady Annette gave him the same unguarded attentions she always had. Her behaviour was without reproof; however, she continued to look at him with the same scrutiny that when single had spurred him on, but while married made him uncomfortable. Her father and brother did not seem to notice, so Darcy began to suspect that maybe he was imagining her covert flirtations. He was interrupted from these musings by Lady Annette's saying, "Darcy, how long will you be staying in town?"

"My plans are not fixed."

"Then you will have to come back to visit us." Darcy could not understand why she would want such a thing. This evening had so far been most uncomfortable. He gave her a small smile and took a sip of wine. Then having his attention, she began talking about the theatre. He mentioned the two shows he and Elizabeth had recently attended and asked if she too had seen them and what her impressions had been. The conversation continued, Lady Annette finding no reason to contradict and saying all the words expected, designed to make a man feel superior. He found the whole exchange rather dull.

Then he contentedly recalled the meals taken with Elizabeth. Darcy found his wife's ideas challenging and even exhilarating. Elizabeth rarely agreed with him, and sometimes even seemed to contradict him just to vex him, but then her eyebrow would shoot up with that impish smile, and he would know of her little treachery. He smiled to himself. Dinner had never been dull with Elizabeth, not even from the time prior to their formal meeting, if a collision in the woods could be called formal. He remembered thinking at the time that Elizabeth was uncouth and impertinent. That sentiment grew throughout their engagement; however, somewhere along the way, he had begun to enjoy her banter. It was not until this moment that he comprehended his growing admiration for his wife's eccentricities. As Lady Annette continued on in her sedate and amenable fashion, Darcy's mind began to wander towards conversations he and his wife had enjoyed about the theatre, books, politics, a vase. Elizabeth had a way of making any subject amusing or provocative. *How have I missed her value as a companion these past two months?* Darcy had the dawning of understanding that perhaps he was not seeing only himself anew, but also his wife.

He was interrupted in his reverie by Lady Annette's saying, "Would you not agree, Darcy?" He looked sharply to her, obviously having wandered from the conversation. She leaned forward, showing herself to greatest advantage and whispered, "Where have you been, sir? We were asking you about the partridges."

Embarrassed to be found daydreaming and even more so, having her cleavage not a foot from him, he said, "This is a fine meal, thank you."

Lady Annette leaned in even closer, pretentiously suspecting that his daydreams pertained to herself. "Save room for dessert."

Darcy was taken aback. *She is flirting with me! I am a married man, and she a maiden!* It was true, he found her very alluring. The ensemble she wore had done its job. Like any other man, he found her assets to be pleasing, but he was married and no longer available to establish an alliance. What could she mean by tempting him in this way? Darcy then continued his reflections about Elizabeth as compared to his current hostess. Lady Annette was beautiful, fashionable, accomplished and steeped in connections, but he now found her dull, conniving and inappropriately tempting for a lady. He had first seen signs of this New Year's Eve, but his opinion was now decided, so he did his best to follow his strategy at the ball, donning a coldness of manner.

The two women left the men to their cigars and brandy when the meal concluded and the men continued their previous discussion on the war. Before long Langston decided to change the conversation. "Susan and I have been very concerned about you since the ball."

"You have me at a disadvantage," responded Darcy.

"Your wife, Darcy, you must have seen her indulging in wanton behaviour. Why she even toyed with me while we were dancing. How can you bear it? If my wife behaved so shamelessly, I would leave her at my country estate as well," he said with a chuckle.

Darcy, surprised at the topic at hand, could not help but be amused by the thought of Lady Susan flirting with anyone aside from the looking glass. He considered how easily Langston was able to go from his licentious behaviour and encouraging the same in him the other night to now accusing his Elizabeth of no worse, and in an uncomfortably public manner at that. He meant to put this line of questioning to rest.

"I saw my wife dancing with many men. Not unusual for a ball, especially one designed to introduce her. I admit I even encouraged her to do so, for she enjoys dancing more than I."

"Dancing, yes, but she was flirting most shamelessly. You know she was."

Darcy's ire was increasing, but he continued with his mask of reserve. This sounded nothing like his Elizabeth. How dare he misrepresent her? Then it occurred to him that he himself had accused her of the same thing, and to her face no less. He regretted again his shameful conduct after the ball and his shameful behaviour at Madame Karina's. "You are speaking about my wife. Elizabeth is a lively woman. Some may misinterpret her exuberance, but I saw nothing outside of the ordinary. If you have something more accusatory to say, please save it for a time that we might speak in private."

But Langston was apparently enjoying himself. "We are all friends here, at least we used to be. And everyone knows how she came to be Mrs. Darcy. You just don't want to admit your weaknesses." Darcy suspected he was speaking as much about the courtesan as his wife.

"Langston, I could call you out for your remarks about Elizabeth."

"But you won't because you know there is some truth to it." Darcy's mind's eye immediately and treacherously went back to the cabin, seeing her in her wet chemise. "Ah, I can tell I am right!"

"I stand by the truth that I have already shared. However, regardless of how it came about, she is my wife now, and I will not have you speak of her in such a derogatory fashion." Darcy glanced to his hosts who listened most patiently, and then he continued, "I thought you had accepted Elizabeth. You were certainly very gracious at the theatre and at the ball, showing public approval."

"Of course, I do accept her, for your sake, Darcy. And I will continue to show her my support. She can't help that she is a most alluring woman and likely still enjoys the games women play to attract a man. In time she will give you all of her attention. I just don't want to see you deceived by her. She is little different than most other beautiful woman from her same sphere." After a pause, Langston continued, "I suspected that you had come to the same conclusion. And now to show you my continued support, I would like to invite myself to Pemberley sometime in the next two months in order to become better acquainted; that is if it is agreeable to you. Perhaps the more I get to know your wife, the more likely I will approve of her."

Darcy's host finally found his tongue and a smirk to match. "Well, this has certainly been entertaining, but we mustn't tarry; the ladies will be anxious for us to join them." Then he stood, the others following.

After the men entered the drawing room, the ladies took turns performing upon the pianoforte. Both were accomplished at the instrument and both sang remarkably well; however, Darcy now found their performances wanting. Although perhaps better musicians than Elizabeth, neither played with her passion and spirit, and they quickly became no more than background music to his inner thoughts. Not for the first time that evening did Darcy compare his wife to these two ladies and even at times the gentlemen. Elizabeth's conversation, talent, intelligence, and even beauty, if he were completely honest, exceeded that of his company. Add to that, she was humble and sincere. Both Lady Annette and Lady Susan took great stock in their beauty, the real and imagined. Elizabeth never seemed to perceive her own charms, except perhaps in the cabin, but then had she actually used her charms, or was it in his imagination, giving her the blame for his own vulnerabilities?

Darcy was ready to leave. Although enlightening in so many ways, he also found the company tedious and their presence a high price to pay. He decided it was time to go home, to Pemberley, to Elizabeth.

Amazing Grace, how sweet the sound, That saved a wretch like me.
I once was lost but now am found, Was blind but now I see.
Isaac Newton
Amazing Grace

Chapter Sixteen

We can't command our love, but we can our actions.
Arthur Conan Doyle
Sherlock Holmes: Adventure Detective, Book Four

After four days of travelling in dreary, slushy conditions, Darcy finally arrived at Pemberley apprehensive yet eager to begin his marriage fresh. He knew that things would be difficult, but he was hopeful for their future together. While on the arduous journey, Darcy developed a strategy for how he could play his part in the reconciliation. He knew that he could not continue on as things had been and hoped that Elizabeth was equally motivated.

Darcy was greeted by his butler, Peters. "Welcome home, sir. I hope your journey was satisfactory. The weather here has been quite erratic."

"Thank you. I am thankful we arrived when we did. It looks like rain is on the way. While you are here, could you tell me where I might find my wife?"

"I believe she is making a call to one of your tenants."

Darcy could not hide his shocked expression. "How long has she been gone?"

"No more than two hours. Mrs. Reynolds has all of the details."

"Could you summon her please? She will find me in my study," Darcy said as he turned to leave.

A few moments later, Mrs. Reynolds met him with a sincere welcome. "Mr. Darcy, I am glad you have returned. You were missed."

His eyebrows shot up. *Could she have meant Elizabeth missed me? But no, that cannot be.* "Thank you. Mrs. Reynolds, can you tell me about my wife's visit with a tenant farmer? Who is she seeing?"

Mrs. Reynolds spent the next few minutes informing Mr. Darcy of the family's problem and Elizabeth's desire to handle it herself. She explained that Elizabeth had taken a footman and Mrs. Carpenter.

Darcy considered going after her. The storm could arrive at any minute.

"Sir, what has you worried?"

He was shaken out of his reverie. "What? Oh, it is just that we noticed a storm approaching that should soon arrive. I think I will go retrieve her myself."

"She is with Clark and Hopkins as the driver. I am certain they would bring her home should they suspect any danger." She hesitated before saying more, but then continued on. "I do not think she is the kind of woman who would appreciate such attentions. Do you, sir?"

He smiled. "I suppose you are right." He was still concerned but trusted his staff to keep her safe. "I will go up and change and get refreshed. If she returns, will you send me a message?" At her agreement, he continued, "If she is not back within the hour, I will go myself."

She smiled at his concern. *He must care for her after all.*

She was almost out of the door when he said, "And can you have my steward summoned as well?"

While still upstairs he received word of his steward's arrival and Elizabeth's return. He went to his study first to receive Stephens for a quick meeting. He wanted to ensure that the man was able to make it back home before the storm hit. Entering at the same time, his steward welcomed his employer home again. "Darcy, I just met with your new wife."

"You met with Mrs. Darcy? Just now?"

"Yes, she gave me a task that she wished to keep between the two of us, but I thought you should know." At Darcy's raised brow, he continued. "She has set up a plan that would provide a maid for the Smithtons, a daughter of one of our other tenants. She is periodically employed here during the summer months and Mrs. Darcy requested that I pay the girl using her own pin money." Darcy started to speak, but the man raised his hand to offset him. "I know. I told her we have an account for such things, but she insisted that since it was her idea and her plan, that she should pay for it. I agreed with her because I know my place, but I thought you should be aware."

"Thank you, Stephens. You were right to tell me, and I agree. Use the fund designed for that, and I will inform Mrs. Darcy myself. Also, before you leave, I have a few things to speak with you about. But I hope to get you out of here ahead of the storm."

"Yes, it has already begun to rain and the thunder continues to get louder, but there is one more thing I need to tell you about your wife."

"Oh?"

"Yes, sir. Shortly after your leaving Pemberley, your wife asked me to begin sending a portion of her monthly pin allotment to a bank account in town. She would give me no details about the account or whose name it was under; she just asked that I keep the knowledge of the transaction to myself. I could not in good conscience keep it from you, though. I went ahead and sent the first payment as she requested and was going to send you a letter with the details, so you could investigate, but decided against the idea. Since it is her money, I did as she wished, but now that you are here, I thought it best you knew."

Darcy sat in contemplation. *Who could Elizabeth be sending money to? Could Wickham have somehow gotten her to set up some account for him?* "How much is she putting away?"

"Fifty pounds per month."

"Fifty pounds? That's more than half of her allowance!" Darcy thought it best to keep his thoughts and feelings of the matter to himself, and so checked his features. "Thank you, Stephens. You did right to tell me." Then he changed the subject saying, "Let us finish our business, so you can get back home." Within a few minutes, Stephens was able to leave, and then Darcy headed to his mother's former study, where he expected to find Elizabeth. The thought of her putting aside this large amount of money would plague him off and on for the next few months as he considered who might be the beneficiary of her contributions. He wanted to trust her, for there was no other way for them to have a successful marriage, but how could he with secrets between them? Maybe she would share her intentions with him. It was probably best to await her enlightenment on this endeavour, at least for now.

Darcy was walking towards the door to the mistress's study when it opened abruptly. Elizabeth and her former maid came out smiling and holding each other's hands, as if in consortium. She obviously had not seen him; however, upon looking up, she stopped suddenly, eyes like saucers. "Hello, Elizabeth."

She recollected herself and took a quick curtsey. "Mr. Darcy, I was unaware of your arrival. I… I… would have… greeted you had I known, of course," she stammered while looking anywhere but at him.

"Do not be uneasy. I only arrived an hour ago and have since been cleaning up and meeting briefly with my steward." At this, she looked up to him with concern that changed to vexation.

"I see." Laura then squeezed Elizabeth's hands and quietly departed, noting Mr. Darcy's glance her way and obvious desire for privacy. Elizabeth urged her to stay with her quick glance, but Laura wisely felt the couple needed some time alone; and nevertheless, she could not possibly disregard her master's wishes.

Elizabeth stood there appearing uncharacteristically nervous, so Darcy took the lead. "May we go into your study?"

She then turned and walked into her room, finding her mettle along the way. When they were both inside, she walked to her desk, the one her husband's mother previously used, and sat down. Elizabeth was trying to keep calm in response to the unexpected arrival of her husband. Darcy sat nearby. Neither spoke for some time, which just increased the tension that had seeped into the room so recently full of cheer.

Darcy took the initiative. "I see you have had a busy day." Elizabeth looked up, content to remain quiet. "You have already met some of my tenants, I gather." Silence. He breathed in deeply and after releasing the breath, he ventured on. "Elizabeth, Stephens informed me of your wish to help the Smithtons."

"Yes."

"I am sure he told you that we have a fund designed to take care of these types of circumstances. There is no need for you to use your pin money in such cases."

"I wanted to use my own funds."

"I understand that you wanted to help, which is commendable, but you might not have been aware of the system we have in place to do just that. I have ensured that the girl's payment not be taken from your account, so there is no further need to concern yourself."

Elizabeth's eyes flashed in anger. "Am I to understand that at Pemberley the mistress of the estate has no authority to make decisions as I have done?"

"No, of course that's not what I am saying at all."

"Are you certain? Because you have taken it upon yourself to change a course of action that I have already deemed appropriate. Will you always follow in my tracks making sure that I don't embarrass you with a poorly planned response?"

"That is not what has happened here. You will learn with time the systems we already have in place. I recognise that you are new and cannot possibly be aware of how we do things at Pemberley. I wish you would do the same, and stop accusing me of some pernicious intent."

Elizabeth was annoyed with Mr. Darcy, perhaps due to their former disputes, but she was also troubled with her own irrational response. She was a sensible person and saw the justification behind his words, but she found his interference to be intrusive. Yet, this was his home, not hers. She should just let him have his way and be done with it, but she felt like he was attacking her abilities. If she were honest, she would admit that she was doubting herself and likely thought the same of Mr. Darcy based on her own insecurities.

Elizabeth sat in intense concentration as she attempted to keep calm. The clock ticked in the background as each sat waiting for something to occur to disrupt the continued tension.

Darcy stood and said, "I did not mean to offend you, if that is what has happened. I simply wanted to help." Elizabeth nodded quickly and looked away. "It will be time to dress for dinner soon. I would like for you to join me." He would have added, "if that is agreeable to you," but he was certain it would not be, so he left it at that. "I will see you soon then?" She nodded, and he departed.

After Darcy had left, Elizabeth let her emotions run their course from relief that their marriage perhaps still had hope, to disappointment that she now had to consider Mr. Darcy in her daily plans, to vexation for his intrusion into her life. The past month had been full of fond moments and the establishment of new and cherished relationships. She could have easily forgotten the man who owned it all, who indeed made her existence there possible, but now he was back, reminding her again that her life was not the idyllic one she had known recently but the one that brought her grief. Elizabeth began to worry anew that he might come to her that evening. It had been nearly five weeks since he last took his pleasure, and he likely would not wait any longer. She began to fidget with her skirt as her anxiety increased once again at the thought.

Then a dawning of understanding began to intrude upon her. Elizabeth contemplated how long it had been since he had left and realised that she had not had her courses since before then. She had noticed previously that she was late in her timing, but dismissed any speculation she might have, owing to the emotional turmoil she had experienced when she was last due. This had happened in the past, so this was a natural assumption, but now that another month had passed, she could no longer continue to ignore the idea that she might be with child. Elizabeth was an intelligent and astute woman, but sorely lacking in the education that would be useful to navigate such mystical waters. Her mother never actually told her how to know if she were pregnant nor the effect it would have on her courses. Her body had demonstrated no noticeable changes. *Could it be possible?*

Upon speculation, Elizabeth could not decide if this would bring her joy or worry. Her husband would no doubt desire an heir. Indeed for many men that was the sole reason to wed, but he did not love her and very likely never would. Darcy had been gone a month with no letter, no explanation. Did this not portend his complete loss of any regard that he might have developed over the first six weeks of their marriage? Elizabeth decided to dwell on this no more, as she had no proof of such a condition, and speculation could bring no relief to her questions.

After Darcy left his wife's study – the room he had seen so little of these past ten years – he returned to his own. He was reminded why he found her so bothersome at times. Why could she not be like any other rational wife? She should have accepted the direction of his steward, and that would have been the end of it. He could have walked in there and told her how proud he was of the actions she had taken while he was away. Truly, he was shocked that Elizabeth had taken initiative in that manner. He could not have foreseen her gumption. Then it struck Darcy. *Of course! I never once gave her any sign of approval except for a cursory mention of her helping being commendable or something like that. She must have taken my words as censure.* Darcy's ire turned to himself. *Again, I find myself unprepared to manage the complexities of matrimony. I promise, Elizabeth, I will try to do better.*

Then the remembrance of his steward's intelligence about his wife's financial dealings intruded upon him. He decided to get the account information from his steward and then contact his solicitor in London to look into the matter. Until he received any confirmation or proof against his fears, he would dwell on it no more. Surely such musings could not help them resolve their differences.

DARCY HAD INTENDED that he would outline to Elizabeth his plan for them, but then began to think better of it. *What if she thinks I am trying to direct her, or worse, what if she is offended? I cannot always predict how she will respond.* He finally decided to follow his original strategy and adjust his execution as needed. He arrived at her room, through their shared sitting room as usual and at the appointed time, which was an hour earlier than when in London. Elizabeth was dressed in a particularly modest creation, purchased while in town, but by her design. She looked very becoming in a simple and innocent way. The point was clear, and he could not say he disapproved. *Best that she dress this way everyday.*

"You look lovely, Elizabeth."

She regarded him in question. *Is he mocking me for my choice in gowns? Stop it, Lizzy. Just say, "thank you."* "Thank you."

He noticed that she wore no necklace nor did she wear her engagement ring. In retrospection, he had not seen her wear the necklace that he had presented to her at Christmas since the day before the ball. Elizabeth had been able to communicate very clearly in these simple ways her feelings about their relationship. At least she still wore the wedding band, if not the engagement ring, but then he traitorously wondered if she might have given the costly jewellery to Wickham. *Stop accusing her of treachery at every turn!*

Walking with her and sitting with her at dinner gave Darcy the opportunity to explore other aspects of her bearing that he had missed earlier. *Her colour has returned, and she no longer looks to be sleep-deprived as had perpetually been the case. Elizabeth may even have gained a little weight back as she now better fills out her gown, but this could be due to the different style of her dress.* If he had begun to think her lovely before, he now saw that she was even more so. *How could I have thought she was barely tolerable?* Then he remembered more than once since their engagement her reference to that very ill judged comment. Perhaps it bothered her more than she had let on that evening. *I must make a point to express my appreciation of her beauty.*

The dinner conversation was stilted, with each participant unsure of how to begin or knowing which subjects were best left unexplored; however, Darcy, being curious about Elizabeth's other activities while he was gone, decided to introduce the topic of her explorations, and so began, "Which aspects of Pemberley have you become acquainted?"

"All of the ones of which I am aware."

His eyebrows went up in unfeigned curiosity. "Do share."

She went on to tell him of her now familiarity with each part of the house, mentioning her favourite rooms or pictures along the way. Many of the rooms and passageways were closed off due to the time of year and the difficulty heating them, but when walking, this was no deterrent; Elizabeth simply planned her walks at the time of day allowing for the most light. Initially she had employed the use of a footman to make sure she did not get lost; however, she had long since become a proficient and now speculated that she knew her way around better than many servants.

When the weather was fine, she made her explorations on the grounds of the estate. Clark was the footman most likely to head out with her, and they became fast friends. Most women would have preferred her escort be relegated to somewhere in the distance, but Elizabeth enjoyed his conversation and he hers. And although walking was not usually considered sufficient exercise for a man, especially a footman, Clark could not agree. A typical outing took at least an hour and sometimes two to three if the weather was especially fine; thus in less than a month Elizabeth had developed a sense of belonging to her environment and a fast friendship with more than one servant.

Elizabeth elaborated little to her husband and kept her reserve in check. As she was beginning to feel self-conscious about her descriptions, especially knowing her husband's censure of such activities, Elizabeth changed the subject, asking him about his time away.

Darcy provided short answers limiting his comments to his own exercise and visits with his family. Elizabeth suspected there was more to his time in London than fencing and Georgiana, but she was happy to speak of something other than his true reason for travelling there.

When they had completed their meal, Darcy dismissed the servants in order to have some privacy. "Elizabeth, I am pleased that you have taken the time to get to know your new home." He noticed that she seemed to relax somewhat. Laughing lightly, he said, "Why do you look so relieved? Of course I would want you to become familiar with your home. Based on your narrative, you seem to be quite the proficient. Another hidden accomplishment?" he said smiling, remembering their previous banter.

"What was it that you wanted to speak with me about, sir?"

Darcy looked down to his hands, then back up to her eyes before answering, "I have been thinking about how we should proceed. I, well… I think you would agree that we cannot continue on as we have been."

Elizabeth did not respond; she was too apprehensive about what he would have to say.

"I have decided that while you continue with your established routine, and I get back to my own, that we will devote time everyday taking meals in each other's company, and also spending the evenings together in some amusement as we have done on occasion in the past."

"But, what if I choose not to eat or want to eat in my room, alone?" Her voice increased in tone and strength as she asked her simple question.

"Elizabeth, I understand that you might not want to do some things that I ask of you, but if you remember, you promised to obey, and in this I must insist."

She tossed her serviette upon the table and stood up, not liking to be forced into his society and desirous to be alone.

"And no leaving the meal early."

"Why are you doing this? I know you don't enjoy my company. It's not my *companionship* that you have appreciated in the past."

Darcy wanted to retort, but held his tongue. She was expressing her honest feelings, and he deserved whatever she threw at him. Instead he said, "Elizabeth, the past three months have brought each of us frustration and despair. Despite my initial doubts as to your motive, I now have to believe that neither of us asked for this marriage, but at the same time, neither wishes to just give up. I cannot, and will not, live a life at enmity with my wife. We both have issues of trust and resentment of which we need to let go if we are to ever find peace. I don't know any other way to get past our conflicts unless we spend time listening to the other and getting to know one another. As the season continues on, we will both find our days filled with activity, but we can still sit together at mealtimes to find some kind of mutual understanding."

Elizabeth had no immediate response as she considered his words. She disliked the man and found his company aggravating. He seemed to vex her at every turn. However, she agreed that living along side a man whom she could not respect nor like would be an unbearable punishment.

"Elizabeth, many marriages begin as ours has – two people, with no true affection or devotion, who begin a union for familial or financial obligations – but find mutual esteem and fondness. Can we not strive for such a life?"

Elizabeth had remained quiet throughout, thinking of what she had wanted her whole life compared to what she now had, so in a small voice meant for herself alone but spoken aloud, said, "But I had always hoped to marry for love." Tears unbidden sprang to her eyes as she lifted the serviette to hide her weakness.

"And I, to fulfil my duty as a Darcy."

She looked up to him and nodded. "I will try to be open, but on one condition."

"Yes."

"Yes? Is that an answer or a question?"

"An answer."

"You know not of what I ask though."

"I believe I do. I promise to you now that I will wait for you."

"Wait for me?" She blushed as she began to fidget with her serviette. "What? Um ... You must be clearer."

"Elizabeth, I realise now that I have treated you with unmitigated disrespect, behaving dishonourably and in every way contrary to how I was taught. I am truly ashamed of myself. I do not understand my own actions, for I have not done what I want, but I have done the very thing I hate." He looked away. Admitting such failure was difficult for this proud man. "I want to amend our marriage. I hope to wait until you are ready to begin our physical relationship anew."

"You *hope*? What does that mean?"

"I say 'hope' because I acknowledge that I am trusting that you will one day be ready for me, but that depends upon you. I cannot deny that I need an heir, and that my expectation, of course, is that my heir will come through our marriage. But in order for that to occur, we must one day come together as one." Here he looked away, surprised at his own embarrassment. "And I also hope that you will want me to come to you, and often."

Elizabeth looked away now and said, "Your hope is an impressive one, sir, if that is what you are seeking."

"Perhaps, but I am a man, and men hope for such things."

Elizabeth was quiet. She was no longer in tears but was uncomfortable with where the conversation had led. Nonetheless, she could not help but be relieved to hear that he would want his heir to come through her and that he was willing to wait until some unknown time when she might welcome him to her room.

"Shall we go to the music room? I have had a long past few days and would like nothing better than to relax in front of a hot fire listening to you play."

"If that is what you wish."

He stood up and walked over to pull out Elizabeth's chair. "I do wish it."

To say Elizabeth was puzzled at his behaviour would be a gross understatement. Darcy had always been demanding and authoritative and when questioned, irritated and dismissive. Now he was being solicitous and amicable. She did not take his arm, but followed by his side through the house to the music room.

As they walked through the doorway, the south wind was blowing against the windows, competing with the sound of the crackling fire. Darcy walked with her over to the instrument. "What would you like to play for me?"

She hesitated but then said, "I have been working on a piece that the piano master in London gave me to practise while away from town. You may already be familiar with it, as I believe the music has been available for several years now, although I had not heard it before."

"Which is it?"

"Beethoven's Sonata in C# minor *Quasi una fantasia*. Mr. Carrington told me that the first two movements suit my playing style well, and the third would be an excellent tool to practise fingering and quick changes. Would you like to hear me play? I cannot say that I have mastered the piece, especially the third movement, but I do enjoy playing it."

"I have heard the piece before, and I believe that I enjoyed it. You do not mind sharing?"

"I do not mind the first two parts. After that, I have need of more practice before I would feel comfortable playing for an audience." Darcy went to the sofa and sat down ready to enjoy himself; however, the next few minutes truly astonished him. Elizabeth's playing had always been delightful, even before Darcy was willing to admit it, but on this evening, she performed with remarkable skill and perception. It became obvious that she had been practising most diligently since leaving London.

When Elizabeth finished the first two, she stood up. "Mr. Darcy, I find that the melody has made me rather sleepy. If you don't mind, I would like to retire for the night."

Darcy sat up straight; he had found himself lounging as he listened. "Of course. I am rather fatigued myself. I will walk you up."

"No need to bother. I can find my way admirably now."

"It is no bother, I can assure you."

So Elizabeth resigned herself to being in Mr. Darcy's company for a few moments longer. The evening had gone better than Elizabeth could have predicted. She had always found her husband perplexing since his mood changes and solemn manner (that seemed to hide something below the surface) contrasted with his almost untamed quality within the confines of the bedroom. And Elizabeth enjoyed trying to unravel and study an intriguing character, but she had reached her fill of Mr. Darcy's and more than anything wanted time alone to reflect on what this could all mean. Elizabeth looked forward to telling her journal all about the abstruse situation in which she now found herself.

Rather than escort Elizabeth to her own door, he led her to the door between hers and his own, the one that led to the sitting room. They walked in together. "Do you often come in here?" he asked. "As I may have told you before, I have always appreciated this room, actually the entire suite of rooms. I have fond memories of coming in here with my mother as she read to me or played some type of game."

"I enjoy the view and have come in here to write letters or read on occasion. But there are so many lovely places within the house to appreciate that I cannot say I prefer any one to the others. Of course the library is magnificent, but I have found my own chamber to be a place of solace." She looked away, thinking she had revealed too much about herself. "Speaking of my chamber. I do believe it is calling my name. Goodnight, sir." At this Elizabeth left him standing in the room as she departed to get ready for bed.

The night was still rather early, but Darcy was fatigued from days of travel. The evening had gone as well as he could have expected. Elizabeth was by no means warm and welcoming, but he had not expected her to be. Instead, she was reserved, certainly not the Elizabeth Bennet that he had known in the past, but they had avoided an argument, which was a positive.

ELIZABETH SLEPT SOUNDLY THAT NIGHT, knowing her husband had no plans to visit her, but also owing to the luxurious accommodations in her room. She had grown so accustomed to the comforts of Pemberley that she found she was able to sleep more soundly than she ever had before in the entirety of her life, except for an occasional nightmare that would intrude upon her peace. When her head hit the pillow, she did not stir until daylight made its intrusion into her room.

On the following morning, the sun was bright after the evening storm. Elizabeth considered taking her walk outside since the weather was nice, but then she remembered the mud. She had felt guilty the last time she took a morning walk after a rainy night with her petticoat and dress covered in filth. The maids would have a tough time getting her shoes and clothing cleaned up, and since she no longer wore clothes that could take such a washing, she instead chose to enjoy her exercise indoors, which would bring her considerable, if not equal, pleasure.

Pemberley boasted many long and interesting passageways where Elizabeth could take in her exercise without having to regularly overlap her paths. She generally stuck to the parts of the house that were closed off, but often found herself walking past servants in the public areas, who would smile as she passed by. Elizabeth often wondered what the servants could think of such a mistress who shamelessly exerted herself within their view, but as she was not one to worry about others' opinions, she would just smile and carry on. As usual, her indoor path took her down a long corridor, the walls of which boasted portrait after portrait of the Darcy line that had graced England for hundreds of years. She would slow down during this part of her journey to study the paintings more closely before continuing on in her exercise. Elizabeth had noticed her husband's portrait on numerous occasions right next to his parents, but she could never find it within herself to spend much time in its perusal. However, encouraged by the bright light streaming through the windows above the paintings, she stopped to consider the man she had married.

In his portrait, he wore a small smile that she had rarely seen, but recognised it to be the sincere one she had witnessed just the night before and on a few occasions in the past. "Who are you, Mr. Darcy? Why were you sent to torture me so?" she said aloud. A few minutes later she found herself at the end of the hall and coming down the grand staircase. Elizabeth had not been paying attention to the people around her when she suddenly came toe to toe with the very man she had been contemplating.

"Mr. Darcy! Forgive me. I was not paying attention to where I was going!" said a flustered Elizabeth, embarrassed to have behaved so unbecomingly in front of her worst critic.

"Please, do not make yourself uneasy. Even if you did not see me, I saw you, so no harm could have been done. May I join you?" Elizabeth's eyes widened as she looked around trying to come up with a viable excuse to dismiss the idea. "Let me walk with you. It is rare that I am able to see the whole house. You may even be able to show me a thing or two that I have missed in the past."

"Very well." Elizabeth continued her walk but at a more sedate pace for fear of his censure. She had been enjoying herself immensely on this bright and cheerful morning. *Why does he have to ruin my walk?* They were silent as they wandered the hallways. Elizabeth had started more slowly than before, but as they continued on in silence, she became more irritated at him for intruding. This naturally led her to walk more and more quickly as if trying to rid herself of a barnacle intent on sucking her dry.

"Do you always walk so quickly?" Darcy finally questioned her.

"Yes."

"Will you be stopping for breakfast, or will you continue throughout the day?"

She looked at him, wondering if he were criticising her or making sport. "You are free to leave me at any time, sir. Truly I am fine all alone."

"I do not mean to offend. I enjoy walking with you." At her raised brow, he continued, "I spent the past four days confined to a cold coach. I find the exertion refreshing."

"I have always used my walks to restore my equanimity when vexed or as a solace when upset. Sometimes I just use the time to escape. My pace or distance is dictated by my mood or need at the time. Of course, it is also dependent upon the weather!"

"The day we met, what had you out at that hour, and so far away from home when a storm was threatening? What were you escaping that day?"

She peered at him, surprised that he would ask her that question after so much time had gone by. "Well, my mother had insisted that I remain indoors and give up my walks while Mr. Collins was in residence. She did not like my acting like a country hoyden in front of a promised suitor. He was finally persuaded to put his hopes on someone else, so I was again able to take my exercise. A full week of the silly man left me in need of a substantial escape, and so I headed out early and kept walking, unaware of the time or the storm. I suppose in my distracted musings, I did not realise that the poor light was not due to a late sunrise but to the storm clouds! Once I discovered my mistake, I turned to go home a more direct route than that which I had come and began to run."

"So it is true. Mr. Collins had put his mark on you first?"

She looked at him quizzically, "I suppose. But my mother had warned him away from Jane – she had grander hopes for her, you see. Then he turned to me, the second eldest. So, it was my placement in the family rather than any true regard that drew Mr. Collins to me – that and my mother's wish to have me as the future mistress of Longbourn. My mother might not understand estate management, but she is astute enough to realise that Mr. Collins could not possibly take over as master without a supportive and intelligent wife. As my father had included me in his daily estate concerns, she thought that Longbourn would be safe with me."

"Your father taught you estate management?"

"I suppose I was the son he never had. We are quite close, you see. And he always said that I had the mind to learn such things. I was just happy to have his attention, for he rarely bestowed it on the rest of my family, and I could only suffer my mother in limited quantities." She glanced up at him as they walked. "I do love my mother, but even I know she is hard to bear in large doses."

"You've never told me this about you."

"Of course not. You never asked, and even I know that it is unseemly for a woman of any consequence to be learning such things. Why give you more reason to spurn me?"

"But you tell me now."

"I have nothing to lose."

"I see you are full of hidden accomplishments, and I mean that with all sincerity."

Elizabeth regarded him, puzzled, not quite sure what to make of this stranger before her. "I think that I am ready to head back to my room now and prepare for breakfast."

It still took several minutes to reach her chamber. She went in and saw that her maid had already taken the initiative to draw up a bath and pick out her morning dress. "Mrs. Darcy, as you are to have breakfast with your husband, I decided to pick something extra nice for the day."

"Thank you, Janette, but warmth is what I desire most."

"You can be both warm and lovely."

After cleaning up from the exertion of walking, Darcy went to the breakfast room to await his wife while having some coffee. The paper was waiting for him at his seat, as was usual, so he perused the headlines while anticipating her arrival. Elizabeth entered about thirty minutes later. Standing, he walked over and pulled out the seat for her. She gazed his way, eyebrow raised. He decided to ignore her unspoken question, knowing that he had been far too inattentive in the past. He understood that he had offended her many times with his public lack of regard and hoped she would be open for him to change.

Elizabeth had discovered that although her appetite had returned with her increase in activity, over the previous week she had begun to feel sick to her stomach in the mornings; and just now with her husband, Elizabeth unluckily perceived that she was also unable to bear the smell of coffee. She looked away often to escape the scent, causing him to wonder at her odd behaviour. Elizabeth ate very little, but he chose to be gracious and leave her to eat as little or as much as she desired. He would not make the same mistakes again.

The conversation during the meal centred on the plans for the day. "I will be in my study catching up on correspondence but hope to be done by midday."

"I intend to meet with Monsieur Lambert to review the menus now that you are home. Then I may practise a little on the pianoforte. I will be having tea with Mrs. Reynolds and Mrs. Carpenter later." She was hoping he would not object.

"You and Mrs. Reynolds get along well, then?" At her nod, he said, "I had hoped that would be the case. She has been at Pemberley since I was a young lad. Sometimes she seems more like family than servant." He ignored Elizabeth's bemused expression, continuing, "I suppose you are now aware of Mrs. Carpenter's plans to take over Mrs. Reynolds' duties later this year."

"Yes, she is well-suited to the role."

"I suspected you would agree."

"Why did you not tell me this earlier, when you sent her to Pemberley, instead of leading me to believe you sent her solely to remove her from my presence?"

"Elizabeth, you must understand that I am not accustomed to explaining myself to anyone." He paused, and then continued after gathering his thoughts, "I should have said something then. You were owed an explanation as mistress of my home and as you were emotionally attached. Please accept my apology for the way I handled that situation. I should have trusted your judgement, but I did not."

"What happened in London?"

Confused Darcy responded, "What do you mean? I am talking about when I sent Mrs. Carpenter back to Pemberley."

"No, I am speaking of this past month. What happened to cause such a change in you? Why are you trying to earn my favour now?"

"Let us just say that I came to a better understanding of my own shortcomings and began to see my unjustified treatment of you. I am committed to correcting my faults and appreciating your many admirable qualities."

Unsettled and doubtful as to the veracity of his sentiments, Elizabeth stood. "Forgive me if I judge too harshly, but I cannot reconcile your speech to my experience." She quickly left the room, unsure what to believe about the man whom she married but did not know. Elizabeth immediately realised her reaction was rude and unbecoming of a lady and almost returned to her bewildered husband, but she needed time alone and so let her legs carry her away.

Two hours later, while Elizabeth was practising in the music room, Mr. Darcy slipped into the back and sat down, unseen by his wife who was in deep concentration. He watched as she played again the sonata from the night before, but she then moved on to the final movement. He watched as she reviewed over and again the many passages that gave her difficulty. The piece was indeed a challenge. He observed how her brow knitted together in concentration as she attempted the same lines over and over, improving slightly with each successive run. Then when she would get it right, the look of unfeigned delight that overcame her countenance mesmerised him. *Her father likened her to the divine once, and I laughed at him as a foolish, old man. Mr. Bennet said that if I allowed her to thrive under my care, I would discover a charming lady of both intelligence and grace; that I could not in all of England find a woman with more estimable qualities than Elizabeth. But instead of encouraging her, I caused Elizabeth to suffer under my overbearing restrictions and physical assault. Look at her! She's stunning! Her smile is without pretension as she rejoices in her success.*

Feeling guilty for intruding upon her privacy, he stood saying, "You have made remarkable improvements."

Elizabeth, obviously unaware of his being in the room, jumped and stood up. "How long have you been here? You should have made your presence known."

"Forgive me. I was enjoying myself too much to disturb you."

Clearly annoyed, she headed towards the door, and then paused before leaving. "Please, in the future I would ask that you announce yourself when entering a room. I don't appreciate your ignoring my wish for privacy while I play."

This is going to be a long and difficult road. But I am beginning to think she just may be worth the effort, thought Darcy, full of equal parts frustration and admiration. She was a trial to be sure, but spirited and intrepid as no other he had ever known.

DURING THE FOLLOWING DAYS, Elizabeth walked outside as the ground had dried sufficiently to allow the endeavour. The storm earlier in the week, however, had brought a decrease in temperatures that meant each day was below freezing. This was not a deterrent for Elizabeth for she had plenty of warm clothing and shoes to face the chill. As she descended the stairs to get her outerwear for her walk on that first day out, she was disheartened to see that it was not Clark to join her but her husband.

"Are you certain you would like to join me, Mr. Darcy? The last time you walked with me outside in the cold, you complained the whole time about the distance and my speed."

"I am quite certain, madam."

"I will accept your escort, but you must promise me that you will not exert your overbearing dictates upon me concerning how long I walk, where I walk and how often I am to walk. I have done very well without your control and would like to continue to do so." Elizabeth said all of this with such honest conviction that Darcy could not help but smile at her tenacity before him. Rarely did anyone show such mettle in his presence.

"I am your servant."

Elizabeth smiled. "I will be gentle." Elizabeth was mindful that Mr. Darcy did not approve of her exercise and would quickly tire of her before long, putting her back into the care of Clark. She would just plan to be reserved in her enthusiasm for walking over the next few days, so as not to give him any reason to exert his ridiculous rules concerning how a lady is supposed to behave while roaming the countryside.

Elizabeth paid little heed to Darcy's presence as she attempted to concentrate on the terrain before her. She was so caught up in her thoughts that she was surprised to hear him speak. "Elizabeth, thank you for accepting my company. It is rare that I explore Pemberley in a way other than horseback." She looked up to him then returned her eyes to the path. "Speaking of horseback, I was thinking that when the weather warms up in a few weeks we might begin your riding lessons. We have many gentle mounts that would suit your level of skill admirably."

"I told you before, that I have no desire to learn to ride."

"I remember your saying that, of course, but Georgiana had a point. I would not ask you to do anything unless it were a sensible idea, one for your good, and since you are a sensible woman, I thought you might have changed your mind."

"You mean if I disagree that I must not be sensible?"

340

"If you truly have no desire to ride, I will not force the point, but I do believe that if you were to think this through in an unbiased manner, you would agree that learning to ride on an estate such as Pemberley is indeed sensible. There are many beautiful locations that you will be unable to reach on foot or by carriage. And knowing your love of nature as I believe I do, I thought that you would want to learn to ride for that pleasure if no other."

"You make a good argument, but you have not taken into account my great fear of horses. How can I possibly want to learn to ride when the very thought makes me lose my breakfast?"

"What are you afraid of?"

"Everyone has some kind of fear. Mine happens to be of horses. You could not possibly understand, so it is best that we just let it go."

"Are you afraid of falling?"

"Please, just let it go. Surely you have some fear that might not seem rational to others but to you is perfectly reasonable."

Darcy walked in silence as he tried to think of something he might fear, to put her argument into context. "I suppose I fear failure."

"Failure? And when has the great Mr. Darcy failed at anything? I thought you were a man without fault. Miss Bingley attested to it once, so it must be true."

"That is impossible."

"Oh? Well I daresay it is a rare occurrence."

"Elizabeth, I have failed at many things, as you well know. You of all people have seen my shortcomings."

"I guess neither of us has been wholly innocent. I know that I am prone to judge someone's intentions before I have all of the information before me. That is a product of too much observation, I suppose. I tend to confuse motives with actions."

"Mrs. Darcy, are you admitting to a shortcoming?"

"My one undeniable fault."

He smiled at her levity. "I would very much like for you to learn to ride. Not for me, but for your pleasure."

She heard the uncharacteristic sincerity in his voice and could not refuse him outright. "If I can somehow overcome my fear, I promise to give it a try."

"Excellent! That is all I could hope for."

The two Darcys walked everyday together that week. Elizabeth continued on with her slow pace, trying not to do anything that might cause Darcy to limit her exercise. She had also spent the time at meals being the proper lady that she was expected to be. This was not a burden for her, for she was raised as a lady and knew all of the social niceties, but she curtailed her teasing banter and avoided leaving a meal prematurely. She, like Darcy, wanted a successful marriage and was trying to play her own part, as she could clearly see his efforts to do the same.

But Elizabeth could not be anyone but herself, and soon her desire for more exertion asserted itself one morning. Although the sky was an overcast grey, the unusually pleasant weather had continued throughout the week. The ground was now sufficiently dry to provide her with ample paths on which to roam. She had remembered a fine prospect about two, or perhaps three, miles from the house that she headed towards. The path would lead to the top of a hill with a long decline on the other side that would eventually wind its way into the woods. The walk up the hill had her breathing hard, but the feeling was intoxicating to her senses. She smiled as she looked out over the winding hills and valleys below. "This view is beautiful, sir! Enchanting!"

Gazing at her, he agreed that he had rarely seen such beauty.

Elizabeth then surprised him when she surveyed the path ahead and began a quick pace down the hill that soon turned into a veritable sprint. Her arms were out to her sides as she laughed at the thrill of the rush of cold air brushing past her.

Darcy watched her as she made her escape, fascinated with her energy and *joie de vie*. How did merely gazing at her compel him to do the same? However, when Elizabeth reached the bottom of the long slope, she continued on in a run, and then disappeared around the other side of a small hill covered in evergreen. He called out to her, but when she did not return, he became concerned he might lose sight of her within the woodland. So, Fitzwilliam Darcy, master of his estate, erudite gentleman and reserved, grown man took off running down the hill after her.

Darcy became more concerned as he continued to travel along the path without seeing her. He was quickly becoming fatigued since he was running at his quickest pace. Finally, he saw her. She was up ahead on her hands and knees taking in deep breaths and crying, or was it laughing?

Darcy ran up to her, breathing in heavily himself, and started to chastise her for the display, fearing that she had caused herself harm, but then checked himself. No, he would not revert to his previous habits of trying to control her, so with as much restraint as he could muster, he exclaimed, "Elizabeth, are you well? What happened? Are you hurt?" He was trying to see her face to somehow determine what was wrong. "Elizabeth, what induced you to do such a thing?" His words became louder and more intense the longer she went without a response.

While Elizabeth was enjoying the exhilaration that came with a swift descent down a hill of some magnitude and in the purview of such inviting scenery, she experienced the intruding idea that her husband, who was watching her from the top of the incline, could in no way approve of her unseemly performance, not now. Darcy was sure to censure her for the impropriety of her actions. Rather than cause her to halt and apologise for her breach in decorum, she was spurred on for a reason she could not have explained. The elation of the moment invigorated her, thus propelling Elizabeth forward at a more rapid pace. She was somewhere stuck between laughing and crying, laughing for the incomparable feeling derived from such an activity and crying for the upcoming verbal lashing she was to receive – coupled with his certain strictures on her future outings.

Elizabeth had continued to run until she could go no further, collapsing on the hard ground and letting her conflicting emotions have free rein. It was not but a few moments later that her husband caught up with her, demanding that she account for her actions. Elizabeth could not move; she continued on her hands and knees as she attempted to calm her heaves as her lungs cried for air, tears escaping the confines of her eyes.

"Elizabeth, please answer me!" Darcy's clamours finally got through to her.

She turned her head and looked up to him and saw a look of sincere concern upon his face, and then she finally found her voice, "I can't do it anymore!"

"What? What can't you do?"

"I can't be what you need me to be!" She no longer confused her crying with laughter. "I need to run! I need to be Elizabeth Bennet – wild, impertinent, impetuous, impulsive Lizzy! I have tried so hard to be a good mistress, to be respectful of my position, but I cannot. My faults are not just in my harsh judgement of others. How can I possibly place judgement on others' actions when I cannot control my own?"

Elizabeth's emotional outburst took Darcy by surprise. Did she think that he was to reproach her for her spontaneous display? Had he not done likewise many times in the past? Had he not done his best to tame her wild, passionate spirit? Instead of giving her reproof, he reached out and placed his hand on her shoulder, slightly startling her, as though she feared him in some way. "Elizabeth, I have no desire for you to change. I admire Lizzy Bennet Darcy's exuberance for life. You remind me of Bingley and Fitzwilliam in that way. Although I cannot claim such a lively spirit, I can appreciate your great capacity for pleasure." She looked at him as if she were gazing at a great statue, scrutinising every aspect of his countenance.

"You jest."

"No, I am in earnest. I have, well, let me just say that I have grown to appreciate some of your qualities that initially I might not have seen to advantage. Please, Elizabeth, do not change for my sake. I would not have you walk around my home and my life as a puppet, pulled by strings. I have never been good at puppeteering."

"No, but you do enjoy directing."

"I would rather my wife not be one of my play actors, but by my side."

"That is not what you have said before. I remember clearly. You said that we all had a role to play on the stage of life, but that since I am a Darcy now, I could not flirt with chaos and ruin your good name."

"I have said and done a lot of things I regret. Come, stand up." He helped her up and began brushing dirt off the knees of her coat. "Would you like to continue on, or are you in need of returning? That was an impressive race you just ran. I know few men who could have performed with greater success."

She regarded him trying to figure out if he were teasing her or displeased despite his previous words. When he smiled, she relaxed and then said, "I was always the fastest at home. None of my sisters or neighbours could catch me, not even the boys."

"You speak of your youth?"

"No, last summer." He raised his brow at her, which brought out her laughter. Darcy was not to know if she were in jest or sincere and could not find it in himself to mind the difference.

343

Elizabeth was not sure how to take Darcy's words. She could not deny the appeal of the new Mr. Darcy, but she also knew that there was a darker, foreboding man who had made his appearance too many times in the past to forget. She found that she could forgive his physical treatment of her, for he did have his husbandly rights, and he was generous enough now not to make demands. However, his officious conduct concerning her sweet sister and the ill-used Mr. Wickham were never far from her mind. Could she ever hope to truly honour her husband as she had promised on her wedding day?

THIS WAS TO BE THE LAST DAY of walking in the open air, for on the next morning they awoke to a veritable winter wonderland. The two ate a quiet breakfast together – Darcy, a full meal and Elizabeth, bread and tea – while Elizabeth thought about her plans for the day. She was to practise her instrument and chip away at one of the tomes she had begun, hoping for some time alone. Just then, a servant entered with a salver upon which sat two letters for Darcy and one for Elizabeth.

"That is strange," said she. "I have a letter from Lydia. Papa must have made her write for she has always been a poor correspondent. She must have written two pages by the looks of it."

"I suppose she misses you."

She raised her brow at him and smiled. "Or she wants something from me." After a last sip of tea, she informed her husband that she would read her letter in the music room prior to practising.

Before sitting at the pianoforte, Elizabeth stood by the warmth of the fire to see what Lydia found worthwhile to write about. She suspected that there would be much talk of officers and lace, but was perplexed when she unfolded the pages because before her eyes was not Lydia's careless hand but one scarcely familiar to her. Elizabeth's name was at the top, so she began to read.

February 11, 1811
Dearest Elizabeth,

Please do not be unhappy with your dear sister, Lydia, for my breach in propriety in writing to you. I have been so worried about you this past month and cannot go another day without contacting you to ensure your wellbeing. The frightened look in your lovely eyes has haunted me since that fateful day in the garden at Longbourn when D showed his true colours yet again in hurting me, now through you.

Elizabeth stopped there. *What is this?* Then she glanced at the inside of the exterior page where she was able to read a short note from her sister, Lydia.

Lizzy,

Do not be vexed at me, Sister. My dear friend, Wickham, has begged me to include a letter to you. I think it is quite unfair that you are now

344

married and continue to take attention away from me. Wickham assures me that he only wishes to make certain you are well. I don't see how it is any of his business, but I cannot deny such a handsome man. You may send a return letter through me if you like. Won't that be fun? – A secret correspondence! And if you wish it, you can send me a small portion of your pin money, so that I can buy ribbons and netting to rework your yellow muslin for it is so dreary. But please do not tell Papa. He claims what is good enough for you is good enough for me, but Mama agrees with me. So be quick, as there is the winter assembly to be held in three weeks.

LB

Elizabeth could not at first comprehend what Lydia had done in sending her a clandestine note from a gentleman. She was shocked to be included in an illicit attack against her marriage. What could Mr. Wickham mean by writing to a married woman? Surely he could see the unsuitability of such an action. If Mr. Darcy were to see the correspondence, it would only confirm his mistaken suspicions against her and could cause permanent damage to their already strained marriage.

"Elizabeth," came a baritone voice from the doorway, surprising her and causing her to instinctively put her hands and the letters behind her back. "Is everything well? You look as though you have had unwelcome news."

"Forgive me, sir. You just startled me," replied she, turning nervously to fold the letter. "I was just about to start practising," she said as she turned back around, looking towards the instrument.

After Elizabeth had left the breakfast room, Darcy hoped to continue the accord that had begun to take shape by surprising his wife in a way that he thought would agree with her sense of adventure. Before she had a chance to get settled at the instrument, he had followed after her towards the music room to initiate his plans. He had glanced within the doorway and observed Elizabeth in agitation as she held two sheets from her opened letter, one in each hand, looking from one to the other. Detecting that she was in distress and wanting to be of some assistance, he finally interrupted her reading. She obviously did not wish to include him in whatever had disturbed her, and Darcy wondered if she might be hiding something from his notice. As he might have two months ago, Darcy almost asked to see the letter since it upset her so but stopped himself short and instead proceeded with his proposal.

"After you left the breakfast room, I decided on alternative plans for us. I hope you don't mind. But if your letter has upset you, we could wait," Darcy said hesitantly.

Happy to change the subject and equally favourable for an opportune distraction from her own discomposure, she told him that she would be happy to agree to whatever scheme he had in mind.

Content to have her approval and hoping to ease whatever secret burden that had arrived with her sister's letter, Darcy chose to follow along. He would not intrude on her privacy and only hoped that whatever she had read in the letter did not portend anything that might incite trouble. Darcy could imagine that her wild, younger sister had probably done something unseemly and too embarrassing for Elizabeth to share. "Go upstairs then and change into something appropriate for an outing and meet me in the entryway in an hour."

Elizabeth was relieved to vacate the room, but curious as to his mysterious proposition. "What are we to do?"

"You will see, my dear," he said with a small smile. He watched her leave with her secret and was determined to provide the space she needed to work through whatever it was that distressed her.

Elizabeth quit the room with her letter in hand, exceedingly puzzled yet again about Mr. Darcy's unusual behaviour, but pleased to have a distraction. When she reached her chamber, she went straight to the small hearth and dropped the papers within, watching the pages go up in flame. She had chosen not to proceed any further once she determined the author and hoped that her husband would never discover that she had received a note from the man whom he could not abide. Elizabeth did not like deceiving her husband and acutely felt the lapse in accepting such an injurious letter, even if it were by no fault of her own, but could not change what was done. She considered telling Mr. Darcy of the offence, but decided that it would be best to ignore Mr. Wickham's indiscretion and hope that the man would take her silence as disapproval. Elizabeth's relationship with her husband was on shaky ground, and she did not want to do anything that might cause more damage.

Elizabeth had hoped to continue on in her solitary pleasures after her husband's return, for surely the house was large enough to avoid one another. But she did as she was told and changed into warmer clothes, with little expectation from his request. When she descended the stairs and approached the door, she discovered her husband already there and with a smile to greet her.

"Elizabeth, the footman is retrieving your outerwear just now. I hope you do not mind the cold today; we will not be walking."

"You know I enjoy being in the open air. What are you about?"

He just smiled. After donning her coat, mittens and then a hooded cape, Elizabeth joined her husband and then went outside where the air was no longer blustery, as it had been the night before, but was calm and serene. The snow blanketed the grounds as Elizabeth had observed from the windows. Before her, however, was something she had not seen. An open sleigh with two ponies attached, complete with bells and ribbons was waiting for them.

"Would you like to go for a sleigh ride, Elizabeth?"

As much as she would have liked to spurn his belated efforts in their marriage, she was in truth excited and overcome with anticipation. Darcy read the response upon her face and returned the pleasure, but in his own more sedate manner. He helped her in and sat beside her. Warm bricks and rugs had been loaded onto the sleigh to protect the inhabitants from the winter chill. Darcy covered his wife and made sure of her comfort. When he took the reins and flicked the ponies forward, the sleigh lurched with a small jolt causing Elizabeth to laugh outright, and then cover her mouth to subdue her own merriment.

The scene before them could not be compared to that of the previous day, the one with grey skies and bleak landscape. Today, the sky shone a bright blue with a blanket of white fleece covering everything in sight, so that the road could not be easily discerned from the lawn. But Darcy knew these grounds as he knew his own self and guided them flawlessly through the many roads and pathways.

Up until now, Elizabeth had only explored the grounds on foot. She was amazed to see how vast the estate truly was as they glided across the countryside, bells jingling. Elizabeth hung on to the side of the sleigh when they picked up their speed, eyes wide and mouth agape. Darcy looked over at her with a genuine smile upon his countenance. She saw him peek at her, and she closed her mouth quickly, while blushing, but could not help allowing a grin to escape. They spoke little, but Darcy did point out various points of interest including the small river that began within the rocky hills and tumbled down to where the great house stood. They saw rabbits and deer roaming the woodland along with red and blue birds searching for berries.

The afternoon was enchanting for both as Elizabeth quite forgot the unwanted correspondence. She was able to see her husband in a completely different light than she ever had in the past. Even trips to the theatre had been stifled by others in attendance, but here, at Pemberley, while alone, Mr. Darcy allowed himself to relax and take unaffected pleasure in the many delights along the way.

After returning home, Elizabeth went upstairs to get warm, but discovered that her biggest need was for a nap. She was awakened at six to prepare for dinner and was shocked to discover that she had slept for nearly two hours and likely could have continued on for two more.

The evening progressed without any dispute between the couple and ended in the music room again. Elizabeth chose to play the many songs Darcy had enjoyed in the past, while he listened on in contented reflection.

UNABLE TO CONTAIN HER DELIGHT, Elizabeth took pleasure each afternoon going outside and playing, building snowmen and sliding around on the ice. Her husband initially watched her through the window, not having enjoyed such activity in many years, but when Elizabeth saw him staring at her, she motioned for him to join her. At first he just laughed and shook his head no, but she finally unwittingly enticed him during her attempts to build a snowman. Darcy had been observing her through the window as she tried to push the second large ball upon the lower one. The snow was quite heavy, but with her tenacious spirit she would not give up. She was endeavouring to lift the mass once again when suddenly two strong arms wrapped around her to guide the large mass onto its resting place. Upon her husband's arrival, Elizabeth jumped at his touch but soon was able to relax as she found his presence beneficial to her task.

"Wait here, Elizabeth," Darcy said as he left her side headed to the house, returning several moments later with an armful of garments. "Our snowman must be attired as a proper gentleman, my dear."

She laughed at his strange behaviour but then got to work adding a scarf, hat and other accoutrements. Then she noticed Clark, the footman most commonly accompanying her on her long walks, approaching with a large salver.

"Sir, the items you requested," Clark said in good spirit, with a bow and a show of feigned ostentation that was in contrast to the informal scene.

Enjoying his antics, Elizabeth looked over and saw a large carrot, an array of buttons, pipes and spectacles laid atop the tray. "Mr. Darcy, are you always so thorough in everything you do?"

"Does that displease you, Elizabeth?"

"I see that everything in your province receives the same exacting industry." She smiled diffidently. "In truth, I admire that about you."

"Thank you," he said with uncharacteristic shyness, unaccustomed to receiving compliments from the woman before him.

"Don't thank me, Mr. Darcy. I speak as I find."

"But your good opinion is not often bestowed and, consequently, of great value to me."

"Oh my, am I that difficult?" Elizabeth responded while biting her lower lip, showing equal parts levity and worry.

"No, my wife, not difficult. You do not use flattery to gain my approval as so many of my acquaintance are want to do. Instead, you have earned my favour."

Elizabeth was at a loss as how to respond. They gazed at one another for a brief moment while Clark stood watching. Abruptly, Darcy then turned to the footman with the tray and said, "Now about our snowman." So the two got to work adorning their creation. After they had finished, Darcy said, "Elizabeth, I did not realise that you were so accomplished in the art of *snowmanship*."

Laughing at his description of her skills, she replied, "Oh yes, if there was ever snow to be had, I was out in it. Jane and I played as young girls, but then she became a proper lady, so I amused myself or played with my younger sisters or the local boys." At his raised brow, she continued playfully. "That was before my coming out, sir. I have always been the model of propriety since that time. Surely there were young girls around the area with whom you played as a child."

"Only my cousins."

"I suppose with so large an estate, you could not so easily walk to a friend's home for entertainment. Well, now you have me as a playmate, for better or worse." She blushed at her own words, but then directed her attention back to their creation. "I had wanted to name him James, after your cousin, but now I believe he more closely resembles my own cousin." At his questioning look, she clarified, "Mr. Collins."

"Ah, Mr. Collins." He took in a deep breath. "If you had married that man …"

"Please, do not even think such a thing! I shudder at the idea. No, we will call our snowman James. I can well-imagine that as a child he would have been at Pemberley fashioning snowmen with you. – And he has always been gracious to me. He seems to be the kind of man who searches for truth, regardless of where it might lead."

"Well, as you only bestow your praise where there is merit, I suppose I will have to accept James as a fixture on our lawn. I am glad that I have at least one relation whom you can admire." He looked down to his feet and then at the snowman, considering their time in London spent with his family, unexpectedly uncomfortable with the conversation. Just then he was sideswiped with a snowball followed by laughter. He watched Elizabeth bend down to pick up more snow and responded in kind, forgetting for the time about the painful memories of London. And so the building of the snowman soon turned into a snowball fight that had the two of them giggling in unexpected pleasure as they had finally found a more propitious means of waging a battle.

WITH THE GROUNDS COVERED IN SNOW, Elizabeth would walk the passageways of Pemberley house in the morning with Darcy searching her out to take in the exercise with her. At first she was reluctant for him to find her, so she would try to elude him. But then she had begun thinking of her walks as a game, like hide-and-seek. Elizabeth would attempt to stay hidden from her husband in some distant passageway, looking carefully before going around a corner, and running past a particularly vulnerable opening. Elizabeth could not have guessed whether or not her husband knew of her particular game, as she was without need of his consent for the amusement. But he soon discovered his wife's diversion several days into the week.

Darcy was looking for Elizabeth yet again, puzzled as to where she might have gone. Each day it had gotten progressively more difficult to locate her. He was on the top floor and had devised a plan to begin there while systematically making his way down to the ground floor. He was rounding a corner and saw a flow of blue gown disappear around a junction in the far passageway. Not wanting to lose her, he quickly went in her direction. When he turned to where he had seen her go, she was nowhere to be seen.

"Elizabeth," he called, but received no reply. *Could that have been an apparition?* he sceptically asked himself. He called out again while still moving forward, then hearing a noise behind him, he turned and saw the same blue flash by, but this time he definitely saw that it was indeed his wife. She had a look of excitement upon her face that drew him in. He called out to her saying, "I see you, Elizabeth." Then he heard something from her direction. *Was that a squeal?* He then took off at a run towards her. *She is playing games with me.* "I see how it is. Well, I hear your challenge, Elizabeth Darcy, and will do your bidding, but you must remember that I grew up at Pemberley and have played this game many times in the past with James. You cannot win!" He heard her laughter in the distance and quickly went in that direction.

She managed to elude him at every turn. *How is she able to escape from me?* They each covered a large part of the uninhabited portions of the house, as Darcy would hear or see evidence of her presence. What started as a bit of fun on Elizabeth's side turned into a morning of escalating competition. At length, Darcy decided to employ the aid of his first footman, Clark. They formulated a plan of attack to catch her unawares. Clark would feign following Elizabeth as her husband, while Darcy would wait in hiding to pounce on her when she ran by.

Their scheme was a good one, for Elizabeth was taken fully by surprise as she rounded the corner. When her husband said, "I have you!" grabbing hold of her waist, Elizabeth let out a peal of laughter that would have stunned the staff had they not known of the little game going on.

She continued in a fit of merriment the likes of which Darcy had never seen from her before. He was completely caught up in the moment and began laughing himself. "You win!" she said, "which is a good thing because I was beginning to get a little hungry. I almost made my way to the breakfast parlour to await your arrival. How fun that would have been." Her eyes were beaming up at him, and how he wanted to kiss her! She must have noticed his glance to her lips because she looked down and stepped back. "Well, I am truly quite famished. I will see you in the breakfast room after I refresh myself in my own room," said she, looking flustered and nervous before leaving.

The staff of Pemberley talked about the morning's activities throughout the entirety of the day, but never in the hearing of Mrs. Reynolds or Peters, for discussing the family was frowned upon. Nonetheless, the topic was too amazing to so easily let go. Mrs. Darcy had quickly become a beloved mistress. She was kind, humble and altogether lovely, but with good understanding. She had a different way of doing things to what they had experienced before, but they found that they quite approved of her eccentricities. The question everyone pondered, however, was how did the staid Mr. Darcy end up with such an energetic wife? — So unlike all of the others of society, especially those whom he had brought home with him for house parties or in the company of other friends. The rumours had indeed reached Pemberley about the scandal surrounding the marriage, and all but Mrs. Reynolds were prepared to dislike their new mistress, but Mrs. Darcy had arrived and put everyone's mind at ease. And they could not even recognise their master, who seemed completely enamoured with her, while she seemed neutral at best concerning the man whom they admired so greatly.

"OH, JANE HAS WRITTEN AGAIN. I hope she is well." Elizabeth had received a letter from Jane and another thick correspondence from Lydia. The mail arrived and was presented on the salver during breakfast.

"Has she not been?" Elizabeth looked over to him with low spirits, not answering. "Elizabeth, if your sister is not well, I would have you tell me."

"She has no real physical malady. Her sufferings are of a more emotional sort." Then Elizabeth looked away and began to read her letter. She sighed, looked concerned, smiled, then refolded her letter, putting it down next to her plate.

"Elizabeth, I am your husband. You can tell me what affects your sister so."

"No, I cannot. Truly, Mr. Darcy. I think it best that we not bring up things from our past that have given us pain."

"I would have you tell me anyway."

350

Elizabeth took in a deep breath and looked over to the servant standing at attention ready to attend them. Darcy dismissed the man with a nod, and so Elizabeth began, "My sister, Jane, is the dearest of all people to me. Any action done against her is also done against me. I cannot easily forget or forgive what you did to her and Mr. Bingley, however noble you claim your motives to be. And every note, every communication I get from her confirms her continued suffering – and at your hands." Elizabeth looked away and put down the roll she had been holding. Her hands were trembling.

Darcy wanted to reach over and hold her hand to stop the shaking, but he knew that it was not from cold as much as anger and grief, and she would not welcome any comfort on his part. "Tell me about your sister." She looked up at him perplexed. "You say you are close, more so than with your other sisters. Why is that?"

After a few moments of reflection, Elizabeth began, "Jane was always my mother's favourite. For years Mama has praised her excessive beauty, but my mother cannot see what truly makes her special. Jane always thinks the best of everyone, eager to forgive and quick to help, even when doing so causes herself pain or discomfort." Then Elizabeth chuckled as she said, "Having me as a younger sister left her with the task of managing a most unruly, little girl. She many times took the blame for my own mishaps, knowing that my mother would never punish her as she would me. When I would get physically hurt, as often happened while playing, she would be the one to provide solace. And when I was pained by someone's cruel remarks – usually my mother's," Elizabeth said looking down with a blush, "she would soothe my sorrow. My bruised pride oftentimes found healing through her natural compassion.

"Once we came of age, I began to see my role in helping her. Jane's trusting nature makes her vulnerable to others, you see. Men have long admired her – always the loveliest in any room – vying for her attention. Although Jane has ever been the model of propriety, I soon became aware of the need to watch over her, as my father was rarely moved to give his role as protector justice. I feared that a gentleman might appreciate her charms, but because of her lack of fortune, would instead seek to engage her heart for his own pleasure without a commitment."

Elizabeth unwittingly glanced up to her husband's knit brow before continuing, "She has such a gentleness of spirit, I worry about how she will survive the cruelties of this world should something happen to Papa. Jane's physical attractions will become a liability for her, I am sure. But you must know, Mr. Darcy, that I will do everything in my power to protect her. She is worth more than any treasure to me."

"She sounds like a remarkable woman. I have met few so genuine in their innocence."

"Remarkable. Yes, I always wanted to be Jane, to have her beauty and kindness."

"But you are beautiful, Elizabeth. And I know none kinder."

Elizabeth laughed. "Please, Mr. Darcy, don't. False words do not become you."

"It is true that your sister is a great beauty. And I can tell that she is a sweet, mild-tempered girl, but you, Elizabeth, are equally lovely, and if not mild-tempered, you are always sincere and generous."

"I cannot believe that you honestly give credit to what you now say. You mean to manipulate me into accepting your pretty words, but I know your true thoughts. I have heard you say otherwise more than once. I cannot blame you for feeling that way, but for my sake, please keep your false declarations to yourself."

Darcy listened to her open up to him as she had never before and saw at once all of her vulnerabilities that she kept so safely hidden from the world to see. *Can she actually think that she is not beautiful? Did I not say that she wasn't and did she not also hear me? Her mother apparently gives her no credit. Could Elizabeth Bennet Darcy deep down be insecure and uncertain of her admirable qualities? Here she is, a woman of good understanding and profound feminine appeal, who does not see her true worth.*

"Elizabeth, when I first arrived in Meryton, I had come with my friend's welfare in mind. He was to lease an estate and I was to help him in his new role. My sister had a difficult summer, which still greatly troubled me, and I was in no humour for any social obligations. But Bingley insisted I go to an assembly to be held that night in town." Darcy had been looking at his hands as he was talking, but here he stopped and looked up to Elizabeth's eyes. She had a puzzled look upon her face. "While at the assembly, Bingley danced with many ladies, while I stood on the outside of the room, trying to be as inconspicuous as a man of my wealth can be. I still heard the quickly spreading report of my income. I can never escape the rumours that follow me wherever I go, and I would not have anyone suppose that I meant to find an attachment in such a remote location.

"Bingley then came up to me and tried to get me to dance with his new neighbours. He hoped to make a good impression, but I wanted none of it. So, when he pointed out a beautiful, young woman who was sitting alone and told me he could introduce me to dance with her, I very rudely – and with the purpose of being heard – said that she was tolerable but not tempting enough to dance with."

Tears had come to Elizabeth's eyes as she struggled to keep a cool head. For months she had dismissed his words as arrogant, peevish, prideful, misplaced, comical, anything to keep them from touching her, but here Mr. Darcy was repeating what he had said, and she could no longer fight her true feelings on the matter. He had offended her greatly that day, and the truth was that it still stung.

"I never gave the young woman any notice, for if I had, I would have discovered that she was in truth the loveliest woman in the room, and even now is the most beautiful woman of my acquaintance." Elizabeth looked away and began shaking her head. Darcy instinctively reached over to take hold of her hand. "Elizabeth, I am ashamed of myself for such a speech. I was wrong on two accounts. Firstly, it was the height of selfish arrogance to say such a thing, and secondly, it simply was not true."

Elizabeth wanted to disappear. She did not know what to believe or how to respond. How did the conversation about her sister turn into one about herself? "Mr. Darcy, please. I do not want to talk about that night."

"But I need to. I need to apologise to you for my rude behaviour at your expense. No wonder you thought to leave me in the woods to suffer the storm. You would have been justified. Elizabeth, my parents raised me to honour women, to take care of them, but in my pride, I began to believe that the only women to whom that applied were the ones of my choosing. Can you conceive of my arrogance? But of course you can; you have seen it too many times to believe otherwise.

"If it makes you feel any better, you were not alone as the target of my pretension. I have turned away more than one woman by the same pompous method. But you, my dear, were the only one who turned around and laughed at me." She looked at him with furrowed brows. "Up until recently, I had not remembered that you were the woman that night whom I offended, but when I recently recalled the truth, that you, my wife, were then the target of my uncivil remarks, I recollected your making sport with me. No one had ever laughed at me before, but you did. You threw my insult back at me in ridicule. I deserved it, but no one had been brave enough until you. I did not know whether to applaud or scorn you, so I suppose I chose the latter, but conveniently forgot who had made the impression, probably to salvage my pride."

"That was many months ago and much has happened since then. Can we just forget about it?"

"Say you forgive me. I need to know that you do."

Elizabeth nodded that she did, and then said, "I can forgive you for your ill-favoured words that night, but truly, you must stop saying such things to me. You and I both know that I am not the most beautiful woman of your acquaintance. You know many attractive women."

"None so lovely."

"What about Lady Annette?" It pained Elizabeth to speak of Lady Annette, but she wanted some sign to confirm or deny the validity of Lord Langston's claims.

Darcy was startled by the question, but soon recovered. "What about Lady Annette?"

"She is certainly beautiful. In fact, I would have said her loveliness matched Jane's, but she lacks Jane's overwhelming goodness, so could never be as beautiful in my eyes."

"Lady Annette is, of course, an attractive woman. I cannot deny the fact. There are many beautiful women of my acquaintance, but that does not negate your being the loveliest."

"How am I to trust you when you say such things?" His words gave her comfort, but did not appease her.

"Elizabeth, deception is my abhorrence. I would not lie to you. I admit that it has taken me some time to recognise my admiration for you, but now that I see your attractive qualities, I am certain I know my mind. You are very beautiful." He reached up and gently touched a curl framing her face. Then seeming to recall himself, he pulled back his hand and said, "Sometime soon I will share your many qualities that I find enchanting, but not now, not over breakfast, but soon."

Elizabeth then excused herself, without having consumed anything but her tea, to read Jane's letter again and to make a response. She had also taken her letter from Lydia, expressing a wish to read the remainder of her mail in the privacy of her own room.

While reading Jane's correspondence, she had been distracted from the possible contents of Lydia's letter. Like the previous note, this one was two-pages long, and Elizabeth feared that Mr. Wickham might have included his own communication. So, behind closed doors, Elizabeth broke the seal and was disheartened to see the same strong hand written therein. She immediately walked to the fire and dropped both pages into the flames. Angry with her sister for participating in the deception, and with Mr. Wickham for his potential damage, she sat down at her writing desk to implore Lydia to desist from any future correspondence. Elizabeth also wrote to her father explaining what had occurred, so that he might enforce her request. After writing her letters and combining them into one packet with her father's direction on the front, she let her fatigue overcome her and laid down for a nap.

Darcy was becoming increasingly concerned about Elizabeth's poor appetite in the mornings, although she seemed to eat plenty later in the day and had been able to maintain her weight gain. But despite his concerns, he would not push her to eat when she clearly had no desire. He was just glad she had continued to sit with him, even if she just drank tea. So after Elizabeth had left Darcy after breakfast, he removed himself to his study. He sat in stilled reflection, staring at the fire in the hearth as if for guidance. He became aware of the hurt that he himself felt with Elizabeth's own expressed pain. This came as a surprise to him. He could not account for his own disquiet concerning Bingley and Jane when for months he had been in confident opposition to the match.

Discounting Jane's own feelings towards Bingley, if Darcy could do something that would somehow alleviate Elizabeth's burden, he would want to do it. But what could he do? What should he do? He interfered once; should he do so again? Would prompting a reconciliation between his friend and new sister be wise? The reasons for separating the two still stood, but did he have a greater understanding of Jane's character that might shed light on the possible outcome? According to Elizabeth, Jane Bennet had all of the qualities that any man of true understanding and virtue could want. Of course, she had no dowry, no connections, excepting his own, and a mother who would plague the man who chose her. But she was not mercenary herself it would seem, and she was very beautiful. She conducted herself with grace and serenity, which was a benefit. If Bingley could somehow keep Mrs. Bennet in check, the marriage might work.

But was it for Darcy to decide? Yet again, he had been an arrogant, officious fool, playing God with his friend's life and happiness, trying to conform him to his own desires. Jane would make a perfect mate for Bingley. He needed someone who would complement his exuberant character with her own stability and ease. He needed a sweet and kind woman of good understanding, who would not try to lead her husband. Surely Bingley would protect himself and his family from a meddling mother-in-law. Darcy had only seen Mrs. Bennet on one occasion since he was married, and he was able to easily manage her intrusions. Bingley was an amiable, generous sort, but he would stand firm when needed, as seen with Caroline on occasion. With Darcy's help, the two men could manage Mrs. Bennet's demands.

It was decided. Darcy would get more information from Elizabeth as to Jane's immediate plans, then he would help his friend to find her. Bingley would not be leaving for the North until it warmed up in April, so Darcy still had time to reach him before he moved on.

DARCY HAD BEEN SITTING at his desk reviewing accounting records and considering reports from his steward when he heard a soft knock upon the door to his study. After calling for the visitor to enter, he was astonished to see his wife standing in the doorway with a timid look upon her countenance. He stood, walking around his desk to welcome her inside his sanctuary. "Elizabeth, this is a delightful surprise. To what do I owe the pleasure?"

"Well, I was hoping to go for a stroll in the gardens, and I thought, with such a lovely day and the snow now gone, that perhaps you might want to take in the fresh air yourself. That is to say, I thought you might like to join me while I explored the walkways near the manor. I plan to stay on the gravel, so you need not worry about the mud. Maybe you could tell me more about the house?" She paused here and looked upon his desk covered with papers. "But I see you are busy, so you probably prefer staying indoors. Naturally, I understand that you don't want to leave your business unfinished. I'll just plan on seeing you at dinner then." Elizabeth turned to leave, feeling like a nervous schoolgirl being thrown into the company of a man for the first time.

Darcy's merriment at his wife's uncharacteristic discomfiture was carefully concealed behind his composed demeanour – that she would approach him for her pleasure, and that she appeared so timid, brought him pleasure that he could not have predicted. Finally, as she started to turn to leave, he found his voice and said, "Elizabeth, please do not leave yet. I would be happy to join you. Can you give me a few moments to put away some of my papers? Maybe I could meet you in, say, fifteen minutes at the entrance?"

Elizabeth despised herself for blushing so uncontrollably, but was hopeful that her efforts would be rewarded with a delightful afternoon spent in her husband's company. She had awoken from her rest thinking about the handsome man with whom she now shared her life. She considered that had she set out to acquire a more perplexing subject with whom to enter the married state, she could not have found greater success. Theirs had been a rugged course, much like the hills around them full of crevices, turbulent waters and caverns of hidden and unexplored beauties, but with her husband's obvious efforts, Elizabeth determined to play her own part in healing their marriage. At some point over the previous weeks, she had discovered that she experienced no small amount of pleasure when with him. Mr. Darcy was agreeable to look upon, it was true – he had always been so – but her enjoyment went beyond the superficial.

She considered the threats Wickham's letters placed on their shaky marriage and only desired to protect their relationship by freely demonstrating to Mr. Darcy her growing regard. This was no hardship, for she now truly anticipated their time together. And she was finally beginning to understand her aunt's words of wisdom about showing love, even if not fully feeling the sentiment.

They set out in comfortable silence, as they had on so many other occasions. Elizabeth understood that her husband was not one to rattle away like so many others and was glad to finally understand that his laconism did not always portend ill-favour. As this was a slow amble through the gardens, she contentedly took his arm, noticing not for the first time, his impressive form.

"Elizabeth," said he, breaking the silence, "I thank you for your invitation. I apologise if my delay in responding suggested that I was unwilling. In truth, I was just distracted by the charming way in which you made your request."

"Oh, my. So you were entertained by my fumbling words. I was unsure if you would want to come out here with me. I mean, I know that you have taken great pains to spend time in my company, but you were busy and.... " Elizabeth looked away, nervous all over again. Changing the subject, she said, "Did you mind so much leaving your work?"

"No, I was happy for the diversion, especially such a pleasing one." She blushed. "I had been working on my business long enough. A break was just what I needed."

"Is that how you spend your time while we are apart – working on estate matters? Or was it some other business?" As he waited to answer, she stopped walking and said, "Please forgive my impertinence! I should not have been so presumptuous. Of course, your business is none of mine."

"Elizabeth, I am happy to share with you whatever you wish, but I am afraid you might find my concerns in this case rather dull. But I certainly may be wrong about my assumptions. I had forgotten that your father included you in his own estate burdens."

"Yes, he did, but his efforts cannot be compared with your own, I think." They continued walking again. "So do you spend much time working? I was always under the assumption that the benefit of being a master was that you could direct others to do your work for you, leaving a gentleman to his leisure."

"Many do give over responsibilities to their stewards; it is common enough. But I could not in good conscience abdicate all of my own responsibilities to a man under my employ – one who, though loyal, has no actual stake in the matter."

"So, to what extent do you take your role? Surely, you do not pay the bills yourself?"

"No, I do not do that. My steward is a very capable man, as was the one before him." Here, Darcy looked away, but soon recalled himself. "I have hundreds of people whose livelihoods depend upon the dependable management of not just Pemberley, but my other holdings as well. It is my responsibility to ensure that they have a secure future, just as it is my obligation to secure my family's."

"I ruined that for you," Elizabeth said softly as she looked to the distant trees. "You needed to marry an heiress to protect your family's future, yet I had nothing to bring to the marriage. I see that now."

"Elizabeth, you certainly brought no financial benefits, but to say that you had nothing to bring is not so."

Wanting to change the subject to one less painful for her to contemplate, she said, "I commend you for the way you manage Pemberley. Your diligence impresses me."

"Those are panegyric words indeed, for I know that you are not easily affected by anything *I* can offer."

"You make me sound harsh."

"I can assure you that is not my intention. As I said before, your praises are meted out only after due consideration and only when the highest commendation is warranted. My money and homes – which I have only inherited – have not impressed you, I think."

"What, no mention of your fine form?" This brought on a chuckle from her husband. "I will have you know that I find your commitment to all of your responsibilities admirable. My own father rarely stirs to do anything outside of the necessary. I just assumed that was standard behaviour, but you seem to be involved in the minutiae of anything within your purview." He blushed at her praise. "I feel safe and secure here at Pemberley with you in charge. I know that my future is in good hands."

Darcy glanced down at his wife and saw that she too could blush, although much more prettily than he. Darcy shared with Elizabeth more stories of the house and the gardens whose flowers would soon make a showing, pointing out objects of interest as they strolled. His knowledge of the estate continued to inspire her as she considered his great capacity for delivering enlightening tales and anecdotes from his family's past. The chill of the air, once the sun had made its descent behind the hills, finally brought them inside to prepare for dinner and each contentedly pondered many more days shared in like manner.

THE EVENING MEAL WAS SPENT in pleasant but familiar conversation as Darcy questioned Elizabeth about her day while not in his company. Elizabeth had been progressing on her instrument and experienced newfound delight in her improvements. She also told him of her nap that took place before their walk and how well she had slept in her lovely chamber.

"You have been sleeping quite a bit during the day, have you not? Are you unable to sleep at night?"

"I cannot account for it. I am sleeping better than I have in ages. Maybe it is your comfortable beds here at Pemberley. Do you have fairies that come and sprinkle magic sleeping dust on the pillows at night?"

"You have seen them?"

"No, I cannot say that I have seen them, only experienced the evidence of their visits." She smiled becomingly.

"Instead of music, would you like to play a game this evening?"

"Hide-and-seek?"

"No, we will save that one for another time. I was thinking of chess. Do you play?"

"Mr. Darcy, I love to play chess. My father taught me to play when I was six. I think he wanted a ready companion to play with him at his whim, but his little strategy backfired when he found that I came to beat him more times than not."

"I would only want to play chess with a skilled adversary."

"So you asked me despite lacking knowledge of my proficiency?"

"Well, I supposed that if you could not play, I would teach you and then apparently fall into the same trap as your father." He stood up and pulled Elizabeth's chair out for her. "Shall we retire to my study?"

"Only if we sit by the fire, for your desk intimidates me." He smiled down at her. She naturally took his arm as he led her down the passageways.

Darcy was enjoying the game in contented quietude. He had rarely derived more pleasure playing chess than on this occasion. Not only was he well matched with his opponent, but he had a beautiful woman before him to study as much as the game. He relished watching her bite her lower lip as she considered her next move, or how she smirked when he would make an answering manoeuvre just before she would take one of his pieces. Although the game was close, Darcy did pull through in the end. "Elizabeth, again you have surprised me with another accomplishment. If I had known, we could have been enjoying the game for months now."

"I saw no need to tell you. A discerning husband would figure it out eventually. I must say, it did take you longer than I would have expected, since you have been stuck out here in the wilds of the Peak country for so long with no one to provide entertainment except for myself." She laughed. "Next time I shall not be so kind."

"Is that a challenge? Tomorrow night I will be ready for you."

She laughed as she yawned. "Excuse me! I cannot account for being so sleepy! Maybe I should retire for the night even though it is still early."

"No, please stay a little longer."

"If it pleases you. What shall we do now? I cannot read, for I will surely dose off, and then you will have to carry me to bed." The words had not finished leaving her mouth before a large blush spread over her. "Oh my. Forgive me. That was awkwardly done. I did not at all mean what that sounded like."

"I know what you meant, Elizabeth."

She tried to change the subject and landed upon a topic that had been on her mind throughout the day. "Do you think that perhaps one day Jane could visit me here?"

"Of course. Your sister will always be welcome to visit." At her look of relief, he said, "Elizabeth, this is your home now. I know that you love Miss Bennet. I would never exclude her or anyone from visiting you."

"Thank you, Mr. Darcy. Maybe this summer?"

"Summer would be a fine time. By then, Georgiana will be here as well. Perhaps they could travel together."

Elizabeth wanted to say more, but apprehension fed her reluctance.

"What is it?" said he as he noticed her start to speak but then stop.

"Your sister, Miss Darcy, she detests me. I am not so sure that having them travel together would be wise."

"Georgiana loves her brother; she does not detest you. She just needs time to accept our marriage. By summer all will be well. We will have spent time in town together, and she will have come around. She is in truth a sweet-natured girl, much like Miss Bennet." Then he casually added, "Where is your sister now? Is she at Longbourn?"

"No, she is with my aunt and uncle Gardiner in town. She is to spend the rest of the winter months and then the Spring Season with them. I, well … I wish I were there for her, but being at Pemberley has been such a blessing for me, I don't know if I could bear to leave."

"I am glad you are fond of your new home."

"I like Pemberley so well, it almost makes the owner tolerable." He looked at her with brows knitted. She laughed. "That was cruel. I find that the owner has begun to grow on me, despite his officious meddling into my life. Yes, seeing him in his magnificent home has improved his looks and my partiality considerably." This time her laugh increased in volume as she found amusement in her sport and in his countenance. "You have come a long way to accepting a tease, but we still have room for improvement."

Finally he smiled. "I am not used to being teased by anyone but Fitzwilliam. You and he are a lot alike you know. I cannot help but imagine that you two would have been well-matched."

"He is a kind man and his conversations do divert me, but I wonder if he and I are too much alike for a truly happy marriage. No, things are as they should be." Elizabeth blushed again as she seemed destined to continue saying the most discomfiting things. "I think it is now time that I retired before I make a bigger muddle of this conversation."

Darcy walked Elizabeth to her room, all the while thinking about what she had left unspoken. Perhaps there was hope for happiness in marriage. After she had gone to bed, he returned to his study and began planning another trip to town. He was already dreading leaving the life they now enjoyed together as friends, if not lovers. This trip would go over much differently than the last, and when he returned Elizabeth would find comfort in Jane's returned hopes.

Chapter Seventeen

I love you the more in that I believe you had liked me for my own sake and for nothing else.
John Keats

The following day, Darcy meant to break the news to his wife that he must leave for town again, but would return within a fortnight. So during breakfast, he told her of his plans, carefully omitting the reason for his leave-taking. He did not want to increase her hopes in vain should something occur to inhibit his success – Bingley was still the capricious man he had always been. Elizabeth accepted his words in resigned understanding. She could not decide how she felt about his departure. She had felt relief when he last made the journey, but now, she had become accustomed to his presence and actually looked forward to mealtimes and the evenings when they would be in company together. However, she had much to keep her busy. With the change in weather, she had planned on meeting more of the tenants and neighbours. This would be the perfect opportunity to make new acquaintances.

Darcy left three days later, at dawn, with the hope of arriving late the following evening. The days were growing longer and he was anticipating good weather along the way. Although he had made this journey many times in the past, two full days in the confines of a carriage was uncomfortable to bear; however, he kept up his spirits with thoughts of his wife and her joy when she was to discover that her sister would again have her hopes restored. He had sent word ahead on this trip, so the house was ready for his appearance.

The morning following his arrival, he paid a call at Bingley's residence. Caroline accepted his presence with unfeigned delight, as she joined the men in the sitting room. She attempted to play the consummate hostess, demonstrating to Darcy that his loss should be keenly felt. Her attentions were, however, in vain. Darcy indicated to his friend that he would like to meet with him alone to discuss a private matter of some import, so they entered Bingley's study and sat before the fire.

"Darcy, this sounds serious. I hope all is well between you and Mrs. Darcy."

"Yes, things are very well, as it happens. In fact, it is on behalf of my wife that I am in town." At Bingley's nonplussed expression, he continued. "Bingley, I have done you a disservice that I mean to attempt to rectify."

"I cannot imagine what you have done."

"My wife's happiness has become very important to me, and I find that I am responsible for employing my influence in a way that has resulted in her sorrow, as well as the disappointment of two others, one of whom I care about greatly and the other being my sister, my new sister that is."

He now had Bingley's undivided attention. "Go on."

"Bingley I must apologise for stepping into a situation in which I had no place. I gave you advice that at the time I felt to be in your best interest, but now I see that it was misplaced and officious."

"What are you saying? Come out with it."

"I should never have encouraged, no directed you to give up your hopes for Jane Bennet. She is a lovely woman of pristine character who would in truth be a good match for you, if you still would have her."

Bingley sat there stunned. "Are you in earnest? Why the change in sentiment? I thought you keenly disapproved of her and her family."

"My wife, Elizabeth, is what changed. Or rather I changed with her guidance and understanding. Without pushing me, or anything of the sort, she has been able to show me how wrong I have been in judging Miss Bennet. Her mother remains the same obstacle as she always has been, but with me as your brother, we should be able to easily avoid the detrimental effects of associating with the Bennets. Her ties with trade are, of course, unfortunate but possibly worth the benefit of having a wife whom you can love."

Bingley was sitting in quiet contemplation as he listened most attentively to Darcy's astonishing words of advisement.

"So, friend, what do you say? Do you still hold Miss Bennet in high regard?"

"Darcy, I am in a stupor, unable to account at all for what you say. Do you mean to tell me that you have changed your mind, that you are now encouraging me to court Miss Bennet?"

"I am saying that you should follow your heart, not mine."

"You do not think I would be hurting my family in so doing?"

"I cannot tell you what the effects will be upon Miss Bingley, but Miss Bennet is a gentleman's daughter, so her standing in society is in truth higher than Miss Bingley's. She does not have wealth, but her brother-in-law does. No one outside of you and Miss Bennet should have any awareness of her true financial plight, so society would have no actual knowledge to judge her, just speculation. As kind as Miss Bennet is, she will need your protection at first, but I am confident that she will eventually win your friends to her favour."

"Darcy, you were so certain before. How can I trust what you say to be sound?"

"You can't, but I am glad you are questioning me!" Darcy smiled as he shook Bingley's hand. "So what do you say, would you like to pay a call?"

"Pay a call? What can you mean?"

"She is in town as we speak, at her relations', the Gardiners."

"But Darcy, could she forgive me? Do you think she has feelings for me?"

"We cannot know unless you call on her."

Bingley displayed a large, unaffected smile. "I will ring for our coats."

Forty-five minutes later, the Darcy carriage pulled up outside a large, yet comfortable house on Gracechurch Street. Darcy had not taken time on his previous trip to Cheapside to examine closely the home of the Gardiners, but he did so now. The building was covered in red brick with large windows that opened up to the clean street. There were quaint window boxes that contained seasonal plants and would likely be full of colour in the summertime. The small garden at the entrance was well maintained and the porch handsomely set up.

The two men alighted from the carriage and walked up to the entrance. Bingley was fidgeting with his coat as Darcy looked on in amusement. Darcy himself had never felt the anticipation of calling upon a maiden for whom he had strong regard, and he felt a pang of jealousy for his friend, for if Darcy were correct, Bingley was to court a woman who held equal sentiment.

The door was answered by a manservant who took their cards and invited them into the foyer to await direction. Within a few moments, he returned and asked them to follow him to a finely appointed drawing room. They stepped inside and there she was, more beautiful than Bingley could have remembered. Next to Jane stood her aunt, a lovely woman in her own right. They took their bow and Mrs. Gardiner invited them to come in and sit down. The conversation was somewhat stilted at first, as each tried to take bearing on the others. But before long Mrs. Gardiner, who was well bred and an accomplished hostess, had made everyone feel comfortable. She asked Bingley questions about his winter and plans for spring. Meanwhile Jane's serene countenance successfully hid the tumult within her breast.

Mrs. Gardiner, being the astute and guileful woman that she was, managed to steer the conversation in a manner that would put Jane and Mr. Bingley together in like interests.

While Bingley spoke with Jane in rapt, private conversation, Mrs. Gardiner turned to Darcy and said, "Elizabeth has written me of her love of Pemberley. I had told her to anticipate the gardens providing her with unlimited pleasures, and it would seem, though winter, that she is now in agreement. She is most happy when in nature, and I believe your estate will forever satisfy her need for bucolic surroundings."

Darcy looked at her in astonishment, then said, "You have seen Pemberley, madam?"

"Has Elizabeth not told you? I grew up in the town of Lambton, not four miles from Pemberley. I joined my family on multiple occasions to your fine estate. I am sorry; I felt for certain that Lizzy would have informed you."

Darcy recollected that her aunt had a previous association with Laura Carpenter, Elizabeth's original lady's maid. "She did mention something about your childhood in Lambton, but I confess that I had forgotten until now, as she only mentioned it that one time and in context of someone else. Please, if you will, tell me of your family. Who were your father and mother?"

She smiled, knowing she would surprise him if indeed Elizabeth had not yet imparted to him her history with his family and estate. "For years my father held the living at the church in Lambton. We resided there from three years before my birth, until I was but fifteen, when my father died."

"Your father was Mr. Pennington?" She smiled broadly. "He and my father were friends!"

"Indeed they were. My father respected Mr. Darcy immensely, always thankful for having a man of principle as his main benefactor. You see my father had known many profligate estate owners, watching as his flock, in former situations, would be at the mercy of unscrupulous masters. He valued your father's friendship very much."

Darcy scrutinised her countenance as recognition dawned in his eyes. "I remember you! You are the former Miss Margaret Pennington, are you not?"

"Yes, that was my name." She watched as Darcy provided her with a most becoming smile.

"I believe I was about twelve when last I laid eyes on you. You must have been fifteen." Darcy looked across the room, as the recollection came to mind. "I remember thinking you were a remarkably beautiful *older woman* at the time." Then turning to her, he said, "and I can see you have changed little. I am surprised I did not recognise you, now that I know who you are. I recall having a boyhood infatuation with you during that time." Darcy said this with a look of mischief in his eyes. "My father would state that he was to pay your father a visit, and I would tag along, hoping to get a look at you." He laughed at the antics of his own youth.

"You tease me, sir!" Mrs. Gardiner returned laughing.

"Indeed, I do not. I was certain you did not even notice me. Then your father died and you moved away. I thought never to see you again, and now here you are, and Elizabeth's aunt! Whatever happened to you after you left Lambton?"

"After my father's death, my family moved to London to live with my grandfather on my mother's side. I attended a school for ladies to complete my education, for my grandpapa had little use for a girl of sixteen. I eventually met Mr. Gardiner at the theatre with friends and soon became engaged. My family's noble heritage made up for my lack of dowry, for a rector could provide but little by way of financial benefit for a daughter coming out in society."

"Your noble heritage?"

"My father was the second son of a gentleman who was the third son of Lord Pennington, the Earl of Devon." She laughed gently at the look of shock on his countenance. "You look surprised, sir. I am astounded that Lizzy has not told you all of this."

Darcy stood and walked to the window. *Why did Elizabeth not tell me? She must have known this would positively affect my acceptance of her family. Perhaps that is why she did not. She wanted me to value them as her relations, not based on her aunt's breeding. She does not boast of her connections like so many others I know. Elizabeth must find me such an arrogant snob. I am certain she has laughed at me time and again.* "She has never mentioned any of your history excepting the location of your current home."

"That would be like her. She delights in observing people's reactions. She was probably waiting for just the right moment to spring the news on you to see how you would respond!" Mrs. Gardiner laughed becomingly. "Why don't we just not tell her and thwart her plans!" They both chuckled in merriment. Mrs. Gardiner was indeed surprised at her niece's failure to inform Mr. Darcy of her family's origins. It would likely have made the transition into Elizabeth's marriage easier and may have even resulted in more time spent in one another's company, but perhaps Elizabeth wanted Mr. Darcy to accept her family based on his own experiences not Mrs. Gardiner's family name, which would have nothing to do with character or intrinsic value.

"Your great-grandfather was the Earl of Devon, so the current Earl of Devon..."

"... is my first cousin, once-removed," she finished, "Yes. I cannot say we are close, for his propensities are unlike my own family's. My father chose the church, not completely out of necessity, but because he desired to serve God and fellow man. His cousin, who inherited not just the name, but the title, has lived his life as many noble men of our day, with dissipation and waste."

"I am familiar with the man and went to Cambridge with his youngest son, Roger Pennington, who like his father indulges in the trappings of this life. He refused to join the armed services and has sought a life in the church."

"He is a great seducer of this world and will likely, through his connections, find an appointment and bring his form of religion to a naïve and vulnerable flock."

Darcy returned to his chair, and they both sat in quiet refection, Mrs. Gardiner on the injustice and depravity of the world in which they lived, and Darcy on the remarkable connection between Elizabeth and a titled family, seeing that her close relations were by far the more genteel of the noble name, as they were obviously more honourable in their view of the world. They were both roused out of their musings by Bingley, declaring that he and Miss Bennet desired to go for a walk and hoped that the other two would join them. As they all regarded the prospect with pleasure, they donned their outerwear and left for the bustling market street, Bingley and Jane re-establishing their easy rapport, and Darcy and Mrs. Gardiner sharing memories of Derbyshire and of the niece whom Mrs. Gardiner esteemed and Darcy was growing to admire all the more.

"Mr. Darcy, my mother highly regarded yours and was grieved when she died. We were so very sorry for your loss," said Mrs. Gardiner.

He looked on her with new warmth in his eyes. "I have never forgotten your mother's kindness. She arrived at Pemberley the following day with a basket full of breads, sweets and pickled vegetables. I remember that George Wickham scoffed at the offering, questioning why anyone would give food to those at Pemberley; we had the finest kitchens in the land. But I had never tasted fare so fine or so welcome. I discovered that there is no aroma more delicious than the product lovingly made by the sympathetic hands of a compassionate neighbour."

"We mourned in our home as if our own family had died, not knowing that would soon be the case. I believe my own father, along with one of his parishioners, died but two months after your own gracious mother."

"I had forgotten how close together those events played out. That was when you moved away. My father had a hard time recovering from the death of my mother, especially when his pastor and friend died. He had no support after that but a distraught twelve year old boy who missed his mother most exceedingly."

"When your father also passed, I received word through local friends who kept me abreast of the happenings. My heart went out to you as I prayed for your strength and comfort. And now I see that you have grown into a fine man, fully capable of being a master to a large and prosperous estate." Tenderness shone in her eyes as she spoke, and Darcy knew that she spoke from the heart.

Mrs. Gardiner invited the two young men to dine, so that Mr. Gardiner might have the occasion to further his acquaintance with them. The petition was agreed upon with alacrity, much to the delight of Jane who had not had the chance as yet to speak with Mr. Darcy about her sister, Elizabeth. She longed to know how she was faring. The evening was spent in mutual regard and pleasure as Darcy lamented that he had never given the Gardiners an overture into his association. Mr. Gardiner was a man of keen intellect and amiable nature. No one who found himself in the company of the husband and wife could find anything wanting.

As the evening progressed, Darcy found where Elizabeth had acquired her taste for music and the arts. Also, her teasing nature mimicked that of both the Gardiners. Darcy marvelled at the ease and respect each Gardiner showed towards the other, and he realised that this was the type of marriage that he had unknowingly longed for. *How could I have been so mistaken in my estimation of her family?*

Satisfied that he had finally chosen the nobler course, Darcy determined to encourage Bingley once again to follow his heart. So the next morning, he visited Bingley and requested a private conference. Darcy apologised again for having intervened without justification in separating his friend from Miss Bennet, but this time conceded that it was for the sole reason of gratifying his own selfish motives. He professed that he found Jane Bennet to be a woman of grace and honour who would not capitulate to a marriage based on mercenary motives without also having the benefit of respect and love.

"Then you believe she might actually have feelings for me, not just an inclination to satisfy her mother's designs?" Bingley asked with renewed hope.

"I believe that Jane Bennet is a woman who knows her mind, and if you would but ask, you would receive the answer you have longed for since I interfered in your plan." Darcy smiled at Bingley's look of delight, and then sobered. "Charles, again please forgive me for my insolence. I wrongly hurt one of my dearest friends, which has resulted in the deprivation of happiness for more than one person, individuals for whom I care deeply. I will understand if you cannot find it in your heart to overlook my interference."

"Nonsense! You say that you think she will accept me out of admiration rather than just my bank account? Because, I do believe I would offer for her anyway, but knowing she has feelings for me would make it all the better."

"I do believe she does, if her manner towards you last night is any indication."

After a few moments of reflection, Bingley said, "You know, Darcy, I find it odd how the majority of women in your circle marry for avaricious inclinations, and that is acceptable, even to you, as the norm, but when a true lady of value seeks to marry, and she is suspected of mercenary intent, you attempted to thwart her (or in this case her mother's) designs. Do you not find your thinking to be rather duplicitous?"

"Charles, I am learning to examine my own heart and am finding it lacking in many ways. I cannot say you are mistaken, but I hope to finally be rectifying my misjudgements."

"Are you for Pemberley today?"

"No, I am to be here a few more days on business; then I will head home."

"I will write to you then as soon as I have good news." Bingley smiled enthusiastically.

ELIZABETH AWOKE LATE THE MORNING Darcy had left. She had hoped to be available to give her goodbyes, but could not rouse herself for the task. She had been sleeping later in the mornings than even while in town and still needed a nap. When she would finally make her way to breakfast, she could not bear to eat anything beyond a plain roll and some tea. She did find that exercise made her feel better, so when she was able to get herself going, she took her walk, but many times she had to move her exercise to the afternoon.

By now, Elizabeth was relatively certain that she was with child but had no one with whom she could share her suspicions. She had not had her courses since some time in December. Although Elizabeth did not know the symptoms to look for, she suspected that her growing fatigue and decrease in appetite must have some connection. She decided to write to her aunt to see if she could enlighten her as to her experience thus far.

Elizabeth could not decide if the possibility brought her pleasure or apprehension. Of course, she wanted a baby, but she did not imagine it would happen so soon. She now perceived that Darcy would be happy at the prospect, but she feared that once he had his heir, he might leave her to herself more often than he had even since their wedding. She no longer found his company irksome. In fact, she quite enjoyed being with him when there was no threat of any physical demands. She supposed that was one benefit if she were with child; he might find this as a reason to avoid intimacies. Elizabeth had no way of knowing if copulation was even permitted when a woman was pregnant. She had so many questions and only wished there were someone with whom she could speak. Laura had kept her distance since Darcy's return, which Elizabeth understood to be based on her husband's presence, not her own company. But then Laura had never conceived a baby of which Elizabeth was aware and so would have limited knowledge to counsel her.

So Elizabeth wrote to her aunt seeking guidance and hoped for clarification of her symptoms.

Without Darcy around, Elizabeth's mind was left to its own amusement, and it cruelly determined to find pleasure in plaguing her with thoughts of Lady Annette and her husband's intentions upon his removal to town.

Elizabeth had been certain of her own dislike of her husband not one month ago. So what had happened to bring about so drastic a change? For the duration of her acquaintance with Darcy, he had been conceited, selfish, arrogant, officious and demanding, all building a perfect basis for her disapprobation, but then he returned from a lengthy trip to London a changed man, it would seem. Now she found herself not only enjoying his company but missing it as well.

Determined to make the most of her time at Pemberley while Mr. Darcy was away, she met with Mr. Stephens. During the meeting, she collected the names and locations for all of the tenant farmers and their families. Included were also the names and ages of their children. She then requested that a footman be made available for her to make daily visits, hoping to meet as many farmers as she could before the planting season began. She had Mrs. Reynolds assign a servant to make a basket of food and rations as largesse for each family that she was to visit and made drawing books for the children that were similar to the ones she had made for her husband's family.

Elizabeth looked forward to this part of her role as Mrs. Darcy, as she enjoyed meeting people and thanking them for being a part of their great estate. While on her route, she discovered many families and experiences for which to be thankful. She was able to hear how esteemed her husband was within the context of his own realm. The farmers and their wives praised him for his generosity, for keeping their homes in good repair, for paying as well as any farmer could hope to make. They spoke of his time as a boy when his father would send him out to work in the fields, so that he might one day lead his people with a firm knowledge of the land and the difficulties therein.

She learnt that the estate made just as much profit from wool as it did from farming, and that the land at Pemberley was ideal for the raising of sheep. Although prime for mining, the Darcys had chosen not to impose upon their land in order to increase their profits, for many a man and child had died in such occupation, and their wealth was in no way wanting to justify the endeavour.

Unfortunately Elizabeth was unable to visit as many as she had planned, but this was owing to the happy circumstance of extended visits with loquacious tenants, wives, children and shepherds. Elizabeth began to feel a true belonging to her new home during this time, as well as a new and considerable admiration for the man whom she married. She was welcomed with hospitality and kindness by everyone whom she met and made heartfelt promises to visit again.

While Darcy was away, Elizabeth received yet another letter from her sister, Lydia. Before even opening the seal, she tossed it into the fire. She refused to play any role in harming her marriage. She now suspected that Mr. Wickham's motives were not as benign as she had once thought and began to consider that her husband's strong dislike for the man may just have some merit.

THE DAY AFTER HIS CALL on the Gardiners with Bingley, Darcy went to his solicitor's office to sign papers that had been waiting for him. While there he decided to enlist the man's help in investigating his wife's affairs. Since Darcy had learnt of Elizabeth's contributions to an unknown account, he could not stop thinking about who the beneficiary might be. He considered Wickham, but after the past month spent in close quarters with his wife, he had a hard time supposing that she might make such a treacherous move. There had been no indication of duplicity. Of course she may be helping her family, but then why the secrecy?

Darcy gave his solicitor the name of the bank and account number to see if he could discover any information that might elucidate her plans. The next day he returned but found that his solicitor was unsuccessful in his attempts to obtain any intelligence. This left Darcy even more puzzled than before and without his wife there to calm his active imagination, his speculation began to run a course that he had originally instinctively rejected. *Will I ever find peace with my wife?*

367

After surprising his sister that afternoon with an extended visit, he decided to eat at his club that night and spare his staff the effort of another meal before his departure the following morning. "Darcy, man, we did not know of your return to town," said his cousin, Lord Langston.

"I am only here for a few days. In fact I leave for Pemberley tomorrow."

"How's that pretty wife of yours?"

Darcy raised his eyebrow at his cousin's meddlesome question, but as this was his typical style, Darcy did not take too much offence. "She is happily settled at Pemberley."

"So she did not join you, yet again? What brought you here? Don't tell me you needed another visit to Madame Karina's. I would think that your wife would have kept you satisfied enough."

Darcy's eyes darkened at the memory. "No, I have no need for a courtesan. Not then, and not now. Tell me how is your own wife?"

Langston shrugged as he said, "As usual. She has her amusements. She retired early tonight, so here I am. So, you never told me. How was *Aphrodite*?" He asked with a snigger that sounded more like a schoolboy than a viscount.

"I left."

"What? You left. What does that mean?"

"Just what I said, I left. I never got that far, and I would appreciate your not mentioning that night ever again. I left the place before I could make that mistake, thank the Lord."

"I don't believe you, but don't worry. I promised not to tell."

Darcy was getting increasingly irritated with his cousin but thought it best to change the subject. "Have you heard from James? Will he be around anytime soon?"

"I heard that he might be back in a few weeks. Don't you go to Rosings each spring? I suppose you will see him then."

"I have not yet decided if we will make the trip. I have already returned to town two times unexpectedly, and I am not at all sure Elizabeth would be welcome at Rosings in light of Aunt Catherine's disappointment."

"Yes, did she really think you would marry Anne? She is such a sickly creature. She would die during childbirth, I am certain. And who would want to bed her anyway?"

"Langston, do you have to be so vulgar? I warrant you are just like James. Anne is a sweet girl – but you are right about childbirth. Hopefully, she can stand up to her mother and remain single. I fear for her otherwise."

"Your wife seems perfectly capable." Darcy's annoyance was obvious. "Don't look at me so. I mean no harm. She is a lovely woman. In fact, if you remember, I had hoped for an invitation to Pemberley so we could get better acquainted."

"Perhaps this summer."

"Excellent."

"Well, if you will excuse me; I have an early start in the morning."

ELIZABETH RECEIVED HER FIRST CALLERS as mistress of Pemberley – indeed as Mrs. Darcy, for no one had visited her at Darcy House. She suspected that her husband had taken the knocker off the door at Darcy House to avoid anyone meeting his *uncouth* wife. She was pleased to be left alone there, for although she enjoyed meeting new people, especially those of interesting character and disposition, she had no desire of being looked down upon. And she had been diverted concerning her husband's pretensions and his insecurities, despite his appearances. However, here at Pemberley in the neighbourhood of her husband's childhood home, she hoped to make the acquaintance of those with whom she would build lifelong relationships.

After her husband had been gone a week, Elizabeth received a small group of ladies. Two of the neighbourhood's predominant women arrived with their daughters, two or perhaps three years older than Elizabeth's own age, in tow. Elizabeth had entertained many times at Longbourn and even Gracechurch Street, so she had no qualms about the endeavour in her new residence. She welcomed the ladies to her home and sought to learn about their history in the neighbourhood and with the Darcy family in general. She soon realised that their sole purpose in coming was not to greet the new neighbour but to confirm if the spreading rumours held any justice.

The ladies spoke of inconsequential matters – the weather, the current fashions – but then eventually brought the conversation around to her marriage, as she had suspected they might. "Mrs. Darcy," said a Miss Ashby, "you cannot imagine our shock to discover that Mr. Darcy had been compelled into marriage. However did you manage such a feat?"

Elizabeth was taken back by such an impolite question, spoken in an unequivocal manner. "Pardon me?"

The ladies laughed into their napkins, "Come Mrs. Darcy, if the rumours are correct, you were able to entice him away from the beautiful Lady Annette. You, who had no dowry, we understand, or title, were able to lure him away from the much sought after Lady Annette. We must know your secrets."

"It must be difficult for you," Elizabeth said after a pause, with a concerned look upon her countenance.

"What are you talking about?"

"Well, you are seeking to know how someone like me, desperate as I must have been in my oppressive state of singlehood, catches a husband. Have you had much disappointment?"

"I have not been disappointed, nor has Harriett," said Miss Ashby as she looked to her friend.

"I do apologise. I just assumed that with your age and well, other disadvantages, that you might be experiencing some difficulties with ensnaring a man, yourself."

"No, I am having no problems with that, I can assure you, Mrs. Darcy."

"I am glad to hear it. So will you be leaving for town soon?" and so the subject was changed.

Darcy had arrived not five minutes earlier and was searching for his wife. The butler told him that Elizabeth was entertaining in the drawing room, so

Darcy went there to make his presence known. He heard voices on his way in and stopped at the door to listen. He was disturbed at his neighbours' insolent remarks aimed at insulting his wife, but then he heard his wife's retort and almost laughed outright. She truly had no moment's hesitation. Darcy decided to make his presence known in a surprising manner that would be sure to cause talk, for he had perceived there was talk anyway. Why not give them something amusing to spout to their friends?

"Elizabeth, dear, I see you have met our neighbours," he said as he entered and then bowed. "Miss Ashby, Miss Turner, Mrs. Ashby, Mrs. Turner, a pleasure to have you at Pemberley." Then he walked over to his wife, whose eyes were wide with wonder, trying to determine if he had heard her discourteous remarks. "Hello, Elizabeth," said he, with all of the passion he could muster with an audience, and then he leaned over, gazing at her for a brief moment and giving her a quick wink. Then he reached down to his wife's hand and brought it to his lips for an obviously sensual and lingering kiss.

"I hope you will excuse us, ladies, as I have just arrived from town and hope to spend some time alone with my wife," said he without removing his eyes from Elizabeth's own.

The ladies' wide eyes and dropped jaws could not belie their shock. They quickly stood, Mrs. Ashby saying, "Mr. Darcy, please forgive us. We had no idea you had just now returned. We would not wish to impose on your generous hospitality."

"Mrs. Darcy, it was a true honour meeting you, and congratulations on your marriage. Mr. Darcy is a fine man." The younger women kept silent as they followed their mamas out of the room.

"Please come again," Elizabeth was heard to say as they made their exit.

After the door was closed behind them, she turned and said to her newly arrived husband, "You are too cruel. I had no idea that you had such a wicked side to your nature."

"I would not have you think me so."

She laughed. "Welcome home, Mr. Darcy."

"Must you call me *Mister* Darcy? I would be happy for you to call me Darcy as you once did before, or even William, as my family does on occasion."

"I will reward your amusing entrance by endeavouring to call you Darcy for now on. There, will that suffice?"

"Thank you, Elizabeth. So, tell me about your visit."

"Apparently, my reputation precedes me."

"You seemed to handle things well enough."

"You are not vexed with my insults?"

"I am not at all sure they realised that you had indeed insulted them."

"How was your trip? Did you achieve all that you desired?"

"For the most part I did, and so I was able to return home before anticipated." He had not discovered the story behind her secret monetary contributions, but he was determined to learn more in time, even if by a direct question to his wife, but for now, he thought it best to let it go, for he was home and anxious to pick up where they had left off.

THAT NIGHT, THEY ENJOYED DINNER TOGETHER. Neither would at first admit to the other how much each was missed. They spoke of many things, extending the meal for much longer than was usual. Elizabeth told Darcy about each of the tenants whom she had visited, along with little stories meant to amuse and enlighten.

"Elizabeth, I am proud of you."

"Whatever for?"

"I leave for a week, which could have been longer, and return unexpectedly. In the short time of my absence you have visited fifteen tenant families and accepted a call from a most disagreeable group of would-be Darcys. The two younger ladies have been vying for my attention for years, you know."

"I did not know, but of course I suspected. You are a most agreeable man and rich as well. So can I expect this to happen often? Young maidens jealous of my position, attempting to usurp me with offensive insults?"

"I am afraid that is your lot, my dear. If it makes you feel any better, I would not have offered for any of them, regardless of their sentiments."

"Whom would you have offered for?"

"Excuse me?"

"If you had not been *ensnared* by me, to whom would you have made an offer?"

"Why do you ask, Elizabeth?"

Quietly and with uncertainty she said, "Tell me about her."

"Who?"

"Lady Annette."

Darcy took in a deep breath. This was not the conversation he was hoping to have on this, the first evening of his return journey. "Elizabeth, what do you want to know? There is really nothing to tell."

Elizabeth wanted to know if he loved Lady Annette, if she missed her in his life, if maybe she was still in his life. She summoned her courage then came out with the question that had begun to plague her most. "Did you see her while in town?"

Darcy stood up, then walked over to pull Elizabeth's chair out. "Come, let us go to our sitting room."

Elizabeth had a foreboding feeling about her husband's strange behaviour. *Why do we need to go elsewhere?* She stood to follow him, as he took her hand. She looked up into his eyes and then allowed him to lead her out the door and up to their shared room. He walked over to the fire and seated her on the settée, then sat beside her, taking her hand again into his.

"Elizabeth, before coming to Hertfordshire, I had been spending a good bit of time with Lady Annette and her family. Her brother, Lord Wexley, went to Cambridge with me. Last Season I had decided that I would make Lady Annette an offer of marriage." Elizabeth tried to take her hand out of her husband's but he held on. "As you say, she is beautiful, accomplished and well-established in society. She would make an excellent match for someone of my standing. She had many suitors but seemed to favour me. Before I could ask for her hand, however, there was a crisis in my family that interfered with my plans. Then her father left for the North, and I would not make a move without his consent. So I waited. When Bingley called me away, I thought it the perfect opportunity to await her father's return, while limiting the annoying speculation that had already begun on our behalf."

Elizabeth turned her head away. She could not determine why his former relationships should affect her so. "You need not tell me any more."

"When you and I became engaged, I met with her brother to inform him of our understanding and offer my apologies for any disappointment I may have caused. The next time I saw her was at the ball. She was understandably disheartened with our marriage, which may be why she was so rude to you. Yes, I noticed how she behaved, but I also saw that you were able to manage her jealousies on your own.

"When I was last in town I ran into Wexley and his father at my club. They invited me for dinner and that is where I saw her. We had a pleasant evening, and that was the last and only occasion we were in the same company since the ball. That was last month. She has much to offer a man and will soon become engaged; I have no doubt."

"Did you love her?" Elizabeth could not believe that she had asked such a personal question of her husband, but she had to know.

"No."

"You would ask a woman you did not love to marry you?"

"You must know, Elizabeth, that marrying for love is a luxury many cannot afford. I had never planned to marry for love, so that was not a part of my decision to ask for her. Lady Annette had a substantial dowry, she was attractive, she had many accomplishments, and her connections were impeccable. I have also come to realise that she is exceedingly dull and ill-humoured." He smiled at Elizabeth's astonished countenance. "Don't look so shocked. No one is perfect. I am convinced that if I had married her, I would have had a very sedate and tedious existence. She would have been the perfect bride for a man of my station but not perfect for me. No, I am thankful that I was unable to offer for her."

"Maybe she would have changed for the better after you married her."

"No, I would have approved of our very boring existence, not knowing any differently, and she would have continued on as before, or worse turned into someone else altogether after she had secured me."

"Maybe that would have been better for you."

"One thing I know, life will never be sedate or tedious with you, Elizabeth, and I believe I can finally see the merit in such a life."

She laughed, "I have much to offer after all, it would seem."

"Yes, you do," he said as he let go of her hand and then brought his own up to her face for a gentle caress. "Elizabeth, I missed you." Darcy saw that she had an uncharacteristically timid look upon her face. "I confess that I hoped that you might have missed me too."

"I did," she said looking away, embarrassed to have admitted what she had been thinking all along.

Darcy was becoming familiar with Elizabeth's vulnerabilities and thought it charming that she might actually have been a little jealous of Lady Annette, but he wanted to reassure her of his growing esteem. "Do you remember when I told you that I would share with you some of your qualities that I find enchanting?"

"I remember."

"I already told you how beautiful I find you, but it is worth saying again. I was blind when I entered Hertfordshire, eyes clouded by my own conceit. No one could have found favour with me, so please do not let those words you overheard continue to bother you, as I know they have. Elizabeth, you are not only lovely, but also a delightful companion, graceful in your presence, and exceedingly alluring," he said as he glanced to her person. Here she blushed, looking down to her hands. He smiled at her embarrassment. "Do not worry your pretty head; I intend to keep my promise. You are also intelligent, witty, refined and playful. I have never before known a woman to stimulate me in every possible way as you do."

"You cannot mean all that you say. I know you cannot."

"But I do, and I would not lie to you. What could I gain by doing so?"

"You could gain what you want most from me. You promise to wait until I too want to be with you. You are saying these pretty words to seduce me, to try to entice me into favouring you."

"Can pretty words seduce you then, Elizabeth?" His mind had unwillingly gone to Wickham again.

"No, words do not. Sincerity. That is what I desire most from you right now, from anyone." She thought some more. "And I need to feel cherished."

"What else do you need?" he said, drawn in to her.

She looked away considering if she should open herself to him again. In a small voice, Elizabeth finally said, "I need to feel, to feel loved. Unlike you, I always hoped to marry for love, or not at all. I must sound like a sentimental fool to you, but I must speak as I feel."

Darcy had never been in love and could not know for sure if that was the feeling that was budding within. He knew he felt high esteem and regard for her. Maybe one day he could sincerely give her what she needed. "I hope one day you get everything you need, Elizabeth. You must understand that I *want* to make you happy, whatever that means."

She thought of the baby that she was all but certain to be growing inside of her and knew that even if her husband could never love her, that one day she would have a child, his child, who could fill the void within her heart.

ELIZABETH RECEIVED A RESPONSE from her aunt, as well as another letter from Jane, enclosed within. She was sitting at breakfast with her husband when the letters arrived. "Are you not going to read your letters?" asked her husband.

"I thought I might wait until after breakfast." Elizabeth was hoping to read her aunt's response in the privacy of her room. She was quite certain that she was with child and hoped that her aunt would reassure her that her symptoms had been those experienced by women in like condition.

Darcy wanted to see his wife's countenance upon receiving news of her sister's renewed hopes and saw that she had a letter from her aunt and also one from her sister. "I have some letters to read as well. Why don't we retire to our sitting room after breakfast, and we can enjoy one another's company while we read our mail?"

For the sake of harmony, Elizabeth agreed to the scheme. Just because she would now be relegated to her husband's company did not mean that she must share the news contained in her correspondence. Elizabeth had found him quite capable in the past at reading her facial expressions, so she would just have to work hard to control them. So when she had finished her tea and bread roll, Darcy walked with her up to their shared room. They sat by the large fire, he in a chair and she on the settée. Elizabeth settled in comfortably, slipping off her shoes and pulling her feet up and underneath her skirts, prepared to savour the words contained within the pages of her letters. She opened the one from Jane first and silently read.

March 11, 1811
Dear Lizzy,

I have such news to tell! I can hardly write for the shaking in my hands. You will never believe me when I tell you that I had a surprise visitor two days past at my aunt and uncle's home. We had started our day as usual when we were summoned to the drawing room to accept two gentlemen callers. The door opened into the room and who should walk in? Mr. Bingley and your Mr. Darcy! Of course, you must have known that they would be calling, but you did not say. I must forgive you there, for I am the happiest of creatures. They stayed for dinner, but Mr. Darcy did not return again because he said he would be leaving for Pemberley soon. Indeed, he may be with you as you read this. His friend returned the following day and then today he asked to speak with me in private. Lizzy, oh how I wish you could now share my happiness with me, for he asked me to marry him! After my aunt gave him adequate time to propose, she suggested he go to my uncle's warehouse to make it official. I am so happy, my dear sister. If only you were here, my joy would be complete.

Even more so, I wish we could share in your own hopes, for my aunt has told me that I am to be an aunt! Oh, my dear sister, how blessed you are. Since Mr. Bingley is such good friends with your husband, maybe after we are married, he will take me to visit you. How I long to see you and congratulate you in person. Please take care of yourself. I confess that I have been so worried about you since last we met at Longbourn.

Well, I must finish before he returns and write to my mother. She will be delighted about our news.

Much love,
JB

Tears had begun to fill her eyes as she read Jane's letter. *Could this be true? Could she truly be engaged to Mr. Bingley?* The answer to her question could easily be found in the man before her, who, when she looked up to him, displayed a heartfelt smile of true warmth upon his fine features. "You knew? You were there? Is that why you went to London?" He continued staring at her with delight infused upon his countenance.

"Does this make you happy, my dear?"

"I thought you did not approve. I thought you would never encourage the match. What happened to change your mind?"

"I was wrong to interfere in my friend's affairs. He needed to decide for himself, and I simply apologised for my part in separating him from your sister. It was really quite easy after that. One look at them together and I realised my error. He loves her, and I now see that she cares for him. I had not seen it before because I, in my foolish pride, thought that I knew best. I ignored what was obvious to all."

Now Elizabeth was truly crying as she attempted to wipe away her tears with her handkerchief. "Forgive me. I cannot seem to stop crying. I have been so emotional lately."

He reached over to wipe off another tear running down her cheek. "Are you pleased?"

"I hope your friend will work hard to deserve her. She is the very best of women, you know."

"Yes, I do know. If you admire her, she must be a wonderful creature. So, he has asked her then?" She nodded her confirmation. "I knew he would need little time to complete the task."

"Thank you, Mr. Darcy, I mean *Darcy*. How can I ever express to you what this means to me?"

Darcy could think of many ways, but quickly put them out of his mind, for he now understood that there was no physical show of affection that could ever satisfy him without his wife's open and honest devotion. "Your happiness is all that is needed."

Elizabeth stared at him in wonder. Could this be the same man whom she married? And would he change back to that once proud, disagreeable man upon leaving Pemberley and returning to town? She could not bear to return to how things had been. Then she recalled her second letter. "My aunt's letter! I should read it."

"Speaking of your aunt, why did you not tell me her history? I knew that you mentioned that she had been a friend of Mrs. Carpenter at one time, but I did not consider her being from Lambton or who she might be. Elizabeth, your aunt is the former Margaret Pennington. Her father was one of my father's dearest friends at one time, before he died. She comes from a noble family, if now somewhat distant."

"I did not realise her father and yours were such close friends. She did tell me she had known you once, but when you did not perceive who she was, I supposed that the acquaintance was tenuous at best. I did tell you that you would have things in common if you were to give her a chance, but you would not."

"I always wondered what happened to Miss Pennington, now Mrs. Gardiner. I cannot understand how I missed who she was. She was but fifteen when last I saw her. I was twelve, but she has changed very little. She is still just as lovely as she ever was."

"You thought her lovely?"

"Yes! I even had a childhood infatuation with her, until she left." Darcy noticed his wife's merriment and asked, "Why do you laugh?"

"I never thought for a moment that my husband would have had a childhood obsession with my aunt! She is a tradesman's wife, you know."

"Yes, I am aware of her husband's occupation, but at the time, she was the daughter of our rector, one of my father's dearest friends. Mr. Gardiner and I spent time over dinner getting to know one another. Elizabeth, I was foolish to discount your family without getting to know them. You must think me such a pompous simpleton."

"I knew if you gave them a chance that you would come to recognise their true worth despite their being in trade."

"Your uncle told me about his successes as a businessman. When I consider how many of my own friends gamble away the money handed down to them from others' hard work and while away their days in conceited profligacy, and there I was judging your family harshly and by some ill-judged standards of value – I am ashamed of myself. And you, my Elizabeth, listened to me make an absolute arse of myself. How you must have been laughing at me."

"No, I could not laugh. Had you been someone else, anyone else, perhaps."

They continued to sit there in silent contemplation, he of his unseemly behaviour the past four months, and she of her growing admiration for the man before her. But then she remembered her letter again and was anxious to read its contents. "I think I would like to read my aunt's letter now, if that is acceptable to you."

"Of course. Will you remain in here with me while I read my own?"

"If you wish it." He smiled and then began to devote himself to his correspondence.

Elizabeth unfolded the letter from her aunt and read.

March 11, 1811
Dear Lizzy,

You sly girl. You never told Mr. Darcy of my connection with his family, poor man. Well, he knows now, and I imagine he regrets his former views on us, so don't be too hard on him.

I will let you read Jane's letter for the exciting news of the day. She is all aglow and anxious to share with you. So if you have not yet read her letter, stop now and read hers before you carry on here. She quickly forgave Mr. Bingley for his misguided absence and is well on her way to being in love, if not so already. We are very pleased with the match.

Now about your own letter, my dear Lizzy, how happy I am for you! You are indeed with child. I am all but certain. I know because your courses stopped and you have all the classic symptoms of fatigue, nausea and emotional outbursts! All of these are normal for a woman in your condition. When will you tell your husband? I know he will be delighted to know that he will soon be a father, and a good one he will be, if he is anything like his own. I know you might hope for an heir, but I cannot help but say that I do hope for a little girl, one just like you.

There are those who abstain from marital relations while pregnant, but I confess that I see no need. When is your expected confinement? I must know so I can plan on helping you, if you wish it.

I must now write to your mother about Jane or she will never forgive me.

Your devoted aunt,
MG

Elizabeth finished her letter with satisfaction. Her aunt had answered her most pressing questions, and she was now free to let the joy of her condition overcome her, but not now in the sitting room. "I will see you later, sir. I believe I would like to practise the pianoforte for a little while."

"Can I come listen to you later?"

She smiled at his consideration. "If it pleases you."

"It does."

"Then I will see you again soon."

BEFORE DARCY COULD JOIN HER in the music room, however, sleepiness overcame Elizabeth again, but this time, she was contented to know that her sleep was for the baby's sake. She let herself fall into a deep slumber, and hours later she was woken up, not by Janette, but by her husband.

"Elizabeth, Elizabeth, wake up. You have been asleep all afternoon."

She roused at her husband's voice, opening her eyes to see him sitting on the side of her bed. Elizabeth instantly recalled that she had fallen asleep in her chemise and reached to her chest to make certain she was covered; however, she was disheartened to discover that she had inadvertently kicked off her blanket while she slumbered. So she began to look around for the covering, only to discover she had kicked it off the bed.

"Do you always sleep so restlessly, Elizabeth?" asked her amused husband.

"Could you please hand me the throw, *Mr.* Darcy? I seem to have misplaced it while sleeping."

"Oh, I'm *Mister* Darcy again. Are you always so changeable, Mrs. Darcy?"

She breathed in deeply, letting out an exaggerated sigh. "I will get it myself."

"No allow me," said he as they both leaned down simultaneously to retrieve the covering off the floor. Unfortunately for Elizabeth, but equally fortuitous for her husband, she caught her leg on the side of the bed while quickly attempting to jump off to grab the blanket, thus falling straight into his strong arms, who could not have planned a more delightful encounter with his wife. "I never knew you to be clumsy, my dear," he said as he held on to her, a becoming smile gracing his countenance.

He has dimples, thought a distracted Elizabeth, and then realising her predicament, she quickly pulled herself away and snatched the blanket off the floor. "I am not usually so, but I find that my husband tends to have that negative effect upon me." Just then Elizabeth remembered reading her aunt's letter before falling asleep and began searching around to find it. Darcy noticed her distracted perusal of the bed and began to look himself for he knew not what. Just then, Elizabeth snatched the letter up quickly as if she feared he might get to it first.

"I did not know you were looking for your letter; I could have already told you where it was"

"What did you see?"

Darcy had now begun to wonder what she did not want him to regard in the letter her aunt had sent to her. "I did not see anything. I do not make a habit of reading other people's correspondence. I have enough to worry with my own."

She saw her error and meant to make light of the whole notion, so she hastily said, "Of course. I meant no disrespect. I think I am still confused from being woken up. That's all." She then walked over to her writing desk while wrapping herself in the blanket. Elizabeth opened the top and added the letter to a stack of others.

Meanwhile, Darcy was watching her curiously, trying to figure out her strange behaviour. *She obviously did not want me to see the letter, but why? It was clearly from her aunt.*

"What time is it? I should probably prepare for dinner."

Darcy, after a few moments in thought, finally said, "I have an idea. It is getting close to the time you would need to dress for dinner, but you are obviously still tired. Instead of attiring formally, let's take trays in our sitting room. We could spend the rest of the afternoon and evening upstairs and bypass all the fuss of getting ready."

"That sounds nothing like you. Are you certain you would want to have such an informal evening?"

"Only if it pleases you."

The timing of her yawn seemed to answer any question he might have had about her preferences. "I will send word down to the kitchen. Why don't you don your dressing gown and I will get more comfortable myself." A look of panic overspread her countenance as she contemplated what he must have been thinking. "Elizabeth, please do not make yourself uneasy. I can assure you that I have no intentions other than to spend a quiet evening with my lovely wife."

"I am sorry. Having me as a wife must be such a tribulation for you," said Elizabeth, equally embarrassed and relieved.

"A tribulation?" He laughed. "No, I would rather say an advantage."

"Oh, and how is that?"

"You add value to my life, I believe. You are someone who does not accept me as I present myself, like everyone else, but you challenge me to examine my own faults, which I might add that I did not even know dwelt within. I have been complacent my whole life, setting my own standards for acceptable behaviour, but you continue to cause me to question everything I have ever known. You make me a better person. So yes, I would say that you are indeed an advantage."

"How fortunate for me that you would begin to see my vexatious nature as an advantage!" She laughed. "Be careful, my husband, or you might just unleash a monster within your own home, for I feel as though I have held my tongue more often than was bearable."

"I would not compare you to a monster. I am the one who is the beast; you said so yourself and would be correct." Elizabeth looked away, disconcerted by the memory. "Again, you are proven the superior. I will not speak of such things again; instead I will leave you to finish preparing yourself for a relaxing evening." He started to walk towards the sitting room door, but then stopped and turned around saying, "Elizabeth, would you leave your hair down?"

With upturned lips and a slight blush, she said, "If that appeals to you, I will."

"You can trust me. I promise. I will see you in the sitting room."

ELIZABETH OPENED THE DOOR to the shared room and went inside to find her husband sitting by the fire waiting for her. Darcy had removed his jacket and waistcoat as well as his cravat, so that his shirt was opened at the top. He had also removed his shoes and was sitting comfortably while setting up a chessboard. When she walked in, he stood to greet her. She stopped for a moment before hesitantly moving forward again. Elizabeth was struck by how handsome her husband appeared when not puffed up in self-importance, casual as he now was.

"I see that you wish to challenge me again. I will not be so easy on you this time, though," said she as she walked over to join him. Elizabeth sat down, and he followed suit.

"Would you like a glass of wine while we play?"

"So, you desire to dull my senses in order to improve your position? But I will not give you the advantage."

Instead while the game progressed, Darcy spent equal time in admiration of her natural charms while trying to hide his appreciation, so that he was the one at a disadvantage, overwhelmed with the unfamiliar feelings of regard that ultimately distracted him from being able to concentrate on the next move, much less develop any kind of strategy. Elizabeth had left her dark, silky locks down as requested and had put on a linen dressing gown, embroidered with tiny flowers around the feminine collar and tied with a buff ribbon below the bodice. Her unadorned beauty caused Darcy to reflect upon her inherent qualities as the foundation of her true allurement rather than fine clothing or jewels. Perhaps this was what made Elizabeth the more beautiful woman over Lady Annette, that his wife's grace was natural – a part of her being – rather than wanting for enhancement. How blinded he had been in the past!

Of course, while his mind was agreeably engaged in such introspections, his wife took advantage of his distraction and soundly beat him. "Check mate! You, sir, let me win this game, but I will have you know that I can win just as well without your assistance. Truly, what has gotten into you? I almost feel offended at your obviously meagre contributions to the game," said Elizabeth, amused by his look of bewilderment. "What are you daydreaming about?"

"If I were to tell you, I might have the opportunity to enjoy that pretty blush of yours."

"Darcy, I never thought you to be so charming. So will you always be this agreeable? You let me take advantage of your musings while claiming I am their object."

He smiled at her teasing. "Let us play again. This time I promise to give you my very best competitive confrontation. Perhaps you should wrap yourself in this warm blanket," he said as he stood and covered her with it, "so that you can no longer claim leverage over me." Then he looked at her prettily nestled within, and said, "No, I am afraid it will be a lost cause. I will just have to plead for mercy and ask that you not spread word of my losses to our acquaintances."

She continued to laugh, but more openly, retorting, "You are a prideful man! Making up excuses for your losses other than my superior skill!"

"I am afraid we may never know the truth of the matter, for I will always have the disadvantage, unless of course we play independently, taking turns with the chessboard without the other's presence. Of course that might lessen the intrinsic pleasure I would desire while playing with my wife."

"You have become quite the charmer. I will punish you by accepting your challenge for another game. This time, I will do something unbecoming during your turn, so as to avoid any unnecessary upper hand."

"I cannot imagine how you might bring that about."

"I will speak of how agreeable you are to look upon, then simper and coo over your fine home and how very rich you are. That should give injury to my cause." He laughed outright. "And when you make a particularly clever move, I will congratulate you on your cunning and acumen."

"I do believe that we have discovered the very thing that I enjoy most about you: your total lack of veneration for me. If I had only known all of these years that I would prefer such a thing, I would have moved to a faraway land and gone undercover as a poor gentleman farmer."

"But your good looks would have continued to plague you."

"You find me handsome then?"

"I am sure I do not, but everyone else does."

"But I find that you are the only one who matters."

"Oh, dear. Well, then I suppose that I will have to confess that I do indeed see that you have some physical attributes for which to esteem, that are greatly enhanced when you smile rather than scowl as I am used to seeing."

"You think I scowl often then?"

"Yes. Well, not recently, I will admit, but as a general rule, yes. You have always seemed most despondent to me and happy to be thus. However, since your return in February, you have grown complacent, I believe. You almost seem happy."

"And this pleases you?" She nodded that it did as a new blush crept up her neck and coloured her cheeks. Just then the servant knocked upon the door. "Enter," said Darcy and their dinner was brought in and set up upon the small dining table by the window. "You must be hungry since you missed tea."

Darcy then stood and reached his hand down for Elizabeth to join him at the table. They enjoyed the meal, speaking of books and their families and any other topic that seemed to naturally intrude. Elizabeth had more than once thought to enlighten her husband on her suspected pregnancy. She knew for certain he would be pleased, but then decided to await the quickening to be assured. She would hate to cause him disappointment if she were wrong; add to that, she was troubled to discuss such a delicate condition with this man for whom she now had a growing admiration, but around whom she still felt ill at ease reflecting upon such personal matters.

Darcy walked Elizabeth back to the fire when the meal was completed, but instead of sitting across from her in the chair where he had previously been, he sat next to her, taking her hand in his own. Elizabeth's eyes widened at the thought of being so close to him while informally attired as they were. He began nonchalantly rubbing her hand with his thumb while examining her every facial feature.

"You have a way of making me blush, Darcy. I begin to grow afraid of you."

"You need never fear me again. I know I was not to repeat such things, but I feel I must. I am not the same man who treated you with disrespect and without honour. I only aspire to give you the dignity that being Mrs. Darcy deserves."

For the first time of Elizabeth's remembrance, the appellation of Mrs. Darcy gave her genuine pleasure, so as a show of her approbation, she placed her other hand on top of his own, the first manifestation of her growing regard. "That means more to me than I can express. I have a dawning hope that we might find gratification rather than grief in our marriage."

With his free hand, Darcy reached up to one of her long curls and began to wrap it around his fingers, and then let it go only to do so again. The softness of her hair and intimacy of such a moment began their work on his senses. He soon brought his hand up to her neckline, smoothing her luxurious locks behind her back, thus exposing part of her shoulder where her dressing gown unevenly rested. His body longed to taste her skin, but he would not betray his promise reiterated not ten minutes previously. He was afraid that one touch would so easily lead to another. How could he take advantage of her budding trust?

Elizabeth had never felt this way; somewhere deep inside, her body was encouraging her to lean over and kiss this man before her, her husband. She had never actually kissed a man before. The kiss that he had imposed upon her in her room at Longbourn gave her no pleasure, only disgust. How could she want to explore his touch again? Elizabeth had firmly believed that she would never seek her husband's physical presence in her life, and here she was, desiring just that. She giggled as she considered that she very likely was carrying this man's baby and yet had never enjoyed a true kiss of affection. At his puzzled expression, she felt like she should say something and so began, "This is a strange situation in which we find ourselves. You want to kiss me, and I confess that I startlingly wish for you to do so, but neither of us is willing to make the move, despite your former *liberties*. Forgive me for my surprising speech, but I do enjoy the follies that present themselves in my life."

Darcy smiled at her whimsical nature that had always diverted him, if he were to own it. "You are saying that I may kiss you?"

"Do you need my permission?"

"I am afraid that is exactly what I need, for I have set up an untenable situation for myself where I must receive your expressed approval before I enjoy any pleasures which my wife might deign to allow."

"Such power I have! You mean to continue to punish yourself for something which I have given you my forgiveness."

"But you said you will never forget. Nor shall I." Darcy then looked away before continuing, "I will never forget the look of defeat and resentment you presented. I will endeavour to make the remembrance for you a distant one, and a recollection that is used to compare your present happiness, that it might add weight to your pleasure."

"You have my permission."

Darcy needed no other encouragement, but he was conscious of his own vulnerability, while Elizabeth could not believe her own daring. Was this really what she wanted?

Darcy leaned towards her slowly, giving her every opportunity to change her mind or turn away. Instead, she leaned into him and met him part way. *Could this be the same woman who turned her head away in disgust? Yes, she is the same woman; I'm just a different man.* He had begun to berate himself again for his previous treatment of her, but this thought was soon overcome by the exquisite pleasure which a pair of fine lips could bestow on the mouth of an inspirited recipient. Then Darcy noticed a hint of rose and what else was it? *Some familiar spice? Did she wear this for me or does she always wear this scent, while I have missed it? – Like so many other fine qualities.* He breathed in deeply savouring her scent, her softness and her warmth.

There could be no comparison between the two kisses in which this couple had thus far shared. The first had been painful for both, taken by force and with no redeeming intention or benefit. Elizabeth had felt the full impact of the deliberate degradation and despised him for it, but not this time. As his lips gently brushed her own an unexpected feeling of longing spread over her and inside of her. The pleasure was short-lived as Darcy pulled back to look upon her face. Could she have enjoyed the kiss as much as he? He received his answer as she took hold of her lower lip within her teeth and glanced up into his eyes. Then a becoming smile overspread her countenance.

"Can we count this as our first kiss? I did not participate in the last one, and this one was so much more delightful."

His eyes danced, joining in her playfulness. "This *is* a new beginning for us, and as I do not believe that I am the same man I used to be, I would say 'yes,' and a perfect first kiss it was, too."

"I would like to reward you."

"For what?"

"For giving me a perfect first kiss, by giving *you* another." She then leaned towards him, lip again ensconced between her teeth until the last moment when she released its hold and met his own. This one lasted longer than the first, as each savoured the feeling of mutual pleasure and accord. Darcy moved closer letting go of her hand and instead wrapping it around her back while the other continued to caress her face and neck. Although near the fireplace, Elizabeth felt a shiver run down her spine that continued to tingle as her husband gently stroked her back.

Elizabeth had never felt the comfort and solace that she did while in the gentle embrace of her strong husband. She knew he was a powerful man, not just physically but also socially and fiscally. He could provide her with the comfort and security that all women, including herself, might desire, and he was holding her with a tenderness she longed for. She could not have identified what exactly she was feeling towards him, but her regard and affection were now secure.

After a few moments of true bliss, Darcy pulled back and gazed into her eyes. "Thank you, Elizabeth. You have made me very happy." They stared at one another, not really knowing how to proceed, but Darcy, not wanting to ruin a good thing with more demands said, "Now perhaps I will have you at a disadvantage, making even the playing field." At her lost look, he said, "Chess."

She smiled as he moved to the opposite chair to take his place at the chessboard. They played again, this time neither truly able to concentrate, both making nonsensical errors and then laughing at their blunders. "Well, Darcy, you have sufficiently distracted me, which I thought might put us on equal footing, but now I see that neither of us is truly able to concentrate adequately to play in earnest. I will have to challenge you again and hope for better luck."

"Whenever you would like to play, I would be happy to attempt the challenge. Now, you are looking rather sleepy, so I think it is time that you went to bed."

"Thank you, Darcy, for keeping your promise and for allowing me to enjoy your company without fear of further... um, well, demands. Your patience means so much to me, and I hope that in so doing, you will find your reward."

"I want what you want. Now, I must insist you go to your rest, so that we will be able to get in our early walk tomorrow. It promises to be a lovely day and the bulbs should be coming into full bloom."

"I look forward to our walk then."

"Perhaps, since it is getting warmer, we might consider a horse riding lesson, that is if you would like to. There are many areas of Pemberley that I would enjoy showing you, yet they are too far to be reached by foot, and the terrain is too difficult for a phaeton." He looked at her hopefully, wanting her to agree but equally wanting her approval.

"We will talk about that tomorrow." She hated to put him off, but was unsure if riding while with child was wise. Maybe she could put him off for another month until the baby has quickened and she could be sure of her joy.

Chapter Eighteen

Happy is the man who finds a true friend, and far happier is he who finds that true friend in his wife.
Franz Schubert

Over the next fortnight, Darcy and Elizabeth each found that their new understanding had its advantages. The time spent together had become a source of pleasure and joy. Although the Darcys did not share a room or a bed, they would meet in their joined sitting room to blithely while away the evening.

After the couple had taken their beginning steps towards a shared intimacy with their first kiss, Darcy was careful not to impose himself upon Elizabeth, fearful that she might feel uneasy or even possibly fear him. He could never quite forget the look upon her countenance on that horrid day in her bedroom at Longbourn, and Darcy would deny himself for as long as was needed, so that she might develop a true trust in him and possibly even invite him to herself. Darcy would delight in their kisses and suspected that his wife did as well, as she willingly welcomed him. And indeed it was so.

Elizabeth could never have imagined the delight she experienced in her husband's strong arms. When they were close, she would breathe in deeply his manly scents of citrus and sandalwood. His kisses were always tender, but never fervent, and she marvelled at their growing mutual affection, as he seemed to long for her pleasure more than his own. She often caught Darcy gazing upon her in a way that left her without doubt as to his regard, so different than in months past.

Evenings were often spent before the hearth, with each taking turns reading aloud to the other. This first occurred when Elizabeth had picked up Darcy's book out of curiosity and began reading where her husband's marker was left. When he joined her and she apologised, meaning to return his tome to him, he resisted and instead suggested that he read to her as an alternative. In this way, they had begun a nightly routine of sharing a book and then reflecting on what they had read. Elizabeth found their conversations stimulating and insightful, while Darcy found them captivating.

Elizabeth had always cherished these activities with her father, but she had fully expected that her marriage could never provide the gratification found in the sharing of thoughts and ideas with another, when equally valued. Her father had respected her opinion and enjoyed discussions with her about the mundane and peculiar alike. Surely Darcy could not value her observations, she had once thought. Up until a month ago, Elizabeth had held no hope that her husband might contribute to improving her mind in this way, so she was astonished when she began to savour her husband's company just as she had her father's. Darcy's insights challenged her to reconsider her previous suppositions, while her input obviously caused him to weigh his own presumptions.

Darcy had never encountered a woman who took pleasure in discussing topics usually resigned to men's clubs or billiards rooms. Not only did Elizabeth enjoy a discourse on issues in which women rarely held an interest, but she also verbalised her own opinions with vigour and acumen. She did not agree with him in order to gain his favour, quite the opposite; she often countered his views, causing him to rethink his long-held perspectives, despite having been challenged by highly educated men in the past. He had long seen that his preconceived ideas about his wife's having little to offer him, aside from a pleasing figure, had no basis in reality. She stimulated his mind, perhaps even more than his salacity. Usually his pride was bound up in his ability to hold his own in an argument, but she shared her opinions with such sweetness and wit that he could not help but concede to her sentiments. Darcy found his cousin, Colonel Fitzwilliam, a worthy adversary when rebutting a point of contention, but Darcy never enjoyed the sport as much as he did with his wife. *His wife.* She was his. He now saw that without meaning to, he had managed to marry a woman most conducive to sharing his life in contented companionship and delight.

One evening, Darcy was reflecting upon his good fortune as he listened to Elizabeth read from *Poems* by William Wordsworth. Her voice was enchanting and took him to the meadows about which she read, and he had begun to anticipate many years spent enjoying such harmonious evenings. A puppy sat at her side, keeping her warm, as she read aloud. Darcy had purchased for his wife a new companion, a pure bred spaniel whom she called Charlie, much to Darcy's amusement. He had thoughtfully considered that although the dog was a hunter, when grown he would keep his wife entertained on her long walks.

A footman knocked on the sitting room door, and when Darcy gave an answering, "Enter," he came in with the mail atop a silver salver, which had been delayed that day due to an earlier downpour. Darcy took the mail off the tray and dismissed his servant. "Elizabeth, you have a letter from Longbourn and one from Hunsford. Shall we take a break from our poetry and read our correspondence?" Darcy had noticed that he himself had an express added to the small pile and wanted to read it forthwith, fearing that it might portend ill tidings.

"If you do not mind taking a break from the idylls of Wordsworth," replied Elizabeth with a smile.

"I do not mind; however, I would hope to return to our reading."

"Of course, if you wish." Elizabeth was happy to consider spending the remainder of the evening in that way.

Darcy arose from the settée by the fire, which he had been sharing with Elizabeth, in order to move close to the lamplight, while she remained where she had been reading. He opened his letter in concealed agitation, not knowing what to expect, and noted the brevity of the communication and that all too familiar script.

Darcy could not have anticipated the application. He glanced up to see Elizabeth's gaze resting upon him. She looked troubled by his countenance, so he attempted to school himself to have a placid and unconcerned look about him.

"Darcy, I do hope your expression is not indicative of something amiss. You appear as though you have received disturbing news."

Darcy's breaths came quickly as he realised the impact the letter in his hand had on his sensibilities. His affections for Elizabeth had grown over the past two months, and it pained him to consider what tidings were in store for him. Rather than respond to her remark, he walked over to gaze out of the window, so his thoughts could run their natural course without an audience.

Elizabeth had noticed that his letter was written in a decidedly feminine script, and she was curious as to the authoress. She was unaccustomed to these feelings of jealousy, but she experienced a pang of uncertainty when she saw him read the letter with avid dedication, leaving her to recall that they had never shared such devotion in writing while he was away. She hoped that the letter was from his sister, as she knew that he loved Georgiana dearly, but heard little from her – so seldom, in fact, that Elizabeth had never seen a letter from her to recognise her handwriting.

While Elizabeth was contemplating her reaction to his letter, Darcy's tempestuous thoughts overcame his ability to think clearly. *Wickham! Blast him!* To distract Elizabeth from her inquiring looks, Darcy said as he left the room, "It looks as though I have some matters of business which need my attention. Please excuse me." He was unskilled at lying, so he hoped that what he had said was close enough to the truth to elude her curiosity.

When Darcy reached his study, he poured himself a brandy into a crystal snifter and held it up to his lips for a moment before taking a large gulp. He set the glass down as the fire burned down his throat.

He began pacing as he considered his plan. He could leave for town tomorrow at dawn and arrive by the following evening, if he travelled with just his valet and minimised the stops. The days were longer even than just two weeks ago, so in the event that the rain had passed, his plans would have him at his London residence by this time two days hence.

Easter was coming up within the following fortnight, and he had considered taking Elizabeth with him on his annual journey to Rosings, the home of Lady Catherine. He had not yet communicated his expectations to her, in case he changed his mind. Elizabeth's sister resided at the parsonage which abutted his aunt's estate, so he thought she might like to have time to visit there, but he dreaded his aunt's manners and doubtless condescension towards his wife, should he bring her with him. The timing of the letter could not have been worse if he intended to take Elizabeth. Perhaps he should go without her and make the trip to Kent as he usually did, with just his cousin, Fitzwilliam, to accompany him.

He hoped to have the concerns to which the express alluded promptly resolved, so he could appease his aunt by arriving at Rosings the Monday before Easter and staying the week through, before returning to Pemberley – assuming of course that the letter did not portend anything injurious which would require his staying in town for longer.

Darcy's feelings for his wife had undergone a most striking transformation since coming to Pemberley. Since that day in the cabin, which now seemed so long ago, he had been highly attracted to her, but Darcy would not initially concede to her overwhelming beauty – a beauty that grew as he came to know her better. And to his utter astonishment, Elizabeth's intelligence exceeded that of most of his acquaintances. She was not only quick witted, but her delivery was all that was charming. He found himself many times caught in her web, and happy to be there. How he enjoyed the challenge that accompanied their conversations. Darcy felt as though he could never tire of her companionship.

Upon their first acquaintance, Darcy mocked Elizabeth for her energy and vivacity, as the social norm for a lady was serenity and calmness, but now he revelled in her playfulness and her love of life. She had proven herself to be a dedicated and competent mistress of Pemberley. The tenants already had accepted her, and she was known for her kindness towards those beneath her. In truth, had he sat down and considered the qualities most desirable in a wife, surely he could not have developed a more comprehensive list.

The only thing about which he was uncertain was the nature of his feelings. Darcy had never been in love before and had never planned to fall in love. His preferences for a bride did not necessarily include sentiments, but he could not deny the surge of energy he felt whenever in her presence or the longing to hold her in his arms, especially when her eyes lit up with a tease followed by a smile. He had some time ago given up his doubts concerning her part in forcing a marriage. Darcy conceded that his knowledge of her was inconsistent with the possibility that she might be after his money or that she would cause herself to be compromised with the hope of an attachment; but then to whom was she forwarding her funds and what of the express?

He picked up the missive and perused its contents again, saying aloud, "What could she mean by, *'indisputable evidence, some shocking news concerning Elizabeth and GW, which cannot help but have an impact on your marriage'?* I know that Wickham had imposed himself upon her family, and he doubtless attempted to turn her against me. That would be like him; he would enjoy nothing better than to poison my wife. But has Elizabeth not shown herself to be discerning and generous? Surely now she could see through his lies." Darcy had learnt in the past that he greatly erred when reacting impulsively to Wickham's interference in his marriage. He had hurt Elizabeth and was determined to think rationally on the matter and not jump to conclusions that might destroy the relationship he and his wife had built.

Nothing could be gained by ruminating over the letter now; there would be plenty of time for that on the journey to town, so Darcy rang for his butler as he wrote out a quick missive for his steward. When Peters arrived, he told him of his plans for leaving, then said, "Please send this note to Mr. Stephens, then ask my valet to prepare for departure at daylight. I leave for town so have the carriage readied. I'll be gone for at least a fortnight, likely longer."

"Shall I have Mrs. Darcy's lady's maid prepare her trunks as well, sir?"

"No, she will not be joining me on this trip."

"Very good, sir. I will make sure that a full breakfast awaits you before your departure."

"Thank you, Peters. You always think of everything."

As his butler left the room, Darcy considered what he should say to Elizabeth about his plans. He could not tell her about the letter, of course, but he disliked deceit. He would be going to Rosings without her, and although she did not know about the possibility of travelling there, he did not want her to think he was intentionally leaving her off. But the less said, the better.

Darcy remained in his study taking care of any lingering business, while he waited for his steward to arrive. As the hour was late, Mr. Stephens did not appear until Darcy had completed sifting through his papers. Darcy was sitting on his leather chair by the fire when his steward was announced. There was little to discuss, as Mr. Stephens was well acquainted with the needs of Pemberley, so within the hour, Darcy was able to make his way back to his rooms. He needed to tell Elizabeth of his upcoming journey, but she may no longer be in the sitting room. If that were the case, he would need to knock on her chamber door. That thought naturally led to other thoughts. *No, I must not think that way. Whatever lies between us in London must be resolved first, and surely she would not welcome me.*

ELIZABETH SAT UPSTAIRS in the sitting room after Darcy had left. She had a foreboding feeling about her husband's sudden change in mien upon reading his letter. He said that he had business to resolve, and had suggested that it related to his mail, but the only letter he had actually opened and read prior to that was the one that was written by a woman's hand. *So, to what business could he be referring?* Not made for gloomy thoughts, she decided to focus on her own correspondence rather than ponder over something that obviously did not relate to herself.

She started with the letter from Longbourn, which was actually two letters in one. There was a short note from her mother and then one from Kitty. She received letters from Jane regularly, so was happy for the novelty, relieved that Lydia had not included one. She appreciated the fact that her father was concerned enough about her welfare, while far away from her former home, to ensure that her family wrote to her, even though he did not himself. However, sometimes the letters were more of a trial to read than the actuality of being away from her loved ones. Elizabeth had quite begun to think of Pemberley as her home now. When arriving, over two months ago, she did not think that she could ever consider such a grand building to be her home, her place of residence, perhaps; but now things had changed to such an extent that she had begun to feel as if she had always been there.

The note from her mother was a reiteration of sentiments from her other letters exhorting her to keep Mr. Darcy happy at all costs, and since the heir may have been conceived already, she could leave him to his own amusements until such time as she would be called upon for the task yet again. *All great men like Mr. Darcy have a mistress, Lizzy, so you need not suffer through his attentions.* Although she had read her mother's remonstrance before without much heed, this time, she felt a pang of disquiet, first on the realisation that her mother must have learnt from Jane that she was expecting, and second on her mother's assumptions about Darcy. *Surely Mama could not know of what she speaks. I would know if he were keeping a woman.* Elizabeth understood that men had needs, which their wives were obligated to meet; however, he had not come to her chamber since leaving Hertfordshire. *Could he be having relations with someone discretely here at Pemberley?* That same pang returned to her chest, as her heartbeat quickened. *He received a letter from a female hand then hastily left the room, without meeting my eye. Surely not!*

Rather than succumb to these disturbing thoughts, Elizabeth laughed at herself for beginning to listen to her mother. When had her mother's advice ever seemed rational to her? She finished her mother's letter, then read Kitty's, which contained the same lamentations as usual. Kitty lacked for ribbon to re-work her bonnets. Lydia was taking the attentions of all the officers, and without Elizabeth or Mary at home any longer to practise the pianoforte, her mother had decided she should take up the instrument. *That is the first sensible idea that I have read since I left; she could benefit from having something useful to occupy her time.*

Elizabeth then moved on to her other correspondence. Mary had been married now for nearly three months. She had written on only one other occasion, claiming that her duties as a parson's wife left little time for such temporal tasks. Mary had not changed, which surprisingly brought Elizabeth comfort. She broke the seal of the new letter before her and read.

March 31, 1811
Hunsford, Kent

Dear Lizzy,

I hope all is well with you and that being married has been as edifying for you as it has been for me. I find that having a husband who can patiently teach me about his expectations (and Lady Catherine's) makes my life fulfilling. I had never considered that being a parson's wife would be so demanding when ministering to the poor. I had assumed that my duties would be more spiritual in nature, but I find that exerting myself for others has given me a new understanding concerning their failings and subsequent needs.

Mr. Collins has asked that I write you to request that should you join Mr. Darcy on his annual visit to Rosings for Easter, would you please minimise any visible signs of affection towards us while in the presence of Lady Catherine, who never lets me forget that my wanton sister seduced her nephew, forcing him into marriage, while he was engaged to her daughter. Reminding her of our relationship throughout your visit could not bode well for us, as we are dependent upon her mercy and benevolence. She only this week allowed me entrance into her grand house, but her kindness was all I could have expected given my connection to you. She even offered to let me use the pianoforte in Mrs. Jenkinson's rooms (Mr. Darcy's previously betrothed's companion). The instrument is as fine as any on which I have played, excepting perhaps the pianoforte at Netherfield. Mr. Collins was pleased with the advancements we have made into her good favour, and we would not want it ruined by your arrival. I know you understand our predicament, and will not take our request in the wrong light.

Lizzy, before I close, I must again acknowledge your kindnesses in encouraging an attachment between my husband and myself. While not condoning such impropriety, I must thank you for dissolving not just Mr. Darcy's betrothal to Miss De Bourgh in order to marry him, but also your own short-lived consideration of Mr. Collins, thus freeing him of his obligations to his patroness and our family. My life is complete.

Your sister,
MC

After reading her letters, Elizabeth had a hard time determining which one disturbed her more, the one from her mother suggesting that her husband had a mistress or the one from her sister, which told her about an apparent upcoming trip she and her husband were to take, but about which she knew nothing. *Easter is less than two weeks away; surely he would have told me about the trip if we were going. Would he go without me?* Two months ago, she would not have given it a second thought; in fact he had gone to town on two separate occasions, while she remained at Pemberley, but to plan to go to Rosings, on a family visit without her, was somewhat insulting. But no, she would wait and see before judging him. Perhaps the letter he received was from his aunt issuing an invitation. *But then why would it disturb him so?*

Elizabeth decided to put her letters away and instead to read her book. Reading was just the task to stop her ungenerous ruminations. But after an hour or more of reading, Elizabeth had begun to grow tired and had little capacity to ignore her physical demand for sleep. She had hoped to stay up until Darcy's return, but looking at the clock, she had begun to suspect that maybe he had by-passed the sitting room and instead gone straight to bed. He never actually said he would return to resume their reading – once he had finished his letter. She knew that he had planned to read with her before opening his correspondence, but something must have been in his letters that changed his mind.

Elizabeth was just getting up from her place on the settée when the door from Darcy's chamber opened. He looked in her direction and without meeting her eyes said, "Elizabeth, something has come up in town that needs my immediate attention, so I will be leaving in the morning at first light. I intend to be back within a fortnight."

"Perhaps I could join you. I would enjoy having the opportunity to see Jane and the Gardiners in Cheapside."

"I think not – this time."

"Then maybe you could take me to Longbourn on the way to London." Elizabeth waited to see what he might say. She did not necessarily have a strong inclination either way. She longed to see Jane, but travelling, even in such a fine carriage, was not appealing to her in her current state. She found it much easier to hide her waning nausea when in her chambers than she likely could while in an equipage, no matter how fine. As Darcy hesitated, she said, "Surely it could not be too far out of your way."

As Darcy was inexperienced in the art of dissimulation, and due to the loose rein on his imagination concerning the contents of his letter, he responded in a manner that he had not intended, but once said, could not be taken back: "I said not this time, Elizabeth." At her wounded look, he added, "Forgive me, but I intend to travel alone."

"What business do you have in London that would not allow you to bring your wife?" she replied with an edge to her voice.

"Business that does not concern you." Darcy knew that his reply was weak. Elizabeth was not a woman to accept even a hint of prevarication.

"Shall you stay at Darcy House the whole time?"

"Of course, I will stay at my home while in town, as I always do."

"Will I see you before you leave?"

"As I will be leaving early, I suspect you may still be asleep, so I will say goodbye now."

"Will you write to me?"

"Certainly, if you wish." Elizabeth smiled sweetly as she turned to pick up her book that was sitting on the side table.

"Have a safe journey, Mr. Darcy," Elizabeth said as she went into her chamber and soundly closed the door behind her. *He is equivocating, and it has to do with that letter, with the unmistakably feminine script. If he is going to Rosings, why not just tell me? Does he continue in being ashamed of our connection, but not have the cheek to confess his petty misgivings to me? Vexing, vexing man!*

When Elizabeth closed her door with a decided thud inconsistent with her smile and sweet words, Darcy knew that he had offended her, but what could he do? The conversation was over, and he had achieved his goal. He did not have to comment on the letter, and she was letting him go with minimal questions. Elizabeth, being quite clever, could have made this whole conversation rather burdensome, but she did not. He should be thankful. Why he was having these thoughts, he did not know. He was master of Pemberley, and he was her protector, not the other way around. She promised to obey him, and that was that.

AFTER A NIGHT OF RESTLESSNESS, Darcy arose before dawn and after a quick breakfast set out as the sky had begun to turn pink with the rising sun. His journey to London was uneventful, which gave him plenty of opportunity to contemplate the letter and all that it might signify. He had developed a faith in Elizabeth, not based on their circumstances, but on her actions and revealed character.

Although the general populace – and he also, initially – would hold to her having been successful in purposely compromising herself in order to achieve a brilliant marriage, there was no evidence to support this and much evidence to the contrary. Elizabeth rarely spent her pin money and had no interest in the usual social diversions of a woman who marries for status and wealth. Putting aside his knowledge of Elizabeth's sending funds to a secret account, he considered his wife's history. Elizabeth did not need to take part in the desperate act of risking her reputation on the hope that he would have conceded to a union. Her sister's marriage (although then only a suitor) to the heir of her family's estate protected her financially. At that point she had no way of knowing that he would do his duty, unlike so many others. Her father could not have challenged him, and she had no brother or other relation to defend her honour. In addition to all of this, she had not seemed pleased with the match, at all, not even a little. Darcy remembered very well, and without fondness, the first month of their marriage. Elizabeth had avoided him whenever she could without causing servants to talk. She always looked sad, very much unlike her demeanour in Meryton, and also very much unlike the expressions she had worn over the past month. No, he was now quite certain that Elizabeth was not the type of woman to use deception to secure a marriage.

Pemberley had been good for them. Elizabeth had blossomed as a mistress of the estate while under the guidance of Mrs. Reynolds. He laughed as he remembered the local ladies of fashion visiting, in order to assay the new mistress of Pemberley. They thought to embarrass her with mention of the circumstances of their union. Her wit put the visitors in their places, all the while concealing to the victims that she had done so. She was truly remarkable. *How could I not have esteemed her from the beginning?*

Fitzwilliam had seen her charms and tried to convince Darcy of the great possibility for felicity in his marriage if he would just give her a chance to shine. She was everything Darcy could have wanted in a wife. He wondered if their physical relationship could have been satisfying, no exhilarating, if he had not taken her as he had on their wedding night and then with even more insensitivity later after the ball and then at Longbourn. Could she have developed a longing for him, as he had for her, if he had only shown affection and been responsive to her fears? She was enthusiastic about everything in life. Could she have had that same enthusiasm in his bed had he not driven her away with his carnal desires, taking her rather than loving her?

One can never go back, but he could change the future. Whatever he might learn, he would take in with steady discernment, not jumping to conclusions. One thing he knew about Wickham: he was skilled at deceit. Darcy refused to become a pawn in his game of revenge again.

DUE TO THE FINE WEATHER, Darcy arrived when expected. The house had been opened, but did not have the knocker out, so he hoped to have no visitors. He was caught off guard when his sister descended the steps to meet him. "Georgiana, this is a surprise."

"Forgive me, Brother, but I was anxious to return home. James has been here with me since I arrived."

"Georgiana, there is nothing to forgive. I am most anxious to speak with you though, so why don't I go change and meet you in your sitting room in half an hour."

When Darcy entered her room, Georgiana was nervously playing with her skirt as she waited for him to join her. Darcy slowly but purposely crossed the room and sat beside her on the sofa. He waited for her to begin, but all he heard was silence. In light of his long journey, during which his active imagination would afflict him, his patience was wearing thin, so finally he said, "Well, Georgiana, you have asked me to come, and here I am. What is it you have to share with me? I own that I am quite eager to hear what is troubling you."

Georgiana had desired to impart all that she had learnt about Mrs. Darcy to her brother, so she had summoned him to town, relieved that her express had been successful in bringing about a quick journey on her brother's part. She had every expectation that this could be the longed for assistance her brother needed as a way to respectfully get out of his undesired marriage. But when her brother came into her sitting room, fear invaded her mind. Everything seemed so easy before he arrived, but now she was not so sure. As she faltered, her brother had spoken. That was the impetus she needed. "Brother, I...um, thank you for coming so quickly. I had hoped you would, of course, but did not know for sure." Her eyes were cast down at her fidgety hands as they worked the lace on the skirt of her dress.

"Go on." Darcy could tell his sister would need help coming to the point.

She looked up at him and when their eyes met, she gained the strength she needed to tell him what she knew might pain him at first, but would hopefully give him relief in the end. She stood and walked the two steps to the table beside the sofa. Opening the drawer, she took out a white handkerchief; she turned and handed it to her brother. "Do you know whose this is?" she asked softly.

He took it from her trembling hand, mindful that she was in obvious distress, but not yet knowing why. After turning it over and looking at the familiar stitching, he replied, "Of course, this is Elizabeth's. I can tell by her former initials and the pale lavender flowers stitched in the corner. Her sister, Miss Bennet, made her one each year for her birthday since she turned sixteen at her coming out. I believe she has five of them. She used to have five, rather. One was sacrificed to my injuries when we met during the storm."

Georgiana was surprised her brother had such intimate knowledge of his wife's past. "Yes, well, you may be wondering why I have one in my possession now."

"I am."

"You see, this was presented to me by someone." She paused as if to gather courage, taking a deep breath. "It was given to me by Mr. Wickham." She stopped there, looking at her hands again as they had grabbed onto her skirt tightly, as if that would somehow protect her from the explanation to come. After a few moments of silence, she ventured a glance towards her brother's face again. She paled as she saw his stony visage looking at her. She could tell by his increase in breathing that he was affected by what she had said, and that he was steeling himself so as not to lose control. She remembered Ramsgate and shuddered. Realising that he must be thinking that she had somehow fallen into Wickham's power again, she continued, "I was shopping with my aunt, my maid and a footman, and while Aunt Estella went into the milliner's shop, I went with Maggie and the footman into the bookstore there on Bond Street. Aunt Estella said I could go since I had a chaperone, and it was just next-door. I was looking for a new book to read and was walking down the aisle alone; I promise that Maggie and the footman were in the shop with me," she quickly said trying to impress upon him her innocence in all of this. She continued, "And after being in there for a few minutes, George, um, Mr. Wickham approached me from behind. I recognised his voice before I saw him, and he began to tell me what I have wanted to tell you. It has been six days now, and I have been desperate for you."

"Georgiana, get to the point," Darcy said in a clipped tone, anger flashing in his eyes, his attempts at staying under good regulation losing their battle.

She was frightened but continued, certain that he needed to know the truth and would be glad to know, in the end. "He showed me the handkerchief that I have just given to you and told me that Elizabeth had given it to him while she was in Hertfordshire last; that she had given it to him as a token of her affection. Brother, they were lovers!" she exclaimed, her voice rising in volume as her resolve and sense of justice strengthened. Tears came to her eyes, unbidden, as her heart broke for her brother's situation, first having to marry such a woman, and second, to have her shame him in this way. Her brother was too honourable for that, the very best of men.

Georgiana's sobs resounded against the crackling fire in the hearth. Darcy stood quickly, and began pacing around the room, agitation clear. Georgiana continued, "He said that Elizabeth despises you and came to him for solace, that they had been good friends before the wedding. As you and he had many disagreements, it was natural for her to turn to Wickham to provide a diversion from her marriage. He said that she confessed that she purposefully took you somewhere secluded, so that you would have to marry her. Of course, you knew that part, but to have it confirmed...."

"That is enough, Georgiana!" Georgiana jumped, knowing her brother would be angry, but surprised nonetheless. "I do not need your commentary; just tell me exactly what was said."

Georgiana, grabbing her own handkerchief, began to wipe away her tears as she continued, "He said that they have remained in contact, and that she has declared her love for him. And that she...she... is carrying his child." She began crying in earnest and could not bring herself to say any more until she calmed down.

Darcy stopped pacing and leaned onto the mantle with both hands, holding on so tightly that his knuckles turned white. *This could not be! I am certain this could not be! She is not with child, and anyway, she could not be so dishonourable! The woman I now know would never act this way.*

But then, do I truly know her? Could her interactions with me be nothing but an act, a ploy to get into my graces? Could she have used beguilement to manipulate me? She did defend him once. I discounted it at the time as ignorance of his true character, but could she have wanted me to absolve him, so she could see him more easily? But she takes no pleasure in carnal intimacies.

Surely, this cannot be true. But then again, Wickham is skilled at seduction. I did nothing to make her want to be with me. He could have enticed her to accept his advances. Darcy's mind raced to past interactions, looking for proof that Elizabeth was innocent. As soon as he would think of something to show her virtue, he would think of another that might prove otherwise.

His reverie was interrupted. "Brother, I know this is difficult now, but perhaps this is a blessing in disguise. Now that you know about her infamy, you can use this information and proof to divorce her and be rid of her for good. Then you could marry someone whom you can favour in truth."

He looked at her in astonishment. *Is that what she truly thinks, that I could want an escape from my marriage – that I think so little of Elizabeth and our union, to be looking for ways to escape?* As if to evade his fears about Elizabeth's mutiny, his worries went back to his sister, and he asked, "Did anyone see you talking to that blackguard? Did either of the servants catch you talking with him?"

"No, I do not think so, but of course I cannot be certain."

Darcy let go of the mantle with a small push and returned to his sister's side, trying to remain calm so as not to cause her fear. "Georgiana, is there anything else you can tell me? What was his stated purpose in approaching you?"

"He said he wanted you to know of your wife's treachery, that you should always wonder if the child she carried, the heir of Pemberley perhaps, was yours or his."

But she is not with child... is she? She has said nothing to me. We were only together those three times, ... but that would be enough. His mind reeled, as he tasted bile in his throat with the very thought of her with another. Then he recalled his resolve to be wary of Wickham's scheming. There were no limits to Wickham's deceit. He would want nothing more than to put doubts into Darcy's mind about a possible heir. "Georgiana, what else in the way of proof did he give you? He is skilled at deceit. A handkerchief and words, which could be a total fabrication, is all we have. I will not believe anything he has to share until I can know for certain." Even while saying those words, doubts involuntarily returned to him yet again. His marriage was tenuous. For a large portion of their union, he knew that his wife despised him. Why now should he think differently? Could the past two months be an act, a way to take him off his guard? Elizabeth was quite clever, he knew. Could she be fabricating their entire relationship? Her dislike for him was clear when last in Hertfordshire; it was not until seeing Pemberley in its glory that an inclination towards him, small as it was, began to be seen. Then he remembered Hertfordshire, and seeing Elizabeth alone with Wickham in the gardens of Longbourn. It was possible. He remembered her smile as she spoke with Wickham and how quickly it vanished when she saw him. He recalled her tears of heartache when he took her from her former home. He had supposed the distress was related to her family, but could she have been crying for Wickham? This was too much.

Georgiana watched her brother as his face turned from anger to hope to despair. "Brother, you know what George said to be true; I see it in your eyes. She has used you from the beginning. This is your way to escape her clutches.

With your connections and her history, a divorce could be obtained on solid grounds. You will no longer be tied to her and her low connections. Did you know about Lady Annette? She has made an alliance with another man. Please, you must take care of this now before you lose another woman you could love."

Darcy was in a daze as Georgiana spoke, but finally her speech sunk in. *But I love Elizabeth. Could it be true, that I sincerely love her?* "Georgiana, you will cease speaking of my wife in those terms. Without sufficient proof, we must consider her innocent of Wickham's slander. You are not to trust that man, do you understand me?" His anger and frustration were driving his tone, and Georgiana blanched.

Georgiana put her head down and nodded, then softly replied, "I love you, Brother, and I only want the very best for you."

He knew this to be true, the only thing now certain. "I know, my girl." He reached over and hugged her as she began to sob. Knowing Wickham had been near her made his anger swell again. *How could he have gotten so close to her so easily? We must be more vigilant in keeping her safe.*

While Georgiana wept, Darcy continued to contemplate everything his sister had said. *Could Elizabeth be with child? That, I can find out.* He began to formulate his first step towards finding the truth.

"Georgiana, sweetheart, you look exhausted. I know holding onto this burden has been difficult for you, but now that you have told me, you need to learn to let it go. I will take over from here and discover what truths, if any, are to be had in Wickham's account. Go get some rest before dinner."

"Yes, sir." She stood mechanically to walk towards her chamber door. She turned around before walking through, saying, "I am so very sorry."

DINNER THAT EVENING PROGRESSED at a normal pace but seemed interminable to Darcy. Georgiana kept stealing glances at her brother throughout the meal as if to communicate her support. Darcy hoped that she had recovered from their earlier conversation. She was still a young girl in many ways and unable to hold her reserve amidst her troubling thoughts. Colonel Fitzwilliam had noticed that both of his cousins were rather distracted from his account of the previous three-months' events. When he mentioned that Lady Annette had accepted a proposal of marriage from Lord Tessington, a man twice her age, and barely received a glance from Darcy, he knew that his presence was neither needed nor regarded. He was determined to discover whatever it was that had left his cousins distracted so.

Darcy had been debating whether or not to include Fitzwilliam in his private affairs. As Georgiana's guardian, he had every right to know about her contact with Wickham and would not appreciate being excluded from the knowledge; however, Darcy could not want anyone, including his cousin, to be made aware of the assault on his marriage, especially when he had yet to learn the extent of its validity. Nonetheless, Darcy always found his cousin to be astute in his judgement and prudent in his sensible guidance. So when the meal finally concluded, Darcy had determined to share the encounter between Georgiana and Wickham and hope that doing so would somehow alleviate his burden. This was fortunate because, not liking to be in the dark about something affecting his cousins whom he loved, Fitzwilliam was determined to speak with Darcy in private concerning their odd behaviour. He also desired to know why Darcy had arrived in London ahead of schedule and without his wife.

The threesome retired to the drawing room where Georgiana exhibited on the pianoforte for her two favourite people. Although usually reticent to perform, she took great pleasure in playing for those dearest to her, and especially for her brother whom she wished to comfort through her efforts. After close to an hour, Darcy stood and escorted his sister to the door. "My dear sister, you are playing remarkably well this evening. I can tell you have been practising most diligently, but alas, it is past time for you to retire. A girl your age needs her sleep." Darcy then leaned down and gently placed a kiss on her forehead, thus inducing her first smile for the day.

"I am so glad you are here, Brother," said his young sister before demonstrating her affection for each and leaving the two to their own amusements.

Fitzwilliam had patiently waited for the evening to progress to the point when the two men would be left alone. He watched as Darcy walked over to the sideboard and poured each of them a generous portion of expensive brandy. Fitzwilliam raised his brow as Darcy handed him his. "That bad?"

Darcy made no response but instead sat down upon the winged chair by the fire, next to Fitzwilliam's seat as he focused on the dancing flames before him. Each of the men sipped on his respective brandy while waiting for the other to begin. Finally, when Darcy rose to pour himself another, his cousin spoke, "Tell me, Darcy."

As Darcy stood by the sideboard, taking another gulp from his crystal glass while staring into nothingness, he muttered in unmitigated disdain, "Wickham."

His cousin stood, his usual amiable affect gone. "What has that bastard done now?" Then he glanced to the door from where Georgiana had left. "Tell me he has not hurt Georgiana."

"He approached her in the bookstore last week while she was shopping with your mother."

"My mother? I know nothing of this! Where was my mother when this took place? And where the bloody hell was her maid, or the footman? Surely Mother would not leave her alone."

"Aunt Estella had gone to the milliner shop and sent Georgiana on with the servants next door. They were at the front of the store while she shopped the aisles and did not witness his approach. Georgiana suspects that no one saw them together." Darcy went on to share the event in as much detail as he was able, leaving out nothing in the telling.

"Surely you don't believe him!"

"I have learnt to be wary of Wickham's tongue. But his usual method is to mix a few lies in with the truth. The question I have regards where the truth ends and the lies begin."

398

"Your marriage – do you still suffer doubts as to Mrs. Darcy's integrity? I was hoping that while at Pemberley you might have come to understand her better and perhaps begun to see her finer qualities."

"That is what puzzles me. If Wickham had approached Georgiana in January, I would have had little difficulty being convinced of the veracity of his tales. Since the very beginning, I had been unwittingly casting about for reasons to doubt Elizabeth, thinking all along that I was justified in my prejudices against her character. But now that I have gotten to know her better, away from town, I simply can't see it."

"You know her better than I, of course, but I would have to agree with you. If Mrs. Darcy did manipulate the situation to bring about your marriage in order to gain your wealth, I would expect her to have at least seemed rather pleased with her success. On the contrary, she appeared more and more forlorn each time I was around her, which was quite contrary to my initial impression of her unaffected liveliness. Even when under duress, she could find something about which to laugh, but her natural high spirits had begun to fade."

"You think it my fault – that she should suffer under me."

"I mean no offense, Cousin. Your many responsibilities and station in life have shaped you to be the man that you are, but, yes, I do believe that her natural ease had begun to diminish while under your protection."

"You tried to warn me," Darcy said disheartened. "I am not angry with you, only with myself, as regards the first two months. But since our move to Pemberley, so much has changed." Darcy could not stop a faint, but sincere smile from appearing. "I own that my feelings for her have grown beyond my expectations."

"Have you fallen in love, Darcy?" Fitzwilliam asked with amused warmth.

"Love? I hardly know. I've never been in love before. When I am with Elizabeth, I can't seem to pull my gaze from her. When I am away, I wonder, without ceasing, what she might be doing – wondering if she might be missing me as much as I miss her. When I go to my bed alone at night, I dream of holding her in my arms and making passionate love to her. And when we kiss, I feel as though I am a young, inexperienced lad enjoying my first taste of heaven." Darcy's smile had grown as he revealed his heretofore unspoken emotions. "Somewhere along the way, her happiness became more important than my own."

His cousin could not hide his curiosity. "And how does she perform as mistress of your estate? Does she suffer much under the load? She has been without the education and preparation ladies are wont to receive for such a challenge."

"I admit that I did not anticipate her proficiency with such a large estate. Having witnessed her mother's uncontrolled behaviour in Hertfordshire, how could I have expected otherwise? I assumed that she would spend half her time admiring the furnishings of the manor and the other half attempting to replace them. But no, she handles herself with grace and poise. Over the winter months, when little social interaction was possible, she set to work learning all of the inner-workings of the estate. She poured herself into the accounts, which Mrs.

Reynolds has so meticulously kept, wanting to familiarise herself with the details of household management. She memorised all of the names of our servants within a week of residence and has won their favour through her kindness and competency. The tenants have also developed a fondness for her, as she visits them regularly, providing relief as required, and many times when not. Yes, she has performed her role remarkably well. I can honestly say that I am proud of her."

"I knew she was clever when first we met, and she challenged you so charmingly."

As Darcy heard his cousin give praise to Elizabeth, he felt an unfamiliar tinge of jealousy run through him. He knew it was unfounded and beneath him, but he was unhappy that another man, even though his cousin, was appreciating his wife in a personal way. "She does attempt to challenge me, but sometimes it is better to have a wife who admires rather than makes sport."

Fitzwilliam could not let this go and so replied, "Come Darcy, a tease from your wife is worth ten compliments from any other woman."

With a small but meaningful grin, he conceded, "Yes, but a compliment from Elizabeth is more valuable yet." He continued with feeling, "She does not hand out her commendation unless deserved, and that only by superior merit. I have never met a woman less likely to praise me, and I admit that I admire her for it. Naturally, I used to think that her lack of veneration was due to a deficiency in effort on her part. She had won her prize, so why bother? But I recognise that I was wrong in my estimation. She does not perform for anyone. I have always lauded truth and directness, but did not value these traits in my own wife. I attempted to find an ulterior motive for her lack of deference, rather than appreciate her honesty. She did not acclaim anything about me – she considered nothing to be worthy of her applause. I have had to work for every word of approbation from her lips. Without meaning to, she has shown me that I cannot use my worth as a landowner or place in society as a means of earning esteem – from her anyway."

"Does she know about Georgiana's summons as being the reason for your hasty removal from Derbyshire?"

"No, I did not want to alarm her, and Georgiana specifically requested that I not bring Elizabeth along. With so little information to go on and Georgiana's mention of Wickham, I thought it best that she remain at home, safe from Wickham's manipulations. Elizabeth was obviously piqued when I told her that I was leaving, and without her, but it was done for the best. I would not have her worrying over the reason for my trip nor have her suffering through Georgiana's accusations, whether or not there is any truth to back them."

"So what's your plan?"

"I hardly know, but first I must discover if Elizabeth is with child. If she is not, then Wickham's story crumbles. If she is, then the only way to know the truth is to speak with Elizabeth herself, which I cannot do until after we are done at Rosings."

"So we are off to Rosings on Monday? Surely, the sooner we arrive, the sooner you can be on your way back home."

"Whether there is any truth to Wickham's tale or not, I know there has to be financial gain at the bottom of his efforts. I suspect we may be hearing from him before long and so would like to remain in town a few more days, until either I have found him, or he has found me."

"And in the meantime?"

"Perhaps you can help me in my search for the bastard here in town. Do you have any men at your disposal skilled in reconnaissance?"

Fitzwilliam smiled and said, "I might be unable to help you determine if you are in love, but I *can* help you there."

The two stayed up late formulating a plan of action for the following week to ensure the safety of Georgiana and Elizabeth. Finding Wickham remained a priority, but each suspected it more likely they would hear from him first.

Chapter Nineteen

Pride perceiving humility honourable,
often borrows her cloak.
Thomas Fuller

The green of the trees contrasted beautifully with the cerulean sky overhead, as Darcy heard and admired the multi-coloured birds working diligently to maintain their nests. The songbirds serenaded one another with the carols passed down through the ages. A light, pleasing breeze made the warmth of the day dissipate as if wading into a cool creek on a hot summer day. He noted that he was walking along his favourite path through the gardens of Pemberley, the one with the show of roses in full bloom, the one that his mother had commissioned when she first arrived at Pemberley, the one to match the garden of her youth. The colours of the blooming flowers made a sea of pinks, yellows and reds as far as he could see. He closed his eyes to take in the scents around him, and as he reopened them, he realised that he was no longer in the garden, but on a path leading from the manor house and into the woody hills.

Darcy began walking again, as if being lured away, and passed by the tree he used to climb as a boy with his dearest friend, the one who betrayed him. He then noticed that his hunting hound had joined him, quietly keeping pace. The wind blowing the canopy of the forest made a deafening sound that now drowned out the avian troubadour. He continued on up the hill towards the opening that would reveal Pemberley manor in all its glory. How he loved the view that summarised all that was his! He began running, so he could hug himself and triumph in his successes as landowner, lord and master over all that his eyes could see, and then even beyond. He prided himself on his generosity towards his servants and tenant farmers; they worshipped him in gratitude. He laughed as he considered that he had everything a man could want. He was his own man whose only responsibilities were those he wanted. He answered to no one.

When he arrived at the summit, he turned to look out through the clearing of trees. There she was, Pemberley, the sun reflecting off of her stone façade in shades of pinks and purples. As he looked more closely he could see the servants coming outside and bowing towards him. He was well pleased as he noticed that they stayed on bended knee, not daring to look him in the eye. He began to hear a whispering noise all around him and realised that his tenants had made their way behind him, holding out coins and wheat to lay at his feet. He gloried in the adoration that was due him, for his beneficence towards them.

Darcy noticed that the young maidens of the group stared at him and admired his form. Even in his youth, he had been handsome, having young women throwing themselves at his feet, begging him to choose them. But he wore his comeliness with dignity, offended when he was noticed, yet he relished the homage.

However, soon he realised that something was missing, rather someone. Amidst all of his people dependent upon him, he was alone. He felt the loss acutely and shook his fist at the sky as he wondered why he was denied a woman perfectly suited to him. He did not know who the woman could be, who would meet his need, but knew there had to be one. As he was looking up, he noticed something large and white soaring overhead. At first, he thought it to be an angel, but then realised that it was not an angel, but a large white bird, perhaps a gyrfalcon, flying as if searching for prey. The bird was headed towards the manor house, gaining speed.

The sky was now getting dark and the house was no longer lit with the colours of the sun, but was grey as twilight. From behind the house he saw storm clouds gather with streaks of light jumping from one to the other in a display of splendour dancing in the sky. The servants, who had been on their knees, arose and ran into the manor, seeking shelter from the upcoming storm. The clouds by this time had reached him and as he looked around, he noticed that he could no longer see his tenants. He turned back and continued to stare at his home, his heritage, as the thunder now shook the ground.

Still the falcon approached the house, circling in and out of the clouds and crying out in loud peals. As this happened, bolts of lightning began striking the tall trees all around the great house and causing them to catch fire. Then he realised that the falcon was not an angel, but a demon sent to torment him. "No!" Darcy yelled to the large bird, as if hoping it, like everyone else, would obey his command and stop the destruction it seemed to be causing. The bird continued to cry out, the only other sound Darcy could hear aside from the wind and thunder. Then, as if on command, a large ball of fire descended from the sky and slammed into his home. Flames instantaneously grew and reached to the sky. The house and all it contained was consumed in the fire, his servants, his memories, gone.

The lugubrious sound of the falcon cut to his heart and left him grief-stricken, even as he watched his home go up in flames. Darcy's pain could not be measured as he watched all before him burn to nothing. The falcon returned and alighted upon a large rock, not ten feet from him. He cursed the bird and picked up rocks to throw at it, but stopped short as he looked into its expressive, green eyes that reminded him of someone dear to him. He yelled out to her, attempting to undo the power she now held over him. Her doleful eyes never left his as he fell into a trance. It was then that he realised she was neither angel nor demon but his heart's desire. He tried to look away, but her charms held him fast. She finally released the spell as she turned towards the valley below where the blaze destroyed everything that was Pemberley, and she cried a mournful sound. This could not be! How could she destroy everything and then return to bewitch him?

Then he understood that she was not controlling him; she was grieving with him. They stood there alone in a type of companionable peace, staring at the great loss for what seemed like hours, then without warning, his dog turned into a large wolf and coming from behind, sunk its teeth into the luminous bird and dragged her away. Darcy felt the loss acutely, perhaps even more than the loss of his home. With tears streaming down his face, he began attempting to chase *them, but his feet would not move, as if laden with stone. He tried to scream out to stop, but was unable to make a sound, as she disappeared into the bramble.*

Darcy awoke with a start, drenched in sweat and breathing rapidly. He sat up in his bed looking around, half expecting to see his home aflame. As he began to comprehend that he had been dreaming, that he was truly in London safely ensconced in his chamber, his anxiety began to dissipate. The dream, so real, not a moment before began to fade in his memory, as dreams tend to do. He noticed that the tears from his dream had made their way to his eyes in truth. He wiped away the remnants of his slumber and stood, knowing that sleep would not return quickly.

His thoughts returned to Elizabeth, as they had so often done since departing Pemberley. *Could she be with child?* He had decided to send an express to Pemberley in strictest confidence to obtain the information that he needed. He now acknowledged his foresight in requesting that Elizabeth's lady's maid keep record of her courses. He had originally desired this so he could know when he might approach her and when she might be increasing, but had soon forgotten about his intentions when he charged himself with keeping his distance. Hopefully, if he sent a rider out at first light, he could have confirmation one way or the other by the fourth evening hence. What he would do if she were with child, he did not know, but if she were not, that would negate Wickham's claims. It was a first step, anyway.

Darcy paced his room for the next two hours, waiting for a suitable hour to request a rider. Wickham wanted him to doubt Elizabeth's faithfulness; he had always relished causing him pain, but as was also usual, he doubtless desired more. There was sure to be money at the bottom of this, so more than likely Wickham would find him before Darcy could find Wickham, but he could not sit idle in the meantime. He rang for his valet just before dawn, and then went to his study to await the appearance of Jonathon, who many times in the past had been asked to make rounds between London and Pemberley. Darcy was having coffee in his study, trying to clear his head, when someone knocked on the door. "Enter," Darcy commanded.

When the rider appeared, Darcy nodded towards him with an unspoken request to close the door behind him. Darcy had written out a note to Elizabeth's lady's maid requesting that she make a copy of her records concerning Elizabeth's courses and seal them for their delivery back to Darcy House. When Jonathon approached the desk, Darcy handed him the missive and said, "I need you to take this note to Pemberley and privately give it to Janette Salle, my wife's maid. When she gives you a response, you are to make haste to return here to me. My expectation is to see you within four days' time. Do you think you can handle this?" Darcy asked this last question, already knowing the answer. This man had always faithfully fulfilled any previous mission.

"Yes, sir. I do not see a problem. The weather is fair and the days getting longer. And even if that were not the case, you can count on me to see it through."

"That is why I asked for you in particular. If you do make it back within four days, there will be a bonus for you. Remember, you are to speak to no one about this. And please give this second note to my steward," Darcy said, handing over a second missive. "No response will be required from him." Darcy provided no additional explanation to this man who had served him faithfully for years. Jonathon had grown up at Pemberley and like the other employees was dependable to fulfil his responsibilities with vigilance and alacrity.

His servant exited the study as the colonel was coming in. "Darcy, you look dreadful."

Darcy raised a brow at his cousin's honest appraisal. "I feel dreadful. I slept little, and when awake, I kept envisioning Elizabeth in the arms of that bastard." Darcy practically spit out the words.

"Surely you cannot really suspect that she would betray you in that way."

"I have a difficult time believing the woman I left at Pemberley three days ago would behave without integrity, in any circumstance. But I have to admit that I cannot be completely certain of her conduct throughout the beginning weeks of our marriage. Wickham is a practised seducer, and she has proven herself gullible to his charms."

"Could she be so changeable, Darcy? You obviously have found a great deal to admire about her most recently:"

Darcy gave a wan smile. "Actually, I believe I am the one who has changed. The impertinent words she spoke upon first marrying are the same ones that now give me delight. Her wild ways that I once mocked now intrigue me and draw me in. I feel like a schoolboy when in her presence, completely captivated and hanging on her every word. But could I now be the one who is gullible, bewitched by her charms?"

"Bewitched, I have no doubt, but I would not go so far as to say deceived. You never told her about your dealings with Wickham?"

"I thought to, but could not bring myself to lay bare our family's history with him while I did not trust her. Then when I returned to Pemberley in February, things seemed to be improving so amicably between us that I did not want to bring up a subject that had caused us both so much pain."

"Had you told Mrs. Darcy, I cannot imagine she would doubt you, especially in light of hard proof. I would have been more than willing to vouch for your innocence – not that any of that would have been necessary. Your wife would have listened to you. It is true that at one time you openly showed your resentment towards her, but you gave her no reason to mistrust you."

Darcy winced. Had he not? His thoughts went to so many of his mistakes along the way. "Believe me that if it were possible to go back in time, I would ensure that Elizabeth could have no reason to desire another man's embrace, but what was done cannot be changed, and dwelling on my past choices will not resolve anything."

"You must see that even when she disliked you so well, she would not have betrayed you. Darcy, you know this in your heart."

"My heart tells me so, but my head remembers a different story. You did not see the way she was laughing with Wickham when I discovered them at Longbourn. And then he crowed his success at seducing her."

"He is a liar. You know this."

"It is ironic that his lies are my only hope – confidence in his efforts to deceive me." Darcy turned away and walked to the window as dawn had finally succeeded in lighting the way outside his home. "But, if it is true, if she did give in to him in a weak moment, my only hope is that she has regrets. Yet if she carries his child...."

"Have faith in her, Darcy. I have never met a woman less likely to disgrace you and your marriage. She may have abhorred you most vehemently, but I cannot believe she would have given in to another's charms – not in that way."

Darcy gazed back at his cousin. "I pray that you are right because I don't know if our marriage could survive otherwise. And at this point, I'm not certain I could either."

Fitzwilliam had hoped that his cousin would develop a tender regard for his wife, but now that he knew Darcy to be so enamoured with her, he worried about how his cousin might endure should their worst fears be realised – should Elizabeth have been taken in by Wickham to the extent that she would betray her marriage vows. Dwelling on these thoughts would not help their current course, so Fitzwilliam decided to move the conversation along. Darcy needed a focus other than his wife's constancy. "About Rosings, have you decided what day we will be leaving for our visit?"

"I hope for Wednesday after Jonathon has returned. It may be tight on our schedule once there, but with both of us working, we should be done by Easter for an early departure on Monday. I can complete a cursory review of my aunt's accounts, while you canvass the grounds. And Georgiana can entertain Aunt Catherine and Anne."

"Does poor Georgie know your designs? I cannot see her willingness in the scheme."

"We will be there but five days, and it will be good for her to spend time with Anne. But regardless of her sentiments, she has a role to play, and that role is in helping to distract Lady Catherine from our absence."

"Aunt Catherine will not be happy about our removal so soon after our arrival. Of course, nothing will make her happy short of a dissolution of your marriage." Darcy rolled his eyes. "Forgive me, Darcy. I did not mean to suggest that was a possibility. In that, our aunt will be forever disappointed, I am certain."

Darcy suddenly aged ten years as a look of despair descended upon him. "The thought of losing her now is unbearable, James."

"I know. But do not let the unknown discourage you. Trust your heart and your wife, my friend."

"So, will you be able to join us for services today once your commission is completed? Your parents sent over an invitation for tea afterwards."

"Vickie is to be there and would never forgive me if I did not."

"Then I will see you later this morning. Stop by the kitchen and get something to take with you on your way out."

LORD LANGSTON AND LADY SUSAN also attended church and the Matlocks afterwards, along with their sister, Lady Victoria, and her usually elusive husband. Darcy, still agitated concerning his wife, had little to contribute to the gathering until Langston spoke up. "Darcy, I was planning on going to Matlock soon, now that the weather has warmed a bit, and hoped to stop by Pemberley first. I know it is a little out of the way, but I thought that while I was up there, Susan and I could spend time getting to know Mrs. Darcy. Would you be opposed to my stopping over for a few days?"

"You are welcome to sojourn there. When were you planning your trip?"

Langston glanced to his wife and said, "Maybe this week." Susan cast him a sullen response, obviously angry but holding her tongue.

"I obviously won't be there, but Elizabeth will be. I can send her an express to let her know of your plans." Darcy began to think that this might be just what he needed. He could not be in two places at once, and having his cousin there to keep an eye on things would give him the peace he needed to continue with his plans at Rosings and his search for Wickham. The thought had occurred to him more than once that Wickham might have used Georgiana to lure him away from Pemberley in order to have easier access to Elizabeth.

"We truly know so little about your wife, that I thought it the perfect way to improve the acquaintance."

"I thank you, Langston." Then he thought further and said, "Before you go, however, I would speak with you."

Later in the visit, Darcy pulled Langston aside for privacy. "Langston, I am glad to know that you will be at Pemberley while I am gone. It has come to my attention that Wickham has been up to no good, and may be conniving an attack on me through my family; I would have you keep an eye on Elizabeth and the estate."

"You suspect Wickham to go to Pemberley? But why? He knows he is not welcome."

"Yes, but he means to cause trouble. I recently received information that suggests he is actively trying to hurt me through Elizabeth. I have my men out looking for him now, but cannot rule out a possible plan for him to go north. I have sent an express to my steward to take precautions, but I would feel more comfortable with you there."

"You can count on me to keep an eye out for the scum, and I will do everything in my power to protect Mrs. Darcy. She will be safe in my hands. In fact, I will plan to leave earlier than I originally thought to ensure her safety."

"Thank you. That means a great deal to me. Now I can concentrate on my responsibilities here and at Rosings while keeping Georgiana safe."

Early the following morning, Fitzwilliam's emissary returned from Meryton to report that Wickham was no longer in residence and that he had withdrawn from the militia about a fortnight ago, so he could be anywhere. Wickham had met with Georgiana just days ago, so he might still be in London. Of course, there was the possibility that he was, even now, headed towards Pemberley, if his goal in visiting Georgiana had been to lure Darcy away from Elizabeth. But Langston knew Wickham and could keep an eye out for him. Elizabeth needed protection from Wickham's deception whether she knew it or not. Darcy sent an express to Elizabeth giving her advanced notice of Langston's arrival and encouraging her to follow Langston's lead as her protector.

MONDAY EVENING, AS DARCY AWAITED WORD FROM either the colonel and his men or from Wickham, whichever might come first, he decided to attend Whites for dinner to distract himself from the grave musings that plagued him when alone. His sister's continued attacks on his wife were unwelcome and encouraged his absence rather than her goal of providing clarity.

As soon as he walked into his club, he was accosted by his merry friend. "Darcy, I had no notion of seeing you here. I thought you were still at Pemberley."

"Bingley, you are a welcome sight. I assumed you would be spending all of your free time in Cheapside with the lovely Miss Bennet."

"I was, up until today, but she and her relations were invited to a dinner party at the residence of one of Mr. Gardiner's work associates. I could not bear to be at home alone with Caroline, so here I am."

"How does your sister fare? Was she much disturbed by your good news?"

"Caroline responded as expected; however, at my insistence, she will be hosting a dinner party on Saturday for Jane and the Gardiners. Will you be in town? You would be welcome to join us. In fact, I would appreciate it if you did."

"No, I will be at Rosings."

"Say, Darcy, is Elizabeth with you this time? I have not seen her at the Gardiner's home, and I know Jane would have said something if she had visited."

"No, she is not. Business came up that precluded her joining me – that and the fact that I will be going to Rosings. My aunt still has not accepted my marriage, and I refuse to subject my wife to her vitriol."

"Could you not have left Elizabeth in town to visit her own relations?"

"Not this time."

"Is everything well, Darcy? When last I saw you, I believe you were anxious to get back home, but here you are without your wife yet again."

"Yes, now Bingley, please no more questions. I would rather you tell me about your own marriage plans."

Hitting on the right distraction, Bingley spent no little time in sharing details of the proposal and subsequent acceptance. The wedding was to be in June, at Longbourn. Jane would finish settling on her trousseau over the next month, then travel home to complete the preparations. Bingley would follow her to Hertfordshire, opening up Netherfield for the first time since Darcy's own wedding. "You and Elizabeth will be welcome to stay with me at Netherfield. I know that you would not wish to be at Longbourn over an extended time."

"Thank you, my friend; you know me well."

"You will stand up with me, will you not?" Bingley said happily as he contemplated his wedding day.

Darcy smiled at his friend's untainted enthusiasm. "I would be honoured to."

"Do you suppose Elizabeth will agree to stand up with Jane? I know she is married now, but I cannot imagine another in that role."

"Elizabeth loves her sister; I know that well."

"I daresay she does. You know that she has been putting up a portion of her pin money each month in order to secure my Jane's future. Naturally, I told Jane that I would have none of that, for we have no need. Better to save for Catherine or Lydia, but her kindness in caring for Jane could not be more genuine."

"Bingley, I am at a loss. Of what are you speaking?"

"Your wife. Since January, she has been contributing fifty pounds a month to Jane's dowry with a promise of fifty pounds per month indefinitely to help support Jane and her future husband. Apparently, Elizabeth was so concerned about my Jane's future that she set up an account for her. You do not know of this? I was certain you would; that is a lot of money to come from her pin funds."

That is the account? Thank God. "Bingley, thank you for telling me. So she has been giving the money to *Miss Bennet*?" Bingley smiled. "That explains the money but not why she was being so secretive. Do you know why she might have kept this hidden from me? It makes no sense."

Bingley shrugged. "Perhaps she did not know if you would let her continue giving. Or maybe she thought it would prove to you your assumption that she tricked you into marrying her for your money. Would her putting that much money in an account for Jane not somehow prove to you her avaricious designs? At least to your sceptical mind?" At Darcy's look of confusion, he continued, "Come Darcy, don't look at me like that. You know that you were determined to think the worse of her motivations for marrying you. I would think that she would have eventually told you anyway, for how could she explain so much money going into an unknown account?"

Finally a bright light! Elizabeth has not been giving funds to Wickham, at least not this way. She still does not wear her necklace or engagement ring, so I know not what might have happened to them, but in this I know for certain: Elizabeth does not have a current financial arrangement with Wickham.

TUESDAY, WHILE STILL IN LONDON, Darcy finally received a note from Wickham brought to Darcy House by a young street urchin. The boy was instructed to give it to the master of the house, and no one else, but before Darcy could contain him, the boy had made his escape. Angry that he had let the messenger flee, Darcy departed for his study, closing the door behind him for privacy.

Tuesday, April 9, 1811
FD,

By now, I am all but certain that your dear, lovely sister, Georgiana, has told you of the relationship that has existed between Elizabeth and myself for these many months. Your wife has many admirable qualities, Darcy, but as usual you did not think her good enough for you, making her intense affection for me grow all the more. You must realise that Elizabeth has always despised you and still does.

I thought you might want to know that the baby she carries is very likely my own. How does that make you feel? Your heir may be the actual child of your best friend from your youth, the one you discarded because I was your father's favourite. You were always jealous, and now you can truly have something to be jealous over. I have your wife's devotion, and you will always wonder if your son or daughter is truly your own.

You may inquire why I would tell you about your wife's attachment to me. As much as I care for her, I would hate for word of our relationship to become common knowledge, for that would ruin the Darcy name and forever bring into question the validity of your heir. Also, any daughter born would be spurned by the society you value so highly. However, I am willing, for the right price, to give up any claims on Elizabeth or our child. Five thousand pounds should do nicely to keep me quiet.

Assuredly, you may also decide to divorce your wife. You have just cause, and I would not blame you. I would be happy to comfort her should you choose such a course. Either way, I will get what I want.

If you choose to pay the five thousand, I will want it delivered to The Red Dragon on Westover Street by Monday week between eight and ten in the evening. Hand over the concealed funds to same lad who just now brought you this missive. If I receive the money, I will forget your wife and my knowledge of the questionable legitimacy of your child. If you do not give me the funds, I will be forced to regrettably report the whole unfortunate tale to the papers.

One more thing I wanted to tell you, Darcy. Your wife's passionate nature could not easily be contained. Elizabeth was begging me to make her mine. She has loved me since before you married her and took her away. I know I do not have to convince you of the truth of this.

GW

Darcy cursed when he read the letter. He knew Wickham would want money, always predictable in his selfish machinations. He consistently looked for ways to take from Darcy, and now he planned to use Darcy's wife to achieve his desired goal. However, as much as Darcy disliked giving in to Wickham, the question that most plagued his heart regarded the validity of Wickham's claims concerning Elizabeth. At one time, Darcy was certain that Elizabeth had indeed despised him, but that had all changed, had it not? If she were with child when could that have occurred? Darcy and Elizabeth had only been together intimately those two times since her last courses, which was the same week Elizabeth had been at Longbourn. There would be no way to tell who the father was if she had given herself to the man. *But surely not! Elizabeth would not willingly give herself to Wickham, or any man. The very thought frightens her; I've seen the look in her eyes.*

Darcy should receive word from Jonathon by the following evening either confirming or denying Wickham's claim that Elizabeth was with child. If she were not, then he could ignore Wickham's demands. If she were pregnant, then the only way to know the truth would be to confront Elizabeth and hope that she would not prevaricate. Her features were an open book and would reveal the veracity of Wickham's assertions. Darcy thought of leaving for Pemberley this very night. The thought of waiting another week to speak with her was unbearable to him, but he had his duty to consider. He could go to Elizabeth's relations to learn if Elizabeth might have mentioned anything to them about her condition or her feelings towards Wickham but then decided against this to avoid introducing more people to the threatening scandal.

And then he had to decide what he would do if Wickham's claims had true merit. What if Elizabeth were possibly carrying Wickham's child? What should he do? He had acknowledged that he had developed deep feelings for Elizabeth. Could he bring himself to divorce her if she continued to hold Wickham in high regard? Could their marriage survive the scandal, even if she did not admire the man? Should he have told her earlier of Wickham's long history of perfidy, warning her away? Had Elizabeth completely tricked him into thinking she was something she was not? These questions would plague him over the following week. But for now, there was nothing to do but await Jonathon's return and leave for Rosings as soon as he had received verification of Elizabeth's condition.

WITHIN DAYS OF DARCY'S DEPARTURE, Elizabeth felt a strange sensation in her now growing abdomen that she knew to be the baby's quickening. She had gotten up instinctively to share the news with her husband, as she had planned all along, but then stopped herself as she remembered that he had gone. As she now had no doubt in her mind that a baby was growing within her, she was angry with herself for not telling Darcy of the news sooner, before his sudden departure. Elizabeth did not know why the thought wore on her so, but she felt certain that Darcy needed to have known the blessed announcement before leaving. Perhaps he might not have left as he did. Perhaps he would have taken her with him. Elizabeth finally found solace when she resolved to tell him on the first evening of his arrival home, smiling as she considered his joyful response.

Elizabeth had been visiting more tenants since Darcy's departure. During the day she could not sit idly, waiting for her husband's return. It was during the stillness of the night that without permission her thoughts would dwell on her husband's location and the possible reasons for his hasty removal from Pemberley. Unfortunately for Elizabeth, she had an active imagination that would consider all sorts of iniquitous scenarios. She knew that there was no justification for her gross misrepresentation of his well-known character, but her mind would do as it chose, so she kept busy during the day to distract herself from his continued absence.

Elizabeth certainly remembered her husband's past ill treatment of her, but she also had witnessed a most extraordinary change. Yes, he had imposed himself upon her most egregiously on that fateful day at Longbourn, but she could not discount his great distress leading up to and following his vulgar actions. And since then, he had proven himself to be above reproach in his behaviour towards her on every occasion and had been most aggrieved concerning his uncharacteristic conduct. Also, Elizabeth could see her own guilt that day. Darcy had been most adamant that she not have contact with Mr. Wickham – surely there was more to that story than she had originally perceived, especially in light of Mr. Wickham's most inappropriate attempts at correspondence with her. Elizabeth had never seen her husband so oppressed as that moment when he found her alone in the garden with his childhood friend. She had told herself at the time that Darcy had absolutely no justification for his actions. Though valid, she also knew that everyone was capable of regrettably hurting another – even a loved one. Elizabeth herself lamented wilfully disobeying Darcy in order to spend time with another man whose company she coveted – who conveyed to her attentions inappropriate for a married woman to honourably receive. She was ashamed of her own behaviour that day and had long forgiven her contrite husband. Now, if she could only put her foreboding thoughts behind her and make her mind match her heart, she could perhaps find peace.

One morning Elizabeth decided again to use her journal papers to give free rein to her growing feelings for her husband. The traitorous musings of the night opened her eyes to her strong feelings of attachment that were hidden within her heart. The thought of Darcy's being intimate with another woman caused her extreme pain and true heartache. Could she bear a life with a husband who sought the arms of another? The thought had never truly caused her much grief before. She might have even preferred he go elsewhere to meet his needs that she had always found displeasing. But now, for a reason she could account to her own growing regard, the idea of his being with another truly appalled her and made her sick to her stomach.

While writing in her journal, she noticed that she needed another quill, for she had worn hers unusable. Rather than go down to her study, she decided to do something highly unusual. She elected to look in her husband's room to see if he might have an extra in his own escritoire. This decision was made due to her current fatigue and desire to avoid the journey to her study and back, but mostly because she had been missing Darcy and anticipated feeling a sense of his presence while in his room. Elizabeth hoped that she might be able to find his scent in his dressing room in order to dab a little on a handkerchief. She felt a little embarrassed about the whole idea and even worried she might be found out, but Darcy's valet had left with him, and no one else would be around to discover her clandestine agenda.

She quietly made her way through the sitting room and opened her husband's door. She nervously looked around his chamber, but the light was too dim to see clearly, so she opened a window panel. His imposing bed caught her eye before anything else, so she walked over to the side and let her hand stroke the top of the counterpane. She then leaned over to where the pillows lay and breathed in deeply, trying to catch a hint of his presence. Appeased by her success, she next walked into his dressing room to search for his manly scents. She opened two before finding her favourite, the one he wore on that night of their first kiss – the one he wore when her dreams drifted to him. Elizabeth put her handkerchief up to the bottle and, smiling, released a small portion of liquid.

Now that that task was complete, she looked for his small desk, and when finding it, she began her hunt for a usable quill pen. While searching she came across an unusual card in the small drawer. She noticed the card due to the gold lettering embossed on one side that read *Madame Karina's* with an address in town. On the back of the card she beheld the word *Adonis* in a flowing feminine script. *That is strange.* Elizabeth studied the card for a few moments as she considered its possible origins before putting it back in the drawer. She then found the quill, and left the room, resolved to return again during his absence when she had more time to savour her recollection of being in his arms. Coming into his sanctum left Elizabeth missing her husband more than she could have thought possible.

Not long after she returned to the sitting room, Janette brought an express to her. Elizabeth saw from the return address that she had received a letter from her husband and smiled brightly as she considered this was the first letter she was to receive from him. But then she recalled that the letter was by express, and she became apprehensive about its contents, so she quickly broke the seal and read.

April 9, 1811
Darcy House

Dear Elizabeth,

> *Do not be alarmed on receiving this express. I only mean to give you notice that my cousin and his wife, Langston and Lady Susan, will be arriving at Pemberley by Easter this week for a visit to last until my own return. He conveyed his desire to become better acquainted with you, for which I am grateful.*
>
> *They have stayed at Pemberley in the past, so Mrs. Reynolds will know their room preferences, and the cook should be aware of meals to suit them. You need only be the kind hostess that I know you to be.*
>
> *I ask that you show Langston the same deference you would me. While at Pemberley, he will be your protector, so you are to do as he says at all times. I have one more appeal, Elizabeth. Please defer your walks until my return unless escorted by Langston or Clark. I will explain more when I return, which should be Wednesday after Easter.*
> *Yours,*
> *FD*

"He cannot know! I will not be here when they arrive; I cannot!" The shock of the contents of the letter kept her from immediately noticing the paucity of sentiment on her husband's part that would later that night add to her growing distress. She began to pace around her sitting room as she considered her husband's demands, for that is what they were. Darcy could not know of his cousin's treachery. She should have told him. "Lizzy, you need to get control of yourself and think!"

Elizabeth would get little sleep that night or the next. Each day brought more anxiety as she anticipated Langston's imminent arrival. To sooth her foreboding, she returned to her journal and poured out her fears about her husband's past and possible current indiscretions, as well as her fears concerning the viscount. *How can I protect myself without my husband?* Speaking with her journal had the effect of developing the idea of talking to Clark during their walk and asking that he stay by her side, when she was not in her chamber, during the entirety of Langston's visit. She, of course, could not possibly express her concerns to a footman. The viscount was her husband's cousin and was of noble heritage. Elizabeth could not publicly defame his character, especially to a servant.

Elizabeth also decided to ask Clark about how to defend herself. This would be a strange request coming from the mistress of the manor, one who should always have a protector by her side, but Elizabeth would not risk becoming a victim again. She would also ask Laura to attend her during their stay as a companion; she must never be alone.

WEDNESDAY ARRIVED AND WITH IT the hope that Jonathon, the courier, would bring confirmation as to Elizabeth's condition. Darcy expected the man some time past midday, after which they would set out for Rosings. The colonel had been out that morning following leads based on a description of the urchin who had brought the note from Wickham, but with no success. Georgiana made no complaints about leaving so late in the day. The later their departure, the less time she would have to entertain her cousin, with whom Georgiana found nothing in common. Darcy awaited the man in his study and was startled out of his reflections when he heard a knock on the door before teatime.

"Enter," said Darcy at the sound. The door opened and in walked a tired-looking Jonathon, still wearing his travelling clothes, obviously coming straight from his horse. "Jonathon, you are back sooner than I anticipated. Well done." Then Darcy opened his desk drawer and pulled out an envelope. The young man took the offered payment as he handed over the missive sent from Pemberley. "Now, go get some rest. You may take the next two days for yourself if you like."

Not wanting to delay a moment longer, Darcy dismissed the young man, then went over to the window in order to more easily read the contents. Within the note, he discovered that his wife was indeed with child, and that she had not experienced her courses since mid-December when Janette first came on. *Why did Elizabeth not tell me? This explains a great deal – why she has slept so soundly and perhaps why she so often refused breakfast. Damn! How am I to know the truth? How did Wickham know of her pregnancy before I did?* Darcy's mind continued to plague him with questions of how he might proceed from here, unable to take any pleasure in the hope that he would soon become a father.

What was he to do about paying Wickham? Even if he were to leave at first light on the morrow, he would find difficulty in arriving at Pemberley, extracting the truth from Elizabeth, and returning by Monday evening, even allowing for travel over Easter Sunday. Darcy needed to either pay Wickham off, which still would not guarantee his silence, or ignore his request for money and hope for the best – that no one would believe in Elizabeth's betrayal. Yet how could he expect others to dismiss the idea when he himself had doubts?

Now that Darcy had received confirmation from Elizabeth's maid and had discounted the possibility of trying to speak with Elizabeth before the following Monday, he was restless to begin his obligations at Rosings. His yearly trip to Rosings held the purpose of overseeing his aunt's steward. But this trip would hold another lesser-known purpose. About six years ago while at Cambridge, Wickham joined the Darcys on holiday over Easter week at Rosings. While there, Wickham took advantage of the parson's beautiful daughter, seducing her in her innocence and leaving her with child. Before Darcy's father became aware of Wickham's perfidy, he died leaving the younger Darcy to take care of the consequences. Lady Catherine blamed the girl and would have gotten rid of the clergyman had she held that power. Instead, Darcy was able to secure a home for Miss Wainwright in the next county, not ten miles away. This arrangement meant her father could still visit her, but she would be away from the local gossip. Darcy had attempted to marry the girl off to a local farmer, providing an appropriate dowry to motivate a man to take on a wife who carried another's child, but she threatened to run away and go into hiding if she were made to give herself to another man. Because her father could not bear to see her so unhappy, the compromise was reached to set her up in her own small home but nearby her father. After the clergyman's death the previous year, Mr. Collins was appointed as replacement. As she had no other family, the young woman was now without protection.

Whenever visiting Rosings, Darcy made a point to check on Miss Ellen Wainwright, now known as Mrs. Wright, via her father, thus ensuring her needs were being met and that she and her young son were in good health. Few knew of the connection between Wickham and the young woman, assuming incorrectly that perhaps Darcy must be the boy's father. In truth, there was nothing other than Darcy's continued vigilance on the child's behalf that had spurred on these rumours, and few had the gall to speak of the possibility within hearing of Lady Catherine or her family, so Darcy remained unaware of the local chatter. On this visit, however, after hearing of the clergyman's death just after Easter the previous year, Darcy meant to check on her himself to see that she was doing well. He could not leave this task to anyone else due to its delicate nature.

Darcy arrived at Rosings with his cousin, Fitzwilliam, and sister, Georgiana. As it was full dark upon their arrival, Colonel Fitzwilliam was unable to begin his exploration of the grounds, as he had hoped, but Darcy, not wanting any further delays, sequestered himself in the study and began to pore over the books. The colonel's and Georgiana's companionship to Lady Catherine only partly soothed the older woman's irritations, and could not keep her from being an imposing nuisance as the evening progressed without Darcy's attendance to her or his cousin, Anne.

The day after his arrival brought Darcy to the home of Mrs. Wright. He spent no more than fifteen minutes there as he questioned her about her situation since the death of her father. He then encouraged her yet again to consider marrying as a way to obtain a protector. As a single and still beautiful woman, she was vulnerable to men of nefarious intent, and he felt certain that he could find a farmer of moderate means willing to take her, despite her history. Although thankful for his concern, she could not agree to the scheme without further consideration. She knew it was not right to continue living off the benevolence of a man completely unrelated to herself, but she was also reluctant to put herself at the mercy of another, especially when the man would be completely unknown to her upon marrying.

Darcy knew that he put his reputation at risk by assisting an unmarried woman, but there was no one else to help her, and he felt that it was his responsibility, considering it was his family who brought Wickham into her life to take advantage of her innocence. Given her fear of attaching herself to a man in marriage, Darcy suspected that Wickham had likely forced himself upon her. In all likelihood, Wickham had violated the young girl and threatened her to keep his assault against her a secret.

LADY CATHERINE HAD INVITED the Collinses over for dinner that evening, owing to Darcy's now familial connection with Mrs. Collins. His aunt declared that she must help him to meet the demands that his having relations in the area imposed. While at dinner, Darcy noticed that his new sister, Mary, kept looking at him oddly as if she were frowning upon a wayward child; then she would glance to her husband with knowing affection. Finally, Darcy's aunt brought up a subject uncomfortable for all but at varying levels of distress. "Darcy, you are familiar with Mrs. Wright are you not?"

Darcy looked up sharply to her, disturbed by this line of questioning, especially in light of Georgiana's attendance. He knew his aunt was aware of the association, but could not understand why she would bring up the name of a woman who had been seduced by a man familiar to his family – and fortunately unbeknownst to his aunt, the same man who had almost succeeded in seducing his own sister. "Yes, I know of the woman."

"She is a beauty, is she not? It is a shame she refuses to marry, considering she has a son to support, but she continues to hold out for the father."

"Then she waits in vain."

Colonel Fitzwilliam also knew of the woman and meant to help his cousin by changing the subject. "Aunt Catherine, I began an extensive review of your park today. Were you aware of flooding on the west side of your estate?"

"Yes, of course I was aware," said Lady Catherine to Fitzwilliam, but she would not be put off. So turning to Darcy, she continued, "Her son is a good-looking lad. He almost has a noble look to him."

Darcy turned to his cousin and said, "Fitzwilliam, was there much damage from the flooding?"

"One of the bridges is unsafe and will need rebuilding."

"But Darcy, what do you plan to do about Miss Wainwright? You cannot let her continue on in this way. Now that her father is gone, she needs a protector, a man other than her current one." She finished this sentence in a most peculiar way, obviously making a point of speaking of Darcy himself as she stared at him, eyebrows raised. She had purposely used the woman's former appellation.

"Aunt Catherine, Darcy has only three days at Rosings to come up with a plan to fix the bridge, in addition to dealing with the poachers in the south."

"Fitzwilliam, I am the one to determine what is important! And if Darcy would stay as long as usual, he would have plenty of time to address these issues and more." Then turning back to her favourite, she continued, "Darcy, I deem Miss Wainwright would benefit from another protector."

What is she talking about? She knows the woman's history. Why is she bringing her up now, in front of Georgiana, an innocent girl of sixteen? Does she mean to mention Wickham by name?

"Georgiana, have you told our aunt about your progression on the harp? Aunt Catherine, do you have an instrument here? Our dear Georgie plays beautifully. Miss Semmes is known for her skill, but cannot compare to our dear girl," said the colonel, dutifully shifting the conversation away from Wickham's misdeeds.

Two days before Darcy's arrival, Lady Catherine had invited Mrs. Collins to her home for tea. Darcy had sent word that he would be coming with Colonel Fitzwilliam and Georgiana, but that his wife remained at Pemberley. This had interfered with the great lady's plan to suggest to Mrs. Darcy herself that her husband was in an illicit relationship with Miss Wainwright. Of course, Lady Catherine knew that Darcy was not guilty of setting up the woman as his mistress, but the evidence to the contrary was incontrovertible. There had long been subtle rumours to that effect, but she had always quashed them, knowing the truth and not desiring her family to be held in derision, yet now it would work to her advantage if Mrs. Darcy were to hear about them through her own sister. Lady Catherine was well aware of Mary Collins's propensity to examine others against an impossible standard of righteousness, even when she herself could not possibly qualify by her own measure. If Mrs. Collins learnt of a possible inappropriate relationship between Darcy and the young Miss Wainwright, she would be certain to write to her sister and share the rumours, thereby saving Lady Catherine the trouble. She meant to stir the pot of antagonism that already subsisted within the Darcy marriage, with the hopes of bringing about a dissolution of the union. She still held out hope for her daughter and Darcy and meant to do all in her power to force a divorce. This was just one means of making trouble, by generating distrust on Mrs. Darcy's part.

But this scheme was by no means the only plan she had in effect. Lady Catherine also meant to give Darcy reason to leave his wife by confirming the validity of an on-going relationship between Wickham and Mrs. Darcy. Wickham, still under her employ – as much as Lady Catherine was under his deceptive and manipulative spell – had been offered five thousand pounds if he could force Darcy into filing for divorce. Their plan was to provide evidence to Darcy that Mrs. Darcy's baby was likely not his, but Wickham's.

What Lady Catherine did not know was that Wickham intended to secure his success one way or another, by blackmailing Darcy if necessary. If the blackmail to keep quiet did not succeed, he would go to the papers and force the scandal on Darcy, forever calling into question his heir. He suspected that Darcy would have no recourse but divorce in that case, which would satisfy Lady Catherine, thus giving him a payoff through her employ if Darcy himself did not take the bait. And if neither ploy worked to be financially advantageous, at least Wickham knew that he had succeeded in discomposing Darcy with the belief that he had been cuckolded by his archenemy.

DURING THE MORNING, Elizabeth walked out onto the estate with Clark, her faithful footman, her new puppy following happily along. By this time, they had developed a comfortable rapport, sometimes engaging in conversation and at others, quite silent. He was an intelligent, handsome young man not five and twenty and Elizabeth often wondered what his life might have been like had he been born into an affluent family. But as it was, he had chosen the life of a servant, or perhaps it had chosen him. She just hoped that her husband knew the young man's merit and would ensure the footman's future coincided with his potential.

Of course, Elizabeth could not be aware of the man's history, as he too had been in ignorance, for his mother, a once beautiful and innocent girl of fifteen, had herself been victim to the assault of one of the elder Mr. Darcy's schoolmates, a viscount, who had come to Pemberley for part of the summer to take in the entertainment often enjoyed on a grand estate. The indiscretion was hushed up as is often the case, yet instead of the master of the estate sending the traumatised young girl away in shame, a tenant was found willing to marry her, one who had admired her beauty and gentleness. It was ironic indeed that the blood coursing through the veins of Darcy's footman was one generation closer to nobility than Darcy's own. But such were the whims of the privileged to give and take as they willed.

Elizabeth took this time to inform Clark of the upcoming visitors and her desire that he attend her at all times. She provided no reason for her strange request and hoped that he would accept it without question, as was expected in a servant. Since it would not do for Darcy's footman to suspect a connection between the two requests — that she feared Darcy's relations — Elizabeth waited until the latter part of the walk before bringing the conversation around to her desire to learn ways of defending herself as a precautionary measure in case she should ever find herself alone without a protector.

"Mrs. Darcy, part of my job is to keep you safe. There is no need for a lady to learn such a thing, and I am not at all sure Mr. Darcy would approve."

"As Mr. Darcy is not here, we cannot ask him, but I can assure you that he would approve of any activity done with my safety in mind. And if for some reason he does not, I will take full responsibility. Please, I would feel much better with the knowledge."

Although uncomfortable with the idea, not because he felt women should not possess the power of defence, but more related to his belief that Mr. Darcy should be the one to teach her – based on the delicate nature of what he would impart – he proceeded to share with her ways in which a member of the weaker sex might protect herself. Clark knew women to be vulnerable to men. He had lived in the world long enough to know of several occasions during which a woman was imposed upon by a brute, completely at his mercy, but surely this could not happen to Mrs. Darcy. He well knew that her husband would see to her safety, and if not her husband, he himself was dedicated to the cause.

After showing her the vulnerable areas of a person that she might attack if needed, including the eyes, nose, and shin, along with how she might best achieve success, he ventured on to the areas more specific to the male. They both blushed as he explained the vulnerabilities of the male anatomy and how she might best thwart any attacker – no matter his strength – especially if she were to take him off guard.

Elizabeth thanked him for his assistance, despite his discomfort in so doing, and they returned to the house. They had been gone for an extended time, as the day was particularly fine, and Elizabeth had felt a sense of peace while in the company of the strong footman who was dedicated to her continued safety. She now saw the wisdom in her husband's sanction to always have a protector nearby, and she again thanked God for the solicitude and conscientiousness of the man she married, the man whom she had come to view as one of the best of her acquaintance. How could she doubt his fidelity? She laughed at her overactive imagination and insecurities. Had Darcy ever done anything to cause her to doubt his constancy, even in light of his questionable feelings toward her?

Saturday morning arrived and Elizabeth began to think that perhaps Lord Langston and his wife might not come after all. Her husband had said that they would arrive before Easter, so if they did not show up today, they likely might not come at all, and if they did, they would only be here for no more than a few days without her husband in attendance. Elizabeth enjoyed her morning walk again with Clark, then spent the afternoon visiting one of the tenants before practising upon the pianoforte, continuing her attack on Beethoven. She found that when she got caught up in the music that she quite forgot her trials and had just succeeded in mastering one of the many difficult passages in Beethoven's sonata when a servant entered informing her of the arrival of guests. Her heart began to race. *Oh, God, please not the viscount!* But her prayers were not to be answered as she wished, for moments later Langston and his wife were ushered in for a greeting before being shown to their rooms.

"Mrs. Darcy, we did not mean to disturb your laboured efforts at the pianoforte. We know our way around since we have stayed here many times, so can take ourselves up to our suite – that is, of course, if you have managed to secure our usual rooms?"

Elizabeth forced a smile as she responded, "Lady Susan, welcome. You are arrived at a fortuitous time, for I have been at the instrument for hours now and am in need of a break. I do believe Mrs. Reynolds is aware of your preferences and has everything ready for you." Not wanting to show her fear, she turned to Langston and continued, "Sir, welcome to Pemberley. Darcy said that you would be here until his arrival this coming week. How nice not to have to spend the holiday alone. I suppose you will be joining me for services in the morning?"

"Yes, we always attend," answered his wife.

"We will be having dinner at six-thirty."

"Six-thirty? I suppose that will have to do," said Lady Susan, resigned to be back in the presence of the woman for whom she held no fondness.

Happy to be alone, Elizabeth left them to find their own way. She then summoned Laura to ask that she join them for dinner. Elizabeth would loan her one of her simple gowns and ask Janette to style Laura's hair. Although an unusual request, Laura did not question her mistress, whom she knew to be a rather eccentric young lady. What the other servants were to say, Laura could not know, but apparently Mrs. Darcy felt a need for her presence, so she would be there for her. Langston and his wife had never met the woman before and would not know that Mrs. Darcy's companion was in truth the housemaid's apprentice. Elizabeth then called Peters and told him of her desire to keep Clark close by at all times. The butler agreed without question and made certain the valet was assigned as the mistress desired.

After taking care of preparations for her own safety, Elizabeth retired to her room to prepare for the evening ahead. Before long, Laura joined her. Her presence was already having a calming effect on Elizabeth, much like Jane's companionship would have.

Dinner conversation was stilted. Although usually a skilful hostess, Elizabeth found herself unable to move things along. Laura, uncomfortable with the company, had little to contribute. Lord Langston sat quietly, staring at Elizabeth as though she were a piece of sweetmeats. He was careful to hide his attentions from his wife, but could not keep his deliberations from the notice of Clark, whose job was to anticipate the guests' needs. Clark began to discern his mistress's concerns and rationale behind her recent, strange requests. Elizabeth, too, could not miss the covert interest in her person and was thankful for her own foresight in ensuring her safety.

After dinner, they adjourned to the music room for the ladies to demonstrate their skill. Susan was finally able to enjoy herself, for she found her abilities far exceeded that of her host. She could not like the attention obviously placed upon Mrs. Darcy by her husband and was determined to show Elizabeth in a poor light. Her accomplishment was completely lost on her husband, however, for he had heard her play the same songs many times, and Elizabeth's pathos displayed on the instrument had a similar effect on him as it had on others of the same sex. Elizabeth's passionate nature could not be contained, for she had no understanding of the influence herself; nonetheless, Clark was able to discern the essence of her bearing and the possible impact on a man's sensibilities, specifically those of Lord Langston.

The evening came to an early end, and Clark escorted his mistress to her chamber. Langston watched the footman's attentiveness and suspected that either Elizabeth had developed a *tendre* for him as well, or he was given the job of protector. Either way the viscount would find a way of getting Elizabeth alone.

DURING THE NIGHT ELIZABETH heard the sound of the door to the sitting room, adjoining her husband's, quietly opening. She watched as Darcy made his way towards her bed. Remarkably, she felt a sense of anticipation for she had missed him dearly and only desired his comforting presence. He lifted the bed linens and crawled in beside her, then soon began caressing her exposed skin, moving next to her hidden form. Darcy's kisses were gentle at first, but became more passionate and insistent as he moved on top of her. Although overwhelmed by his closeness, she could appreciate the feelings of warmth and desire that she had recently begun to own while in his company.

His hands and mouth continued their explorations as he joined with her in fervent abandon. However, something seemed wrong to her sensibilities. Her husband had said that he would not come to her again without her invitation. When had he returned home? Just then, as these thoughts intruded upon her, she looked up to see Langston's face above her, leering. Elizabeth attempted to push him away, but he insistently continued his assault as he laughed in derision.

Elizabeth began to weep as she considered her predicament. How could she have mistakenly supposed that her husband was home and would have come to her? She continued to desperately fight off the vile man's overwhelming presence, as he forcefully held her at bay. Elizabeth tried to scream, but no sound erupted. The harder she fought, the more helpless she felt.

"Mrs. Darcy, please wake up! You are dreaming!" Elizabeth heard a distraught, feminine voice insistently say near her ear.

Elizabeth opened her eyes to darkness as she slowly came to realise that neither Langston nor Darcy was there, but only Laura Carpenter, who had obviously been attempting to wake her from her nightmare.

To Laura's dismay, her mistress appeared terrified as she hastily looked around to take in her surroundings. Elizabeth trembled and began to cry without restraint as she allowed her companion to provide comfort. Having Laura with her for consolation was a true blessing; nonetheless, Elizabeth was thankful for the darkness, for had there been light, Laura would have seen the scarlet blush upon her countenance as she recalled her disturbing dream. Never would Elizabeth have imagined such recollections – that she would have welcomed her husband in that way was inconceivable to her conscious state; but that her mind would devise the following events was unthinkable. Must she also be tortured in her slumber? Could she not find solace behind locked doors? Why would a dream that brought peace with her husband turn into one of fear and pain? Could it portend future threats emanating from her trust in the man who now owned her heart?

THE NEXT TWO DAYS PROGRESSED without incident for Elizabeth. Her faithful servants stayed by her side and asked few questions, but each suspected the mistress's true concerns. Having Clark and Laura in her presence allowed her to concentrate on being the hostess her husband would have her to be. She noticed the viscount's leers but felt safe with Clark nearby. Laura continued to sleep in Elizabeth's room with her, which ended up being a real treat, reminding Elizabeth of the days when she and Jane shared a room at Longbourn.

In the meantime, Elizabeth missed her husband's company exceedingly and eagerly anticipated his return on Wednesday. Although she had once felt only distress while in Darcy's company, it had been many weeks since Elizabeth had come to regard him as the very best of men and longed for his comforting presence.

Tuesday morning arrived and while taking breakfast with her guests, the mail was brought in on a salver. She saw that she had received another letter from Mary. Elizabeth had written to her sister in Kent asking for any interesting happenings, hoping that Mary might inform her of whether or not Darcy had made a showing at his aunt's. She excused herself after the meal and went to her sitting room to read in private, dismissing Laura until she was done.

April 12, 1811
Hunsford, Kent

Dear Lizzy,

I have missed you and must wonder why you have not joined your husband on his annual trip to Rosings. I thought you would want to see me and my new home, but perhaps Mr. Darcy had not included you for a reason. I dislike the news that I feel obligated to share with you, but this is what comes of sinful impurity, for the Bible says in Ephesians that sexual immorality and all impurity or covetousness must not be among us, as is proper among saints – that everyone who is sexually immoral or impure or is covetous has no inheritance in the kingdom of God.

God's judgement might now be affecting you and your peace. Mr. Collins was at Rosings earlier this week and came rushing home to tell me the most shocking tale. Then I too was invited for tea and also enlightened as to the truth of his claims. His patroness, Mr. Darcy's own aunt, entrusted Mr. Collins with the secret sin that now ensnares your husband. She said that Mr. Darcy has a mistress that he keeps near Rosings and whom he visits at least once a year to her certain knowledge, but likely more. They have a child together, a son, who favours him and precludes all doubt as to his parentage. Lady Catherine told Mr. Collins the scandalous news, I believe, so that I could warn you to keep vigilant care to satisfy Mr. Darcy's lustful inclinations. He will not inherit the Kingdom of God if he continues on in his sinful state, and it is our duty to free him of the chains that bind him.

The shameful woman was once highly regarded at Hunsford, for she once dwelt in this very house as daughter to the former rector! I am certain that I may not be able to sleep tonight with the thought. How easily a woman of virtue can slide into disgrace. At least Mr. Darcy married you and saved you from your ignominy, so that now you can find salvation, but not this girl who continues in sin.

Last night we were invited to Rosings, and I myself saw his discomfort when the name of his mistress was mentioned, a Miss Wainwright, otherwise known as Mrs. Wright, since her fall from grace. I will pray that the woman and her illegitimate son are driven away from our God-fearing neighbourhood. Although my husband was sworn to tell no one of Mr. Darcy's defiling behaviour, I cannot in good conscience remain silent when I can help you to see the truth of his dishonour.

Your sister,
MC

"What can she mean writing me such a letter!" exclaimed Elizabeth out loud. "There can be no merit to this!" Elizabeth began her internal re-evaluation of her husband's character and could not reconcile this letter with her experience. But the longer she considered the unlikelihood of its having any basis in truth, the more she began to doubt him. Had he not treated her as an object of lust in the past? If he had a child with this woman, he would have seduced her years ago, at a much younger and less judicious age. He might even now regret his behaviour, but if this were the case, might he also now continue his obligation to her while enjoying the fruits of his past debauchery?

But perhaps if he did have a child with this woman, he no longer wants to see her. He is married to me now; would he not give her up in light of this? But then why is he going to Rosings without telling me? And didn't Lady Catherine allude to his taking a mistress when she attempted to thwart our wedding plans at Longbourn? Elizabeth could not find peace as her mind continued to condemn him more readily as the morning continued on. She pictured him in another woman's embrace, kissing and touching her as he had kissed her most recently. It had been days since Elizabeth had actually lost her breakfast, but she could not stop the nausea that had crept into her stomach. She ran into her dressing room and grabbed a chamber pot.

Wiping her mouth with the handkerchief that she had nestled up her sleeve that morning, she got a whiff of her husband's scent that she had just reapplied before attending breakfast. This time, the smell held no allure for her. She threw it down onto the floor and staggered back into her room and crawled onto the bed.

Elizabeth did not want to believe her husband could be guilty of such dishonourable behaviour, but it was Darcy's aunt who told her sister. For what reason would she say such a thing if there were no truth to be found? Even if there were but partial truth, would that not show him to be a different man than she had envisioned? *How can I bear to see him again?*

AFTER AN EXTENDED TIME IN HER ROOM, Elizabeth decided to go out again for another walk. She had already been out earlier that morning, but needed to work off her distress with exertion. She had always found a good walk to be just the thing to help her towards a rational response. Elizabeth had considered avoiding her walks while Lord Langston was in residence, but her uneasiness required that she expend some energy; and with Clark in attendance, she felt safe, for the footman was almost the size of her husband and seemed more like a bodyguard at times than an unassuming, pleasing companion. So she summoned Clark to join her yet again. The day was especially warm for the season, and the sun was shining brightly, so Elizabeth was able to get away with only a spencer jacket for her warmth.

"Are we to bring the puppy?" asked Clark before heading out.

"No, not this time. I believe we wore poor Charlie out earlier today. I spent more time carrying him than not, and what I need most is a long and arduous walk. I hope you are ready for some exertion," she said with a waning smile.

"Yes, ma'am. As you wish."

And so Elizabeth and Clark headed out in the usual direction. They spoke little on their journey as Elizabeth attempted to work out how her husband could be blameless despite the information relayed in her sister's letter.

When the two had departed, neither noticed the viscount watching from his window. He had seen them together often and suspected the handsome footman was taking advantage of Darcy's absence. Elizabeth seemed plenty happy to be in the company of the servant, this being the second occasion to be alone today. The viscount laughed as he considered that it was not just men who took advantage of the availability of servants. However, today would not go as the footman might have intended. Langston summoned a mount to be prepared and quickly set out after them.

The viscount was surprised at how far the two had travelled on foot before he was able to overcome them. They were at least three miles from the manor house, which suited the viscount well enough for his purposes. He approached them, noticeably startling Elizabeth. "Hello, Mrs. Darcy; I did not mean to interrupt." He looked to the footman in unfeigned judgement as to his suspicions regarding the encounter.

"Clark always accompanies me on my walks, when my husband is not available that is. Mr. Darcy insists on his presence wherever I go."

"As Darcy has charged me as your protector while he is away, I can take over from here." Then he looked to the footman, "Clark, is it? You may leave us. I will see to Mrs. Darcy's safety."

Neither missed the look of panic on Elizabeth's countenance. "No, Clark, I wish for you to stay. Surely a woman cannot have too many men at her disposal. Perhaps you could give the viscount and me a little distance, but your presence is most welcome."

Langston turned his attention back to Elizabeth, "Now, Elizabeth, surely there can be no occasion for taking up your servant's time when he could be needed at the house. I insist that he leave us to ourselves. We have much to talk about, do we not? I will return you to the house before long. Susan was hoping to explore the gardens with you. Clark, you are excused."

Elizabeth hated to put the servant in a difficult position but could not bear being left alone with Langston who would most certainly take advantage of their solitude. If Clark stayed, he risked disciplinary action by the viscount who was charged by Darcy himself with her safety. Her husband had specifically sanctioned Langston's escort.

Clark also thought through this but then continued the possible scenario. If he were to leave Mrs. Darcy alone with the viscount, he would be responsible for any acts of aggression that the viscount might press upon his mistress. He could not miss the licentious look in the nobleman's eyes, despite the woman's being the wife of his cousin. Clark wavered, unsure of what to do, but Langston had a plan. "Clark, I know you would hate for me to tell your employer that I found you out here in an inappropriate embrace with his wife. I have no doubt you would lose your position and be left without a reference. As a matter of fact, I am quite certain that Darcy would destroy you and your future hopes."

"Langston, you would not get away with such a lie. Darcy would not believe you. Clark has always been a faithful servant, and my husband trusts him implicitly."

"But does he trust you? He has told me more than once that he suspects you have had liaisons with other men. In fact, he sent me here to ensure that you not engage in extramarital activities, but I do not believe that he suspected you would have designs on his servant. He would not believe *your* story if I told him that I saw you with my own eyes." Then he turned to Clark and said, "Forget you saw me, and I may let you keep your post, otherwise I will be forced to divulge your clandestine rendezvous with Mrs. Darcy, and not just this one. You have walked her to her room each night since I have been here. My wife has suspected a close relationship between you two, and she has a hard time holding her tongue, but I could keep her quiet unless forced to do otherwise."

Elizabeth took courage. She could not in good conscience force Clark into an untenable situation such as this. Although without merit, she could see how her actions could have the appearance of impropriety, and she would not see Clark losing his position over her poor judgement. She would hope that the viscount meant her no harm, and if he did, she would employ the skills that Clark had shared. "Clark, I will be safe with Lord Langston. He is Mr. Darcy's cousin, and it is true that my husband sent him for my safekeeping; he wrote me that same message days ago. Please, go back to the house and await my return."

Elizabeth could see that the footman was torn as to his duties. She took a step towards him and placed her hand on his arm. "Truly, Clark. I will be fine. Lord Langston is Mr. Darcy's cousin. He can have no harmful designs on me." She knew this to be a falsehood, but could only succeed in protecting Clark's position if he were to leave. Finally the young man reluctantly turned towards the house and left Mrs. Darcy to the viscount's care. He looked back several times to see Elizabeth and the viscount begin to walk slowly back towards the house. This at least provided him with the comfort of knowing that they were headed home rather than further away. He had no recourse but to hope and pray for the best.

"Elizabeth, you made the right decision. Shall we walk?"

"I prefer heading back towards the house, if that is acceptable to you."

"By all means." Langston set a slow pace, taking her hand and placing it securely on his arm. After a few moments of walking in silence, Langston said, "You have done an admirable job avoiding being alone with me, but truly, I cannot account for your evasion. You are my cousin's wife; I would not cause you real harm."

Elizabeth did not respond, hoping to discourage this line of talk.

"I had hoped for some privacy because I have something about which to speak with you that you might find interesting, even beneficial." She refused to take his bait, but he continued on anyway. "I don't judge you for meeting up with your footman friend. I know many men and women who enjoy the benefits of attractive servants – as long as no issue comes of the dalliance, that is. Clark is a handsome man; no one would blame you, except perhaps your husband, but then again, he has no room to judge."

His words had hit their mark. Elizabeth stopped and looked up at him with anger in her eyes. "I would ask that you not suggest anything of the kind about me or my husband. What happens between us is none of your concern."

"I only mean to help, my dear." His words of endearment sickened her. "I just thought that in your naïveté you might be under the misunderstanding that your husband has been and will always be faithful to you."

Elizabeth felt as though she had been punched as she considered his words and the pain they invoked within her. "You are speaking only to hurt me."

"Can you in all honesty discount what I say? I have proof you know." She could not speak for the quickening of her breaths. "Did your husband ever mention to you about his visit to Madame Karina's?"

Elizabeth struggled to remember where she had seen that name. She searched her memory and recalled that just the other day she had come across the same name on the card in her husband's escritoire, but she would not give in to his incitements. However, deep inside, feelings of panic began to make their assent into her consciousness.

"I only know about it because I was there with him. I believe it was at the end of January, in town. A group of us decided to go to the woman's establishment. She caters to gentlemen and her services are extensive. But do not concern yourself; she is very discreet, even going so far as to assign pseudonyms to her customers. I believe she gave Darcy the name Adonis, for she had paired him up with Aphrodite. Fitting, I thought, since Aphrodite is the goddess who incited adultery thus bringing on the Trojan War. If I remember correctly, the love story of Adonis and Aphrodite ends with a tragedy." Langston laughed at Elizabeth's unaffected look of despair. She could no longer hide her inner turmoil as she considered her husband's treachery.

Elizabeth felt as though she had been struck to the core. *Oh, my God, no! No! This cannot be. How could he? Just when I know my heart, am I to be so cruelly tortured?* She now remembered very clearly the card having the name *Adonis* written in a flowing and feminine script on the opposite side.

"You see the truth in what I say. He was anxious to arrive; I just wish I could have seen his face when he looked upon Aphrodite. She is a beautiful girl, looks a lot like you actually, if maybe a few years younger."

"Enough! Say no more! Your words are poison, and I will not hear another thing you have to say!" Elizabeth attempted to pull her arm from his, but she could not make it budge. "Release me, sir." She said this in a low voice, but the outrage was clear.

"I think not. We are not done here. If your footman can get in on some fun, surely a viscount can too." He leered at her and grabbed her other arm holding her in a harsh grip. "Now we can enjoy each other's company or not. Either way, I will find *my* pleasure. No one is here to stop me this time." He then picked her up and carried her off the path and into the trees.

Elizabeth knew her danger. Her only solace was the thought that if Lord Langston were successful in overcoming her, then she could not become with child by him, for she carried her husband's own. While in his grasp she could do nothing to effectively fight him. Certainly, she kicked and screamed for help, but Clark must have been too far away to hear her for no help was to come. Langston then stopped at a tree and pinned her against it with the weight of his large frame.

"Elizabeth, don't fight; you cannot get away from me, and if you just try to relax, you might find that you quite enjoy it." She spit in his face, causing him to strike her on the side of her head before grabbing her wrists and putting them into one of his hands in a strong grip. Then he covered her mouth with his other hand and began to speak in her ear, slowly, almost as if to soothe. "Elizabeth, my dear, calm down. I mean you no harm. I know how to please a woman and would like to please you. Once you see how things can be, you will welcome me to your room when the family gathers together. Darcy need never know. And what could he say anyway. Has he not also broken his marriage vows at Madame Karina's? That was not the only time either. Let this be an occasion to be avenged of his intimacies with other women. This is the way of the world, my darling. You must see the possibilities for pleasure."

She could not believe her ears. While he spoke she thought back to her simple life at Longbourn, her peace and comfort. *What has wealth given me? What has being a part of society done for me, and what has it done for my husband?* She began to cry, treacherous tears pouring down her cheek, which only seemed to spur the man on.

Langston laughed at her, as she seemed to give up her fight. "Yes, just relax, my Elizabeth." He removed his hand to take off her bonnet, while still holding her wrists with the other, then he began kissing her mouth, gentle at first but then more demanding as he pushed his tongue in to explore. While kissing her, his hand began its intimate explorations. He started to unbutton her spencer, but in his impatience, he ripped it open, not caring at the moment how that might look on their return. His passions took control of his better judgement as he reached his hand down her dress to find her breast. She was not fighting him and he began to think that she might be enjoying the excitement of the moment, for he certainly was. In one swift stroke, he tore open her bodice revealing her stays. His mouth immediately went to her milky skin as his hand then moved to pull up her dress. He had let go of her wrists as he pulled up her dress, so he could reach for his own buttons. He was certain now that she had given in as she put her hands on his shoulders to feel his strong muscles.

He smiled to himself as he was finally going to be able to savour his passion as he had thought about for months. Darcy was indeed a lucky man, but his fortune would have to be shared on this day. Any apprehension about Darcy's finding out about their current escapade dissipated with her willing consent, which would preclude Darcy's learning about their encounter, for what could she say if she herself enjoyed the venture? Although the thrill of taking a woman by force had its merits, he found even greater pleasure in causing a woman who once spurned him to now want him. And this would not be the only time.

The viscount, in his musings, was soon brought to his knees in a sudden and equally violent blow to his nether regions. Elizabeth had been waiting for the right moment to catch him off guard. She knew that she had only one chance and was willing to expose herself to his disgusting explorations if she could, in the end, make her escape. Years of walking did their work as she, with all of the force she could muster, kneed him in his groin. The effect was immediate, almost taking her off guard as well. Clark had told her that she would find her success if she were to employ such a tactic, but Elizabeth could not have imagined a more compelling and expeditious result.

Elizabeth found her freedom and took off running at a speed beyond any race she had ever run before. His wails from behind followed her as she saw that she was at the hill that she had traversed with Darcy on that day that he told her she was not to change; she got to the top and immediately ran down the other side and into the woods below, veering off the path. She knew that Langston had been unable to move when she first struck him, but she feared that he might even now be chasing her, perhaps on his horse. The blackguard would be certain to punish her if he were to find her, so she ran with all of her might, not letting herself give in to fatigue. Her breaths were deep and burning her chest, but on she ran. Her tears had stopped, as she had no room for them in her attempt to escape. She could hear Langston in the far distance yelling at her, as she continued to try to put a span between them. Finally, after she knew not how long or far, she collapsed onto the floor of the woodland deep within the park and far away from any path or any familiar marking. She had run more than twice the distance she had ever run in her life, when her legs and lungs had finally given way. She lay there heaving for air resigned to whatever fate Providence had deemed fitting, as she had not an ounce of energy left in her to bring about a true escape.

LANGSTON CURSED THE WOMAN over and over as the sharp pain brought him to his knees and left him lying on the ground in a powerless heap of excruciating agony. After several minutes of recovery, he was finally able to pull himself to a stand and look around for direction as to where she might have gone. He swore that he would make Elizabeth pay for her duplicity. He attempted to get on his mount, but the pain was still unbearable, so he started on foot and began in the direction that he thought she had gone. Although minutes behind her, the viscount thought that he would be able to catch her, for she would be unable to match him by speed and strength, especially when he could search by horseback.

He crested the hillside and looked around for any movement in the distance, but seeing nothing to indicate her presence, he continued onward, limping at first but gaining momentum. Langston could not contain his anger as he thought about how he would make her suffer for her attack. "Elizabeth! I will find you, and when I do, you will pay!" He was running now and upon cresting another hill, stopped to look out, but missed her just as she dropped to the floor of the forest. Since there were still few leaves on the trees, he was able to look far into the woodland for his prize. Seeing no sign of her, he continued on, but fortunately for Elizabeth, he had chosen a different path than her own.

Had Elizabeth still been running, he likely would have seen her in the distance, but her fatigue had saved her. She lay there for she knew not how long listening for signs of the man's presence, daring not to move. She no longer heard his shouts or expletives, and without meaning to, eventually fell into a deep slumber, too tired and too afraid to sit up.

ELIZABETH FINALLY AWOKE to the encroaching darkness when she heard a rumbling in the distance that could not be mistaken. She sat up and tried to get a bearing as to where she might be. The sounds of the trees and bushes blowing in the wind and of the advancing storm were all she could hear. The viscount must have wandered far away from her, for she had likely been there for hours. As she stood, Elizabeth could feel the chilly, blustery wind blowing at her torn clothing, causing her exposed skin to appear as gooseflesh, so she tried to pull her spencer tight, buttoning the only remaining button that had not been ripped off. She had to find shelter from the approaching storm before the sunlight had completely disappeared, so she began to walk. Although tired from her run, as well as from her two long walks that day, she had recovered sufficiently to move forward at a good pace, but she could not find shelter before complete darkness hit. With the light show that had begun in the distance, Elizabeth had occasional glimpses of her treacherous path ahead.

The trees and ridges around her hid the majority of the storm that was now quickly approaching. Elizabeth had been crossing the crest of a hill when a large bolt of lightning struck in the far distance causing her to jump and lose her footing on the loose gravel beneath her feet, thus inducing her to stumble forward, slamming her hands against the rocky terrain. "Blast!" came unbidden out of her mouth, which had the strange effect of amusing her, for never in her life had she uttered such a thing.

Elizabeth sat there considering what she might do next. Thoughts of Langston intruded upon her as she considered his vile assault. She remembered vividly how he had violated her. She could not bear the thought of ever being touched that way again, even by her own husband. All men were beasts, she now knew. And where was she to go? She could not possibly return to the main house, for Lord Langston might be there to meet her. Without Darcy around, she would have no protection, for he had given instructions that Langston was to act on his behalf. She knew that her actions at the tree would forever make her vulnerable to the despicable man. He was certain to denigrate her to all of Darcy's acquaintances and even to Darcy himself. Would her husband believe the lies Langston would tell at her expense? Then without consent, her mind recalled Langston's account of Madame Karina's. Elizabeth would not have believed him but for the gold embossed card she had found just this week that stood as proof of Darcy's faithlessness. Tears were running down her cheek as her mind took her down the road of her husband's infidelity. Elizabeth had keenly felt the possibility of her husband's having a mistress from his single days, who may even still continue in his life; but to know that in addition to this that he sought out a paramour to satisfy his lusts, even after their marriage had taken place, made her truly ill.

Pulling herself together, she said aloud, "Come Lizzy, I need shelter before the storm hits." She stood up, wiped her eyes, and saw that her fall had resulted in her gloves being ripped on each of her palms. The dull pain stayed with her as she continued on, but now that it was full dark, she no longer looked for a building but perhaps a canopy from a large tree to sit under. However, with so few leaves to act as a shelter, she would be drenched through. While her mind could not easily leave her husband's treachery, she considered her current options as she struggled on in the darkness. Unfortunately, her blurry eyes, coupled with nightfall, caused her to trip upon an unseen tree root, resulting in her falling again, but this time her tumble took her down a steep hillside. Elizabeth instinctively huddled to protect her unborn baby, but to no avail. She hit several trees and rocks along the way down and would have felt the pain of each had she not been knocked unconscious about halfway down the steep slope.

The rain began its own descent as the cold winds from the north burst through the hollow of the valley. The storm hit hard and fast as torrential waves of rain and gusts of wind came down on Elizabeth while the temperature dropped considerably. Although she had landed by a ditch that had quickly filled with water, fortunately for Elizabeth, she landed just above the water line, but the cold, wet effects of the rain would seep into her core. As she lay there, eventually returning to a conscious state, her thoughts went to her baby within while she prayed earnestly for its survival. Despair and hopelessness threatened to overcome Elizabeth, and if not for her child, she truly would have let herself be defeated, even then, by the welcome numbing effects of the cold.

Chapter Twenty

An excellent wife who can find?
She is far more precious than jewels.
Proverbs 31: 10-11

After searching for Elizabeth for over two hours, Langston finally gave up his efforts and began his journey to the house. By now he was able to ride and so quickly travelled the distance. During his return, he attempted to come up with a viable excuse for why Elizabeth had not joined him. Remembering Darcy's fear of Wickham's being in the area, he decided to say that he had been attacked from behind by the man, who then escaped with a willing Elizabeth heading south.

As he came towards the house, he noticed the flashes of the storm in the distance. *This should delay the search for her. With any luck, she will get lost in the woods north of here and perish before she can be found.*

After taking his mount to the barn, Langston walked to the house. When he entered, Peters and Clark approached him and asked for Mrs. Darcy's whereabouts. "I have no idea where she is now. We were walking together in conversation when I was struck from behind. Next thing I knew I was on the ground looking up to see her running off with Wickham headed south. After I was able to stand, I went after them, but after two hours of searching, returned here. There is a storm coming and it will soon be dark. We will have to search again in the morning."

"Wickham?" said a distraught Clark.

Langston looked to the meddlesome footman and said, "That is none of your concern. I suggest you get back to your duties."

Then Peters chimed in, "Clark means no disrespect. He is naturally worried about our mistress. Clark, go prepare for dinner." Then turning to Lord Langston, he said, "Sir, forgive my presumption, but Wickham has not been seen around here in four years. Are you certain that he was the one with Mrs. Darcy?"

"I know what he looks like."

"The man is not welcome at Pemberley and no one has seen him, of which I am aware." Then the butler paused in thought before continuing, "I will begin to question everyone. Hopefully, we will be able to find some clues to help in the search."

"With the storm approaching, I am afraid we will accomplish little tonight. Darcy will be here sometime tomorrow. He will be devastated that his wife has left with the man," Langston said quietly, looking around as if to ensure privacy.

"Do you think she left willingly?" asked the concerned butler.

"I am afraid she did. I could hear her laughing in the distance as they left me there. Darcy had asked me to keep an eye out for him, as he suspected Wickham's return to Pemberley. Apparently, he and Mrs. Darcy were friends in Hertfordshire."

"Oh my. That does surprise me. She has such openness about her. Wickham must have taken advantage of her kindness."

"That will be for Darcy to figure out. As for me, I need a hot bath. And Lady Susan and I will eat in our rooms tonight. Without our hostess and with this knot on my head, I would prefer not having to dress for dinner. Could you send for my valet to attend me? I will tell my wife of our changed plans this evening."

Pemberley was subdued as each of the servants fretted over Mrs. Darcy's absence. They looked to Lord Langston for leadership but only found a man who seemed content with her desertion. Few believed that Mrs. Darcy would have willingly left with Wickham, for many had known the man and his profligate ways. Elizabeth had earned the respect of every level of the staff through her kind attentions and understanding nature. If she were with Wickham, that meant that she was in trouble, but they needed a leader to organise the search. It was true that the weather and dark night would preclude any kind of effective search this evening, but Peters wanted to organise a team to head out first thing in the morning. In light of this, he met with his staff to come up with some plan of action, despite the viscount's lack of involvement.

DARCY WAS PREPARING TO LEAVE ROSINGS early Monday morning, planning to stop at Darcy House to change horses and eat a quick meal. After that, he hoped to continue on to Pemberley late that afternoon with the expectation of putting at least four hours of road behind them. He and his cousin decided that it would be best for Georgiana to travel with him to Pemberley while leaving Fitzwilliam in London to deal with Wickham. Since receiving the letter, Darcy had continued to struggle with how to handle Wickham's demands. The two cousins set aside little time to discuss the possibilities while at Rosings due to their taxing schedule. They had been either hard at work completing their respective responsibilities or entertaining Lady Catherine and their sickly relation, Anne. So before breaking their fast, Fitzwilliam came to Darcy's room for a private word and discovered that his cousin had almost come to the decision to pay off his former friend and nemesis.

"Darcy, this is ludicrous! Your wife is not the kind of woman to be unfaithful! I would bet my life on it. Wickham is lying in order to extract a sizable sum from you. Just the other day, you were telling me of your wife's many fine qualities. How could you possibly think otherwise just because of Wickham's account? He has never been worthy of trust."

"I know Wickham's faults; I can assure you. But everything he has written has some merit. How could he know of Elizabeth's pregnancy without her having told him, and why did she not tell me? The truth is she despised me at one time – and not that long ago. And then there is her last trip to Longbourn. When I arrived, I found them in private conversation, walking in the garden together. Elizabeth was openly showing him her regard. She claimed that nothing happened between them, but of course she would not have told me otherwise. But even then Wickham made reference to seducing her. And how did Wickham get Elizabeth's handkerchief?"

"Darcy, I know it looks bad, but do not commit to anything until you have spoken with Mrs. Darcy. Give her a chance to explain."

"That is exactly what I plan to do and as soon as possible, but I am supposed to give Wickham the money by this evening. Do I give in and be done with it, or do I take my chances and hope he is bluffing? No matter the truth, I must do something today or risk a scandal that would forever call into question my progeny."

"By giving him the money, do you avoid a scandal? And does giving him the money not confirm the validity of his claims? Who is to say that next month he won't come back with another bribe? You must take no notice of his demands; don't even acknowledge that you received the letter."

"But what if it is all true? What if Elizabeth carries his baby?"

"You will have two days to consider that option, my friend. But if she did give herself over to Wickham, you can be certain she regrets it. You will have to decide whether you can love her anyway. Can you accept her in your life even if she has made mistakes? Would she accept you if you had been the one to betray her trust?"

The two men sat in silence as Darcy thought about his own hypocritical failings. "We had better say our goodbyes. Thank you, James. Your guidance means a great deal to me."

"So, you recognise my superior judgement then?" the colonel said with a smile.

"I would not go that far, Cousin." Darcy took in a deep breath as he considered Fitzwilliam's argument. It certainly had merit. Darcy in no way wanted to give Wickham any compensation, whether there was truth in his claims or not, for how could he financially reward the blackguard for taking his wife? "You have a plan should I not pay Wickham?"

"I always have a plan; I am a trained officer in His Majesty's Army," Fitzwilliam said light-heartedly, but then became serious yet again. "We will use tonight as an opportunity to ferret him out. He will not get away with his treachery; that I can promise you." Thoughtfully he continued, "At one time you were purchasing Wickham's debts in order to keep his gaming obligations from your father's notice. Do you still have those?"

"Yes, I have kept them all. They span over ten years now."

"Good. Do you know their combined value?"

"Somewhere upwards of five thousand, I suppose."

"And he is asking for five?" Fitzwilliam smirked. "How apropos. Once he is in my grasp, I can assure you that he will no longer be a threat."

Darcy contemplated what he was implying. "You plan to turn the tables on him by threatening imprisonment?"

"You have far more control over him than you realise. Trust me to take care of him, Cousin. It'll be a piece of cake."

"I pray you are right." Darcy stood and picked up his gloves. "Come, we should go. We both have a long day ahead of us, and I am already weary."

The journey to town passed quickly as the weather had been dry since the previous week. Each sat in quiet contemplation about recent events. Georgiana had been exceptionally subdued since Darcy had arrived from Pemberley, feeling the full weight of her brother's wife's treachery. She could see the stress that her revelations had inflicted upon him. Darcy had not told her of Wickham's demands, nor had he consulted her regarding any part of his plans, but she could see a change in him from the night of her disclosure. "Brother, you say that I am to travel with you to Pemberley?"

Georgiana's voice startled her brother as he had been deep in thought, but then he said, "Yes. I prefer that you join me. That does not present a problem does it?"

"I have not packed. Am I to stay there for long?"

"That, I cannot say, but you will be there until I return to town again at the earliest. There is no need to take time today to pack beyond what you brought to Rosings though. We can leave Maggie at Tromwell House to prepare your trunks, and she can then travel with my servants. Mrs. Annesley can remain in town at Tromwell until then."

"Will Mrs. Darcy be at Pemberley?" she asked in a small voice. The question surprised her brother, as he considered all that she might be asking behind the words.

"Yes, Georgiana, Pemberley is Elizabeth's home now. She will be there."

Georgiana looked to her cousin who seemed to be asleep. "Will you let her stay though?"

"I want you to stop worrying about my marriage. We will not conjecture until we have all of the answers, and I will certainly not judge my wife without them."

She glanced again to her cousin before continuing softly but insistently, "But Brother, you cannot deny that she and Mr. Wickham have been in a relationship. He had proof of her affections."

In susurration, yet also with resolution, Darcy responded, "Desist, Georgiana! I will not have you speaking so. Now, Elizabeth is my wife and I will not have you speculating about the truth or falsity of her fidelity. We will go to Pemberley and discover the veracity of his claims. I have known Wickham longer than you, and I can assure you that his false words will poison you. I will not have them poison me against my wife without knowing the whole story. We will talk of this no more."

At Darcy House, the threesome went inside to refresh and eat. The Darcys would stop for no more than two hours before setting out again. During that time Darcy and Colonel Fitzwilliam met in Darcy's study one last time to confirm how the next week would play out. It was determined that Fitzwilliam would have some of his men stationed undercover at the proposed drop off sight, keeping an eye out for the young boy whose description Darcy relayed. That would be easy enough. After handing over a satchel, seemingly filled with funds, the boy would be followed to determine Wickham's hiding place, which would then be under close surveillance until a time when Darcy or Fitzwilliam would confront the miscreant.

"Please write should there be any public report. I would like to know as soon as possible. And, James, should that happen, can you reassure our family that I, well, I suppose tell them that I will get to the bottom of Wickham's claims and will do whatever I can to protect the family."

"I will take care of everything here. I have leave until the beginning of July, and I will devote whatever time is needed for your cause."

"Thank you. I know that I can count on you. I will send over a missive to my bank giving you leave to take out whatever funds are necessary should it come to that."

Fitzwilliam raised his brows. "So I will have full access to your account? I must not let such an opportunity pass me by, Cousin!" he finished with a smile.

"I trust you with my life. If I cannot trust you, my dearest friend, with my money, then I have no hope."

"Then count yourself most fortunate, for I will guard all that you have as if my own."

Soon Darcy and Georgiana were on the road again with fresh horses and food for later. They would travel approximately thirty miles today, helping ensure that they made Pemberley by mid-afternoon two days hence. The weather could change quickly this time of year with rainfall on most days. Since it had been dry, Darcy suspected they would be in for some showers along the way.

DESPITE A CHANGE IN WEATHER, they were able to make good time. Finally, on the third day they approached the lodge that marked the entrance into the Pemberley estate. The sense of relief was palpable for Darcy, but his sister had become more somnolent as they journeyed. She dreaded the confrontation with her brother's wife and wished that Elizabeth were anywhere but at their family's beloved home.

As they pulled up to the grand house, two servants rushed out to meet him. When he first descended from the coach, before he could hand his sister down, Peters said, "Mr. Darcy, sir, we are glad you are finally home. We have grave news to impart."

"Follow me to my study." With foreboding, Darcy left Georgiana to be escorted in by a servant, much to her vexation. After closing the door behind him, Darcy turned to Peters and the footman, Clark, who had accompanied them. "Tell me."

"I suggest you sit down." Seeing that his master had no inclination to sit, Peters began, "Your wife, sir. She is missing."

"Elizabeth is missing? What do you mean, she is missing?"

"Yesterday afternoon she was walking with Lord Langston when your cousin was hit from behind. All he could determine after that was that Mrs. Darcy left with a man, Mr. Wickham, if he saw him correctly. She has not been seen since." Darcy apparently decided that sitting was a good idea after all. He mindlessly made his way to the chair in front of the chimneypiece and sat, eyes wide, mouth agape.

It is true! Blast! How could I have been so foolish? He must have scheduled Monday night for payment to keep me in town. Or perhaps, he suspected that I would not pay after all and so chose to come up here to abduct Elizabeth himself, hoping for an even greater payoff. "Tell me everything."

436

The next thirty minutes were spent in narrating the events of the past two days, how Elizabeth had been walking with Clark until Langston relieved him, how Langston had returned three hours later without her and how the search had so far come up without a clue as to her location. "Where was she last seen?"

Clark spoke up, "I left her with the viscount on the path leading to Lake Merimar. We had been walking for about three miles when he crossed our path. I reluctantly left them there, following his orders that I leave. That was the last time I saw her. You will have to ask Lord Langston yourself about his experience, for I cannot reconcile his tale with what I know about Mrs. Darcy."

"Clark, are you accusing my cousin of something?" Darcy said, his anger finally finding an outlet.

"No, sir. I meant no disrespect."

"What is being done? Where is my cousin?"

"He is out with the search party, but he does not think they will find success," said Peters. "The staff, including the footmen and stable hands, was ready at dawn and had begun the search when your cousin called them in and directed them to the south. Mr. Wickham is well acquainted with the grounds of Pemberley, and Lord Langston suspects they are long gone."

"Damn! If she is with Wickham then I have no doubt that they are no longer in the area, but I do not think she would have left willingly, which would likely have slowed him down. Did Langston say if they were on foot or horseback?"

"He did not say, only that he saw them walk away from him."

Darcy sat there considering his servants' report and trying to decide what course of action he should take. "Has anyone gone into the towns nearby to ask if Wickham has been seen?"

"We sent men out this morning, but there is no indication that he has stayed at the local inns or visited the alehouses."

Darcy stood. "I am going to change. Clark, meet me at the stables. Have a horse ready for each of us. I want you to take me to where you last saw her."

"Yes, sir." The look of relief on the footman's face was palpable, and Darcy considered what else the man might know.

Georgiana had entered her family's home with little fanfare. She had not been in residence there for nearly a year and keenly felt the disappointment in how she was left in the hands of a servant. She had wondered about her brother's hasty removal from the front entrance and was curious to know what could have disturbed him so. She had observed him for the past several days in subdued but clear agitation. Georgiana suspected that her brother's wife was at the heart of the matter, and hoped that it was so. She knew that her story about Wickham, nearly two weeks ago, had a profound effect on his peace and was likely now the catalyst for his disquiet, but she also suspected that more had taken place since that time, about which she was left in the dark. Before she had gotten to the stairs to the upper floors, her cousin's wife, Lady Susan, approached her.

"Georgiana, you have arrived just in time for all the fun."

"What can you mean by fun? I was under the impression that something was terribly wrong."

"Well, I guess it all depends on your perspective," replied Lady Susan who grabbed hold of Georgiana's arm and led her upstairs. "Follow me to my rooms and I will tell you what has happened."

When they entered Lady Susan's chamber, Georgiana walked over to the hearth, so that she might warm up a bit. The air around the peaks was much cooler than even a few hours' carriage ride away. "So, do not keep me waiting. What has occurred?"

"Your sister-in-law has run away! Is that not delightful? It turns out that she and that Wickham fellow – you know the one who used to live here at Pemberley, his father being your father's steward – well anyway, apparently he and Mrs. Darcy had been acquainted, very acquainted it would seem, from her time in Hertfordshire. She had wanted Wickham all along, but must have gone through with the marriage to your brother in order to get control of money, maybe even by selling the jewels." She said all of this in whispered tones, as if fearful of being overheard in her private room, yet satisfied with her tale, nonetheless.

"I knew it! My poor brother was used by that, that … strumpet!"

"Georgiana, dear, do calm down. What do they teach young girls now? Such language!"

"Forgive me. I am just outraged that anyone could be so cruel to my charitable and generous brother. He gave up all of his hopes, for her, and then she treats him this way. How dare she!" Georgiana began to pace, a trait reminiscent of her brother. "What can I do? How can I help him?"

"He will likely be angry at first and then perhaps saddened as anyone of Darcy's kind nature might be, but when he is ready for comfort, you need to be there for him, for we are likely to be at Matlock House. As much as I enjoy your company, I cannot bear to be in this house a moment longer with the memory of that imposter in our midst."

Georgiana continued to pace, considering what she might do to assist her brother in this altogether horrible affair. She knew Elizabeth would one day regret her decision to leave with Wickham, for she knew him to be a selfish and deceptive man, only interested in how he might use her for money and whatever else men of his ilk wanted. She just hoped that her brother would not fall for any duplicity on Elizabeth's part when it came to it.

After the enlightening conversation, Lady Susan claimed she needed solitude for some beauty rest before preparing for dinner, so Georgiana left her alone. She went into her own sitting room and called for a substitute lady's maid to help her change out of her travel clothes. When the maid arrived, Georgiana said, "I do not believe I have seen you before. How long have you been employed by my brother?"

"I arrived shortly after the new Mrs. Darcy married Mr. Darcy. I serve her."

"I see," said Georgiana coolly. She knew that oftentimes, loyalties were formed between the servant and master, or in this case mistress. "So, do you believe that my brother's wife has left for good?"

"I hope she will be found soon. I cannot imagine what has happened to her, and I begin to fear for her."

"I am sure that she is safe enough. What is your name?"

"Janette, Ma'am."

"You will be my lady's maid until my own arrives. Help me change."

And so, Janette continued her duties, but employed on another. She had served many ladies in the past, but Janette had never enjoyed the peace and comfort that she had while with Mrs. Darcy. The young woman before her held the usual air of privilege that was missing in her mistress, and she suspected that the young Miss Darcy was likely predisposed to think ill of her new sister. She had clearly been relegated to her relations all these months; and Janette, like everyone else, knew the scandal concerning Darcy's marriage. That was old news as far as she was concerned, however. Janette had only known Mrs. Darcy to be a kind mistress who had been good for Pemberley and good for her husband, as she saw it. But she suspected that his younger sister might see things differently, especially in light of the new rumours related to Mrs. Darcy's absence. Janette completed her new duties and was given direction concerning Miss Darcy's expectations.

TWO HOURS AFTER THEIR DEPARTURE, Darcy and Clark returned as twilight set in. They had canvassed the entire area where Clark had last seen Elizabeth, and there was no evidence of anyone's having been there. When they entered the house, Darcy saw that Langston had also just returned.

"Darcy, you are home. I was told that you had arrived a few hours ago. I guess you know about your wife."

"I know that she is missing. Come into my study and tell me everything." Langston followed his cousin, and going straight to the sideboard, poured each of them a brandy. Handing a glass to Darcy, he walked over and sat down upon one of the chairs by the fire.

"Come sit with me, Darcy, and I will tell you what I know." When Darcy had seated himself and taken a few sips of his liquid, Langston began, "Mrs. Darcy is with Wickham." Darcy looked up sharply at him, a pained look upon his countenance. "They went south, so that is where we have been looking, but I have no hope of finding her. She wanted to leave with him. I heard her laughing as she walked away."

"That cannot be! Even if she had wanted to leave with Wickham, she would not have laughed while you were injured."

"Oh, Darcy! Don't be so naïve! She is a tart who has been using you for your money. I tried to be kind to her, but she did nothing but spurn my friendship. She probably planned the clandestine meeting with the help of that footman, Clark. No wonder he was reluctant to leave me with Elizabeth. He was probably assisting her in her rendezvous with the blackguard after enjoying his own. I wouldn't trust the man. Check the Darcy jewellery collection to ensure nothing is missing because I would wager she took the lot and made her escape."

Hearing his cousin say such vicious words about his wife gave Darcy a sickening feeling in his gut. *Could any of this be true? No, this sounds nothing like her! But do I really know her? Could she in fact have taken advantage of my accident in Hertfordshire and planned to steal from me all along? I would rather have given her half my fortune than go through this.* And then there was Clark. Could Darcy's trusted employee have been deceiving him as well?

"Darcy, I am leaving in the morning. I suggest you dissolve the marriage as quickly as possible. You cannot salvage it, and you need to move on. You have already given up on Lady Annette; perhaps you can soon find another woman of pristine character, one from your own set, not the daughter of a poor gentleman. You have noble blood in you and must act like it in order to salvage your family."

Darcy had no response, for at this moment his heart was breaking in two. He loved Elizabeth. He knew that now with all the certainty that one could have in a situation such as this. He downed his drink and stood up to pour another. "Will you leave before breakfast?"

"At first light. Poor Susan has had to deal with Mrs. Darcy's rude overtures and now her disappearance. I need to get her to Matlock."

"I will see you off then, but as for tonight, I am exhausted. I really must have time to myself. Georgiana is here and will attend you and Lady Susan at dinner."

"Darcy, I am sorry about all of this, but your family warned you."

Darcy stayed in his study for a while longer. He sat in the leather chair by the fire, looking at its twin, the one Elizabeth preferred. He imaged her scintillating eyes, teasing him with raised brow and upturned full lips. He was a puppy, lost when she looked at him that way. How many times did he want to kiss her pouty mouth but was stopped by her melodious laugh when he seemed to forget that his words had just been turned against him – as she had yet again shown her intellectual prowess catching him off-guard in his adolescent musings. What had become of Fitzwilliam Darcy? How did this woman of little consequence take so much control over his sensibilities? Even now, she affected him physically as he meditated on her fine attributes.

He stood up to walk around the room trying to shake his reflections. Now was not the time to get sentimental. His duty to his family demanded a clear head. Two piles of mail had been left on his desk, one with only four pieces and the other with at least two dozen. Darcy carelessly picked up the smaller of the two stacks tapping them upon his desk as he considered Langston's words. Darcy felt the full weight of Elizabeth's disappearance and peril, whether she was with Wickham or alone in the wilds. He glanced down to the papers in his hands and realised that he was holding Elizabeth's mail. Apparently, since her disappearance, his staff had decided to bring her correspondence to him rather than her own study.

He mindlessly flipped through the letters but was arrested by an all too familiar script. *Wickham!* Darcy stared down at the sealed parchment before him, familiar resentment and fury welling up inside. He broke the seal without thought for preserving his wife's privacy and opened the page to read what Wickham had written to his wife. The brevity of the note in no way diminished its significance.

440

April 13, 1811
London

My Dearest Elizabeth,

How I have longed to see you once again, to hold you in my arms. I am finding it more and more difficult to bear the separation that has been imposed upon us. Your sister may have told you that I have left my place in the militia and hope to find a situation that will better suit my education as a gentleman, with the wish that we can finally be together, if only on occasion. London holds many possibilities for me. I am much encouraged and hopeful for support – that perhaps even Darcy will one day see how I can play a positive role in his future. Do not give in to despair.

I know you did not wish that I write you, but knowing Darcy was away, I thought it to be safe. I find that I cannot stay away from memories of us together. I continue to see your beautiful face in my mind's eye and only hope that you remember me the same way. Thank you for getting word to me about your condition. I realise that I might not have the freedom to claim you and the baby as my own, but that can in no way diminish my affection. Please write to me soon through Lydia.

With loving remembrance of our brief time together,

George Wickham

Darcy's hands were shaking as he read Wickham's deceptive words. By the end, he was breathing in quick succession as he crumbled up the paper ready to throw it into the fire. He stopped himself just short of destroying proof of Wickham's artifice in the flames, but only to preserve the letter should it be needed later.

Was Elizabeth so blinded by continued hatred for himself not to see through Wickham's machinations and pretence? Had Darcy not just been reflecting upon Elizabeth's quick wit and insight? How could she be so addled to believe in the flattery of a scoundrel such as Wickham?

Wickham's words pained Darcy more than he could have anticipated – that his wife would prefer the profligate to himself. *But that cannot be!* Darcy reminded himself yet again of the depraved man's cunning and propensity for deceit. Darcy had no way of knowing the validity of Wickham's implications. Indeed, the outlook for Darcy's marriage was bleak. His wife either ran off with a libertine who would ruin her good name and crush her spirit, or she was taken against her will to face the same fate. Elizabeth had been missing for over a day now and might even at this moment be abandoned somewhere in the elements. Could Darcy let her face the consequences of her actions at the hands of a man who would shatter her?

Darcy could not reconcile the evidence with his heart. Somehow, he could not bring himself to believe in her guilt and felt most acutely the danger that threatened her, either from Wickham or the elements. Regardless, nothing could be done this night towards restoring Elizabeth to her home. Darcy had to decide his purpose and possible outcome should his wife be found with Wickham, but he still could not let his mind meditate on the painful possibility. Regardless of her desires or the events leading up to her disappearance, she was his wife. He must do everything within his power to recover her. And then anything beyond that hope would be tied to her wishes and expectations.

THAT NIGHT, DARCY SLEPT LITTLE as he contemplated what his cousin and the footman had told him. He continued to review the words from Wickham's letter, unable to find rest from his painful speculations. He had the nagging feeling that he had not heard everything and hoped that the next day would bring answers. He planned to send more men out to explore the towns, going as far as twenty miles in each direction. It had been raining, so the roads would slow things down a bit, but he could hopefully get news by the following day. Then he remembered his cousin's recommendation to check the Darcy jewels. He never could have conceived that Elizabeth might steal from him, even if she preferred Wickham, but he had to look for himself. He planned first to go into her room to see if there were any clues as to her possible location – a letter, a map, anything that might give direction.

Darcy walked into Elizabeth's dark chamber, lighting some candles along the way to illuminate the area. He had rarely been in this room over the past ten years. He had a strange, dual feeling of comfort and loss. This had been his mother's chamber, so as a child, he would come to her side when afraid or sad, seeking her soothing words, but that was years ago. Now, he felt a sense of regret for the past six months – all of his mistakes, the pain he had caused, giving Elizabeth reason to hate him. If she were with the blackguard, Darcy was certain that he himself drove her there. In the presence of her own bedchamber, he remembered her to be a kind-hearted, lovely woman, who must have been pushed towards Wickham by Darcy's own malignant pride. Darcy had tried to repair the damage, to atone for his sins, but it must have been too late – too late to prevent her pregnancy anyway. *It must be true that she carries Wickham's child, or why else would she have left? She has everything a woman could want here at Pemberley – fine clothes, elegant surroundings, the very best food, a wide-open park – but she did not have love, or so she thought. That is what she wanted most, for she said so. Elizabeth did not care for my wealth. That is why she left to follow a pauper like Wickham. He made her feel loved. I should have told her that I love her! But was it already, even then, too late?*

Darcy sat on the floor leaning against the side of the bed and wiped tears away with his shaking hands. He then prayed out loud, something that even now, he had rarely done, but that seemed right. Darcy asked for resolution, for elucidation, for hope. He prayed for Elizabeth, that she would finally find happiness, and for his family who would suffer with him. Then he made an appeal for wisdom and clarity, so that he would know the next steps to take.

This was an odd prayer for Fitzwilliam Darcy. He had always felt confident and secure in his own merit, but he had finally come to see his failings and needs. Since his time in London alone during the winter, Darcy's faults plagued him more each day; however, at the same time, he found solace in finally being made aware of these weaknesses. He acknowledged that he was not perfect and was not expected to be so. Elizabeth had certainly known his faults but seemed to care about him anyway. Darcy had begun to trust in a plan bigger than himself – that perhaps Providence had caused his marriage to come into being, but now his doubts seemed to torment him.

How long he sat there, he could not know, but he felt a peace come over him that he could not have explained. He stood and walked over to Elizabeth's writing desk and opened it, then sat down on the dainty chair – that was made more for a petite woman than a statuesque man as himself – and began to sift through her papers. He felt a stab of guilt at first, for he was a firm believer that private correspondence should be kept confidential. He bristled at the idea of anyone reading his own mail, even letters of business, but he could not overcome the feeling that there was more to know. He had already read the one letter from Wickham; could there be more?

He pulled out all of the papers and divided them into letters and what appeared to be journal entries. *She keeps a memoir?* He decided to avoid reading her journal unless absolutely necessary. The first letter he opened was the one from her aunt, received on that day that she learnt of Jane's engagement to Bingley. He read in her aunt's own hand that Elizabeth even then had suspected she was with child, but there was no hint as to why she kept the information hidden. Her aunt seemed to believe that Darcy was the father, but then why would she suspect otherwise unless Elizabeth had told her so? *And why did she not want me to read it? I guess she wanted to keep her pregnancy hidden, but then why is that?* He next opened Jane's letter and shared in the joy of her happiness. He smiled as he remembered Elizabeth's tears of joy when she read it. That was no affectation he beheld that day. *I feel certain she had forgiven me of my officious meddling into Bingley's affairs.*

He then moved on to more recent correspondence. There was a letter from her mother, written just over two weeks ago. He read aloud, "*All great men like Mr. Darcy have a mistress, Lizzy, so you need not suffer through his attentions since you are with child.*"

"What could she mean by that? 'All great men have a mistress!' That fool of a woman is filling Elizabeth's head with aspersions on my character! Surely Elizabeth does not believe that drivel!" He continued on with the letters. Mary had written Elizabeth, telling her about his trip to Rosings. Checking the date, he surmised this must have been the letter that Elizabeth had received the night before he left. *But Elizabeth said nothing about my trip. Could she have wanted to come? Or at least have been asked?* Then he saw his own hand – the express that he had sent just days ago. *She crushed the missive into a ball, it would seem, and then spread it back out. What could that signify?*

He saw another from Mary and two from Miss Lucas, which he did not read. He knew Wickham's writing well, but saw no other letters to match. He was beginning to grow sleepy as he sat in the darkened room. Rather than walk to his own, he crawled into Elizabeth's bed, gathering one of her pillows into his arms. Her floral scent permeated his nostrils as he breathed in deeply. *Oh, Elizabeth, where are you? Be safe, my love!*

Chapter Twenty-One

"Only a man who has felt ultimate despair is capable
of feeling ultimate bliss."
Alexandre Dumas
The Count of Monte Cristo

Darcy awoke with a start when sunlight beamed down onto his closed eyelids. The overcast skies hopefully were gone along with the despair of the previous day. He sat up, disoriented as to his location, and remembered that he was in Elizabeth's bedchamber. Glancing at her escritoire, he saw that he had failed to put her letters and papers back where they belonged. He thought to look through them again, but remembered that his cousin was to leave at first light and so hastened to his own room and called on Nelson to dress him, as he anticipated a long day ahead.

When descending the stairs, he overheard his cousin and Lady Susan as they were preparing to leave. "Really, Husband, I have been trying to leave for days, and now you want to make me leave before we have even had a chance to eat. You are too cruel." Then she spoke more softly, "Do you suppose Darcy will find his wife? I think she is gone for good, and I say good riddance. I couldn't stand the sight of her. If you had not sent that footman home the other day, I would swear that she ran off with him, the way she shamelessly flirted with him. I told you that I saw him walk her to her room each night and station himself outside her door. I think he probably went in once the house fell asleep."

Darcy had heard enough of Lady Susan's speculative slander. "Langston, Lady Susan, I see you are ready to leave. Has the kitchen packed you a basket for your journey?"

"Darcy, we were just saying that we wish you luck with your wife. I do hope she is found," said the woman, oblivious to his poorly disguised vexation before taking a quick glance in the mirror on her way out the door.

"Forgive Susan; she has been worried the past two days, you see. Give us word on your success," Langston finished as he went out the door.

Good riddance was the thought shared by all.

Darcy went to the breakfast room to get some coffee before heading to the safe to ensure the Darcy jewels were still enclosed. When he entered the room, the footman who had been most solicitous of Elizabeth entered. When Darcy acknowledged him, he said, "Sir, I would speak with you of a matter of some importance."

"Not now. I have some business I must complete before beginning today's search. I would have you accompany me again today. Summon a group of men to meet us at the stables in an hour's time." Clark made no motion to leave. "Well, get to it. We have a lot to do and little time."

"Please forgive me, sir, but this cannot wait."

"Follow me." Darcy, irritated, led him out of the room and to his study where he shut the door and walked to his desk to sit behind it while directing his footman to the seat before it. Darcy knew that Lady Susan had been speaking of the man who sat before him. Elizabeth and Clark had spent much time together, especially on her walks, and if there were any truth to Lady Susan's claims, Darcy meant to get it out of the man now. So concealing any expectations he might have, Darcy said, "I am listening."

The man looked nervous sitting in front of the imposing desk, but he would not be deterred, "I am concerned about Mrs. Darcy's welfare, sir. I have reason to suspect that she is not with Mr. Wickham."

"Go on."

"Two days ago, when I was walking with Mrs. Darcy, Lord Langston approached us and asked me to leave. Mrs. Darcy had a look in her eyes that I can't get out of my head; she was afraid. She tried to get me to stay, not to leave her alone, but the viscount persuaded me to go. To be honest, he threatened me."

"He threatened you? How?" said Darcy, his calm failing him.

"He said that, well, he said that if I did not leave, he would tell you that he had found us in an inappropriate embrace," said Clark blushing, fearful of the outcome but determined to try to help his mistress.

"And were you? In an inappropriate embrace?"

"No!" he cried. "I have never done anything improper towards Mrs. Darcy. I swear that I have not! I respect her too much to even think of such a thing. She is the finest lady I know, and regardless of any sentiments I might have, I would never hurt her in that way."

Darcy could see the impassioned vehemence in the man's eyes, and he continued to bait him. "Have you or have you not been sitting outside my wife's bedchamber door each night while she slept within?"

"I have."

"Did you ever enter her room?"

"No, I swear it!"

"So my cousin accuses you of an inappropriate embrace, you have been so devoted that you cannot leave her side as she sleeps, and you tell me that you cannot get her look out of your mind, *regardless of any sentiments you might have*. And I am to believe that nothing untoward has happened between the two of you?"

"Please, let me explain from the beginning, sir. It will all be clear."

"I am listening but please be quick. I need to find *my* wife."

"Last week, Friday, I believe, Mrs. Darcy and I were walking as usual. She told me that she was to have houseguests and then asked me to stay by her side while in the public areas. Later in the same conversation, she asked me to teach her ways to defend herself." At Darcy's creased brows, he continued, "I told her that you would be the best person to teach her, but she insisted most firmly. She was so adamant that I gave in and taught her some general protective measures, but then I told her how to protect herself specifically from a man.

"I know you are unhappy with this; I did not want to be the one to teach her something better left to her husband, but she seemed almost desperate to know. When Lord Langston arrived at Pemberley, I began to watch them both closely.

446

I was always around and found that I could easily do my duties while keeping an eye on her." Clark paused here, not knowing how to speak his fears. "Well, whenever she looked at him, she looked rattled. She was very good at hiding it; I doubt others could tell, but you see, she and I had spent so much time together that I felt like I could perhaps read her subtle changes. I stayed outside her chamber door because she asked me to. Mrs. Carpenter slept with her each night and acted as companion during the viscount's visit. She was never alone. Mrs. Carpenter can confirm this for you."

"Are you saying that Elizabeth was afraid of my cousin?"

After a moment of hesitation, Clark said, "I am. At first I did not know why. I thought maybe it was because he was a peer; however I didn't think that she was the type to be intimidated by rank, but then I saw how he looked at her, as men do when they desire to have physical relations. Then when he threatened me... Well, I begin to think that he meant to harm her." He finished this in a softened, subdued tone, well aware that he could be writing his own dismissal papers.

"Why did you not tell me this last night?"

"Lord Langston was still here. He threatened me before, and I was hesitant about what he might do if he found out. He has rank and is a member of your family, and I am a footman. Who could I expect that you would believe? But I see that I was being a coward. I will never forgive myself for leaving her with him. She appeared at ease at my leave, except for the look of panic in her eyes that she tried, in vain, to hide from me."

"Tell me, has she ever said anything to you about Mr. Wickham?"

Clark looked uncomfortable at the unexpected question. He hated to share a conversation held in confidence, but he knew it was important to be completely up front. "Yes, she did twice."

"Recently?"

"Once in town and then again here at Pemberley. In town she asked if I knew the man and when I said that I did, she asked if I knew why the animosity subsisted between the two of you. I told her what I knew, which was very little. I said that he was your friend growing up – your fathers' being close – but then he moved away after school. The second occasion was when you were in town last month. She asked what kind of man Mr. Wickham was, and I told her that he had a reputation with the staff of being a libertine. This troubled her; I could tell. She asked a few more questions about how he made a living and whether he was liked. I again told her what I knew. He did not have a profession of which I was aware and that he was liked well enough by some, but that he was trusted by none."

"And how did she respond?"

"She said little, just thanked me for my honesty. That's just it, sir. I cannot believe she would have left with him. She is not the type of woman to trust a man like that. I remember that she had seemed unsettled at my description of him but then quickly recovered, expressing her appreciation." He looked at his master in the eyes and continued, "Mr. Darcy, I am confident that she did not leave with Mr. Wickham, not willingly."

"So, if you were to look for her, where would you go?"

Clark breathed in a deep sigh of relief. Mr. Darcy trusted him enough to help anyway. "North."

"And my cousin said south?"

"Yes, sir."

"Then we go north. I have much to do before we leave. Have everyone ready in an hour. I will see you at the stables."

Darcy did not look at the jewels; instead, he ran up to Elizabeth's room to look again at her papers in the escritoire. He opened the windows fully to let the light in. Then he pulled out the papers that appeared to be a journal. He was looking for some clue to validate Clark's report. He did not know whether to be relieved or even more worried. His cousin was about his size, maybe a little shorter, and could do damage to a woman if he so desired. Darcy saw now that Langston never did like Elizabeth. *Maybe he meant to hurt her in some way, and has been lying to put obstacles in the search. My own cousin! How could I not see it? Or maybe Clark is the one who lies? But what of Wickham's letter? I will find out one way or another from Elizabeth herself.* And so, he began to read from the page dated the day before her disappearance. It did not take long before the proof was before him.

Monday, April 15, 1811

L continues to leer at me as he always has. I know not if he just means to frighten me or if he plans another encounter. I could not bear the latter. C has been faithful in his role as protector. If I were not so alarmed, I would find his constancy diverting. He would make a good husband someday to a young lady, if he could somehow find a situation. His wife would always be happy and feel safe, for he would dote like a puppy, but protect like a lion.

I hope that D returns in two days as expected, for I know that he is the only one who can truly protect me. But I fear that D would never suspect his cousin to be the profligate that he is – nor believe me should I speak my fears – so I will not even be able to rely on D to safeguard me. I suppose I will have to count on my newly learnt skills of defence. Why are women left in the dark about such things? D would be appalled at my new accomplishment, so I will not tell him, unless he finds out the hard way! I jest. I would never do anything to hurt the man. I can tell that he has been hurt enough – he has been so lonely. No, I mean to do everything in my power to make him the most cheerful of creatures, even more so than B! D tries so hard to be miserable, but I am determined. He will have cause to show those handsome dimples at least once an hour while in my company!

Oh dear, I have rambled again. You have done your job, dear journal, for I am no longer afraid. I will meet my guests today with confidence! -EBD

"Another encounter? What can you mean, Elizabeth?" He pulled out another sheet, dated the previous Saturday.

Saturday, April 13, 1811

They came. I had prayed they would not, but Providence apparently thought it wiser that they come, although I admit to having my spiritual doubts. I could deal with Lady S's condescension; she is no different than Miss B, but with a title, sans beauty. Of course, I would never admit such a cruel thing aloud. She would not believe me anyhow for her best friend apparently tells her otherwise – her looking glass! Enough Lizzy! I must move on. She must have other attributes on which to find diversion. But there can be no mirth when it comes to L. I am thankful that I am never to be left alone with him, but I cannot help but feel vulnerable. Why did D charge me to obey him and give him rights as protector? L could so easily dismiss LC or C and then I would be alone with him. I still cannot forget the last time as the nightmares persist. Without even trying, he continues his assailment on my marriage! How can I be intimate with my husband when the very remembrance of L's liberties makes me panic? D must never know. What if he were to blame me? I could not bear it. He could never love me and would surely think it my fault. -EBD

Langston has violated my wife? This cannot be! I don't want to believe it, but it must be true. What has he done to her? She's been gone for days now. And what have I done by putting her in danger – my kind and beautiful wife? "I'll call him out, I swear it, but first I must find her!"

Darcy wanted to read more of his wife's journal, to find out about Wickham – if she carried his child, and what she thought of himself, but not wanting to intrude upon her privacy any more than he already had, and equally wanting to get started in the search, he put her papers and letters away, and prepared to head to the stables, newly determined to find her.

As planned, a group of men set out from the Pemberley stables on horseback to peruse the countryside looking for Elizabeth. Darcy decided to keep all of his men nearby in the search rather than ride out to the towns, for he no longer feared she was with Wickham. Until now, the search had focused on the south side of the estate at Langston's direction. Darcy's anger intensified more with every moment as he considered his cousin's wilful subterfuge of the search efforts. He likely even knew where she was all along, but guided the men away. However, Darcy tunnelled this anger into action, directing his staff in the pursuit of his wife. He divided the men into groups of two, and they spread out going in different directions. He sent two men, including his steward, to check all of the tenant houses or any other structure where she might have found shelter. Darcy knew his wife trusted Clark, so he sent him with another man whom Elizabeth might not be as familiar. Darcy went out alone, for he did not feel equal to being with another, as he felt the full weight of her disappearance and danger upon his own shoulders. Elizabeth had told him that she felt secure under his protection, yet he had failed her.

The team had gotten out by eight-thirty in the morning and searched throughout the day. If someone were to find her, he was to shoot into the air twice with his pistol to alert the rest. While the others took breaks, Darcy continued his search without stopping except to rest his mount as he sought clues. As Darcy had feared that morning, clouds moved in and threatened rain again. The temperatures continued as usual for the season, and Darcy did not want to consider what could happen if Elizabeth was still out there without shelter.

Darcy became more and more frustrated as the day wore on. Elizabeth had been out there for two days. The past winter had been exceptionally cold, even in town, and since his arrival, he had noticed that the air was chilly at night with only a modest increase during the day. Darcy knew Elizabeth to be an intelligent, resourceful and active woman; if any could manage in the present circumstances, he felt she would be the one. But then, he considered the baby. Darcy knew little about the stress that might be placed upon the womb in such conditions, this lack of understanding inclining his thoughts towards even greater fears.

While riding down a path that would have been familiar to Elizabeth, Darcy noticed something on the ground blowing in the wind, perhaps a ribbon about twenty yards into the trees. He approached and soon saw that it was indeed a ribbon, green satin, attached to Elizabeth's bonnet that she most often wore when walking on warmer days. He jumped down from his horse to retrieve it and look for any signs that might give direction. Perhaps she was nearby. Darcy scanned the area for clues while calling out her name but could not determine anything to enlighten him. But then he saw something shiny on the ground a few feet away from where the bonnet had lain. Walking over, he reached down and picked up a button. Turning it over in his hand, he tried to recall if he had seen it before on one of Elizabeth's garments. Then he noticed two more nearby. Putting them into the pocket of his overcoat, he made a comprehensive search of the area, trying to find clues that might alert him to where she might have gone, or been taken. His mind took him to one horrible scenario after another as he considered her danger. Darcy shook his head as he attempted to focus on the task at hand, but his mind would torment him as he imaged what might have happened to her, as he considered why her buttons might be strewn upon the woodland carpet. After an hour, or perhaps two, of canvassing the area, he finally came to the conclusion that he could find nothing else of benefit, so he moved on, resolved to come back if his continued search brought no success.

Although still two hours before dark, the grey sky became even more overcast, blocking the sun and its limited warmth. Darcy had Clark describe to everyone what Elizabeth had been wearing and was disheartened to learn that she would easily blend into the environment. Fortunately, the still mostly bare trees allowed him to scan large areas of land at a time; however, in so doing, he risked missing her in a hasty perusal.

He was about five miles out from Pembcrley house nearing the boarder of the estate, farther than Elizabeth had ever gone, where a deep ravine cut through the landscape in this rocky terrain. Darcy had always thought this area of Pemberley to be dramatically beautiful, although not suited to farmland or shepherding. The steep inclines made traversing the grounds treacherous. He thought it unlikely that she would have come this way, and this far out – and was not even certain what led him here – so was turning around when he caught with his eye, far down below him, a small mound of green against the brown of the winter grasses. He called out her name as he kept his eye on the colour, but there was no response.

Darcy dismounted; it would be too dangerous to attempt to ride his horse down the slope. He removed the blankets and saddlebag that he had brought with him in case they were needed. He was not at all certain that the colour he saw could be Elizabeth's clothing, but he wanted to be prepared if it were. The saddlebag contained his ration for the day that he had been unable to consume for his anxiety over his wife's disappearance. He made his descent without difficulty and coming closer to the mass, he began to see that the bundle was taking the shape of a person. With greater momentum, Darcy began to stumble down the hillside, but kept his footing enough to remain upright. Once at the bottom, he took off at a sprint, as he felt certain that it must be Elizabeth who lay before him, puddled on the side of the ditch that ran at the base. *Oh, my God! Please let her be alive*! He knew beyond a doubt that he loved her; his whole being cried out in supplication for her health and wellbeing. He reached her in an instant, although it seemed much longer to his afflicted patience.

Falling down to his knees before his wife, for indeed it was she, he turned her body to get a better look, almost too afraid to discover the truth of the situation. Elizabeth's clothing was soaked through, still wet from the rain two days previously, likely owing to her layers of clothing and lack of direct sunlight. A lone button held her jacket together, and Darcy cursed Langston for whatever occurred to bring that about. Elizabeth's skin was pale; however, she had sweat beading on her forehead, indicating a fever. *She's alive! Thank God.* He removed his gloves to touch her skin and confirmed that she was hot to touch, despite the cold. She was shivering; he saw that now. "Elizabeth, my love, it's Darcy. I'm here and will take care of you. Can you hear me?"

He heard a moan deep inside of her just before she opened her eyes. Seeing she had little strength to even accomplish that, he said, "Do not exert yourself; everything is going to be alright." He covered her with the blankets, and removing his greatcoat, he wrapped it around her and then looked about as he considered how he might get her to safety. The side of the ravine was steep to descend but would be near impossible to traverse up while carrying his precious burden. This area of the park, although well admired, was largely unknown to Darcy.

The rumble of thunder in the distance alerted him to the coming storm and the need to quickly make a move. His horse along with his pistol remained at the top of the ravine, so Darcy was unable to alert the others of his need for assistance. He decided that going up the way he came down was not to happen.

Of course, he could go back to his horse on his own to call for aid, but he could not bear to leave Elizabeth's side. He looked up and down the water line and saw that he might be able to carry her up the hill further along the way. Darcy must do something, and this plan seemed as good as any, so crouching down, he put his arms underneath her shoulders and knees. "Elizabeth, I am going to pick you up. We need to get you out of here before the rain begins."

Barely opening her eyes, Elizabeth reached her hands up and grasped the lapels of his waistcoat. She held on tightly for but a moment and then seemed to lose her stamina as she fell limp in his arms.

Although a strong man, owing to many hours at Antonio's and on horseback, the incline and distance began to work on Darcy's endurance. And as Elizabeth, though a slender, petite woman, carried the additional weight of her waterlogged clothing, Darcy began to feel the fatigue that would soon leave him incapable of continuing on at his set pace. The sky was growing darker as the sun began to wane, and the clouds continued to thicken. Darcy realised that they needed to find shelter rather than attempt the journey home. He began searching his memory for buildings that might be nearby. Although there would be no tenant homes around, there may be lodgings used for hunting now and again. On he walked, his precious bundle close to his chest. Along the way, Darcy began speaking to Elizabeth about whatever came to mind, not knowing if she even heard him. "I saw Bingley while in town. He asked that I stand up with him and hoped you would do the same for your sister. I told him that I was certain you could not refuse, as close as you are. Truly, I have never seen the man happier. They should be very content together. She is just what he needed to make his life complete. My sister joined me this trip. I cannot wait for you and she to become better acquainted. I think you will be good for her, actually. Your confidence and high spirits will be a fine example for a vulnerable young lady just coming out into society." On he spoke in like manner, expressing his hopes and expectations for the future, but she continued in silence.

A particularly bright flash of light erupted followed by a loud thunderclap, and Darcy knew their danger. He hoped his mount had given up on him and returned to the safety of the stables, alerting his staff that he was still out in the elements. Darcy began to recognise his surroundings and recalled a small but adequate cottage somewhat nearby. As far as he was aware, the building had not been in use for some time, but Darcy recalled exploring it in his youth and hoped it was still functional for shelter. He would have to traverse another quarter mile or so to reach it. His arms and legs were burning, having walked up and down the hilly countryside for close to an hour as he searched for passable routes home. Then the rain began, a steady downpour that would soon have him drenched without his greatcoat, but he had no concern for himself, only his precious cargo. His greatcoat would keep her from accumulating any more water, but underneath, she remained soaked through.

Then he saw it up ahead, the shelter for which he had been searching. He attempted to pick up his pace, but for naught. He had reached the limits of his endurance and just hoped it had been enough to get her to safety in time. He approached the door and attempted the handle with his foot, but without success.

452

"We have shelter, my love. I am going to set you down for just a moment while I open the door." The old latch relinquished its hold easily enough, and Darcy pushed the door open. The darkness of the approaching night made it difficult to discern the contents of the small building, but it was dry and contained a hearth to build a fire. So he returned to his wife and carried her over the threshold, gently setting her down on the wooden floor.

His first task was to build a fire, so he got to work. There was firewood by the hearth and coal in a basin nearby, so perhaps the cottage received some use of which he was unaware. Although still warm from his exertion, his hands were shaking, likely owing to fatigue. Darcy found the flint and began the process of lighting the fire. It had been years for the young man, but he soon had a small blaze going. He continued to add fuel to dispel the chill in the air.

Then he returned to his wife who had not moved. Darcy carried her closer to the fire and then lifted the greatcoat and blankets that had protected her in the rain. She was still shivering underneath. *She must get out of those wet clothes.* Reaching down, he unbuttoned the sole button holding her spencer in place. Removing that, Darcy was more able to see that her bodice had been ripped. Anger and remorse fought equally to take control, but he had to stave off those emotions and concentrate on the task at hand. He pulled off her jacket and turned her to the side in order to reach the back where he unbuttoned her dress and untied her stays. He had many times dreamt of a scenario such as this, savouring his wife's femininity, but the reality of this day caused him to forget any such aspirations. He removed her dress, petticoat and stays, revealing the sight he had come to know in his mind as well as any. But this time, he noticed the small swell in her abdomen, their baby. It struck him that her fight was not just for herself, but for their child as well. Darcy had to believe in Elizabeth's faithfulness to their vows – that she had not succumbed to Wickham's charms.

At the same time, even in the limited light, he was able to notice her wrists that held the remnants of bruising brought on by Langston's violent grip, in addition to the many other blemishes from her fall. This reminder of his own cousin's treachery increased his fury at Langston's gall and sympathy for his wife's undeserved suffering. The irony of all that he had once previously held dear, versus his current understanding, struck him like a lightning bolt from the storm outside. He had always valued those of consequence more highly than the lower classes, even the gentry. Add to that, his familial connections, his name and heritage drove his obligations and sense of duty. How wrong he had been to place significance on the very virtues that now threatened his wife's life and honour. In this one moment he discerned how hypocritical his existence had been. He thought that he had put his faith in all that was right and excellent, but now saw the deception. Could money and name actually make one superior over another? Could there be any inherent worth presented to a human being who had the advantage of birth into one family versus another? Was his cousin more valued in the eyes of God than his precious Elizabeth, owing to his title and wealth alone? It could not be so. He had been deluded his whole life and now saw his error.

Although he knew Elizabeth would in no way want him to remove her chemise, he truly had no other choice. The wet garment had to come off in order for her to have any hope of finding warmth. But mindful of her modesty, he reached over to the woollen blankets in which he had previously wrapped her, and as he lifted the shift, he covered her with the blanket, easily overcoming his own longing to see her bare. It would not be today; he now understood that loving her made him less likely to take advantage of her vulnerabilities, not more so. His only desire was to care for her. Yet again, he comprehended his previous inadequacies as a husband and protector.

He remembered that her stockings would also likely be wet, so he lifted the blanket to remove her shoes first. Darcy noticed that her ankle was blue and swollen, which would explain in part why she had lain where she was. She had apparently fallen down the ravine and could not then get to safety. She must have lain in that same location for two days without aid. *Blast!* He knew not what to do about the ankle but put something below it for a cushion and support, so he rolled up his greatcoat and placed it underneath.

Darcy was finally able to examine her face more closely. She had some bruising on her brow and dried blood in her hair. If she had fallen down the ravine, she may even have some broken bones. So he checked her arms and legs for any obvious fractures, and excepting her ankle, she seemed intact, but still he must remember to be gentle when moving her in case she had any internal injuries that were not apparent.

Darcy was able to look around the room to take stock in its contents. He was relieved to see more wood, since any other options outside would be waterlogged. He found a pot that he decided to use to collect rainwater for drinking. She needed fluids, as he well remembered from his own illnesses. The pot was dusty, as was everything else, so he had to first clean it. There were no towels for such a job, so he removed his cravat. Once the pot was relatively clean and collecting rainwater, he returned inside, beginning to feel his own effects of being cold and damp, but before considering his own predicament, he checked on Elizabeth. She had begun to moan, shifting around, almost uncovering herself. "Calm down, Elizabeth. I'm back."

"Say no more! Release me!"

This took Darcy by surprise. *Does she think I am Langston?* "Elizabeth, this is Darcy. I won't hurt you"

"Lies!" Although with great intensity, her actual volume was difficult to hear.

Darcy leaned close to her and began whispering soothing words of comfort as he smoothed back her hair, wet from her perspiration and rain. The effect was evident as her breaths calmed somewhat. *So it is true; she does talk in a restless sleep.*

"Papa! I want my papa!"

His heart broke for her. He knew he had been a wretched husband. She did not want him, but her father, as protector. Darcy had sent her own tormentor into her midst despite her wishes for him to stay away. *I made her dance with him at the ball and chastised her for not wanting to. My poor dear wife; she deserves better than me.*

Darcy continued on with his ministrations as she fell back into a slumber, but he soon became aware of his need to get out of his own wet clothes. Earlier he had hung Elizabeth's clothes on nails and over chairs near the fire to begin the long drying process. Darcy removed his coat and waistcoat and pulled his shirt out from his trousers. He then stood by the fire for the warmth to let his remaining clothes dry while on him. The room was warming up nicely since he had plenty of fuel for the fire and worked to keep up the blaze. After a short while, however, fatigue from having too little sleep and too much exertion, without eating, hit him. He sat on the floor next to his wife and let his eyes close.

DARCY AWOKE TO A DARKENED ROOM. The fire had dissipated, and the room was growing cold again. At first he was disoriented as to his location, but then realised that he was lying next to his wife who was sleeping soundly. He got up to stoke the fire and add wood.

When he began to warm up again, he sat back down and considered their predicament. How ironic it was that they would find themselves back in a cabin during a rainstorm; only this time, it was he who was the caregiver.

Darcy had vague recollections of the time spent in that cabin months ago, but what he most remembered now was the soothing and gentle touch of the then Miss Elizabeth Bennet. She despised him then, yet she showed kindness. She too felt it wise to remove some of his clothing to get him warm, and he accused her of nefarious purposes. She too took pains to try to get warm herself, and yet he saw her efforts in light of seduction. *What a fool I am. She has always been so gracious to me considering my failings, yet I found only stratagem to ensnare me.* He laughed outright, not a laugh of mirth but irony. Fate was cruel to him, mocking. But no, it could not be fate, but Providence, and He was not laughing but teaching, rebuking. *My lessons have been difficult, as well they should, but I will forever be grateful.* Then he began a prayer of sorts, asking for the restoration of Elizabeth's health and for the health of their child. He felt the comfort that comes to those whose hope rests in One stronger than themselves.

ELIZABETH BEGAN TO STIR. She was burning hot, no longer looking pale, but crimson with fever. Darcy stood and rushed out the door to get the water bucket and then poured some into a bowl. He then reached for her petticoat and tore off a strip, dipping it into the water. "Well, my dear, it looks as though your petticoat will not survive this outing either." Darcy then began a nightlong vigil of wiping her brow and soothing her distress, periodically getting her to drink some of the collected rainwater.

At length, Elizabeth awoke again and began looking around. She could not recall where she was or how she had gotten there, but she saw her husband looking across the room, as if in a trance, with worry in his eyes. The fire illuminated his handsome features and she wondered what had been happening. She recalled having woken up near a ditch at the bottom of a ravine after a fall;

she had tripped. A deluge of rain fell around her, but she could not move owing to some kind of injury to her ankle and spells of dizziness each time she sat up. Elizabeth had continued to worry about Langston, but her biggest fear at the time – aside from her baby's safety – had been that she might not be found and had no way to alert anyone as to her location, for she was a long way from the house and any discernible pathway. When Darcy finally arrived at home, the viscount would likely tell him some false story about her being gone, perhaps some fabricated tale of abandonment. After hours of lying there in the dark, Elizabeth had become so very cold and felt slumber take control of her sensibilities. And that was the end of her remembrance.

Apparently her husband did eventually find her. "What day is it?" she faintly asked aloud. He started and turned towards her.

"Elizabeth, you are awake. Thank God. Here let me get you some more water." He reached over to the small bowl and brought it to her lips, while gently lifting her neck with his hand. She drank a small sip, and with further encouragement, took more. Darcy tenderly laid her head back down onto his rolled up jacket that he had turned into a makeshift pillow. "How are you feeling? We have some bread and cheese. Are you warm enough?"

Elizabeth became aware of her state of undress. Her eyes opened wide as she looked down to her body where the blanket lay. Feeling underneath the covers, she realised she was completely naked. In tears of shame and anger, she said, "How dare you undress me!"

A startled Darcy looked kindly at her saying, "Elizabeth, just relax."

Just relax. Hearing the same words Langston had used, Elizabeth became defensive, saying, "What did you do to me?"

In confusion, he said "Nothing! You were wet and cold and needed to get out of your clothes. I was only trying to get you warm. I swear that I did not so much as look at you. Although as your husband, I had every right." Then taking a deep calming breath, he continued, "Please Elizabeth, settle down. You can trust me."

She covered her ears in lament. "Please stop!"

Darcy was thankful that Elizabeth was no longer in a senseless fever. Seeing her alert and speaking to him was an answer to his prayer spoken throughout his vigil, but he could not understand what had gotten into her to make her so piqued. He did remove her clothes, but then he just told her that he had been mindful of her modesty. She was his wife; he was just taking care of her. Surely by now she knew of his high regard. Had they not come to care for one another?

Then presently, Darcy came to grasp her plight. His cousin had violated her; with her ripped clothing, the evidence was incontrovertible. Elizabeth must keenly feel her distress. Darcy recalled what she had written about Langston's advances and her fears for his response – that he, as her husband, might not believe her or worse, might blame her. So as encouragement to share what distressed her, Darcy said with a calm he did not feel, "When you are ready, I want you to tell me."

"Tell you what?"

"What truly disturbs you," Darcy said, looking kindly at her. "Your chemise is dry. I would have dressed you before now, but I did not want to disturb your rest." He reached around her for the bowl, saying, "Here, take some more water, and I'll get it." He helped her to sit up to take another sip, but as soon as she was done, she made a face as if in pain. "Does something hurt?" Darcy had been worried that she had some kind of internal injuries of which he was unaware and became rather alarmed.

In obvious embarrassment Elizabeth said that she needed the chamber pot. She was in unconcealed physical discomfort. Darcy smiled and reached up his hand to her face, saying, "I will look for something." Elizabeth watched as he searched the small building for something suitable for the task, and when he found an appropriate container, he came over to her side and asked what she needed him to do.

"I suppose that I am getting my just deserts, for I was not a very compassionate nurse that night in the cabin, was I?"

"You were much more patient than I deserved. Now, please do not be uneasy. Shall I leave for the other room, or would you rather I carry you in there for your privacy? You will have to tell me what you are able to do."

"I would like privacy in here; you go to the other room, but close the door. And don't forget to give me my chemise."

Darcy was showing a side of his nature that she had not had the opportunity of seeing before. He was sympathetic and kind, showing evidence of having the heart of a servant – not an overtly proud master. After he re-entered the room, Elizabeth told him that she was unable to handle putting on her chemise alone, so with gentleness and with understanding of her modesty Darcy assisted. After that was put behind her, she ate some more of the bread and cheese and then fell back asleep, as her fever persisted, going from shivering to a heated restlessness.

"MY BABY! OH GOD, THE BABY!" Elizabeth said in a panic as she reached down to her abdomen to touch the swell. She had awoken abruptly from a disturbed sleep.

"Shhh, calm down. You must save your strength."

"But, the baby!" At his concerned but unsurprised look, she said, "You know about our baby?"

Our baby. He smiled, "I do know. Why did you not tell me?"

After a time she summoned her strength to speak, "I was going to after I was certain – after I felt the quickening – but then you left. I know I should have. How did you find out?"

"I will tell you another time; right now, I want you to eat the remainder of the food and then get some more rest."

Elizabeth was curious as to what he was not telling her but had no strength to pursue it, so she finished what Darcy had given her to eat and then closed her eyes, falling back asleep. This slumber was not a restful one, as her mind would torment her with visions of Langston in communion with her husband. They were at Madame Karina's holding paid whores, laughing at their wives' ignorance. Her fever had returned with a vengeance, but she only knew sorrow and emotional pain. In essentials, her husband was no different than Langston. She truly thought he had changed, or that he was not the man she had once thought, but no, he had deceived her, taking his pleasure elsewhere like every other entitled reprobate.

ELIZABETH OPENED HER EYES to more darkness, apparently another day – or was it more? – had come and gone. The fire continued to burn steadily. Elizabeth saw that her husband was asleep next to her, enveloping her in his arms. The feelings of comfort and regret fought for dominance, as she lay there. She loved him; this she now knew, or the pain would not be so great, but then how could she love a man who could behave so dishonourably in their marriage, deceiving her as he had? How many other women did he hold like this? Or did he just take and then leave as he had always done with her? She had not the strength to push him away or to even try to stay awake, but her mind held no such lethargy, as it would continue to plague her with painful musings as she slept again.

Darcy had worried about his wife during the first night and then throughout the following day. He kept expecting that they might be found, that someone would see the smoke from the chimney top, but no help arrived. Elizabeth needed nourishment and attention from a doctor. He could not know if their baby lived or if indeed Elizabeth would survive. All Darcy could do was try to keep her comfortable, so when the fire, though robust, was inadequate to keep her warm, he used his own body to give heat. Lying there with her had brought him both joy and pain. He loved Elizabeth and relished being next to her, nurturing her, but then he knew that she was not safe. Elizabeth's fever could quickly cause her health to tailspin into her own demise.

IT HAD BEEN NEARLY FOUR DAYS since her last full meal; and subsequent to being found, she had consumed all of Darcy's rations, but that was not enough to meet her needs. This, coupled with the fever, left her exceedingly fatigued. Darcy noticed Elizabeth awake again in obvious, though subdued distress. "Why the tears?"

She looked over at him as he watched her closely. "I have not felt the baby."

"But you had?"

"Yes, but not in days now," said Elizabeth, her grief palpable.

Darcy lay next to her again and pulled her into a firm embrace. She wanted to push him away and punish him for his infidelity, but she needed to feel his strong and comforting arms. He had saved her life; she was quite certain she would have perished if in the elements another night. And he had been so kind to her, but she could not forget his inconstancy. Nonetheless, at this moment her need for him won out over her anger.

"Elizabeth, our baby is in God's hands now. But whatever happens, I am here for you." Elizabeth continued to shed tears until she fell back asleep, exhaustion consuming her. They both continued to sleep arm in arm, giving and receiving comfort. Darcy had had less than a fortnight to consider Elizabeth's being with child and even then, the days were filled with doubts as to the true parentage, but regardless of his previous misgivings, his sense of loss was severe. He imagined that Elizabeth's pain would be so much more difficult to bear; therefore, he meant to give her as much comfort and solicitude as he was able.

Time slowly progressed; Darcy could not imagine why they had not been discovered during the course of the previous day. His sister must be worried to distraction, consequently he reluctantly decided to prepare for the journey to the house; he did not like the idea of leaving his vulnerable wife there alone, but she seemed to be out of any immediate physical danger, so putting on his vest – but leaving his coat in place as it was still being used as Elizabeth's pillow – he prepared to leave. Elizabeth had remained in no more than her chemise underneath the woollen blankets throughout the past day, but when she saw Darcy begin to dress, she too wanted to put on her clothes, so her husband retrieved her now dry corset and gown. "Your petticoat did not quite survive fully intact; I had to use some of the fabric, but it will be under your gown and may provide some level of protection."

She sat up and when he handed her the gown, they both stopped short as each recalled simultaneously that her dress had been ripped open in the front. Elizabeth looked away ashamed and embarrassed at what her husband must be thinking.

"Here, Elizabeth, let me assist you."

Darcy had moved forward ready to help, but Elizabeth pulled back. Every kindness had suddenly become like a cruelty to her sensibilities as she recalled his treachery, thus needing an outlet, she replaced her feelings of shame with those of indignation. "Please, do not touch me, I beg you."

"If that is what you wish, but I only mean to help you." Then he took a deep breath before continuing, "Elizabeth, you can tell me about Langston." He awaited her response, giving her time to compose herself and to consider her words. As she was obviously alarmed and unwilling – or unable – to share any part of her distressing ordeal, Darcy pressed on, "I know that he has hurt you somehow, and I am willing to listen, but you seem angry at *me*. You cannot compare us, do you?"

"I do. You are no different," Elizabeth said before turning away, her tears saying as much as her words. Her hands trembled as she reached up to wipe her eyes.

"I don't know what he did to you, but Elizabeth, does my recent abstention not prove to you that I have changed, that I have only your interests at heart? I hope that I have somehow redeemed myself in your eyes, if even just a little. I thought that you had forgiven me."

Elizabeth became provoked as she considered his activities during his *abstention*. "You are both made from the same mould. I speak not just based on my own experiences, but also based on others' recitals of you."

"I would have you tell me, for I cannot at all account for what you say. I have tried my best to become a husband who shows you esteem and forbearance, but I suppose that may not be good enough for you," said Darcy, becoming exasperated at the direction of the conversation.

"Your form of esteem puzzles me exceedingly, and as for forbearance, it comes at a high price."

"How can you say that? I spent the entire day looking for you, and since, I have dedicated my complete attention to your care." As Darcy tried to calm down, he continued more gently, "Elizabeth, I have a deep regard for you not just as my wife, but as a dear friend."

She looked at him afflicted. She wanted to believe in his regard, but the evidence to the contrary was too great. In the past he treated her like a possession, and since then had given himself over to other women. He was manipulating her into believing he cared when he did not. "You have no honour. You may perhaps be trying to convince yourself, but you will not convince me."

She could not have caused more physical pain if she had smacked him across the face. "Madam, I demand that you speak plainly with me. I would have you tell me whatever it is that troubles you, so that I might defend myself. I cannot believe you are saying this based on what happened months ago. I had assumed that we had moved past that, but perhaps I was mistaken."

"I speak of you and your despicable cousin, and of all of your allegedly illustrious peers, for your standards of righteousness have no merit with me." She was obviously agitated, but he would not respond, rather he sat there staring at her, indignant at her unmerited attack. "Tell me, how many women have you lain with since our marriage began?"

That question brought Darcy unmitigated shock. "Pardon me. What are you talking about? Elizabeth, you offend me and my honour." He looked away, clearly shaken, and then turning back to her said, "I demand an apology for that question, Elizabeth. You have insulted me completely and utterly."

"But you do not deny it."

"I have been with no other. I would add *since our marriage vows*, but I could speak of much longer than that."

"You lie."

"I demand you tell me what you think you know."

"Is *Aphrodite* a friend of yours? Or perhaps you make it a habit of visiting whorehouses in order to obtain intellectual stimulation?" If he had been shocked before, it was nothing compared to now, and his expression could not hide his distress. "You cannot deny your *knowledge* of her."

"How...? Elizabeth, please let me explain...."

"There is nothing you can say that can absolve you of your iniquity, so please save your breath to cool your porridge." Tears of ire and of heartache began their descent anew, as she looked away to hide her vulnerability.

"I am sorry if I have hurt you with my actions, but please listen while I explain, I beg you." He reached over to touch her arm, and she pulled away with a jerk that belied her weakened state. "When I left here in January, I was exceedingly despondent and not at all hopeful. While in town, I took time considering what needed to be done. I admit that I had reached a low point in my expectations of our marriage. One night, while at my club, I was speaking with some acquaintances, including Langston." He stopped here and looked at her, knowing that his cousin's name would cause her grief. She made no movement, still facing away from him. "Well, the group alighted upon the topic of Madame Karina's, a bordello that caters to the elite. The group decided to go, and I went with them." Elizabeth then became noticeably agitated; her hands trembled as she continued to wipe her eyes. He wanted to reach out to her, for his own sake if not hers. He would not have said this much, but he needed to be completely honest with her. She knew of his visit to the establishment, but she did not know all.

"I spent the whole of the short journey there telling myself why going was a good idea. I had convinced myself that the scheme was perfectly acceptable, even respectable. Aphrodite was the woman to whom I was assigned."

"Stop! I beg you to stop!" she cried covering her ears.

"Elizabeth, while in the holding room, I began to have second thoughts and had resolved to leave the place altogether, but then the proprietor came to get me and take me to the room. I told her that I needed to leave, but she led me on, and I obediently followed." Darcy was speaking quickly now, trying to get out his story before causing greater distress. "When the door opened to the room, a woman, no a girl, was there who greatly resembled you. I felt like I had been in a trance, but when I laid eyes on her, I knew I had to leave, but I must confess that I did not want to." She looked at him horrified, wet faced. "I asked God to deliver me, for on my father's grave, I wanted to stay and would have, I am certain, if not by some kind of divine intervention.

"Elizabeth, I am thankful beyond my own understanding that I did not linger, but it was not by my strength, for I had never felt weaker. Please believe me when I say that I had never in my life visited a brothel before. I have always thought them to be beneath me, but I was disenchanted with our marriage and had begun to think, like many others of my peers, that given our circumstances it was the only possible way to contentment. Now I know that it would have been the path to destruction and to the ruination of our marriage."

"Do you expect me to find comfort in your desire to hire a whore only after being married to me? Am I so disgusting to you that you would be driven to a trespass you had never considered before – if what you say is indeed the truth?"

Darcy could not stop the tears that came to his own eyes as he saw the hurt in hers. "I am not the same man, Elizabeth. Something happened to me while in town, even that night. I know this sounds odd, but it was as though Providence was showing me that I had nothing to offer anyone, that even my best intentions were based on a vicious pride. I learnt that in truth I was no better than any other profligate. It was a lesson that I needed, I must have." He tried to reach over to her, but she pulled away yet again. "I am so very sorry for hurting you. When I got home, I thanked God again and again for delivering me from my weaknesses, from my perversity. I would never hurt you purposely, and I would not hurt you now. I had hoped you would not learn of my transgression, since nothing came of it. But Elizabeth, you need to know that it was never about you or any deficiencies on your part. I was the one lacking. You are a beautiful and very desirable woman; you must know that I feel that way. I even then came to the conclusion that I could not – I would not – come to your room without your invitation and willingness, and I had begun to lose heart, fearing that you would never want me, so I gave in to my vulnerabilities – but no, I have never once found you lacking."

"And what about your mistress?" Elizabeth said in anger and heartache.

"My what?"

"Miss Wainwright."

At this he looked utterly puzzled. "Miss Wainwright is not my mistress."

"Your aunt seems to think she is for she told Mary, and that you and she share a son. Can you expect me to believe that she would spread such rumours about her own family if they were not true?"

"I cannot tell you what my aunt might do, but I can assure you that Miss Wainwright is *not* my mistress. I barely know the woman."

"Then how do you explain going to see her, an unmarried woman, with a child who favours you? How do you explain supporting them financially?"

This story, he knew would also cause her pain, but her discomfort could not keep him from telling her, so with renewed vigour, he said, "Six years ago, my father and I visited Rosings on our annual trip at Easter time. We brought my friend, George Wickham with us." Darcy paused her, looking for some evidence of her regard. He saw that he had surprised her and was now utterly determined she know the truth of her favourite. "While there, Wickham seduced a young woman, the daughter of the rector at Hunsford, and she became with child. Truth be known, I have every reason to believe that he had not actually seduced her but forced himself on her, although she would not admit it. Miss Wainwright was ostracised by the community and had no choice, for her father's sake and position, but to leave. My own father died before he learnt of Wickham's vile act, so the obligation fell to me. I set her up in a small home, after she refused to marry. I check on her each year to ensure her continued comfort if not respectability. Her father, up until he died last year, always acted as liaison, but without him, I went alone. I realised, even at the time, how it might look to an outsider, but I could not in good conscience ignore my continued duty to her care.

"I must say that I am shocked my aunt would spread a falsehood such as this, not only because I am her own family, but also because she knows it is blatantly false. She knows that Wickham is the boy's father. I cannot understand why she would say such a thing, to your sister no less." Seeing the disturbed look on her face, he recalled how she must feel now knowing that her friend, Wickham, could be so cruel, if she even believed him. "Forgive me, Elizabeth. I know that you have kind feelings towards the man, and surely I should have told you some of his history sooner; however, I could not bring myself to share my painful history with him. There is more to tell, but that will have to wait for another time."

"So you think that he imposed himself on the young woman? Why? What would make you think that?"

"She was but fifteen. She has refused to marry – says she cannot bear to be with another man. Her father was adamant that he would not force her. I think he knew the truth."

"I cannot believe…."

462

"But you can believe that *I* would, that *I* was the father?"

She looked up at him with sadness. "Your aunt, she said that you were the father. Why would I doubt your own relations?"

"Because, I hope that you know me well enough not to believe such a story."

"I don't know that I *do* know you. There are such mixed accounts of you that sometimes I am unable make you out."

"I think you do understand me, Elizabeth. You knew me well enough to be hurt by the possibility. You must have thought it unlikely at some level. Surely you are not so deceived by Wickham that you would believe him innocent and me guilty."

"I noticed that a female had written to you, and you left so quickly without even telling me why. What was I supposed to think? And then you have not come to my room. I thought that maybe you had been meeting your needs elsewhere. My mother...." At that she stopped. Her mother's words had always lacked wisdom. Elizabeth had known this.

She then began to cry, tears of relief or pain, she did not know. Elizabeth had not wanted to believe her husband capable of any misdeed. She had grown to admire him as a landowner, gentleman and husband. To have thought him capable of such offences had afflicted her, but now she felt saddened by her own lack of faith in him. She wanted to believe him about the brothel, and that he had not followed through with the transgression, but she was pained that he had gone there in the first place. *Langston! The vile man, trying to poison me against my husband! He delighted in tormenting me with this story and with Lady Annette as well. And I let him.* She looked to Darcy who appeared truly worried for her and said, "Do not fret over me. He has hurt me in almost every way possible, but I will prevail."

"You speak of Wickham. Elizabeth, I must know – how has he intruded upon you? Has he ever laid hands upon you? — With or without your consent?" Darcy turned his head away as if doing so might somehow change her response.

"Wickham? No, I do not speak of him. He was nothing but kind to me while at Longbourn. That must have been the surest way to torment you; I see it now. Though had I been in love with him, I could not have been more wretchedly blind. But vanity, not love, has been my folly," she finished quietly, ashamed of her credulity. "I speak of your cousin, Lord Langston."

"Please, do not conceal what he has done."

Elizabeth closed her eyes shut, as if to disappear, but she knew that she had to confide to her husband what had happened. It was his right to know. And otherwise he would guess and likely come up with worse than was true. Nonetheless, she feared his judgement upon her for the viscount's misdeeds. "Your cousin hates me, Darcy, and has tormented me since we first met but making it seem as though he was being solicitous to my needs. He was deceiving you with his false kindnesses." She took in a deep breath and turned away as she spoke, "The first time was Christmas at Tromwell House. If you will remember, your cousin told you that Georgiana was looking for you. He offered to return me to the family, but after you walked away, he led me to one of the bedchambers, instead, and locked us inside." She glanced back to see

Darcy's look of shock and confusion and then with emotion continued, "He began trying to kiss me and to touch me; he eventually picked me up and carried me to the bed." Tears were flowing down her face as she recalled the scene that she had tried so many times to forget. "If not for his brother, the colonel, coming just at that moment, he would have succeeded in … violating me. Colonel Fitzwilliam was looking for me, knocking on doors and calling my name, so Langston let me go, promising to finish what he had started another time. He said you would not believe me if I told you – that you did not trust me."

"But, that is not true. You should have said something!" Darcy said with vehemence that soon lost its zeal as she continued.

"Darcy, you thought I had taken advantage of you in order to make you marry me. Can you honestly say that you would have believed me over your own cousin? He would have denied any wrongdoing. I told you I did not wish to dance with him at the ball, and yet you made me. What was I supposed to think?"

"I don't know. I would like to think that I would have believed you, but it pains me to say that I might not have. I just don't know."

"He joined us at the show and sat next to me in the carriage and at the theatre. He kept whispering words of seduction and malice, rubbing up next to me, yet I could do nothing to stop him. And at the ball, he told me about you and Lady Annette, suggesting that you still had feelings for her. And then you proved his point by dancing with her and dining in her company without me." Her voice gave way here. She could not have known how much that event had injured her those many weeks ago.

"Langston took your seat, so you would be forced to sit elsewhere; he did that to hurt you. Elizabeth, I let him." Darcy said, distressed at his own insensitivity. "But you must know, I never truly had feelings for the woman. She was a good match; that is all. Once you and I were engaged, my connection with her ended."

She looked away again, her feelings too raw to even comment. "Then I received word from you that he would be coming here, and I panicked. I tried to protect myself, even going so far as to ask Clark to teach me methods of defence, which was fortuitous for I eventually had to put what I learned to the test. Langston found Clark and me while we were walking and threatened him, finally convincing the poor man to leave. But I found my escape and ran. You would have been even more proud of me than before," she said with a little sparkle in her eye, "for I ran faster and longer than even the day of our walk. Indeed, I ran twice as far as I ever had in my life – until I could go no further and fell to the ground. I know not how long I lay there trying to catch my breath. I feared for my life at that point, for I had behaved most unladylike, I am afraid, causing a great deal of pain for your cousin. I could hear him yelling in the distance, threatening me. I was truly at the mercy of Providence."

"Elizabeth, please speak plainly to me. Tell me that he did not succeed in forcing himself upon you."

"He did not prevail, but doubt not that he would have. I am afraid of what might happen should I ever see him again. I feared coming home that day, unsure of what he might do to me without your protection. The servants had no choice but to obey him; he could have defiled me without recourse had I returned home. I was looking for shelter, somewhere he could not find me when I tripped in the dark."

"Your dress is torn. I have been in agony thinking of what he did to you."

With more emotion, she continued, "I had to let him think that I was giving in to him, so I could take him by surprise. He let up his grip and began to lose control of his desires. He never expected what I did; I have no doubt. That was the only thing that allowed me to escape. I am quite certain he was unable to ride, or he would surely have caught up with me. Husband, he did assault my mouth and touched me inappropriately, but it went no further. I am fine. I did not want to be exploited in that way, but no true harm was done."

"No true harm, Elizabeth? He violated you, even if you were able to stop him! And you were left out in the wilderness for two days! I will call him out to defend your honour!" he said heatedly. Darcy had been growing more and more agitated as she spoke and could hold back no longer.

"You will do no such thing! You would cause a rift in your family that would never heal. I could not bear to think that I played a role in the destruction of your relationship with them."

"That would be an unfortunate consequence, but can in no way keep me from seeking satisfaction. You have been completely innocent. Langston is the one who deserves punishment, and I mean to mete it out." Darcy stood, pacing while he ran his hand through his already tousled hair.

"But if you were to lose, if he were to succeed, I … I could not bear it. And then I would have absolutely no protection from him. I shudder to think what he might do to me without your presence. Please, Darcy, I beg you, do not fight him." Although weakened by her fever and days of little nourishment, her voice gained momentum as she spoke to him across the room.

He turned to her abruptly. "I thought that I had lost you. While searching for you, I felt the full weight of what that loss would do to me. Elizabeth, can you really ask me to forfeit my right to fight for you? It would be a privilege for me, I can assure you." Then he stood up straight, eyes penetrating. "I have every reason to expect I would win any challenge."

"I have no doubt, my husband, but please, do not say such things. Just let it go. God will take care of vengeance as he sees fit. I have read that we are never to avenge ourselves, but to leave it to God. Darcy, are *you* to play God?"

He looked away. Had he not spent his life doing just that? — Playing God by praising himself for his status and accomplishments, placing judgement on others, relying only on himself alone. And where did it get him? "I will consider your request, Elizabeth, but I make no promises. I cannot let him just get away with what he has done to you, to our marriage."

Darcy continued to pace as he pondered the repercussions of Langston's perfidy upon their marriage thus far. Unable to ignore the increasingly unbearable thoughts that intruded, he spoke on what might distress her, but could not be helped. "Elizabeth, when we were intimate after the ball, that was after my cousin had assaulted you at his parents' home." Elizabeth nodded; she could not bear to look at him in the eye, mortified with the incident. "You were very upset that night. At first, I thought that I might have hurt you."

Elizabeth was shaking her head. "You did not hurt me," she said trying desperately to contain her emotions.

"You were thinking of him, of what he had done to you." She nodded quickly without words and could no longer hold back her tears as she brought her hand up to cover her face. "I didn't know. I should have paid closer attention." He then sat down upon the floor of the cabin beside her, pulling her to himself.

This time, she let herself be held by her husband as she gave in to her grievous emotions. After months of fear concerning how he might respond if he learnt of the viscount's attack and efforts to put the dreadful ordeal behind her, the floodgates of her emotions opened. She had not yet allowed herself to dwell upon Langston's most recent attack, for in her escape and injuries, she had other troubles to weigh on her mind, but with her husband now holding her in an embrace, her distress had free rein. "You were so much like your cousin! — Your size and bearing are like his, and you were holding me and touching me the same way. I kept envisioning him pressing on me. I could not escape, so I just closed my eyes and tried to disappear!"

"My God, and then I afflicted you at Longbourn!" Darcy's anguish was much less overt than Elizabeth's but terrible, nonetheless.

"It was very wrong of you, but you did not hurt me. I felt a betrayal of our wedding vows, but in truth neither of us had fulfilled our promises to the other that day. I know that I selfishly chose to disregard your strictures in order to feed my own pretentions." Elizabeth was taking deep calming breaths trying to gain control again, as she continued, "But regardless of my own error in judgement, the whole ordeal truly frightened me. I have felt oppressed not just since your cousin's attack, but since our marriage began." She looked up to his eyes, pained at her own confessions. "Darcy, I have tried to move past my reticence, to somehow be the wife you need me to be. Recently I thought that perhaps I would finally be able to find contentment in our time alone, but your cousin – I just don't know if I can. What if I never desire what you want? That is not fair to you. I was so afraid you had taken a mistress or had a paramour, but surely if you did, it would be my fault."

"No! You have never been the one deserving blame, and I will not hear of it again." He gazed in her eyes as he said, "My dear girl, you have been nothing but courageous and blameless in every way. I will forever spend my life making up for all of the sufferings my family and I have inflicted upon you."

"Please, don't say such things. I should have been more welcoming to you from the beginning, but I followed my own inclinations rather than my obligation to you, as your wife. Perhaps we could have found some kind of truce earlier if I had only trusted you." Elizabeth reached her hand up to his face and said, "You are an upright man; I see that now, and I have no doubt that you will do whatever is best for my welfare, as my protector."

"You call me upright. But how can you say that after how I treated you? — After hearing of my weaknesses in London?"

"I am disturbed by your confession, but a truly immoral man would have continued to hide his guilt, I believe. And *I* am guilty of taking other men's words over my own husband's based on nothing but comments meant to stoke my vanity or bring me fear. For months I held onto feelings of righteous indignation about Mr. Wickham when your only faults were to withhold your side of the story and to refrain from feeding my own self-importance." She looked down to her hands, away from his gaze. "It is true, that I did admire Mr. Wickham. I coveted his compliments and words of appreciation – and at your expense. I let him manipulate me into hurting you. I even gave him reason to suppose that I would accept an on-going correspondence from him. I am so ashamed of myself, so you see we each had our temptations."

"Elizabeth, …"

"And Langston's ignominy was ever before me, and yet I took his word over my trust in you. I regret my lack of faith. You would have every reason to be offended by my unjustified judgements."

"I gave you no reason to think otherwise. Wickham told me on that awful day at Longbourn that you cared more for him because he flattered you, while I despised you. I would not say that that was my intention, but he was right in that I did nothing to gain your approval." Darcy reached up to her face and then looked away as he said, "So he has been writing to you? Elizabeth, when I arrived at Pemberley, there was an unopened letter from Wickham with your name on it. It must have come while you were missing. I broke the seal and read it."

"Oh, my. I have received letters from him through Lydia. But I can assure you that I have not read nor answered them. When I opened the first letter, I did not know who had written it, and as soon as I discovered who had, I burnt it. I received one other, which I also burnt before opening it. I do not even know what the letters said, but I wrote to my papa and told Lydia to desist from helping him."

"Did the first one arrive with the letter from your sister – the one that had you upset that day in the music room?"

She nodded. "I was afraid to tell you – afraid that I would damage our marriage even further than I already had. Now I see that I was wrong. I should have confided in you." Her eyes grew wide as she looked at him.

"What is it? What's wrong?"

"The baby! I feel the baby, right here." Then she rubbed her midsection where she felt the baby move. She gave her first true smile for him in weeks. "I feel him, *or her*."

"Do you think I could feel it?"

"No, I cannot feel with my hand, only on the inside right now."

"What does it feel like? I would like to know."

"Well, I suppose it feels like a tickle from the inside, but not the kind that makes you laugh, rather the kind that makes you sigh." She smiled up at him.

"Elizabeth, I am so pleased that we are to have a baby. I could not say it earlier, not with the fear of disappointment, but truly..." He looked away. "I thought that, — I was told that the baby might not be mine."

"What? Who would say such a thing? You never told me how you knew I was with child. Tell me now."

"Wickham."

"What does he have to do with anything?"

"He informed me the baby might be his. That you loved him and had been with him, and that you continued to despise me."

How did Wickham know about the baby? Elizabeth searched her mind for some recollection to enlighten her. *Mama! She must have said something. I knew Jane should not have told her.* "You believed him."

"Elizabeth, we have both been mistaken about so many things. We have each thought the worse of the other. Can we please learn to forgive one another and start fresh, again? I can assure you that I did not want to believe him. I have never been a vulnerable man. I have kept people at a distance, never showing my weaknesses, but with you, my dear, I have found myself to be susceptible in so many ways. I knew at one point that you did not care for me, much less like me. It is natural that I would consider the validity in his claims."

"The great Mr. Darcy has been foolish, vulnerable, prideful, weak and perverse. I seem to have a negative effect upon you. Are you certain you wish to forgive me?"

He smiled at her ability to disarm him. "I am certain that I need you in my life, and as forgiveness will make it all the sweeter, I suppose that is exactly what I wish." They stared at one another for some minutes, the firelight playing off their features as each became mesmerised by the other. He wanted to kiss her, to replace the feelings of distress with those of affection, and had been leaning forward, hoping she wished the same, when without warning, a loud knock sounded at the door, startling them both.

Darcy reached his hand out to caress her face and said, "It looks like we may have been found. Here, let me help cover you." Then, after wrapping the blanket around her shoulders, he stood and walked to the door, taking one last glance back to her before opening it.

"Mr. Darcy, thank God! We have been looking for you for two days. We thought for sure you were injured somewhere in the wilds of the estate."

"I am well. Come inside where it is warm." He led the two stable hands into the room. "My wife is also here. I had expected that someone might have found us yesterday."

"We were looking in the wrong part of the estate apparently. Also the rain has not let up since you went missing. We saw the smoke from the chimney as we came up, but the mist and rain kept us from seeing it before now. When Hermes came to the stable without you, it was too late to begin a search. The men had been coming in from their own searches for Mrs. Darcy and said that they had not seen you since morning. We searched all day yesterday for you and Mrs. Darcy and then picked back up this morning."

468

"I was just about to head out walking, so your timing is perfect. Instead, I will send you for provisions and a cart to transport my wife since her injuries keep her from walking."

"We are supposed to send out two shots if we found you, so I'll just do that now."

The man who had been talking walked outside and a few moments later two loud shots were heard. He re-entered with food and wine. "I brought some food for you, knowing you would be hungry."

"Thank you, Parker." Darcy took the food from the man's hands and walked over to his wife who had been watching the interactions. "Elizabeth, here, I want you to eat something." He opened the sack and took out the provisions, making certain that she had begun to take in some nourishment before returning to the men. "I would like for you to make haste to the house and let everyone know that Mrs. Darcy and I are both well. Bring back some more food with the cart, and have my wife's maid pack some warm clothes for her to change into."

"Shall we bring the maid with us, sir?"

Darcy turned back to his wife who was listening intently to the conversation. "Yes, thank you for your suggestion. Oh, and tell my man to have bath water drawn for each of us when we return. One more thing; send someone for the doctor. I would like him to see my wife today."

"Yes, sir," the man said before walking back out the door.

"Darcy, please, come sit down and have something to eat as well," said his wife.

"No, I want you to get what you need first."

"But there is more than enough for the two of us."

"As you are eating for *two*, I think that what you have there should be about right. Truly, I am fine waiting. What's a couple of more hours?"

"Well, I can assure you that I am incapable of eating this much! So, when I have had all I can possibly consume, you will eat what is left. I know you are hungry, for I heard your stomach telling you, not ten minutes ago."

"It seems that we are both rather stubborn. Clark wanted to call you stubborn when he told me that you *insisted most firmly* that he teach you means of defence, but I believe he thought better of such strong language; however, I have no qualms. You *are* stubborn, and I wouldn't change a thing about you," he said smiling.

"Nothing, sir? Are you certain? My impertinence must give you grief, I believe."

"Impertinence? — No, rather your lively nature. I have never had to wonder what your true feelings have been towards me. I believe that you are the only person, outside of James perhaps, who would have the strength of purpose to tell me that I am a liar and without honour."

"But I was wrong to say that," Elizabeth said, alarmed to have her cruel words repeated to her.

"You may have been mistaken in your assumption, but your audacity was no less magnificent to behold."

"You are making fun of me."

"I can assure you that I am not. Elizabeth, everyone venerates me. I can never truly know a person's true impressions. I am a man with a great deal of financial power and as such, I have few true friends. My status and money have always affected my relationships, keeping me from knowing for certain if people speak from their heart or their purses. Not with you, my dear. You have never once, since the Meryton Assembly, treated me with obeisance."

"But surely a wife should hold her husband in esteem."

"Obeisance and esteem are two different things, though. I would not have you fawning over me like a rapacious upstart."

"I do, you know."

"You do what?"

"Esteem you," answered she, almost shy to say such a thing to her husband. "That is part of why it hurt me so, to think that you had...." Here she stopped as tears came back to her eyes. She wiped them away with the blanket. "I had come to see you as an admirable man, and to have your character called into question, ... I could not bear it."

Darcy reached over to hold her hand, gently caressing it within his own. "Elizabeth, we both know that I am not perfect, but I can promise you that I have every intention of remaining faithful to my marriage vows, and would even if I had not grown to cherish you as I now do." He looked into her eyes still moist from verbalising her fears. "But I must tell you that my feelings of sincere regard inspire me to speak plainly. There is no other woman in all of England whom I esteem more than you. Having you as my wife is the greatest thing that has ever happened to me. I say happened to me, because, I had no choice in the matter. It has been as if someone other than myself has been directing my life for the past six months, with my being dragged kicking and screaming to a paradise, for which I have always longed, but in which I never dreamt of sharing."

Then he declared softly but with feeling, "Elizabeth, in vain I have struggled. It will not do. You must allow me to tell you how ardently I admire and love you."

Elizabeth's astonishment was softened by the great joy that she felt upon hearing such a heartfelt declaration from her husband. She had not dared to hope that he could ever express such romantic sentiments, or that she should be the receiver of his declarations of love. She blushed prettily, unable to immediately speak. At first, he had assumed in his modest and vulnerable state that she had been distressed by his heartfelt words, but then he saw a smile overspread her face, which could not conceal her joy. She looked away, embarrassed. "Darcy, you have made me the happiest of all creatures. Could I be naïvely lost in another dream, only to awaken to a cruel reality of despair, or did you really confess your affection for me – I, who have done nothing but cause you grief and pain?"

"No, my love, you know not of what you speak. You are the only one I have known in the entirety of my life who has been able to use the grief and pain, which came by my own hand, to transform me, to bring me to a joy beyond measure. For how can one be truly satisfied in this life without a true understanding of oneself, without the lessons learnt by the gentle reproach of another?"

"Sir, you can hardly call my reproaches gentle!" Elizabeth replied with a slight smile. "Truly, I do not deserve your love, I who have done nothing but cause you trouble since the first of our acquaintance." Then laughingly she continued, "But by all means turn my faults into virtues."

"Elizabeth, you are the most virtuous woman I know. I am the one who has antagonised you; I wanted to believe the worst in you, to vilify your conduct, despite all of the evidence contrariwise. You have represented yourself admirably well. I know of no other, man or woman, who would have stood up to me with such courage and conviction. I, on the other hand, have deserved every reproof that you have sent my way. When you were hurting, I salted your wounds. I cannot think about my actions towards you during those first months of our marriage without abhorrence."

"Think no more of our past words and actions. The feelings of the people who married are so widely different from what they are now, that even unpleasant circumstances attending it ought to be forgotten. You must learn some of my philosophy. Think only of the past as the remembrance gives you pleasure."

"I cannot give you credit for any philosophy of the kind. Your retrospections must be so totally void of reproach that the contentment arising from them is not of philosophy, but what is much better, of ignorance. But with me, it is not so. Painful recollections will intrude, which cannot – which ought not – to be repelled. I have been a selfish being all my life, in practice, though not in principle. As a child I was taught what was right, but I was not taught to correct my temper. I was given good principles, but left to follow them in pride and conceit. Unfortunately an only son (for many years an only child), I was spoilt by my parents, who though good themselves (my father particularly, all that was benevolent and amiable), allowed, encouraged, almost taught me to be selfish and overbearing, to care for none beyond my own family circle, to think meanly of all the rest of the world, to wish at least to think meanly of their sense and worth compared with my own. Such I was, from eight to eight and twenty; and such I might still have been but for you, dearest, loveliest Elizabeth! What do I not owe you! You taught me a lesson, hard indeed at first, but most advantageous. By you, I was properly humbled. I came into the marriage certain that you were the one to receive the advantage, that you should be grateful of my condescension, for saving you and your family, when all along, I was the one unworthy. But I know that you discerned this, for I held it before you like a trophy throughout our time in London and Hertfordshire."

"Sir, please. You must not speak this way, for it pains me. My feelings forbid it." With a blush, Elizabeth spoke her heart, and his name, for the first time. "William, I love you. I honour you with my mind and cherish you with my heart. I did not at first understand why Providence brought us together in such an unconventional manner, but I now know that we were meant for one another. Could we have found our way together without God's intervention in our lives, I who despised your hauteur and you who found me intolerable?"

With her declaration of love, Darcy's heart soared, but was tempered by the realisation that had they not met on that path on that stormy morning, they likely would not have reached an understanding. He had longed to hear his name upon her lips. Few called him by this name; even his sister called him Brother as a rule. This simple, yet powerful evidence of their changed understanding and the thought that they might never have found love if not for Providence, spurred him to lean in closer to her, so that their faces were mere inches apart.

"Well, William, if you don't kiss me, I will have to kiss you. And I would hate to instigate another scandal within a secluded building."

He needed no other invitation. Too elated to smile, or do anything other than comply, he leaned in to touch her lips with his own. They tasted of wine and cheese, thus reminding him of her need for sustenance. He pulled away regrettably and said, "My love, I will have to consider the best means of beginning a scandal later, for I absolutely insist you continue your breakfast. But don't mind me, for I can happily sit here and watch you. In fact, I will do more than that." Thus saying, Darcy grabbed an orange that had been sitting on the napkin on which her food lay. He peeled the rind away and then separated a segment from the rest, bringing it up to her mouth.

She laughed at his gallant show and dutifully ate. "Mm. I've never tasted food so delicious. Tell me, are you always so good at feeding others?"

"I cannot say I have ever fed anyone else before, excepting Georgiana when she was an infant. I used to enjoy feeding her and doting on her. I suppose that I am a natural, for we see that she grew up to be a healthy, young lady." Elizabeth continued to eat in contemplative silence, considering Darcy's sister and her obvious, vehement dislike.

"How is your sister? Did you see her in town?"

"I forgot that you were unaware when I told you. Georgiana has joined me and is even now at Pemberley. She must have been overwhelmed with fear when I did not return two days ago."

"Is that how long we have been in the cottage?" At his affirmative nod, she continued, "You must be starving! And I cannot eat another bite. Here you take the rest. I confess that I am feeling very sleepy all of a sudden. Although much better than before, I need to lie down again." And so she did.

Darcy saw the fatigue in her eyes and posture and so allowed her to suspend her eating for a little while. He leaned over and kissed her forehead, "You rest, but when we get home, I expect you to eat a veritable feast."

"I will do my best; I promise." She closed her eyes, initially in contemplation of how the reunion with her new sister might play out, but then she drifted off into a quiet slumber.

Chapter Twenty-Two

Let your fountain be blessed, and rejoice in the wife of your youth,
a lovely deer, a graceful doe.
Let her breasts fill you at all times with delight;
be intoxicated always in her love.
Proverbs 5:18-19

Elizabeth was awakened about two hours later by the entrance of a small group of people from the main house. Darcy had lain down next to her, carefully putting his arm underneath her head while draping his other around her waist, resting his hand gently on the swell of her abdomen.

The Pemberley entourage walked in without knocking as Georgiana burst into the room anxious to see her brother well. Darcy jerked his body up, disoriented by the loud bluster, while Elizabeth ducked down trying to protect herself from Darcy's hasty movement.

"Brother!" said Georgiana as she entered the darkened room. Then she looked down at the scene before her. She could not have missed the intimate attitude that she had witnessed, as her brother awoke with a start and came to his feet before her.

"Georgiana! You see that Elizabeth and I are safe."

His sister looked back and forth to the room's two inhabitants with equal parts outrage and relief displayed for all to see upon her countenance. "What is *she* doing here? Do you not remember that she left you?"

"Georgiana, hold your tongue!"

His sister pointed at Elizabeth in indignation. "She is the cause of all of your troubles, not me!"

Darcy took the few steps to his sister and, grabbing hold of her arm, led her out of the cabin. He turned to Janette and said, "Please help my wife change into clean clothes. I will be outside with the men." He continued on with Georgiana as they stood several yards away from the group.

"Georgiana, what was that about? Can you not see that Elizabeth is unwell?"

"But, Brother, she is using you! Are you so blinded by lust that you cannot see that she is using you? That woman in there is in love with another man, and you know it, yet you take her back."

"Enough! I do not know all that you have heard or what you think you know, but I can assure you that she is not interested in any other man, including Wickham, and I will have you keep quiet about any speculation that you might have on the matter. You are being watched by our servants, and I will not have you making a public spectacle."

More quietly, but just as vehemently, she continued, "She has poisoned you against your family. Do you not see it? You have changed. I can see that you are more yielding to the weaknesses of others. You bring her into our lives – no not our lives, your life – and expect your family to accept her. Well, I will not.

You may let her make a fool of you, but I will not help her!" Georgiana finished with great emotion, as she ran back to her own mount and rode off.

Up to this point, Darcy had not realised the emotional strain he had placed on his little sister. However, he now saw his error in this and in many other ways; he had not actively brought the two women in his life together. He expected Georgiana to now accept Elizabeth after he himself had perhaps unknowingly and unwittingly led Georgiana to believe the worse possible scenario. After calming down, he walked over to his men to retrieve more food. Darcy ate in silence as he awaited Elizabeth's preparations. When Janette appeared in the doorway, he re-entered their haven of the past two days. Elizabeth was sitting on the floor by the fire wrapped in a shawl. Darcy was adamant that she cover herself with his greatcoat as well. Although she was not certain she needed it more than he, she was thankful for his thoughtful attentions.

"Elizabeth, my love, I am going to carry you out to the cart. Janette will ride with you while I am on horseback. I will never leave your side."

"Do you expect danger on our way to the house, Darcy?" she said not in fear but mirth.

"My only concern is in being away from you any longer than I have to be. When we reach the house, a bath should be awaiting each of us, and I am afraid our time together will be less constant. Of course that may sound pleasing to you, but I hope for as much time as you will allow." She smiled at his open words of affection.

"I look forward to your continuing to be my nurse, if you would wish it, but for both our sakes, we will leave the more unpleasant duties to my maid."

He extinguished the fire and then glanced around the cabin to take in the memory of the location of their first declaration. Walking over to his wife he bent down, easily picking her up. He was still somewhat sore from the journey of two days past, but revelled in his lovely burden this day.

ALTHOUGH MUCH IMPROVED, Elizabeth still had the lingering effects of a fever. Her body was sorely bruised and her ankle was still black and blue. After arriving home to a subdued, but heartfelt, reception, her husband carried her to her chamber, so that she could take a bath and eat a hearty meal before she was relegated to her bed. Darcy reluctantly left her in the care of Janette, who had been beaming since seeing her mistress for the first time. Laura and Mrs. Reynolds had also been summoned to help transport Elizabeth to the copper tub and back, so Darcy had no charge left but to await her summons.

The doctor arrived about an hour after the Darcys. Elizabeth had completed her bath and meal and was lying in bed when the man was escorted in by her maid to examine her. When his examination was completed, he called in his patient's husband, who had been waiting anxiously in the sitting room for a report. The man told Darcy that Elizabeth was still feverish but not in any danger. Her foot likely had no broken bones but was sorely bruised and sprained, and Elizabeth had to stay off of it for the following fortnight. Darcy well remembered his own similar injury and thought that Elizabeth, like himself, would find two weeks a challenge to bear. The doctor was also able to give his opinion on the baby. Darcy learnt that the female body is very protective of the infant, and the baby, by God's grace, likely knew nothing of the week's trials. A relieved Darcy walked the doctor out and then went to his study to await his sister while his wife was left in the capable hands of her maid.

Georgiana and he needed to talk, and without an audience. Darcy still could not believe Georgiana's response upon entering the cabin and her words before she had made her hasty exit. After he was unable to find her elsewhere, he entered his study, asking Peters to send Georgiana in when she returned. While there, he sent an express to his cousin, Colonel Fitzwilliam, who had remained in London, informing him of the events of the past week. Darcy was happy to be able to assure his cousin that Wickham had no foundation for his claims and asked him to deliver that message post-haste to the miscreant, letting him know that he would receive nothing from Darcy, regardless of his threats.

Darcy had begun to worry when two hours later Georgiana had not yet arrived. Just as he was about to call for his horse, a light knock was heard on the door. "Enter."

Georgiana slowly opened the door, looking fearful but resolute. Darcy had spent most of his time waiting in contemplation about what he might say to his sister in order to put the past ungenerous thoughts behind them. He had determined to be compassionate but firm; he could not abide his sister continuing her antagonistic words aimed at turning him against his wife. He understood that Georgiana had been deceived yet again by Wickham, but once Georgiana learnt the truth, he would demand that she begin to show charity, if not true affection. He knew in time, with an open mind, that Georgiana could not help but love Elizabeth, even as he did.

The conversation that took place between brother and sister left Georgiana in tears of anger and frustration. She argued in support of the obvious conclusion – the one that held Darcy in chains for months – that Elizabeth had taken advantage of his kindness, that she had seen Darcy as a means to raise herself in society. Everyone knew the truth of the matter, why could he not? Georgiana was certain that Elizabeth had used her arts and allurements to take control of Darcy's rational side. Darcy was patient and unruffled, even in the face of her vehement arguments, for he too once believed as Georgiana, but he was determined that his sister show Elizabeth the respect due her as Mrs. Darcy and mistress of his estate.

Not having the energy to argue any more, he dismissed his sister and retired to his own room, hoping that Elizabeth might have requested him; however, he soon discovered that his wife had already fallen asleep. Unable to stay away, he opened her chamber door and walked over to her bed. The fire from the hearth was the only light, but it was bright enough that he could regard her face. He sat on the side of the bed and took her hand in his own. Much to his dismay, he noticed that her fever had returned. He retrieved some water and a cloth from the washbasin and began the task of keeping her cool. Elizabeth slept soundly during his ministrations, occasionally speaking in her sleep. Darcy heard his own name, but she became more agitated as she began to speak his cousin's name as well.

Initially, she pushed him away when he tried to comfort her, but his soothing touch and words again calmed her troubled spirit. After hours of attending her, sleep attempted to subdue him, but he could not leave her side in case the fever returned, so unsure if Elizabeth would approve, he removed his shoes, topcoat, cravat and vest and lay on top of the counterpane next to her.

DARCY WAS PLEASANTLY SURPRISED TO FEEL tickling upon his face. Opening his eyes he beheld a sight that warmed his heart and relieved his worries. Inches from his own face, he saw Elizabeth's, demonstrating a tender look of peace. In a groggy voice, he said, "You are awake. I was worried; your fever came back."

"I feel better now, though I am a little cold."

"I'll add wood to the fire," he said as he jumped up and went to the other side of the room. After a few moments, he came back and sat next to her reclined form.

"I know that I said we would leave the unpleasant business of my caretaking to Janette, but I do not want to summon her and the others just to take me to the lavatory. Do you mind carrying me in there? I promise that I only need transportation."

"You can ask me anything, my dear. I am at your disposal." After he took her to her dressing room and then brought her back to bed, he asked what else she might need.

"You must be careful, Husband, for I do enjoy being spoilt. Before you know it, I will have you running down to the kitchen to make me some chicken soup, then feeding it to me while rubbing my back."

"I would be happy to do any of those, although my cooking skills are highly overrated. In fact I will offer to rub your back even without the soup."

"Would you indeed? I confess that the floor of the cabin, coupled with my fever, has left me with several pains in my back."

"Sit up and I will get behind you." Darcy assisted her to a sitting position, and then he leaned on the backboard of the large bed. His gentle ministrations soothed Elizabeth, and she began to wonder what it might feel like to have him touching her this way during intimacies instead of the way he had in the past. Elizabeth's experiences had all been unpleasant and disgusting to her, but now, while receiving his tender touches, she could imagine the pleasure that closeness with her husband might afford.

Darcy too was thinking of touching his wife. She was so fragile yet strong. How could someone with her small frame be so spirited? He considered how she had defended herself against Langston. He was nearly twice Elizabeth's size, yet she courageously took him down. Elizabeth felt so right in his hands as he continued to rub her back. The intimacy of the moment worked its magic, and both Darcys felt a longing to touch and be touched by the other.

Of course to Darcy's understanding, this made perfect sense. He loved her; he longed for her. He had dreamt of lying with her so many times that he had a difficult time differentiating between dreams and reality. His visions had changed, however, from those early fantasies where he took and she gave. They had evolved into an emotional exchange of physical touches and pleasure. It was no longer a longing for sexual gratification but now a longing for a physical expression of an emotional bond, not an act of selfishness but an act of serving, and of intimate oneness. But now was not the time. Elizabeth was still ill and in pain. The emotional trauma of her time with Langston still plagued her. Darcy could and would wait for her.

Elizabeth soon became drowsy again and expressed her desire to lie back down. "But you need not leave, William."

"It might be better for both of us if I do."

"You know best, I suppose, but I would prefer that you stay. I found your presence in the cabin, and even now, to be comforting for me."

"I can deny you nothing," thus saying he lay back down upon the counterpane.

"Not there, in here," she said lifting the covering to invite him in.

"Elizabeth, I am only human. How can you tease me so?"

"I surely don't know what you are talking about. I mean not to tease; I just want you by my side."

"I cannot be by your side without wanting to be *with* you, and since you are ill, it will not, cannot happen today. I can contentedly join you while you sleep, safe from me under the covers, but when you invite me underneath there with you, well, it makes me want to get closer, as close as I can get."

"I see," said Elizabeth contemplating if she should say what she was thinking or let it rest – but she knew what she wanted. He was her husband, and she his wife. "I would have you sleep here with me anyway." At his look of indecision, she said, "William, for the past week, I have been fearful of your cousin and his veiled threats. Then with his actual attack, I had to endure his vile assault. I spent two days in vague recollection of my plight, not knowing if I would live or die, and then the baby...." At this, tears threatened to spill down her cheeks. "I do not want to be alone. I feel safe in your arms. Please, just stay and hold me."

He could not argue against such a plea, and so he got under the covers with her, his shirt and pants securely on. Darcy put his arms around her and she instinctively nestled in close. She fell quickly into a slumber, but Darcy lay there for a while before falling asleep again, savouring the moment in contented delight. Her need for him gave him the strength he required to subdue his own natural desires, yet he could not help but anticipate one day soon that they might find comfort without limitation.

THE FOLLOWING FORTNIGHT WAS A TIME of frustration and felicity for the couple. Elizabeth, never one to truly enjoy idleness, became more and more intent on leaving her room and moving about. The rain had brought with it an increase in temperatures, and spring was promising to burst forth in colour and show. Elizabeth's only experience at Pemberley had been winter, and although lovely in its own way, could not compare with the promise of the rebirth of the regional verdure. However, Darcy was equally insistent that she not leave their suite, for fear of causing more damage to her ankle.

"My love," said he, "I find your eagerness to move about endearing. You certainly never waste a moment in frivolous inactivity, but I desire that you recover without incident, so that we can more quickly get back to our walks."

"You will be joining me? I thought you would prefer riding."

"I will not leave to Clark the care of my wife if I can help it. I look forward with pleasure showing you the gardens and grounds of Pemberley as spring makes her show. We will be obligated, much to your satisfaction, I believe, to go to Hertfordshire in June for your sister's wedding, so our time here will be limited. I must insist that you hasten your recovery by following the doctor's orders, so we can have plenty of time together to enjoy the mild weather."

"I thought you might want to spend the Season in town."

"No, I have had enough of society in town and only desire your own."

"Are you certain that you are not ashamed of me? Perhaps you are embarrassed to introduce me to your world." Elizabeth said this in jest, as communicated by her arched smile, but Darcy could not let such a statement go without a response.

"Elizabeth, do not say such things. I would be proud indeed to have you on my arm at any event or gathering in town. I simply do not want to share you with anyone else, especially those who are prone to think ill, with no provocation except tales of a non-existent breach in propriety. No, I prefer we spend as much time here, at home, before conquering the wilds of London society."

After this conversation, Darcy began to consider a more strategic means of introducing his wife into society that would put to rest, once and for all, the negative aura surrounding his marriage. He wanted Elizabeth to be accepted as the accomplished, lovely, kind and elegant woman that he now knew her to be. He acknowledged the blame in her previous, less-than-welcome reception by his family, acquaintances and society at large. It was obvious, based on the timing, that their current hope of having a child did not have its origin until more than two months after being confined in the cabin. Darcy wanted everyone to know that he married a virtuous woman of grace, for her sake as well as his own, and would do so again if given a choice.

Also, there was the matter of Georgiana. Darcy's sister was disinclined to spend any time in Elizabeth's presence, and as Elizabeth had not been able to leave their suite, there was no hope of reconciliation between the two women Darcy loved most. Darcy had chosen to take meals in their shared sitting room so that Elizabeth would not have to eat alone; however, this left his sister with only her companion, Mrs. Annesley, as she would not consider joining them. The conflict that naturally arose, as Darcy seemingly had to take sides, left him remorseful again for failing to encourage the relationship while in town, shortly after his marriage. He would not force Georgiana to join them, but he would not leave his wife either. Darcy openly and affectionately invited his sister to meet with the couple to partake in meals, but Georgiana would have none of it, until one evening during dinner.

Darcy and Elizabeth had just begun their meal when there was heard a tentative knock upon the door. "Enter," said he. The door opened slowly to reveal Georgiana whom Elizabeth had not seen since the day in the cabin.

"Brother, I was wondering if I could eat with you?" Georgiana had been quite lonely during her refusal to be in Elizabeth's company. She had every expectation that her brother would soon tire of his wife, seeing the nonsense in relegating himself to their rooms, and then come eat with her, but she had given up hope of this occurring as time went on, for it had been over a week with no sign of his giving in.

Since arriving back at Pemberley, Georgiana had noticed several changes that had left her mindful of Elizabeth's intrusion into their lives. The pianoforte had been shifted slightly, and unfamiliar music lay on top of the stack that once only contained her own. The menus had changed from what they once had been, and a new puppy had been introduced into the home. All of these, though insufficient and unreasonable to oppose, had vexed Georgiana, nonetheless. She did not see that her biased judgements lacked merit, except in that they had left her feeling a stranger in her own home, the fault belonging to Mrs. Darcy.

So Darcy and Elizabeth were surprised to receive Georgiana into their sitting room that evening. "Please, Georgiana, we would love for you to join us, wouldn't we, Elizabeth?"

"Of course. William, let's move to the table, so that there is room for all three of us." Because she was unable to move herself without aid due to Darcy's strict standard of adherence to the doctor's guidelines, Darcy picked her up and carried her to the table. He had taken into habit the gallant approach in transporting her, as he took delight in any opportunity to pick her up and hold her close, if even for the purpose of walking across the room. Elizabeth laughed at his antics, equally enjoying the chivalrous display. "You must forgive your brother, Georgiana. He cannot help his audacious command of my person," Elizabeth said giggling.

Darcy smiled at her, saying, "Indeed I cannot. I have few pleasures with you locked away in here; I must take them as I can." After setting his wife down in her seat, he pulled out another for his sister. "Here, Georgiana, please sit here," said he. She timidly walked over and sat in the chair that he indicated, next to Elizabeth.

"Georgiana, I am so pleased that you have joined us. I had hoped that we might have an occasion to become better acquainted. William has told me so much about you that I feel as though I have known you for years, yet have no actual time to justify the idea. Have you enjoyed being back at your home?"

Georgiana had come into the sitting room with the only purpose of seeing her brother, not Elizabeth. She had no desire in the least to carry on a conversation with the woman who had invaded her family and pitted her brother against her. "I cannot say that I have, seeing so little of my brother and experiencing the changes you have put in place."

"Georgiana!"

"No, William. I would have your sister tell me what bothers her. If there is anything that I can do to make her feel more welcome in her own home, I would do so. Of course, until *you* allow me to leave my room, I have no choice but to hope for her comfort." She turned to her new sister, continuing, "Tell me, Georgiana, what changes have disturbed you so?"

When it came time to speak them aloud, Georgiana felt flustered and embarrassed that she had so little to go on. "Well, the menus have changed."

"Which foods do you not care for? I would be happy to have them changed to accommodate your preferences."

Georgiana tried to think of the ones that she had disliked and coming up with little to say, she added, "And you have been playing my instrument. Your music is in the way." Even to Georgiana's ears, this sounded absurd and juvenile. "I suppose that is not really a problem, but you have brought a new dog into the house. He barks incessantly."

"That is true; he cannot bear being away from us. I would be happy to keep him with me if that would help."

"No, it is a bother, but he is a nice puppy." Georgiana would not admit that she had enjoyed his play every bit as much as she disliked his noise.

"What else can I do?" Elizabeth said as she reached over to place her hand gently on Georgiana's arm. This surprised Darcy and his sister who gently pulled away.

"That is all I can think of for now."

"Well, I am glad we could easily resolve those issues. If you think of anything else, you know where to find me, in my turret guarded by a dragon," said Elizabeth in jest as she gave a sidelong glance towards her husband. The conversation flowed readily between Darcy and his wife as Georgiana listened in.

She could not believe how her new sister teased her brother, but even more so, how he seemed to enjoy the banter, doting upon her and savouring her every whim. It took only two or three more meals in their company before Georgiana came to realise that her brother seemed genuinely happy, more so than she had ever seen him before. His eyes lit up with each word Elizabeth spoke. He reached over on several occasions to touch her hand or face, which always brought about a poorly concealed blush and smile for her husband's delight. Not once in the whole of the conversations did Elizabeth say something that called into question her character. At first Georgiana just listened, but after a few days, she began to chime in, sharing her own accounts to add to the topic at hand.

By the time Elizabeth was allowed by her husband to leave their chamber, Georgiana had developed a tentative fondness for the time spent in her company. The two new sisters tarried in the music room or on the portico in relaxed chatter about nothing and everything. Although unskilled herself at entertaining exchanges, Georgiana came to appreciate and enjoy listening to Elizabeth. As predicted by Darcy, the two women soon developed a comfortable relationship built upon mutual regard. After observing her brother's obvious joy in Elizabeth's presence, and Elizabeth's esteem for her husband, Georgiana decided to let down her guard and try for acceptance instead. Being away from her relations at Tromwell House provided Georgiana with an openness that she had yet to bestow, so that now, she was able to see Elizabeth without bias.

Darcy had refrained from sharing with Elizabeth Georgiana's near elopement with Wickham, so one day when Georgiana mentioned the man's name in order to judge for herself Elizabeth's involvement with him, the conversation naturally made its way around to Georgiana's past feelings and disappointments. The two women had each been deceived in their own ways by the profligate and were able to commiserate and also comfort one another. A bond of sorts began to subsist between the two, thereby giving Darcy all that his heart could desire.

"William," Elizabeth said later on the same day, following the revelation of Wickham's corruption, "Georgiana told me about her time at Ramsgate. Why have you never said anything?"

"At first, I felt uncomfortable sharing an occurrence that brought me and my sister pain. I knew you so little, and could not predict your response. You admired Wickham, I well knew. I could not bear the thought of exposing Georgiana to one of Wickham's sympathisers. I see now that my fears were groundless, but at the time I was apprehensive about where your loyalties lay."

"I know that I apologised before, William, but please let me say again how very ashamed I am of my behaviour during our engagement and on my return to Hertfordshire. I see now that I gave you every reason to doubt me and my integrity."

"Elizabeth, do not be hard on yourself. He is a well-practised deceiver who played on your kind heart. And I gave you no reason to suspect his story might be false and every reason to censure me."

"While in the cottage, you told me that you would share with me some of your history with him. Will you do so now? Will you tell me what else he has done? I had heard his side of the stories for so long, that I truly cannot discern truth from fiction."

Darcy then told her of his father's favour bestowed upon Wickham for nothing other than his friendly and engaging manner. Darcy had grown up seeing his father's kindnesses paid to a boy who would soon grow to mock the very man who admired him. Darcy had never been convivial like his once close friend had been. Mr. Darcy rarely summoned his son for his entertainment, as he had always done with young Wickham. Instead his father would take him on the estate and into his study, grooming him to one day take over as master. Darcy knew rather than felt that his father loved him, but he could not have missed his father's respect towards himself that he never witnessed being imparted to Wickham. When his father died and left Wickham a living, the deceiver refused, accepting a reasonable monetary recompense for his trouble. He later returned, having supposedly changed his mind. When he received nothing but a denial, Wickham decided that revenge was the better course and so took his chances with Darcy's sister.

"I should have suspected he would take such a path. He always did go after younger, less experienced females. Georgiana's naïve heart made her his perfect prey. Elizabeth, I never could have forgiven myself had he succeeded."

"And I gave you every reason to think that I admired him, for indeed I did. My vanity has ever been my one weakness."

"Perhaps you would not have been so weak in this instance if I had not said things to cause your vanity to need stoking. I essentially told you that you were no more than tolerable, and he, well, I do not care to know what he told you, but

I hope you believe that no matter my sentiments before, they are only of adoration now."

She smiled at his sweet words. "In the cabin, you said that he told you about the baby. I suspect Mama was the culprit there. She never could keep her tongue, but why did he tell you the baby might be his? What could he gain by a fabricated story? And why did he continue to write me, do you think? I had made my sentiments on the matter clear, I thought."

"Elizabeth, I have not wanted to tell you."

"Please, you know not what you do to a curious woman such as myself. I must know."

He paused as if to consider whether or not to share with her Wickham's designs against their marriage, but seeing the anxious look on her face, he realised that he could not subject her to the discomfort of always wondering. "Blackmail." At her look of distress, he reached his hand over to hers before continuing. "He requested money in order to keep his silence, otherwise he would share the story with the papers that you were carrying another man's child."

"I cannot believe it! But it must be true," said she. Then turning a pained look towards, him, she continued, "Did you pay him? I hate to think what my friendship with him has cost you."

"Do not be uneasy. I did not pay him."

"But does that mean he has spread the lies? Oh no! Everyone will think that I am a, a harlot! We will never have peace, and our poor child...."

He reached over to calm her, and then said, "Fitzwilliam took care of everything. He gave no details in his express, but apparently, we have no reason to concern ourselves with Wickham's threats anymore. When we next see my cousin, he will share all. Apparently, Fitzwilliam desires to enjoy the tale in person."

"But why did Mr. Wickham write to me? Surely by then he knew I was not accepting any correspondence from him."

"That I do not know, but maybe Fitzwilliam will give us some insight when next we see him."

"DARCY! THIS IS A SURPRISE. Had you come next week you would have missed us. The Season is underway, you know. We were just making our plans to return to town."

"Lady Susan, please forgive my unexpected intrusion, but I was hoping for some time alone with your husband," Darcy said as he looked towards Langston. "Perhaps in the library?"

Langston glanced nervously at Darcy, unsure what to expect from the visit. He had spent no small amount of time considering what might have come of the search for Elizabeth Darcy. He had heard no announcement of her demise. In fact, Darcy had been eerily silent on the matter, thereby leaving his imagination to run its course. Langston considered the possibilities should Darcy find his wife, but he knew that his position in the family would protect him from Elizabeth's accusations should she overcome her reticence. The viscount

482

planned to deny whatever Elizabeth might allege that he did; the family would not believe the tart over himself, and from his experience, Darcy did not truly care about what happened to her anyway.

"Susan, please have a place setting added at the dinner table," Langston genially said to his wife.

"Please do not bother on my account. I will not be staying."

Darcy had travelled to Matlock by horseback, leaving early that morning before Elizabeth had woken up for the day. He lamented having to depart without her knowledge, but he knew that his wife would disapprove of his mission, and he hoped to spare her any more worry than she had already experienced. He had left word that he had pressing business that must be dealt with, but he expected to return that evening shortly after dark.

After Langston closed the door behind him, he was taken completely by surprise when Darcy landed a fist squarely across his jaw sending him to the floor. Holding his face, he turned back up to his cousin whose eyes were aflame with pent up fury, relieved to finally have the outlet for his anger before him.

"What the hell was that for!" cried his cousin.

"You take me as a simpleton, Patrick. You are mistaken if you thought that your betrayal would go unnoticed or unpunished."

As Langston stood, he said, "I have no idea what you are talking about." Just then and without warning, another punch landed to his gut, buckling him over as he fell down to his knees.

"I did not come here to discuss what happened between you and Mrs. Darcy. As far as I am concerned, I have heard enough from her own report."

"You can't believe anything that chit says, Darcy. She is seeking to preserve herself by pitting you against your family."

"Quiet! I am well aware of everything you did to harm *my wife* – whom you should thank by the way, for her peace of mind is the only thing that has kept me from calling you out," Darcy said ominously. He rarely lost his composure, but when he did, he was a fierce sight to behold. "You will stay away from Mrs. Darcy. If we are required to be in your company in the future for family matters, you will keep your distance from her. If she feels any threat from you or any discomfort while in your presence, I will not hesitate to rethink my promise I made not to challenge you."

"Darcy, she lies!"

"My wife told me how she defended herself when you were out in the woodland with her." Darcy could not stop his upturned lips at the thought. "My stunning bride took you down, a man twice her size. Now, consider this to be a delayed response to your attack against her at Christmas." Just after these words were spoken, Darcy kicked him in the groin with his riding boot, satisfied when his cousin sucked in his breath, no longer able to throw defamatory accusations.

Darcy stepped over Langston and stood at the door. Before opening it, he turned and said, "Your father will be informed of your treachery, as will James. I cannot know how Uncle might respond, but James will support me. I have no desire to acquaint your wife with your faithlessness or to let any of this be made public, but be warned, I will defend my family whatever the cost to you or Matlock."

Langston lay there, seething, but unable to get up. While in their youth, he had always been able to impose upon Darcy or James without recourse. They were much younger than he, but now he was wise enough to realise that should it come down to a challenge, Darcy was the better shot, and swordsman for that matter. James was equally as dangerous but in a far less gentleman-like manner. Although full of pride and pretension, Langston knew that if he wanted to spare his own life, he would have to let his cousin have his way. If there was one thing the viscount knew about Darcy, it was that he never made idle threats.

When Darcy arrived home, he went straight to Elizabeth's chamber through the sitting room. As he opened the door, he saw that Elizabeth was sitting by the fire with Georgiana and Charlie. Elizabeth's eyes were red as she took in his appearance. He had been in the saddle all day and had not yet taken time to change. The weather was warm for the season, and the scenic ride had lifted Darcy's spirits considerably – that and the long-awaited thrashing upon the viscount. Though despite his own relief, he saw that his wife's mood was far from his own.

"Elizabeth, are you well?" He glanced to his sister. "Georgiana, could you take the puppy outside?" After Georgiana had left, Darcy knelt down next to his wife. "My love, what has you in tears?"

"How could you?"

"Elizabeth, please …"

"You could have been hurt or something terrible could have happened to you!" She covered her face as she cried in frustration.

"You have so little faith in me?"

"But he is vicious and without integrity."

"He is a coward, and anyway, I took him quite by surprise. I know he is a physical threat to you, but it has been long since I have had the advantage over him. The last time we fought, I soundly thrashed him, but that was years ago. He fears me much more than I fear him."

"I thought you would stay away from him."

"I could not let his assault against you go without recourse, Elizabeth. I did not challenge him, for your sake, but I had to ensure that he would no longer be a threat to you."

"What did he say?"

Darcy smiled at the remembrance of the debilitated heap he had left on the floor in the library of Matlock Estate. "He said very little, actually."

"Did he not deny what he did?"

"Truly, my love, he was given very little opportunity of saying anything. He will no longer be a threat to you." He squeezed her hand as he stood up. "Now, allow me to go to my room to change into something more comfortable, and then I will return and spend the entire evening turning those tears of worry into laughter."

"You defended me to your family."

"Something I should have done long ago."

THE DARCYS DID NOT HAVE LONG to wait to hear from the colonel, for about a month after Elizabeth's illness, when she had recovered fully, the Darcys received a surprise visitor. They had just sat down to dinner when Colonel Fitzwilliam walked into the dining-parlour and took a bow. "James!" exclaimed Georgiana as her face lit up upon his entrance.

"Don't get up on my account. I just wanted to alert you to my arrival. Peters will be setting a place for me so that I can join you after I clean up a bit."

Twenty minutes later, Colonel Fitzwilliam returned looking every bit the gentleman that his heritage had taught him to be. "My timing is impeccable. I have eaten very little today and have been daydreaming of Lambert's roasted lamb and potatoes." He sat down and joined the conversation, while taking in all of the subtle and extraordinary changes that had taken place in the relationships before him. Elizabeth was all smiles and blushes as she spoke with her husband and new sister. Darcy was obviously a lovesick puppy, reminiscent of Bingley, as he himself had spoken of Miss Bennet. While in the carriage with the Darcys on the way from Rosings to London, he had heard every word that Georgiana had spoken against Elizabeth and was pessimistic about his young cousin's acceptance of Darcy's wife. However, here she was, not only seemingly accepting, but in high spirits.

Fitzwilliam brought liveliness to the party that resulted in a convivial evening of animation and good humour. The time came for the traditional separation of the sexes, and although Fitzwilliam had much to share privately with Darcy, they all chose to stay together, retiring to the music room. The two women took turns entertaining the gentlemen, and Darcy had never felt more contented. His three favourite people in the world were in his home, sharing his life. Darcy knew why Fitzwilliam had come, likely deciding to bring the valuable package himself rather than trust it to servants. Based on the tone of the express that Fitzwilliam had sent to calm his fears about Wickham, Darcy also suspected that he came in person in order to enlighten him about the steps taken to protect Elizabeth's reputation, but for tonight, he was satisfied to let that wait for the morrow.

On the following day, after breakfast, Fitzwilliam approached Darcy requesting time alone with him in his study. "I had hoped to do just that. Elizabeth plans on taking Georgiana with her to visit one of the tenants who recently had a baby. She has decided to introduce Georgiana to the duties of being mistress to an estate by letting her join her visits. I thought at first that Georgiana might somehow take offence, but she seemed quite excited by the idea."

"It is remarkable the change that has come about. I suppose Georgiana just needed to see you happy – that and to see Elizabeth away from my family. My mother had shown your wife a great deal of civility, at least by her own standards, but the rest have been much less kind in their judgements. I am afraid they may have tainted our dear girl's receptivity until now."

Darcy looked away, but not before a flash of anger crossed his countenance. "Your family has been nothing but caustic to my marriage, except you, of course, and perhaps Vickie, although her husband was nothing but rude," he said as they entered his study. He walked over to a chair by the hearth, motioning for his cousin to join him. "Would you like tea or perhaps something else?"

"No, I had plenty at breakfast. I suppose you know why I have come."

"I suspect you are here for two reasons, and I hope one was a delivery."

Fitzwilliam reached into his pocket and retrieved a small box, handing it to his cousin with a smile. "You are correct. I had thought to send it with your courier as you had requested, but decided to come myself with the further inducement of sharing my tale with you sooner rather than later. I suppose you received my express?"

"I did. Thank you, and although it put my mind to rest, I admit that I have been most anxious to hear how you brought everything about. There are so many unanswered questions."

"Let's just say that I was able to convince Wickham the foolhardiness of attempting to extort money from a man of your character and means. The bruising took a while to come down, but when he was finally able to see the paper before him, he signed a statement saying that he was mistaken in his memories – that in truth he had only dreamt the story while in a drunken stupor. He wrote a promissory note of one thousand pounds – to me of course – should the story find circulation."

"Where is he now? Are you still keeping an eye on him?"

"That will not be necessary." At Darcy's raised brow, he continued, "He decided to take a trip to the former colonies. He set sail the other morning, just before I left for Pemberley."

"How did you convince him?"

"I prefer to keep that to myself, but let us just say that he preferred going to the alternative."

"Thank you, James. Your support means a great deal to me."

"Seeing you pleased as you are is all the thanks I need. I am happy for you. From your express, I assumed that you and Elizabeth worked through all of the suspicions on your end, but from experiencing you together last night, I would say that you did more than just resolve your doubts. How did everything come about?"

"I think you might change your mind about a drink. Perhaps something stronger than tea may be in order." Then Darcy went on to describe the treacherous deeds of Langston. "I had every intention of calling him out, but Elizabeth convinced me otherwise. Anyway, having his brother as my second seemed somewhat extreme."

"So you are just going to let him get away with it? I am surprised. He deserves whatever you might do to him. I might call him out myself if you do not."

"Elizabeth reminded me of where my true duties lie. Langston will one day answer for all of his deeds, but not by my hand, or yours. At any rate, I did end up paying him a visit. Although he got far less than he deserved, I was clear on my sentiments and expectations for the future. I plan on using his treachery to weigh on your parents. They will not be able to censure Elizabeth again with this hanging over them."

486

"I always knew that he could be self-indulgent, but I had no idea he could be this dangerous."

"I spent so much energy trying to help Elizabeth adjust to me and my family that I did not consider my own family's need for change, or mine for that matter. I trusted Langston based on nothing but his standing in society and as a member of my own family. I knew him to be an unfaithful husband and judgemental peer, but I sent him to be my wife's protector anyway. I have been a fool, but no longer."

"You are the best of men, Cousin. Elizabeth is lucky to have you."

"No, I am the fortunate one."

Darcy noticed that his cousin was fidgeting with his sleeve as he looked into the fire, a sure sign that something else was on his mind. He patiently waited for his cousin to speak.

"Darcy, about our family, there was one more thing that I discovered. I could not decide whether or not to tell you, but since you have opened up about my brother, I feel that I must not hold back."

"What is it, James?"

"Aunt Catherine."

"What does she have to do with anything?"

"Apparently Wickham has been under her employ for months now. She first paid him to attempt to break your engagement."

Darcy stood abruptly and leaned against the mantle as he considered Wickham's interference those many months ago. *The notes in Elizabeth's reticule.*

"That is not all though. Apparently, she promised him five thousand if he could somehow dissolve your marriage. Not knowing if he would be successful, he decided to try for the five thousand from you as well. He thought it was a win-win situation – that he would either earn the money from you to keep quiet or from her by forcing a divorce."

"Damn him! Well, he was unsuccessful on both counts. He wrote my wife letters, hoping I would see them. Now we know his goal. What I don't understand is how my aunt could have devised such a plan. Surely she knew her efforts would not find success. A divorce could only hurt the family."

"It would seem that Wickham's charms are not relegated to just the young. Apparently, he was able to convince Aunt Catherine that he could bring her success – that you would be free to marry Anne. She was likely desperate enough to fall under his spell. I swear he could talk a street urchin into believing she could one day marry the prince."

Darcy was deep in thought, about what to do concerning his aunt, when his cousin continued, "Will you confront her? Aunt Catherine remains unaware of our knowledge of her deceit."

"Why does it have to be so difficult? Why must my family behave like vultures? They have everything; why must they try to destroy Elizabeth?"

"I am just a lowly soldier. I cannot understand the inner-workings of the elitist's mind. Through my experiences though, I have come to realise that status does not determine a person's value, nor does money. I am a much happier man than I would have been as first born."

"You would have been a most worthy earl."

"No, I am thankful that is not my lot."

After a few moments of reflection on both sides, Darcy asked how long his cousin would be visiting. "I leave tomorrow for Matlock, but don't worry, I will be in Hertfordshire come June."

DARCY FELT THE TIME WAS RIGHT, and knowing that he and Elizabeth needed time away from the ears of servants, but in a setting that carried a different meaning than their private rooms, he invited his wife to take a turn about the gardens. "Elizabeth, as this is a fine day, and spring is making a pleasant showing, would you be agreeable to join me for a walk outside to explore the beauties of Pemberley?" She readily assented.

"Excellent. Thomas, please retrieve Mrs. Darcy's outerwear for her." He put out his hand for Elizabeth, who smiled demurely up at him as she stood. Her hand was without gloves and soft to touch. Darcy had rarely in his life felt the nervous rush of excitement that he felt as they awaited her jacket. Darcy had planned this day to complete a task that was long overdue. In so doing, he would be declaring to her in as sincere a way as he could his changed feelings.

Elizabeth chose not to wear her bonnet, as it would only be the two of them walking outside. She despised the social necessities of town and rarely joined in when she could avoid it. This freed Darcy from his own conventions, and they set out arm in arm to explore the burgeoning spring within the Pemberley landscape. They walked at a leisurely pace, which was much unlike Elizabeth's usual preference, but perfect for today's object, which would be revealed in time.

Elizabeth could tell that Mr. Darcy had something on his mind. For the past week, she had caught him staring at her with his dark features more than once. The corners of his mouth would go up slightly and his eyes would soften, as his personal thoughts ran their course in his enigmatic mind. Elizabeth had long become used to being the object of his gazes, but lately her heart would flutter when confronted with his stares. His admiration was apparent; his affections lay bare.

Once out of the view of the manor, Darcy took Elizabeth's hand off his arm, choosing to hold it within his own. As they now wore gloves, he felt that this was another social necessity that they should have chosen to do without. After several more minutes of walking in companionable silence, when his courage had mounted sufficiently, he stopped abruptly. They found themselves on a well-kept path that went through the woods, silent except for the rushing of water and the sound of birds within the trees preparing their nests for their own upcoming season.

Taking both of her hands in his own, Darcy confessed, "Elizabeth, six months ago, I had the then unknown privilege of requesting your hand in marriage. In my arrogance, I wrongly assumed that you were the one to receive all of the benefits inherent in our union. I accused you openly, and silently, of actively taking advantage of me and my interests. I didn't even have the strength of character to ask for your hand properly."

"Please, William, do not say such things. We have moved past that, have we not?"

"I had spent my adult life fending off women of my own social circle who wanted me only for my money, estate and family name. I had lamented the social climbing intentions of not just female admirers but also of other men who befriended me for what I could give them. I despised their assault and yet revelled in it as my due. Then unbeknownst to me, the one woman in all of England who was unimpressed with Fitzwilliam Darcy came into my life, and I was at a loss. I spurned you as I fabricated sins to mimic every other facet of society, actually more so, for I accused you of the iniquitous crime of trying to protect your family through our marriage. I had longed for a woman who could look past my fortune and care for me as the man that I am, and there you were before me, but I did not recognise you. I could not see at the time that you were exactly the woman I needed, the one who was most worthy of my own adoration.

"You suffered at my hands and my words, but courageously stayed strong. I admire your fortitude more than any other of my acquaintance. I tried to make you change, all along not conceiving that I was the one in need of change. I am relieved to admit my lack of success. By you I was properly humbled and was able to finally see my own deficiencies. I thank God everyday for bringing you into my life."

"William, please, you speak of deficiencies, but you have always been a man I could look up to, one whom – though trying for my natural liveliness – I could admire."

"You are too kind, my love. I know my faults well enough; and I know your virtues," he said, stopping and looking around for a moment before proceeding. "I notice that you do not wear the engagement ring that I gave you, nor the necklace."

Blushing, she answered his unspoken question, "When I overheard your conversation with the colonel about Mr. Bingley and Jane, I naïvely resolved never to accept another gift of any worth from you and so left the two pieces of any value at Darcy House. I was angry at your ungracious remarks about my family and my dear sister. I know it was childish of me, and I have regretted especially leaving the necklace behind, for I did admire it and knew that you had thoughtfully picked it out for me. I planned on retrieving them when next we went to town."

He smiled. That explained so much. How unjustified he had been in his quick judgement of her actions. "Elizabeth, the engagement ring that I gave you was purchased for that purpose. I was unwilling to give you the ring that you deserved, the one that my mother and my grandmother each wore when married into the family. I am ashamed to say that I feared your relationship with Wickham, that you might do something to the ring. When I saw that you no longer wore your engagement ring, in my lack of trust, I feared that I had been correct, that perhaps you had in fact given the ring away for Wickham's financial gain. You once called me a fool and now I see yet again that you were justified, although I could not see it then in my pride. I am ashamed of myself, but I mean to amend my mistake."

Then getting down on one knee, he began to remove her gloves, one finger at a time. While so doing, Darcy said with feeling, "Miss Elizabeth Claire Bennet, you have stolen nothing but my heart. I am yours and at your mercy." He paused as if to gather his thoughts. Tears had begun to fall from her eyes as her small hands trembled. "My pride led me to offer for you before, my pride for my family name, my false sense of honour based on how others viewed me. I claimed that I had offered for you to save your family, but now I see that it was not so. I have been humbled by you, and now I offer for you again not based on my pride or the scandal, or anything other than my great and abiding love for you and for you alone. Please say that you will accept this ring as a heartfelt token of my affection."

Then he pulled out of his pocket a diamond of such magnitude that Elizabeth gasped. It was a radiant emerald-cut stone flanked on either side by two equally brilliant diamonds of about a quarter the size and cut in like manner. He held her left hand within his own and slipped the ring upon her finger."

Elizabeth's tears were flowing uncontrollably, as she could not bear to remove her hands from his own to wipe them away. So instead, she wrapped her arms around his shoulders as he stood to embrace her. How long they stood there, Elizabeth could not say. She felt bereft when he pulled away, but that feeling soon fled when he bent down and claimed her mouth. The kiss started gently, more of a caress than anything else, but his not-yet-expressed need for her soon overcame his usual reserve in her company. She sensed his passion and could not help but respond in kind. Finally, he slowed down his exploration of her sweet mouth and finished the kiss. "Forgive me, my love, but I find that my control while in your presence is waning. I, I... I need to show you how I love you."

"You mean more than kisses, do you not?"

"Of course not here, but you must know that I long to be in union with you, as a man in love, not a man who takes and uses as I have in the past. I want to make you feel as gloriously satisfied as I." At her look of panic, he asked, "Do I scare you?"

"Yes, I am afraid. But I trust you. I cannot claim to equally want what you want – too much has happened. I can only say that I long to feel closer to you than I do now."

He smiled. "That is exactly what I want. Elizabeth, I will not hurt you; at least I will do everything in my power not to hurt you. I just want to love you physically and with my whole heart." Blushing, Elizabeth nodded her head in understanding. "But I will not come to you until you want me to. I promised that before, and I plan to hold to my word. I just hoped that maybe you might now want me to." He reached his hand up and moved a stray curl that was blowing in the breeze.

Elizabeth knew what he was asking of her, and although fearful – for she had only known pain and humiliation in the past – she could no longer deny him.

490

She loved him and wanted to give him whatever it was he needed from her, whatever he might ask of her. She had enjoyed the few times that he had slept in her room during the initial days of her illness, and she longed for him to do so again. "Will you come to me tonight?"

"If you will welcome me, then yes."

"Will you kiss me as you just did?" she asked with an arched brow and a hint of playfulness.

"I will kiss you like this," he said as he lovingly kissed her mouth again. "And like this," as he moved to her cheek. "And like this," as he kissed behind her ear, lingering until she shivered. His breath overwhelmed her.

"Well, I would by no means suspend any pleasure of yours, sir," Elizabeth said after she had caught her breath and was able to look into his eyes again. "Will you stay with me?"

"Of course, if you will have me," he said as he gave her an affectionate embrace and whispered in her ear, "Thank you, my sweet Elizabeth." Then he gave her another light kiss to seal the deal before they continued their walk.

DARCY, ELIZABETH AND GEORGIANA enjoyed dinner together in the dining-parlour. Elizabeth had asked Janette to take extra care in designing a playful, but alluring hairstyle. Elizabeth chose one of the gowns that her husband had picked out for her when she first arrived at Darcy House. Although she felt exposed, especially with the augmentation of her bosom owing to her pregnancy, she was not bothered by the idea, as she had been in the past. She knew her husband loved her and would enjoy seeing her dress especially for him.

Janette suspected something was different with the Darcys. A lady's maid was privy to many secret affairs of her mistress. She knew that Darcy had wanted records of his wife's courses at one time. Although unfamiliar with the details of the matter, she knew that the Darcys had, generally speaking, been in a platonic relationship since arriving at Pemberley, and she was certain that this could not be healthy in a marriage. Janette had come into Elizabeth's room more than once during her mistress's illness to find Mr. Darcy in bed with her. He was always dressed, and Mrs. Darcy had seemed too ill to do anything of a physical nature aside from sleeping. But things would be different tonight. Janette had already picked out a suitable nightdress and planned that her mistress's hair would be left down rather than plaited as usual. Also, when bathing, her maid had added extra rose water and spent additional time in her meticulous preparations.

After dinner, the threesome retired to the music room where Elizabeth and Georgiana took turns entertaining a distracted Darcy. He enjoyed their display but anxiously awaited the night ahead. Darcy was glad that he had been able to wait for Elizabeth's invitation, but now, when the time had finally come, he could not bear to delay another moment longer than necessary. Towards the end of the evening, Elizabeth chose a song that Darcy found most stimulating to his heightened senses, and he wondered if she had chosen it for that purpose. Regardless, when she was done, he stood, saying, "My dear, that was beautifully done, but on that note, I suggest that we all retire for the night." No one would blame him when he could not suppress the look of desire that had decisively and pertinaciously taken control of his mien. Elizabeth blushed, hoping her new sister had not noticed, as she herself had.

Before escorting Georgiana to her room, Darcy took his wife to her door and whispered for her ear alone that he would see her in half an hour's time. She smiled shyly at him before closing the door behind her. Darcy could not miss Elizabeth's enticing dress and coiffure. She had obviously gone out of her way for his sake, making herself appear to greatest advantage. He quickly went to his own room and called for Nelson to prepare him for the night ahead. Rather than don a nightshirt, he kept on his pants and shirt, but removed the rest of his clothing. He did not want to intimidate her before the night had begun.

How differently Darcy felt tonight than on their wedding night. In November, he had thought of himself alone, the pleasure he would experience and the future conveniences of having a wife available to meet his needs. Add to that, he cared nothing for his new, young and fearful wife. Elizabeth, though brave in so many ways, was frightened, lonely and distressed, yet he took her anyway and told her she was obligated to make herself available for him. In his distorted mind, she had nothing else to offer him. However, now, he wanted nothing more than to give her pleasure and to be available to her for comfort and to meet all of her physical needs. Darcy wanted to remove her fear and would even forego this evening if he felt that she was not ready to consummate their marriage in true love and affection. Now he saw that she offered him everything that could bring him true happiness, and that no one matched her ability to do so. How arrogant he had been, but he would spend the rest of their days together ensuring that she knew how valued and loved she was, how worthy of his adoration.

Elizabeth's thoughts tended towards a similar train. She, like her husband, found herself distracted while her lady's maid worked her magic. As Janette brushed out her long, thick locks, Elizabeth remembered her wedding night – as well as their other encounters – with trepidation. Could she bear another experience as she had undergone before? She recalled his animalistic inclinations; she thought of Lord Langston's vulgar advances. Nothing in her could anticipate with pleasure the night ahead, and yet, perhaps she did. When Darcy held her during those nights of her illness, Elizabeth felt a true peace of mind and comfort. She imagined, while in his arms, his gentle caresses and tender kisses. She felt a longing, deep inside of her, to be loved by him, but she could not reconcile those desires with her experience.

In nervous agitation, she bit her lower lip as she strummed her fingers on her now curved belly. "You look lovely this evening, Mrs. Darcy. Your husband will find himself bewitched by your charms."

Elizabeth's eyes widened as she blushed yet again. "You must find me quite diverting with my unreasonable fears. He is my husband, and I am carrying his child, for goodness sake!"

"Mrs. Darcy, you have nothing to be frightened of; your husband loves you."

"Yes, he does."

"Would you like some wine?"

"I think not."

Elizabeth continued in silent contemplation of the night ahead until Janette left her to herself. She entered her room and waited for Darcy to join her. It did not take long before he knocked gently on the door and opened it. She was standing by the fire, shivering from the cold ... or was that fear? She could barely look at him as she nervously glanced to the bed and then the floor before her.

When Darcy opened the door into Elizabeth's chamber, he stopped short. There she was, just as he had remembered from the cabin, backlit by the fire, but instead of a wet shift, she wore a silky dressing gown of creamy white. Her hair cascaded down her back, soft curls framing her face. Elizabeth had briefly glanced at him, and in her eyes, he saw an array of emotions. He smiled fondly as he considered how well he had come to know this woman before him. Darcy saw embarrassment, apprehension and something else. He had seen it before, even earlier today, and he understood the disturbance of her mind to be passion, though she did not.

He walked up to her and took her hands in his. When Elizabeth continued looking down, he lifted her chin up to behold her continued look of trepidation. She was unknowingly biting her lower lip, a gesture that he always found fetching, but her obvious discomposure reminded him to show restraint. "You are so very beautiful, my love." Then he reached up further to caress her cheek, as she instinctively leaned into his touch. "Are you cold? You tremble." He rubbed her arms as he gazed into her eyes, which had now found an object in his own.

"You will think me a coward, but despite carrying your child, I find that I am rather uneasy. Please forgive me; I am trying not to let my past experiences affect tonight, but I...."

"Shh," he said as he leaned down and kissed her gently on her cheek where his hand had just been. She felt the now familiar tingling down her back, as she closed her eyes to his tender touch. Darcy moved to her ear with his soft lips, whispering, "I love you, my darling."

"I know."

He smiled and lightly kissed her behind the ear. "You sound rather confident."

"I am, you see," she sighed contentedly, "for it is in every touch, kiss, gaze, word, and caress that you give me."

She stopped speaking as his mouth had slowly made its way to her own as he lingered there to savour her welcoming lips. Darcy explored her mouth as his arms wrapped about her waist. He noticed her legs giving way, so in a fluid motion he picked her up as he had on that nightmarish night when he had carried her to safety, but tonight he need only cross the room to her canopied bed. His bundle was no less precious tonight as he laid her down on the feathered bedding.

The initial agitation upon her countenance had disappeared as the passion became unmistakable. She shared equal delight in his ardent kisses as he had hers. Darcy left her mouth and began to trail kisses down her neck, always gentle, always loving. He tasted her ear, her throat, her neck again as he untied and opened her dressing gown. Her nightdress was modest, yet still enticing, in the satiny silk that hugged her skin. His kisses dared to go lower as he longed for more of her. But he held back, greatly desiring her, but more so desiring her accord. He lifted her torso off the bed as he pulled the dressing gown off his wife's shoulders, her smooth, milky skin drawing his mouth to her yet again. More than once, he felt himself losing control, but then remembered the trepidation in her eyes, and so restrained his passion.

What he could not fully fathom was that Elizabeth, too, felt an undeniable desire building within her. She longed for his exquisite touch and began to wish most fervently that he would lose himself to caressing her. She had never felt so wanton, as her timidity had given way to desire. So, almost without thought, Elizabeth boldly took his hand in hers and brought it to her breast. The invitation was clear, and he could not refuse.

The next moments were spent in physical giving and taking. Elizabeth of course had nearly no experience in the art of lovemaking. She had never known that the feelings, which she now possessed, were even possible. One moment she felt ever so naughty and the other completely consumed by feelings of rightness. She knew not how to give him the same pleasure, but soon found that, on this night anyway, she need only accept his ministrations to bring him enjoyment.

Before Elizabeth knew what had happened, her husband had divested himself and covered them with the blankets. Her only thought was to be ever closer to him; indeed could she feel close enough? That question was soon answered as he made love to her in truth, speaking the silent language of shared intimacy. Elizabeth suffered no apprehension; in truth, she would have been pleased had she been able to capture the moment to revisit whenever the fancy took hold.

Darcy could never have imagined such bliss. If he had considered their previous encounters satisfying, he now knew his error. His wife's wilful giving of herself to him, her own pleasurable responses, provided him with profound transport and gratification. How wrong he had been to consider their previous moments of intimacy to be sufficient. But then Darcy noticed tears streaming down her face. "My love, am I hurting you?"

She shook her head as she tried to speak. "No, I just, I just never knew."

He looked in her eyes in the darkened room. "What did you not know?"

"That it could be like this," she replied clearly overwhelmed by the moment.

He kissed her forehead, then her lips before saying, "Neither did I."

The two continued in mutual sharing of each other, as he fulfilled his vow on their wedding day to worship her body. Darcy expressed his love for her as God intended in marriage, and she him. The fears and pain of the past were forgotten as Elizabeth was enveloped in the love of her husband. As promised, he stayed with her. In truth, he could not have left had she asked him to. His demand for her had grown beyond the intense moment of copulation. He too needed to hold and to be held. With contented satisfaction, he bundled her in his arms as they

494

drifted to sleep, each with a new appreciation for the marriage bed and the one who brought exceeding fulfilment.

Chapter Twenty-Three

*Now to him who is able to do far more abundantly than all that we
ask or think, according to the power at work within us, to him be
glory in the church and in Christ Jesus throughout all generations,
forever and ever. Amen.*
Ephesians 3:20-21

Darcy and Elizabeth had never experienced a honeymoon; neither had even considered the idea of secluding themselves in some distant county or land to block out the stresses of life while learning the physical intimacies of marriage. Of course, with many marriages of convenience, couples might take a companion or even family for the new wife on the journey, so that she should not find her husband's constant company a bother. But even that had not occurred to Fitzwilliam Darcy during the first few months of marriage. He had spent much time alone with his wife, but he had never truly appreciated the need for withdrawing from society for the purpose of intimacies, until now. Unfortunately for Darcy, the time was quickly approaching that they should leave Pemberley for Hertfordshire for Jane and Bingley's wedding preparations. Jane greatly desired her sister's presence in advance of the wedding, and Darcy could deny his wife nothing that would bring Elizabeth happiness, and indeed Jane's joy was her own.

Darcy and Elizabeth now had appreciated several weeks of exploring the physical – and spiritual – blessings of the married state. Although at first modest in her dress, Elizabeth soon saw her gown as an impediment to their union, and after perceiving the influence that her bare shape had on her husband, she gladly refrained from wearing anything unnecessary. At first she had been embarrassed, not just about baring all, but also about her now rounded frame, but Elizabeth quickly overcame such emotions as passion seemed ever more in control of her sensibilities – and the effect upon her husband could not have been more supportive, for he had never seen a vision more captivating and exquisite than his disrobed wife, tousled hair cascading down her feminine figure and a gentle blush for his eyes alone.

Elizabeth had never looked at her husband's naked form before. In the past, she would squeeze her eyes shut, so as not to be intruded upon by disturbing visions of the male physiognomy, but no more. Her husband's fine composition became an object of much scrutiny and admiration to the young bride's eyes. Although she had seen pictures in books of famous artistic renderings depicting some Greek or Roman god of old, Elizabeth had never considered the magnificence of the reality and found that her curiosity far outweighed her apprehension.

Elizabeth had worried that her lack of experience would somehow take away some of her husband's pleasure. She knew married men often took on mistresses or visited courtesans, and although she no longer dwelt on that possibility for her own husband, she did consider that a man must want something more than a wife could provide. However, nature took its course and she soon learnt the art of giving as well as taking, that she too derived much enjoyment when able to stimulate in her husband such fervour and delight. Although not on the first night of their newly consummated union, Elizabeth also found her own apogee, surprising them both in rapturous gratification. Darcy had discovered yet another accomplishment of which his wife could boast, perceiving that the more public talents – that he had once openly lauded in the female – held no advantage over the more private variety.

Darcy often recalled the conversation months ago with his cousin, Fitzwilliam, who had said that Elizabeth was a lovely woman with a true passion for life. Fitzwilliam had suggested to Darcy that he consider the benefits to such a wife. "Her passionate nature could mean many nights of pleasure for you." *Indeed.*

"HUSBAND," ELIZABETH SAID ONE MORNING while nestled underneath the linens on Darcy's spacious bed. He was sitting at his escritoire jotting down a quick note to leave next to her on the pillow before his morning ride. He was hoping she would sleep in, for she was in much need of rest. "You are headed out?"

He looked up from his writing. "Lizzy, you are awake. I hope I did not disturb you."

Her drowsy eyes had been watching him intently as he exhibited the same exacting standard writing a short note as he would a letter of business, only on this occasion, his lips were upturned as he was obviously contemplating some pleasure he had known. Yet, unhappily Elizabeth remembered the last time she had been at his small desk while looking for a quill pen. "Why do you keep that card? — The one from that brothel. Surely you have no need to keep it, do you?"

Darcy took in a deep breath, recalling how his wife must have felt when she had first learnt of his inconstancy, but he desired to put her mind at rest now – to leave no room for misunderstanding. "When I arrived home that awful night, I had planned on burning the blasted thing – to rid myself of the reminder of my guilt, but I stopped myself. I realised that the reminder might serve me well." Darcy twirled his quill pen as he purposely spoke. "You see, when a man is his own master, and of a grand estate such as Pemberley, it is easy to fall into the misapprehension that he has somehow earned the praise that naturally accompanies such a position – to by some means suppose that he deserves the blessings bestowed upon him. I never want to forget that I am vulnerable just like any other man, whatever his station.

"When I left town, I decided to bring the card with me rather than leave it behind. I returned to Pemberley determined to resolve our differences, and I thought that having the card might be a tangible reminder of my own errors to help me to overcome my previous resentment that I had let come between us." Darcy saw Elizabeth's brow crease at his words. He did not mean to pain her. "I would open the drawer to look upon the card each morning and determine to show you the grace that I myself desired. The card would admonish me."

"You must have used the card often then?" Elizabeth asked as a sad look overspread her sleepy countenance.

"At first, yes. But soon – not more than a few days really – I no longer needed its constant reproof. I had already and quite unconsciously developed a tender regard for you, my love. I understood that you had every right to be piqued; I just wanted us to move beyond our differences. But I will destroy the card; I would not wish to cause you pain."

"As much as I dislike your keeping your little memento, and agree that it should be destroyed, I am grateful for your dedication towards improvement. It shows a real strength of character I believe, not often witnessed."

"Now how am I supposed to work on my humility when I have you praising me? It was much easier when your approbation came so seldom."

"I just did not know you then. Now I see many things for which to admire you," she smiled, "not the least of which is your uncanny ability to make the argument of carrying a calling card to a brothel seem noble."

THREE WEEKS BEFORE THE BINGLEY and Bennet wedding was to take place, the Darcys packed their trunks and began their journey to Hertfordshire. They were to stay at Netherfield, at Bingley's invitation and Darcy's relief. The couple, with Georgiana in tow, arrived in Meryton just before dark three days after their journey began. Darcy had offered to take Georgiana to London instead, since he was concerned that she might not appreciate an extended stay with the Bennet connection; however, she told him that she would like to get to know Elizabeth's family before making a judgement on them, as she had so erroneously done with her new sister. Indeed, Georgiana had come to love Elizabeth as a dear friend. When Darcy was answering mail or taking exercise, the two women were rarely apart, even if only in quiet companionship. When the ladies of the Derbyshire neighbourhood called, Georgiana openly showed her approbation for her new sister, thus making a public declaration of her support. So she felt that meeting the Bennets, about whom she was so curious, would be yet another show of acceptance into her family.

The day after their arrival, the Darcys travelled the short distance to Longbourn giving true joy to everyone, especially Mrs. Bennet who had longed for another occasion to boast of Mr. Darcy's company. Two days after they had arrived, while visiting the Bennets yet again, Mrs. Bennet pulled Elizabeth aside in the garden for a chat. "Lizzy, you look so well in your expensive clothes. I can barely tell you are with child."

"Thank you, Mama," answered Elizabeth, resigned to her mother's continued distractions.

"I am glad you are no bigger than you are, for people might think that you had anticipated your vows. You know how people like to talk."

"I am well aware of that practice, for that is why I am now married," answered she, her mother oblivious to her daughter's subtle allusion to her own contribution to their marriage. Although frustrated by her mother, Elizabeth could no longer take umbrage, for she never would have married Mr. Darcy if not for the woman's meddling ways.

In hushed tones, very unlike her usual, her mother then said, "The baby is your husband's is it not? Wickham was spreading rumours, you know, that would suggest otherwise not two months ago, before he suddenly disappeared."

"Mama! Of course Mr. Darcy is the father! How can you think that I would do such a thing? Wickham is a villain and should not be trusted. I believe Mr. Darcy wrote to Papa telling him of the man's corruption and deceit."

"Yes, your father told me, but I had to ask myself. Don't take offence, my dear. I meant no harm. Mr. Wickham was so charming, and your husband, so severe." Then a few moments later the conversation continued on, shocking Elizabeth even more. "I do hope you carry your husband's heir, for your sake. And at least until the baby comes, you are able to make excuses for retirement."

Elizabeth was afraid to ask and felt it best not to know what her mother could mean. However, her mother's cause only gained momentum. "I am sure by now you know that men desire more than what a gently-born lady can provide by way of corporeal attentions. To your benefit, Mr. Darcy can afford an alternative. As I have said before, all great men have mistresses, and I would bet my pin money for a month that Mr. Darcy has one in town. I know he has one near his aunt's home, for Mr. Collins said so."

"Madam!" came a deep baritone voice from behind them startling both the older woman and Elizabeth. "You know not of what you speak. I demand that you cease filling my wife's head with tales of despicable behaviour that have no basis in truth. Your son-in-law, Mr. Collins, has no understanding and is spreading lies that besmirch my character. I insist that you keep your misplaced assumptions and unverified lies to yourself. If you were a man, I would have to call you out for such a speech."

Elizabeth was mortified that Darcy had to witness her own mother's uncouth remarks. The sad truth was that her mother likely saw no harm in her words.

"Mr. Darcy! I intended no disrespect! Oh my, I just meant that men of your means have…"

"Silence, woman!" Then looking to his wife, his countenance softened. "Elizabeth, my love, please go inside." Elizabeth's eyes grew large, as she knew not what her husband would then say to her mother. She was not to find out; however, from that point forward, she never heard a disparaging remark from her mother about her husband, herself, or her marriage. Mrs. Bennet, at least while the Darcys were in residence, with obvious trial, held her tongue much to everyone's surprise and considerable comfort. And although it took away some of Mr. Bennet's entertainment, he was happy to see that his favourite daughter found peace while at home.

When Mr. Collins and Mary arrived for the festivities the week of the wedding, Elizabeth's sister showed open judgement on Darcy. Elizabeth had written her to correct her mistaken intelligence on the matter, but apparently she had not believed her. Elizabeth was ashamed of her family's cold welcome towards her husband, but Darcy was quick to soothe her, for who at Longbourn could compare to his own relations? The benefit was that Mr. Collins kept his distance from the "dishonourable" couple, giving them the pleasure of time alone in the gardens or shrubbery where they were enthusiastic in their explorations of the many places to hide in togetherness amongst the boughs.

One afternoon, while Mr. Bennet sat in his study, he heard a knock upon the door. After bidding entrance, Darcy walked in and requested an audience. "I wondered how long it would take for you to tire of talk of frippery and lace. As there are few places to provide sanctuary, I expected your arrival at some point and fairly suspected it would be sooner than this."

After sitting down, Darcy began, "I rather thought I was paying my due. I feel that I deserve whatever trials come by such domestic clamouring." At his father-in-law's raised brow, he continued, "In truth, I came to, well, to offer my sincerest apologies that are long overdue." Darcy shifted in his chair, uncomfortable with admitting his faults, but determined to make amends. "I arrived at Longbourn that day last autumn and offered for your daughter's hand in marriage, completely confident in my own merits and Elizabeth's deficiencies. I thought that she was to receive all of the benefits of such a union. I am certain that you laughed at me and my conceit," he pondered. "But no, how could you laugh when such a man as I was to marry your daughter?

"I have since come to regret my arrogance at your family's expense. Your gracious daughter taught me her true worth. I am indeed indebted to her! Elizabeth was instrumental in my improvement. By her I was properly chastened. I came to you without a doubt of your family's inferiority and my self-importance, but Elizabeth showed me how insufficient were all my pretensions to deserve a woman as worthy as she."

"Mr. Darcy, it takes a strong man to admit his shortcomings."

"On the contrary, sir. It is through my weaknesses that I have been able to see clearly to my faults. Admitting them to you has been the least challenging part of the business. With your daughter by my side, I feel as though I am becoming a better man."

"I see that Lizzy has indeed improved in your estimation?"

"It has been many weeks since I have admired – more than that – have loved Elizabeth. You once compared her to the divine, and I thought you foolish. Now I see I was the fool, yet again." Darcy sat in contemplation as Mr. Bennet watched on, not daring to interrupt such a heartfelt and entertaining speech, hoping there was more to come. He was not disappointed. "She called me a fool once, while teasing, you see, but her intentions were clear. You were correct when you said that there was no other woman in England who could match Elizabeth's estimable qualities. I now say none within the whole of the Kingdom. She is without equal, and she is mine." Darcy provided a broad smile to Elizabeth's astonished father as he contemplated the woman with whom he was joined for life. He could not help himself, so happy was he.

"I see. So, does that mean that Elizabeth is now more than tolerable? I would hate for you to find such exceptional qualities joined to a face lacking charms. But then, to have such perfection in person and character united cannot be common."

"Mr. Bennet, your daughter is extraordinary in every way; I do not deserve her love, but she has bestowed it upon me nonetheless. I will forever spend my life repenting of my behaviour the first few months of our marriage."

"As Elizabeth has forgiven you, I suppose I have no choice. She is happy, more so than I have ever seen her. I cannot deny it." Mr. Bennet then reached over across his desk from where he had been sitting and shook Darcy's hand. "Welcome to our family, Darcy. We are honoured to have you. Of course, Mr. Collins will remain as my favourite son-in-law, but I believe that one day you may surpass him, if what I hear about your library at Pemberley is an accurate account."

"You are most welcome to our home whenever you wish to make the journey, to town or Pemberley." A comfortable silence then set the stage for mutual reflection upon the path to their current felicity until a smirk crossed the face of Darcy's father-in-law.

"My Lizzy called you a fool, eh?"

THE DAY OF THE WEDDING ARRIVED with a rush of excitement. Elizabeth had chosen, much to her husband's vexation, to stay at Longbourn the night before the nuptials, to be there for her dearest sister. Elizabeth had promised Janette's masterful talents to be practised upon Jane, not that she needed any such expertise to highlight her graceful beauty. While Jane wore a dress to match the blush of her cheeks, Elizabeth wore a lavender silk creation covered with a sheer, white overlay. As her bosom was now even more ample than usual, she chose a squared neckline that highlighted the pearl necklace her husband had presented to her near Christmastime, while in town. They each manifested a picture of comeliness not often witnessed outside the enhanced portraits hanging upon the walls of society's drawing rooms. Each carried a bouquet of white roses with lavender and thyme interspersed within to mark the virtue and courage so often witnessed by their beaux.

Elizabeth stood up with her sister, as Jane had wanted, but only after much pleading on her sister's part. Elizabeth was embarrassed to stand in front of the church in obvious gravid display; however, her husband had the final say and exerted his right as husband to insist she acquiesce.

"Darcy, what are your relations doing here?" asked a puzzled Elizabeth as the Fitzwilliams entered the church.

"Hmm? Oh, perhaps they considered your sister family enough to attend."

"I think not, since if I remember correctly, they missed my own wedding. I will greet them and find out the truth."

"No, my dear, you can speak after the wedding, it is time to take our places."

After Bingley and Jane had spoken their vows, however, Elizabeth was completely taken by surprise. As the newly married couple stepped aside, Darcy took the two steps over to his wife and took her hands in his, saying, "My dearest Elizabeth, will you do me the greatest honour of marrying me?"

Elizabeth's eyes became like saucers as she looked up into his face. "What can you mean, Darcy? Are we not already married?" She leaned in close to finish, saying, "I certainly hope so, for we have a baby between us."

He smiled as he explained for her and the rector alone, "Seven months ago, we stood here and made wedding vows that neither of us had any desire of keeping. That has changed. And I want you, your family, my family and all of England to know that I, Fitzwilliam Darcy, love you and would marry you again if given the choice."

Elizabeth smiled a large becoming smile and said, "You seem to be staking a lot on the assumption that I would marry *you* again. Well, I suppose since you are so rich, *and handsome*, that I will comply with your little exhibition." She looked out to the congregation to see the whispering taking place, and then continued, "Last time I married out of love for my family, but this time I marry out of love for you. I would be pleased to accept your offer."

And so, in front of all those congregated, Fitzwilliam Darcy married Elizabeth Bennet Darcy, again. A public display such as that could not fail to make its mark in the society papers the following day. Although still not accepting of the match, the earl and countess could not deny the invitation to come. Darcy had written to his uncle telling him of the viscount's treachery and attack on his wife. He threatened repercussions that would forever divide the family unless they were to, in all ways required, show public support and affirmation for his marriage. The earl and countess brought with them their daughter, Lady Victoria, whose husband had again chosen not to come, but whose presence was not missed.

The wedding breakfast, held at Longbourn afterwards, was a scrumptious affair and truly highlighted Mrs. Bennet's one true accomplishment. She was subdued in the presence of nobility – perhaps in part out of reverence, but certainly a direct layover from her private conversation with Elizabeth's husband.

Colonel Fitzwilliam attended the wedding and breakfast afterwards but had to make a hasty retreat to Brighton on war business. However, he would not have missed the renewal of the Darcy vows for a house in town off Grosvenor Street. "Darcy, my friend, you have made a wise decision marrying up as you have," said he as he leaned over to kiss Elizabeth's hand.

"I am well aware of the great advantage that has come my way in securing my wife's hand in marriage – again, no less."

"Elizabeth, you are radiant, but you know that in marrying my austere cousin again, you put yourself at risk of renewing the jealousies of all the women of the *ton*, reminding them anew that you were successful in securing one of the wealthiest men in England."

"Is he that rich? I had no idea, I am sure."

"Indeed he is. Now do you regret your decision?"

"Hmm," said she as she tapped her finger to her cheek, "I suppose since it is too late to change my mind, I will have to accept my lot without regrets, but I shall not marry the affluent man a third time."

The three laughed at the absurdity of the conversation, but then the Colonel became more serious when he said, "Elizabeth, I want you to know that I am pleased you are in the family. I have never seen my cousin happier. He verily glowed when repeating the vows, in earnest this time."

"Your cousin is a superior man, and I would marry him as many times as necessary, if it pleases him."

Before leaving, Fitzwilliam pulled Darcy aside to tell him what had happened with Langston while at Matlock. "Darcy, I too spoke with Langston about his dealings with your wife."

"James."

Holding up his hand, the colonel continued, "I just made certain he knew that you love your wife dearly and reaffirmed your strictures on him. He also knows that I would support you in whatever way you deemed necessary in order to secure your wife's safety. I left him fearful of your changing your mind one day, for he knows your skill at sword and pistols. I assured him that I would second you without a moment's thought. He tried to blame Mrs. Darcy at first, but I disabused him of the notion. Truly, I never knew him to be such a coward."

"He has always been so. Only a coward would treat a woman, the weaker sex, as he does. I would say, 'the sex unable to defend themselves,' however now I know differently."

"What do you mean?"

"Let me just say that my wife is quite accomplished in the skill of defence against a man."

Fitzwilliam laughed, "You don't say. You told me she got away but did not tell me how, and Langston certainly did not say anything. You must be careful in the future not to say or do anything to make her angry."

"There was something else that I meant to ask you while at Pemberley, but it quite escaped me when you mentioned my aunt. Did Wickham happen to say how he obtained my wife's handkerchief? That is the one part of our dealings that has me confused."

"What are you two men whispering about?" asked Elizabeth, stepping up and putting her arm through her husband's. "I promised to love, honour and obey, but I do not remember saying anything about keeping out of your private conversations."

"It is nothing, my dear."

"I heard you mention my handkerchief, so it must concern me. Please, do tell."

Fitzwilliam looked over to Darcy and said, "If you will excuse me, I must say goodbye to my parents and Vickie."

They said their farewells, and when Fitzwilliam walked away, Elizabeth turned to her husband and said, "Darcy, what is the matter? And what were you saying about my handkerchief?"

"Curiosity is your true fault, isn't it, my love?" Darcy said smiling fondly at her. Then he continued, "When I went to town at my sister's summons, she gave me a handkerchief, specifically one of yours that your sister had made for you. Georgiana told me that Wickham had shown it to her as proof of your affection for him."

"But how did he get it?"

"That is what I had hoped Fitzwilliam would tell me."

Then Elizabeth recalled having left one in Hertfordshire on her last visit. "Darcy, I am only missing one. Do you remember the day that you arrived and found me with Wickham?" He looked at her, eyebrow raised. "Of course you do. Forgive me. When I left my room, I went to Lydia's. I was very upset and must have left it in there. I suppose she gave it to him herself."

"But why?"

"She has had an infatuation with him for some time, and she is not the brightest girl." She stood contemplating the idea. "I will ask her."

"No, please do not. I have no doubt in your innocence. I was just curious. Let's just drop it."

"If that is your preference, then I will think on it no more; but you do still have it?"

"Yes, it is at Darcy House."

"Then I am satisfied. Jane's gifts mean so much to me that I would hate to no longer have it in my possession. I already sacrificed one to your wounds that day in the woods."

As if on cue, Jane and Bingley walked up. "Oh, Lizzy, I am so happy for you."

Elizabeth laughed, "Only you, Jane, would think of me and my pleasure on your own wedding day. But as happy as I know you to be, I think that I may be more so."

"I would have it no other way."

"But, dear sister, I cannot help but worry that we intruded upon your own special day. Did you know of my husband's secretive designs to take over your wedding?"

"Oh, Lizzy, do not think that way. When Charles mentioned the idea to me, I fondly remembered the many times of our youth when we had spoken of a double wedding and how perfect it would be for us all."

Bingley then went on to say how grand it was, for the two sisters who loved each other so well, that their long hoped for double wedding would be realised on that day, even if a little unconventional in its execution.

"Bingley," said Darcy as he shook his hand. "I thank you for accommodating us, my friend. Also, I must wish you congratulations! You look well pleased. I do not think you could have chosen a bride more perspicaciously," he finished with all sincerity.

"I am sure I know not what that means, but I can say that I have never been more pleased, and now we are brothers!" Then turning to Elizabeth, he continued, "and you are my dear sister. Thank you for taking such good care of my Jane all these years. She has told me time and again about your kindnesses towards her."

"She has? But did she tell you of all the times that she had to take care of her overly zealous sister? I certainly owed her a great deal of recompense for her efforts during our growing up years."

"I know nothing about that, but I do know about your recent generosity in securing my angel's future. However, I can no longer let you continue on as you have. In fact I plan on putting the money thus far given into an account for your other sisters. Perhaps Darcy would like to help as well."

504

Elizabeth's eyes widened as she realised that Darcy was likely just now learning of her contributions to her sister's dowry fund. Turning to him, she said, "I can explain."

He held up his hand, "No need to. I know all about how you have been sending your pin money each month to help your dearest sister and friend. You are most generous and an example that I mean to follow. So yes, Bingley, I too would like to add to their dowries, if it is acceptable to Mr. Bennet, that is. I will speak with him before we leave Hertfordshire to set up the details."

"Thank you, Fitzwilliam. You are most generous. I had no notion of your ever doing so, I can assure you."

"I know, and I also know that you did not marry me with that expectation. I want to help." This earned two lovely smiles from the eldest Bennet sisters.

"You are truly a good man, Mr. Darcy. I knew when Lizzy married you that you both would somehow find contentment, but now I see that you have found so much more."

"We are now brother and sister. Must you call me Mr. Darcy? Please, call me either Darcy as everyone else, or perhaps Brother, as my sister does."

"Very well, Brother, and you must call me Jane."

Bingley and Jane soon departed for town. Darcy had offered his home for the following three days before the couple would catch a boat to the continent. The Darcys would stay on at Netherfield until that time, giving the newly married couple time to become better acquainted without his sisters around. Unfortunately for Darcy and Elizabeth that meant that they, in turn, would have the tiresome pleasure of Bingley's sisters' company without the benefit of Bingley's presence, but each would take it in stride. It had been quite scandalous upon their arrival when Darcy requested his former room for both him and his wife.

"But Mr. Darcy, we have a room for your wife just across the hall from you. I am certain that you both will be much more comfortable that way, for I recently realised that your former room has not the space for two," Miss Bingley had said.

"And where is Georgiana to stay?" asked he.

"Just two doors down from your own chamber."

"I see. If it is acceptable to you and to Georgiana, put her in the room across from me and my wife."

"But there is only one dressing room, Mr. Darcy," said Miss Bingley as she had continued to attempt to change his mind. "And the bed is too small."

"Thank you, Miss Bingley, for your kind attentions, but we are happy to share accommodations, especially in light of the bed, are we not, my love?" he said turning to his wife who was trying not to let out a giggle. Elizabeth had developed a real fondness and appreciation for her husband's dry and subtle humour. The look on Miss Bingley's face almost caused her to lose her countenance while her husband appeared as serious as he ever had been. Elizabeth had come to realise that Darcy had a knack for holding in his true feelings when it served his purposes; however, now she could read him and all of his previously indistinguishable nuances as she had her father. *How like my papa this man is!* But as with Mr. Collins was with her papa, the novelty of Miss Bingley as a source of entertainment had soon worn off.

While at the wedding breakfast, Miss Bingley stood off to the side with her sister, Louisa, and her husband, Mr. Hurst. She found plenty to talk about as she attempted to disparage Mrs. Bennet's choices, but even her sister could not agree this time. Everything about the day had gone smoothly and without blemish. Louisa had even found Mr. Darcy's impromptu sharing of vows romantic and touching. If only her own husband adored her has Mr. Darcy had so obviously adored his wife, she would be more than pleased. Louisa saw Caroline's words for what they were – the green monster of envy.

The Gardiners were also at the wedding, delighted to witness the nuptials, and renewal of the same, respectively, of their favourite nieces. They had been at Longbourn since two days prior, spending as much time as was possible with the Darcys. Mrs. Gardiner was able to share some stories with Georgiana about her parents from times past. "I once held you in my arms, Miss Darcy, when my father came to visit Pemberley. I begged him to take me to see the new baby. I was but fourteen. I remember that you were so small in my arms." Then reaching over to her and touching the young woman's arm she said, "Your mother was so proud of you; I can still remember. She loved you so." This brought Georgiana both joy and pain as she considered a life without a mother, but was pleased that she now had a sister in her life and a whole new family to love. During the visit, Georgiana had come to respect the wise and comforting words of Darcy's former infatuation, the *older woman* from his youth, as they recalled yet again the stories that had already been shared with Darcy, but without Elizabeth's or Georgiana's presence. The Gardiners were to leave in the morning with a promise to have dinner at Darcy House the following week.

The wedding and subsequent breakfast were splendid successes. The day ran long as the Darcys remained at Longbourn until most all of the guests had departed. The Fitzwilliams left for London shortly after the colonel had gone, happy that their obligation had been fulfilled with as little trouble as possible. They had spoken politely to Elizabeth and her family hoping to appease Darcy and his justified entreaty for restitution for their son's abhorrent actions. Lady Victoria, who was soon to be known as *Vickie* to Elizabeth, took time during the festivities, before their departure, to become better acquainted with her new cousin. Her brother, the colonel, had high regard for Elizabeth, which was enough to open her heart towards the younger woman. She found a most agreeable companion who would one day, with time, become the closest of friends. As Elizabeth and the colonel shared a liveliness of spirit, his sister, who also shared that same trait, could not help but love her.

That night Elizabeth slept soundly in her husband's arms as she dreamt of the events of the day. She had never been more hopeful of her life as Mrs. Fitzwilliam Darcy.

ELIZABETH HAD CONTINUED her morning walks with her husband by her side. Miss Bingley, who had now finished her tenure as mistress of her brother's home, sniggered behind Elizabeth's back, wondering if Mrs. Darcy would ever become a true lady. Mr. Darcy seemed to have been roped into her wild ways, or perhaps attempted to limit her uncivilised excursions by keeping watch. Had Miss Bingley known Darcy's true pleasure derived from a morning walk with the woman he loved, she might have felt more jealousy than disdain, but she would remain in preferred ignorance. Early, on the morning following the wedding, shortly after dawn, the couple found themselves near the setting of their infamous meeting.

"William, do you recognise this place?"

He looked around, the woods seeming as similar here as anywhere, but then understanding dawned on his face. "Is this where I practically ran you over?"

She laughed, "I am glad you now see the truth for what it is. Yes, this is the place. I was walking, or perhaps running, this way, and you came galloping up the path from over there," she said while pointing down the way. You fell off your horse right over there," she said as she walked in that direction. "Your horse dragged you a good distance into the woods that way. I will show you where you were finally released."

Darcy followed her past the bramble and mature oaks until she stopped. He stood behind her and so could not see her expression as she looked onto the spot where his foot had found its freedom. Her hand reached up and covered her face as she began to cry. He had become used to the emotional outbursts that accompanied the state of being with child, but he could not account whatsoever for her current spontaneous display. "Lizzy, are you well?" he asked gently, walking up and touching her shoulder with his right hand. She turned halfway towards him, which allowed him to see her tears. Rather than ask again, he just took her in his embrace and soothed her while she cried.

"Don't you see?"

"No, my love, I do not. What has you so distraught this morning?"

She pulled back wiping her eyes and pointed to a large oak that had fallen to the ground. The sight was no different than another along their walk. Elizabeth's father had mentioned that during that awful storm some trees had found their demise, which had yet to be removed. "It was over there that you lay, where that tree is now. If I had done what I had originally desired, if I had left you there while I sought help, you would have surely perished. But something inside of me demanded that I get you to safety. For months I cursed my decision to move you to the cabin, and now I understand. If I had left you there you would have died!" Speaking her thoughts aloud brought on an even greater display of affectivity.

"Are you certain? Maybe this tree fell at a later time."

"No, I remember clearly my papa saying that a few trees had fallen around the area and that we were fortunate not to have been hurt during the storm."

"Well, my sweet wife, you did get me to safety, and I am fine. Please, no more tears," he said as he rubbed her back.

"I know you think me to be emotional like so many other women who cry over silly things, but I can assure you that I am not. Since January, I find that my sentiments have no boundaries! But, the thought of something happening to you overwhelms me."

507

Her husband continued to comfort her as she let her feelings play out, until he asked, "Where is the cabin? I would see it if we can."

Elizabeth pulled away and smiled, saying, "You wish to distract me, and I cannot oppose the idea. I believe it is in this direction." Elizabeth reached over and took his hand as they worked their way through the woods. The distance was greater than Darcy could have thought. There were small hills, ditches and brush along the pathway. Indeed, it was not a pathway at all.

"Elizabeth, is this the way you took me?"

"Mostly, although I had to bypass some of the steeper hills. There it is," she finished, pointing ahead.

Darcy looked back from whence they came, then forward again. "You jest."

"I do not, sir."

"You expect me to believe that you dragged a man of my size, over rough terrain, that distance? Elizabeth, I know you are an active woman and likely more capable than most, but I cannot believe that you were able to accomplish that feat."

"Do you still think I had an accomplice, Husband? Perhaps Mr. Wickham helped me?"

"No, of course not, but you must be mistaken."

"I am not. I remember the journey quite clearly. You were in and out of consciousness, the rain was coming down, and I nearly missed the sight of the cabin. Water filled those ditches over there," she said as she motioned towards the trenches, now dry. "The lightning was what frightened me most, for I had heard of people being struck down. Halfway here, I began to wish I had gone for aid instead. Thank God I did not."

"Perhaps that is our answer."

"What do you mean?"

"You do believe in divine intervention, do you not?"

"I do, but I thought that a man of your intellectual prowess might discount such an idea."

"At one time, you would likely be right, but I have come to see that there are many things in our lives that cannot be explained by chance alone, that forces outside of our control might be at work, deciding for our good. I now see that a keen intellect and spiritual awareness are not mutually exclusive. I told you about my time in London, back in January." He blushed. "I know this might sound odd, but I suspect someone was taking care of me, despite my continued will to the contrary. I believe that I was somehow changed for the better. My eyes were in a way opened to my weaknesses that I had not seen before. That even though *you* were not concerned about my eternal whereabouts, someone else was." Then Darcy reached for her hands and said, "Elizabeth, think about it. Here we stand as husband and wife, overcoming all odds, even our own wills, to get to this point. There can be no other explanation but Providence. Certainly, I could never have conceived of such an enigmatic journey.

"And when I consider how I have afflicted you in so many ways, and yet you forgive me – I am overwhelmed. What did I do to deserve such grace?"

Elizabeth laughed. "Grace is not something you can earn, William. As I had been pardoned, I chose to pardon you, despite your many faults," she said, her eyes sparkling, either from emotion or amusement.

"You are a remarkable woman, Elizabeth Darcy; your generosity overwhelms me. I have many times wondered why you did not leave me in the storm to fend for myself. I certainly gave you no reason to help me."

"True, but you were so very rich." This caused Darcy to laugh outright at the absurdity. Then he looked upon her radiant features, suddenly overwhelmed with emotion.

"I thank God everyday for the accident that brought us together. And although the road has been hard-won, the blessings that you have brought to my life far outweigh any strife." Darcy leaned down and kissed her on her forehead as she contentedly leaned into his gentle and loving embrace.

"I came that they may have life and have it abundantly"
John 10:10b

Epilogue

The warm breeze was blowing across the portico as Elizabeth Darcy sat sipping lemonade. She was looking down upon the lawn at her husband, who was entertaining – or perhaps being entertained by – their daughter, Margaret. Elizabeth could hear the young girl's laughter rising up in the wind. Across the lawn ran Margaret's younger brother who wanted in on the fun as well. "You must wait your sister's turn, son," she heard Darcy say.

"But Father, she has had your attention all morning, and now I want some of it too."

"You do have a point. Alright, my young man, go get your own foil and we shall see which of you is the superior fencer."

"But Father, she always wins for she is two years older."

"One day, my son, you will be the one to protect *her*. You must be ready, and seeing how Margaret is a worthy adversary, I do bclicvc that the best course of action now is to try your luck with her. I will be here with you should she become dangerous," his father finished with a grin.

"I want Mama to come play," Elizabeth heard the little girl say enthusiastically.

"Your mother is much too accomplished to fight children at your level of skill. She shows little mercy."

"Then you can play with her, Father," said the one, as the other chimed in his agreement.

Just then, Elizabeth heard someone come up from behind and turning she saw Fitzwilliam approach. "James, you made it! I am glad you were able to get away. How is your brother?"

"He will not be with us long, I am afraid. It's a damned shame to die in that way and for such a worthless cause. Excuse me, Elizabeth; I don't mean to be so indelicate with my words in front of a lady. But surely his exploits could not have been worth that kind of torment."

"And how is Susan? Does she suffer much?"

"She is mostly angry at Patrick for bringing the disease home with him from, well, from wherever he contracted it. They say there is no cure, that there will be a long road of affliction before it finally takes them. My parents have asked that Rose and I take the children. They are old enough now to know something is horribly wrong, although they have not been told what, and my parents hope to shield them from the truth. This autumn, they will return to school, so it is just while they are on holiday."

"Is that what you will do then? Will you take them in?"

"Rose agrees. Our own children are so much younger and may not understand why their cousins come indefinitely. In truth, Langston's children beg to come live with you and Darcy," he said smiling. "As much as their

510

parents disliked the idea, those children have come to adore you as their favourite aunt."

"But I am not their aunt."

"They want you to be; therefore you are," he returned. "Is that my cousin down there fencing with his children?"

"Indeed it is," said she. "I never thought I would see the day that Fitzwilliam Darcy let his daughter fence, but there you see for yourself. After he taught me, I thought he would have given up on the idea altogether!" Elizabeth laughed at the memory. What she would not say – but was remembered with equal fondness – was that oftentimes when Elizabeth attempted her fencing lessons with her husband, they would end up back in their chamber, bypassing the endeavour altogether, thereby impeding her proficiency; but neither had felt inclined to complain. In fact, to make the process run much more smoothly, they soon decided to begin the sport while in their rooms, thus bypassing the contingent transit up the back stairway. As it turned out, her proficiency at swordplay had greatly improved during that adventurous time in their marriage.

"James, you have been a dear friend to me since the very beginning. When William married me, I anticipated a life full of grief and despair. You were the only person in his family who gave me a chance, at least at first. Your support during those dark days meant so very much to me.

"If I have not said so before, I want you to know that I thank you. William has told me, on more than one occasion, how you defended me to him during the first, sombre days of our marriage. I think we would have eventually fallen in love, for I believe with my heart that we were destined for one another, but had he not come home to Pemberley when he did, had you not stayed in town to deal with Wickham, I would not have survived that day."

"And had my family not been the one to send you out into the wilderness, you would not have needed him home. Please, Elizabeth, think nothing about it."

"Had you not come looking for me on that first Christmas at your parents' – Well, you have protected me more than once, and I thank you again and again."

"Fitzwilliam, are you flirting with my wife again?" came a voice from below. "I demand you come down here and defend yourself for your treachery. I will pit you against Bennet. He will fight you bravely, sir."

"Tell him to prepare himself for battle!" Then turning to Elizabeth, he said, "You have done wonders for Darcy. Not in my wildest dreams could I have imagined him so happy. He truly is a different man. Thank you."

"I really had no choice in the matter. Either I must live with a conceited, prideful man, or I had to tease it out of him. He resisted at first, I believe, but soon gave way when he realised the great pleasure that could be gained by falling in love. And I soon learnt that my true accomplishment has been to love and be loved by Fitzwilliam Darcy."

FINIS

ABOUT THE AUTHOR

Georgia McCall resides in the city of Memphis, Tennessee where she practices as a registered dietitian/nutritionist. She enjoys many pleasures including jogging (the slow variety) whence she derives all of her creative ideas. The quote, "Write drunk, edit sober" has often been attributed to Ernest Hemmingway. While that has its own merits, Georgia must add, "Write while under the influence of physical exertion." Of course, the benefits of this tack are lessened in that many of the details are lost once the writer is showered and dressed and ready to sit back at the blessed computer. But overall, most creativity stems from such activity, as an abundance of oxygen to the brain has proven its worth!

It has been the greatest pleasure to wake up in the morning, excited to get to the story and express to the reader a tale rich in truth and diversion. The characters that Jane Austen developed are extraordinary – too perfect not to revisit again and again. So after reading no less than three hundred of such variations, the author decided to throw her own story into the mix. Of benefit, Georgia tends to throw herself into all of her pleasures with zeal – or what some might call obsession. Nonetheless, this has the advantage when writing a book.

In addition to jogging, Georgia also enjoys her many acquaintances, church family and most especially her own family. She is the mother of two delightful girls, ages fourteen and nine, who love to watch the Jane Austen movies almost as much as their mother. She also enjoys camping, visiting coffee shops, eating delicious food, music, hanging out with her steadfast friends, reading, and date nights with her husband and best friend. She loves her Lord and hopes that in some way, He is glorified in the writing of the story.

514

ACKNOWLEDGEMENTS

The author would like to thank Kaye Ford for the many hours of support, reading, editing, and *Skyping* from around the world that were instrumental in completing this work. I could not have produced my story without your constant encouragement and professional insight.

I would also like to acknowledge all of my friends and acquaintances who graciously gave of their time to read my story and give me the needed assistance and assurance to publish, including Jennifer Velazquez, Dena Teague, Kathy Scott, Jennifer Wallace, Melanie Howle, Diana Neel, Becca Papachristou, Jennifer Jung, Yvonne Wells, Brandie Ivers, Pam Craig, Jay Vaughn and Christine Shih. I would also like to thank Dianne McCaulla for coming in at the tail end of the project and developing the cover that I wished for but was unable to create on my own.

I would be remiss without also acknowledging Jane Austen and her genius in writing *Pride and Prejudice*, whose characters and plot were the inspiration for writing this tale. Her capacity to create a timeless story of trials and love, that even now brings joy to her readers, cannot be overlooked.

I also thank my God who has given me all things, the least of which being whatever skills I have brought to this endeavour.

I would finally wish to acknowledge the sacrifice of my family who unwillingly had to endure a year of distraction and disorder. Your forbearance did not go unnoticed.

Made in the USA
San Bernardino, CA
16 August 2016